THE SIREN OF GOOD INTENTIONS

J. E. Mooney

To Patti & Jim

You set me on the path
that led to this self-
published novel
Thank you both!

Ted 14 Dec 19

Althea Publishing
St. Augustine, Florida

Book design by Sagaponack Books & Design
Cover design, illustrations, and map by Sam Christiansen

Based on a true story.

ISBN 978-1-7331829-1-1 (softcover)
ISBN 978-1-7331829-0-4 (hardcover)
ISBN 978-1-7331829-2-8 (e-book)

Library of Congress Catalog Card Number: 2019915309

Summary: In search of medicinal plants and adventure in Western Africa, Victor, a former Peace Corps volunteer and Doria, an aspiring botanist, as well as those around them, face danger and death from tribal healers, diamond smugglers, and more.

FIC009100 Fantasy/Action & Adventure
FIC027260 Romance/ Action & Adventure
FIC061000 Magical Realism
FIC002000 Action & Adventure

Althea Publishing
Saint Augustine, Florida

Printed and bound in the United States of America
First Edition

*To the men and women of the OMVS
Environmental Impact Assessment Project*

Contents

Part 1: How It Begins 1

Part 2: Doria and Nigel Blake 95

Part 3: Lessons from the Interior 191

Part 4: Confluence 287

Part 5: Discovery. 379

Part 6: Untethered. 407

Part 7: Event Horizon 453

Part 8: Intersection and Collision 477

PREFACE

The Siren of Good Intentions is an exploration of my past in an alternate universe. Memory and imagination commingle naturally and the more time passes, the more imagination intrudes on the memory. Fiction is therefore the safest and most authentic form of memoir—at least in my case.

Fiction is also a great vehicle for exploration. How do conflicting character traits manifest in one individual under stress? What are dreams? Why and how do some human beings bond to each other? What forces and elements surround us every day but have defied our science to detect, let alone understand? These are among the questions asked in this book.

I've also tried to recreate a place and time that changed my life. Senegal was intoxicatingly different from anywhere in North America I had ever been. Chaotic, hot, multilingual, part French, part African, it consumed me. This is why I've spent such effort to create a sense of place. This part of West Africa is, in a real sense, a character in this novel.

I hope you make it through to the end. I know it's long, but I promise you the ride will be worth it.

Thank you to all my readers.

J. E. Mooney

Part 1
How It Begins

1. Victor Gets a Job

I came here to the westernmost nation of West Africa to do volunteer work in the bush. It seemed like a good idea since I had graduated from college with no valuable skills (a philosophy major with a minor in self-medication isn't exactly preparing for the world of work), nor any idea what I wanted to do next. After two long years of digging wells and building irrigation systems out of car parts along the length of the Senegal River, I had decided to stay in Senegal for the foreseeable future. It was less a real decision of direction and more of putting one foot in front of the other. I had a shot at a real job now: to make sure small groups of scientists were able to do their fieldwork in the bush. More specifically, my role was to assure their lack of bush experience did not jeopardize their safety or their sanity.

These scientists had been assembled by a former US Army colonel named Derek Planck, to conduct the primary environmental research required to justify the commercial interests of a handful of Western industrialists and West African plutocrats. This design included the displacement of more than 12,000 people, mostly Malinke, in the Fouta Djallon mountains of Guinea and the upper Senegal River basin around Manantali in Mali. It was the Malinkes' misfortune to inhabit their ancestral lands of the last 10,000 years, which harbored some of the largest deposits of rare metals on the planet, including the occasional vein of diamonds. Colonel Planck worked for a consortium of international resource development companies called Industrial Minerals and Mining Enterprises, whose obscenely ironic acronym—IMAME—was just another thumb in the eye of the West African people. The project, however, was organized, not to study the mineral wealth abundantly documented for decades, but to define those difficult and politically sensitive parameters ignored for centuries of foreign rule—cultural displacement and disintegration, plant and animal extinction, environmental degradation, and the unsustainability of life as we know it. Little issues like that.

* * *

When Planck contacted me via a friend of mine who worked for the US Agency for International Development, I had finished working on a well-digging project that had taken ten months of gritty work along the Senegal River, from Saint-Louis, Senegal, to Kayes, Mali. USAID had helped fund the project. I was staying at the Hotel de la Poste for some R&R before I headed south to Dakar, where I had just rented a small bungalow. I relayed the message for Planck to meet me in Saint-Louis in the bar of the hotel.

He was impossible to miss. Planck was barely six feet tall, but people would easily mistake him for six foot three. His thin physique was the product of a lifetime of fitness training and his stiff gait shouted his military past. In khaki from his perfect canvas shoes to his floppy desert hat, Planck strode into La Poste at 7:00 p.m., probably to the second. I had gotten there three beers earlier, swapping West African stories with Claire and Lamine Volant, a Canadian couple from Montreal contracted to teach at the local trade school, L'École des Ouvriers Méchaniques (LOM).

Claire spotted Planck first and said to me, *"Ta blonde est arrivée."* ("Your date is here.")

I laughed, excused myself, then walked to the entrance to greet "my date." I gestured toward a table at the corner of the patio where our conversation would be private—for the most part. Before moving, Planck confirmed, "Victor Byrnes, right?"

"So far." I shook his hand. "And you're Derek Planck. Any relation to Max?"

"No," he said.

I should have known better.

We sat at the far end of the patio after I bought 200 CFA francs (about 75 cents) of roasted peanuts—Senegal's major cash crop— from a girl squatting against the rattan wall of the entrance. She was light-skinned, probably from one of the nomadic tribes, and wrapped in an extraordinary fabric: a riot of purple and red stripes with orange and green amoeba-like shapes, and stars of different sizes. I had lived in West Africa for many years and never ceased to be amazed by the collision of colors in which West African women dressed. My new acquaintance took no notice that I could tell. We both sat facing the entrance. I asked if he was a beer drinker, which thankfully he was, and ordered two Storks, locally brewed and bottled.

"Mr. Byrnes, we've got one helluva project for the development of some very isolated … let's call them deposits, in Mali and Guinea. We need someone like you to help make sure our various teams get to where they need to go and get their jobs done."

What, no small talk? No, You're a long way from Ithaca? He was getting right down to business. "What kind of jobs?"

"You name it, we've got it," he said.

I covered my mouth with my hand to stifle a laugh.

"There are three geologists, two for minerals and one for petroleum. There is an exploratory drilling team, a hydrologist, a public health team, a forestry specialist, and at least four, possibly five environmental biologists."

"The environmentalists, are they coming as tourists?" I deadpanned.

To his credit, Planck laughed. "No, sir. These folks have real jobs. In fact, we couldn't have gotten this project close to this stage without them."

"Why's that?"

"This project is sponsored by four African countries—Mali, Mauritania, Senegal, and Guinea—and four Western countries—the US, France, Belgium, and Norway. They formed an international government organization called—and excuse me if I butcher the French ...." He pulled a card from his shirt pocket and read: "Organization pour l'Exploration et l'Utilization du Fleuve Senegal, OEUFS. Did I say that all right?"

This made me laugh out loud. "Eggs! Really? The acronym in French means 'eggs.' Wow. Who was the brainchild who came up with that?"

"Marketing, Byrnes. I suspect so that people could remember it?" Planck's smile recoiled into his tight lips. "So, in order to provide the $625 million for the first phase of the exploration and the construction of a hydroelectric dam, these governments—OEUFS—require that we provide environmental impact studies on virtually every aspect of the project."

"Didn't Glen tell me this was a private consortium?" I could already smell the corruption from the African capitals to Paris to Washington, DC. This was going to be more interesting than I'd thought.

"As a development project," Planck emphasized, "this venture has the interest of government officials in a variety of industrialized countries. IMAME is actually contracted by OEUFS. And IMAME itself isn't just private money, Byrnes. Our government and the French government, in particular, have a vested interest in stable countries that have untapped and strategically valuable resources."

There it was—the recurring theme of the last three hundred years. I could only surmise that it was beyond Planck's imagining that a fellow American might have views of international exploitation different from his own. Could I blame him, though? There was, in fact, considerable upheaval and risk in these small African countries for whom self-government was not an evolving, progressive political experiment, but a clan feud.

Nor did it surprise me that center stage was actually not regional economic stability, but access to resources. Guinea was a perfect example. Even before Guinea's first president, Sékou Touré, died, Guinea's foreign allegiance pendulum swung back hard from the East to the West, with the new government now firmly in the hands of the military whose tribal loyalties required purging of certain officers and bureaucrats. But Sékou Touré himself had learned the hard way that not all colonialists were Western.

Immediately after Guinea won its independence from France in 1959, President Touré banished the hated French colonialist rulers and invited the communist countries of the era to help him develop his young nation. USSR, East Germany, and China sent technical assistance of various kinds and, in a replica of Western aid, made sure that 90 percent of the financial assistance went to purchase Russian, East German, or Chinese goods. It took Sékou Touré a few years to learn that the Soviets and Chinese were as rapacious as the colonial French or the imperial British ever were, and far more devious.

One legend concerned a Russian rock-sorting machine for diamond mining that broke down every six months. Each time, a Russian technician was summoned to fix it. He pronounced it irreparable in the Guinean jungle, so the huge machine was shipped back to the Soviet Union. This happened three times over a period of thirteen months.

During the third repair transport to Russia, the transporting ship suffered engine trouble in Dakar, so the Russians decided to transfer the machine onto another vessel. While the diamond machine was in mid-transit to the departing ship, the supporting crane cracked, dropping the machine onto the wharf. It split open, revealing a cache of the largest diamonds ever mined outside of Southern Africa. Hearing the news and assuming the first two "breakdowns" had been identical scams, Sékou Touré gave every Russian in Guinea exactly twenty-four hours to leave the country by any means they could. Though likely an exaggerated account, like all legends, there was truth of some kind behind it.

Western governments these days acquired Africa's resources with far more stealth. Whatever the confiscation IMAME carried out, it would leave the government officials, if not the ordinary people of Guinea, Mauritania, Mali, and Senegal, thankful for our presence.

"What is it you want me for, exactly, Mr. Planck?"

"Logistics director."

"I like that. Do you have some details for me?"

"Five Land Rovers, a mobile laboratory, two river research boats. We figured you'll use military-type tents and there will be a fair amount of scientific equipment that will need care and maintenance."

"Are we going to be in the bush for weeks or months at a time?"

"Probably both, but that will depend upon what disciplines need to be where and when. You'll plan that with the scientists themselves."

I could see the squabbling already. Some biologist will need to be in Tougue, Guinea, because it rains there in October, but the geologists or the insect team will have to be in Segou, Mauritania, in October because the rains there will have stopped. They're frickin' 300 miles apart, with no known roads—dirt track or otherwise—connecting them. We would need an airplane, at least, and a helicopter, preferably. I was already thinking of ways to divide the disciplines and the trips.

"Any chance of getting a company chopper?" I asked.

Planck flashed a sympathetic frown. "We thought of that, but the airlift capabilities will only be available for the next phases of the project."

The raw materials extraction, I thought. It made sense, of course. Why waste money on the feasibility study when you really need to invest in the heavy lifting for getting the mineral deposits out.

"One of the projects is to build a hydroelectric dam. It's the best way to provide power to the remote mining sites. The dam, however, will flood a valley for 200 kilometers and potentially change an area the size of New Jersey down the length of the river."

The Bakoye. Since I'd gone on my first trip outside Dakar I'd heard rumors about damming the Bakoye River. It was the major tributary feeding the Senegal River and carved through the most rugged terrain in all of West Africa—the Fouta Djallon mountains. Damming the Bakoye was akin to some great quest, a prophesy, even, that would bring extraordinary economic benefit or decades of devastation, depending on your perspective. If that river was dammed, it wouldn't just affect the region Planck was talking about. It would affect the population living along the entire Senegal River and beyond. I was beginning to understand the enormity and the risk here.

I said, "I'll need to do all the hiring of the drivers, cooks, and workers. And I'll need to carry both a rifle and a handgun."

Planck arched his eyebrows. After a long pause he asked why.

"Rifle for food, primarily. And the handgun, protection, mostly."

"You aren't going to have permission to carry weapons across international borders, Byrnes. This project doesn't work like that. We're not army or law enforcement."

"Of course," I said nonchalantly, "only the corrupt local police, the rebel groups, the drug dealers, the smugglers, the poachers, the government officials, the unemployed mercenaries, and the French sportsmen are allowed to have firearms." The French sportsmen being the most dangerous. I pushed away from the table.

Planck chuckled. I was actually starting to like the man.

"Point made. I'll look into it," he said tersely. "Do you know how to use firearms?"

It was a legitimate question, particularly considering my recent do-gooder past. I was raised by a father who loved and respected hunting. I owned a .22 caliber pistol when I was twelve, a 12-gauge shotgun at fourteen, and a .30-30 rifle at sixteen. I could take all three apart and reassemble them with ease.

"I can hold my own with most nonmilitary types." Planck was former military. I didn't doubt his experience with guns was far greater than my own.

We settled into a lengthy conversation about the logistics for the various parties, where they would need to go, for how long. He asked me about stocking provisions, gas, potable water, first aid, and safety. I told him about the terrain, how it changed from desert steppe to savannah to jungle. How the rains turned passable dried streambeds into impassable quagmires. I also told him that most of the risk and danger came from things we couldn't foresee.

Planck nodded, I expect, because that's exactly why the military prepares so thoroughly, so continuously. When unexpected events overtake you, a person needs to be able to react instinctively with the right moves. Thinking is great if you have time and if your fear and adrenaline haven't completely immobilized your brain.

I asked, "Just how experienced are these scientists, anyway?"

"None are ex-military, if that's what you're getting at."

"Exactly. Soldiers, trained security people—you folks come prepared. These academics will be coming from some sleepy Midwest or New England university whose fieldwork has been 100 miles outside Omaha or Hanover, where their greatest danger was missing the last filling station or being a whole day's drive from a pharmacy." I wasn't shouting, but I was excited.

"Stop negotiating, Byrnes," Planck said, as if he were bored. "We know the risks. That's why you and I are talking."

I chuckled to myself. Yes, indeed. This was going to be a lot more fun than digging wells in the desert. "And exactly what am I to be paid for taking these risks?"

Planck let out a breath. The discussion was coming to an end.

"Twelve hundred a month, plus forty dollars a day," he told me with ease.

Considering that I had just finished two years of work at $100 a month as a volunteer, and that my prospects of other work as a liberal arts college graduate seemed dim at best, I said I would think about it. This was 1978, after all. That was real money.

"Don't think about it too long, Byrnes. You were first on my list. You aren't last."

"I've got some more logistic questions before I decide anything."

* * *

When Planck left thirty milnutes later, I had accepted his offer without any other salary negotiation. We agreed to meet in Dakar in three days, at the IMAME offices. I rejoined Claire and Lamine.

Claire was in good spirits. "It's a pity your date didn't want to join us," she said in a mocking tone. "Was he afraid his trousers would lose their crease?" She laughed languidly and stretched her arms around Lamine, who leaned in and kissed her.

"Tell us, Victor," he said, "what did the soldier want with you?"

I told them about the corporate treasure hunt that needed the sanction of an independent impact study so all the interested parties could feel good about divvying up the region's wealth for the next twenty years. My role would be to lead the parties into and out of the bush safely.

Lamine seemed more than a little intrigued. "So, you're going back and forth for weeks or months at a time between Dakar and Kankan? What about getting all those trailers and people across the borders?"

"We could be going a lot farther than Kankan," I told him, "but that decision won't be up to me. As far as getting across the borders ...."
I laughed. "Maybe I'll have a universal 'get across borders free' card. We're supposed to have permission to cross the borders freely."

Lamine laughed out loud. "There is no such thing as 'freely' when you are dealing with the *douaniers* and border police. Is your new company funding your *baksheesh*?"

Of course I knew that bribes would have to be paid to get through the major border crossings, irrespective of any documentation guaranteeing unmolested passage.

"My new consortium, Lamine. I'm not worried about that just yet. Besides, since we're probably going to some of the least traveled parts in four countries, I expect we'll find plenty of borders where nobody's there."

Lamine's eyes grew wide. "Are you crazy, man? These borders aren't your normal Frenchman's line on a colonial map. There are serious rivers and mountains that divide Mauritania, Mali, Senegal, and Guinea. You're going to drive your Land Rovers across them all?"

"I don't know. We'll figure that out. Probably map out the best places to cross once the dry season starts. Maybe we'll find some crossings that the locals will be able to guide us to."

Claire unwrapped herself from Lamine and yawned. She looked around the bar, then rose slowly and sauntered over to where a group of teacher friends were standing. Claire put her arm around the shoulders of a male colleague and joined their conversation.

Lamine hadn't looked up, even as I followed Claire's sashay over to the group of chattering expatriates. He said, "I have some talented students in my senior auto mechanics class. Maybe there's an opportunity for us to help each other, Victor."

"Maybe … sure … uh … we'll see."

He went on and asked me questions about the terrain, the project vehicles and equipment, the type of work the studies would involve, none of which I could answer.

When I left the Hotel de la Poste, Lamine rejoined Claire with their friends. I needed to get down to Dakar early the next morning. The project was headquartered there, as were the embassies of the sponsoring countries and the offices of every major company doing business in West Africa. Besides, I needed to return to my place, get into some clean clothes, take a swim, and hang out at one of the cafés on the tiny beach on the island of Gorée. Now, that was a lifestyle worth supporting.

I was staying the night at Lamine and Claire's apartment. Before heading there, I took a walk to the monument circle that welcomes everyone to Saint-Louis center after crossing the 1920s-era bridge across the Senegal River. Around the circle were the decaying, mold-covered government buildings of this former capital for all of French West Africa. I walked down a side street where children were playing. Charcoal fires in hibachi-like urns were lit on porch steps to make tea or roast corn. There was a slight stench of sewage and used wash-water. I passed a hut built of old planks and corrugated steel that was a small convenience store for anything a local family might need—a tube of tomato paste, a tin of Nescafé instant coffee, a can of concentrated milk with enough sugar to bake a pie; batteries, pencils and pens, cold drinks, loose tea, soap cakes, charcoal by the gram—a veritable you-name-it of daily essentials. Most of these shops throughout Senegal were run by the Mauritanians, referred to by the Senegalese as Nars. Most of them were surly and suspicious shopkeepers, on guard against petty thievery and keeping their money always on their bodies. They didn't seem to care much for any of their customers, who returned the sentiment.

Eventually the street ended at an open sewer that extended about a mile along the back of the city. I scaled down the near side, jumped over the streaming effluent, trundled up the other side, and continued walking in the sand toward a row of palm trees about 50 meters ahead. The palms were aligned like a parade, all arched back from the years of incessant offshore winds. Feeling and hearing this evening's steady yet gentle breeze, I listened for that other deeper sound, the roar above the wind. I could hear it now, undulating and vast, growing louder and louder as I approached. The Atlantic Ocean.

I needed a walk along the shore to actually think about the path to which I was now committed. The truth was that I didn't know even a third of the places I was supposed to take those academic thrill-seekers with their instruments, their self-assurance, and their preconceptions. Suddenly I was dreading the thought of being responsible for these people in the desert or in the savannah, or, God help us, the rain forest. Of those researchers I'd met in Senegal, most were well-meaning, hard-working scientists from developed countries—the US, Canada, England, Italy, Germany, France, Denmark—accompanied by outsized egos and a tourist's sense of adventure. Oblivious to their ignorance, many posed a real danger to themselves. I'd have to be on my guard with them all the time.

The sun was below the horizon, yet a few pink-fringed clouds lingered, settling toward the ocean's edge. I heard the solitary cry of a seabird. Not a seagull, maybe a tern, I couldn't tell. I walked toward the call, seemingly straight ahead of me, where the whitecapped waves sank into packed sand. I had a sense this bird was trying to tell me something. Something important, something close. But of course it wasn't. It was only my own sense of uncertainty reflected by a mindless creature of the sea.

2. On Gorée

When I woke, the sun was already a yellow crown over the ocean. Claire and Lamine's fifth-floor apartment sat across the bridge from the Hotel de la Poste and had a great view of the river and, beyond the city buildings, the ocean. It made me long to get back to Dakar, to my apartment on Gorée Island. Filling my lungs with salt air and the scents of morning charcoal fires, I climbed out from under my mosquito net, pulled on some clean clothes from my pack, and headed to the taxi center (called a *gare routière* in French), the main transportation hub where the bush taxis picked up and dropped off their fares. Most of the bush taxis making the four-hour ride to Dakar would leave by 8:30 a.m., only after they had filled all eight seats in the Peugeot 505 station wagons. I was eager to get to Dakar, but just as importantly, I was keen to claim a window seat.

When I arrived at the dusty parking area it was teeming with morning travelers, drivers, and vendors. I bought some guavas and mangoes from a young girl who approached me as soon as I walked into the crowd. I picked up a loaf of bread from a young man who actually had loaves spread out on a table and let you come to him. Very odd. From one of the Nar shops on the edge of the *gare* I bought a can of sardines and a bottle of Vittel water.

I listened intently to make out the individual names of the various destinations as they were cried out: Dagana, Kaolack, Matam, Podor, Dakar, Nouakchott. It wasn't difficult locating the next taxi leaving for Dakar. I maneuvered over the three people already settled in and plopped next to a window at the back. This time of day it would take only fifteen more minutes to fill the taxi and we'd be on our way to the capital.

I was getting comfortable, in a manner of speaking, when a young man came up to the driver, carrying an overstuffed cardboard suitcase and towing a sheep—the short-haired, floppy-eared variety found everywhere in Senegal. The young man and the driver bound the legs of the creature together and hoisted the sheep onto the roof rack of the 505, where they put a net over it. The sheep cried in protest, squirmed and tried to escape, until the two men tied the animal's legs to the roof rack. The sheep fell silent. The dust slowly settled back to the ground. The taxi now full, we sputtered out of the *gare*, onto the only paved road connecting Saint-Louis with Dakar.

I am always in for a thrill when hurling down a two-lane West African highway. What has always amazed me is that, as a people, the Senegalese, like most West Africans, are patient to a fault, often impervious to the passage of time as though there was never a reason to hurry for anything—anything except driving. Passing another vehicle is such a reckless pursuit that it remains a mystery why there are not more accidents and fatalities on this road. I swallowed a guava in three bites, washed it down with some Vittel, and set up my pack against the window for a pillow. Sleep amid the heat and the hissing wind would be fitful at best.

My mind was restless. I was excited by this new adventure, but also nervous, even frightened. Having responsibility for myself alone traveling to these uncharted places was dangerous enough. But the thought of taking the responsibility for the safety of ten or more West African novices dried up my mouth. I'll need to cultivate this nervousness, I thought. It may be the most critical asset to keep us out of danger.

My half sleep was shaken off when we screeched around the traffic circle in Thies, the last leg of the journey. Ninety minutes to go. I tried to let my mind wander into the half sleep. When will Jetset Jensen be back in town, I wondered, and then dozed. I awoke abruptly in the bustling *gare* of Dakar.

Dakar, a port city on a paddle-like peninsula, juts out from the rest of Senegal and provides sunsets and sunrises over the water depending upon where on the peninsula you happen to be. I could see the sun slightly low in the west and knew I had some time to get to the port, where I could catch the regular commuter ferry, a *shaloupe*, over to the island of Gorée. I was looking forward to some downtime in my small apartment. Unfolding my legs from the back seat I wiped the dozing from my eyes.

As soon as I stepped out onto the sandy parking area I was surrounded by children and women selling everything from bread to blankets, fruits to fish. When I spoke Oulof to them, they cackled and laughed, pressed forward not only to sell me something, but to test the white man, this *toubob*. I played a young children's game with them. They made me laugh and I made them laugh. However, this ruse could not keep them from the task at hand. These were not street waifs. These were determined, focused businesspeople competing thickly and raucously for every sale, refusing to give up or be deterred by a not particularly clever diversion.

Dismissing them with a wave as I headed for one of the local taxis, I bought five mangoes, five packets of roasted peanuts, and another baguette. I stuffed them into my duffle and got into the cab, telling the driver to take me to the Gorée Ferry. Soon I would be somewhere familiar, tranquil, and cool.

The boat ride to Gorée is one of the few things in all of West Africa that runs regularly on time. I flashed my pass at the ticket window and received a familiar, unconcerned wave forward. I joined about twenty other people in the waiting area. This time of day, about an hour before dusk, most of the people going out to the island are either residents or planning to stay the evening. There was uncharacteristically little chatter among the patrons this evening. I surmised it was relief from the heat provided by the permanent offshore breeze and the shade of the waiting-area canopy.

The twenty-minute ferry ride was bumpier than usual; a stiff wind stirred the bay with a steady chop. Though I was accustomed to the ride, it wasn't the calm, droning start to my unwinding that I had in mind. In hindsight, it was an alert.

With a nod to the policeman on duty at the end of the ramp, I descended the gangway and headed off to my apartment: past the small white beach and the cafés, up the sandy road about 50 meters, taking a left at the small shop that sold cold beer and fresh fried fish; right at the next corner, and then up past the coral stucco walls to the fifth door. As I fumbled for my key I smelled marinara sauce and heard Carlos Santana, both coming from my apartment. My plans changed instantly.

Once through the door, I stepped onto the slate patio and stared angrily at Amelia Jensen, who threw up her hands and screamed.

I yelled, "How in blazes did you get in here, Jetset, and how could you possibly have known when I'd be back?"

She recovered quickly and brushed her chestnut hair off her face. "In fact, I had no idea when you'd be back. I was hoping to have at least one more night of peace." She turned away from me, laughing to herself, and walked into the kitchen.

"Excuse me!" I exclaimed with frustration. "Just how long have you been staying in my apartment?" When she could have stayed anywhere in Dakar, including her own apartment!

Amelia Jensen was director for African projects for the Cunningham Foundation, whose third-world philanthropy was atoning for five generations of robber barons. Jetset had written her master's thesis at Johns Hopkins School of International Diplomacy, on the predictable failure of large project aid to developing countries by Western governments and how it actually precipitated the very instability the aid was designed to avoid. She was offered an internship at US AID headquarters where she—and I'm guessing, here—pissed off every indentured bureaucrat with whom she worked. She was a natural for the $4 billion Cunningham Foundation, who needed real iconoclasts to burnish their image.

"This is only my second day here, so don't panic, Byrnes," she said as she uselessly stirred the sauce on the cool stove top.

"Jules let you in, didn't he?" My good friend and trouble-making companion who lived alone, also on the island, Jules Tamara was a French citizen watching over the family business interests in West Africa.

"Of course he did," she admitted. "Do you imagine I climbed up the bougainvillea and dropped in like 007?"

"So why didn't you stay with him, with all the rooms he has? Or at the Taranga, or any of those diplomatic expense account hotels, or that new flat you found months ago?" I felt invaded. My duffle was suddenly way too heavy and I threw it down onto the tiles.

"Let me get this straight, Byrnes." She came out of the kitchen to face me. "You just got back to your place after, what, a week in the bush? To find, instead of an empty apartment, a home-cooked meal and a friend you haven't seen in over a month, and this displeases you?"

I offered my only excuse. "You ... startled me."

"Clearly." She pointed to the table on the patio on which had appeared a vase of gladiolas and irises. "When was the last time anyone brought you flowers, Mr. Byrnes?"

"Jetset, I'm really—"

"Don't call me that, Victor, please …."

"Amelia, I'm an idiot. You're a wonderful, irreplaceable friend, and I *have* missed you. Truly." Really? Had I really missed her? I sounded to myself as if I missed her at some point. "Did you actually make spaghetti sauce?" If I knew Jetset, she had used fresh tomatoes and basil from the Marché Kermel and probably some other experimental ingredients.

"I was thinking Italian couscous, actually. But we have lots of time before we have to decide what dinner is." She took two steps toward me. Her hair partially covered her right eye and she looked as though she sensed my submission, her lips curling in a victory smirk that I found irresistible. I took two steps to her and hugged her gratefully. She pinched my ass hard and I yelped.

"I deserved that."

"Uh-huh." She nodded slowly.

When I finally kissed her, we were both sliding toward that familiar release, that sense of comfort and ease discovered when we first met that was molded from friendship before dissolving into passion.

"You've been eating well," I teased her.

"Your turn," she replied.

3. At Work

Ineeded to start figuring out right away how I was going to get five or ten or fifteen scientists of different disciplines into parts of West Africa about which I knew little or nothing. Three team leaders were arriving today. Amelia was up and dressed as early as I. She was meeting with World Health Organization (WHO) officials regarding an early detection and intervention project for cholera epidemics—a regular scourge found anywhere on earth where high-density populations and seventeenth-century sanitation converged. Amelia was going to be busy for a few weeks in the Ivory Coast. That was good because I could focus completely on this new gig. It was bad because she's great downtime company, even if I can be slow to see that.

Our ride on the 6:30 a.m. *shaloupe* was both peaceful and expectant. She and I spoke of the unknown few months that awaited us, and how we were each a key piece in something we didn't fully understand but hoped was meaningful; of how we fretted that we were not adequate to the possibly important tasks we would face. And even if we and our projects were successful, what impact would all that leave? It was easy for me to encourage her. The WHO was defeating smallpox, cholera, and other diseases nearly everywhere it engaged, even with a bureaucracy that hamstrung energetic scientists with byzantine politics. Amelia had the less easy task, of making me believe that the IMAME project would have a positive effect on the lives of the West Africans. Fundamental research about insects, birds, trees, and weather was only beginning to influence policy in developed countries. How could this science possibly be used for anything other than to justify the decisions already made? My goals had to be narrow and personal.

"That shouldn't be hard for you," she said, poking me in the side at the same time.

I kissed Amelia before she jumped into a cab to take her to the Cunningham Foundation's office in the heart of the Dakar business district. I decided to walk the kilometer to the converted warehouse along the Port Access Road, which IMAME had secured as the headquarters. The morning air, clear and dry, was already hot enough to steam the draining sewer water off the road into fetid clouds. I hurried even though I risked breaking into a sweat before breakfast.

Each warehouse I passed was surrounded by a 3-meter-tall chain-link fence with spirals of razor wire at the top, testifying to the pervasive theft in Dakar. These warehouses didn't store automobiles or firearms. They stored rice, peanut oil, hand tools, blankets, and cement—items of real value in a poor country. The pink stucco building of IMAME was differentiated by a small bronze sign next to the entrance: INDUSTRIAL MINERALS AND MINING ENTERPRISES – ENVIRONMENTAL DIVISION. The building was further distinguished because it had windows, most of which had air conditioners in them, caged by padlocked metal bars. Someone was thinking ahead.

I pushed the button by the plaque and heard a buzzer squawk deep in the compound. After two more pushes at the button, an old Senegalese man in a faded purple kaftan and knitted cap shuffled to the gate. He glanced at me with a puzzled grimace. As he opened the gate, he asked me my name. I told him in Oulof my name was Iba Diouf. This made him laugh. We then proceeded through the long traditional greeting—how was my wife, how was my family, how were my brothers and sister, etcetera, etcetera—to which the unchanging answer was "Peace only" (*"Jamme reck"*). Finally he opened the gate, still laughing, and told me to go straight ahead.

Derek Planck stood hunched over a desk with maps overflowing its top, and pointed to one map in particular, practically stabbing it. Looking over Planck's shoulder was a pensive man with long white hair which he unconsciously pushed back as it fell over his eyes. He was shaking his head, apparently disagreeing with Planck. They both looked up as I entered the room.

"Victor. Good morning. Welcome to headquarters." I shook Planck's hand as he introduced the older gentleman. "This is Doctor Stedman. He's heading up the medical survey team."

I turned to him as he extended his hand.

"Call me Lee," he said quietly.

Lee Stedman was dean of tropical medicine at Baylor Medical School and apparently a much sought-after developing-world health specialist. I, of course, knew nothing of this upon first meeting him.

"We were just going over the topographical maps to see where Lee's teams should work in the next six months. Maybe you can give us a hand."

"Glad to," I said.

"Derek tells me you know the Senegal River basin geography pretty well, Victor," Lee said.

"Up to a point, I know it very well. I've spent the last two years digging wells from Saint-Louis to Bakel in Senegal. I've worked in Kayes, Mali, and in Sedougou, in Mauritania."

"What about Guinea?" Lee asked.

"What about it?"

"Guinea is the home of the Fouta Djallon mountains where the headwaters of the Senegal River are formed. The dam will be built only 100 kilometers downstream from what Derek has shown me, so we will have to journey as far up to the source waters as possible to baseline at least one village in the area."

"Guinea will be new for all of us." I hoped the truth still rang with confidence.

Stedman didn't seem to think so. "What exactly, then, do you intend to do, Mr. Byrnes, to assure we arrive where we need to conduct our research?"

It was a fair question, delivered without emotion, and one I myself had fortunately been pondering. There was only one answer. "I'll be traveling there by myself first to make sure we have a safe route."

"That's the right idea, Byrnes," Planck's singing tone told me I was slightly off base. "But there are a few other options for reconnaissance we probably should consider. I'm thinking your first trip could include more team members."

Puzzled, I looked at him.

"Victor," Planck said, "we have a lot of planning to do in the next sixty days. I like your idea of scouting out the path in Guinea, but first we need to look at the needs of all the teams and put our project plan together as a group, in context of the needs of the team leaders."

"When are the rest of the team leaders supposed to arrive?" I asked.

"Siegfried Mueller and Alan Broca arrive today. Mueller heads up the geophysics team—geology, hydrology, forestry, and agronomy. Five people, total. Broca is the head zoologist. His team will be six at full complement. Dr. Stedman's health team is the largest, with eight."

We agreed that the most practical way for the team leaders to understand where they had to go and decide on the best tools and expertise at various locations was for me to take them on a three-week reconnaissance mission. That was just enough time to travel the length of the Senegal to where it is formed by its two tributaries in Mali, and, depending on the available routes, travel all the way to the Mali-Guinea border. Regardless, we had to be back onto dirt roads before the rainy season started in the mountains or we would be stranded. It didn't take an expert to know that. We would have to leave within the next ten days.

"Derek, have you got the Land Rovers cleared through customs?" I asked.

Planck put down the map he was holding and waved for me to follow him as he strode out through the office and toward the back of the building. He led me past a storeroom with an abundance of equipment on shelves and on the floor in boxes, then through a large set of double doors, into a paved courtyard with a giant acacia tree in the middle. In a perfect circle around the acacia tree rested four gleaming, gray Land Rovers. They still had the plastic covers on the black leather seats. Impressive. I walked around these beauties for a good fifteen minutes, opening and closing the doors, popping the hoods, checking out the dual spare tires. I started to feel like a fleet captain.

"What else have you already taken care of?" I asked.

Planck said to follow him back into the storage area, where he handed me a list of the gear that had cleared customs and was now stowed, or rather, splayed about the facility. Tents, stoves, shovels, cots, sleeping bags, portable toilets, mosquito netting, and on and on. My first job was to check the inventory and then come up with a list of what else we needed.

"But before you spend the rest of the day with that," said Lee Stedman, from the hallway entrance, "I'd like you to see one more thing and give me your opinion."

Planck rolled his eyes only slightly, saying, "Lee, can we do that later?"

"I would like Mr. Byrnes to give me his opinion now, Derek. Please."

"Fine."

Dr. Stedman led me to a parking lot. I looked at him, puzzled, beholding a white Winnebago camper.

"This is our mobile laboratory for serology and parasitology," he said. "Let's take a look inside." He opened the rear door and we walked up the three stairs into a very hot mini-laboratory.

It had all the conveniences of a small medical lab. I looked at Dr. Stedman but couldn't tell if he was proud or looking for me to notice some imperfection or fault. "I hope there's air conditioning." I headed for the exit.

Outside, I paced slowly up one side of the converted camper. The wheels were not nearly the size of those on the Land Rovers and the clearance couldn't have been more that 14 inches. Then it struck me that this laboratory was going to the end of the graded road and no farther. There was no chance this camper was going to cross silty riverbeds, or travel through the desert, or negotiate the steep gorges into the highlands of Mali and Guinea. I smiled that ironic, disillusioned smile we all find when some absurdity overtakes our planning.

I shook my head. "I'm afraid, Dr. Stedman, there's been a miscalculation." My amusement at the glaring oversight quickly turned to concern.

"What sort of miscalculation?"

I told him my thoughts and pointed out the differences between the Winnebago and the Land Rovers. Stedman wasn't worried.

"I think you'll find that Derek had this re-equipped with a four-wheel-drive transmission."

This made me laugh out loud. Not Derek, the military logistics master! How could he make this kind of mistake?

"Lee, I don't care if the thing has a hyperdrive, it simply can't get around except on well-maintained roads. And you must believe me. Where you're planning to go—remember, on the map just now—there are no roads at all! You're going to have to put this on the frame of a Unimog—a big Mercedes flatbed truck with a three-foot ground clearance."

Dr. Stedman's face morphed into a scowl. His eyes narrowed and I thought I saw him clench a fist. Suddenly he turned and walked purposefully past me, back into the courtyard. Following a few paces behind, I heard him call out, "Planck, we need to talk about the lab."

This was not a great start.

4. Preparations

Planck's military stiffness was a mint julep in a hammock compared to the trifecta of scientific pomp, posturing, and one-upmanship displayed by Stedman, Broca, and Mueller. There is no doubt all three were highly qualified and knowledgeable. And there was ample reason to debate the route and itinerary since the three disciplines of earth science, life science, and human health required much different data, sampling logistics, and geographical areas of interest. But standing in an office barely cooled by an overloaded air conditioner, with the three of them hunkered over four large topographical maps spread across two folding camp tables, each of them arguing why his route was so critical that the others had to change their plans or sit this trip out, was incessant exasperation.

Mueller broke out of the angry huddle first. "There is no other solution," he announced. "We will all take separate vehicles and go each where we must. Byrnes, you will have to make sure we each have a Land Rover and a driver qualified to take us where we want to go."

"Herr Mueller," Planck said. (Mueller's degree entitled him to be called "Dr.," which he preferred to "Mr.") "That's not possible. That would bust our gas budget in the first month and put additional wear and tear on two additional vehicles simply because the three of you have different agendas. We haven't yet hired additional drivers, and none of the ones I'm considering have ever driven in Mali or Guinea. Nor do they speak English! Byrnes is planning to leave tomorrow in order to have as much time for each of you as possible in the field before the rains get here. And please keep in mind this trip is for site selection, not conducting your studies."

"This is not acceptable," Mueller stated. "We have been looking at this for hours and there simply is no other solution."

"While I'm surprised to hear myself say this," Alan Broca said, "I agree with Siegfried. We should each have our own car and driver. I don't care if he knows the way. We'll figure out how to get to where we need. And how to communicate."

"Really?" I'd raised my voice more than I wanted. "So, when you've told the driver to go left and he drives right across a ravine and you break an axle, what then? When that ravine turns into six feet of roaring river after two days of heavy rain 70 kilometers south of your position, what's your plan?"

"Enough with the histrionics, Byrnes," Broca said. "We're not new at this. Each of us probably has more experience than you have."

I could not let such crap go unchallenged. "So you have each lived in a remote village in this region for the last twenty-six months, speak two of the local languages, and know the weather patterns by the smell and direction of the wind?"

Broca looked at Stedman for support. Planck smiled at me.

"Victor," Stedman said. "Alan simply wants you to understand that we are smart enough and experienced enough not to take chances that might jeopardize our work. We're having difficulty arriving at any other sensible plan."

So there I was, a twenty-six-year-old liberal arts major, doing this kind of work for the first time, while trying to corral three renowned PhDs who each had led field studies of various types in many different regions of the world. Putting myself in their place, why should I listen to this kid fresh out of the Peace Corps? Yet for all their erudition and experience, they were acting like children. I had provided a common target which had at least brought them together, but some parenting experience on my part would have been very handy.

Derek continued to smile, so I again took up my cause. "The drivers aren't available and the rains are coming." Then I had an inspiration.

Our sponsoring agency, OEUFS, had divided the entire river basin into 100 square kilometer sections—364 of them. Getting to eighteen of the grid areas in three weeks, even if they weren't too far flung, would still be a real challenge. But this suggestion had the benefit of both dividing the trip equally among the three team leaders and giving them each complete control for certain portions of it. "We'll use the OEUFS grids. Three each for half a day."

Mueller and Broca stared at me. Broca raised his eyes as though weighing the idea, and Mueller put his hand to his chin. I hoped was this progress.

Stedman spoke up. "Half a day seems like too little time, Mr. Byrnes, if we're to explore 100 square kilometers per discipline."

It was a geometry problem in time. For the next twenty minutes we argued and brainstormed until we hit upon a grid and time-sharing solution.

I completed my thinking out loud. "We may have to limit the total time and maybe the number of grids you select, to stay within our three-week window. And we have to schedule travel between grids." It was like explaining a new game at summer camp.

"That sounds reasonable to me, Byrnes. Alan? Siegfried?"

"I will of course need six complete sites," declared Mueller. "But I think this could work. Thank you, Lee," he said to Stedman as though I had nothing to do with the agreement.

Broca had made the full calculation in his mind and likely thought that anything would be better than the stalemate endured since the day began. "Let's get this done now," he said.

The final plan of sixteen days of work and five of travel was all doable, so long as we could be back on real roads by the time the rains arrived. However, the only paved roads for this route were in the central and north of Senegal. Every other part of the journey would be a rutted dirt path or a dried streambed or mountain pass. And then there were the river crossings. If we did not get through these before the rains began, particularly those farthest away, we could be trapped God knows where while easily forded tributaries turned into deep rapids. How would this "team" react in such a situation? The only solution is to head to the farthest destination first and then come back. With any luck, we'd beat the rains back to Senegal even if we had work left to complete. It was a minor miracle that we achieved consensus on this itinerary.

The team leaders tabled their arguing over grid control and set themselves to research planning. This gave me the opportunity to do my own work.

Unlike the team leaders, I had no individual office. I had a desk in the main conference room and access to all the maps and records I needed there. The three PhDs liked to joke that I got the biggest office. While each of them self-sequestered into their respective office, I buckled down to plan the trip.

After about fifteen minutes Planck came back in, pulled a conference chair up to my desk, and sat with the back of the chair facing me and his arms crossed on top of it. He rested his chin on his arms and broke into a toothy grin. I had no idea he was capable of such mirth, but I had a feeling it was at my expense.

"So, which doctor gave you that throbbing vein in your forehead?" he said with way too much pleasure.

"All three are witch doctors, if you ask me." I tried to sound more displeased than I actually was. "How are you getting on with providing me a rifle or a handgun? I've already decided on my first targets." More calmly, I said, "We're going to have to work together and I hope we've learned a bit about how to do that. What do you think?"

Taking my initial questions seriously, Planck told me it was not going to be easy getting the permit for a weapon and that we may need to have an OEUFS official along with us regularly if we were to carry a handgun. He added, "Look, Byrnes, what you just went through with these doctors is very likely only a taste of what you'll go through this next month in the bush."

"Three weeks," I reminded him.

"Are you taking bets? Anyway, you did fine. But out in the field you will need to make decisions quickly and be prepared to stick to them. If you don't, they'll lose respect for you."

"I would say that respect for me is already in short supply." I tried not to sound petulant.

"Don't be fooled because these hardheads won't admit you saved their bacon just now. They all know what you did. But they're used to being in charge. Out in the field, you're the expert. Look for ways to show them your expertise and your ability to help them get their jobs done. And remember, you're not trying to win them over, you're trying to keep them safe and productive. And, very importantly, keep them from interfering with you doing your job."

I nodded. "Thanks, Derek. And you're probably right about the time frame. I'll plan on thirty days. So long as we are long gone from the Guinea highlands and the Manantali mesa before the rains come, we'll be good."

"Are you going to drive or put the vehicle on the train?"

I hadn't thought of putting the Land Rover on the train, but it was an idea worth considering. The train left Dakar and, though it made a number of stops, scheduled and unscheduled, it would take us all the way to Mahina, from where we could pick up the trail to the site of the hydroelectric dam, Manantali. The main road through the center of Senegal was the fastest route to our destination, but a good 150 to 200 kilometers south of the river basin where we needed to be. There was no advantage to putting 300 kilometers of dirt-road wear and tear on the vehicles. I told Planck the train sounded like a good idea, that I'd look into it and get back to him tomorrow.

If for this trip I would be the driver, I needed a second-in-command to keep the preparations moving forward. This task fell to the first driver I hired, Mammadu Omar N'Diaye. I knew Mammadu from my volunteer days, when he was the only driver of six—in a large UNDP regional well-digging project—who could be counted on to show up on time every day, do whatever task the job required, and use his own judgment to the advantage of the program. It was Mammadu who bargained with a local transport company to loan him a truck to take the masons and supplies to a remote jobsite after his starter motor fell out from underneath the project's truck. He also had this knack for fixing anything, with something in his pocket or whatever he could find on the floor of the truck or on the side of the road. This ranged from flashlights to transmissions. But the real reason I hired Mammadu was because I trusted him.

On the downside, he may have been the most stubborn male the Djiolla clan had ever produced. Between his hard head and my volatile nature, it's a wonder we stayed as close as we had.

I didn't know if Mammadu had any experience transporting trucks via the train. Still, he was the first person on my list to ask. He was scheduled to come by before lunch for an orientation of our project, along with his role as the chief driver, and I thought that would be a great time to pick his brain and delegate some of the start-up projects.

Rather than wait in my office, I went back to the reception area to check in with Miriam, the project secretary. I had requested quotations from local metal workers for building a flat galvanized water tank and a substantially reinforced roof rack. I hoped at least one of them had been eager enough for the business to provide me a proposal.

Mammadu had already arrived when I went to see Miriam. The two of them were shamelessly flirting and laughing like children on a playground. Mammadu's hulking frame nearly bent the metal desk where he sat.

In Oulof I said to them, "Stop that now, or I'll tell both your spouses!"

Mammadu turned to me and said, through his broad grin, "But this woman is my wife."

Miriam howled and looked at me as she became crippled with laughter. She wagged her finger. "*Deddet, Deddet, Victor, bul ko le degg!*" ("No, no, Victor, don't believe him!")

"But you already have four wives, Mammadu, so that means you must divorce your first wife."

"Yes, you're right, Barbu," he said, referring to my bearded face as he always did. "Will you take her?"

"Of course. She cooks the best *chebugen* in all of Senegal."

More roaring laughter from the two of them, and Mammadu slapped my opened palm. He gave me a big hug and a handshake. "Are you sure you're not a Djiolla?"

"No, no, my friend. You know I'm descended from the clan of the river kings. I just pretend to be a Djiolla."

Mammadu and I had had this exchange many times before and we always loved it, as did any Senegalese who was part of our theater. Miriam applauded and then shooed us out of her office.

I switched to French. We both understood French was our business language, and for work details I was far more comfortable speaking French. "There are a number of projects, Mammadu, before we set out for Mali. But I want to ask you: What do you think about transporting a Land Rover to Mahina on the train?"

He took about five seconds to look at me to be certain I was serious and then settled into his business mode. "It's done all the time," he told me. "But I don't like the train. It never runs on time and it smells."

"Given those objections, do you think it would be worth the savings of wear on the truck and the cost in gas and maintenance? And time savings?"

"It's possible."

"Please look into this for me, Mammadu. Don't forget we're crossing the border into Mali and getting off in Mahina. I need to know how much it will cost to transport the truck to Mahina and the paperwork and logistics requirements."

Mammadu chuckled. "We will only have to worry about Dakar and getting the Rover onto the train. They will never ask us for anything except a few dollars in Mahina."

Of that I was fairly certain, but Mammadu's confirmation allowed me to think mainly of getting the Rover to the train station, loading it onto the train with nearly all of our gear, and making sure none if it was stolen. Did Mammadu think that someone would need to ride in the truck to prevent theft? Yes, it would be necessary and so he volunteered for the job.

"Thank you, my friend, but I need you here for a while, to take care of business while I take these first-timers out into the bush."

"No, Barbu, you need me with you."

"No, really, I need you here in Dakar. You will need to make sure the inventory list is correct, and to test anything we'll need when we are out for two or three months at a time. Test the fire extinguishers, the tire repair kits, the tools, the camping stoves, the radios. I will need you to inspect every piece of this inventory personally. There is no one better for this work."

"Barbu, most anyone can inspect equipment. I'm needed in the bush, where you will meet hunters who only speak Malinke, or you will need someone to drive all day and not ever get tired."

Mammadu played to his considerable strengths, language, and stamina. Nevertheless, I had no choice and needed someone I could trust to complete the critical items back at headquarters.

"Who will repair the tires or change the oil?"

His arguments for going on the expedition were degenerating. He and I had repaired many a vehicle and twice as many tires together, mostly Peugeots, but also the occasional Volvo truck and, of course, Land Rovers. He knew this was not a reason for him to come with us.

"I must travel with the scientists," I said. "For both of us to go in one truck is not the right decision. Soon we will be traveling with four trucks and you will lead us. But until then, you must complete the work here. That is your job and your duty."

Mammadu began to sulk ever so slightly. He was silent, unable to give up his desire to be in the field while knowing that I was not going to change my mind. "As you say, Barbu."

"Now please get us the information about putting the Land Rover on the train."

I dispatched him in one of the gleaming new trucks, and he seemed, if not content, resigned and focused as he got behind the wheel of a vehicle with which he had an intimate relationship.

Who can say who their true friends are until they have been in life-threatening situations together? Mammadu and I had confronted thieving government officials, corrupt police, poachers, locust clouds lasting two hours, and border crossings lasting days. We'd had our shouting matches and our fallouts. Yet there was no man in all of West Africa or anywhere that I would rather have working with me as we went into the unknown.

5. Getting Started Is the First Test

The train to Mali is supposed to leave at 7:00 a.m. It never does. But we four Americans were there, ready to go, at 4:45 a.m. with our Land Rover packed to the gills, our paperwork in hand, second in line behind a vegetable transport truck that had come over from the port. It had to be going all the way to Bamako since there was no other town large enough between the two capitals to have a community willing to pay top prices for South American peppers or US cauliflower.

When our turn came to board at slightly after six, I drove the Land Rover up two steel-mesh ramparts and parked the Rover as directed by a uniformed Senegalese. We used the chained hooks to connect to the Rover's undercarriage. Once this flatbed had its full complement of vehicles, it would be moved into the last section of the train. Not one to assume this would all go exactly as it was supposed to, I stayed to watch two other trucks behind us load. Only when the signalman waved the utility diesel engine to move the flatbed to its place at the rear of the train did I actually believe we and our Land Rover would be traveling together.

My three charges had been ready to go at four in the morning. I joined them on the passenger loading platform. It turned out that Broca had three years of field study in India and had many train travel stories that rivaled any we had heard about West Africa. Mueller stood stoically in line without interacting with anyone. And while I was aware that he had similar developing world travel experiences, he decided to keep those stories to himself. I was grateful.

When passenger loading was announced, we were lifted along in a wave of other business travelers. We picked out four seats in the business car and stowed our personal luggage in the racks above. I excused myself in order to return to the vehicle flatbed and make sure it was attached to the rest of the train. When I got to the end of the business class car, the door to the next car was locked. I was able to get off the train and walk down past the four "sardine class" cars, to the flatbed.

Railway safety in Europe, Japan, and the United States is understood and respected everywhere one travels. People generally obey signs, sit where required, and pay for their ride. People taking the train from Dakar to Bamako are often 0 for 3 in these categories. This fact could, in part, account for the hazardous overcrowding of the railcars in both passenger and cargo cars. Arriving back at the flatbed on which our Land Rover was secured, along with the vegetable transport and other freight trucks, I found at least twenty "passengers" sitting on the hood and the roof of the Land Rover, as well as on the edge of the flatbed itself. It was thirty minutes before our scheduled departure time. I climbed onto the flatbed and told the freeloaders they could not ride anywhere on the truck. There was plenty of room on the flatbed itself. They paid as much attention to me as would crows around a carcass. It took three tries, each louder and more gesticulating than the last. The recumbent young man on the spare tire moved almost too slow to be deliberate. With perseverance buoyed by indignation, I cleared the Land Rover of the travel urchins. Were I to have left at that point, it would simply have been like chasing away the aforementioned crows. To emphasize my commitment, I unlocked the driver's side door and hopped in. As I did this, to my amazement, a conductor appeared, walking along the ground next to the car and carrying a stick akin to a long Billy club. He began chasing away the hitchhikers. As the vagabonds scattered, he called to me and asked me to please take my seat in the club car. He never questioned that I was a passenger, nor where I belonged.

Sharply at 8:15 a.m. the train pulled out of Dakar station, a mere hour and fifteen minutes late. Our first scheduled stop was only twenty minutes away at the town of Rufisque, whose claim to fame is the largest cement manufacturing plant in West Africa. Before dozing off I had noticed bushy-tailed Broca studying a small map of the area of Mali. Stedman was intently engaged with a pencil, writing in the margins of some manual he was reviewing.

When the train stopped in Rufisque, I decided to check out our equipment. I got off the train and walked down the siding, then climbed aboard the flatbed. Gazing back up the length of the train I remarked on the old rust-brown train-cars sitting each with a different tilt to one side or another, joined together as if they were toys from different kits. They were lined with broken windows, peeling clapboard, and dented roofs. Before I verified the stanchions holding down the Land Rover, I decided to visit the first passenger car attached to the flatbed. I estimated at least one hundred people in a car designed for half that number. Chickens and ducks were stuffed in the overhead compartments. Children were sleeping two abreast in the aisle. Through the rear I encountered three gentlemen hovered over a small charcoal burner, making tea. I turned and went back to inspect the Land Rover.

On the flatbed all seemed as it should. I sat down on the railcar's edge to take in the scene and get some fresh morning air into my lungs.

The view facing me was that of the cement factory, apparently in full production, spewing steam and particulates from four giant smokestacks. On the other side of the tracks, a landfill was giving off a stench you could walk on. I decided not to spend any more time outside, particularly when I could, hopefully, be sleeping in the business class car. Then it struck me. Where was the Rufisque rail station? I couldn't see it from the flatbed, so I climbed off and looked down the tracks, past the engines. No train station on this side. I scrambled over onto the other side and scanned the forward vista ... with the same result. We had apparently stopped far short of our first destination, which was only 30 kilometers from our start.

Glancing over at the landfill I noticed it was covered with an undulating blanket of thousands of mottled seagulls. They constantly bickered and poached from one another, diving like kamikazes, only to pull up at the last second. They formed instantaneous hierarchies of ownership around a piece of spoiled meat or fish, making the young and the infirmed fend for themselves. Darwin's natural world seemed sadly congruous with the waste of the city. I could only marvel at the survival gene that allowed them to thrive in such decay.

Having alerted the team leaders to our current situation, I tracked down a conductor who informed me that one of the two engines had broken down. He offered no additional information on the breakdown. I considered the possibilities around the repair of the train like I did the alternative strategies for our travel. The only choice was to sit tight, relax, drink bottled water, and let the situation work itself through. I've made better decisions.

Though we frequently moved outside the railcar for short periods, we had no understanding of how long it would be until the breakdown was resolved. Staying put in our seats seemed the best course. As the hours lumbered on, the problem soon became not simply discomfort from the heat and humidity, but hallucination. With flies descending through the open windows, there was a constant din of buzzing, swatting, grumbling, moaning. Every one of us in the business class car constantly adjusted our semi-recumbent bodies in vain attempts to get comfortable. Our sweat was an adhesive to the ancient leather seats.

Dr. Stedman rose zombielike from his seat and began lashing out at the flies, then punching and kicking at much larger villains that only he could see. Perhaps he was lashing out at fate itself. Had that been the case, I would have advised the doctor to save his strength. We were, after all, only at the beginning of a journey, at the very beginning of a two-year project. Without getting out of my seat I reached over and grabbed his shirttail to bring him back to the here and now. At first he swatted at my arm, and then looked down to see my grip and reproachful stare. I signaled with my eyes for him to retake his seat, which he did without protest. The flies were a terrible nuisance, but it could get worse. Night would fall in a few hours and the flies would be replaced soon with West Africa's greatest nemesis, mosquitoes.

I hate mosquitoes. Africa has over nine hundred species of mosquitoes, nearly all of which carry some nasty, blood-loving disease that emerged at the dawn of time and continues to prey on new life. Though few of the microbic hell-raisers traveling in mosquito bellies are harmful to people, West Africa has nearly all of them. King of these is malaria; yellow fever is a close second. The good news for us was that we were taking anti-malaria medicine and had inoculations against yellow fever. We had no inoculations against the mosquitoes themselves, however. It occurred to me that if we did not start moving in another hour, I would have to unpack at least two mosquito nets so that we could hang one on each side of the aisle. I mentioned this to my seatmate, Alan Broca.

"Don't wait," was his advice. "We could use them now for the flies."

Of course! I dragged my butt out of the sticky seat and hurried back to the Land Rover to fetch four mosquito nets of the six I had packed. I passed them out, advising my companions that it might be better to use one for the two seats since the more taut it could be stretched, the more likely the mosquitoes could be kept at a distance. Broca and I managed to rig the net on the overhead rack and attached it to one arm of my aisle seat, creating a tenting effect. This arrangement restricted our movement, yet would most definitely keep the mosquitoes at bay. Stedman and Mueller did not share our good fortune.

I asked to help, but Stedman and Mueller assured me my intervention wasn't needed. They struggled through a number of iterations that provided me, if not the groggy Broca, no small amount of theater. As the net collapsed around them or as they both pulled in opposite directions, other passengers sat up to take in their performance.

Much as I wanted this slapstick to continue, it dawned on me that Herr Mueller might be more comfortable by himself in the Land

Rover, which was certainly not guarded by a conductor to prohibit him from riding inside. I made the suggestion to him.

Stedman exhaled noticeably when Mueller said, "You might have a decent idea there, Byrnes. I'll take one of these nets and see if it makes a difference. Lee, will you be OK here, dealing with this by yourself, or do you want to try the Land Rover?"

"I think I'll give this another try here, Siegfried. It might make a difference with just one of us."

I slipped out from underneath the net and handed Mueller the keys to the Rover. Then I offered to give him a hand.

"I'll be fine, Byrnes," he informed me. "If I have any problems, I'll come back and get you."

My concern was not only his well-being (which, liking the man or not, was my job), but also his care of the Rover keys. I reminded him to be careful as he was walking off to the flatbed, and he assured me, without turning around, with a simple wave of his left arm jingling the keys high on his forefinger in mock acknowledgment of his responsibility. He was a piece of work, Herr Mueller was.

I awoke, after some time of fitful sleep, next to Broca. The light slowly faded to gray and to black. I decided I would check up on Herr Mueller.

I crawled from underneath the net, descended the train, and walked alongside the passenger cars. It was pitch dark. The lights of the cement factory were clear in the distance, as was the pale glow in the sky in the direction of Dakar. Stench of the landfill was as strong as earlier, but the wind had ceased and the night's resulting calm felt peaceful.

I made my way along the track bed, stopping to look up two or three times to take in the palette of stars that shimmered with its own life in the black Sahelian night. Even through the gauze of humidity foretelling the rains, I could see the Milky Way arching across the sky. I stumbled more than once as I kept my neck craned upward, hoping to see a meteor or some celestial event that would mark this time and place—to give some out-of-world significance to this otherwise meaningless excursion.

Arriving at the flatbed, I climbed onto the platform and heard muffled curses coming from inside the Land Rover. It rocked, then stopped as the hulking Herr Mueller continued to adjust his sleeping position. I could faintly make out the occasional flash of white mosquito netting thrown against the window. I hoped he had remembered where he put the keys.

Back inside business class, Stedman had figured out his mosquito net and rested against the window, arms folded on his chest and legs bent up on Mueller's seat. Broca was actually snoring, he, too, leaning against the window. Again creeping under the netting into my seat, I took a nearly fetal position and slept.

Jarred awake by what must surely have been an earthquake, I thrashed at the netting down around my face before any recollection of where I was could inform my reaction. It was still black outside, but quickly I understood: the train was moving. Others were jolted awake as well, as we rolled steadily, gaining speed and creating a welcome breeze through the open windows. I looked outside at the sky for an indication of the time. Eastward, away from the cement factory and away from Dakar, there was a hint of light on the horizon. Daylight was near.

After about five minutes the train began to slow down, and I thought our restart had been too good to be true. But I was mistaken. We were simply making our scheduled stop in the city of Rufisque, a mere twenty-two hours late.

The remainder of the voyage by train was remarkably uneventful. We made two additional stops in Senegal and one in Mali, before we reached Mahina, fourteen hours after leaving Rufisque. Mahina isn't much more than a train stop. It has two paved roads and, unlike the cities and areas we had passed through, Mahina had the shroud of the rain forest. Dense green trees lined the dirt streets and the compounds of shopkeepers or fenced yards. Most buildings were constructed of cinder block and plaster, with corrugated steel roofs. There were also the homes and lodges with mud brick walls and dark thatched roofs. The humidity was thick and in my bones I could feel the rains coming.

Our train crew hooked up the ramparts to off-load our vehicles.

I asked Herr Mueller, "Would you like to drive?"

He looked at me as if I had asked him to jump off a building. "Not on your life, Byrnes. I've already spent more time in that damn truck than I ever wanted to."

"Then I'd consider it a favor if you gave me the keys so that I can."

Now he understood the reason for my question and fumbled in his trouser pockets just long enough to make me nervous. He pulled them out and handed them to me.

I backed the Land Rover down and parked in the dirt staging area. The three scientists, looking a bit ragged, trudged over to the truck, bags slung over their shoulders not unlike hitchhiking college students. Before I could start searching for my maps and other information about Mahina, the young train conductor came over and asked me to please park farther down the staging area so the next truck could get off. To my amazement, the Unimog carrying the fresh vegetables from the port of Dakar rolled speedily off the flatbed and, without bothering to park, sped away, kicking up a cloud of dust and disappearing into the jungle tableau—my preconceptions again obliterated.

Dusk was settling. We agreed to set up our camp right there on the railroad staging area, at the far end that bordered the forest. Our first test as a team had arrived. After repositioning the Rover and climbing up the back on the three ladder rungs we had installed, I untied our four-person tent and started to let it down to see who would help.

Broca stepped away from the group first and grabbed the end of the bundle. As he began to understand the weight of the tent, he yelped, "Siegfried, give us a hand here!"

Mueller shrugged and moved too slowly to prevent the tent from overwhelming Broca. It fell to the ground with a thud.

"Jesus Christ, Siegfried! How about a little more pitching in, huh!" Broca wasn't happy.

Mueller yelled back, "You should have waited, Alan!" He picked up the opposite end of the tent from Broca and stood there. "Well?"

I intervened, telling them where the tent needed to go and giving directions as I unpacked the green monster. This was *my* expertise. Learning from the brief dustup, I gave them each separate jobs: stake assembly, peg placement, guylines, etcetera.

"Gentlemen, it's just us for the next three weeks. Let's please keep it calm and work together, OK?"

It was possible that group interest overcame individual annoyance. We managed to erect our sleeping quarters and set up our cots and the infamous mosquito nets with coordination and without further argument.

I offered to cook us a meal of freeze-dried Texas chili, served with two-day-old baguettes and a bottle of Algerian wine called Valpierre that I had stashed into the food trunk. There were plenty of oranges, mangoes, and guavas, and I promised them we would scout out Mahina first thing in the morning for fresh bread and any other provisions they thought might be useful.

Mahina, it turns out, was scouting us. It wasn't hard to see the four silhouettes making their way over to us, our camp lights providing more illumination than the few shop lights glowing from town. Two of the men wore knit caps and one a baseball cap. The fourth and tallest was hat-less and hairless. He walked into our camp area while the three others remained a few paces outside.

"Inni tchay." I greeted him in Malinke, which made him smile.

"My name is Soula Swaray. I'm the chief of police for Mahina."

I noticed he was dressed in what must pass for a uniform here. Swaray had on a dark blue or black jumpsuit with his name above the right top pocket. In daylight I would easily have mistaken him for an auto mechanic. His minions may have been similarly dressed, but for all I could make out in the dark, they could have been in black tutus. Their only discernable features were their vacant eyes.

I held out my hand. "Pleased to meet you, Captain Swaray," I said, assuming a title for him that wouldn't offend. "My name is Victor Byrnes. My colleagues and I are on a research mission from your government."

He shook my extended hand. "I see," he said. "And has my government given you rights to camp wherever you want?"

Our first shakedown was in progress.

"Yes, in fact they have," I said without revealing, I hoped, the steady increase in my pulse. "Here are their orders."

I turned briefly to get the OEUFS authorization papers from my travel bag. With only our kerosene lantern to help him read the papers in the near dark, he glanced up at me a few times. There was no specific mention of our camping wherever it suited us, of course. But there was sufficient language granting things like travel privileges, freedom from customs, and other expansive rights that I had enough to argue our position into the next morning.

"We presumed this lot to be government property since it is part of the rail yard. This is government property, isn't it?" I knew it was. All the land in Mali was government property unless it was specifically granted under a tight and very rare gifting.

"It is not as simple as that," Swaray said. "This is not a permit to camp here, it is only a notification that you will be working here."

We danced like this for a good ten minutes. Swaray was getting frustrated but he wasn't going to leave empty-handed in front of his men. I had an idea. I raced back to the kitchen trunk and grabbed six apples. These were rare in this area and very prized. I asked Swaray if he would take these as a show of good faith. Without a smile he took the apples from me and tossed one to each of the three men behind him. Not one of them saw it coming in the dark and the apples fell on the ground. Swaray chuckled.

Once his men had retrieved their prize, Swaray stared at me for a few moments. "You should stop by my office tomorrow morning, Mr. Byrnes. Are you planning to be long in Mahina?"

"Just long enough to do some simple soil and water tests," I lied. "Then we will be traveling down to Manantali. Then back to Senegal."

"Ah, yes, Manantali, the mythical dam. Please tell my government they have studied this too long already. It is time to build the dam. Be sure to come by my office tomorrow."

He flipped his apple in the air, caught it, and took a large bite. Turning to the troopers he gestured to them to return to wherever they had come from.

"Where is your office?" I asked as he strode away.

"Ask anyone," he said. "They will point you the way."

The scientists hadn't moved a muscle among them. Lee Stedman spoke some French and probably understood much of the encounter. But Broca and Mueller could only surmise what occurred in the little play they had witnessed.

"I'm not that fond of apples anyway," Stedman said.

I explained the gist of the encounter, including that we would be making a visit to our new friend, the chief of police. Mueller grunted his understanding and Broca wanted to know if I thought Swaray was dangerous.

"Not to us." I worked it out in my mind as I spoke. "He's probably more dangerous to the government of Mali." I recalled his cynicism—so easily displayed to foreigners. That was enough information for Broca to abandon any further worry and start rummaging around one of the food trunks for a snack. I didn't quite share his peace of mind.

6. The Road to Manantali

Sunrise came well after the roosters crowed. The vehicle fumes and the clank of rail work awoke us far earlier than we'd intended. But waking again at 4:30 a.m. seemed now routine—even if none of us actually arose from our cots until six.

Breakfast conversation centered on our route to Manantali. We finished our meal, broke camp, and managed to pack the Land Rover as efficiently as we had in Dakar, perhaps more so.

We headed into Mahina for additional provisions and to visit Chief Swaray. The constable was easy to locate. Mahina has one main street that had been paved once upon a time but now was a wreck of dirt, rocks, and holes. On either side of us were dark cinder-block buildings saturated with moss and mold. Round black trucks of Russian or Chinese manufacture rumbled by, carrying cement, wood, and charcoal.

In our effort to locate a store to find something useable for our journey, we passed the police station, distinguished from the other buildings for its chain-link fence topped with barbed wire and a sign over a wooden porch: GENDARMERIE. Four men in blue jumpsuits were sitting on the porch, with the same number of young men standing close by on the ground. I pulled the Land Rover into a space that may have been for parking, outside of the fence, and asked Stedman if he wanted to accompany me. He agreed and then asked Broca and Mueller to do a town reconnaissance. Mueller snarled something about an errand boy. His shoulders slouched and he shuffled to catch up to Broca, who had practically leapt out of the Rover, rubbing his hands eagerly.

Stedman and I walked through the gate to pay our respects to Captain Swaray. As we came up the porch stairway, the uniformed men watched our approach without moving their heads. I asked if our host was available. One dour young man stood and opened the front door, then signaled for us to proceed.

Through a room strewn with plastic chairs, benches, file cabinets, and file folders everywhere, we entered Swaray's office. He rose, shook our hands, and gestured for us to sit.

"Tell again, please, what brings you to this forest town," he asked.

I gave him the standard lines about primary research in public health, fisheries and wildlife, hydrology and geology.

When I was finished, Swaray asked, "And what will be done with all this information you are gathering?"

"It will be used to determine if the dam should be built and what plans may be needed to help lessen any undesirable effects."

"If the dam is ever built," Swaray stated, "it would be a good thing for this area. There will be jobs for years and people from outside will spend money here. We are told there will be money to rebuild the hospital. But so far, there has been only talk from the government."

"This is a serious and important project, Captain Swaray," I told him. "Many people living in Mali, Senegal, Mauritania, and Guinea are committing time and resources to this. The dam will provide electricity and will allow cargo ships to come up the Senegal River as far as Kayes."

Mali is a land-locked country and, like all such countries, considers a port city a matter of self-preservation.

"Will this be so we can easily get goods from far away, or will it be so that our resources can more easily be taken out?"

This was another good question. Our constable was beginning to strike me as more politician than police officer.

"Both, no doubt," I said. The question wasn't what was going to happen, but rather, who would actually benefit.

"How long will you be in Manantali?" Swaray asked.

I translated for Stedman.

"Not long, perhaps three days," Stedman said. He declined to elaborate.

"Do not spend more than a week in Manantali," Swaray said. "Once the rains come, only on foot will you be able to make it back to Mahina." He rose and, in two long strides, was pointing to a map on his wall. "Take this route today and you can be in Manantali before sunset."

It was only 30 kilometers away and still early morning.

I thanked him for his advice and asked him where the road started to our destination.

He laughed slightly as he said, "At your campsite."

The three of us agreed it would be wise to check in with Swaray as soon as we returned from Manantali.

Back outside, I noted the sun had risen thoughtlessly into a cloudless sky. The air was humid. The rains would come soon. Stedman and I left the parked car to round up Broca and Mueller.

We found them a short walk away, negotiating for a case of canned pineapple juice and canisters of bottled gas, with a merchant who clearly knew he had captive buyers. I had a good idea of what a fair price would be for these commodities, but I wasn't about to spoil Mueller's fun as he refused to believe whatever price the merchant told him. The merchant, a small man with a pockmarked face and jagged yellow teeth, refused to sell his week's supply for anything less than full retail. The only language between Mueller and the merchant consisted of numbers and gestures for "Yes" and "No."

We needed to be on the road. Pulling Mueller aside for a moment, I told him why the merchant likely wasn't going to budge. I told him to make a higher offer, but slightly under the price the merchant was sticking to, and ask for a little something extra, like bread or tea or Nescafé. Mueller concluded his deal using my suggestion, and we loaded the extra provisions into the Land Rover.

The start of the route to Manantali was exactly where Swaray had indicated, assuming the footpath with two overgrown tracks on either side was the route. Broca wasn't so sure. I steered the Rover resolutely down the path, keeping the wheels on the insinuations of prior vehicles.

"How can you be sure this is the right way to Manantali?" Broca wanted to know.

"The combination of our compass direction," I replied, "the fact that this is the only path remotely resembling a road from this point—and the green sign reading: MANANTALI, 30 KM. PLEASE DRIVE WITH CARE."

"Very funny, Byrnes."

"Think of it this way, Alan. Wherever we end up is bound to be an interesting area for you to scout. There are plenty of reptiles, birds, insects, and mammals everywhere." I had no notion if this was true or not. I was certain, however, we were on the right ... trail.

"That's fine for the animal scientist," Mueller said, "but I have to be at the dam site."

"Gentlemen, do you recall the bridge we crossed over while on the train?" I asked. Of course they had. "That bridge crossed the Bakoye River." Exactly where we needed to be.

Broca got it. "Then make sure we follow the river and we'll be fine. We're in grid 122 for the entire journey."

* * *

Our road became increasingly challenging. Large rocks jutted up on either side and many directly in front of us. I actually shifted into third gear while we were still within a kilometer of Mahina, but now I was alternating between second and first gears. My travel companions sat mute, save for the occasional grunt as we bumped around.

Our first river ford was at the edge of a cliff, looking into a 50-degree drop for about 10 feet. The path seemed unobstructed, so I told everyone to hold on as we went over the edge, down, and into the river. With the low flow just before the return of the rains, we easily crossed the shallow span of water. I crossed it a bit too fast, however, and we jolted hard up and down twice in rapid succession. On the other side we had nearly the same wall to climb up as we had run down. Fearful of slowing down and not making it over the top, I pressed the accelerator, and we became airborne as we breached the top. Again we came down hard, bouncing twice. I decided to stop and inspect every inch of the Rover, giving the three scientists a chance to stretch and take stock of where they were. We had been traveling for a mere ninety minutes.

"Jesus H. Christ, Byrnes! That was terrible!" said Mueller.

"A little respect for these old bones, please, Victor," came from Stedman.

Broca looked at me and shook his head. "You have to do better, Byrnes. I need to take an internal organ inventory!"

Once out of the truck, we were attacked by a cloud of flies. Not the black housefly types we were used to and expecting, but flies about the size of a finger digit. And these flies weren't content to land and lap up surface residue on our skin. These flies wanted a blood meal. These were tsetse flies.

When I was a child and heard of sleeping sickness delivered by the tsetse fly, I envisioned an insect rather like a gnat: small, and spreading disease in a furtive, painless bite. It turns out that the tsetse fly has mouth parts like a mine borer, which can deliver a bite through your blue jeans deep enough to draw blood. Our yelps were likely heard for miles up and down the river. Fortunately for us, human sleeping sickness was extremely rare in this area. But the disease these tsetse flies did carry, equine trypanosomiasis, was the reason no horses or donkeys were used as transport.

I completed my inspection while the beasts buzzed like high-voltage static. Our Rover was in good shape, but I noticed a crack already in the upgraded roof rack that held our tent, camp tables, and camp chairs. I'd have to drive more carefully *and* more slowly. We hurried back into the vehicle and continued on our way.

We encountered no more steep ravines, but the road worsened overall. Clearly, the path hadn't been used by a motorized vehicle in more than a year. A few times I had to stop, consult the map and compass, as well as scout out ahead to assure myself we were on the path toward our goal. My traveling companions didn't say much now; they seemed to struggle to stay hydrated in the heat and keep the insects at bay.

As I was completing my road assessment during the third stop, folding the map on the hood of the Rover, I looked toward the river. Seven very hairy heads peered out from the foliage. Baboons. Baboons are not the nicest of creatures. They are strong, occasionally aggressive monkeys with very large canine teeth which they display often to warn or injure rivals and other enemies. These baboons were only observing. We stared at each other for a few seconds.

Then I got into the car and fired up the engine. As I did, the baboons slowly came forward and simply crossed in front of us. Except they weren't only seven. There were at least two hundred of them. Little ones carried on the backs of their mothers jumped from one adult to the next. The entire troop climbed right over our vehicle, not stopping to inspect, handle, or steal anything packed on the roof. They simply traveled over us as if the Land Rover was an odd-shaped boulder.

Broca was fascinated, and Mueller asked, "What should we do?"

"Nothing, I think. Right, Alan?" We had reached the realm where one of the scientists had some useful expertise.

"I'm not a simian expert, but it seems a good idea to just let them continue on their way. They aren't likely to threaten us. We probably appear too different from anything they know to really consider us threatening." Broca gave the passing troop his full attention.

"Baboons are hunted pretty relentlessly. They are kept as …"— Broca was searching for the word—"slaves, I guess, would be the best description. They are smart animals, but not predisposed to much training, particularly the coercive, violent kind they would likely get from local captors. I think we're just novel enough to get a pass from them."

Broca never took his eyes off the primates. They made little noise on their way to a destination deeper into the woods. As they thinned out and the stragglers disappeared into the bush, one decided to give us a more thorough inspection. He jumped onto the hood of the car and parked his pink butt right on the windshield. We all laughed. I motioned to Broca that I was going to honk the horn, silently asking him if he thought it was a good idea. Broca shrugged, distancing himself from my decision.

Wanting to get on the way without this extra passenger, I leaned on the horn. Our guest shot up into the air as if I had stuck him with a pin. He came down with a thud onto the hood and, baring his battle teeth, he started a loud rhythmic barking. Then he started to jump up and down on the hood, to the point of shaking the vehicle from side to side. Suddenly, three other baboons were barking on the ground on both sides of the Rover. One climbed up the side and began jumping on top of our roof-stowed gear. This went on for about thirty seconds, but seemed much longer. Then they stopped and ran away to follow their community into the jungle.

I got out again to inspect, hearing from Stedman as I did, "Are you sure that's wise, Victor?"

Broca said it was fine, so long as there were no tsetse flies. There weren't. The young stragglers had scampered off, clearly wanting to catch up with the rest of their group. Getting up onto the roof, I discovered the only damage was two piles of baboon shit. Broca got out and looked at the stinking piles curiously, and concluded it was a sign of their dominance and displeasure of our fouling their space. I grabbed a stick to wipe the fresh crap off our belongings. We would wash them before we unloaded and set up camp. For now, getting to that site was more important than completing the cleanup. I fired up the engine and got us back on our way.

For the next four hours the trip was more of the same, minus the baboons. I got out the map when we stopped for lunch. In five hours we had traveled slightly over 20 km. Someone on foot could have passed us. On the bright side, we were less than three hours away from our destination. We stopped for a lunch of sorts.

After eating my peanut butter and baguette, I noticed Stedman sitting on the back bumper of the Land Rover, an unopened can of pineapple juice at his side, fanning himself with a paperback and staring blankly into the forest. His checked shirt was drenched with perspiration, his face bright red. I grabbed a bottle of water from our store at the back of the Rover and handed it to him.

"Drink, Lee," I commanded. He cocked his head to look at me blankly. "This will keep you hydrated better than the sugar water in the can." I pointed to his juice.

"Of course," he said breathlessly, and reached for the water bottle.

I left Stedman and walked around to see Mueller and Broca poring over the map, pointing at various coordinates and deciding where to venture first thing in the morning. I herded them all together for our final push south.

Until now, the terrain had been rocky, overgrown with dense grasses, bamboo-like shrubs, trees with vines dangling like ropes, and relatively flat. That changed abruptly. Our path came through a meadow, then stopped and utterly disappeared in front of a plateau that rose vertically about the length of a football field straight up.

"Oh shit," I declared.

"You have a gift for understatement," Broca said as he craned his neck trying to see the top of the plateau.

We had both recalled the topology lines on the map but were really not prepared to encounter this mass of earth rising like a fortress.

"Do you see the road?" Mueller asked.

"I do not, but I do have an idea. Let's fan out in both directions along the bottom here. Siegfried, you and Alan take the east and Lee and I will walk west. You're looking for any indication of the road, obviously, and a potential way through this plateau. Walk no more than fifteen minutes, then come back."

The foliage had thinned out considerably, unable to hold water in the volcanic iron slag that had become ground at the base of the plateau. That made it very difficult to find anything resembling a path. Stedman and I had been progressing slowly along the wall for about five minutes, when I heard a shout behind us. Mueller and Broca had found the pass through the plateau.

"Pass" was too strong a word. Our route was not a road in any sense. The only indication any vehicle had been here before was that some of the oxblood-colored rocks had been pulverized by something of considerable weight.

Back in the Land Rover we grumbled and shook, turning onto the plateau and heading steadily upward.

"This is no man-made path, Byrnes," Mueller said. "It's totally volcanic. This can't be the road we want."

"It's pretty straight so far and nothing is blocking our way," I said.

"Looks more like the plateau of *The Lost World*," Broca said. "Minus the shroud of fog."

Mueller stared out the window. "This looks like a massive primordial slab, with distinct signs of hydrologic wearing. Very fortunate for us, Byrnes."

Broca shouted, "Shut up, Siegfried, before you jinx us!"

Not soon enough.

As we made a very tight turn through a cluster of large rocks, the pass took a steep vertical climb and the Land Rover started to slip. Small stones spat out from our sputtering tires. I shifted down to first gear low four-wheel drive, and we made some progress. But the terrain continued to get steeper, to the point that our incline resembled a carnival ride to the moon. The tires slipped again. I stopped the Rover.

Though we were prepared for near vertical travel, I had hoped we wouldn't encounter it on our first trip out. On the other hand, it was probably good to practice so the team leaders would understand our limitations before the rest of their teams came out. I couldn't help thinking that if Mammadu had been driving, he would probably have kept the wheels going steadily and made it up to the flat peak without incident. Silently cursing my lack of skill (or was it courage?), I got out a sledgehammer, along with a steel pinion a meter in length, and headed up the incline on foot.

Mueller followed. "You're going to winch up," he observed.

"Ah-huh," I answered.

We had to find an area where the Rover could regain the traction to complete the trek upward. I asked Mueller to go back to the Rover and lift the secure lever on the front-mounted winch, and then bring the line to me. Although he looked at me puzzled, he eventually understood. He managed to unlock the winch cable and bring it up to my position. The line reached my spot easily, so I looked to see if there was a place farther up that gave us a better chance for success.

"Probably not," I mused out loud, confusing Mueller.

I explained my thinking, and we agreed the key was to establish a spot where we could pound the iron pinion deep enough into the ground to sustain the pull of the loaded Land Rover. This took three tries to locate. I swung the mallet at half strength for the first three blows as Mueller warily held the stake in place. After about fifteen minutes, we managed to imbed the stanchion deep into the ground so that only the grommet eye of the top was showing. Sweating like a faucet, I began to wonder how the hell I was going to get it out! I decided to worry about that later. I connected the winch line to the stanchion and then rambled down to the Rover. We unloaded the heaviest pieces of gear from the roof rack—the tent and the camp locker—and the two jerricans of fuel on the back. I directed the three to move up the slope. Using the winch controls, I pulled the line taut and released the Land Rover handbrake.

Instead of just going up the mountain as the winch pulled the line in, the Rover also slid sideways. Before I could take my thumb off the "Wind" button, the Rover moved like a slow pendulum off the side of the pass and started to dangle along the edge. I was speechless and, for the first time, frightened.

I heard shouts of "Whoa! Whoa!" above me from my companions.

But there was only one thing to do: keep pulling the Rover up. Now the Rover was being pulled up a far steeper path where it had almost no purchase against the rocky plateau. When I stopped the winch and let the Rover stabilize, it was clear our transport and contents were in real jeopardy. I motioned for Mueller and Broca to come down to me.

"You see the problem here, ya?" Mueller asked.

"Yeah, *we* sure do," I emphasized. We were, after all, in this together.

"Do you know what you're doing here, Byrnes?"

I expected this from Mueller, but it came from Stedman. Hell no, I had never been in this situation before! I was completely winging it. That may be great when you're trying to keep a college professor from knowing you had not read any of the last two assignments, but this was ... how should I put it ... more serious. But if I were to admit this and relinquish control to the group, my job was effectively over. And I had no intention of letting that happen, having banked some hard-earned credibility up to this point.

Without answering his question, I began simply to direct. "Alan, you take the winch control and keep it at this speed."

I showed him the control and where I wanted it.

"Siegfried, you and I are going over to that outcropping, and as the Land Rover moves when Alan begins to wind it up, we're going to push it as hard as we can so that the Rover regains a foothold on the road."

In unison, Stedman and Broca turned their heads and looked at the outcropping next to the Rover.

"One thing is certain," Broca said, "if we don't get it back onto the shallow incline, once we release it from the stanchion it will fall like stone for about 20 meters."

"No kidding." I heaved with exasperation. "We're not going to release it from the stanchion until we're sure it is solid."

Stedman still wanted some verbal assurance. "Do you think this will work, Victor?" Without any alternative ideas of his own, Stedman's tone had turned deferential.

I took another calculated risk. "Good question, Lee. What do you think, Siegfried?"

"To be honest, Byrnes, I'm not keen trying to push a heavy vehicle while stretched out on that spit of rock." He gestured toward the outcropping. "But I think it is probably what we have to do to get back on track."

Ineloquent but right.

"OK then, let's get to it," I said, mustering my courage.

I dispatched Stedman to monitor the anchored stanchion. Mueller and I slowly made our way to the craggy escarpment next to which the Rover hovered. The two of us climbed slowly, grabbing purchase on sharp-edged juts and wedging ourselves between the Rover and the rocks. I found a place to plant my feet, then turned around and placed both my hands on the Land Rover passenger-side front door. Siegfried did the same just below me. I called to Broca to start the winch, and as he did, Siegfried and I pushed hard as we could to direct the Rover onto solid footing. Slowly the Rover moved both up and sideways, back onto the pass.

After about a minute we were only partially successful. As the Rover increasingly attained the solid footing we needed, it became more and more difficult to move sideways. I yelled to Broca to stop the winch. The Rover was no longer dangling like a free weight, but was still riding on an incline that could cause it to slip back at any time.

The next try, we had to use a combination of the winch and turning the wheels. I asked Stedman how the stanchion was holding.

"Looks good," he yelled over. "Vibrating but holding steady."

Though we all sighed with some relief, we knew we could not take it for granted. With continued vibration the stanchion would eventually work itself loose.

Mueller and I remained stationary as we slowly took our hands off the Rover's position.

"I'm going to get into the Rover and steer it to the side as you winch it up," I said to Broca. I motioned to Mueller that we should go down to Broca's position.

"Byrnes, I'm not too sure about this idea. If that spike gives way, you and the Land Rover could end up as another debris pile down this ravine."

"I'm open to suggestions, gentlemen," I told him and Mueller in all sincerity.

Silence.

Though the Rover was steady and motionless, we all knew it was unstable. I asked Broca to increase the winch speed now and to start it up as soon as I got into the truck. Half on my hands, I spider-walked up to the driver-side door and opened it. Trying to move lightly to minimize the rocking and the potential for the Rover to move back into a pendulum, I stood in the driver-side doorway, held on to the steering wheel, and leaned my weight in the direction I was steering. I told Broca to winch away.

The Rover started to climb, eerily, almost noiselessly, without an engine noise ... just the sputtering of the stones and steady whine of the winch. I bent my knees and turned the wheel slowly to the left, onto the path. I could feel the road underneath becoming steadier. After another thirty seconds without any sense of the Rover slipping, I pulled myself into the seat. Assuring I was in the lowest gear possible, I slowly accelerated.

Stedman called out, "The stake is vibrating badly and bending. I think it's coming out!"

I could see the winch line vibrating as well. Crap!

Though I desperately wanted to gun the engine, I knew if I gave it too much gas I'd lose traction again. I gave the Rover a little bit of gas and eased off the clutch. The Rover started to increase the speed of the climb, adding the incremental engine power to that of the winch. I turned the wheel harder to the left now, trying to position the Rover almost sideways along the mountain. It was working. The winch line went slack as the Rover was climbing and moving on its own faster than the winch was pulling. I yelled for Broca to stop and I pressed slowly on the accelerator. Gravel spat out from underneath, and my heart skipped. Yet the Rover grabbed hold of the path as I steered back to the right.

Stedman, still watching the status of the stanchion, had to jump out of my way as I passed him, maintaining movement until I had gone just far enough not to overdrive the length of the winch line. Or so I'd hoped. I stopped like I hit a wall when the winch line went taut again and yanked the Rover to the right. I had nearly reached the flattened area above the stanchion. Feeling a small sense of triumph, I pulled up the brake, turned off the engine, and jumped out of the car.

"Release the winch line. Red button on the right," I yelled down to Broca, who had been walking up steadily to keep the remote-control cable in reach. As I watched the winch line go slack and the Rover remain stationary, I let out a breath I must have been holding for an hour.

"How's it going?" Mueller wanted to know.

"Seems like we're out of danger for now," Stedman told him.

"Let's get the gear," Broca reminded us.

Mueller lumbered over to meet up with Broca, who dropped the winch control and then bounded down the ledge to the off-loaded equipment. I was on my way to collect the jerricans. Broca and Mueller hoisted the tent onto their shoulders.

"My God," yelled Mueller, "what stinks so horribly!"

"Baboons' revenge," Broca muttered.

Before we started down, I had to stop at the peak of our plateau and gaze over the valley into which we would be plunging. In the distance, the view of the Manantali dam site was unmistakable. Two large buttes, higher than the plateau on which we perched, stood on either side of the Bakoye like guardians to an ancient kingdom. Off to the left we could see plumes of smoke from the fires in a small village, tiny clusters of thatched roofs barely visible. A deep green forest canopy spread out to the vast horizon, where we could see dim outlines of the Fouta Djallon mountains. All four of us got out of the Rover and took in the sight of our goal.

Stedman slapped me on the back. "Well, Byrnes, you earned your day's pay," he said.

Mueller laughed as I've never heard him. "I didn't think we'd make it. Ha-ha! No time to rest on our laurels, Byrnes."

"Let's savor this moment, shall we?" Broca offered.

We fell silent.

After a few moments I spread the map over the spare tire on the hood to confirm our location. Thinking on the challenges of the last three days, I couldn't speculate on what awaited us at the dam site.

7. A Welcome Party

Aforest path resembling the road we were on before climbing the plateau emerged as we reached the plateau's bottom. We resumed our slow and steady pace through the jungle. About 200 meters from the river's edge at the dam site, we drove into a clearing that extended to the tree-lined riverbank. I put my foot down on the accelerator. The bumps were nothing in comparison to those on the road behind us. Determined to get into fourth gear, I let the engine run out like it hadn't since we had left Dakar.

I heard a "Yippee!" from Broca, riding shotgun, and an "It's about fucking time!" from Mueller. Stedman, sitting behind me, stuck his head out the window, letting the speeding air blow his silver hair back like a sheepdog's. I pulled the Rover right up to the trees, turned it parallel to the river, and stopped.

Each of us simply wanted to soak in our arrival as we watched the powerful river flow past us. We stood like pigeons on a wire, gazing over the flowing water. Mueller walked forward and climbed down the embankment until he reached the water's edge. The bank continued to drop off steeply, so there wasn't an opportunity to walk into the river. But Broca, who was looking downriver, motioned for us to go in that direction, where a clearing sloped gently into the river and transitioned to a set of smooth volcanic rock shelves over which ran the clear waters of the Bakoye.

Soft and clear today, I thought, but in less than a month the very spot where we stood would probably be under two meters of fast brown water.

Stedman walked over to Broca and asked, "Who do you think cleared all this brush, Alan?"

This area, the size of a small city block, was matted down. All of us knew we weren't the first ones to visit and work here.

"I'll bet it was the French geologists," I guessed out loud.

A large splash got all of our attention. On the far side of the river, a group of hippopotami slid into the water. It was impossible to tell if we had startled them or if they simply were going about their watery ways. What I knew was that hippos are very intolerant of man. There are many stories of biologists or zookeepers trying to get close to a hippo in the water, only to have the beast turn on them and break their arms or back. And as mean as they are in the water, hippos are terrifying on land because they are more easily spooked. I've never asked anyone who knew for certain, but the rumor was that if a person managed to get between a land-foraging hippo and the river of its choice, the person had better be extremely fast. Otherwise it was likely the frightened hippo would trample him or her to death on its frantic race back to the river. Hippos, it turns out, kill more people in the wild than any mammal on earth. This made me think that we'd better camp away from the riverbank, closer to the forest.

"Feel free to explore, gents," I told them. "I'm going to set up camp back where we entered this clearing."

They thought I was kidding them, so I explained.

"Good call, Byrnes," Broca affirmed.

My footing with the trio was getting firmer the farther we traveled.

As I finished setting up the gas stove and was moving the food locker into a handy spot, Stedman walked over.

"Victor, it really is quite scenic along the river's edge. I understand why we should have our camp away from the river, but surely we could have dinner there." He pointed to a spot where the trees separated and opened westward across the river, holding the promise of a spectacular sunset behind the far-side mesa. It was a great idea.

When Broca and Mueller ambled up, Stedman explained his idea. Immediately the four of us set to hauling our kitchen and dining gear down to the river's edge.

Before dinner we needed to wash up. The volcanic rock jetty Broca took us to earlier was ideal. Only a foot above the waterline, the rocks extended like a platform into the river. It was serene and inviting, even though it was a bit far from the camp. Stedman pronounced the water running swift enough to not harbor the snail vectors of the dreaded bilharzia—a nasty debilitating urinary parasite. Having grabbed some sweat-free, if not entirely clean clothes, we stripped to our shorts and washed in the Bakoye. It was a great feeling. The water was cooler than any of us expected. But this was a wide and deep river, even here at the end of the dry season. I wondered if it had already rained in the mountains.

Cleansed and refreshed, the four of us settled back at the table. Though the air temperature was hotter than a San Antonio summer, we agreed that hot food was the right call. I was preempted by Mueller, who came over to the stove table and rubbed his hands as if in preparation for some work. "Let's cook up a nice juicy steak," he said earnestly.

"You're a funny man when you've just had a wash," Broca said.

"Well, Alan, after the day we've had, you can't expect us to settle for the same old thing. We had some challenges today, and now we're actually in Manantali. So let's celebrate in some way."

"Siegfried," Broca shot back, "why don't you swim across and bag us a hippo? I'll bet a little one would be pretty tender."

"I was thinking that our field leader would hunt us a wild boar or an antelope or something."

"Still waiting for my right to bear arms," I said with a shrug. "And I don't recall seeing a lot of game along the route—unless you think cooking up some baboon would be the way to celebrate."

Broca told us, "I saw some droppings of small ruminants. Duiker, maybe. Could be a tasty treat, but hard to come by because they're so small and shy."

Mueller's food locker rummaging produced a bag of freeze-dried beef stroganoff, which he raised in victory. Stedman clapped, and Mueller, instead of handing it to me to prepare, went to the stove himself and shooed me away.

"Just show me where the utensils are, Byrnes," he said.

This was a moment to savor. Having been at the brink of disaster, we were now relating like a team of equals. Mueller's playful side was new to all of us and that he manifested it in service, preparing our meal, was plain enjoyable. Stedman joined Broca, making fun of Mueller's meticulous inspection of the cooking materials. And Mueller reciprocated by dismissing their pedestrian understanding of his art. We could have been college buddies getting together for a guys' outing.

As the sun set behind the buttes of Manantali, we shared the feeling of a sensitized life and an awareness of its intensity. I brought out some kerosene lamps as we sipped our post-meal coffee. I put the lanterns at each end of the table and sat back at my place. Simultaneously, the four of us felt the same thing. Our feet were being bitten.

We reached down to scratch our feet. I was wearing sandals, and the tops of my feet and ankles were starting to burn. Stedman started to swat at something, but the poor light wasn't helping him locate exactly what was attacking. He yelped, as did Broca.

My reaction was less polite. "What the fuck …?" I screamed and jumped up.

Mueller was muttering and swearing in a low voice. Without getting out of his chair, he picked up one of his feet and put it on the table. He too had sandals on, but I couldn't see a sandal or, for that matter, a foot. What I could see was a black mass of … something. Specks of the black mass started moving up from his foot to his ankle. Ants. Mueller wiped his foot, but he succeeded only in taking off a single layer and hadn't removed the ones biting his flesh.

In the meantime, of course, we were all experiencing this intensifying burn as the ants moved from our feet to our calves. Out of our chairs now, we danced in pain and confusion in the dark. Stedman pulled a flashlight from his jacket pocket and switched it on. The ground was a shimmering black surface undulating like the back of a stretching beast. However far and in whatever direction Stedman trained his beam, the view was the same. The ground had been displaced with a devouring shroud of ants. Mueller turned over the lantern and poured out the kerosene onto the ground. He lit it. It burnt in a small area, but had no effect on the ants. They were up to our knees.

I sat on the table and lifted my legs, indicating to my comrades to do the same. With my bare hands I wiped off layer after layer of ants. When I reached my skin, I could tell that my entire lower leg had been turned into a wound. Meanwhile, the ants on my other leg were over my knee, scattered up my thigh. Broca was in worse shape. The ants were up onto his thighs like stockings, eating him as he flailed to get them off. I pulled one of his legs toward me on the table and twisted him around. I rubbed off as many ants as I could, looking over my shoulder at Stedman and Mueller, who were bordering on panic as they, too, tried to clean their legs off the little meat-eaters. Sitting on the table we at least were not being swarmed anew each time we were able to remove some ants from our legs. But each of us shivered as we stared at each other.

When we reached the point of picking off stragglers, we stopped and listened. Amidst the eeriest mechanical rhythm any of us had ever heard were the sounds of other creatures dying. Slight squeals, deep moans, and hisses pierced the night as life was sucked out of rodents, frogs, other insects, snakes, God knows what else. Stedman started to shake beyond his shivering.

At that moment Broca noticed it wasn't likely that our flimsy camping table would sustain the weight of four grown men for much longer. "We've got to get into the river," he said with utter conviction.

"You're crazy," Mueller told him. "It's five meters to the river." He grabbed Stedman's light out of his hands, then directed the beam toward the water. The black wave rolled completely to the riverbank.

"These are army ants. Though which subspecies, I have no idea," Broca stated in a calm that helped us. "This species may not have ever been studied or even discovered." He pinched a few ants between his thumb and forefinger. "These might even qualify as the smallest army ants on record."

"Alan," I asked, "what does this mean for our chances of getting to the river?"

"Nothing, really. I'm just stating what I believe about our discovery. What I also believe is that we need to make a run for it before the table gives out. Once we get into the river, we should be able to stay in it and get downstream, past the end of this swarm."

"How far would that be?" Stedman asked, having regained some body control.

"Lee, I really don't know."

I said, "We also don't know how long this will last, do we?"

"It could be an hour or two or it could be two days."

"I'll go first," I said. "I'll take the flashlight and shine it back up here when I'm in the water."

"Victor, once you make it to the water, you'll be down that embankment. You won't be able to shine the light back this way."

Broca was right again.

"OK then, you keep it steady for me to that clearing. Once I make it I'll shout back, and you can all come together with the flashlight."

The three of them looked at each other questioningly. I was starting to hyperventilate. I knew I needed to go. My pounding heart accelerated. I let myself down slowly as not to rock the already shaky table and as soon as I felt the hive beneath me, I ran straight for the clearing. Each time I put my foot down it was as though I was running on a layer of tiny raisins. The ants crunched slowly beneath my steps, and I had no idea if I was successfully running on top of them or that they were attaching to me at every footfall. Although one of the three behind me was shining the light, my body blocked it from illuminating the path directly ahead. I could only see right or left as I ran. Unable to see the approaching bank, I ran over it and fell sideways, banging my head and left arm on rock and sliding headfirst into the water.

I took a body parts inventory. Pain ran through me from my feet to my crotch, from my left wrist through my shoulder and neck. I started treading water. Nothing was broken, it seemed. But I could feel tiny creatures on my neck and in my ears. I flailed at them, slapping my neck and head. I heard Broca yell my name two, three times.

"I'm all right," I managed to call out. "Be careful of the bank. It disappears quickly."

"Are the ants covering the slope of the riverbank too?" Mueller shouted.

"I can't say, Siegfried," I replied slowly, mindful of the waning breath I was expending. "It's slippery rock, so probably not."

I could feel ants biting my upper lip and nose. I straightened my legs and let myself sink to try to touch bottom. The bank continued steeply down, enough so that it was not possible to stand at the edge. I swam out a few meters and tried again. This time I was able to touch the bottom, but my head was underwater.

Surfacing, I called out, "We'll have to swim downstream for a bit, but it shouldn't be too bad. We'll swim over to where we cleaned up."

"OK, Victor, we're on our way to you," Mueller shouted.

I heard the thud of the table turning over and then the huffing breaths of the three men.

Then, something else. Something behind me in the river, displacing a lot of water ... then, a series of deep, wet snorts. Hippos.

8. Survival of the Fittest

Stedman, Broca, and Mueller crashed down the side of the riverbank. One of them, I could not tell which, lost his footing in mid leap and tumbled down the bank into the water. Someone landed directly on top of my head and left shoulder, leaving me dazed and aching. I moved farther into the river. They were gasping when they surfaced, flailing as though they couldn't swim.

"Is everyone all right?" I asked.

Behind us were an unknown number of unfriendly and possibly frightened hippos. Mueller and Stedman gurgled some affirmative response, but I heard nothing from Broca.

"Alan? Alan, where are you?" I yelled.

Mueller started swimming toward the riverbank to find Broca. Stedman, who had fallen on top of me, was still recovering, so I left him and swam to my right to look for Broca. I continued to call out "Alan! Alan!" I heard a moan almost directly in front of me.

"Siegfried, he's over here."

Broca was huddled against the steep bank and wasn't moving. When I was close enough to touch him, I could see his breathing was very short and his eyes were closed.

"Alan, what's wrong?"

"I-I ... my chest ...." He tried to speak and breathe, but it was clearly painful for him.

Mueller and Stedman both swam over slowly.

"I think he may have broken a rib, Lee," I said, to which Broca painfully nodded.

Stedman asked, "Can you float on your back, with your arms at your sides?"

"I ... don't know, Lee. Let me see...." Broca put his head back and tried to bring his torso up, but he yelped in pain before he could complete it.

Stedman said, "Just relax your head, and we'll pull you horizontal from your shoulders."

He motioned Mueller to move along the other side of Broca. They took Broca by the armpits in one hand and sidestroked away from the bank, dragging Broca into a back float.

"Guys," I said, "we've got company on the other side of the river. Hippos. Let's try to move close to the riverbank. Remember where we bathed? That's our destination."

"Sounds good," Mueller said, spitting water.

"Alan, we're going to pull you along slowly," Stedman said. "Try to keep your head raised enough so you don't get water up your nose."

"OK. … I'm OK like this. I can kick my legs. Let's get moving."

The pain in my feet, groin, and stomach reminded me that we still had hundreds of the tiny carnivores eating us. My ears were tingling and I couldn't tell if it was the water or if the ants had made their way to my auditory canal on their way to my brain. I dove underwater and shook my head. While there I took each leg, one at a time in both hands, and moved up and down trying to mow off any straggling ants. When I came up to the surface I wiped my neck, arms, chest, face, every part of me that I could reach, hoping to drown any remaining insects I had carried into the water. I could still feel the creatures biting my face in the corners of my eyes. I suggested to Stedman that I should take Alan's shoulder for a bit and let him clean himself off. Mueller was simultaneously trying to swim, hold on to Broca, and wipe the ants off his face. Broca was trying to move his arm up to his neck, but it was clearly painful. With one hand still under his armpit, I kicked hard with my legs and took my swimming arm to brush away ants I couldn't see on Broca's neck, forehead, and cheeks. Slowly we made our way down the river in this torturous water dance.

I heard no big splashes from the other side of the river, only the occasional snorts indicating multiple hippos. It was impossible to know if they were keeping to one place, shadowing us down the river, or moving toward us. But we had no alternative. We had to make it to the ledge that jutted out into the river. Since the ledge was barren rock, I thought it unlikely to be swarming with ants. But I didn't know. We would have to see once we got there.

After about fifteen minutes of painstaking water treading and cautious swimming—not knowing what was unseeable in the river—Mueller was able to put his foot down onto a hard surface, and said, "We could be there."

We were. The sense of dread and mouth-drying fear gave way to a tiny wave of relief. The jagged edges of the iron rock were remarkably welcoming. We managed to locate a smooth area that rose as a small mound out of the water. I climbed up the mound and put both my arms under Alan's shoulders, pulling him up. Broca let out a few cries of pain, and eventually sat low and rested on his elbows.

"See any ants?" Stedman asked.

Standing firm, I rose and took in the scene. "Not so far. But I want to take a look."

A palette of a billion stars lit up the African night, bright as a moon. My eyes had adjusted to the dark, and I could see an outline of the rock ledge and where the trees began, some distance beyond. I inched toward them, aware of the sounds of my own breathing … listening for the snorts of the hippos and hearing none … listening for the wind and hearing none … listening for the other sounds and hearing the machine-like buzz of a billion ants chewing whatever they encountered.

My adrenaline spiked. Where the rock ledge stopped and the soil bank began, the din of a conquering insect civilization continued to rise. I stopped to calm myself with a few deep breaths and ventured to my left to see if the feasting bugs could be flanked. Not so. Before I could even get to the bank, I could feel the scouts on my feet and on the rock ledge. I took three steps back, hoping their chemical communication hadn't noted a meal along the iron rock. Moving a little faster, I returned to the spot where my colleagues were resting.

"We may be safe here, but only here, from what I can scout out. The ants have moved out this way. How far along the bank I can't tell, but they're farther down the river than we are."

"Guess we stay put for a while," Alan said.

No one argued.

"We should get out of the river and wring out our clothes to dry off," Stedman said. "I don't think hypothermia is likely, but the drier we are, the more comfortable we'll be."

"Comfortable" being highly relative this night.

Suddenly a loud, snorting breach in the river's surface boiled up behind Stedman, who was climbing out of the water. Then came a loud, low roar like a gurgling diesel engine. A hippo was no more than a man's length away, heading toward the ledge. In the starlight its head shone like a wet leather sofa. Broca yelled. Stedman grabbed Mueller by the arm. I ran up behind Broca, bruising my feet, and yanked him back by his shoulders. His weight and momentum overcame my balance and I fell backward with a thump, onto the ledge.

I looked back to the river and the hippo was gone. Had he just wanted to scare us? Good work! Stedman and Mueller struggled to their feet.

"Alan! Is that hippo going to follow us?" I asked.

"Probably not," he said through clenched teeth.

We stood up together while he said, "But let's not take the chance. And here I was, really looking forward to seeing the beasts close up."

"Tomorrow, Alan. We'll figure this out after we get some sleep," I said, trying to believe my own words.

Broca put his hand around my back, and I put my arm around him as we started to follow Mueller and Stedman to the forest's edge.

Broca stopped. "You're bleeding, Victor." He unwrapped his arm from my waist and smelled his arm. "We should stop here and collect ourselves a bit."

"Yeah, good idea. Let's hold up a second and pull ourselves together."

Stedman and Mueller had already halted.

"How badly are we hurt?" Stedman asked.

Broca could walk, but couldn't move his upper body much. Stedman and Mueller had abrasions on their legs and ant bites everywhere, yet nothing to keep them down. My back was on fire, apparently having scraped it from the backward fall I took with Broca's weight on me.

We took off every stitch of our clothes and wrung them out. We cleaned out any remaining ants from our crotches, navels, ears, and elsewhere. The night air was mercifully warm, but we were chilled from both the evaporation as our bodies dried and the reluctant acknowledgment that we still had much to overcome through this night.

We listened for the sounds of our enemies. The incessant cries of small animals succumbing to the death march kept us frozen on the ledge for what must have been hours. Exhaustion at some point overcame fear. On that jut of iron rock we each found some time to nod off as we sat on the least uncomfortable spot we could find and leaned against one another. The hippos didn't come onto our ledge; however, we could hear them occasionally on the far side of the river.

After a nap that could have been five minutes or two hours, I snapped awake. The first thing I noticed was that the waning quarter moon was up into nearly its zenith and poured enough light to outline the contours of the ledge and of the forest behind the river. I noticed sounds next. New sounds: the water lapping against the stone, and animals deeper in the jungle—monkeys or birds—far away and chattering. And no teeth-clenching din of insects. The jungle immediately in front of me was different: no sound of any kind, quiet to the point of oblivion.

Leaving my semiconscious companions, I ventured into the jungle to determine if we could get back safely to the tents. Advancing a short distance, I stopped. Moonlight or not, I couldn't see once I entered the jungle canopy. I hadn't felt a single bite, though. I paced off a few more meters toward our dinner area. Nothing.

I went back to retrieve my three charges. Mueller was already on his feet and appeared relieved when he saw me return.

"Gentlemen, I think we have an opening. The ants seem to be gone. I think we should try to reach our tents as soon as possible."

"Can you be sure, Victor?" Stedman asked.

"I'm sure we have a path for about 15 meters and that the chomping sounds are gone."

No one spoke for a few seconds as the scientists listened intently for corroboration.

Broca was the first to rise. He was unsteady. "Let's give it a try, Victor. Lead the way."

It was remarkable how good this statement made me feel. But as soon as I understood that my ego was reacting to Broca's simple desire to get to comfortable refuge, I was pissed at myself. How can I be so fragile around these guys? Why should their acknowledgment of my leadership be so damn important? Were they all my father? Son of a bitch!

"Let's try to retrace our steps from this afternoon," I told them. "How's your memory holding out?"

Broca replied for all three. "We will be fine. Go!"

We put our still-damp clothes back on. Broca was on his own power, though his arms remained wrapped around his body, like holding his guts from spilling onto the jungle floor. He and Stedman walked about four paces behind Mueller and me. After about thirty minutes of stumbling shoeless in the dark, stepping on sharp stones and something that felt like mulch, we got to our dinner table without incident.

Unfortunately, the kerosene lamps were useless and, after five minutes of fruitless groping around the table and nearby ground, no flashlight could be found. Nor could any of us locate our shoes. Nevertheless, we had a good sense of where the tents were and tramped over to them like wounded soldiers returning to base. I scrambled around for my pack and found a flashlight. Nothing in our camp had been so much as scratched. It was impossible to be sure, but it looked like the ants never made it this far back from the river. All three scientists were rifling their packs, swigging deeply from their canteens, and heading immediately into the tent. Stedman assisted Broca, who was breathing in short, shallow bursts.

I made sure all three were settled, then went back to survey the landscape for signs of the ants. The moon was heading down into the lower western sky. It would be daybreak soon. Adrenaline was dissipating from my system and exhaustion was taking over. We had all survived this first twenty-four hours of fieldwork and without further reflection, survival would have to be the success criterion for now.

I ducked into the tent, stripped to my shorts, and curled on top of a sleeping bag on the ground, under a cotton print sheet that Amelia gave me months ago. For this moment it was more than a sleep cover. It was security. My back felt like I had been clawed by a leopard, so I curled onto my side, unable not to listen. Had the feasting ants returned? It was the first time since I was a child that I mistrusted the night. Perversely recalling the day's events I remembered how often I had tasted fear, all salt and thick, like nausea before you vomit. Exactly when I found sleep, I don't remember, but it was brief, punctuated with shivers of cold and dread.

Before I opened my eyes to the ripening light outside the tent, I heard: "Jesus fucking Christ!"

It was Mueller.

Throwing off the sheet, I was awake quickly, rushing through the tent's screen door. Mueller was standing in his boxer shorts, staring toward the river. I could not believe what I was seeing. Beginning a few meters from our campsite, the grasses, shrubs, small trees, wildflowers, plants of all kinds which had populated the jungle meadow just yesterday had completely vanished, replaced by a gray-green ash. From a point maybe half a football field length upriver to as far as we could see downriver, the only remaining vegetation were the stalks of formerly strong young trees, denuded of bark and standing like wire props. Had I seen some residual smoke, I would have thought I was viewing the aftermath of a horrific fire. Transfixed, I moved out into this landscape before I knew what I was doing, staring down and sideways, feeling the soft, cold powder beneath my toes. Small skeletons spread out in all directions: rats, snakes, lizards, voles, and some larger skeletons, maybe a civet, a duiker, a hyrax. My God, I thought. Any one or all of us could have, would have ended up as skeletons. This killing field was terrifying, yet utterly fascinating. The larger trees had been defoliated for about the bottom three meters. The silence was perfect. No bird calls, no monkeys, no hippos pounding their tugboat bodies through the river.

I stepped slowly to our dinner table and gathered in the sight. The cans which once held tomato sauce or beans had lost their labels.

I saw something glimmer on the ground. It was a buckle which had been attached to one of my sandals. The leather had been eaten away from it, leaving only the indigestible metal. The sight was almost incomprehensible, the stuff of science fiction. Nothing that one might think of as organic remained. Our leftover food, garbage, parts of our shoes, pages from a book—all gone.

I sensed Mueller coming up behind me, but I still shuddered as he drew up to my side.

"Good Christ, Victor! Have you ever seen anything like this?"

"No," I muttered. "Not ever. No."

Mueller bent down, picked up some of the putrid mulch and rubbed it between his thumb and two fingers. He sniffed it. "Interesting. Looks like the little fuckers digested, then regurgitated or shat out most of what they ate."

I repeated Siegfried's gesture and looked at the small smudge on my fingers. It had the smell of blood in garbage. My mouth filled with saliva, and I spat out. "Help me with the table and stove, will you?"

He remained still, looking wide-eyed at the destruction, his mustache twitching like a bug on his lip.

It took us two hours to regain some semblance of our group's former dynamic, such as it was. Broca awoke, or rather he rose from his cot and stood in place for what must have been five minutes. He looked down at his feet, smudged with clotted blood and cuts. When I asked him how his ribs felt, he looked perplexed at first, then silently started to rub where he had been injured. He attempted a deep breath, wincing in pain almost immediately. Still without a word and holding his lower chest, he moved slowly past Mueller and me, stopped at the edge of the ant residue, and peed directly into it. It was as though he'd been saving it for the last three days. He let out a snorting laugh.

"You creepy sons of bitches," he said through his teeth. "I hope you're back in hell!"

"Easy there, Alan." Mueller came up from behind Broca and put his two hands onto Broca's shoulders. "Aren't they just nature's fascinating creatures to you biologists?"

"Yes, they are, Dr. Mueller, absolutely. And I'm sure their desire to devour my flesh and turn me into Formicidae detritus—ant turds, to you laypeople—was not the least bit personal. Nevertheless, they're ferocious little devil spawn that belong in myth and history, but not to us here."

"You just had a really bad dream, Alan," I joked.

"Is that what you think, do-gooder, which clearly you are not?"

Was Broca losing it or was this sideswipe simply part of his way of coping with the fact that we were in the middle of nowhere in very dangerous circumstances, and perhaps in peril? He was making me nervous.

"I think," said Stedman, emerging from his slight slumber full of grace and leadership, "that we have witnessed a remarkable, unique, and rare event from which we were lucky to escape. Alan, have you considered how few men manage to see such a phenomenon firsthand?"

"Really, Lee? Oh, sure! This was a remarkable and significant event—in a natural history, zoological fucking academic sense. I suppose the devastation could have been more consequential than the simple elimination of every forest creature within a swath over a kilometer long! Of course, the hippopotami left us alone, if you don't count that little encounter along the rocks." He broke into a giddy laugh and then peed out onto the devastation.

This new Alan Broca was getting dangerous.

Mueller was annoyed. "Give it a rest, Alan. Let's get on with some breakfast."

"Of course, Siegfried, there isn't any worry that they'll return. I'm sure they went back to hell and are hibernating for—"

"Alan, are you a scientist or a scared little boy?" Stedman raised his voice in a way I had not heard before. "Stop this histrionic prattle. We've got work to do today, and you, especially. What on earth has come over you? Please settle down. We know you were hurt badly last night. We were all hurt and frightened. But we're fine today. You need to be sure you take care of your ribs and if you've got any lifting or tough physical work as part of your plan, I'm sure Victor can help you. Now please ... please let's do our jobs. Entomology may not be your specialty, but you are the head of the zoological team. Can you put this behind you and get to work or not?"

Broca started to shake and beads of sweat popped onto his forehead. I could see his legs wouldn't hold him much longer, so I grabbed the sheet from the nearest cot in the tent and rushed to wrap it around him. He collapsed into my arms, burning with a fever. Perfect.

Stedman moved swiftly to help me and cradled Broca as he began to shiver. Stedman muttered, "I should have known it was something like this."

"Something like what?" Mueller asked before I could.

"Alan acting so strangely. It wasn't him, it was the onset of this fever that was pushing him to lose control and lapse into some form of disassociation. What has he contracted now, damn it?"

"Can you tell what he's got, Lee?" I asked. "Is it malaria, do you think?"

"It could be a reactive fever that will pass or it could be something worse, like meningitis. Let's put him to bed, keep him hydrated, and see if he gets better or worse in the next hour or two."

Mueller shook his head and shrugged.

That's all the concern you could muster! I shouted in my mind.

Broca continued to shake. Warned by a gagging sound, we jumped out of the way before he vomited like a broken sewer pipe.

Stedman continue to hold him. "Victor, help me get him onto a cot."

He wiped Broca's mouth with the sheet. I held on to him as well, mimicking Stedman's moves.

Stedman went into the tent just as Siegfried emerged from it, carrying the cot and a small foam pillow. Still holding onto Broca, I motioned to Siegfried with my head, where to place the cot. By the time we had Broca lying down, Stedman returned with his doctor kit. He knelt by Broca's side and measured his pulse. He pulled up Broca's T-shirt while unfolding a stethoscope. Broca's breathing was very short and raspy. This reminded me of the time my friend Tabor nearly died.

Tabor Millhouse and I were in the same volunteer cohort. When I arrived at his post after a project, he complained he was coming down with a cold. But thirty-six hours later he was thrashing on his bed and couldn't recognize me. I got him into a bush taxi to Dakar, forcing him to drink water. When we arrived in Dakar twelve hours later, the medical officer put Tay on an IV and rehydrated him. Tay had typhoid and amoebic dysentery together and was dehydrating faster than if he had cholera.

This, however, was different. Even though Alan Broca looked very much like Tabor Millhouse when I had pushed him, fever-wracked, into a bush taxi, we weren't anywhere near a paved road. And we were not twelve hours from Dakar, we were thirty-six hours from Dakar and that was pushing it.

Our opportunity to explore this key site was disappearing. I needed Stedman to help me make the call.

"Lee, do we need to get him to Dakar right away?"

The doctor looked deep in thought and then said, "Anywhere else, Victor, I'd be inclined to monitor Alan for a day and then decide. But we are so far from anything resembling even minimum medical care. Yes. We should get him a real medical facility immediately."

"What the hell are you talking about!" Mueller roared. "We just got to the most important site for our entire project! We cannot leave before I at least do a preliminary survey!"

"Siegfried, I don't think we should take a chance with Alan's health here, maybe even his life," Stedman said.

"Bullshit! You don't know what he has. He could be fine in an hour or two!" Mueller was turning red.

Stedman seemed fired up. But as he steadied himself to come back at Mueller, I put my hand on the doctor's chest and stood in front of him.

"This is now my call, Herr Mueller. There is too much risk to Alan and, ultimately, to the project."

Mueller took a step closer to me. I didn't move.

"So," I said, "either you can stay here yourself—we'll leave you everything except the Land Rover, and we'll back here when we can— or we all go and get Alan the care he needs, now!" I was shaking.

Mueller clenched his fists and started to sweat. We faced off like that for a few seconds ... until Mueller abruptly turned and kicked my exposed duffle bag off a camp chair and then again into the dirt. He stormed off without another word.

I asked Stedman to be sure Broca was stable, and I started the work of decamping. After nearly ten minutes Mueller returned and started to pack up as well. We didn't so much as look at each other.

Stedman reported, "I've given Alan something for the fever, Victor, but this doesn't look very good. His pulse is nearly ninety. If it is bacterial meningitis, he doesn't have more than forty-eight hours, if that, before it's irreversible. I'm monitoring him for headache. Have we got enough water to keep him hydrated? How fast can we get to Dakar?"

"Even if we get the train—which we shouldn't count on—there isn't any telling how long it will take."

Stedman nodded, remembering our train ride fiasco.

"Driving will take us the rest of today's daylight to reach the Senegal border," I said. "Then we should try to keep on going straight to Tambacounda. That road is flat and straight, but also, it's pitted laterite, so it will be a slow slog, day or night. We'll have to stop in Tambacounda for gas. From there it will be another ten hours to Dakar. If we keep moving, we could make it in thirty hours, maybe faster. But I gotta say, as fucked up as this excursion has been, I wouldn't count on anything going the way we want it to. Let's get moving. Are you ready?"

We packed together.

I was tempted to thank Mueller, but I said, "Let's get on the road."
Mueller sniffed and dismissed me with a wave of his hand.

Broca was conscious but incommunicative, other than an occasional moan and contorting face. He was in trouble.

9. Bugging Out

The ride up to Mahina was slower yet steadier than the ride down. Knowing a bit of the terrain we would have to cover and where the problems lurked, I was able to make a few course and speed adjustments. Ascending the other side of that plateau where we had been stuck yesterday had proven far easier than climbing the Mahina side. Trying to navigate the steep slope down was still tricky, but easier than slipping and winching our way up.

When the dense forest cleared and I saw the meadow where we had camped by the train tracks, I sighed with relief. But it was only the first and shortest part of the journey. The next phase was more than 200 miles over routes I had never taken. I decided to check in with our new friend, Soula Swaray, for directions.

It had taken us nearly five hours to get back to Mahina, and by the early afternoon the sun was bearing down like an angry god. Stedman had taken to wetting one of his T-shirts and keeping it on Broca's head and neck. Mueller was sullen and sweating profusely. We rode into Mahina proper, halting in front of the police station.

Mueller was out of the Rover before I had set the handbrake and announced that he was on a mission to get the coldest, safest drinks he could find. Safest? Beer was the first thing that came to my mind, but I let it go.

"Victor, we'll need to get moving soon," Stedman said. "Why do you need to see Swaray, exactly?"

"I'm getting directions," I told him.

"If you must. But please hurry, goddamn it!"

I was hoping that sleepy Mahina was not having a crime wave or other event that might occupy the local lawman. It wasn't. Swaray sat at his desk, eating, and reading from a stack of reports.

He looked up at me and showed not the slightest trace of surprise, or, for that matter, interest. "You've returned earlier than you told me, Mr. Byrnes." He continued reading.

"One of our group has become very sick, Captain, and we need to get him back to Dakar for treatment as soon as we can."

"Bad luck for you, sir. Your train is two days from its return."

"So we will drive. And here, Captain, is where I need your help. Can you show me the best way to Bakel from here?"

I took out the map that depicted various paths from Mahina to the Senegalese border, none of them actual roads. But I didn't spread the map out. I kept it folded in my hand, waiting for Swaray to give me some sign that he was in fact in a mood to help me. He made no change to his eating and reading.

"Captain, our colleague could be dying. I really need your help now, please?"

Swaray took a towel from the desk, wiped his hands, and said, "Sit." He went to an adjacent room the size of an outhouse. He took a black kettle from which he poured water into a basin and washed his hands.

"Show me your map," he said, returning to his desk.

Why couldn't he share my sense of urgency?

I spread the topo map out and held my breath. Swaray ran his fingers over the map, studied it silently for about a minute, then rendered his judgment.

His directions were clear, even if the routes on the map were not. He gave me names of villages that I wrote down. He told me to be sure and confirm the routes with the people in the village. This was not going to be easy.

He pointed to a spot at the river not far from our first destination in Senegal—Bakel. "There are no ferries, no barges. You will have to drive across. Leave now. The rains have begun in the mountains."

I was right. We had to stay ahead of the rising river. On the map I circled the villages of Kuladabou and Diaoula, estimating that the entire route to the river crossing was considerably less than my earlier estimate. A small bit of luck: 80 kilometers, tops.

"What is wrong with going up to Kayes and using the bridge crossing there?" I asked.

"Kayes is chaos, Mr. Byrnes, and the *douaniers* will keep you at the border a long time while they steal everything they can from you. Go through Kayes when you have more time."

"What can I bring you from Dakar, Captain, on return."

Without hesitation Swaray said, "Mahina needs a doctor, Mr. Byrnes. Bring me a doctor."

A great, seemingly unrealistic request, yet one I could possibly deliver, given that Stedman was one of three medical doctors on the project. But I knew we could only deliver some miniscule, fleeting fix for a few people. Was some tiny assistance, regardless of how small or temporary, a step to something better? Or was it an empty attempt to fulfill a cry for help?

"I will return with a doctor, Captain," and extended my hand to seal my word.

As he took my hand his lips curled into a smile. "God willing," he said.

Our different understanding of God was immaterial. We shared the understanding that neither of us could control events determining if we would see each other again.

10. A Dash to Safety

Mueller asked if he could drive. I was happy to let him. I concentrated on the navigation and he focused on driving rather than his bitterness for leaving Manantali unexplored. As Mueller eased the Rover onto the Mahina bridge across the Bakoye, guiding it across the narrow trestle, I looked below and was certain the waters were moving faster and higher than when we had crossed only two days before on the train. I pulled a compass from my shoulder bag and set it on top of the map on my lap.

Broca was still wrapped in the sheet with the wet T-shirt on his forehead, looking like a mummy. Stedman checked his pulse. From my perspective, Broca was next to comatose. His shaking had subsided, but his head bobbed uncontrollably. How the hell were we going to get to a hospital in time?

Mueller followed the dirt road for the next 50 kilometers. The land was still parched and worn by many vehicles in the last six or eight months of no rain. And just five kilometers out of Mahina, the steep hills and rocky terrain dissolved into flattened red clay and sand track. Mueller was steady at the wheel.

"Keep your foot to the metal as long as you can, Siegfried," I said.

He shot me a glance with a curled lip. "Don't you think that's what I've been doing?" he shouted. "Jesus, Byrnes!"

"I'm just saying go fast when we can, 'cause we know there'll be times when we can't."

"I've got this, Mr. Field Guide," he said.

At the fifth village, we stopped and asked for directions to the Bakel road. It was difficult at first since no one in the village spoke French. But our common lexicon of the place names allowed us to understand we were on the right route. I peered regularly at the odometer to calculate the distance we had traveled, comparing it to Swaray's points on the map. No road veered west at the sixth village, nor the seventh. By the eighth village, we had traveled nearly 70 kilometers and I was certain we had missed the turn. *Shit!* We stopped again and asked. The villagers came out, as they always did, curious and talkative among themselves, speculating on our purpose. Children in rows of crusted bare feet and wondering eyes surrounded the Rover, forcing Mueller to stop abruptly.

I got out and asked the crowd, in French and my very limited Bambara, for directions. The women cackled at my clumsy use of their language and my question seemed to stir more discussion than decisions ... until an old man with a gnarled cane and an army cap limped purposefully to the front of the crowd.

"I speak French, Monsieur. I was in the war. I fought Rommel in the desert with the French army. You see these medals? I am a decorated veteran."

There was no denying his French was better than Swaray's. And he could easily have been as he claimed. But we needed information. In French, I asked him about his family. He held up his cane to stop me.

"All fine, by the grace of Allah," he said. "What are you doing here?"

I let out a huge breath I didn't know I was holding. This man had indeed been in the military.

"We need to take the road to the river crossing to get to Bakel," I told him.

"You are on the road to Kayes."

"Yes, but I was told there was a turn to Bakel near here and that we could cross the river when we got to the border."

The old man laughed with a smile of yellow-brown and most of his teeth.

"That road goes from Selekane, not Diaoula," he told me as if I would know exactly what he meant.

"Where is Selekane, sir?"

"Selekane is back the way you came, through Birabi and Khotseme."

We were definitely in trouble. I couldn't keep the names of all these villages straight. I reminded myself never to travel deep inland again without Mammadu.

"What is the next village in that direction?" I asked, pointing to where we had come from.

"Diaoula."

Aha!

"And from there, how do I get to Selekane?"

He smiled and shook his head. "You continue to Birabi, then go to Khotseme." I decided to draw in the sand at my feet and I had to move the children back to create my canvas. The afternoon sun was blistering. Stedman and Mueller were sweating through their clothes, just like Broca.

Stedman called out, "Victor! Hurry the hell up. Need I remind you …!"

I ignored Stedman and finished my discussion with the old vet. I offered him some francs, but he shook his head. I offered him the two apples in my shoulder bag.

"Please give one to the chief," I told him.

"I am the chief," he informed me.

"I'm grateful for your help, Chief. May Allah be with you."

"Go with Allah, white man." He had no trouble taking both apples and promptly gave one to the small boy.

I jumped back into the Rover and consulted the map.

"Victor, do you know where we are?" Stedman asked. "And more importantly, do you know where we're going?"

"Come on, Byrnes, what's the fucking program?"

Mueller was just as nervous as Stedman, and more belligerent.

"We're going back three villages and ask for the road to Selekane. The road to the river crossing starts at Selekane."

"Of this you are certain?" Stedman said.

"Hell no, Lee. I'm just trying to get us there the fastest possible way. We've got plenty of daylight left, but we'll need all of it just to get across the river!"

Locking eyes with Mueller, I said, "Siegfried, let's get going back the way we came. If it doesn't pan out in the next two hours, we will head directly for Kayes."

"Victor. Get us to the river. Just do it." It was Broca, barely awake. "Lee, some water, please?"

He didn't look any better, but this was the first coherent thing he'd said since last night. I took this as a good omen. Apparently, Mueller did too. He put the Rover into gear and turned it around with a jerk and spinning tires.

"Your fever is still significant, Alan," Stedman said.

"This I could have told you myself," said Broca, squirming to get comfortable. "Just don't catch whatever this is, heh?"

"Byrnes, where in God's name are you taking us now?" Mueller wanted directions he could trust. "Have you finally got this route figured out or will we be chasing our tails until after dark? You can't keep on *exploring*, you know. Alan is in desperate shape."

Now he worries about Broca, I thought. But I needed to concentrate. I had to get us through this confusing intersection of villages and navigate to our next milestone, the river at Bakel.

At the third village we stopped and quickly confirmed we were in the right village and that the road we needed headed west on the other side of the village.

We encountered some luck at Khotseme. Tacked to a stick leaning out of the earth like a burnt sapling was a hand-painted sign in black lettering on corrugated cardboard, with the name of the village. We stopped and confirmed the road to Selekane from the first adult we saw, by simply asking, "Selekane?" and pointing up the road. Head nods were all the confirmation we needed.

Mueller accelerated over the sand, swerving and careening like a getaway driver. After another five kilometers, he jammed on the brakes and brought the Rover to a wrenching halt. A huge erosion crevasse sliced into the middle of our path. It was deeper and wider than two car lengths. The jamming of the brakes produced no squeal of tires, just a cloud of dust that blew storm-like around the Rover. I bumped my head on the dashboard and Broca fell to the car floor behind Mueller.

"Mueller!" Stedman cried out.

Though the wheels had stopped, the chassis rocked like a porch swing before settling. I jumped out to assess our route. Mueller got out to make his own assessment. I started to growl at Mueller, and then noticed tire tracks that led the way around this small canyon.

I raced back to the Rover to check on Broca. Stedman was having difficulty pulling him up into the seat. I opened the rear door and put my arm around Broca's hips and hoisted him up. He let out a low wail, full of pain and little energy. Stedman and I exchanged glances. Though our faces were caked with sand and sweat, our eyes said it all: Broca was getting worse.

Lee said, "He won't make it another sixteen hours to Dakar at this rate. Is there anything before we get to Dakar, maybe in Tambacounda?"

"A clinic, yes," I told him. "How well-equipped and staffed, I wouldn't dare guess. It'll be your call when we get there."

No time to waste. I shouted to Mueller, who was about to climb into the driver's seat. "Siegfried, do you see the vehicle tracks off to the left?"

"Of course I see them," Mueller snarled at me.

He swiveled back to the Rover, mounted the driver's seat, and slapped the gearshift into reverse. Then he ground the gearshift into first and, with a hard turn left, spun the Rover onto our bypass.

Let it go, I told myself. Let it go.

As we approached the next village, we came across the second sign of the day. This one was far more encouraging and far less useful than the last. The sign read: SENEGAL, but as far as we could discern, there was no road or direction indicated. Just another cardboard sign announcing the country as if we had just landed there.

I took a compass heading and, with the map, determined we were indeed on the road to Bakel. "The border can't be more than ten minutes away," I surmised aloud.

"Double that, Byrnes. At least, yeah? And help me out here. Do you see the road?" Siegfried asked.

I pointed to the tracks in the sand. Mueller followed them through the trees, hunched over the wheel, wide-eyed. As we approached the river, the road was turning from the occasional semihard iron clay and dust, to deep sand.

"Siegfried, try to keep as even and steady a speed as you can. We don't know what we're getting into yet."

He glanced at me. "You thinking maybe I don't know we can't afford to get stuck, heh? Is that it? Of course I'm going to be careful. But we have to make time. We probably haven't got more than three or four hours of daylight left, and we don't even know how to cross this river once we get there, do we?"

"All I'm saying is that I thought you were going a bit fast for the conditions. Please be careful."

He ignored me, refocusing on driving, though he decreased our speed for the conditions. Mueller may not like me much, but he wasn't stupid.

Forty-five minutes from the last village, we saw a row of trees on the horizon. Mueller knew what it meant.

"The river is close, Byrnes. It's about time."

The path became clearer and the soil harder. Our road twisted through a stand of acacia and baobab trees and finally to a soft sloping riverbank. We had reached the second major tributary of the Senegal River, the Baffing, the river forming the border between Senegal and Mali. Siegfried eased the Rover down the bank on an angle, carefully following the track which was no longer sand but hard clay and loose rock. The river was flowing steadily and looked as wide as a football field is long. We saw women and girls on both sides of the river washing clothes and gathering water. On the Senegal side we could see the roofs of several huts up and over the riverbank. Where the road led straight into rushing water, Mueller pulled up and stopped. I noticed two vultures floating high in the distant sky, making lazy spirals.

"Go ahead and kill the engine, Siegfried. Let's see what we're dealing with. Lee, how's your patient doing?"

"Status quo for the moment. The ride could have been worse, and I've been able to keep him cool. But his fever is persisting and he's barely conscious. How far to Tambacounda?"

"I'll know better once we're across the water hazard."

I waded into the river to see how deep the water was and how fast. For more than halfway across, the water came barely to my knees. Then the river bottom slid down and I was up to my chest. The bottom was soft. A vise gripped my stomach. Then I saw it. The road actually emerged about 10 meters upstream from where I was headed. I waded to where the road rose out of the water and I waded back to our expedition. This time the rushing water never got higher than mid-thigh and the river bottom was rock. The Rover would do fine at a smooth, steady pace—so long as we stayed on the rocks.

Mueller thought he should continue driving and that I should lead the way like a Sherpa.

"Sorry, Siegfried," I told him. "I'm the designated driver. If I screw up, it's only my ass. If you screw up, it's both our asses."

Stedman clarified for us. "If either of you screws up, we may have a dead colleague on our hands. Settle this now and get on with it!"

Before I could say "Out, Herr Doctor," Mueller had descended from the driver's side.

"Don't fuck this up, Byrnes," Mueller muttered.

Now I was pissed. "Thanks for the confidence, jerk-off! How on earth can you say such a thing? How about you help and walk in front so I don't lose the path? How about it, Siegfried? You want to lead the way? Or should we just wing it?" This was not like me. Or so I hoped.

Mueller was stationary. I could tell he was fuming.

He was also thinking, and said, "So long as you are confident in your route, let's get across quickly." He waded into the river along the path I had paced back.

I shook my head.

As I eased the Rover into the water, a crowd of children appeared from nowhere, completely surrounding us. The boys cheered and laughed and splashed the car. Some decided to run in front of us. I envisioned inadvertently gunning the engine and drowning one of these urchins under a wheel. I shuddered and honked the horn.

In West African culture a blaring horn is completely contextual. It could mean "Greetings"; it could mean "I'm on your left"; it could mean "Do you want a ride?"; it could mean "We just won!"; it could mean "Do I know you?" In our case it clearly meant "Let's make this into a party."

One of the braver boys jumped onto the running board and grabbed hold of the rack to ride with us. Soon, boys behind us were running through the water to catch up and jump a ride on the back where one of the spare tires was attached. I hit a large rock under the water going at a speed faster than I wanted. The resulting jolt knocked the rear-riders off, face down in the water, causing their comrades to howl with laughter. Frightened as I was for their safety, it never crossed my mind to stop for them. On the positive side, this clearly dissuaded others from catching a ride. But the throng only held back; it didn't disperse.

Around my wet feet I began to feel a steady slosh of water by the brake and the accelerator, reminding me that even if this crossing route was the shallowest, it still was deep enough to submerge our tailpipe. The only way to protect the engine was to keep my foot pressed in one position on the accelerator. I held firm until my foot ached.

We reached the other side and drove out onto the dry land of Senegal. I didn't stop until we were up and over the riverbank, passing a bemused yet probably relieved Mueller. After coming to a halt, I looked at the setting sun. At least two hours to Tambacounda. No victory yet.

"No time to congratulate yourself, Byrnes. Alan's fever is rising. We must get to that medical facility in Tambacounda *now*!"

Despite the sweat and cold compress partially covering Broca's face, I could see he was sunburn red.

"And Victor, we don't know if what Alan has is contagious. We should assume that it is and check ourselves as well."

I was suddenly cold in the searing heat, looking at Stedman's eyes.

The road from the river to Bakel was worn and rutted. We reached the town in fifteen minutes, driving without stopping. Two hours later, along a wide, flat, graded dirt road, we pulled into Tambacounda and saw the signs directing us to the medical facility half a kilometer off the main road. Halleluiah!

It was a physically modern building from the outside and with pale green walls, rolling beds with IV masts, a reception desk, and signs indicating various departments. Clearly, this facility had been constructed by the enormous goodwill and financial resources of people who hadn't the slightest idea of what they were doing. The equipment, covered in dust, looked as though it had never been used. Even if there were technicians who knew how to use an autoclave or an X-ray machine, there didn't seem to be any electricity to power them. We postulated there must be electrical generators which, in all likelihood, had no fuel.

Soon after we entered, we were greeted by a smiling young man who introduced himself as Dr. Fobekun. He and his colleague—who was attending a patient—were medical doctors from Nigeria, here at the request of the Senegalese government, and paid by the government of Belgium, who had built the facility.

Grateful for the opportunity to speak English to a fellow professional, Stedman spoke for us, explaining our predicament and requesting assistance in diagnosing and treating Broca. Our host shouted for some assistance to a nurse, whom none of us had noticed standing next to a hallway door. He spoke to her in a language I didn't recognize so I assumed that she, too, was Nigerian. She quickly disappeared down the hallway. A lengthy conversation ensued between the two medical men as Siegfried and I stayed next to Broca, who was slumped in a chair, semiconscious, and, like us, dripping sweat and caked with sand. Siegfried asked if we could take Broca to an examination room and get him cleaned up.

"The nurses will be here momentarily," Dr. Fobekun assured us. "We will give your companion all our attention and care."

Two nurses appeared with a gurney, a stack of linens and towels, an IV mast, and a small box with medical supplies. They moved methodically to get Broca onto the gurney, stripping most of his soiled clothes and getting him wrapped in a never-been-worn hospital gown. He groaned and winced.

One of the nurses produced a bottle of water from the box of supplies and tried to get Broca to drink. He waved her away deliriously, shaking his head and refusing to drink. She asked if either Siegfried or I could get him to drink. We looked at each other, willing to give it a try. Siegfried shrugged his shoulders, moved behind Broca, and held him up by his armpits on the inclined gurney. I pushed Broca's flailing arm down and put the bottle to his lips, tipping it slowly. Broca's resistance weakened and eventually he drank. The four of us produced a collective sigh of relief.

In the meantime, Drs. Stedman and Fobekun had a plan.

"Gentlemen," Stedman said, "we may have some good fortune here. Dr. Fobekun has told me a great deal about these facilities and his specialties. He's an internist and will be very valuable in helping Alan's diagnosis and treatment. Also, the reason there are no lights or electricity is that they conserve generator fuel whenever possible and only start them at the end of the day or when essential equipment is required. The facility has been here for only eight months."

"We will start the generator now," Fobekun explained. "And we will set up the lab and a room for your distressed colleague right away. We will conduct both blood work and a spinal tap to know if we're dealing with meningitis. Dr. Stedman and I will perform these tasks together."

"What about treating him, Lee?" asked Mueller.

"Dr. Fobekun and I will discuss the availability of various options, but first we need to know what we're dealing with. Do the two of you have your vaccination cards?" he asked.

Our dumfounded expressions produced a deep sigh from Stedman. He scowled.

"Do either of you know if you were inoculated against *Neisseria meningitis*?" His voice was raised.

I'm sure he used the full name just to impress upon us that we needed to come up with our vaccination cards.

"I did have a meningitis vaccination," I said, "but I have no idea if it's what you're looking for."

Stedman nodded knowingly, without saying any more to me. "Siegfried, what about you?"

The big German produced his vaccination card as if he'd been waiting for the moment. Stedman flipped through the pages of the yellow pamphlet, huffed, and handed it back to Mueller. Then Broca rolled to the side and started to cough and dry heave. Stedman and Fobekun moved into action—directing the nurse and moving the gurney toward the hallway. Mueller and I followed. As we moved down the hallway, the lights came on and a whir of electronics buzzed to life. Finally!

The next few hours felt like geological time. Mueller and I were not needed. I wondered where we were going to spend the night. If Stedman and Fobekun decided it was necessary, we'd be off to Dakar, driving nonstop through the night.

Stepping outside alone, onto a terrace at the back of the building, I could hear the drums of Tambacounda in all directions. Fires flickered in family compounds. Dinners of millet porridge with beans or a local tree leaf believed to be edible, if not nutritious, were being prepared and consumed. Life in West Africa was proceeding normally despite all the disease, the droughts, the plagues of locusts or ants; despite the legacy of colonialism, or the death of a child, or the stain of corruption. The night air was clear, though it held the faintest whiff of moisture. The rains were on their way.

The night sky was a swath of stars shimmering like a bride's veil. I felt as if I were on the other side of the galaxy, looking at Earth's solar system—as though the sun was just another of the millions of impossibly distant fireballs around which circled worlds upon worlds, lifeless or teeming, shut off from any galactic family by space and time so vast as to defy comprehension.

Mueller interrupted my reverie to let me know we had some new information about Alan. Stedman and Fobekun determined that he had viral meningitis. He'd been treated and would heal with rest, liquids, and sleep. Now I could concentrate on setting up camp in the hospital compound. I suddenly felt very, very tired.

11. Catching a Break

Before leaving Tambacounda for Dakar in the morning, I phoned Planck from the hospital. He was waiting for us when we pulled into the IMAME courtyard around dinnertime. After an hour to settle Broca at the embassy infirmary and the unpacking of necessities, Stedman, Mueller, and I went our separate ways.

I was spent. I hadn't so much as bathed for a week and my mind was reeling from the strange events we four strangers had suffered together. It was too much to think about. As the ferry to Gorée rocked on the ocean swells and the beat of its engine lulled me with its monotonous rhythm, I was ready for a long sleep, dreading tomorrow's work: to recount our adventures and account for my decisions.

My friend Jules Tamara was waiting for me as I disembarked with the few tourists and locals.

I said, "Don't you have anything better to do than hang around the dock, preying on unsuspecting visitors?"

"If I did that," he said without looking at me and grabbing one of my bags, "I'd have no friends on this island at all. And what kind of person would that make me?"

"You didn't need to meet me, Jules."

He looked at me as though I was not the person he knew. "It's not in your nature to be just a tiny bit gracious when someone does something nice for you? Amelia was very right."

"Jules, don't act like you think I don't appreciate this. I really do, and you know I do. It's great to have you meet me when I get home after a really tough week."

I couldn't possibly be ungracious enough now to tell him how I really felt: that all I craved was some downtime with a gin and tonic, a joint, and Jimmy Page wailing from the speakers. But guilt coerced me to do the gracious thing. Not that I was insincere with Jules. It's just that I had little confidence in my own feelings of needing to be alone right now. This need seemed adolescent and self-centered in light of Jules' friendship. I was undeserving.

Jules accompanied me up the narrow streets to my apartment, and I invited him in for a drink. He accepted, splashing a wide, closed-mouth smile and a single raised eyebrow. Did he have something he wanted to share with me? I easily relaxed on the patio and Jules was part of the reason. Left to my own devices, there's no telling what demons I might have summoned.

"Young Victor, I have to tell you, you were not missed at all. Life went on normally on the island and, in fact, without your input, the Gorée swim team won the national championship."

I didn't even know there was such a thing, but it wasn't a surprise. From the time they could walk, the boys of the island were diving for cowry shells and swimming races past the outer ferry buoys and back.

"Congratulations to my neighbors," I said, and raised my gin and tonic in an absentee toast.

Jules clinked his glass to mine, then sat back and sighed. "So get it off your chest, my friend. I can see it in your shoulders and your neck. It was a difficult trip, yet so short."

"Jules, *mon ami*, I'm not ready. I want to kick back, not think about the past or the future. I need to listen to some good music." I stood and put a cassette into the player. Not rock, jazz.

With a nod, Jules acknowledged my need to unwind.

As the second song began, he said, "You know, Victor, I'm a lucky man. I windsurf and spend time with whomever I want. The family business practically runs itself. I have money, lovers, invitations, and interests. And still I work to have my friends. You, on the other hand, live like you are still an impoverished volunteer, save for this glorious little hideaway. You leave for long periods of time, you barely say hello before you are gone again, and you have more people who care about you than the Fatou herself."

Jules was referring to the most revered Gorée village elder and head of the Senehole clan, Fatou Tioubaba. Everyone loved her. Was Jules just observing out loud or was there more I should understand? It's so impossible to see yourself as your friends do.

I replied, "I'm a lucky man too. My friends are real and tell me like it is. They meet me after a long, difficult journey and ask only to spend time with me. So I don't need to live in a lavish house because I am rich with what matters. Wouldn't you say that's true?"

"Indeed, young adventurer, I would. Does Amelia know you're back?"

"Jesus, I didn't think anyone knew I was back. I wasn't sneaking in or anything, but Christ, I haven't even slept a single night in my own bed yet."

"She's quite taken with you, Victor."

"You say this like I haven't noticed. Look, Amelia is terrific and I care for her, really. But please let that work itself out between us. I know you think we're great together, and sometimes we are. But neither of us is changing our life to be with the other, you know? I'm not changing me."

"You say that as though you could, Victor."

"Touché."

"Actually, I envy you, you know. Just exploring and letting the wind take you wherever. You've no deep ties to West Africa, really. Just a set of experiences, like photos in an album. Great memories and all, but then what?"

"I don't know, Jules. On to the next photo album, maybe? I honestly haven't thought or even fantasized past tonight."

"And what did you fantasize for this evening's entertainment? Latin jazz, Tanqueray on the rocks, and Dakar prostitutes?"

"Since when did you start reading my mind!"

"You see, I know you better than you think. You may want to be a dissolute neocolonialist, but your heart is much too large."

"That's why you hang with me, Jules? My goofy heart?"

"You think, Victor, it's guilt that drives you, but I know better. We—your friends—know better. Guilt is a Western construct to keep people from accepting themselves. It isn't guilt that drives you, you recovering Catholic. What drives you is your big restless heart."

"Are you trying to seduce me?"

"That ship certainly sailed some time ago, didn't it?"

"But please, what about you? What drives you? You could sell that family business and buy an island in the Seychelles."

"*My* roots are here, dear boy. Where else would I go that I know as well, where I am as comfortable and have so many friends whom I have diligently cultivated over the years. Why in heaven would I start that from scratch? And even you must admit, Victor, that you come to Gorée to be here, to be close to the sea, to be in a small, tight community with us frogs, the Senegalese and the few other strangers that drift to this oasis, away from work and pressure. Yet never too far away."

I finished my gin and tonic and asked Jules if he wanted his Chardonnay refilled.

"No, thanks, Victor. Thiery will be on the last ferry this evening and we'll probably cook in."

As he got up to go, he handed me an envelope.

"Your patron, Planck, asked me to give this to you. He didn't know yesterday if you would be stopping by the office, so he had a messenger drop it off. It's an invitation to hobnob with the chichi of commercial society!"

"What are you talking about? Did you open it?"

"Of course I opened it. It wasn't sealed, and I wanted to be sure it was something you should be doing. I wholeheartedly approve."

I opened the letter inviting me to the home of Nigel and Doria Blake, as a welcome and a getting-to-know the community barbecue. I knew of Nigel Blake, of course: Barrow & Bean International's top man in Africa, dealmaker, and socialite. His spheres and mine did not intersect. He had ministers visit him. Dignitaries from other countries paid courtesy calls on Nigel Blake, lest they be overlooked for lucrative trade deals. IMAME and BBI, I thought. What a perfectly exploitative partnership.

I needed to lie down. I thanked Jules and asked him if it would be all right if I popped in to visit with him and Thiery if I promised to bring a bottle of single malt scotch, Thiery's drink of choice.

Jules put his right hand on my left cheek. "You are always welcome, Victor. But don't bring Scotch. I've got that covered. Bring your stories."

Senegal green-headed parrots were landing and congregating in the acacia trees overhanging my veranda. A flock had begun to socialize noisily and soon it would be raining guano on my tiles and outdoor furniture. We both looked up and laughed, knowing there was nothing to be done. I hugged Jules and closed the door as he left with a wave.

I turned on the air conditioner in my bedroom, made another gin and tonic—mostly tonic—and switched the music to Ravel.

*

The next day was a day of recovery. The Land Rovers needed maintenance from the winch to the tires, from the air filter to the exhaust pipe. Mammadu had already started the work by the time I arrived.

"Barbu," he said, "you are not permitted to damage these vehicles before I have a chance to lead a caravan to Mali. One trip only and the winch is bent like a ribbon. What have you been doing?" He flashed his big smile at me as he attacked the dismantling of the winch, straining to loosen the twisted mounting bolts.

"I was testing how strong this truck is, Mammadu. We want to be sure we have trucks that will stand up to mountain climbing in Mali and Guinea."

"Did you get into trouble, Barbu? You need to take me with you always. You know that."

"I do, Mammadu, I do. I'll be right back."

I went over to Planck's office and found him on his way out to pick up newly arriving scientists at the airport. He said he was looking forward to my full report and asked if I had received my invitation to the Blakes'.

"I did."

"Great!" he exclaimed, and disappeared into the waiting Land Rover.

Our secretary, Miriam, came to the conference room as I was writing my report. "Victor, you have a friend here to see you."

"Don't you mean friends, as in plural, you know, more than one?" I asked Miriam. She couldn't understand my self-mocking joke.

"No, Victor. There is one man outside and he said he knows you from Saint-Louis. Monsieur Volant."

I thanked Miriam and asked her to show my visitor into our office.

Lamine was the product of a Senegalese mother and a Quebecois father, Raoul. They had met in Senegal after the end of the Second World War, when Raoul was making his way slowly back to Canada from the northern Sahara. He had been a gunner-mechanic on a half-track. More than half the men who had stood on those gun turrets battling Nazi soldiers, debilitating heat, and sand storms, died.

As Lamine tells it, Raoul, feeling blessed, ventured across the oasis of Tunisia, the restless expanse of Algeria, the chaotic yet beautiful Morocco, and then down the Atlantic coast to Saint-Louis, Senegal. There he met the woman who would become Lamine's mother. I'd seen photos of her. She was half Oulof, half Toucouleur, with high cheekbones and flawless chocolate skin. Lamine was born in Saint-Louis, but grew up in Montreal after his father took his fledging family back to Canada and a solid, middle-class Canadian life. Raoul bought a filling station and a garage just as car ownership was expanding in southern Quebec's postwar economy. As Lamine tells it, his father flourished due to his hard work, blunt honesty, and a genuine fondness for his fellow man—a family culture that young Lamine learned early on. Growing up on Montreal's Rue Saint-Denis North before it was packed with restaurants and shops, Lamine suffered all the tribulations of mixed-race children in a predominantly white neighborhood. Lamine had graduated from Montreal University with a degree in mechanical engineering and knew he didn't want to preside over a car repair business. He was teaching undergraduate calculus as a graduate assistant, and met Claire. She was one of those few students who did astoundingly well with little effort, but could not have cared less. It was easy to see what she saw in him—a partially forbidden adventure packaged in a toweringly handsome body and an unassuming, almost shy disposition. What Lamine saw in Claire, I imagine, was a type of freedom.

It was good to see him. He shook my hand more vigorously than I expected, and I asked him to have a seat in my conference room office.

Down here for work with a Dakar trade school, Lamine came to ask me about employing one of his top students as a driver-mechanic. I was inclined to help him out but wasn't about to jeopardize the safety of our team—to say nothing of my own—on a favor for a friend, regardless of how professional and well meaning. I told him I would like to hire his protégé, but he would have to pass muster with Mammadu before he could even meet with me.

"Victor, this kid can build an Indy car from discarded bicycles. He's the best mechanic in the country and he's only twenty-two years old. And because he's still young, he's willing to work hard."

Working hard was not a trait I normally associated with young Senegalese men. Senegalese women, absolutely. Senegalese men, not so much.

"We'll be up to Saint-Louis in two weeks, so Mammadu can check him out then."

"No need. He's in Dakar for the next two days. You can check him out today or tomorrow or Saturday morning. Then we're headed back."

"That could work," I said, rising from my chair and beckoning Lamine to follow me to the staging area where Mammadu was adding recent supplies to the inventory sheet. When I introduced the two of them, Lamine tensed noticeably, probably at Mammadu's imposing build and his practiced glower, which he used to wonderful effect on nearly everyone. Lamine could tell how difficult Mammadu would be to impress or even admit that he was impressed.

The arrangements made, I asked the two of them if they'd like a quick coffee at the patisserie around the corner. Mammadu demurred, having more paperwork than he was used to, and Lamine accepted, looking relieved.

The patisserie was called La Paradise and was owned by a Lebanese family, the oldest daughter of which was a stunningly beautiful girl with an ice-water attitude. However, she made a perfect café au lait and the *pains raisins* were, as far as I was concerned, the gold standard for the francophone world.

After we ordered from the counter, Lamine and I took seats around an umbrella-covered small table. After some easy talk about each other's work, we fell silent until the coffees arrived.

Lamine looked sullenly into his cup, gripped it in both hands, and said into the steaming liquid, "Claire's cheating on me."

I stopped in mid-sip, put my cup down, and thought what to say next. Finally I said, "Lamine, how do you know?"

"She told me."

"She what? She told you? I mean, had you caught her or suspected her or something?"

"No idea. I had not even an inkling. She wanted me to know. Apparently, she was uncomfortable doing it behind my back. Now that I know, she wants it to be OK."

I was out of my depth. As in, way out. Eventually, I stammered, "She told you in order for her not to be guilty and she's going to continue?"

Lamine nodded.

"Shit soup. I ... Lamine, I ... I'm sorry, man. I don't know what to say." Obviously.

"That's pretty much the way I reacted, too. I asked her if she was going to stop and she said no, she wasn't planning on it. Then I asked her who was the guy and she matter-of-factly told me it was that Ukrainian football coach for Saint-Louis High School, Darius."

I liked Darius. He was funny, spoke English, French, and Russian, drank like a lord, and was dangerously unattached.

Lamine continued. "I started to get terribly angry and terribly frightened at the same time. I was shaking and crying, thinking I was going to hit her or break something. She came up to me and kissed me and hugged me and told me she loved me and that she didn't want this to hurt me." Lamine finally looked up from his coffee. "Victor, what kind of woman is this?"

The answer that came silently to my whirling brain was "porn queen," but I sure didn't say this to my friend. All I could come up with was, "I guess she's a woman for whom sexual fidelity is not something she feels bound by."

Lamine looked at me as though I had just made insect noises. I felt obliged to dig my way out.

"Had the two of you every discussed fidelity or did both of you assume you felt the same? Had you felt jealous before or given this subject much thought? It just seems to me, Lamine, that Claire didn't suddenly wake up and decide that she was going to throw her moral code out the window, no?"

"No, ... no, not likely."

"Don't try to figure her out now, man. Let's work on you. What are you going to do?"

"I don't know, Victor, I just don't know."

I was concerned for Lamine and didn't think he should be alone. He had been living with the revelation, apparently, for a few days. We left La Paradise and went to our separate responsibilities, agreeing to meet that afternoon at the trade school workshop.

I was off-center the rest of the morning, trying to think of what it must be like to love someone who you discover is from an alternate universe. Does love actually keep you from knowing someone because the image we have of our love is too wonderful to taint? Or do we see our own reflection in the object of our love? I had no idea. I hadn't been in love since freshman year in college, with an older woman who treated me like a pet. Every encounter after that was another version of friends with benefits. To be totally in love with a person who did not share your ethical foundation would be hell.

The rest of the morning went by slowly. Mammadu and I discussed future routes, the inventory, and inspected the Rovers. I heard voices in the office and went back there to find Miriam greeting our latest arrivals. Denali Tekkendil, head microbiologist, was one of those people who looked as though he could be twenty-five or forty-five. When I extended my hand to shake his, he looked at it for a second as though trying to remember the customs of the common folk and then took it in a robot-like grip. His hand was cool and dry. When he spoke, it was with an unsettling tone that made me feel as though he was giving a lecture.

"These offices seem rather small, I think, but then, we will be spending most of our time in the field, is that not so, Mr. Byrnes," he said before I had introduced myself.

"That is our plan, Dr. Tekkendil. That's where the work is."

"Indeed, it is."

I moved on to the forestry expert, Orson Limber, a block of a man, mustached and sun-cooked, clearly a man who spent most of his days outdoors. Though four inches shorter than me, he must have weighed 15 kilos more and it was all solid. My hand felt small in his enthusiastic handshake.

He had a broad smile and said simply, "Happy to be here, Mr. Byrnes. Looking forward to getting out."

Roger Gracie, about my height but thinner and slightly pale, struck me as unsure of his surroundings. Tentative, almost suspicious. His eyes roamed around the office as I greeted him.

"Oh, yes. Mr. Byrnes, yes, of course. You are to see to our safety, right?"

"That, and other issues all critical to your productivity," I said, smiling.

He cocked his head quickly, like a perplexed rooster. "Oh, you mean like food, transportation, sleeping arrangements—"

"Dancing girls, government bribes, fair weather. You name it, I'll make sure you have it." I started to laugh at my joke, but since no one else had joined the mirth, I stopped.

I introduced them to Mammadu and took them to their work areas. Tekkendil had one of the few semiprivate offices, which he would be sharing with another health team specialist. I was sure this would elicit some complaint, but he simply acknowledged the arrangements, asked where the reference materials were located, and went off to begin work. Impressive.

Around 12:30 p.m. I reminded them about lunch over at the hotel. I decided not to go with them. Mammadu and I still had much to do and we wanted to get over to the trade school to interview Lamine's prize student.

After our hurried lunch, we walked quickly to the trade school. We had been expected and were led to a large workshop-classroom where Lamine was sitting on a mat on the floor with a group of students, finishing lunch around a communal bowl. He stood when he saw us, smiled, and asked us to join them. We shook our heads and said we would come back later.

Lamine arose, wiping his mouth. "No need, gentlemen."

He waved to a student still sitting on the floor and motioned for him to stand. Dante Sen had a lithe build and a big, confident smile. While I warmed up to the youngster, Mammadu kept his stern game face. I was going to enjoy this test.

Young Dante showed us the project that currently engaged him. He and another student were rebuilding the transmission of a Peugeot 404 pickup truck. Not as complex as rebuilding an automatic transmission, but there were precious few of those in West Africa. He picked up small pieces on the worktable—pitted bushings, bolts, and gears, some with missing teeth—and showed us how and where each was used. He turned around and showed us where he was actually making some new parts. There was an impressive array of cutting and polishing tools, welding equipment, and so on, and we saw some of the detailed work that student Sen had produced.

Mammadu sniffed. "When we are in the bush," he said, "there are no fancy tools. We don't carry torches for welding."

"Maybe you should," was the young man's quick reply.

Showing no reaction, Mammadu continued. "What's the most likely failure of a starter motor?"

"The Bendix, the spring that engages that starter shaft with the engine. Often, though, it's only a case of lubrication. The springs themselves, particularly on Land Rovers,"—he smiled at being able to show us he knew our vehicles—"are coiled 14-gauge steel and not likely to fail."

As he and Mammadu continued their tête-à-tête, I started tuning out and looked around the garage-classroom. My eyes rested on the frame of an old motorcycle. It was dusty and missing its engine, but I could tell from the gas tank it was a Norton 750—a classic. How the heck did that get here? Who owned it and what was going to happen with it? I tugged on the brakes and the clutch, checking if the cables and disks were all in place. They were frozen. The conversation stopped over at the workbench when they noticed I was no longer paying attention.

"Victor, what are you doing?" Lamine shouted.

I beckoned them to come over to the Norton.

"Lamine, what's the story with this shell of a motorcycle?" I asked.

"I don't know, Victor. Frankly, I don't get here that often. Dante, do you know?"

Dante shrugged his answer. We set to querying all the students, and after about ten minutes one of the instructors found us and gave us the story. The bike had been there for at least a year, dropped off by the son of a Danish diplomat. The son hadn't taken care of the motorcycle at all, not even an oil change. When he brought the bike in, the engine was frozen and needed a rebuild. The instructor showed us where the old engine was stored—in about twenty pieces on a shelf in a cabinet that probably hadn't been opened since the engine was placed there.

"Who owns the bike?" I asked.

"No one, I suppose," the instructor answered. "The diplomat and his family were posted to Madagascar and we never heard back from them."

This gave me an idea. I conferred with Mammadu to see if he liked it. He thought about it seriously, asking me some questions, when Lamine interrupted our sidebar conversation. Dante stepped up beside him.

Lamine said, "What are you conspirators dreaming up?"

"Dante, I have just thought of a test for you. I would like you to get this motorcycle working by Saturday morning. By working, I mean road worthy—brakes, transmission, wheels, everything. Lamine, what do you think?"

"I think that is maybe too much to ask. Are there manuals anywhere to be found, I wonder? Are all the parts we need here? What if parts are corroded or lost? Even if we can make them here, I'm not sure you've given us enough time."

I again directed my question to the student. "Dante, what do you think?"

"I think it will be difficult. Maybe impossible. But I would like to try."

The kid, no more than five years my junior, rose significantly in my estimation.

"I'll tell you what. Get it running, and then we'll decide if 'road worthy' is too much to ask. And I'll put 5,000 CFA into the mix for any purchases you might need to make. I'll need the receipts, naturally."

Lamine looked over at his protégé. "Are you sure about this, Dante?"

"If I succeed, will you guarantee me a job?"

"That's the deal, right, Mammadu?" I said.

Mammadu nodded his consent.

"Victor, how much am I allowed to assist? I mean, this needs to be fair on both sides."

Thinking that it was important now for Lamine to have something he could concentrate on and possibly set aside the demons plaguing him, his assistance could only improve the outcome.

"Your call, my friend. It has to be a true test of Dante's ability, but you're his mentor. I trust you. Besides, if the bike turns out to be a winner, the project might buy it from the school."

I meant myself, of course, since I was finally making enough to afford a used motorcycle.

We all shook hands.

12. Nice Ride

On Friday, I met the five additional team members that Planck had picked up at the airport. In the blur of our first meeting and the planning now going on in earnest for our next foray into the bush, I formed no vivid impressions, save one—Leah Genescieu. Hair the color of midnight, piercing gray eyes, with the body of an athlete, this ornithologist from Rice University was unapproachable and fascinating. Romanian by birth, she grew up in a Romanian neighborhood in Queens, New York. She made it through Fordham University as a biology major and then to Rice for graduate work, earning her PhD in ornithology at twenty-seven years old. I had to pry this out of her when I introduced myself.

Of the others, I took less notice. Doug Borden, the geologist. Hamilton Laird, or Dr. Ham, as he introduced himself, was the clinical MD who would be treating people that the health team studied. Gwen Wong had an MD in epidemiology and was the head of the field team Stedman had assembled. Dolores Knapp was the nurse / medical technologist assigned to the team; her experience in Ivory Coast and Cameroon eminently qualified her. She had originally studied nursing, but her true interest was held by the tiny creatures that caused disease, not the large creatures who contracted them.

At lunch Planck announced the invitation by the Blakes, for all of us to attend a Saturday afternoon at their villa. Planck arranged transportation for everyone to be picked up at the hotel. I declined to be included, knowing I had a mission on Saturday morning and saying I'd get my own transport over to the Blake residence.

What should I have expected of a student, talented or not, from the impossible task of rebuilding a motorcycle in fewer than two days? If he failed to have it running, what criteria should I use to assess if I should take him on? I knew I wanted to hire Dante as a favor to Lamine. But could I? Had I boxed us into a corner with my overly clever, self-serving test?

I met Mammadu at the IMAME office around ten. He greeted me with his normal broad-smiling energy.

Walking over from the office to the trade school, I asked him, "Have we made this test impossible, Mammadu?"

He looked at me, then straight ahead. "We have made it, Barbu. Difficult, impossible, or easy. Let's see the results. Then we will know."

I nodded.

The door to the trade school was locked, and it took a few minutes of knocking for Dante to come and open it. He wasn't looking as happy and confident as two days earlier. He led us back to where he was working on the motorcycle. I scanned the area and could not find Lamine.

"Is Professor Volante here, Dante?" I asked.

"He is gone back to Saint-Louis, Monsieur. Yesterday evening."

It wasn't odd that he went back, but why hadn't he sent me a message to let me know? Oh, well.

When we saw the bike, still on the half-meter elevated workbench, it was clear that Dante was having some problems. The engine had been cleaned and mounted, but the gearbox was still apart and on the floor. The clutch and brake cables were dangling like dead tentacles and the gauges, though in place, had not been tightened down.

Dante explained, sheepishly. "We could not find the parts for the gears, Monsieur, so we had to take measurements and make them. It was not so easy. Also, we had to buy new cables because the old ones were rusted and frayed, very unreliable. The engine has been tested on the bench, but ... well ... we could not do everything in the time you said." Dante looked at me blankly, having no idea what was to be done next.

Mammadu squatted to inspect the work in progress. He peered around the frame, the wheel mounts, and the shock absorbers, picked up a few of the parts awaiting their turn in the assembly.

When he rose, he looked square at Dante. "Do you have everything you need to make this motorcycle run?"

"I ... think so, Monsieur."

"You think so or you know so, student?"

"I-I know so, Monsieur. Everything we need has been fabricated, purchased, or repaired."

"Do you think that you and I can assemble all this in the next hour?"

Dante did not understand what Mammadu was asking. "I haven't tested the electrical system, Monsieur, and the gearbox here will take an hour just by itself, maybe two."

"Barbu, can you assist us?" Mammadu asked me.

Then Dante understood. Mammadu was offering our help to assemble the motorcycle together, however long it took. But the young mechanic still couldn't be sure if this was a good thing or a bad thing. He scratched his head and gave me a smile of confusion.

"Absolutely," I replied. "How else are we going to get this baby running?"

Mammadu's expression conveyed instantly the opportunity he had created. He wasn't simply doing me or Dante a favor. Assembling the motorcycle as a team was a golden opportunity to evaluate the young man's skills as well as see how well we could work together— all of us. I loved this guy.

"Student Dante," Mammadu said as he moved to the workbench and picked up a wrench to strike a workman's pose. "Put us to work."

Dante's furrowed brow and roving eyes told me his brain was clicking into a higher gear. He turned to the standard-height bench behind him and, without making eye contact, beckoned us to come around the bike and look at the drawings. Remarkably, Dante—apparently with a good deal of help from Lamine— had developed a reasonable set of diagrams for the engine, the transmission, and the electrical system. Some elements of the brake assemblies were absent, but then, brakes are about the easiest component of a vehicle to repair and assemble. Scrutinizing these drawings made without reference to a manual of any kind, that I could tell, I gained a better understanding of the time it took to get this bike running and the professional approach that Lamine had instilled in Dante.

Dante divided us up. He took the gearbox, gave Mammadu the brake and clutch cables, and I would test and assemble the gauges and the electrical system. The tools were spread around like debris from a bomb blast (I made a mental note to work on that with Dante), so we put everything on the bench next to the drawings and took our direction from the energized student. We asked many questions, and when each of us got into a task with sufficient understanding, the workshop resounded only with the sounds of tools and their work, and the occasional grunt or sigh. Whenever one of us got stuck, the question or need was spoken aloud and whoever was in the best position to help, did so. Mammadu questioned Dante's order of assembly, and the student took the time to explain why the gear shaft had to fit through the clutch bearing first, even though it meant a more awkward assembly of the initiating cables. And so it went for over an hour. I had the easy part, even though I had to calibrate the fuel gauge and retest it three times. The lights worked fine, and we decided not to work on the electrical ignition in order to save time. Then, quite suddenly, there was no more work to do.

Dante and Mammadu guided the bike down the ramp and off the bench. They put gasoline in the tank, choked the engine, and Dante motioned for Mammadu to give it a kick start. Mammadu looked at me and I nodded. He was the strongest of us and if that kick start was going to need some torque, Mammadu was our best bet.

The first kick was dull and lifeless. As was the second. And the third. The fourth produced a brief sputter. It eventually took eight more strong kicks, each one getting more turnover, to ignite our bike to life. Dante now bent down to make some adjustments to the idle control. He inspected the gauges, checked the tires and brakes. He asked me to take it for the first spin, but again I declined.

"You should be the first test driver, Dante. After all, it's mostly your work."

The young man smiled sheepishly again. "I've never driven a motorcycle before."

"Have you driven a moped?" I asked.

Every student his age, and particularly an auto mechanic, must have driven if not owned a moped—the dangerous half-breed of a bicycle and a motorcycle, with the worst characteristics of both.

"Yes, I have."

Mammadu laughed. "You can do it, student Dante. And you should."

That was enough to give the young man the extra shot of confidence. Mammadu and I unlocked the garage door and raised it high and fast. Sunlight rushed into the shop in a torrent. Music filtered in from the stores lining the street, as did the scents of the city, overcoming those of oiled metal and burnt petrol inside the workshop.

Dante straddled the Norton, pulled the clutch, and snapped down the foot pedal into first gear. There was a grinding noise, and Dante stopped. I looked at Mammadu, who shrugged. Dante snapped his foot down, harder this time. The grinding gear noise made us all wince. Dante maneuvered the clutch and gearshift together slowly, and the gear engaged with a stiff *ka-CHUNK*. When Dante released the clutch, he wobbled so much that Mammadu and I rushed to his side to keep the bike from falling over. Slowly, Dante got control by speeding up and heading out into the street. Before he lurched into the Dakar traffic, he grabbed onto the brakes. He stopped so fast he started to go over the handlebars. He recovered his balance, but clearly this challenge was beyond him for the moment. I ran to his side and steadied the bike, holding onto the handlebars. I asked if I could take the bike from here. He nodded quickly, and we switched places.

It had been a few years since I had been on a decent bike. I'd owned a BSA in college and had driven dirt bikes with a bunch of hotshot British and French riders who worked at the sugar plantation up north. But this big street bike was an unexpected gift. I gunned the engine a few times to listen to it purr. The exhaust clearly had some baffle issues; that made the experience more visceral. I eased the bike into the slow Saturday traffic and sped off for the industrial park road by our office and then over to the port, where traffic would be lightest. I pulled my sunglasses from my shirt pocket as I started to gain speed, and then hunkered down with my chin nearly on the speedometer, giving the accelerator another turn.

What a sense of freedom! And so tenuous. The wind pushed my hair and beard back across my head with a hot slap. I leaned to one side or the other, weaving my way along the back street to the intersection at Place de l'Indépendance. Once into the stadium-sized four-lane traffic circle, I powered the bike past every car in front of me until my turnoff at the far end of the Place. Down by the port the air cooled slightly beneath the giant palms lining both sides of the avenue. Yes indeed, Dante had a job with us, if for no other reason than this exhilarating ride.

On the return to the trade school workshop, I had a bit of trouble downshifting to third and second gears. Mammadu was standing on the street, clearly anxious as he awaited his turn on the Norton. We switched places, and Mammadu roared off before I could warn him about shifting. Dante and I heard him grind the gears and eventually take off. I told Dante he had to adjust that tomorrow, but that I needed the bike for the rest of the day.

"Monsieur, you paid for most of the parts. I don't know who owns the bike, but it is definitely not me. Perhaps Professor Volante?"

It was inconsequential; I would take it and we could settle matters on Monday. Dante showed me where to wash up and by the time Mammadu returned with my trophy, I was ready to appear at the villa of "Lord and Lady" Blake.

Part 2

Doria and Nigel Blake

13. Doria Blake Serves

Doria Blake paced slowly around her swimming pool. Even in the hot Dakar afternoon she wore makeup, an exquisitely fitting flower-print dress, and toeless pumps. A single barrette held up her blonde hair. Although she was preparing for a late luncheon requested by her husband Nigel, for some colleagues, she had other things on her mind. She signaled to her maid, Ahminta, to set out the freshly cut flowers on the poolside table. She placed them as Doria directed and then retreated to the kitchen. Doria liked Ahminta Mbodj. She took training well and was eager to please. Holding a steady, decent-paying job was important to the young Senegalese single mother. Doria had even allowed Ahminta to bring her two children to work occasionally, surprising Doria with their cheerful laughter and politeness. They were healthy, at least, Doria remembered. She wondered if that would always be so.

Nigel often brought businesspeople to their beautiful home for all kinds of occasions. Doria unerringly fulfilled her role as hostess: luminous, gently commanding, and gracious. Their home was owned by Nigel's employer, London-based Barrow & Bean International. A showplace for their vice-president and director for African and Middle East business, the villa sat off the main coastal road into Dakar—Route de la Corniche Estate—along which could be counted the homes of international dignitaries, businesspeople, diplomats, and celebrities. The Blakes' house, like nearly all the villas along the corniche, was surrounded entirely by a two-and-a-half-meter concrete wall on top of which were large shards of broken glass imbedded in the concrete. As a security measure, it was more aesthetically pleasing than razor wire. Doria detested it even though she could barely see it from the ground.

Inside the walls, Doria conducted the lavish, orchestrated beauty. She walked out the front door and scanned the brick semicircular driveway. She shook her head as her gaze lingered on the Volkswagen-sized sundial surrounded by tropical flowers. She again thought how ostentatious it was and resumed her stroll. Along the sides of the house, well-kept bougainvillea and hibiscus spread in front of the stucco walls and occasionally intruded onto a few of the many first-floor windows. She took a pair of shears sitting in a box beneath the window and clipped some stems, keeping the blossoms in a bouquet in her left hand. When she tightened her grip on the bouquet, the thorns of the bougainvillea drew trickles of blood from her fingers. Doria looked at them with curiosity and continued her walk. She bent down to inspect the orange bromeliad and the calla growing almost wild across the unpaved patches of earth. Doria smiled at this tiny bit of floral chaos.

She sighed and strolled back into the house, through the sunroom, and onto the veranda. She dropped the cuttings in a corner for Ahminta to place in a vase. Crossing her arms, Doria stared across the outdoor dining area to the papaya-shaped pool. The early afternoon sun shimmered jewel-like off the water. How long had it been now? Five years? Or was it six years that she and Nigel had lived in Dakar? Had she really been playing the dutiful wife that long? Or had she actually *become* the dutiful wife? Where was the person she had believed herself to be or could have been? It was all just fantasy now, a dream that she allowed herself to imagine was somehow still possible, making her current life bearable for its impermanence. Today that dream-self seemed too distant and vague to sustain her.

How wonderfully exotic it all appeared when they first arrived in Dakar. Doria vividly recalled the road from the airport lined with tiny wooden shops overflowing with produce, clothes, car parts, butchered livestock, drums, and cooking pots. Whizzing over the road in BBI's Mercedes, there was much she didn't recognize: sculptures of twisted industrial metal, a tower of mud bricks the size of an apartment building. Troops of small children marched along in their school uniforms, without an adult in sight. Men and women labored on bicycles overburdened with sacks of everything from flour to cement to goatskins. From the very beginning it had been excitingly strange and compelling.

The people at the British embassy could not have been friendlier—at first. Doria would always remember Pamela George, an oddly brash woman by British diplomatic standards, whose quick wit tempered by an aristocratic grace gave her all the latitude she needed to skewer her fellow Brits, whom she reveled in calling "colonialists."

At the usual parties, Pamela took Doria aside in a deliberate effort to rescue her from the European diplomatic swarms whom Pamela knew would try to absorb the new arrival into their peckish tribes.

"Olivia Crabtree is as progressive a thinker as Idi Amin. When Olivia's not dispensing her toxic opinions about the 'negroid race,' you find her hidden away in only the finest restaurants in Dakar. You'd think the woman would at least try to learn French, but that, too, is probably beneath her. You cannot avoid her, Doria, but you can limit your exposure to her. Here, let me introduce you to …" and taking Doria by the hand, Pamela would introduce Doria to nearly every woman and gentleman at whatever event they attended. Most introductions were accompanied by some commentary, but some did not.

Doria most valued Pamela's friendship. Pamela seemed interested in what made Doria tick and never discouraged her. Doria could rattle on for several minutes about some strange flower or plant species about which Pamela knew nothing.

So Pamela asked her new friend a question. "You and Nigel seem very nice together, dear, but it isn't until you begin speaking about your plants and their—what did you call them—'their little biochemical engines,' that I see your pretty pale face flush with excitement. Why have you subjugated your passion, to traipse around Africa with this man?"

"You know, Pamela, I'm so very grateful that Nigel's work took us here. I honestly don't think I would ever have even seen such beautiful tropical flora in person, let alone have the opportunity to cultivate it. I've had this passion all my life, it seems." She stopped there and sipped her tea. "I actually majored in botany at the university."

"Good for you, dear. Don't lose that, and promise me you won't let yourself get bored. Boredom will rip your heart out as thoroughly as any man. It creeps up on you, stalking like a slothful ghost, stealing your will, diluting your passion, until you wake up one day to look into the mirror and not recognize the woman staring back at you."

"So," Doria said, "aside from my keen desire to explore the world of these tropical plants that I find everywhere, what advice have you to keep me from becoming bored?" She chuckled slightly as she asked this, thinking Pamela's dramatic warning was exaggerated yet amusing.

"Take a lover, preferably someone outside the diplomatic community."

Doria coughed on her tea and laughed. "That's not the second hobby I had in mind. Is it one of yours?"

"Heavens, yes! I'm not a professional woman like you, dear, and after three children, one needs to rejoin the land of the sexually attractive before it's too late. Or even after it's too late!"

"Pamela, that's so … so un-British of you." Doria was serious and joking at the same time.

"If by 'un-British' you mean unwilling to die that slow death of endless, dull functions, vapid conversations, suppressed intentions, and willful denial, then yes, I suppose it is."

"Is that how you think of us?" Doria asked calmly. "Of yourself?"

Pamela reached over and patted Doria's hand. "Stereotypes became such because they are true, dear. We British are the bulwark of rectitude on the surface because we secretly loathe ourselves for the grubby, mire-seeking animals we all are. And I dare say that present company is *not* excluded. Though I haven't sorted out what your dark-side desires might be. Have you?"

Doria was surprised but not offended. This was Pamela at her most interesting: commenting on human frailty with a coarse wit and a deep sense of her own imperfections. Holding her teacup in both hands, under her chin, Doria responded, "I suppose you'll just have to be my friend long enough to find out."

But that was not to be. Ten months after Doria's arrival, Pamela's husband was assigned to the embassy in Ottawa, Canada. Pamela quipped that it was perfectly proper that they should go from one of the warmest French-speaking capitals on earth to the coldest. After Pamela's departure, Doria missed her deep-sensing, protective friend and found all the other women dull in comparison. It was only a matter of time before the beautiful young bride of the new director for Barrow & Bean was thought of as a haughty loner.

Since those early days, it seemed to Doria that her life in Dakar had been one long period of stasis, punctuated and even mercifully disrupted by her charitable activities. She recalled her energy during their second year in Senegal when she led the spouses of the British embassy corps on a drive to "adopt" the children of a primary school in the local village of Ouakam. To this day the school continued to receive supplies and food every three months that it never would have otherwise. But what had happened to those first children when they reached middle school age? Many had dropped out of school altogether to try to find work, to raise their own siblings. Most were simply lost in an ocean of poverty, where the malnourishment and disease that Doria's small school program had forestalled for a few years eventually prevailed. What path was left to her to do something meaningful?

These days she went regularly to St. Joseph's Orphanage in Yoff, not far from the airport. She adored seeing the children and bringing them gifts. But they too were malnourished, ill, their potential obliterated. Drawn, as many of the children were, to this gentle white lady, others shrieked at the sight of her or sat in corners, mumbling incomprehensibly. The problems of the population around her were so large, so implacable, powered by the forces of culture, geography, and history—the very reasons she wanted to leave England in the first place. How could she ever help them?

And now, of course, she was preparing to entertain Nigel's business network. She snorted involuntarily as the irony bluntly hit her. A palm frond floated down into the pool, breaking the dance of sunlight on the water. Doria shivered. It was an unexpected and eerie feeling. Shaking off the goose bumps, she refocused on Nigel's gathering.

* * *

In his incessant quest for expanding both commercial growth of BBI and his own personal network, Nigel courted as many influential people as possible, even those with no discernable commercial interests. When he wasn't traveling to set up distributorships, negotiate purchase agreements, or oversee a new office, he was constantly hosting events large and small at his home. Doria had, in the past, enjoyed these gatherings with their smart conversations and interesting people. Lately, however, all topics seemed banal and the chatter distracting. It was, in the end, just wind.

Today's lunch guest list was typical of a Nigel networking event. It included a noted botanist from France who was teaching at the University of Dakar, Alain DeLevres; head of the Port of Dakar Administrative Authority, Alioune Djiop; and Nigel's longtime friend at the British embassy, Tony Hume. Doria had no notion of how or why Nigel knew Alain DeLevres, but she was glad to have someone out of the mainstream commercial interests participating. She was particularly excited that he was a botanist.

The Blakes' security guard held open the two passenger-side doors of the Mercedes as Doria greeted her husband and guests by the driveway.

"Mrs. Blake, it is a pleasure to see you again," intoned Djiop, dressed regally in a traditional Senegalese boubou and slacks of pale blue, embroidered on the wide cuffs and the collar with gold thread.

Hume kissed Doria on both cheeks and whispered how he couldn't wait to relax with Doria's great cuisine.

Nigel, standing still next to his Range Rover, spoke seriously to DeLevres. He looked up at his wife, stopped his conversation short, and walked up the stairs with his guest.

"Sweetheart, please meet Professor Alain DeLevres, renowned tropical botanist and visiting lecturer at the University of Dakar."

Doria extended her hand and with a soft, almost sly smile, she said, "I've been looking forward to meeting you, Professor."

DeLevres, a round man with a thick mane of salt-and-pepper hair, kissed Doria's hand perfunctorily. *"Merci,* Madame Blake. And to Monsieur Blake, for your hospitality."

The party moved through the open villa, to lunch near the pool.

"Is it true, Monsieur Djiop," Nigel asked before Ahminta served the first course, "that Dakar is now the third most important port for exporting West African diamonds?"

Djiop inhaled deeply, choosing his words. "That, Monsieur Blake, is a curious way for a food company executive to begin a conversation."

Nigel looked at Djiop unfazed.

The minister continued. "One would think that Freetown or Monrovia or even Conakry would be more likely choices, as these are the port city capitals of the key West African countries with diamond resources."

"Yes indeed," Hume chimed in. "But those ports simply haven't got the security capability, nor the access to brokers—honest brokers, I'm talking about here—that can be found in Dakar."

"Besides," Nigel added, "Sierra Leone, Liberia, and Guinea are in terrible shape compared to Senegal. Their infrastructures are ten times worse than here."

Doria, who normally listened absentmindedly, began to wonder how the conversation had become about diamonds. Her hands began to twitch.

The Frenchman entered the discussion. "I understand the political situations are beyond reckoning in those former English colonies. I tried to secure travel into Sierra Leone and Guinea to research native medicinal plants, and the French embassy advised me that there were rebel groups controlling the area I intended to visit. It was shocking news, and nowhere could I read about it in the journals. Apparently, there is a dispute over the very resource you're speaking of—diamonds."

"We know something about this at the embassy, of course," said Hume. "So far, there isn't a lot of news coming out, I'm afraid. But we have heard, and I think Mr. Djiop can confirm that much of West African diamond traffic is now going through Dakar, as Nigel said."

Djiop shifted in his seat. "There is no truth whatsoever to rumors that illegal cross-border diamonds are laundered in Senegal."

Tony pushed his chair back and curled his lips into a smile. Nigel looked at him and frowned.

Doria turned her attention to DeLevres. "Can you tell me, Professor, what are the properties of the plants you were looking for? You said they were medicinal?"

"Yes, I can, Madame. I am specifically interested in what is commonly called *banjeau* root in Guinea, which is purported to be a powerful muscle relaxer and helps to relieve arthritis pain. There is another, called *osimious*, a tree whose bark, when dried and made into a tea, is supposed to reduce fever and stop diarrhea."

"Are hospitals and doctors using these, here in Dakar?"

"I very much doubt it. There have been some local remedies that I believe have been investigated by the Institut de Louis Pasteur for their curative qualities, but to my knowledge they haven't been approved by the medical profession—unless you mean the traditional healers plying their native cures outside of the hospital's oversight. Then the answer is, of course, yes."

"Actually, I was thinking of Western-trained doctors knowing about and using local medicines wherever they can. I'm certain they are more readily available to the general population and, presumably, at prices these people can afford."

Nigel sniggered. "I'm sure the drug companies would be mounting their own expeditions if these jungle plants did what the professor here says they do."

"Not necessarily," DeLevres said. "Most, if not all the European drug companies rely on primary field studies from researchers such as me and others, for information regarding curative and other properties of tropical flora. They are not like oil or mining companies, who know exactly what they are looking for and how to find it. The pharmaceutical scientists are chemists, not botanists."

"Do you not think, Mr. Djiop, that more should be done for the suffering here in Senegal?" Doria asked. "I've seen many children here in Dakar that have skin lesions and distended bellies. Many have misshapen arms and legs from un-knitted broken bones." She put down her fork and smiled as she blushed slightly. "Perhaps more is being done, and I'm simply unaware of it."

"Madame Blake," Djiop said, "we all wish there were more we could do for our poorest citizens. We are grateful to have the benefit of Western medicines and knowledge here in Dakar and elsewhere in our poor country. We will need many decades, I think, to reach even 50 percent of our citizens with health resources."

"Well," Hume interjected, "I'm sure the medical community is grateful for the work of Professor DeLevres and his colleagues, since they are the ones finding the cures and figuring out ways to make them available. Am I right, Professor?"

The Frenchman tilted his head and said, "We botanists find plants and investigate their properties. The chemists and the medical doctors make medicines."

"I truly believe," Hume said, "that if Senegal or Guinea could take advantage of their natural resources and use that wealth to educate and build the economy, other benefits would flow. Don't you agree, Monsieur Djiop?" Hume looked directly into the minister's eyes.

"We in West African countries have only recently liberated ourselves of colonialism." Djiop held Tony's stare. "Our resources have been making others wealthy for nearly three hundred years. I hope it does not take us that long to reap the benefit of what is left to us."

"But even you must admit, Monsieur Djiop," Nigel said, "that without Western knowledge and Western markets, your natural resources would not have nearly the potential and the value that they do."

"This is why we have remained friends with our former colonial adversaries." Djiop smiled.

Tony Hume spoke of the IMAME consortium and how they had partnered with three country governments and helped them form a multilateral agency, the Organization pour l'Exploration et l'Utilization du Fleuve Senegal. It was quite the collaboration. A hydroelectric dam would be in Mali, the mineral mines mostly in the Fouta Djallon mountains in Guinea, and water for agriculture for Mauritania and Senegal, as well as a navigable river for cargo vessels as far inland as Kayes, Mali. Nigel was keen to learn more about this venture, but neither he nor the other two men could provide any more information. The conversation turned to the Senegalese national football team.

Doria finished her lunch in silence as she pondered her own situation. She had adored Nigel from the first moment she saw him. He was gregarious and gracious, always smiling, she recalled. Back in Manchester, his heart seemed as expansive as the world itself. She remembered as their courtship began in earnest when she, as a staff researcher at Barrow & Bean's food laboratory, and he, a young account executive fresh from taking his honors at Oxford, had walked her home in the rain. He saw a kitten sitting, drenched, in the middle of a side road and rushed to pick it up. Surprisingly, the tiny creature did not try to run away, tired and hungry as it must have been. They brought the kitten back to Doria's flat and adopted her, naming her

Stella. Nigel continued to bring milk and cat food to the office to make sure Doria wasn't supporting the little feline on her own. As Stella grew and settled in, Nigel had reason to visit regularly, having taken a genuine interest in Stella's well-being.

Had Nigel's heart contracted over time? she wondered. Had his love for his career, living in neocolonial splendor, meeting important and connected people, turned him away from what she believed was his true and generous nature? It felt like that sometimes. She looked at him across the cleared table; he appeared animated and confident. She banished these thoughts for now.

A slight breeze came up from the ocean and lifted the palms' boughs, disturbing the green-headed parrots. They rose in tight formation and flew down quickly, squawking and taking refuge in a large, out-of-place rhododendron, the only vegetation BBI had imported for the villa—a reminder to the Blakes of the better part of England. Though it was a specific hybrid chosen for its heat resilience, it required special care that Doria personally lavished on it. To see the parrots making themselves at home in this foreign shrub filled her with a sense of accomplishment. Small victories, she said to herself. My life is a necklace of small victories.

As the dessert of homemade mango and guava sorbets was served, Doria put her hand on DeLevres' arm as she asked, "Do you think, Professor, I could come by and, well, learn about your research and these local plants and herbs? I'm truly fascinated by some of the things Ahminta has told me about her family cures, *garabu bok*, I think she calls them."

Hearing Doria speak Oulof made Djiop laugh. "Excellent translation, Mrs. Blake."

"Oh, I didn't translate, Monsieur. It was Ahminta. These are her words. She tells me that her grandmother used to make a compound with bark and leaves that could help knit broken bones, though whether the bark and leaves are from the same tree or what plants they do come from, I haven't a clue. I would be ever so grateful, Professor, if you could guide me." Doria looked straight into his eyes.

"It would be my pleasure, Madame Blake. Since my trip to Guinea was postponed, I will be spending more time than usual at the horticultural center at the university, updating my class notes. Next week will be best for me. When would you like to come by?"

"Monday morning. Thank you, Professor. Say, around nine o'clock." She never doubted the Frenchman's answer.

"Fabulous, darling," Nigel spoke up. "Have we found you an outlet for all that pent-up energy you've been storing? You know, you've been like a cat in cage ever since you stopped going to the Ouakam hospital every week." He laughed gently and sat back in his chair.

Doria didn't bother to correct him. It had been a school, of course.

Tony was compelled to add, "Wouldn't it be grand if she came up with a cure for gout from sedge grass!"

Doria laughed good-naturedly. "Your sarcasm does not become you, Tony."

He was well aware that Doria had finished second in her class at Chelsea College and had, as Nigel liked to say, sacrificed her career as an underpaid plant researcher for the burden of traveling the world with him.

She added, "Besides, it can't hurt to learn more about the country and region we live in. And we know very little, really, about Senegal."

"It would be wrong to take such things too lightly," DeLevres said directly to Hume. "What we do *not* know of healing and other properties of tropical flora is quite vast. I dare say we have not even cataloged, let alone investigated, all of the plant life here. My own research hopes to take advantage of the knowledge of the people who have been here for thousands of years and use their acquired wisdom. Perhaps Madame Blake might even consider accompanying me on some of my field research."

This suggestion caught Doria by surprise and she quivered at the thought. It was the perfect next thing for her to try. She was about to say how wonderful the idea struck her when Nigel spoke first.

"One step at a time, I dare say. Right, darling?" He flashed her a quick smile. "Going to the laboratory at the university, Professor, strikes me as a perfectly intriguing and perfectly safe first step. I'm not sure my wife is up to fieldwork in the open savannah or the rain forest just yet. Hell, I'm not even up to it!" He laughed with his lower face while his eyes stared at Doria.

Doria looked straight at her husband. "Let's indeed start at the laboratory, Professor. And if we both find that I could be useful to you in some fieldwork, that could work out as well. We'll take it one step at a time, as Nigel said."

While Ahminta began clearing the table, Doria rose gracefully and asked the guests if they were ready for coffee.

* * *

After the guests and Nigel left the house, Doria was once again alone with her thoughts. She wanted to do some gardening, so she went to the bedroom to change. Carefully she undid each button of her dress and lifted her shoulders and arms out of the sleeves. Pulling the dress down, she did not allow it to touch the floor. She looked at herself in the mirror. She wished she had been more athletic looking and slender, less round. It had taken her years not to feel awkward about her breasts. She had always tried to flatten them with her choice of clothes, but that too was uncomfortable. When Doria was in her teens, her mother had tried to help her understand and appreciate her body, had always wanted her to dress flatteringly, yet always with care, being proper and attractive simultaneously. It bothered Doria that her mother seemed preoccupied with the attention of others and particularly of men. Doria had resented that her mother prodded her to dress and act not for herself. And yet she did as her mother asked, until her mother didn't have to ask. At what point did those behaviors stop being the wishes of her mother and begin to be a part of Doria herself? She couldn't say.

But the Rousseau family code of decorum had its desired effect. Throughout her college years, Doria was pursued by mostly earnest young men who hadn't the slightest idea who Doria was, what she believed, or what was important to her. They only knew how she looked and, even more simply, how she dressed. Love enters in at the eye, Doria had said to herself, and laughed. She had always been more bemused than flattered by their attention, thinking not so much that she didn't merit their sideways glances or stuttering sentences as they tried to strike up conversations, but rather how strange they acted for no reason she could fathom. She selectively accepted offers to date, but never felt she came to understand and feel what these men must have felt—a physical need.

Nigel Blake was the only man who had stirred in Doria Rousseau what she called "need." That feeling was closer to security and warmth—being with a man who could be passionate about small things as well as big. Nigel laughed easily and would seldom get cross at anything. And he was very clever. No one had ever made Doria feel more out of herself than Nigel, and for that she had decided to love him.

She changed into loose-fitting dark slacks and an old casual shirt of Nigel's, left unbuttoned and worn on top of a T-shirt emblazoned with the Senegalese flag and Union Jack, crossed at the staffs, with the BBI logo beneath. Perfect gardening clothes.

By 3:00 p.m. her gardener would be gone, the heat would be at its peak, and the plants she tenderly cared for in the shade of her palm trees would need her the most. Or was it the other way around? These were all individual and special plants in one way or another. Aloe vera was easy to care for, though not native to Africa, and she used it frequently for salves and ointments that she gave to the Senegalese who worked for her. The bundle of Greek allium, with cheerful white blooms atop the slender, leafless stalks, was a dry-weather flower that Doria loved to cut and place in clear vases against a multicolored African cloth on a table or next to a window. Yellow clusters of Ferula blossoms had an incandescent quality that illuminated the path through the garden at dusk. And many others, most of which came from places other than Senegal, but none more interesting than kachura. It had shiny broad leaves with clusters of purple-and-white funnel-shaped flowers that protected a yellow center where bees gathered. She had discovered it by accident as she passed the home of the Indian ambassador. She had asked the ambassador's gardener about it, who generously pulled a few rooted sprigs from the ground and gave them to Doria with instructions of how to root, plant, and care for them. "It is fussy," he told her. "But if you are good to kachura, she will reward you one hundredfold." It was a wonderful addition to her landscape and, she discovered, had properties that had been used for centuries in India for reducing swelling from bruises and infection.

All these plants provided Doria with an outlet for her nurturing, a feeling that she needed deeply to express. Children would have been the natural subjects for such focus, but Doria, unable to conceive, and Nigel, as yet unwilling to adopt, found other, separate outlets for their parental instincts.

Doria's pursuit of botanical charges was more than a vestigial force of biology. She loved how the plants adapted and grew, changed and developed. There was so much to learn from them, so much they could teach us and help us lead better lives. Their natural beauty and strange, wonderful capabilities, born of secretive chemical engines too complex to duplicate, awed Doria. She hummed an old English folk tune as she sank her trowel into soft earth while thinking of her upcoming visit to the French botanist's lab. In the palm trees above her, crows gathered, chasing away the parrots, and spoke to each other in deep, inquisitive calls.

14. Purpose Rising

Nigel's morning ritual had never varied since his arrival in Senegal, at least not that Doria could recall. Once awake, he would swing both legs to the side of the bed and place both feet into the slippers he had left meticulously placed the night before. With a stretch of his arms into the air, he stood upright in his slippers. He remained still at the bedside, erect like a diver, sometimes yawning as he brought his arms perpendicular to his torso, and let them fall to his side. When Doria was awake, watching him through one eye over the pillow, she would count to herself how long Nigel stood with his arms straight in the air before lowering them to become a crucifix, and then to his side to start his day. One, two, three, four; one, two, three, four. ... Nigel must be counting to himself too, she surmised, though she never asked him. Once this small exercise was complete, Nigel strode into the bathroom for his morning toilette. Rectitude regained.

Doria would most often take this time to drift in and out of sleep, trying consciously to craft a new dream from the shifting wisps of dream images she could recall, sometimes from the prior night, sometimes from nights long ago. She loved remembering a dream of being in a college laboratory, where she was no longer the student but the instructor. She was standing in front of a class that included her mother and her uncle Jonas. But she was more than an instructor. She was the head of a research team and she was sharing with them all her discoveries: a way to duplicate photosynthesis, or maybe something else ... a treatment for radiation sickness. Her test subject mice had all survived and one had even obeyed Doria's verbal commands to flip in the air and open the cage latch. Doria laughed softly in her half sleep as she envisioned the obedient, healthy mice. But now the sun was rising, piercing her window shades with rays of clear heat. Day had begun its full intrusion.

By the time Doria had donned her robe and descended the marble stairway to the kitchen, Ahminta had arrived and was preparing the couple's breakfast.

"Here, Minta, let me help you," Doria sang as she took the dripping juicer to the sink to be washed.

A bemused smile crossed Ahminta's face and she moved on to setting the table. When Doria took the fresh baguette and began to cut it into thin slices, Ahminta rushed quietly in from behind her and put her hand on Doria's arm.

"This is my work, Madame. Thank you." She moved to the counter and took the knife from Doria's hand.

Doria blushed and stood some steps away, watching Ahminta, who looked over her shoulder and smiled.

It was another beautiful morning in Dakar, in a blistering succession of hundreds of beautiful days. From the wide double-framed window by the kitchen table, Doria peered out over the terrace pool to the garden that stretched the length of the security wall. She gazed at the ornamental shrubs and flowers. In her mind they started to change into something different: plants of imaginary origins and shapes, vegetables with leaves like wings, or flowers with blossoms the size of beach balls. Plants that could, if they existed, grow only in wild places and be harvested at the peril of the local men and women—the kind of plants that resist cultivation by any hand other than God's own. Doria imagined herself exploring the forest and discovering such wonders. Suddenly her garden seemed quite small and tame. I must learn more about those curious spices and odd-smelling plants in the market, she thought.

Nigel glided into the kitchen, imperially slim in his handmade suit. Doria thought it odd that Nigel kept the same morning eating habits from home: his timed egg, his thinly buttered toast. Had he no sense of personal adventure, other than to throw himself into those consuming business deals? Doria eagerly experimented with the local fruits: guava, papaya, ugly fruit, tamarind. Each one had been a revelation. They were always fragrant and as accessible as air itself. Doria joined Nigel at the table as Ahminta placed the palette of colorful fruit in front of her.

"I need to go to Rotterdam for three days next week," Nigel announced. "Clive has finally got the Bahn-Denzir Group to negotiate distribution rights for their entire line of biscuits and preserves. I have no idea how they can produce them so cheaply and keep up their quality. But lucky for us, they haven't nearly the international network we have."

Doria looked at Nigel, smiled pleasantly. As she regained concentration on her plate she said something that had not remotely come into her mind. "Must you?"

"Heavens, Doria, I'll only be gone three days, total."

She reconnected her mind with her speech. "I … I realize that, of course, Nigel. But you know, this is such a large place, and I rattle around frightfully when it's only me."

It was Nigel's turn to smile and shake his head. "You're a funny girl, my dear. You'll be fine. You always are. I expect you'll be taking up Alain's offer to see his laboratory one of those days. Oh, I expect I'll be preparing for that trip most of the day in the office, so expect me home at a decent hour."

"No dinner with Tony?"

"Not tonight, certainly. I think he's down country in the Casamance until Saturday, anyway, dealing with some trade issue that only an attaché could love."

"Will you be home for dinner then, Nigel?" Doria asked without looking up. "Or should I join you for dinner downtown?" Finishing her last slice of mango, Doria looked up with an expectant smile.

Nigel was touched and confused. Doria would graciously come down to Dakar's diplomatic district when invited, but never had she invited herself during Nigel's business week. Realizing Doria was waiting for his answer, Nigel patted his mouth nervously with his napkin.

"Well, I suppose we could arrange something. Would you like to meet at Le Lagon?"

"That would be lovely, dear. Shall we say eight o'clock?"

"Doria, you've made my day," he said, standing up from the table and leaning over and planting a gentle but sincere kiss on her dutifully proffered cheek.

Amazing, he thought. This is indeed new!

* * *

Of the many open-air markets in Dakar, Doria's favorite was Marché Kermel. Like a colossal gazebo, the grand pavilion of the market stood three stories above the local shops and warehouses that congregated in a hive just north of the main commercial entrance to the Port of Dakar. Hundreds of clustered vendor stalls, each one no more than a meter square, radiated like shallow bleachers from the outer perimeter of the pavilion. In every stall was a woman wrapped in a chaos of colors, squatting behind her wares. For sale were imported tulips, zinnias, and other flowers; red and yellow peppers; water; cantaloupe and casaba melons; green beans, white beans, red beans, beans in pods and beans in baskets; green and yellow squash, okra, and eggplant; rice from China, rice from India, and rice from

California; peanuts; palm oils; fresh fish, dried fish, catfish, red fish. And flies. Everywhere, tiny clouds of flies hovered.

As Doria and Ahminta descended into the market area from the Blakes' white Mercedes, the smells of the market again accosted her. Fragrant and pungent, the scents of everything fresh blended with those of the rotting. And the sounds: percussive, humming rhythms of the market. Often there would be young men at the entrance, beating away on talking drums. Young women on their way to their stalls might stop, put down the large sacks they carried on their heads, and dance a few feverish steps, then laugh brightly before continuing off to work. The sounds of bargaining were everywhere, as were the sounds of chopping and slicing, weighing and counting, cursing and cackling: a concerto of commerce at its most basic and energetic.

Doria enjoyed her immersion into this wealth of human activity, buoyed and a bit disturbed by her distance as an expatriate white woman. Upon her arrival, Doria was again surrounded by all manner of young women selling blankets or sweet potatoes or bread. Today she purchased green peppers from a very young girl who said nothing and could not look up at Doria. Ahminta took the peppers into her basket. The wave of young merchants dispersed into the din. The white lady and her servant continued their search for the day's groceries.

Ahminta's great aunt Bydee kept a small kiosk in Marché Kermel. Doria always made a visit to her before she left. She visited the old woman because Bydee was a traditional apothecary and always had dozens of interesting and challenging concoctions. There was a sticky substance the color of unripe peas and the consistency of damp talcum powder that Doria had purchased last year for a headache. It was called *mendech*. Though it stuck to the roof of her mouth and tasted like burnt grass, it was every bit the anodyne Doria had hoped, giving her the courage to procure other, less benign-looking cures to keep but not always to try: a black goo with a scent and consistency of rotting cheese that was rubbed on bruises; a light brown liquid with dark seeds spewing tiny tendrils in all directions, to cure insomnia; a chunky whitish paste that Bydee swore would not only help Doria get pregnant, but guarantee her a son, when applied right after her "moon cycle." Doria was fascinated by all of them.

Today Doria thought she might buy some *ndaymou gar*, a sticky yellow compound that was mixed in water and was supposed to provide energy and focus. Doria had tried *ndaymou gar* many times before and found it not only pleasant tasting, but rather like caffeine in its effect, and without the attendant withdrawal headaches. What she really wanted, however, was to make some for herself—grow whatever herb or tree this came from and test out her own mixture. But when Ahminta, on Doria's behalf, asked her aunt how it was made, Bydee looked at Doria sternly and wagged a long, wrinkled finger at her, saying in Oulof, "That is not for you to know, young woman. You do not have the need, you do not have the gift." Ahminta translated this slowly into French for Doria.

"But I do," protested Doria, smiling, "I do, Bydee. I want to help make the children of Yoff learn better in school."

After Ahminta's translation, Bydee held up her hand dismissively and told Doria, "You think this is for children, yes? You are a crazy woman. You can buy what you want from me."

"Please, Bydee. I know this would be so good for children in the proper amount. I have to learn how these wonderful medicines are made."

"Why not buy them from me?" she asked. "Why not let me sell you whatever you need?"

Ahminta was starting to tire from translating.

"Can I at least watch you make them, Bydee? May I come to your home and learn? I'll pay you two times what you would normally get."

If she would pay two times without bargaining, Bydee considered, what would she pay after a day or two of negotiations. "Come back another day," the old woman said. "I cannot do what you ask today."

"But soon you can," Doria replied.

Doria was encouraged, though she knew she was engaged in a transaction that might take days or weeks to complete. Yet it would be complete at some point and this made Doria smile crookedly and look at Bydee. Bydee waved Doria and Ahminta off, to let her get on with the day's business.

Ahminta was glad to be moving on. This aunt was not her favorite person.

* * *

Doria's white Mercedes rolled slowly up the drive of the University of Dakar. Students were milling around recently-erected buildings in a dense, transforming throng like groups of clouds. They stared curiously at the slow-moving vehicle, wondering perhaps if it carried one of the many diplomats or politicians who frequently descended upon the campus. They swirled around and crossed in front as if the car presented no more risk to them than a tree. Doria thought this must be what if feels like to be a dignitary—secure but unsure of the crowd.

She rolled down the window and warmly asked where she could find the graduate botany lab. She asked a dozen students, none of whom could help.

Finally, a tall young man with a skin-tight rayon shirt and powder-blue bell-bottom slacks spoke. Not to her, but to her driver, Iba.

"It is in the old section of the university," he told him in Oulof. "When you arrive at the statue of Leopold Senghor, go left, then right, down the unpaved road. It will be the second building you see."

Doria thanked the young man who was already walking away.

Alain DeLevres worked in the part of the university where windows stayed broken for years and where carpets of dust draped classrooms and labs. It was built in the early twentieth century. Today, in 1977, neither students nor faculty cared to spend much time there. It felt and looked more old France than modern Senegal, with Christian religious symbols throughout the grounds and European artwork in the corridors and classrooms. A fountain in a small courtyard that had not felt water running since independence held an imitation Rodin sculpture pondering its loneliness.

The "unpaved" road turned out to be a formerly paved road that simply had been neglected for decades and was more treacherous for the unconnected patchwork of aging asphalt and ravines. It declined steeply as they traveled down to the second building, where the ground leveled.

The drab edifice, light gray and a single story, spread like a small warehouse, and was bounded by a gravel-on-concrete walkway. By the time Iba parked the Mercedes, Doria was already outside the car, thanking him. She let him know she might be a while, offering Iba and Ahminta the opportunity to explore the university. They both politely declined, preferring to stay until she returned. Doria entered the building hoping to find not only Alain DeLevres. She wanted to restart a journey she had imagined since college.

While the university could attract competent and occasionally excellent instructor talent from Africa, Europe, and the Americas, administratively it was a wreck. Budgets were routinely overrun. Instructors often went without critical materials for years. Academic rigor was by happenstance since the well-connected could count on passing grades regardless of performance. Interdepartmental battles disrupted class schedules, and research almost never received peer review. Oddly enough, this suited Alain DeLevres just fine.

Dr. DeLevres wasn't malicious, incompetent, or pathological. He simply preferred to build his own world amid the chaos. The environment wasn't merely permissive, it was feudal, providing an excellent backdrop for DeLevres to develop and preserve his self-image as a survivalist and a problem solver. It also eliminated the likelihood of scrutiny, academic or otherwise, into his work. He was not an academic hack, having published many reputable papers and a textbook on medicinal plants, and edited a long-regarded anthology of biomedical botany. But he did fear his current research direction would get him thrown into a West African prison.

When he received the phone call from Doria Blake confirming his offer to visit his lab, DeLevres wasn't sure how to react. He could think of no more pleasant diversion than to spend a few hours puffing for the beautiful and serene Mrs. Blake, but he was concerned that she might not content herself with the standard ethnobotanical jabber that second-year students accepted as cutting-edge knowledge. She might try to learn more about his work than would make him comfortable. He suppressed this concern by the thoughts of escorting an appreciative Mrs. Blake through his sanctum.

He was waiting for her in the lobby, perched casually in an ebony chair made a century earlier in the Congo, reading *Le Journal de Mycologie Tropicale*. There were no students or signs of other activity.

He rose as Doria entered. "Madame Blake, how kind of you to visit."

Doria extended her hand to be shaken by the Frenchman, who kissed it politely.

"It was kind of you to allow me to invite myself, Professor."

"I could not refuse such an earnest request to peer into my life's work," he said.

"Yes, well …. Dilettante though I am, I feel there are such wonderful curative secrets in plants around us. Your work intrigues me so."

They walked down the corridor toward DeLevres' office. The midday sun streaked through arched windows illuminating the swirls of dust that looked like steam.

"I must be honest with you, Madame Blake. Our work can be quite painstakingly dull. We collect hundreds of samples from our fieldwork, as you can imagine."

"Are you referring to whole plant collections?"

"Mostly. We are interested in both cultivated and wild species of all manner of plants, used for everything from spicing food to … curing sleeping sickness."

"What do you gather from the local markets?" Doria asked, thinking of her own experiences. "There are so many interesting samples and concoctions sold there."

"Indeed there are, yes. But so much of what you find here and in the city markets close by, such as Kaolack or Saint-Louis, are tainted with European plants or, sometimes, even medicines. For example, we discovered pulverized aspirin in a so-called traditional cure for fever, in five different markets."

Doria nodded as she processed this information. When he opened the door to his office, Doria wouldn't sit. She walked over to a bookshelf stuffed with reference books. With her back to him, she made her request. "Please tell me about your work, Professor. Which local plants do you think are the most ... important?" Regardless of his answer, she knew that part of the truth would be found among his books and notes.

"Many are important, Mrs. Blake, and some are truly useful. I presume you are most interested in medicinal applications. Let me think." He crossed his arms and tapped his forefinger on his lips. "*Erythrina senegalensis* is widely used for a variety of conditions and in a variety of ways. It is used to relieve dysentery or malaria, depending upon whether you drink the infusion of the pulverized leaves, as used by the coastal Senegalese, or you ingest the powdered flowers, as do the Malinke in eastern Senegal and Mali. We grow it in our garden, but it's a fussy weed."

"It's actually a small tree, isn't it, Professor?" She continued to scan his reference library. "With tiny bell-shaped red flowers?"

DeLevres viewed Doria with much more curiosity now. "Very good, Mrs. Blake. It takes three years for the mature plant to develop flowers. We are just starting to uncover the active compounds that *Erythrina* manufactures."

"Does it work, Professor? Or would I be more precise in asking, how well does it work?"

"My work is not on the clinical side, Mrs. Blake, so I don't have perhaps the best answer for you. Anecdotally, I can say that *Erythrina* is effective in reducing the symptoms of dysentery."

"Could it be used to treat cholera?"

"Theoretically, yes, I suppose." DeLevres shrugged. "But we have no evidence it's been used in this manner. You might ask this question at some of the clinics farther in-country."

Doria turned from the reference bookshelves to face him. "Do you work with anyone conducting trials? I mean, do you work with any clinics you mentioned, in rural areas?"

"I'm afraid you do not yet understand the nature of my work. I am examining the biochemical nature of traditional healing plants to both understand and potentially synthesize their curative elements.

I'm also attempting to produce cultivars that could be either more potent or have other enhanced qualities, such as additional drought resistance or more prolific reproduction or less susceptibility to bacterial infections. How any of these plants actually perform in trials is a question for other researchers. Not for me."

An idea was germinating within Doria. "I have to believe, Professor, as you produce these hybrids, regardless of what you create and discover in your laboratory, that actual field trials to test the efficacy of some of these enhanced compounds would serve your research, would it not?"

"Assuredly, they would. But I'm not necessarily at that stage in any of my current projects," DeLevres said, looking away from Doria.

She tilted her head and smiled. "Please show me the lab itself. I'd love to get a feel for how you break down the compounds and what constituent elements you're searching for."

"I'm searching for anything and everything, Mrs. Blake. When I see something I recognize, I know what stage I'm in. But truthfully …." He paused and led Doria through the door of smoked glass, into the lab. "I prefer finding things I have not seen before. For example, when an alkaloid compound shows up where none was foreseen."

Isn't that interesting, Doria thought, knowing if DeLevres was discovering and working with alkaloids in these plants, then he might be exploring their psychotropic effects. Alkaloids were complex compounds that reacted easily with brain chemistry and produced varying effects, from euphoria to hallucinations to psychosis. Such plants were rare on the planet and had not been well researched in West Africa—or even well catalogued, as far as Doria was aware. If DeLevres was uncovering alkaloids in his research, he might well be exploring some very interesting, potentially useful and potentially dangerous flora. Doria's senses now seemed heightened as she was taking in details she might otherwise have missed. It was very appealing.

DeLevres frowned and said nothing for a minute. They proceeded to one of the many workstations along the long Formica bench. Doria sensed DeLevres perhaps revealed more than he had intended. She watched him take a deep breath and let it out in a long sigh.

"Has your research uncovered anything that might be used to treat more elusive diseases? I'm thinking not of the physical problems like diarrhea or ringworm, Professor, but of a scourge like mental illness. An herbal medicine that could positively affect brain chemistry."

DeLevres stopped and looked directly at Doria Blake, finding no trace of irony or acknowledgment that she believed she was unlocking the secret at which DeLevres had carelessly hinted. She had affixed a perfectly soft smile to complement her steady blue eyes and looked back at him as mother might look at a child, knowing utterly and without judgment.

"Certainly … err … West Africa has its … err … share of mental illness," he said. "But from the little I know of the subject, it's difficult to diagnose, it carries significant social stigma, and is treated more like religious exorcism than an illness."

"You know more than you credit yourself." Doria looked away from him and to the laboratory bench where DeLevres had been conducting his private tests only hours before. "I have seen many of the children at the Ouakam orphanage clinic whose emotional instability alone makes it impossible for them to live normal lives. They suffer far worse from mental illness than from the other physical diseases. So bad is the mental affliction, in fact, that they cannot be treated even for the simple things. They cannot eat food when they are near starvation. I've seen these disturbed children eat sand and feces, speak gibberish, and shrink from the touch of another person. No one, not even the nuns can reach them."

"Your heart is big, Mrs. Blake. Is that what draws you to this field of study?" DeLevres had averted her original question.

"What draws me is that nature has provided for us in ways we have yet to comprehend, and the most vulnerable among us are in the greatest need."

"That has always been the case, I'm sad to say," DeLevres said with sincerity.

"Where one finds the root of disease, Professor, there, one also finds the cure. What afflicts these people springs from this tropical land, as do answers to their suffering. From the rain forest, or savannah, or wherever these plants grow. If we can find such natural medicines, shape them, and administer them before we destroy them, then I believe we can accomplish great things. Do you wish to accomplish great things, Professor?" Doria asked.

"I, Mrs. Blake, seek to understand what these people have learned from over fifty centuries of living here. Greatness is not anything I understand, nor to which I aspire. Besides, it is always the judgment of others that determines greatness, is it not?"

Doria nodded. "And time." She picked up a glass bottle half filled with a clear liquid and silently read the label.

"Please tell me more of how you are isolating specific compounds and how you test to find which of them are the active agents."

"How well do you remember your college chemistry and botany courses? Much of what I do are basic analyses. For example …"

DeLevres was quite happy to move the conversation to the mechanics of his work, and though Doria was genuinely interested and would pay close attention, she had already learned much regarding the potential to learn from Alain DeLevres.

15. Dinner Date

Nigel stood in front of one of his six office windows where the radiant fever of the sun was only partially mitigated by industrial blinds. He returned to the memo he had been reading. BBI was looking for better operating margins from its international subsidiaries and would rely on the parent company's overseas executive officers, of which Nigel was one of two dozen, to step up their activities. The execs were directed to concentrate their business development on partnerships and low-cost producers, rather than internally developing new products or new distribution channels. This directive meant the deal with the Bahn-Denzir Group became a high priority. There was urgency to travel to Rotterdam for contract negotiations, and such a trip could be easily extended to pursue a critical component of the side venture he and Tony Hume had conjured.

Although he never considered himself a particularly ambitious man, Nigel was nevertheless eager for the approbation and respect of his superiors. Not in the sense that they should value his work or even his loyalty, but that they should see him as a potential equal. That need might never be fulfilled, Nigel considered, in the unspoken caste system of corporate England. He moved from the memo and on to the Bahn-Denzir contract draft.

Born to parents of moderate means and indeterminate lineage, Nigel had distinguished himself in public school and then at Oxford. His half-Irish father, William, a bright, entertaining man whom everyone in Reading called Billy, had always seemed satisfied with his job as a construction engineer, if for no other reason than he seemed to get so much of life from his family and friends. Nigel received his gregarious nature and self-deprecating humor from Billy, who loved to entertain and often played the family's old spinet piano for guests as well as for Nigel and his younger siblings—two sisters and two brothers. Glenda, Nigel's Scottish mother, was the grounded, practical force of the family. Though Billy was a good provider and a devoted husband, Glenda had never seemed at ease or secure with their solidly middle-class status. As her firstborn, Nigel was the recipient of her regular tutelage in responsibility, hard work, and dissatisfaction with anything except perfection. She, like so many mothers, believed her son must surely be destined for finer things, even greatness, and she schooled him relentlessly on perseverance and leadership, fueling his ambition.

Lifted through childhood by the life-forces of his parents, Nigel developed a self-confidence that comes with successive accomplishments. He excelled in his studies and explored the piano and theater. Though not much of an athlete, he competed fiercely in football and was valued as a stalwart if not a star. Nigel had been bothered throughout his school days, though, by the notion that some of the boys not nearly as academically successful as he, acted superior and condescending because of their "family standing," a term Nigel came to use in derision. As a youngster Nigel simply couldn't understand why these boys refused to be friends. Later, when he better understood the stilted framework of class distinctions, Nigel's desire to prove his own worthiness became increasingly consuming. It was a lesson long in coming that accomplishment was not the currency of those considering themselves upper class.

An energetic and creative apprenticeship at Barrow & Bean International made Nigel a rising star. In handling difficult negotiations, he developed a disciplined understanding of the details and nuances, yet he remained affable and approachable to the other side. His success came about not because his charm disarmed people, though it often did. It was because Nigel made it appear as if he had no agenda other than mutual success of whatever endeavor or deal was taking place, and his deft handling of facts and motives could only have been the result of sustained effort and thought. It made Nigel a particularly useful worker bee at BBI. For all his successful works, however, Nigel felt like he was on a trampoline, rising and falling, never launching.

Nigel wanted to speak with Tony Hume as soon as possible before leaving for Rotterdam—the next stage of their side business depended on it. Trade deals had been Hume's specialty with the British Foreign Service ever since leaving Oxford. He was certainly the best person with whom to brainstorm the upcoming Bahn-Denzir talks. More critically, Nigel needed to consult Hume on the opportunity to travel to Antwerp to set up the critical next step in their personal diamond venture.

Recalling the rendezvous with his wife, Nigel was at once pleasantly excited and vexed. Doria would be fine company, and he hoped his wife's new desire to spend time together in town indicated a crescendo of her interest in him and perhaps even her sexual appetite. But his excitement to establish a cutter and dealer for their smuggled diamonds made him impatient to convene with Hume. Rationalizing the difficulty of contacting Hume today, and picturing his alluring wife shimmering in the ocean dining room of Le Lagon settled Nigel's decision. He made plans to leave work and arrive at the restaurant slightly ahead of Doria. Before returning to his contract review, he sighed with satisfaction.

Of all the amenities that Dakar offered to the well-heeled Senegalese and expatriate community, Le Lagon was among the finest. The restaurant was tucked into a rocky inlet on the tip of Dakar, just minutes from the busy downtown. Guests entered through a gated fence overgrown with different shades of red bougainvillea and hibiscus that spread an intoxicating tropical perfume. It had a perfect unobstructed view overlooking the bay and a glittering Gorée Island.

True to his plan, Nigel arrived ahead of Doria. He alternately smiled and rubbed his chin as he walked down the enclosed gangplank lit by a score of gas torches. He settled at the bar after confirming his dinner arrangements with the maître d'. At seven fifty there were already a few diners and two other bar companions who appeared to be, like him, awaiting the arrival of a significant other. He ordered a gin and tonic and tried to clear his mind of business in order to think of Doria.

She arrived almost at the stroke of eight. Nigel saw only her legs at first as she walked carefully down the gangway. He recognized everything about those legs: their shape, the length and narrowness of the step, the rhythm as they swayed ever so gently, the slight, smooth knees folding like wings. Good God! Nigel thought.

As she arrived at the bar Nigel rose instinctively, wondering how this mythical creature could be his wife.

"You look fantastic, Doria, as you always do," Nigel said as she leaned in to kiss him hello. He cursed himself that his greeting had sounded perfunctory, almost offhanded. Nigel's talent to say the perfect thing in an ordinary way had always confounded him.

"It's a beautiful evening once again, Nigel. I'm so glad we could share it before you had to dash off. And yes, I'd love a white wine, how did you know?" she said, teasing him for not having preordered the only alcoholic drink she ever had.

"It was for thoughts of your company that I neglected your refreshment, dear," Nigel said. He ordered her a glass of Pouilly-Fuissé and then turned to her, resting an elbow on the bar.

Doria slid into the bar seat next to him.

He said, "I have to tell you, love, that I was so pleasantly surprised by your offer to have dinner with me in town. Have I forgotten some special event? Your mother's release from the hospital, perhaps? Your father's gout cleared?" Nigel felt a bit clumsy for some reason and his humor, though perhaps appreciated, didn't have its desired effect.

"Let's not speak ill of those not here, Nigel," she told him with a slight smile.

Nigel relaxed.

"We haven't taken the opportunity to do this in such a long time, with your business dinners and travel and all. And I wanted some time to be with you and catch up on a few things before you left for the Netherlands."

"I'm here and you're here and we have the whole night, this boringly beautiful night like nearly every other night in Dakar. How shall we make it last?"

Doria tilted her head and regarded her husband. "It *is* beautiful to us, sitting here like ... like royalty, gazing out to the horizon without any care to our well-being or our next meal—"

"Oh, but I do worry about our next meal. I'm told the cuisine here has taken quite a tumble."

Doria smiled in spite of herself. "I'm serious, Nigel. You must know something of my heart. It is difficult for me to live in such plenty, with so much need all about, wherever you turn."

"And yet you've done so admirably these last, what, six years?"

"And so have we both, my husband. But I really don't want to speak about our past uneventful years. Is that all right?"

He could see that his challenging barb had struck a chord. He melted. "Darling, of course it is."

Her wine arrived and he handed it to her and offered a toast. "To the future only. May it lead us both to our hearts' desire."

"To our futures, Nigel, that we live the lives we were meant to live." She clicked his glass and looked into his eyes.

"Indeed, darling." He wasn't sure what brooding sentiment lay beneath her words.

The maître d' came over and led them to a table at the water's edge. They sat silently studying the menus they already knew well. The ocean waves softly turned beneath their feet like sleepy orphans.

"I must say that Professor DeLevres is doing some very interesting work," she said into the menu. "His work with indigenous plants, to produce medicines, is quite fascinating and even admirable, considering he's not collecting money from Novartis or any of those drug companies."

"No?" Nigel asked without looking up.

Doria needed to think for a moment. "Well, he certainly seems free enough to pursue his own line of research. Wouldn't research for a drug company come with strings attached?"

"Though I can't say for certain, darling, I suspect Dr. DeLevres is not funding his lifestyle nor his research through his stipend from the university."

Though Nigel had a point, it wasn't important to Doria. "Nevertheless," she said, "it's possible his work will benefit hundreds of thousands of African children if it can produce medicines made locally and for little money per dose. If the hospitals are able to use them."

What is she thinking? Nigel wondered. He refocused on what to order.

"I'm thinking of asking to be his assistant, as a volunteer," she said.

He lowered his menu to see his wife's eyes. "It's been a while since you've been in a laboratory, dear, talented as you are. What do you think the professor's response will be?"

"For one thing, I'd rather like to do fieldwork for him. You're right about how rusty I would surely be in the lab. My hope is to start out traveling to the different areas of Senegal and Guinea, collecting plant specimens. Learning the plants from the natives ...."

The waiter arrived and took their order.

A few seconds seemed like many minutes before Nigel voiced his fomenting opinion of his wife's new plan.

"That's extremely ambitious of you, Doria. The Senegal-Guinea border isn't just unsuitable for the faint of heart, it's genuinely danger-ous. Why on earth would you want to venture into such an area?"

"You must understand, Nigel, that this is an incredible chance to explore a dream I've had since I was a little girl. There are natural medicines out there that we don't even know exist. I believe that somewhere, nature provides the cure for every disease she inflicts. What modern medicine has relied on mostly up until now are distilled spirits and sublime accidents."

"And those sublime accidents, as you refer to them, all happened in a laboratory, didn't they? Not in the jungles of West Africa."

"That is the point. There is a real possibility we are simply missing so much of what can help us because we are tied to our laboratories, to our beliefs in our science, and too dismissive of what millennia of living on the land has taught people."

Nigel noticed a light in his wife's eyes that, although not familiar, was instantly recognizable—passion. "Have you thought how you might accomplish this, assuming DeLevres shares your enthusiasm?"

"Not completely, not yet. But it can be done. I know it. And I will need your help and your support, Nigel." She reached out and touched his hand.

Though Nigel might have thought this touch to be a transparent gesture, he welcomed it and wrapped his fingers around hers. He shook his head in abdication. "If you are as determined as you say, dear, then I'm sure there will be no stopping you. In which case, I'd be a fool not to lend a hand." To himself Nigel was thinking that a good dose of mosquito-infested rain forest and a few nights away from toilets and decent food would be all that was needed to deter Doria from her quest. He patted her hand.

She smiled, withdrew her hands, and folded them in her lap. "I have to thank you for this Nigel. I didn't know how you would react, and I feel much better knowing you will support me."

Nigel didn't disagree and wondered if now was the time to change the subject and speak to Doria of his illicit diamond venture with Tony. He thought not. "You're most welcome, darling. How could I do anything but what you ask of me?"

16. Preparing for a Journey

Before the sun hinted its inexorable climb, Doria was up. It felt strange how convinced she had become of the meaning and importance of what she was planning to do.

In earlier times, explorers had discovered that quinine warded off malaria, that the bark of a tree produced aspirin, that aloe vera coagulated blood and healed wounds. She saw herself as one of those early pioneers, a person of commitment and drive to discover and learn the knowledge hidden in the cells of plants—neglected knowledge from which she could end suffering. A chill of excitement coursed through her body.

Putting on a robe rather than dressing, she switched on a light at her desk, took a clean sheet of paper, and wrote a list.

Ask Professor DeLevres: Leading authorities? Under-explored plant families.

Research botany texts from library.

Map out the region for specific plants.

Bydee.

This last entry made Doria think at bit. Would Ahminta take her to see Bydee at her home? Doria amended her last entry.

She looked over at the bed she had slept in alone. Nigel had left yesterday on his trip to Rotterdam and instead of being away two nights as he had originally indicated, he would now be away for five. Apparently, he had some business in Antwerp totally unrelated to the contract he was working on for BBI. Realizing she was looking forward to this unencumbered time, she shook her head and chuckled with self-reproach.

Stars were receding into dawn by the time Doria dressed. She put on a pair of slacks suited for working in the garden. With their deep pockets, comfortable fit, and khaki color, they were perfect for her fieldwork frame of mind. Doria bounced down the stairs with her notepad.

When Ahminta opened the back door to the kitchen, Doria was humming. She placed breakfast for the two of them on the table. Doria asked Ahminta to sit and eat with her. Ahminta shook her head, looking confused. Doria pulled the chair out and nearly ordered Ahminta to sit. She did so, hands folded in her lap.

Doria realized she was being silly, which made her feel awkward. They ate their fruit in silence.

Before either of them rose, Doria asked, "Ahminta, do you think you would take me to visit your aunt Bydee?"

"Of course, Madame, she will be at the Marché Kermel, as always."

"I meant, take me to visit her at her home."

Ahminta didn't respond.

Doria continued. "I'm sure she won't mind, Ahminta, when all is done. We'll make a good deal between us and it would be very, very helpful."

Ahminta did not want to visit her aunt's home for many reasons— Bydee's husband regularly made sexual advances toward her, which caused the women of the compound to dislike Ahminta intensely. Nevertheless, it was not possible to say no indefinitely.

"Aunt Bydee will be surprised and suspicious, Madame," she said.

This made sense to Doria. "Then, let's meet her at home for lunch and bring a gift!" The gift Doria had in mind were shoots of kachura, the medicinal plant from the Indian ambassador's residence.

The servant girl nodded silently.

Two hours later they were in Doria's car, headed for Little Dakar, a massive sprawl of small block buildings and corrugated roofs stretched in all directions adjacent to one of the more prosperous neighborhoods of the city. Many buildings were unfinished, had openings for doors but no doors, had three exterior walls instead of four, had roofs that covered only half of the openings to the sky. And there were people everywhere, walking, cooking in outdoor kitchens, gathered in front of small shops, hunkered around a game in the sand, waiting in a queue for water from a communal faucet. This road apparently divided an impoverished hive of humanity from the community of privilege. They saw open sewers into which people were pouring waste. Doria noticed that the power lines, which had been a consistent, if chaotic companion to the roads they had traveled, had vanished. A speeding taxi beeped at them from behind, swerved in the sand as it accelerated past the Mercedes, and then, in a dust cloud, turned left into the hive without slowing down. It had been absorbed into the expanse of Little Dakar.

The diminutive name belied the enormous population of this section of the city. Much more than a neighborhood, Little Dakar was an enormous borough, home to nearly a third of Dakar's two million souls. It was compressed onto perhaps one-twentieth of the land that comprised the city.

Ahminta guided Iba onto sand paths barely wide enough for the Mercedes. A herd of a dozen sheep scattered in front of the car, chased diligently by a young boy brandishing a stick. Ahminta motioned for Iba to pull into an opening in a cinder-block wall which was an entrance to the family compound of Bydee Mbodj.

The scene in the compound, only one neighborhood away from the presidential palace, could easily have been from a village at the other end of the country. Two women with infants wrapped to their backs crushed sorghum or millet in thin wooden caldrons that resembled African drums. The batons they used were shaped like giant cotton swabs, longer than a Western broom and as thick as the business end of a cricket bat. The women wielded these heavy instruments in a classic Senegalese syncopated rhythm while they hummed or sang. The younger girls, also clad with infant children, clapped, sang, and learned the duties of preparing the grain to make porridge.

Iba brought the Mercedes to a halt. Instantly it was surrounded by seven children ranging in age from four to thirteen. One of the older boys wore a Mickey Mouse T-shirt and dark shorts. Another was dressed in long, slightly tattered trousers and a plaid shirt, unbuttoned to his belt buckle. None of the children wore shoes. The women grinding the millet looked over at the Mercedes, but didn't stop what they were doing. Ahminta didn't move.

Grabbing her purse and slipping in the soft sand, Doria refused Iba's help as she left the car and informed him, "I don't know how long we'll be, Iba. Please turn off the engine until we know what's happening."

Doria pulled out a small plastic bag with a bowl partially filled with water and two of the sprouted roots from the kachura. Doria's idea was to present her gift to Bydee and explain the plant's significance. Once Bydee understood Doria's thoughtful generosity and the plant's intrinsic value, Bydee would be moved to help Doria learn to make *ndaymou gar*.

Bydee was not at the family compound, as Ahminta knew. Doria asked her to inquire if her aunt had come back from the market for lunch.

Ahminta approached the two women preparing the millet and said to them in Oulof, "My mistress is here to leave a gift for Bydee. I'm going to tell her to put it in her room."

Ahminta glanced back over her shoulder at Doria. She wanted to ask her cousins a question in Oulof that Doria couldn't understand

and that would make them respond negatively—the one thing Doria would understand and hopefully call the visit off. But that question couldn't be "Has Bydee come back for lunch?" since Ahminta would already know the answer to that question.

She hesitated, then asked, "Have you been giving your children any of Bydee's medicines?" She said this loud enough for Doria to hear her aunt's name and focus on the negative response from the two women.

The elder of the two snarled, "Of course not, stupid girl! The children are not ill!"

This response was more shrill than Ahminta had anticipated. It surprised her, as it did Doria.

Ahminta turned to Doria, about to "translate" that Bydee had not come home for lunch, when a woman's voice yelled out in Oulof from one of the rooms behind the two women: "Those medicines do not belong to Bydee, and you know this, little girl."

Ahminta shuddered at her miscalculation. The voice belonged to another aunt, Mady Toula, who must have traveled up to Dakar this day from her home in the Casamance, to provision her half sister's stores of traditional medicines.

Mady emerged abruptly from behind an orange tie-dyed doorway curtain and walked, with arms pumping, around the two cousins and directly to Ahminta. "Why would you ask such a silly question, girl?" Mady asked just as she noticed Doria silhouetted before her luxury car. "And who is this you have brought with you?"

Ahminta was cornered. Mady spoke French better than Ahminta herself. Ahminta steadied herself with her matter-of-fact reply. "This is my employer, Madame Blake."

Mady, hands on her hips, regarded Doria with squinted eyes. She then looked at Ahminta's rigid posture and averted eyes. Mady tapped her foot rapidly in the sand. She brushed past Ahminta and strode, with her arms pumping, right up to the point where her breasts nearly touched Doria's navel. Mady was a good half a head shorter than the British woman, but equally slender.

When she stopped, she tilted her head and extended a hand in greeting as she said in perfect French, "Good afternoon, Madame Blake. I am Mady Toula. Bydee Mbodj is my half sister. What brings you to our compound this afternoon?"

Ahminta came up behind Mady and tried to speak. Mady Toula looked at Ahminta with scorn, and the young woman cast her gaze down without a word.

Doria took Mady's hand into both of hers and introduced herself. Happily surprised that Mady spoke French, she said, "We came to speak with Bydee. Or rather, *I* came to speak with Bydee. Ahminta was helping me find her during the lunch hour."

"Minta told you Bydee would be here for lunch, did she?" Mady asked with innocence, and then shot a glance to the young woman.

"Oh, we knew it wasn't certain she'd be here," Doria said, "but it seemed a worthwhile gamble."

"I don't understand, Madame. What is a worthwhile gamble?"

"You see, I was hoping to offer Bydee a trade for some of her home remedies."

"What sort of trade, Madame?"

Doria took a step back and crossed her arms. "You know— Meedy, is it?"

"Mady. Mady Tou-ou-la."

"Mady, I think my business is with Bydee and seeing as she is not here, perhaps we should go." Doria waved to Ahminta to walk to the car with her.

"Madame, Bydee does not have these medicines to take to the market unless I give them to her. She sells them and brings the money to me. The medicines are mine," said Mady with a Cheshire cat smile.

"Is that so," Doria said. "Is this true, Ahminta?"

Before the young mother could speak, Mady chastised Doria.

"Don't ask the girl, Madame. She may clean your house, but she is not your friend."

Doria covered her mouth with one hand. When she dropped her hand, she said, "Ahminta and I have a fine relationship, Mady Toula. Ahminta, please tell me, does Mady own the medicines Bydee sells?"

Mady crossed her arms.

"She does, Madame Blake."

"Then you, Mady Toula, are the person I've really come to speak with."

Mady flashed a near-perfect smile.

Instantly, both of them saw good fortune in the woman standing before her. Mady believed she was looking at an uninformed customer whom she could charge four, five, or even ten times the going rate for a simple headache paste or muscle salve. Doria's expectations were filtered through the prism of her new mission and the chance to fulfill a childhood dream. She saw a tutor in the ways of traditional healing and knowledge of the plants and other ingredients, to create medicines. Though such high expectations may have been misconceived, they set a stage for achieving the impossible.

Mady motioned for Doria to follow her, which she did without hesitation, back to the small room with the orange tie-dyed curtain door. When Ahminta tried to follow them inside, Mady swatted at her to wait outside.

Doria first noticed how much cooler it felt inside the dark room than in the shade outside. Nothing in the room had any substance or shape as her eyes took time adjusting to the near absence of light. The next thing Doria noticed was the smell, or rather, smells, like passing by a farm or a landfill, so strong was the odor of deterioration. Despite this, like her eyes adjusting to the light, her sense of smell became accustomed to many layers of odors. Not only pungent sweet, but nutlike sweet mixed with overripe cherries. Other smells, like meat and blood combined with burnt grass, and the smell of earth mixed with bitter tamarind, the smell of rust, and the smell of decaying squash and fermenting fruit. Doria was amazed at how many different odors she could differentiate.

Against the cinder-block wall, Doria could now discern well over two dozen wooden and metal bowls of various sizes, each filled to a different level with all manner of mixtures. As her eyes adjusted further, she could see these were organized—four came together at one end, each bowl with something different—a green powder, a lumpy black paste, twigs tied in small bundles, a white liquid with the consistency of a sauce. After a space along the wall, three more bowls lined up together, then another three, then two, then another four. Doria surmised that these were the ingredients and maybe even Mady's products. In the middle of the room sat a squat wooden bench. And along the other wall was an assortment of sacks, bundles of sticks, and large colorful bowls with lids on them.

Mady gestured for Doria to sit on the bench. The only light in the room filtered through the doorway.

Mady sat next to Doria, put her nose within sniffing distance of Doria's, and said slowly, "What have you come to trade, Madame?"

Doria suddenly realized she was still clutching the kachura, but wasn't sure if she was ready to explain its significance to Mady—until she knew more.

"I want to learn how to make *ndaymou gar*," Doria told her.

Mady knew exactly what she heard, but wasn't prepared to believe it right away. "Do you mean you wish to buy *ndaymou gar*?" she asked.

"No, Mady Toula, I wish to learn how to make *ndaymou gar*. I want to learn what plants and minerals are used, how they are prepared and in what quantities, where to find them—all of it. I want to '*build*' *ndaymou gar*," Doria replied.

Mady told her, "You cannot make *ndaymou gar*, Madame. You are not Djiolla."

"Why must I be Djiolla, Mady Toula? I can learn just like a smart child, only better. Teach me, Mady Toula."

"I can show you *ndaymou gar*," Mady told her. "I can mix it here today. But you cannot learn here today."

"Why?"

"You must be of the land, you must know the story, you must know the care, you must know the respect needed to make *ndaymou gar*."

"Respect for what, Mady? Respect for the plant that gives us such special gifts? Respect for the ground that gives life to the plants and animals? Respect to your ancestors who discovered how to make *ndaymou gar* and passed down its secrets to their daughters and to their daughters' daughters?"

"Yes, Madame," Mady conceded, nodding her head, "and respect for me and my living, my work, my money."

"I do have respect, Mady Toula." She lifted from her side the pot holding the kachura. "I have brought you this gift to show you my respect. Do you know what this is?"

Mady took hold of the pot with both hands and squinted, turning it counterclockwise. She shook her head "no" and handed it back to Doria.

"This is kachura and it comes from India. It takes great care to grow successfully here in Senegal. In India it is used as decoration, but most importantly, it is ground into an ointment that, when rubbed on your body, will ease muscle pain." She handed the plant back to Mady. "This is my gift to you, Mady Toula, to show you my respect."

Mady again took the small pot in both hands and this time studied the succulent with the purple-tongued blossoms even more closely. She sniffed it, then she broke a tiny piece from one of the green limbs, ground it between her thumb and forefinger, sniffed that, and put her tongue to it. She rubbed the remainder on the back of her left hand. Mady nodded and set the plant down between them. She stared intently at Doria, who had tilted her head to see better. There wasn't enough light to fully grasp the meaning of their body language. After a few seconds, Mady breathed deeply and turned to the wall behind her.

"This is *ndaymou gar*," Mady said as she collected a set of four of the bowls. There was a yellow powder in one, some seeds in another, a brown liquid in the third, and the fourth bowl was empty. "You must pay me 10,000 CFA to teach you how to make it," Mady declared.

This amounted to forty dollars.

Doria considered the substances in the three filled bowls. "Mady, you must teach me where to get the ingredients you have in your three bowls. Teaching me how to put them together doesn't help if I don't know what they are."

"You can buy them from me."

"No, I will not buy them from you. But I will buy your time and your knowledge." Doria added quickly, "And I will never sell any or simply give it away when you or Bydee could sell it. I will not take away your customers or hurt your business, Mady Toula. Of this, I am completely certain." Doria *was* completely certain. She could not conceive how providing this cheap, locally produced, mind-clearing mixture to the orphans of Ouakam might upset some ancient balance to which she was oblivious.

"For my mind, my knowledge, you must come to Ziguinchor, Madame. You must come to where I live, where I work."

Doria knew of the regional capital city of the Casamance, but had never visited.

Mady was saying, "There is no *tenzi* to harvest here, no *golo sang*."

"What are those, Mady? Is one of these *tenzi* right here?" She pointed to the bowl with the yellow powder.

"You will pay me 500 CFA every day we are together and I am teaching you."

Doria started to smile and then stopped. Ziguinchor had a climate of its own, where it rained more than anywhere else in Senegal, making it a jungle enclave in the surrounding savannah.

"How long will we work together? How long will it take me to learn what you know?"

"What you say, woman? How long to learn what I know? Two lifetimes are not enough for you."

"I will teach you *ndaymou gar*. That is what you have asked."

"When are you returning to Ziguinchor, Mady Toula?"

"When these supplies are all sold," Mady informed Doria as she stood with an outstretched arm and drew it in a circle around the entire room. As Mady did this, Doria noticed a bundle of clothes and a pack near a mattress at the far end of the room. Doria stood up herself and went over to the bed, curious to see a bit more. Mady walked at her side. At the end of the mattress, Doria noticed an animal-skin sack sewn with leather laces and tied with multiple bands at the neck. Thinking this was perhaps water or some other drink, she picked it up to see if it had a stopper at the mouth.

Mady gently took the skin out of Doria's hands. "You want to know what this is, Madame? Heh?"

"Well, maybe. Can you drink it?"

Mady howled with laughter. "No, you cannot drink this. In this skin is something more precious and more potent than you know."

"What ... what is it?"

"This is what you will pay me for, Madame. This is the energy that makes medicines strong. This is the life that mixes with the dirt and makes new life."

Doria shook her head in confusion.

"This is moon blood," Mady said with a wide grin.

Still, Doria shook her head.

Mady repeated herself. "This is moon blood."

Doria raised her arms, palms up, and looked blank.

Mady grabbed her own crotch for a few seconds, then she reached over and cupped Doria's crotch, holding her hand there as she recited "moon blood."

Doria's first reaction was to take two steps back, but she stumbled at the bedside and stopped as Mady kept her hand between Doria's legs. When Mady pulled her arm back, Doria understood.

"That flask contains menstrual blood, doesn't it? A woman's menstrual blood."

Mady nodded and put the flask back in its place. But Doria's curiosity was now piqued. Mady was very likely postmenopausal, so it probably wasn't hers. Whose might it be? Did she go collecting it around the village? Doria started to get disgusted with the idea.

Mady saw Doria's squinting eyes and pursed lips, and chuckled. "You do not understand, Madame, do you?"

"No, Mady, I don't think I do, but ..." she said, "I want to learn. Whose moon blood is this and how do you use it?"

"When you come to Ziguinchor, Madame, if you come, you will learn then."

Doria nodded. Suddenly the smells and the experience overwhelmed her. She felt faint. She pulled herself together and clutched Mady's arm for a moment as she walked to the door and back outside.

The onslaught of light gave Doria an immediate headache. Putting an arm to her eyes, she stumbled once, turned to the wall of the hut she had just left, and rested her forehead on the hot cinder blocks.

Ahminta, who had been sitting under the millet-stalk canopy where her cousins had been grinding the millet flour, arose and watched her mistress. "Madame Blake?" she said. "Madame Blake, are you hurt? Are you sick?"

Doria composed herself, waving to Ahminta that she was fine, though she continued to keep her head on the hot wall. In the acacia tree between the small buildings of the compound, mourning doves had gathered in the slight shade. They cooed in a harmony that Doria recognized from the earliest hours of the morning. Their unexpected chorus soothed her.

Mady emerged from the working room, also squinting. She walked over to Doria and put a hand on her shoulder. Without stirring from her position, Doria put her opposite hand on top of Mady's.

"You will come to Ziguinchor, Madame. I see that in you. But will you stay? That is what we must find out together."

Doria turned her head to look at Mady. "I will come and I will stay, Mady Toula," she told her.

"Perhaps," said Mady. "Perhaps you will come and perhaps you will stay. Or perhaps some other thing will happen." Mady noticed Ahminta staring from her shady perch. "Minta, get your mistress something to drink. Now, girl."

Ahminta went to another building in the compound and returned with a glass and a can of pineapple juice.

Doria drank slowly, quenching a thirst she hadn't felt until that moment. "How do I find you in Ziguinchor, Mady?"

"You will not have to find me. You have to take me."

"Take you? Really. ... How long will it be until all you have made is sold?" Doria's mind was racing: how long she might be gone; where she would stay; what would Nigel do.

"It could be twenty days, it could be one hundred days." Mady spoke like an oracle.

Doria let out a sigh. "Of course," she said. "I'll be by every two weeks to see how your sales are going. Is that all right?"

"Of course, Madame," Mady replied. "And I can also send a message with the girl."

"Yes, quite. I'll see you in two weeks, Mady Toula. And be sure to keep the kachura watered and give it some compost or fertilizer. Will you do that?"

Mady scratched her head, then she nodded and smiled.

"In two weeks," Doria said again as she extended her hand to be shaken. Mady took Doria's hand in a limp grip. Though it made Doria uncomfortable, she smiled back and pumped Mady's hand up and down energetically.

17. Aligned Interests

The city of Antwerp, in 1978, was very much like the Antwerp of 1958 or 1858. One of the key continental trading ports with England and Spain in the era of exploration and conquest, and later the US and Africa, it owed its recent growth not to the fact that it was the second-largest port in continental Europe, but because it became a domicile to the largest industry of post-World War II society: international bureaucracy. Home to many of the United Nations' organizations and a budding pan-Europe shadow agency, Antwerp's main thoroughfares were lined by gray stone buildings with sharp, steeple-like roofs.

Since the bust of the great tulip speculation market in the early 1400s, risk mitigation in commodities has been an industry unto itself. Diamonds, unlike gold, were rare and not used as currency by either banking systems or countries. They had far more investment potential since the commercial diamond market had been tightly controlled and a healthy black market had emerged. Diamonds became a substitute currency for the merchant-jeweler class of Antwerp, comprised mostly of Syrian and Lebanese Arabs, Jews, and Armenians whose wealth could never be determined by looking at their material possessions or bank accounts.

It is a testament to the vision and ruthlessness of Cecil Rhodes, the businessman who bought the South African farm of the de Beer brothers after the discovery of diamonds there, that diamonds are not nearly as rare as their price would indicate. It took Mr. Rhodes a mere seven years from that original purchase to become the sole owner and operator of diamond mines in South Africa. Rhodes also moved the company into diamond distribution and sales, thus controlling 90 percent of all diamonds mined in South Africa. By the 1920s, however, other sources of diamonds had been discovered, most significantly in West Africa and Australia. The president of De Beers at that time, Harry Oppenheimer, understood the potential market chaos and formed a cartel that to this day is the most successful in capitalist history. If "excess" diamonds came onto the market, the cartel bought them up and tightly controlled the flow and price of diamonds. This practice was so successful that in 1978 De Beers alone controlled more than 88 percent of all mined diamonds in the world. Into such a monolithic industry did Nigel Blake plunge himself with his dream to have financial security that was beyond his means.

Nigel concluded his rocky but successful negotiations with the Bahn-Denzir Group. He had locked in BBI's distribution rights for all of Africa, including North Africa and Madagascar, for their full line of confectioneries. It had been a good match going in. His only rival had been Nestlé, which actually competed with Bahn-Denzir in many products. BBI was the only other European company with a distribution network throughout Africa, making Nigel's work much easier. But he took neither his potential partner nor his adversary for granted. Nigel researched every aspect of the Bahn-Denzir Group, from its Dutch family origins to its contractual relationships with farmers, to its labor practices, to the technology its competitors were using, to its financial records, all to make certain he had the knowledge to give him an advantage of his own making, not just one of circumstance. Nigel needed to know their business in order to penetrate the differences between fact, exaggeration, and fabrication in negotiations.

The outcome of Nigel's personal venture was much less clear in his mind. This frustrated him. He and Hume, along with an extremely clever Guinean from Hume's earlier work, named David Semba, had developed a conduit for smuggling diamonds out of Guinea. David procured the diamonds and, via a mule, smuggled them to Senegal where Hume could arrange for them to be legally exported from Senegal. Nigel was to develop their market.

Although he had spent time researching the diamond cartel's central selling organization, he was quite certain an opportunist such as himself could not penetrate it. This meant he had to find a diamond dealer who would get the stones cut and polished, ready for sale at the Antwerp diamond center. The diamond dealers, Nigel learned, would be reluctant to purchase diamonds that had not been produced by the cartel—unless they were at extremely favorable prices. Even then, how many would be likely willing to defy the cartel? To find such a dealer, Nigel had contacted Heinrich Rudden, a broker who traded commodities, products, services, and information in four continents. Having worked with and learned from Heinrich Rudden, Nigel was certain Heinrich was the man to assist at this critical stage. He also considered that Rudden's curiosity and deductive thinking could lead him to try to take a more active and decidedly unwelcome role in Nigel's venture. It had taken Nigel over a week to track Rudden down and get him on the phone before leaving on his trip to Rotterdam.

"Heinrich, it's Nigel Blake. How have you been, old man?"

"It is you, Nigel! Ya, I am quite fine. Though I wish we could do something to raise the price of coffee beans! Would Barrow & Bean be interested in 130 tons of excellent Ethiopian coffee? Why don't you open a chain of coffeehouses? Africans are coffee mad, and that Nescafé is pure shit, you know."

"Yes, it certainly is. Heinrich, look, my friend. I tracked you down in Addis because I need your advice."

"It will cost you, my friend. Are you sure you're not interested in the coffee beans?"

"Not right away. Though I will ask around. Seriously."

"Seriously and, if I may ask, quickly. How can I advise the super deal maker of Barrow & Bean Africa? And, tell me, how is that glorious wife of yours?"

"How thoughtful of you to ask. Doria is indeed the reason I'm calling you." Nigel could hear Heinrich's breath deepen at the mere mention of Doria's name. "I've bought an anniversary present for Doria, an uncut diamond."

"Really? Good for you. Those aren't so easy to come by. Did you buy a lot or just a single?"

"I got a single from a guy who told me he bought a lot. He's left Dakar now, so he's not around to give me any direction. I'm heading to Antwerp in a few days and I'm hoping to locate someone who could cut and polish it for me."

"Is this a mine-certified stone? Have you got all the paperwork certifying its legitimacy?"

"The truth is, Heinrich, while I've got a write-up, I'm concerned this alone might not pass muster. I'm no expert, but any of the diamond dealers would be able to tell me. But if there were a problem, Doria's present would in the dustbin, I'm afraid. I was hoping you might be able to recommend me to a dealer-cutter that may be less fussy about the certification."

"Nigel, you crazy man! Only that fantastic wife of yours could possibly make you fudge the rules, hey? Yes, my old friend, this will cost you!" And Heinrich let out a burst of laughter.

Heinrich told him to go see Simon Lasry. He was a young and talented cutter who fancied himself a rebel and would enjoy working on a diamond that was below the radar of the cartel. Nigel would have felt more comfortable with someone who was simply interested in the money, but Heinrich assured him Lasry was the right man.

Nigel had phoned Lasry the day he arrived in the Netherlands.

"I'm a friend of Heinrich Rudden, Mr. Lasry," Nigel said from his hotel room. "My name is Nigel Blake. Heinrich recommended you to me."

"Heinrich Rudden, you say?" was the accented response. "Heinrich Rudden is a fox in wolf's clothing."

"I-I don't quite follow, Mr. Lasry," Nigel said.

"People believe Heinrich is a predator they recognize, but he is more clever, more sly than they see. Do you not see this, Mr. Bleak?"

"Heinrich is, as you say, cunning and stealthy, to be sure. But he is an honest businessman, Mr. Lasry. He doesn't cheat and you always know what he wants."

Nigel couldn't determine if the short silence meant that Lasry agreed or that he did not. Whichever the case, Nigel knew that Lasry had to speak next.

"What is it you want of me, Mr. Bleak?"

"I would like to discuss a business proposition with you, if I may."

"That I knew when you told me you were a friend of Heinrich's," Lasry shot back. "What kind of business do you want with me?"

Nigel thought hard to form his next response. "I'd like you to help me find a way to enhance some private raw diamonds."

"Private raw diamonds, you say. Rogue diamonds, then."

"Well, I'm not sure I know what you mean when you say—"

"There are three types of raw uncut diamonds, Mr. Bleak," Lasry said. "Most are controlled by the nasty De Beers company and their proxies. Some few others mined in Russia or Sierra Leone arrive at Antwerp via known merchants in New York or Sydney. Everything else is a rogue diamond. Is that what you have, Mr. Bleak?"

"That's one of the things I'm hoping you'll tell me." Nigel stopped and listened.

A shorter silence this time. "When are you expecting to be in Antwerp?"

"Next Tuesday. May I come and see you in the late morning, say eleven o'clock?"

"I will be here, Mr. Bleak. We will have fifteen minutes. My workshop is 18 Gwendenstaat, off Lombardonvest. Eleven o'clock."

"I'll be there," Nigel stated.

* * *

Simon Lasry's workshop was one block off Lombardonvest and ten blocks from the train station, in the heart of the diamond district. The walk in the June morning air of bustling Antwerp filled Nigel with belief. The temperature was still brisk, but not cold. The sun blinked regularly between the rows of small dark clouds in between the mixture of eighteenth-century stone buildings and twenty-first-century glass buildings. The farther from the rail station he walked, the fewer tall buildings he encountered. He found 18 Gwendenstaat, rang the bell on the old building front marked "18," lifted the latch, and walked in. Nigel stopped and stared.

Simon Lasry's workplace was part art gallery, part tech laboratory, and part loft apartment. There were three oscilloscopes, a laser-guided lathe, and other precision cutting tools, Nigel guessed, set up along three workbenches. He also noted the three large green screen monitors, keyboards, and cables. To see it all, Nigel had to look over a reception desk and two file drawers. And the light. Though Nigel couldn't see any overhead lighting, there seemed to be an abundance of natural light coming from large pipes overhead, illuminating the work space almost like a window. On the walls hung paintings, possibly prints or reproductions, of artists Nigel recognized—Kandinsky, Miró, and Pollock. In a corner near the entrance, a detailed wood sculpture of a rabbit stood at least six feet tall, more than half of it ears. Nigel saw no signs of a human being.

So he called out. "Simon Lasry, Nigel Bleak is here to see you."

From very close behind him Lasry said, "I'm glad you found my place, Mr. Bleak. You are even a bit early."

Catching his composure, Nigel relaxed as much as he could. "Yes, that I am," he said. "Just trying to make sure I knew your address."

"No doubt," said Lasry as he walked around Nigel, into his work space.

When he reached the bench of electronic equipment Lasry turned and faced Nigel. Lasry was of average height and build, though his shoulders were large compared to his slender waist. He sported the tendrils and yarmulke of the Chasidic Jewish community, though he was clean-shaven rather than bearded, and wore a blue print shirt when Nigel would have expected the traditional white shirt.

A true rebel, Nigel thought, also taking note of Lasry's long, thin fingers.

Nigel said, "Yes, well, thanks very much for allowing me this visit. Heinrich Rudden, as I mentioned, told me you are a diamond dealer and cutter with a reputation for quality and integrity in your dealings."

"As are many of my colleagues and competitors, many of them a stone's throw from my workshop."

"Yes, quite. I understand this, Mr. Lasry. But their names were not provided to me by someone whom I trust, and yours was. I have come into possession of a number of raw diamonds that I would like your assistance with perfecting and marketing."

This made Lasry chuckle, but he stopped abruptly. "You mean you want me to fence stolen diamonds for you."

"Not at all, Mr. Lasry. I want you to cut the raw stones and either I simply pay you for your work and you hand them back to me, or you can market them yourself and we can agree on the split of the proceeds."

"Where are these diamonds from?" Lasry asked.

To Nigel he seemed almost disinterested.

"They are from West Africa, from a private prospector who is quite anxious that as little information as possible escape regarding where his mine operates or its possible productivity."

"Such discretion must be very difficult to assure, Mr. Bleak. Have you a stone to show me today so that I might actually believe you?"

This is a very good sign, Nigel thought. He reached into a buttoned pocket on the inside of his suit jacket, retrieving a handkerchief folded into the size of a matchbook. Nigel unwrapped it carefully and revealed the four small gray stones, each about the size of an almond and rounder. He extended his hand over the bench to show Lasry, who bent from the waist to look at the prize, without moving his hands.

After getting to within a nose length of the stones, Lasry straightened up and asked if he could examine one with his equipment. Nigel nodded, and Lasry picked one of the stones and placed it on a small black platter in the middle of a staging area on the bench, with at least four different electronic components surrounding it. Lasry put on a headset to which was attached a set of eyepieces. From switches under the bench he powered up three very narrow beams of white light and a fourth of incandescent blue. Lasry then turned a small wheel mounted on the side of his bench, like that of a table saw, and raised the platform holding the diamond. As it intersected with the narrow beams, reflected and refracted light seem to scatter in all directions. Nigel unconsciously drew in a deep breath and held it. But it was not the reflected light which interested Lasry. He lowered himself to get a very close look at the specimen stone, noticing how the light was behaving inside the crystal … then quickly straightened and turned everything off.

"I'm afraid I can't help you, Mr. Bleak. This stone has deep fissures which would very likely require cutting it into many smaller stones. Plus, the clarity concerns me."

Nigel's shoulders slouched as he reached to take back his stone.

"If that is your opinion, Mr. Lasry, I will conclude that my friend Heinrich was mistaken about you. You are not the first to examine this stone, you are the last. It strikes me as odd that your assessment should be so different from those who preceded you."

Lasry then spoke more candidly. "It is very important in this business that you know the value of what you have and how that value is derived."

"This is true in all business projects with which I have been a part."

"But you are not a diamond merchant. And diamonds are very special. Most people think their stones are worth far more than they truly are. Do you know what this diamond is worth?"

"As is, maybe two thousand pounds. Cut and polished, perhaps 10,000 pounds. Set in a platinum necklace, perhaps 22,000 to 25,000 pounds."

"High, perhaps, but not unrealistic. Tell me, why don't you just sell these stones as is and save yourself the time and trouble to deal with another partner?"

Was he asking to buy the raw stones? It didn't matter to Nigel, who responded, "For the added value, of course. I represent more than just myself, as I told you."

"How many stones are you considering, Mr. Bleak, and in what time?"

This was the best question Lasry could have asked. But Nigel himself had no firm idea. It depended solely on what they got from Tony's contact in Guinea.

"We are speaking of enough raw diamonds to invest in the right partner and the right protections," Nigel told him. "Probably twenty-five to thirty stones, three times in the next year."

"Can you come back this afternoon at four o'clock so that I can consider what you are asking? I may have more questions."

"I would prefer, Mr. Lasry, that you come to my hotel. The Hotel de Cigne. Do you know it?"

"I do."

"Please come by at 17:30, then. We will discuss this opportunity and have an early dinner."

Nigel stuck out his hand to shake. Lasry cocked his head slightly, pursed his lips, and extended his own hand to seal their next meeting. Nigel felt Lasry's long fingers in his firm grip, his skin smooth and soft, his musculature and bone structure uniform and hard. These hands, Nigel determined, were not those of a craftsman, but of a surgeon.

18. HICCUP

Tony Hume had a dilemma—in fact, a number of them. Most immediately, the ambassador was huffing because they had been blindsided. The Canadians had just signed a preferential produce trade deal with Senegal that included provisions granting Canada access and ownership rights in local companies that England had been maneuvering to acquire. The Canadians had enormous stockpiles of wheat that were thrown into the bargain, and the British ambassador blamed Hume for not knowing about these provisions sooner in the negotiations so that Britain might have countered with an offer posing as an important and begrudged concession. Of course, Britain had no comparable offer, and Hume needed to so inform his ambassador.

"It was unfortunate that the Canadians locked in this deal before the Senegalese gave us notice. But I don't believe, Ambassador, that we could have done anything but postpone the inevitable."

"That's a bit defeatist, isn't it, Anthony?" the ambassador shot back. "Those rights will not be offered equally to the rest of the international trading partners, will they? No, they will not. And we had our dairy products package on the table, didn't we? We could have made a bold offer and kept our dairy farm lads smiling back home, had we known the timing of this transparent Canadian move."

"I doubt, Ambassador, that the Senegalese would have thumbed their noses at a grain deal that essentially guarantees them food subsistence for most of the country, just to secure from Britain a refrigerated warehouse packed with double cream Gloucester." It was insolent, but Hume was not in the mood to be lectured by his boss, who clearly was not nearly the strategist he would have his staff believe.

"You should not dismiss this failure so easily, Anthony."

Hume hated being called Anthony. It reminded him of his strict boarding school masters who insisted in using his full given name.

"Ambassador, we were not going to get those rights. The Americans and the Russians both had large food deals ready to move. The Canadians' ace in the game was that they can pass themselves off as a francophone country with both the food aid capability and a sensible trade policy. They don't subsidize their agriculture nearly to the extent the French do, nor, for that matter, to the extent we do. It's all in the brief I've put on your desk. Do read it when you have the opportunity. Thank you, Ambassador."

Hume excused himself rather than wait to be dismissed. He had little interest in this petty trade deal. There were other issues requiring his attention. The British ambassador watched Tony's exit, his face reddened and swelling.

More important to Tony was the issue of cross-border transport of small bundles of purloined gemstones. Their diamond mule, Issa, had disappeared. Issa used his capacity as a cargo inspector to travel on ships to Dakar and put the stones directly into Hume's hands. Project Blueprint, as Nigel had dubbed it, had an emergency: how to get the diamonds to Dakar. His contact, David Semba, a consultant to the Department of Transportation in Guinea, had worked with Tony for three years, when David was assigned to the British consulate in Conakry, and was now a partner with Tony and Nigel. Semba had provided Tony the latest information regarding the vanished carrier. This was fearful, breathtaking news. David believed that the ports of Conakry and Dakar were no longer easy to move through. If the governments weren't watching you, the organized crime rings from Marseille, Casablanca, or Freetown were. The sea routes had become too hot for fledgling amateurs like themselves to risk their new venture.

They would have to find something overland, something unobtrusive. That standard posed its own set of solution-resistant problems: finding the trustworthy mule, getting across two or three borders without government suspicion or discovery, putting the mule in touch with David. This was going to take time, and Tony Hume was not feeling patient. They had to figure out how to get the operation back on track immediately.

* * *

Nigel was feeling full of himself, having returned from Europe with a trade deal for BBI and a cutter-fence for their raw diamonds. Settling into the back seat of the Mercedes taking him home from the airport, he looked forward to seeing Doria and wondered if she was still thinking of that silly plant hunt into the rain forest. He returned to his thoughts of how to get the stones into Antwerp undetected and how many stones would comprise the right balance of detection risk, cost of the trip, and speed of reward.

Nigel went directly to his office and called Doria. Unsurprised to get no answer he left a message on the machine that he was back safe and at the office. Next, he called Hume and got the news that siphoned off his euphoria.

"Issa did not show up in Conakry, Nigel. David thinks he's been hauled off by one of the mobs. Who the hell knows!"

"Did he have any stones on him when he went missing?" asked Nigel nervously.

"No. David hadn't given him anything since his last trip to Dakar. Issa was supposed to be connecting in Conakry with David. He never showed."

"Shit!" Nigel exclaimed. With only two shipments delivered and their mule missing, how many more stones could they reasonably amass? More importantly, what did this mean for the confidentiality of their enterprise?

"Look, we'll be fine," Hume said, trying to calm his friend. "Did you connect with a cutter and a buyer? Tell me you were successful." Hume needed to get some balance from Nigel's successes, assuming he'd had some.

"Yeah, Tony. I located a good stonecutter and we hit it off."

"Nigel," said Tony, with mock exasperation, "this guy is just a hired gun, a whore. I hope you didn't 'hit it off,' because it's going to be very tough to kill him if you need to."

Nigel shot up from his chair like he had been set on fire. He yelled into the phone, "Goddamn it, that's not funny! There will be no killing of any kind, not even in joking." He stopped abruptly, realizing his office door was open. He walked to the door and, after assuring no one had been close enough to hear him, closed it firmly. "This is serious business we're in and you know that neither of us is prepared to take a life just to expedite our cargo or keep our work secret."

"*Du calme, mon ami,*" Hume said slowly, nearly laughing.

This agitated Nigel further.

"I'm trying to impress upon you," Hume said, "that you can't go about building heartfelt relationships with our business partners since the nature of our enterprise is highly cautious, stealthy, and ... illegal. I'm sure you recall that bit. There could easily be some very hard choices to make down the road."

Correct though Hume was, Nigel did not feel like relinquishing his righteousness so quickly. "Tony, you and I are doing this for the money and the independence that money will buy us. I will not for a single second countenance covering our tracks with a murder or anything like it. My God, think of what it would be like, constantly wondering if we might be caught at any second, always looking over your shoulder. What kind of life would we have traded for then, tell me."

"You didn't have sex with the cutter, did you?"

"Stop your confound joking, Tony!"

Hume ignored him. "Let's consider where we are this very instant, Nigel. We have two shipments totaling fifty-three stones. We have this little hiccup to deal with, losing Issa. But authorities aren't breathing down on us, and you scored our key middle person. Things are nearly on track. That's damn good for West Africa, wouldn't you agree?"

"And your point?" Nigel could barely speak.

"My point is we focus on the issues at hand—stay prepared, stay flexible, and stay in business. It's economic maths, Nigel. Please don't get upside down because you saw the truth in my joke and didn't like it. Are you still with me?"

"Of course I'm with you. Again you've missed the point."

"I think not, old friend. We have to replace Issa very fast or we will have no business. And, by the way, what if he tells whoever is responsible for hijacking him, about us? Granted, he knows only my face and your voice on the phone. But we have to think this through and figure out a new method of how to get the raw stones to us."

"Yes, yes. This is a critical hiccup. I'm not questioning that. But it isn't yet a setback. Let's think this through!"

Nigel asked Hume about replacing Issa with another man from the mining operations in Guinea. "Replacing Issa won't be simple, Tony, or quick. Issa knew the people, the protocols, and the terrain. How in hell are we going to plug someone back into that network and environment, particularly someone we can trust? Or worse, how the hell are we going to recreate it from scratch?" Yet, as Nigel threw the question out to Hume, he believed he had a potential solution.

"Fuck all," Hume said. "We have to make some luck, and fast. Meet me at the Café de la Sirène at six this evening."

"I'd prefer something a bit less conspicuous, Tony. Any of the expat crowd could stop in there."

"Precisely. Just a normal end of the day."

Nigel thought about this and replied, "See you at six, then. And we'll keep it low-key."

"That's the British way, isn't it?"

When Nigel hung up the phone and sat back in his chair, he became excited about his solution. Though he didn't know well any of the individuals involved—something he would begin to rectify today—the very idea that the engineers from the IMAME project had essential carte blanche border privileges for their work gave Nigel hope. Could they place a cook, a driver, or even an expatriate who could get to a drop-off point in Guinea and transport the diamonds back in their research caravan? There was much to learn first: where they were going, when, for how long, their level of authority, and more. But unless Tony had something better in mind by six o'clock, Nigel was convinced that using a group of scientists headed down the river basin into remote, rural Guinea seemed a near-perfect solution to their dilemma. But who could they get and how would they recruit this person? There was now much to discuss at Café de la Sirène.

19. EXPLORING OPTIONS

In the solarium cooled by the shade of six coconut palms, Doria sat at her desk and wrote down her experience with Mady Toula. She wanted to gather the disparate pieces into a meaningful whole. It was impossible to recall the Oulof or Djiolla names of the different pastes, liquids, and spice-like ingredients. Still, she was able to draw the layout of the baskets and other containers and label each by color, smell, shape, or some property she could recall such as wet or dry, and so on.

The little bit she had learned from her soon-to-be tutor of West African herbal medicine was the window she needed to see through her own heart and into a world she believed she was meant to inhabit. The biological components of the earth were powerful and priceless. Doria had the need and, perhaps the ability, to discover and set free that power. She shook her head as she realized how grand and prideful her thoughts were. But she could stifle neither the anticipation nor her giddiness.

She paused to remember that Nigel should be home today. Her watch told her he would have landed over two hours ago. Thinking that he may have called while she was out and that he most certainly had gone straight to the office, she decided to call him there. He picked up on the first ring.

"Nigel. You're back safe. How did everything go?"

"Hi, darling. Thanks for ringing back. I called you when I arrived, of course, but you were out."

"Yes, yes I was. But I'm home now. Tell me how you got on. Did you get your contract from the dreaded Bahn-Denzir?"

"Well, in fact I did. We had a true confluence of need and opportunity, and I was there at the right time to bring it together."

Doria had always found Nigel's modesty about his success to be genuine. But at this moment his voice seemed to have a distant, almost hard edge.

"Minta hasn't been in all day, so I thought I would cook dinner for us. Something simple, of course," and she laughed slightly, thinking how rusty her culinary skills were. "When do you think you'll be home?"

Nigel's mind was moving quickly. "I'm meeting Tony at six tonight to discuss some of the results of the trip and some ideas I have for the 'greater commercial interests of the Island.' So I'm thinking dinner around eight. Is that good, Doria?"

"Eight will be fine, Nigel. We'll catch up then."

"Right. Cheerio, love." He hung up the phone.

This was the first time Doria could recall when Nigel's boyish energy seemed completely suppressed, even though his words were pure Nigel. Perhaps she was imagining it. If something was truly troubling him, she would be able to understand it when they were together. She had much on her mind as well. With more than three hours until Nigel was home, Doria had time to tend to her plants.

* * *

When Nigel arrived at the café, Hume was comfortably sitting at one of the small interior tables, puffing on a cigarette and nursing a Pastis. Nigel ordered a Kronenbourg draught as he pulled out the chair next to his cohort.

"Considering you just got in from Amsterdam this afternoon, Nige, I'd say you look remarkably fresh. Damned annoying, if you ask me."

Anxious as he was to discuss his idea to solve their diamond transport crisis, Nigel was charmed by his friend's unflappable humor and glad for a chance to relax a bit.

"Not as fresh as I look, Tony, but you know how important appearances are. It doesn't hurt that Dakar is in the same time zone as Amsterdam. I think of it as traveling from Edinburgh to London by train."

"Without the heat when you disembark, heh?"

Nigel's beer arrived. He took a long gulp.

Then Nigel asked, "Have you thought any more about how we're going to replace Issa?"

"Naturally, I've thought it about it, but blast if I can come up with a reasonable solution. I was thinking perhaps of paying off some of Diouf's people down at the port. But that would mean cutting Diouf himself in. He might well go for it, but at what price? The advantage could be that he keeps someone he can trust at the docks at all times. Even so, that still doesn't address the problem of who brings the stones up from Guinea."

"And Diouf might not go for it, Tony. He may not be a straight arrow, but he's a sly politician. Our operation is probably too small for him to stick his neck out."

Hume nodded. "Yup. The ol' boy would much more likely be cutting deals directly with De Beers or Kimberley. So, what about an overland solution?"

"That's what I've been thinking. Listen to this. The IMAME project pretty much goes from Saint-Louis all the way to Kankan in Guinea, am I right? Doing all manner of research for those dams to be built in God knows when." Nigel paused to see if Hume made the connection.

"So, your idea is to somehow get Semba to make contact with …"—he struggled to figure out the next puzzle piece—"with whom? Do you know somebody on the project you can trust?" Tony leaned across the table to be sure he had heard Nigel clearly.

"I know *of* a number of people on the project, but I don't know anyone—*yet*."

"So, Nigel, just what is the opportunity here?" Hume leaned back and crossed his arms.

"What we do know is that there are Americans, French, and British people, as well as a good number of Senegalese, working on the project. I have no idea who is here when, who does what, how long they are here, and so forth. But it should be an easy matter to find out."

Hume inserted not so much as a grunt, so Nigel pressed on. "I'll extend to all of them an invitation to a get-together at my place. A Barrow & Bean International welcome for the new expatriates. We'll get to know them, find out how they operate, and see if there might be a suitable person—or persons—to approach with a business proposition. Someone who could take a package from David in Guinea and bring it back to Dakar without any interference from customs or port authorities."

"I suppose with six months of schmoozing and socializing we might find someone. But really, Nigel, we don't have that kind of time. Who knows if there even is an opportunity?"

"Listen to me, Tony. When expats are thrown together into this caldron of Africa, they bond much faster than they ever would back home. And those with a sense of adventure might be willing to pursue a side project. We could tell them almost nothing of the purpose of meeting our man in Guinea. And we may need even more than one person from that team. I'm thinking of backup."

"But that's too risky, Nige. We don't know enough to plan this out properly."

Nigel rested his elbows on the glass table and covered his face with his hands. As he drew his hands down, he looked at Hume.

"Right as rain, Mr. Hume. But we need a plan of some kind, don't we? Neither of us is prepared to toss in the towel. Do you want to travel to Conakry yourself and carry stolen diamonds, as a diplomat? Can you find enough pretext to travel to Guinea and the time to meet with our man Semba in the interior? You said yourself there is going to be increased security around the diamonds, and we still don't know exactly what happened to Issa. I think it's too dangerous for either of us to get directly involved, don't you?"

"How quickly could you pull off this soirée with the IMAME team?" Hume had measured all the alternatives as Nigel was speaking and could not come up with a better idea.

"I'll ask Doria tonight, but it should go as quickly as we can make it go. The only person I know on the team is their project manager, a man named Darrin Planck, I think. I can contact him as soon as Doria and I agree, by which I mean first thing tomorrow."

Hume extinguished his cigarette and sipped his Pastis. "I need to contact David. I'm sure he's sweating bullets in Conakry, trying to find out what happened to Issa and wondering, like us, what the hell we're going to do."

"I know you have to get in touch with him, but there isn't a whole lot to say until we have a solid plan in place."

"Nigel, he's got to know that we're working on something promising. He's got to be able to trust us and believe we will figure this out. If he gets too worried and flees, or if he makes a mistake waiting for us, we're out of business—or worse. I'm going to call tonight and hope he gets the message to contact me tomorrow."

"I'll give you a call as soon as I make contact with IMAME," Nigel assured his friend.

* * *

Doria failed to see the reason for Nigel's insistent urgency in having a party for people they didn't know, Americans at that. "Nigel, you know I'll be happy to host your get-together, but can't it wait until I come back from Ziguinchor?" Doria was concerned the timing might interfere with her commitment to take Mady Toula back to the Casamance.

"That's exactly the point, Doria, my love. These people are scientists, heading off into the bush at various times, and we have an opportunity for them to be together and show them our hospitality, but only for this short interval when they are all here in Dakar."

"Why must you fête these Americans all of a sudden? What are they to you?"

Nigel was taken aback by his wife's reaction. Never before in their marriage had she been other than accommodating and gracious when it came to supporting Nigel's business interests. And this new attitude of hers could not have occurred at a less opportune moment. With his own agenda in play, his natural ability to empathize with his spouse was compromised.

"Not only are the IMAME people some of the most interesting Anglophones to land in Senegal since we've been here, their work on mineral exploration and public health is quite aligned with BBI's plan to grow our operations into commodity development. These people are potentially very important, Doria."

"I don't doubt that. They're Americans, after all. I just don't understand why your party has to be this weekend. For heaven's sake, you don't even know if they will all be available on Saturday."

But Nigel did know, having tracked down Derek Planck via telephone, after leaving Hume at the Café de la Sirène. They got along well over the phone. Planck thought a gathering at the Blake residence would be a nice opportunity for a group of scientists who didn't know each other. But it had to be this week, or else many people would be on their way into the bush for extended periods.

"But I do. I mean, we do. This Saturday may be the only time for months that most of their teams are in Dakar. We haven't entertained many Americans over the years, love. You know how badly they speak French."

Doria chuckled at this bit of common knowledge. "It's very short notice, Nigel, and if I am to agree, this must not—it cannot interfere with my plans to go to the Casamance. You know how important this trip is to me."

Nigel let out an exasperated breath and wiped his hand over his head. He knew Doria's trip was important to her, but he did not understand why.

"Then, bloody well figure out if you're going this weekend or not, Doria," he shouted.

She was silent for a few moments as she absorbed the short outburst.

"Please calm down," she finally said.

They had never argued in real anger with each other before.

"Yes," he said, mocking himself. "Calm down indeed. I-I apologize, my sweet."

They fell silent again. Doria could not fathom what was so important about honoring a group of Americans, but she did not want to let her husband down.

"I'll do my best to arrange my trip for Monday, Nigel. We'll plan for the Americans to come over for a late lunch Saturday afternoon. Will that suit?"

"Yes, of course, dear. What can I do to help you prepare?"

Resigned to entertain this Saturday, Doria switched into planning mode and gave her spouse a list of things he would have to accomplish in order to help her. It was familiar ground. The civility that stitched their relationship was restored.

20. A Gift for a Gift

Doria had two mechanisms for contacting Mady: the half sister Bydee at the market who had been decidedly distant since Doria's encounter with Mady, and the faithful Ahminta, who had become sullen and monosyllabic since their encounter with Mady. Neither seemed trustworthy at this point. Therefore, Doria had Iba drive her to Mady's residence to check on her new mentor and gather what information she could for a departure day.

The white Mercedes drew little attention on the day she pulled into Mady's family compound. Doria disembarked and walked through the family group, smiling and saying *"Bonjour"* as she went. She knocked on the door of the concrete building that housed the apothecary, hoping Mady was there. But she was not. Using Iba to translate into Oulof, Doria asked every family member in turn where Mady had gone. No one knew.

Disappointed, she walked back to Mady's shed and banged on it a few times, hoping not so much that Mady would answer and invite her in, but that the door would suddenly open and allow Doria an unfettered visit to the secrets within. She knocked louder and faster, until the skin on her knuckles broke. But the lack of response never changed. Doria stopped banging on the door and, cradling her fist with her other hand, looked around.

Twenty pairs of sullen eyes were staring at her in the late morning light. They stood in silence looking at Doria, then at each other.

From behind the streaming beaded curtain of one of the huts, a preteen girl with a shaved head and hoop earrings the size of a large coin came out and approached Doria. When she was within a meter of the stranger, the girl stopped and said something in Oulof.

Doria shook her head and bent down with a smile on her face. "I don't understand you, little one."

The girl turned to Iba, repeated her message, and held out her hands, revealing a wad of paper. She turned back to Doria and held her hands above her head.

"Her grandmother, Mady Toula, wants you to have these," Iba translated.

Doria held out a hand, into which the girl dropped the paper ball. As she carefully unwrapped it, Doria could smell a pungent sweetness escape from the package. Inside she saw two beige, gooey marble-sized balls.

"What are these?" Doria asked to one and all.

Iba translated and the women giggled.

"These are special treats, Madame," one of the older girls said in French. "They are special *bonbons* for you."

Doria wasn't certain what to do with them, so she asked, "Should I eat these? Are they sweets after a meal?"

The women and girls giggled again. "No, Madame," the older girl said. "They are sweets before the meal. Grandma Mady said that if you come by and she was not here, you should have these as a gift."

"Tell your grandmother I thank her. Do you know when she will be ready to go back to Ziguinchor?"

The girl shrugged her shoulders and looked around. No one knew anything about their grandmother's plans. Doria put the candies into her purse and withdrew a pen and a small notepad. She wrote a message for Mady, saying she was ready to go to Ziguinchor on Monday, and included her address and phone number so that Mady might contact her. Doria believed that to be unlikely.

In the back seat of the Mercedes, Doria again unwrapped the candies and inhaled their fragrance. It was like submitting her senses to an exquisite red wine. Only the artist knew for certain how the spell of pineapple, mango, cardamom, and ginger came together. Yet for each recipient, the experience was unique and penetrating. It was an act of will for Doria to wrap them up again and save them for later.

21. Assembling the Pieces

At 12:30 p.m. Tony Hume went to the one public phone on which he could rely, at the Rue Liberté Bureau de Poste—the one at the director's office that Tony paid an extra 1,000 CFA to have to himself every week. It was of no concern to the director whom Hume called or why; the diplomat needed a private line for personal business, perhaps family. The reality was different. Hume had a standing call to the third partner of their diamond business, David Semba.

It was always a relief to Hume when David answered. Tony would call, ring twice, and hang up. He would call back and if David did not answer by the third ring, Hume was to hang up and try the next day. The fact that Tony was to call a police station in Conakry made him nervous. But David's half brother was the deputy commandant, and the commandant was content to spend his time away in the town attempting to be a politician. David had convinced Tony that this was the safest and most reliable way to communicate. Because the lunch hour always included wives with energetic children delivering meals to their police husbands and other officers breaking and heading home or to local restaurants, it was the ideal time for the coconspirators to speak.

Without bothering with pleasantries, Hume said, "Have you found out any more information about Issa?"

David responded in English. "If he were dead, someone would have reported his body by now. My brother knows of no such report. Nor do we believe the authorities have him, since my brother would have been able to get news. It is puzzling, Tony, and worrying."

"You're damn right it's worrying! So long as we don't know what's happened to Issa, we need to be extremely cautious. Nigel and I have come up with a possible way to restart the operation, but you must tell me if you think it's a good one."

Among the reasons David worked with Hume in the dangerous enterprise was that Hume treated David like a partner, not an African national of convenience.

Hume explained the overland route for the stones and acquiring a contact from the IMAME team.

"Who are those people? Tourists? Researchers? At the first sign of difficulty they will desert us. They will give us up to save themselves."

"I'm just as concerned as you are, but we're running out of time and options. We can halt the Blueprint until we've replaced Issa, which may be never! Or we find a better plan. What do you think, David?"

The governments and the mine operators knew that theft of raw diamonds was increasing. Therefore, so was mine security. Guards were beating workers to death for just appearing guilty of theft. Gun trafficking, a constant but tiny issue in the mountains, had been increasing to provide tribal dissidents with the means to try to reclaim their land from the mine owners. Civil penalties for those caught smuggling diamonds were also on the rise. The situation was becoming ever more difficult and dangerous. The longer they waited, the higher the probability of failure. Their window of opportunity was through the next six months. And that was optimistic.

"We can't wait," David said.

"We all agree, then, this overland transit becomes our new plan for now."

"It is critical to get the right person for this work. He must be knowledgeable and not too greedy. Who have you identified?"

"That's where we still have work to do. We know that IMAME will pass freely across borders, but we don't have the right individual identified yet."

"And if this individual cannot be found?"

"We go to our backup plan, which is to cultivate a separate individual and try to attach him to the IMAME team. The truth is we might find the right individual and not even tell him what he's really doing. Nigel and I are working out the details."

David was silent for a few seconds. "Have good news for me about the transport on our next call, Tony. I will have a shipment ready in two weeks and I will need another 10,000 CFA and $1,000 US."

"If I have to ride along myself, we will get this done."

David never minced his words. "This role needs someone a bit fearless as well as cunning. Someone with a strong stomach, Tony. We both know that's not you. We need someone who has the goodwill of the gods."

* * *

"David is OK with the idea of the overland route, Nigel," Hume related over a late lunch on Thursday. "Apparently, moving around the interior is much safer than at the ports. Issa's disappearance smells very bad, so we have to be extra careful. David has some stones to get to us." He sipped his espresso and asked, "How are you getting on with the IMAME bloke?"

Nigel smiled slightly, then drew a breath. He had success with Derek Planck getting the rundown on the project, and most especially, the personnel.

"We're on for Saturday, Tony, and I believe we'll have the opportunity for some very interesting conversations."

Nigel went on to describe the project with all the details he had gathered during his meeting with Planck. He had been so forthcoming that he had provided Nigel with a target. Though most of the scientists were coming and going for trips sometimes months apart, only a few would be staying for extended, multiple trips. Because of their work and academic backgrounds, and the fact that they had little real experience with this region of West Africa, none of them were really good candidates as a mule. But there was one individual who might be. He was the young American who had already been working in the region for the last two years and was responsible for the logistics for all the expeditions. He spoke more than one of the local languages and had already led a rather precarious and eventful mission to the Guinea-Mali border.

"Did you meet this fellow?" Tony asked.

"I didn't. He was busy at the airport picking up some new members of their project. If this American is our guy, we have to get to know him quickly. And we don't have much time. Can you find out anything from your contacts at the American embassy, without raising suspicion?"

"Seems straightforward enough, Mr. Hume. The United States and the United Kingdom are donors to OEUFS, making us cosponsors. It's in our interests to know what's going on, isn't it? And to know the key players. I have the IMAME file here. Not much in it. The personnel files are one-pagers. I'll get you a copy."

* * *

There was ample information on Derek Planck, Vietnam War veteran with two duty tours. He was certainly not Nigel's first choice. Hume was convinced he would be a poor backup as well.

The trouble was, however, that there was virtually no information available on this Victor Byrnes fellow. All USAID could report was that he had been a Peace Corps volunteer for two years, with little distinguishing activities other than he remained in the northern Senegal bush nearly the entire twenty-five months. He had been a liberal arts major at Cornell University, which Hume thought might work in their favor. Young liberal arts majors had such mutable ethics. This, however, afforded no additional insight to his courage, his creativity, or loyalty. Hume ruled out the only other two members of the team that he could get information on: a medical doctor, older, a former dean of the School of Tropical Medicine at Baylor University, and a reptile specialist, Alan Broca, who was recovering from viral meningitis.

Hume hated this short time frame to try to do a thorough job of research prior to meeting and selecting a potential partner. No—not a partner, for God's sake. A transporter, a mule, a higher-order pack animal. If they did select one of these Americans, Hume would use as much of his time in the next few weeks to find out what made the individual tick. But until then, it was still a crapshoot. Hume shivered whenever he considered the increased risk they were supporting.

22. Come Together

Nigel knew Doria was attending to the preparations of the party on Saturday morning. He was not aware that she was attending to other preparations simultaneously. In the Marché Kermel as she searched with Ahminta for the ripest papayas and mangoes, Doria's thoughts were not as focused as her husband had credited her.

Wanting to be certain she was getting exactly what Doria wanted, Ahminta presented Doria a bundle of carrots in each hand. Doria decided instantly on those in her left hand, with barely a glance to see if they were the better selection.

She asked her servant, "Is there any chance your aunt Mady is at the market today, Ahminta?"

Ahminta shrugged. "Maybe," she murmured. After a few seconds of standing awkwardly together, Ahminta thought out loud: "Perhaps, Madame, you could visit Bydee, and she will know."

The thought of visiting Bydee did not excite her. And it was useless to meander through the four-acre market teeming with shoppers, kiosks, and all. She would never find Mady, even if she were here.

"I'm not sure Bydee will give me an honest answer," Doria told Ahminta.

The bustle of the market, normally an attraction for Doria, was now a distraction. Trying not to resent Nigel for his last-minute, inexplicable need to entertain a group of American researchers, she focused on her task of fulfilling her list for the event, while at the same time trying to uncover a way to contact Mady and plan her trip to the Casamance. Doria stumbled as she looked around the galaxy of produce and trinket vendors.

"What is the matter, Doria?" she muttered. "Stop this foolishness and concentrate!"

By force of will, she attended to her duties rather than her desires. Difficulty controlling herself was new to Doria and very disconcerting.

Her inner thoughts became spoken ones as she and Ahminta wandered through the market.

"Where could that woman possibly have gone, and why hasn't she tried to contact me? We really should be getting on next week, but I don't even know if she's sold all her medicines. Maybe I should contact DeLevres and see what he knows about traditional plant medicines from the Casamance. Of course!"

Ahminta asked which of two bowls of melons was right for their basket. Doria waved a hand, authorizing Ahminta to buy whatever she thought suitable. Doria absentmindedly put her hand into her purse, pulled out her wallet, and gave Ahminta a large bill for lettuce. The merchant cursed in Oulof since he could not make change. They left the market thirty minutes later than normal, packed their purchases into the white Mercedes, and headed to the European grocery store.

Doria gazed out the car window, watching the buildings change color and century as Iba drove her and Ahminta from the market area to the modern high-rises of the Place de l'Indépendance, and then to the northern Rue de la Paix where the French, Italian, and Scandinavian boutiques lined the boulevard as chic as any in Beverly Hills or La Rive Gauche.

Walking into La Groceria, Doria suddenly felt out of place, as though some transformation had taken place only moments ago and she no longer belonged to this strange world of pristine counters, air conditioning, and attentive clerks.

With the last purchases complete, Doria wanted to use what time remained to find and speak to Alain DeLevres. Would he be at the university or at his home on a Saturday morning? Even though there was little the botanist could do for her now, she needed to connect to the blossoming new side of her life, the one which DeLevres and Mady had helped her construct.

When the white car made its way to the aging laboratory building on the university campus, Doria saw an old Citroën parked in the driveway in front of the laboratory. She knew instantly it belonged to DeLevres.

Her servants waited, and she entered the building. The entrance door made a scratching noise as it closed across the floor behind her. She heard a rustle of papers from DeLevres' laboratory. The lab door opened and the rumpled DeLevres stood holding it open slightly, just enough for him to see out.

"Madame Blake," he said. The composure in his voice was not conveyed by his shaking hands and wide eyes. "A most unexpected and ... pleasant surprise. To what do I owe this honor?" He did not move to ask Doria into his space.

"I'm so glad you're here, Alain," she said with more familiarity than she felt. "I wanted to tell you that early in the week I will be traveling to Ziguinchor. I've met a most interesting concoctor of traditional medicines, and she's agreed to show me what it takes to make them. I don't know at all what they are, but I want to study them. I was wondering if you had any reference materials that I could borrow for a few weeks."

DeLevres came out into the hallway, closing the laboratory door behind him. "I must have at least a few illustrated texts that you could have. Let's see, here in my office ...."

"I was hoping you might have something of your own notes, as well," she said without having thought it until she spoke.

"Well ... I ... I'm ... I'm not sure that lending out my notes is the best for either of us, Madame."

"Alain, you need fear nothing from me. I would never take anything from you. I would only hope to provide you with new information. And I would never reveal the direction of your research to anyone. I know you must take great care when exploring the world of hallucinogens."

She said this so matter-of-factly that DeLevres knew she had made that deduction during her visit to his lab. Now what was he to do?

"The compounds I'm researching, Madame Blake, are referred to as psychotropics. My private research, dear lady, is unique and not ready for public eyes."

She stood closer to him and he backed up slightly. "I'm not suggesting sharing anything with another soul. I'm looking for your help during this first field trip of mine, and in return I will invite you to visit and help me sort through what I've learned and what I cannot understand."

DeLevres was a statue.

"And surely, Alain, the opportunity to work with a traditional healer who knows what these plants do, how they go together, and where to find them, is not to be missed."

"You ... you are a very determined woman, Madame."

"I think that working together will be a great benefit to us both."

DeLevres walked around Doria, back to his lab door, which he opened slowly. He motioned Doria to follow him. She lingered in the doorway, not wanting to intrude further than she had already insinuated herself.

DeLevres waved back to her. "Come, come. You have a point, Madame. This is very risky for me, but ..."—he shrugged—"it is surely an opportunity as well." He went to a glass cabinet on the wall opposite the lab bench and pulled out a pile of notebooks. No dust had gathered on these.

"Is there anything specific you'd like to see?"

"Only how you've organized your thinking here, so I could find what I'm looking for quickly."

DeLevres showed Doria how each book was labeled by date and region of the country, and each had a small table of contents that had been pasted in as an afterthought. He opened one that was labeled SOUTHWESTERN SENEGAL. February to May 1977. In the book she noted intricate drawings of plants, leaves, trees, shrubs, flowers, and so on, very few of them named and all of them described where they had been found and what he understood as the plant's use. Beneath a few were later markings regarding compound discoveries made in the lab.

"Good gracious, you've already done so much of the work!" Doria exclaimed. "And these drawings are so well done. Are they yours, Alain?"

"They are mine," DeLevres stated with pride. "Do you recognize the French names, Madame Blake?"

"Some, I believe I do, and others, surely not. And it looks as though you don't have the French names for a lot of these." Toward the end of the first notebook were descriptions of what a particular plant was supposed to do, but there was no name nor any drawing. Doria asked why.

"I could not find any plant to match the description I'd been given," he replied. "I went there with a cab driver / tour guide, not an expert traditional healer. You are about to engage in … what did you call it? An opportunity not to be missed. Yes?"

"Then … I may … take this one notebook with me? Oh my! I-I cannot thank you enough for this, Alain." Her voice quivered. "I will be in contact with you as soon as I reach Ziguinchor. Are your phone numbers here in your notebook?"

"Yes, yes, Madame Blake," he said, escorting her out of the lab. "Please take very good care. That notebook contains the original notes. I have transcriptions of the data with my laboratory notes. This is a field notebook."

"I will, Alain, I swear." She turned to go, then instantly turned back and planted a thankful kiss on the professor's cheek. She turned again and walked outside.

Professor DeLevres, still motionless in the hallway between his office and his laboratory, slapped his forehead and then shook his whole body. As loud as he could, he shouted, "My God, am I complete fool?" In a lower tone, he exclaimed, "God help me!"

* * *

If Doria felt light-headed from her success, she contained herself, walking calmly to the Mercedes and clutching the notebook in both arms like a schoolgirl. As a present to herself, she decided she would not look at them further, until she was preparing for her journey.

It was five past noon when she returned home, so Doria quickly marshaled her household resources for final preparations. Nigel was relieved to see his wife immersed in her conductor role, directing Iba, Ahminta, and Nigel himself in readiness activities.

By 12:45 p.m. Doria had inspected every detail and found them ready. Except for herself. Going into the bedroom, she closed the door behind her and went to the dresser drawer where she had placed DeLevres' notebook. Eyeing it with a sense of guardianship, she again reminded herself not to think about the notes until this event was behind her.

Next to the notes sat a little ball of tissue that Doria had forgotten. She picked it up and carefully unwrapped it. She lifted the two homemade candies up to her nose. Their sweet-spicy scent was intoxicating. She closed her eyes and smiled as she considered eating one right now. Picking up one of the two gooey balls, she nibbled at it and was instantly seduced by a mix of indescribable spice flavor and the sweetness she could smell but barely taste. There was a fire like a hot pepper. It was an easy decision to pop the rest of the candy into her mouth and savor the sensations. These are absolutely amazing, she thought. I must have this recipe. Wrapping the remaining candy back into the tissue, she replaced it in the drawer next to the DeLevres notes. A wonderful sense of anticipation and fulfillment built inside her as she undressed for her shower.

23. BAIT

Derek Planck was the first to arrive. With him were two other men, older than Planck, who were dressed as if they were about to play golf.

Nigel was at the front entrance to greet them. "Gentlemen! How nice of you to grace this tropical bungalow." He shook Planck's hand heartily, who then introduced Nigel to his compatriots.

"Nigel Blake, this is Siegfried Mueller, our team leader for hydrology and geology."

"You are one of the team leaders who went on the first trip in the bush?"

Siegfried smiled and nodded.

Nigel led his guests to the patio, where Hume was standing and sipping his first gin and tonic. He smiled.

"The others are on their way. I think at least two more carloads. We're nearly at our full complement of experts," Planck explained.

"Well," Hume chimed in, "it's only a short time before the hard work begins, so you'd better make the most of the downtime you have here in Dakar, heh?"

Nigel offered drinks and all three requested beer. "I'll show you to the bar the first time, gentlemen. After that, you're on your own. Sound right?"

The Americans nodded and, as they moved along the side of the pool to the bar, Nigel looked around for Doria. Not seeing her, he called out.

"Doria, love. Will you be joining us soon?"

As though she had been waiting for the request, Doria emerged from the darkened house dressed in a sheer white linen blouse under which one could faintly see her green-flowered swimsuit top. Her safari shorts were cinched at her waist with a braided cord. She had done her hair up with only a few golden tendrils hanging down like feathery earrings. The three guests turned to greet their hostess. Their ability to move left them for an instant.

She smiled slightly, not fully comprehending her effect on men, while appreciating it for the ease it gave her in the world. She shook each guest's hand and asked them what they did. They stumbled over themselves to speak to her. Nigel and Hume nudged each other.

Two more Land Rovers pulled into the circular drive, and Hume and Nigel both went to meet them. Knowing his duty for the introductions, Planck followed closely, beer in hand.

Doria asked to be excused, to put music on the stereo. She selected the album of a local guitarist, feeling the buoyant rhythms of Senegal were appropriately festive yet relaxed. She felt unexpectedly light and cheerful.

Nigel shepherded the guests through the house to the patio, and let them introduce themselves to Doria. It was impossible for the hosts to remember everyone's name or the reason each came to be in Senegal. They proceeded through the protocol with grateful humor.

The drinks and music nourished conversations, especially among the team members who were together socially for the first time as a group. The early afternoon heat was already searing bare skin, but none of the guests had taken advantage of the chairs underneath the umbrellas.

Beside the barbecue pit, Nigel chatted with Planck. The conversation revealed Planck's faith in hierarchy, the rule of law, and the restraint of citizens' unbridled rights. Was he at least a capitalist?

"Isn't there another American in your group?" Nigel asked. "A young man who's actually been here in Senegal for some time? You mentioned him when we spoke the first time, right Derek?"

"Sure," was the reply between sips of beer. "Victor. He said he would be here a little later. Something about errands at home and catching the ferry in time. He lives on Gorée."

"Interesting." Not really that interesting, but it did say a bit about the maverick nature of young Mr. Byrnes.

The forestry expert, Orson Limber, came up to Nigel's side. "Nice setup you have here, Mr. Blake," Limber said from the side of his mouth, as though he were sharing a secret in public. "You been with Barrow & Bean a long time?"

"Too long, it seems," said Nigel truthfully. This man had a conniving way about him, thought Nigel, which, though right for certain aspects of a potential ignorant soldier, were not the signs of someone who could stick through adversity. Nigel moved on to another guest.

With stealthy coordination, Hume pulled aside the medical doctor who had been telling his public health teammate about his work in the slums of Rio de Janeiro and how tending the poor people had jaded him to their economic plight. Though they were splendid people, of course.

Doria realized that everything was under control for the next hour or more, particularly with Nigel and Tony working the crowd to such great effect. But it was very hot, and Doria wanted to cool off in the pool.

"Thank you all for coming," she announced. "The pool is open. Please do jump in and escape this heat! I'll be taking the plunge myself. Please join me."

She disappeared into the cabana at the far end of the patio, emerging in a short white robe. She walked delicately yet purposefully to the end of the pool where the stairs were shaded. Every man, Nigel and Tony included, snapped to attention without realizing it. Dolores Knapp and Leah Genescieu could only roll their eyes.

Doria smiled at the grateful onlookers as she took off her robe, set it on a pool chair, and walked waist deep into the shimmering water. She pulled an inflated inner tube into the pool and plopped her bottom into the middle of it, splashing and sinking a bit. When the pool calmed, she closed her eyes and floated in the water.

Dr. Ham went straight for the changing cabana.

A throaty engine noise burst from the front of the house. Everyone save Doria turned their head toward the entrance, though they could see nothing. Hume put down his tumbler of gin and tonic and went to the front to learn what was happening.

Iba had let pass through the gate and into the Blake compound a man with rangy red hair and beard, riding a Norton motorcycle. The newcomer, wearing sunglasses but no helmet, parked the bike in back of one of the Land Rovers and climbed the stairs toward Nigel. Pushing the hair off his face with one hand, he stuck the other out to shake Nigel's hand.

"Hi there, I'm Victor Byrnes."

"Pleased to meet you, Victor Byrnes," Nigel said. "I'm Nigel Blake. Welcome to our home. We have been expecting you, naturally."

Victor pumped Nigel's hand and thanked him. As he strode into the house, he gazed around like a child entering a toy store. "Nigel, you have a terrific place here. Been here long?"

"Almost six years, Victor. Come on, let me show you to the party." He put his arm on Victor's shoulder and led him to the back.

When they passed Ahminta, standing obsequiously awaiting instructions or the opportunity to clear dishes, Victor greeted her.

"Sama jigen, nanga deff?" ("My sister, how are you doing?")

Ahminta laughed.

Victor extended his hand to shake hers. She took it shyly and told him she had never heard a *toubob* speak Oulof.

He asked her name, and Victor was able to recount a short version of her family's claim on the Senegal River basin below Podor.

Nigel became impatient with Victor's attention to his servant and grabbed him by the elbow. Allowing himself to be led once again, Victor waved to Ahminta.

"Glad you could make it, Byrnes," Mueller called as he saw the two men descend the patio stairs.

"Herr Mueller! You're looking much too relaxed for a man that just cheated death!"

This made the rest of the guests wonder what Victor was talking about. They gathered almost in a circle around the two men and asked what had happened on the five-day journey into the bush. Nigel, too, was intrigued.

"No, no," Mueller said, trying to demur. "It's too long a story. Alan, maybe you can tell them. You were the closest to death, after all!"

Broca merely held up both his hands and shook his head in refusal.

But when Leah Genescieu batted her eyes at Mueller and said, "Pretty please, Siegfried," he puffed up and began.

"Well, you see, our guide put us all in great danger, leading us up a mountain with no road and no idea where he was going. Then ..."

It had started. Victor couldn't bring himself to shrug off the insult, comical though it was. However, he didn't retort. He simply walked away as Siegfried regaled the throng with his account of the trip to Manantali.

Victor saw a woman in the pool he didn't recognize, so he went over to take a better look and to keep himself from getting into an argument with Mueller.

Doria had been in a glorious state of lassitude, drugged by the soft motion of the water and the shaded heat.

From behind her, she heard, "Good afternoon," in a new voice. She paddled herself around to face the voice.

"Hi, there, I'm Victor Byrnes."

She beheld a young man with a rust-colored beard and bright green eyes. Doria continued to stare. Victor tilted his head and looked at her curiously. Their eyes locked for only a few seconds. Then Victor knelt by the side of the pool. Doria's curiosity was enhanced by a tingle she couldn't explain.

"That water looks pretty inviting," Victor said. "May I join you?"

Victor pulled his shirt over his head. He stood and, walking over to the stairs, undid his belt, dropped his shorts by the side of the pool, and revealed his very American swimsuit that looked like baggy boxer shorts. Doria laughed and then blushed. Victor, who was turned sideways in the shade, didn't notice. He awkwardly pulled off his hiking boots and sat on the pool stairs, looking straight at Doria.

She still had not said a word, but she started to realize that this young man had an effect on her she could not remember feeling before. A tremble like a chill came over her and the butterflies in her stomach spread.

Before she could move another muscle, Nigel came up behind Victor.

"I see you've met my wife," he said.

"Actually, I haven't," Victor told him. "She seems more water sprite than human at the moment. Does she speak?"

Puzzled, Nigel went to the other end of the pool and said to her, "You mustn't be so rude to the guests, Doria. I'm sure Mr. Byrnes was only trying to be cordial."

Her husband's voice broke the spell, and Doria returned to the world. She remained slightly confounded by her own feelings.

"I do apologize, Mr. ... Mr. ..."

"Please call me Victor."

"Mr. Byrnes ... Victor," Nigel said. "Yes, yes. Here, let's get you a drink, shall we?"

The same friendly arm that had led him through the house, now pulled Victor up by his armpit in the direction of the drinks. Victor cast one last glance back, then moved toward the other guests. Over his shoulder, Nigel shot a scornful, questioning look at his wife. She saw it, but paid no attention. She decided to get out of the pool and get dressed. As she headed to the cabana, Dr. Ham was making his exit.

"Oh no! Leaving the water so soon?" he asked.

"The water's become quite warm, I'm afraid," Doria answered.

24. Hook

Nigel recognized the bolt of lust that singed his wife, but he chose to think of it as a moment of awkwardness. Without proper introduction, Mr. Byrnes hardly knew his place with the wife of the host. Now that the two had been separated, they could get on to business. Nigel thrust a beer into Victor's fist and began his research.

"Tell me, Victor. What's it like going deep into the real West African bush? I don't get there, save for the occasional visit to a banana plantation. And that just can't be the same at all, compared to what you encounter, yeah?"

Encouraged by his second beer, Victor launched into his stories.

Doria came up beside her husband without a glance at Victor and asked Nigel to introduce her to the other guests. Nigel did so without hesitation, signaling for Hume to take up the conversation with their bearded target. Victor watched Doria walk into the middle of the gathering, arm in arm with Nigel.

From behind, Hume rested a hand on Victor's shoulder. Victor barely noticed.

"She is quite spectacular, isn't she?" Hume said, grinning at Victor.

"What? ... Oh. ... Yes, she's quite, ahh, quite ...."

"Stunning, I think you were about to say. Well, don't think you're alone, my friend. She has that effect on every normal man who meets her."

Victor gazed at his beer for a moment.

Tony continued. "I understand you travel regularly across the borders of Mauritania, Mali, and Guinea. That must be quite a hassle. Dealing with the border guards searching your vehicles, knowing that you have to bribe them."

"I suppose," Victor replied evenly.

"You suppose?" Tony said, his voice raised slightly. He let out a laugh that was at once disarming and oblique. "Tell me, then, what's the going rate for a customs inspector in Kayes or Sélibaby?"

"We probably won't be going through the big towns," Victor said. "When we crossed the border from Mali into Senegal, we drove through the river and there were no customs officials, and literally no border delineation at all. I'm pretty sure it will be the same for Guinea. I mean, we were probably not more than 50 kilometers from the Guinea border, and I promise you there were nothing but rarely traveled dirt paths through the forest. Unless there was a border guard who lived in a village near the area, the government couldn't possibly afford to keep a real border post out there."

Hume nodded.

"I know those borders pretty well. With some greetings in the local language and a small bit of cash, you can get across without much hassle." Victor took a swig from his third beer, and added, with a laugh, "As long as you're prepared to bargain for an hour."

"Really? How interesting. And how far into Guinea do you expect to be exploring?"

"Probably only as far as the outskirts of Kankan. And mostly in the mountains."

This continued for twenty minutes. Tony pumped information from Victor, who was content—relieved, even—to talk about it. He spoke of splitting up the teams and how their schedules would depend on the work the team leaders needed to accomplish, the weather conditions, and so on. When Nigel looked over from time to time, Hume raised his glass with a smile.

The party settled into that easy rhythm that comes with a few drinks and hospitable surroundings. Nigel rejoined Victor and Hume. He wanted to confer privately with Hume about best to plant the seed of collaboration today. The two excused themselves and ambled into the house, leaving Victor alone.

* * *

From Nigel's introductions, Doria realized she might in fact have some interesting guests. She joined a conversation with three members of the public health team, in whose work Doria was genuinely interested.

After learning of their plans to look for diseases and treat as many villages as they could along the way, Doria asked, "Will you be considering the availability and use of traditional healers and healing methods?"

"That's not part of our brief, as of the moment," said the Indian microbiologist Denali Tekkendil, "but in India we have many local cures based on ancient plants that have been used and perfected over thousands of years of our history. I would not be surprised to find the same here, though I don't believe that Africa has yet achieved the level of sophistication in its approach to traditional pharmacology that has been reached in India."

"Perhaps," Doria responded, "but you may be surprised." She spoke about the traditional cures in the marketplace and her own desire to explore these in a scientific manner.

Tekkendil said, "That seems a bit ambitious, Mrs. Blake. Are you a botanist?"

"In a former life," she said with a turn of her head. She noticed Victor standing alone and she involuntarily turned her shoulders to look at him.

He was watching Nigel and Tony walk into the house. Victor then turned his whole body toward their group and looked at Doria again, directly in the eyes.

Her stomach tightened.

"Would you excuse me, please?" she requested. "I have some things to check up on in the kitchen." She turned gracefully, walking up the wedding cake stairs and into the house.

As if by quantum transport, Victor Byrnes appeared at her side. Tentatively, he said, "Mrs. Blake?"

"Y-yes, Mr. B-Byrnes?" she replied, looking past Victor.

"Please call me Victor." He extended his hand to shake.

Looking at her own hand with uncertainty, she nevertheless placed it in his. Both pulled away quickly.

"Doria," she told him, looking again into his eyes.

"I-I wanted to apologize for my behavior earlier. I didn't mean to be rude. I just hadn't expected ..."

Doria rescued him for the first time. "Please, Mr.—I mean, Victor. No apologies required." After a pause, she asked him, "Are you enjoying yourself?"

"I am now," he replied. He blushed and looked down. "I mean, you have a lovely home and all. You're very kind to have invited the entire team."

"It was my husband's idea, but I'm only too glad to help out." She smiled.

"Remind me to thank him again. But, really, large gatherings aren't my thing. It's not when I'm at my best."

"And when are you at your best, Mr. Byrnes?" Good God! When had she become so bold?

"Victor, remember? Um, probably when I'm out of the big city, working in the desert or the jungle. Probably when I'm out on Gorée, diving for cowries, or hanging out on my patio with my friends, talking to the parrots."

Doria laughed. "You talk to parrots, do you?"

"Sure I do, and they talk back to me. They like my little outdoor buffet when I bring them guavas or oranges."

"And what exactly is your role on this project?"

"I'm supposed to get everybody where they need to go, safely, and get them back safely."

"You're the safari leader, are you?"

"My official title is chief of field logistics, but, you know, I'm pretty sure I like safari leader much better."

Even now, as their conversation stopped and they thought of what to do next, it felt relaxed and nourishing standing next to one another.

"I need to check up on some things in the kitchen, Victor. I'll see you in a bit, yes?"

Victor nodded. His gaze followed her up the stairs.

She turned and looked back at him before she entered into the shadows of the interior. The rush in her stomach had returned. She thought, I have no idea what's happening. Have I turned into a flirt just because a handsome young man has paid me some attention?

Coming out of the house at the same time Doria was entering, Nigel stopped her. "Darling, would you be averse to having Mr. Byrnes over for lunch tomorrow?" he asked.

"Sunday? I'm over at the orphanage until one. Can we do it later in the day, perhaps?"

"I have a small business proposition for him and I'm hoping to get his decision before he gets on his way back into the heart of darkness."

Doria was curious. "Business proposition? You only just met the man, Nigel. What sort of business could this American adventurer be in, that could interest BBI?"

"Information, my dear, information. And truly, Doria, you needn't concern yourself with my transactions with Mr. Byrnes. What about a late lunch tomorrow, then?"

"Why don't you find out first if it will be convenient for V—him before we settle on plans."

Nigel was practically smiling as he assured his wife, "I'd be shocked if he didn't accept."

Doria shrugged. "Fine, I'll ask Ahminta to prepare something today so she won't have to come in on her day off."

Hume flashed by them and bounded down the stairs to the patio. "Got to refresh this drink," he said, pointing to his empty tumbler.

Nigel kissed his wife on the cheek, thanked her for accommodating his request, and followed after Hume. The two of them looked like schoolboys. Doria couldn't remember the last time Nigel seemed so animated. What a strange day this had become.

The two comrades found Victor in another conversation. Nigel asked if he could interrupt for just a second and placed his hand on Victor's shoulder. Hume, seeing that Nigel was in control, returned to the bar and, from there, watched the two men.

"Victor, I have an idea for a way to help each other. Would you be interested?"

Victor thought for a moment. "I can't see why I wouldn't be interested, Mr. Blake. But what could the director of BBI Africa need from a nomad like me?"

"Nomad, indeed. That is precisely what I need from you. And please call me Nigel. Look, I don't think we need to discuss any details today, but I was hoping you could drop by tomorrow and have lunch with us so that we could discuss my idea."

"Wow, sure. That would be great." Victor was thinking of the Sunday ferry schedule from Gorée Island. "I probably couldn't be here before one thirty, though, if that's all right."

"We'll try to stay hungry until you arrive. I've invited Tony Hume over as well. He's an old African hand and can help us think through my ideas."

Victor nodded.

"It's settled then." Nigel sipped his gin and tonic, looked intently at Victor, and walked over to Hume.

Victor, again alone in the small crowd, joined a new conversation.

The rest of the afternoon passed pleasantly. Victor was surprised when Lee Stedman joined him poolside.

He said, "This group of strangers really needs this, Victor. You know, this slight bit of bonding. It could be the glue that keeps them working together once they've traveled hundreds of miles through the desert and the jungle. Endured insect hordes together. Fell ill, became bored, became terrified. Like the four of us last week, yes? But maybe even better."

"I like your optimism, Dr. Stedman." Victor smiled. "I hope you're right."

The company departed as the sun fell below the western wall of the villa. Nigel and Doria said good-bye to everyone individually.

When Victor approached to leave, Nigel shook his hand firmly. "I'm looking forward to our discussions tomorrow, Victor. I appreciate you making the time."

"You've piqued my curiosity, Nigel, that's for sure." He withdrew his hand from Nigel and extended it to Doria. He presumed it was still too soon to engage the double-cheek air kiss that is customary for international bi-gender greetings.

Doria, enjoying his touch, looked at his mouth and said, "It will be a pleasure to see you tomorrow."

Victor bowed and kissed her hand. This time her shiver was unmistakable. It could have been confused for revulsion, save for the slight blush in her cheeks. She pulled her hand away slowly.

"You have been a gracious hostess, Mrs. Blake," Victor said. "I promise not to be such a rude guest tomorrow."

"That should be easy," Nigel said with a laugh. "All you have to do is stay dressed until after lunch!"

"No swimming tomorrow. Business only, I promise."

"Not to worry, young man," Nigel said. "Drive that machine of yours safely, will you, please? There are very few motorcycles in Senegal, and the folks driving cars and trucks don't always know how to react when they see one. It's not a moped!"

"Yes, sir." Victor saluted as he bounced down the stairs.

The hosts turned to go inside when the blast from the motorcycle engine gave them a start. They pivoted together to see Victor speed away. The sound of the motorcycle grew quieter with distance, but still pierced the sounds of other traffic, the sounds of wind and crashing waves, the cries of flocking gulls. Again, Nigel turned toward the house, but Doria did not ... until he pulled her gently back, when the engine drone, like a faraway bagpipe, disappeared.

25. A Simple Plan

This particular Sunday at the Sisters of Tiny Lights Orphanage was not like Sundays past. To Doria Blake, most of the children—boys in particular, but little girls as well—seemed hyperactive, unable to settle or concentrate on even the simplest games. She believed some of the reason lay in their diets, which was why Doria always arrived with chicken or fish and fresh vegetables. She wasn't sure that any of her gifts were making it to the children's plates after the first meal, which she normally supervised. The orphanage cooks were all local Senegalese and faced their share of poverty. She had no doubt that much of her weekly charity was siphoned away from its intended beneficiaries. This can be better, she thought.

Then there was this strange feeling of energy caused by the appearance of a green-eyed American. Not ever could Doria recall this rush of ... of ... what, exactly? Was it desire? Doria felt a noticeable biochemical response to Victor's presence that was both pleasurable and disconcerting. But at this very moment she willed herself to focus on the chaotic scene of hyperactive or inactive tykes before her, channeling her adrenaline to clear her head and see the children individually. Her adrenaline—if that's what it was—helped her see hundreds of details about each child, from the tiny moles on this one's neck to the slight discoloration on that one's shin, to the inability of another to focus her eyes. If only I could bottle this awareness! she mused.

Her senses remained heightened even as she prepared to leave the orphanage. For that very reason, she became despondent walking away from the group home. As hopeful as she was for her new enterprise, she understood she could not rescue nearly as many as she could see, smell, hold, and hope for. Maybe none of them.

The ride home provided time to calm her thoughts, or at least redirect them. Doria had become impatient to meet with Mady, whom she hadn't seen or heard from in two weeks. Could it be that her plan to go to Ziguinchor and apprentice to the inscrutable herbalist was just some fantasy? Would she truly be able to decipher Professor DeLevres' notes and mount local expeditions to retrieve plant samples—*meaningful* samples? And if she did, then what? She'd have to transport them back to Dakar for DeLevres to analyze, to know if they were worth anything. Mady would really have to help her learn the local flora. Would it be possible to set up a small lab of her own in Ziguinchor? It didn't have to cost much for basic reagents, a Bunsen burner, centrifuge, microscope … what else? She looked into her purse for a pen and paper to start another list. She was still writing when Iba pulled the car through the gates and around the half-moon driveway.

Opening the car door, she saw the Norton parked directly in front of the stairs. A rush of excitement stole into her abdomen, rose into her throat, and refocused Doria from her thoughts of a grand experiment to thoughts of chaos and plunging into the unknown, which had returned as inexorably as an apple falls to earth and not to the stars.

Nigel and Victor were seated around the dining table, and Hume was grabbing three large bottles of Sibras beer from the refrigerator. When Doria entered the dining area, Nigel and Victor rose. Victor smiled broadly. Nigel approached his wife and held her by the shoulders and kissed her on the cheek. Over Nigel's shoulder she and Victor locked eyes. As Nigel disengaged his perfunctory embrace, Hume walked into the room and clanked the beers onto the table.

"We've only just started our business, love. So nice to have you back home. How were the urchins today?" Nigel said.

"The *orphans* were a delight, Nigel. Though I must say I'm worried for them."

"You're always worried for them, dear. Since you've been going there—how long has that been? Three years, at least? And they've been so much better for your attention. Doria, I won't let you continue visiting them if, each time you return home, you're in a funk."

"I'm not in a funk, Nigel. But seeing the same children getting older and their promise of a better life evaporating, I'm just so—"

"But that's it, isn't it? They never had any promise of a better life. In fact, just the opposite, which is why you go and why you care for them. Yeah? You personally, you Doria, are not their promise of a better life."

Nigel was right, of course, but she would not give up. "I know there's more I can do for them. They get so little attention of any kind—medical, social, physical."

"You can't save all of them, love. You may not even be able to save one of them," said Nigel. "But we've had this conversation before, haven't we?"

Doria allowed herself a small smile. Nigel's concern for her emotional state was genuine enough. But it seemed to Doria it served more to keep his own life sensible and upright. It felt clumsy.

Victor said, "Maybe it's enough that you make them happier for a short period of time."

Nigel looked at him curiously. "Well, there you are, Doria. An accomplishment just by the mere fact of your presence."

She stared wide-eyed at her husband.

"West Africa will get you like that," Victor said. "The things we want to change are so much larger than any of us. But the individual fleeting moments ... most times, that's all we affect, really."

"How bravely philosophical, Victor," Hume said. "And simple. But what does one do to tackle the big issues? You know, the real meat of existence—world hunger, global war, how to make the perfect martini. This is where we all must put our best efforts."

"Hear! Hear!" Nigel said, raising his Sibras and knocking the bottle against Hume's.

Ordinarily, Doria would smirk at the schoolboy humor. Today, however, their disinterest in her internal struggle made her sad. She tilted her head toward Victor and said, "At least, one of you has a sense understanding ... and care. Thank you, Victor."

The American blushed above his beard. He said, "You-you're welcome ... Doria."

"We'll have to save the children another time, love," Nigel stated. "Tony and I have business to talk over with Victor."

"Please. Do get on with your schemes and deals. I'm sure it will all be great fun for everyone."

Instantly she was worried for Victor. Into what web were Tony and Nigel drawing him? But these were three grown men, at least to the extent men can ever be "grown." Doria went into the kitchen. She wanted to develop the idea that had come to her while in the car.

* * *

Nigel's plan was simple, derived from Hume's knowledge of a new law in Guinea against exporting traditional artifacts of a certain age and style that represented the country's history and cultural heritage. The existence of this "unjust" law became the foundation for their "situation."

Hume laid it out. "We're trying to assist a fledgling co-op of West African artists *cum* entrepreneurs. They're Senegalese and Guineans and they buy and resell African art, mostly carvings and traditional jewelry, the majority of it made in Guinea. Nothing terribly fancy or expensive, but some of it quite good. However, as you may have heard, Guinea has just passed a new law requiring enormous taxes and duties on these crafts."

Nigel jumped in. "The justification for the law is to protect the traditional history and culture, Victor, but they will let anything out if the price is high enough. It's appalling."

Hume continued. "So when you couple the exorbitant export fees with the bribes of the customs officials, our group is having a very difficult time."

"Can they source from other countries?" Victor asked.

"Possibly. Over time," Nigel said. "But that would also increase their expenses significantly, and since they operate on razor-thin margins, they would most probably collapse."

Hume said, "At the British embassy, we're trying to promote small business and entrepreneurship whenever we can. We've helped this co-op with a small bit of technical and monetary assistance. They've been doing a good job of local marketing to the shops and they have their own street vendors, but with their costs now more than doubled for these artifacts, they're at risk of collapse. They're trying to source more here in Senegal, but honestly, it isn't that good or unique."

Shifting his gaze from Tony to Victor, Nigel said, "Tony came to me because the British embassy can't be helping a local co-op get goods duty-free from Guinea. He was thinking that perhaps Barrow & Bean's network could assist. But in fact, we can't either. We have trade contracts with the government export authority that are very narrow, specifying agricultural commodities. While we're trying to add the artifacts to our list of exempt goods, that will not only take time and *bribes*, it won't be looked on nearly as favorably by the government with this new law in place. We might not be able to negotiate these artisan works into our contracts at all."

Nigel and Tony were now silent, looking at Victor as he puzzled his way through to what they assumed would be a most logical conclusion.

Victor only looked back blankly.

After a few moments he said, "That's a tough story, I'll admit, but that's life here in West Africa. This shit happens a hundred times every day in one way or another."

"Granted, but not to men like *us*," Nigel stated. "If you want to be successful at anything, Victor, you have to find ways to overcome big obstacles, even insurmountable ones. Were this your personal enterprise, would you give up if there were other solutions, maybe difficult ones that remained unattempted? I don't think you would.

So, consider the plight of this small group. If we had the means to help and didn't, are we not perpetuating that energy-sucking fatalism that you seem to have picked up a small dose of yourself?"

All three were silent for a few heartbeats.

Victor swigged down his Sibras and spoke. "This is the same false hope that got me to volunteer in Senegal in the first place. I'll give you one example. I helped a group of villagers get a pump to irrigate a vegetable garden. The project failed because the pump cylinders were stolen to make cooking pots." He paused. His face contorted as if his cheeks were wrestling with his mouth. "But I get how critical it is to help any group of West Africans believe in their ability to build better material lives. To do that, though, it has to succeed. It *has* to!"

Silence again.

Then Victor said, "So what are you proposing?"

"We would like you to transport a small shipment of these artifacts back to Dakar each opportunity you have to cross over from Guinea."

There was simple and illegal, yet with an ethical justification that made it rational and perhaps even appealing. As Victor considered the risks, he had many questions.

"You want me to smuggle artifacts out of Guinea."

Hume said, "Trinkets, really, not the national treasure Sékou Touré babbles on about. But bluntly stated, yes, that's what we're asking you to do."

Nigel and Tony knew the next question or statement from Victor would tell them whether or not they had their man.

"How and where would I gather this small shipment, and exactly how small are we talking?"

Nigel looked at Hume and both their shoulders relaxed. Only the details remained.

Small was the size of a duffle bag. That might be too large, according to Victor. They could make it smaller, but not much smaller. How would Victor meet the contact person and where, exactly? Nigel would contact Victor with details for their man inside. The conspiracy came together like dust and water vapor become rain clouds.

Victor asked the question that the British men had been expecting from the moment of his consent. "And what exactly do I get out of this, Nigel? Tony? You've got to know that I could potentially put our whole project at risk for some shoe-polished, termite-ridden wood carvings."

Nigel was prepared. "Victor, let's not exaggerate the risks. You stated what we all well know: that the borders you are crossing are so

undermanned and remote that even if you were to be discovered—
which is highly unlikely—a small bribe will be all that is needed. And
all you have to do is tell us of that expense and we'll reimburse you
without question."

"Yes, but I still don't see what's in this for me," Victor said. "Aside
from the thrill of it all, naturally."

For all his adventurism, Victor still might have refused. He had
his adventure already as the safari leader for a group of scientists.
To jeopardize this for a heightened fear when crossing the Guinean
border or for pocket change was hardly rational, even to a twenty-
seven-year-old male. But keeping his association with Nigel Blake so
that he could be close to Doria was different.

Nigel said, "As you can imagine, Victor, this is not a huge
moneymaking enterprise we're speaking of here, but we wouldn't
expect you simply to do it from the goodness of your heart. Tony and
I have discussed this. Tell me what you think. For each delivery here
to the house, you get a wonderful dinner and 10,000 CFA—about
five hundred dollars."

Even though bargaining was a way of life in West Africa, it was
not a way of life for Victor, particularly when he had all he wanted.
The deal was struck.

The three men were discussing the weather of the target areas
when Doria poked her head into the proceedings from the kitchen.
"Have you gentlemen eaten lunch yet?"

They had not. All four went to the kitchen, where they took
Ahminta's prepared plates from the refrigerator. They ate heartily
while Doria sat with them and watched. Hume and Nigel kept asking
Victor for stories about traveling through the Sahelian bush. During
his stories Victor turned to look at Doria, a politeness she returned.

At the meal's conclusion Hume excused himself to leave for a
later engagement. Nigel walked him to his car in conversation. Victor
and Doria stood alone in silence as the two coconspirators edged out
of view. Smiling, Doria moved to clear the table.

"What? No dessert?" Victor said, feigning disappointment.

"I'm afraid you voracious Americans ate it all yesterday," she said
with a laugh. And then she remembered something. "But you may
be in luck, young man," and she scooted away to another section of
the house.

Into the empty kitchen Victor said aloud, but only for himself to
hear, "Oh, I am so in luck, I am."

Doria returned with a wad of tissue in her hand, which she held
steadily in front of Victor and carefully pulled back the paper as though

lifting rose petals. Even before the gooey ball was revealed, Victor could smell the aroma and his mouth watered. Without thinking, she lifted the rich mass between her thumb and forefinger and proffered it to an expectant Victor. He opened his mouth and Doria plopped the candy in. What a delightful, exhilarating sensation—for both of them. Then, realizing the intimacy of this act, they took a quick short step away from each other.

Victor, still chewing with a big smile and wiping around his mouth, managed to say, "Doria, this is wonderful! Where did you get it?"

"A Senegalese friend of mine makes them. Aren't they divine?"

"Spectacular! You need to get more."

They heard Nigel's footfall through the dining room as he returned.

Victor said, "Please let me help you with the dishes," as Nigel entered.

"Nonsense. The dishes can wait until I get to them later. Or tomorrow, for Ahminta," she stated.

Nigel, in excellent spirits, put an arm over Victor's shoulder. "I want to thank you for your offer to help, young man. Let's make sure we meet later this week, as your travel plans firm up."

Still savoring the candy and his proximity to Doria, Victor realized it was time to go. He shook Nigel's hand, turned and thanked Doria with a kiss on the cheek, and left the kitchen with Nigel at his side until they reached the doorway.

The sound of the Norton firing up spooked the lark sparrows outside the kitchen window, who chattered their annoyance. Doria asked them to calm down as she listened again to the engine noise fade.

26. Cross Currents

Doria sat at her dressing table in her pajamas, brushing her hair. Nigel came up behind her and put his hands on her shoulders. His hands were small but firm, always gentle. He kneaded her muscles slowly, relaxing her neck until she let out a slight coo and placed a hand on top of one of his.

"You smell so wonderful, my Doria," he said as he continued his massage of her neck.

He bent down and kissed her neck … kissed it softly, lovingly, hopefully. Doria could not help the tingle that rushed through her, and she closed her eyes, tilting her head to allow Nigel that wider expanse of tender skin that led over her shoulder and delicately down to her goose-fleshed breasts. He moved his lips up the back of her neck, over her ears, lingering playfully, and down to her cheek. She turned toward him and met his anxious mouth in a deep kiss. Moving apart slowly and opening her eyes, Doria rose and faced Nigel, who cupped her face in his hands and kissed her again. Moving his hands over her shoulders and down her arms, he began to unbutton her pajama top. She looked her husband in the eyes as he opened the satin garment and moved his fingers in a circle around her erect nipples. She stepped into him and he held her breasts firmly, massaging them gently, moving his hands to her behind, pulling her into him. Their kisses became ardent, and Doria's pajama top fell to the floor.

Nigel had sensed his wife's heightened sexual tension and knew it was likely due to the presence of the young American. But she was his wife and he needed to channel that energy to him and to their joint passion. He had to make his wife want him and know that his love for her was present, accessible. Not churning in an unrequited dream.

For Doria, Nigel was her outlet and her haven. Her feelings for Victor had been so intense that even hours after he had left, she still felt the pull, the rush, the sense of letting herself give in. To let that urge soar, she would be with her husband who cared deeply for her, protected her, loved her more than she could love him in return.

Their lovemaking was long and experimental. Doria, moving her spouse and herself in ways she had not before thought she wanted, was eventually depleted, as most certainly was Nigel. As they lay together in the postcoital blush, Nigel needed something more.

"Were you making love to him, Doria?"

It was not Nigel's way to be so open and to tread such potentially dangerous ground. But he couldn't help himself. Nothing like this had ever come between the two them and the shock of her sexual fearlessness moments ago frightened him. She would not pretend she had no notion of what he meant.

"I was not fantasizing, Nigel." She reached over and touched his damp chest. "I was feeling. Feeling free and flying."

Neither of them could recall when their lovemaking had been as pure, as exciting, and as fulfilling for them both.

"And I felt you fly," Nigel said as he kissed her good-night.

Later, in a deep sleep, Doria journeyed to Ziguinchor in a dream. *She was traveling by boat through a mangrove swamp. When she disembarked, a tall black man took her by the hand and led her to a path in the forest. A woman behind her was pushing her forward and steering her. It started to rain and gangly bald birds with huge beaks and sagging throats clacked her along, speaking in a strange language. The unseen woman steered Doria to a clearing where she saw a plant like a multicolored cabbage. The plant slowly opened, revealing a light that hurt Doria's eyes. When the light faded, inside the plant was a glass of milk. She grabbed it without thinking and drank it to the bottom.* Doria awoke quickly but incompletely, only long enough to realize she had been dreaming. But the dream did not disturb her and she returned easily to a deep sleep.

* * *

Getting away seemed like a good idea to Victor. It must have made Mrs. Blake feel great, flirting with him, seeing how he felt about her, and just toying with him, egging him on with no intention or real desire to … to …. But how could she *do* anything? "She's married, you idiot," Victor said aloud. "How stupid can I be? Of course she'd never want to be with me. We just both like this attraction, but nothing's going to happen." It had been painful to leave the Blake residence, but it was equally painful to realize what an adolescent he was, pining for an unattainable older woman he had met only one day earlier.

It was midafternoon on Sunday and he had no intention of squandering the rest of the day. Victor needed to be active. Would he return to Gorée and go diving? Do some body surfing up the coast? And where is Jetset? he wondered. He hadn't seen or heard from Amelia since he had returned. He couldn't believe that he hadn't contacted her before now. He felt guilty and energized at the same time. Jules had even mentioned her, and Victor had let the idea of her wash over him like he was a river rock. Could he find her this afternoon? Now he had a destination—Amelia's flat just off Avenue Pompidou.

The Sunday afternoon traffic was uncharacteristically heavy, and Victor was tempted to weave the Norton through the string of slow-moving automobiles in town. But recalling how moped riders were regularly rammed by oblivious drivers of cars and trucks and sent hurtling like sacks of rice across the tarmac, he decided on a careful approach.

Even if traffic was unusually dense, parking was not. Having left the Norton a few meters away from the entrance to a café on Avenue Pompidou, Victor bounded up the four flights of stairs to Amelia's flat and pounded on the door. As he suspected, there was no answer. Hell, the only reason he himself would be home is because he lived on Gorée—*the* destination on a perfect summer Sunday. ... Was that where she was? Had she got tired of waiting for him and, putting her better judgment aside, gone off to pursue him? Without a telephone, all anyone could do to contact an island resident was to leave a message with another islander or visitor and hope it got delivered.

Victor reached into his pocket and pulled out a scrap of paper. He had no pen, but he wanted Amelia to know he had thought of her before she contacted him. The paper was a receipt from one of the cafés near the port. Not knowing how else to identify the note or otherwise make it distinguishable from a scrap left by a vagabond, Victor folded a 100 CFA note into the receipt and folded it four times to give it enough thickness to wedge firmly into the doorway. Then he hurried back down the stairs.

What to do with the Norton, though. He couldn't take it to Gorée and wouldn't dare leave it overnight in the lot for the ferry passengers. He could, like last night, leave it at the IMAME offices. But to do that now would only make him miss the next ferry. Of course! He'd leave it right where it was. Another message to Amelia that he'd been there. Happy with himself, he hurried off to the ferry dock.

The 3:30 p.m. arriving boat was easing its way into the passenger berth. With his monthly pass he avoided the lines of tourists and entered the shaded waiting area. He wondered if Amelia would be among those getting off. And as though his will had forced the reality, after most of the passengers had left, Amelia sauntered down the ramp. She was in a sleeveless yellow top and short flower-print skirt that waved and shimmered with every step. Her straw hat knocked against the bag she had slung over her shoulder, a cloth sack with bulging contents.

"Amelia!" Victor shouted.

She didn't hear him at first, so he tried again. "Amelia Jetset," he called, hoping her hated nickname would pierce the noise of the terminal bustle. It did.

She stopped and looked into the waiting area with a cold stare. Victor walked quickly up to the rail separating the debarking passengers from those awaiting the next ferry out. "Amelia, I've been looking for you," Victor shouted even though he was now only a meter from her nose.

She said, "Have you, now? Really?"

As if he could not understand why she might take this disparaging attitude toward him, Victor looked at her earnestly. "Absolutely, I have. I can't believe we missed each other. Man, that's just too ironic." Victor wanted to slap himself sometimes for the things that came out of his mouth.

"I'd say it's more pathetic than ironic, but then, we haven't really seen things the same way much, have we?" She turned to continue her exit from the terminal.

"What the heck are you talking about, Amelia?" he cried. He ran along the rail parallel to her path and bounded around the ticket window to catch her on the other side. He turned quickly and stood directly in front of her, blocking her exit.

"You can get out of my way anytime now." She moved to go around him.

"I don't have any idea what's wrong with you, but I was just at your place looking for you, and I was really happy to have found you here. Actually, hoping I would find you here, and you act like I've just run over your dog. What the hell is up with you?"

"Nothing's up with me. It's OK. It's fine. I thought that since you've been back in town for nearly a week you might have tried to contact me or come to see me before the end of the weekend." They were now walking side by side out of the terminal. "It was silly of me to have thought that. Christ, I feel so stupid."

"Amelia, what are you going on about? I've had all this stuff happening since I got back. I was working most of the day yesterday and in fact I was even working a few hours today. I just came from your place, for crying out loud."

"Oh, you were not. Don't lie. It's OK if you weren't thinking of me right away. I get it."

"You get it, do you? OK, smart lady. I left a piece of paper in your door with a 100 CFA note in it. Not more than thirty minutes ago. And something else. Something only I will recognize."

"You did not," Amelia said.

"Let's go to your place together and find out, then."

"Don't you even think of coming with me if you're lying," Amelia said in a last effort to protect herself.

"You know, Ms. Jensen, we'll see what the truth is together."

Victor grabbed the bag Amelia had slung over her shoulder, and he hailed the next cab in line as they approached the public lot. She let him as though she was distracted by something distant and odd.

Amelia insisted on paying for the cab. Victor waited to see if she saw the motorcycle, but it might have been a cigarette butt for all the notice Amelia gave it. They trudged up the four flights of stairs and waited together at the top to catch their breaths. Facing each other, chests heaving slightly, reminded them both of their occasional lovemaking and they laughed in short bursts. Amelia regained control and, with her face twisted in determination, walked stiffly to her door. A few centimeters above the lock where she inserted her key, a folded paper was jammed between the door and the frame.

Victor leaned against the wall, arms crossed, as she unfolded the paper, withdrew the 100 CFA note, and read, "Four Sibras, 460 CFA. Café Durant. How romantic! Do you think I'm a moron, Victor Byrnes? Do you?"

"Is that a rhetorical question?" Victor answered too quickly for his own good.

"I'm sure this was stuck there by one of my loyal patrons, you know, with the 100 CFA for services rendered. You had nothing to do with it."

Victor was getting exasperated with his penance. "Amelia, I told you exactly what was here. Even if I didn't put it here myself, and I absolutely did, it proves I was here. And, by the way, that motorcycle we passed on the way up …"

Amelia looked at him quizzically, then stepped toward the balcony and looked down. "What about it?" she asked.

"It's mine. Well, I've got it for a while, anyway. I rode here and it's further proof I was here looking for you! I finally had a break from all the work at my job and I came here. Tell me that doesn't count for something."

She opened the door and walked into the flat. Victor remained at the threshold.

Putting her purse and her cloth sack down on her sofa, she looked back at him. "Are you coming in?"

"Am I invited in?"

"Don't be a dope. Of course you're invited in."

She disappeared into the kitchen. Victor plopped himself down on the couch, next to the bag, and peered into it: a fresh baguette, packages of Camembert and Saint-André cheese, a chunk of *pâté de campagne*, and two bottles of red Côte de Nuits Burgundies. She had gone to Gorée to find him, prepared with a picnic full of his favorite foods. His stomach sank. Victor slung the sack over his shoulder and went into the kitchen.

Amelia was sitting on the counter, sobbing quietly. Never had Victor seen her like this. She was always the controlled professional, not aloof but not vulnerable either. He went over to her and bent his forehead to touch hers, his hands at his side.

"Victor, we suck together," she stated.

"So far," he said, making her chuckle through her drying tears.

"Why are you such a shit?" she said, hitting him in the chest with a balled fist.

"I'm not a shit, Amelia. I'm an idiot. I'm a careless guy with a reptilian brain. And sometimes I'm selfish and oblivious."

"That pretty much defines a shit. And what do you mean, 'sometimes'?"

"What do you want from me, Amy? I'm ready to give you more, but … what exactly is that, and would it be enough?"

"What 'more'? How about 'some,' just some times, could I ever come first?"

He kissed her on the tip of her nose. "How long would 'some' be enough?" he asked.

"I don't know, Victor, but it would be nice to find out, don't you think?"

"I do think." He kissed her on her mouth, and she kissed him back but only briefly.

"And I don't mean, just for now or for tonight. I need to know that you care for me, that I'm not always the one chasing after you. That you want to be with me."

"So, my little payment for 'services rendered' didn't convince you that I want to be with you? Jesus, Amy. What I can give, I'm giving. You've got to see that. And you know I care for you and I want to be with you."

"Since when have you started calling me Amy?"

"Since two minutes ago, when I needed something short so I could hold a thought together."

"I like it." She picked up his left hand, held it to her cheek, and kissed the inside of his palm.

He put his right hand to her other cheek and bent to kiss her again. It was a long lingering kiss that kept going deeper, stronger. From her perch on the counter Amelia wrapped her legs around Victor's waist. Then they were kissing each other all over, moving their hips tightly together, taking off each other's shirt. Slowly, Victor slid Amelia's skirt up to her waist, tickling the inside of her thigh. She hiked herself off the counter with both hands, and Victor quickly slid her panties down to her ankles and onto the floor. Amelia undid Victor's belt, his zipper, and dropped his jeans to the tops of his knees. When he entered her, it produced a phenomenal release in both of them, as though this sexual gravity was itself forgiveness—a determined wish cast into the void.

When later they sat next to each other on Amelia's living room couch, opening the picnic she had prepared, they talked of work, of how it made them feel. They agreed that something about working in Africa heightened one's senses and awareness. It provided a sense of life and liveliness unmatched working in the States, so far as either of them knew.

Amelia, with her graduate education, had much more experience than Victor in working with large development organizations. But Victor's experience living in the most remote areas of the country, contracting dysentery, dealing with the frustrations of helping a people with a four-hundred-year history of servitude and slavery, this was the experience most organizations needed and many people coveted. Most, however, had neither the courage nor the stamina to endure. Victor saw it differently. He had simply put one foot in front of the other with one rule: Don't give up.

In Amelia's world, international assistance turned into a ravaged carcass picked bare by government officials and other thieves. Courage and stamina were required in many forms to keep the emerging dreams from becoming banal excuses.

The couple laughed as they compared stories. What made them go on working in these conditions, seeing so few results? Whatever it was, they seemed to have it in common.

As early evening waned into night, their conversations drifted, truncated by the wine, by weariness, and by a small measure of peace between them. They drifted off to sleep on the couch, only to awake and realize they should be in bed. As they rose from the couch in total darkness, Amelia could see that Victor was looking around trying to collect his belongings.

Amelia touched his arm. "It's too late for the ferry, Victor. Stay. It's OK."

He turned to Amelia and nodded. A sheepish smile was pasted to his face. When he put his arm over her shoulder, they prepared for sleep together.

Late in the night, Victor had a dream. *He was traveling by boat down the Senegalese coast. The large boat became a dugout canoe, in a mangrove swamp. When he disembarked, a stocky black woman took him by the elbows and led him to a path in the forest. A man behind him grabbed his waist and began pushing him forward, keeping him off-balance. It started to rain and two tall black birds with huge beaks cackled at him as he stumbled along, and then spoke to him in Malinke: "Di qua sanichei niya." ("Hunger drives the hunt.") The unseen man pushed Victor into a clearing, where he saw a plant that looked like a multicolored cabbage. The plant slowly opened, shining a beam of light straight up. When the light faded, inside the plant was a small gray stone. He grabbed it without thinking and ate the stone, feeling it drop to the bottom of his stomach.*

Victor turned over in bed. His rest remained fitful until the horizon changed from deep black to matte gray and the roosters of the alleys crowed their scratchy Angelus.

Part 3:

Lessons from the Interior

27. To Ziguinchor

The rains had started in the Casamance, yet Dakar remained sunny and hot. The only indication of seasonal change was the increase in humidity. It was a strength-sapping beast that wrapped itself around the city and held tight. The overcrowded panel buses—normally bustling with conversation—transported their charges who, in near silence, fanned their faces with basket tops, old magazines, or a hand. Thoroughfares remained crowded but quieter: sultry to the point of despondence, awaiting the release of rain. Street vendors moved off the sidewalks, into the creeping shadows of buildings. Those shopkeepers fortunate enough to have air conditioners had difficulty keeping them running—and from being stolen. The humidity clogged them with floods of condensation that spilled onto the streets. All those compressors and fans put a strain on the city's rudimentary electrical system, causing frequent and widespread power outages. Life continued more slowly, more deliberately. Walking to the local Nar shop to pick up bread, catching a taxi to go to work, sweeping the compound—all the routine activities of everyday life required more effort and more force to overcome the torpor levied by the weather.

Not everyone complained to see this season, however. Farmers everywhere prayed that the rains would begin early, arrive daily, and stay long enough for them to have an ample harvest. Along the great river in the north, farmers planted melons, millet, and beans, hearty crops that withstood the inconsistent rains on the edge of the desert. East of Dakar and south of Saint-Louis, groundnuts were going into the earth as fast as the farmers could plant. And in the Casamance, fields of manioc, sorghum, and upland rice were already sprouting.

Other plants were growing, as well, in the dense moisture of the Casamance forest. Plants were working their magic, turning sunlight, water, and minerals of the earth into food and other life-supporting components: chemicals that protected from predators, compounds that built immunity, colors and scents that attracted birds and insects to assist with pollination. Dynamic processes were occurring in the grasses and weeds, the mosses and mushrooms, the trees reaching skyward. The flourish of fertility appeared everywhere in the south of Senegal.

The Casamance was a new land for Doria, so much more like the Africa she had imagined than the Africa she inhabited. Only 250 kilometers south and yet so different. It had been a difficult journey, made more so by her quirky travel companion and apothecary mentor, Mady.

On the Sunday after the IMAME event, Mady sent a message to Doria that she wished to leave the next day. While Doria had been looking forward to contact from Mady, the idea of giving one day's notice to prepare seemed impossibly rude. Mady's message ended that if Doria could not be ready then, Mady would go by taxi, on her own. But Doria had been preparing in her mind since she and Mady had struck their bargain. All she needed to know, which she could not, was how long she would be there. If she needed and wanted to be there longer than two weeks, she would make the journey back to collect whatever else she might need.

Nigel was more direct than usual. "Doria, really! Traipsing off by yourself to a place you've never visited, with a woman you barely know, could be a disaster. Injury, failure, unscrupulous characters! This is a dreadful idea!"

"Dreadful for whom, Nigel? Don't you travel to all manner of places in pursuit of BBI business? I manage here alone, don't I? Now this is reversed. I'm sure you'll mange just fine, at least for a short time, without me. And please do not do this, when my journey is finally happening. Be happy for me. I'll look out for myself, and Iba will be with me." She touched her husband's cheek. "I'll be fine and so will you."

Nigel kept his frown throughout the morning.

Doria learned that Iba was more than a competent chauffeur. He had spent a good part of his youth in the Casamance, working as a driver for the Ministry for Water and Forestry. Nigel asked his secretary to make reservations for Doria at the Hotel Du Sud, the best hotel in Ziguinchor.

Doria and Iba left to pick up Mady the next morning before seven. Reaching the family compound, Doria saw a gathering of women and girls around a pile of bags and suitcases as tall as the car and nearly as wide. Was Mady expecting Doria to arrive in a lorry to transport all of these things? As the white Mercedes pulled up, the women all waved, gave big smiles, and indicated where the car should park. Doria had only a carton of bottled water, two suitcases, and a large handbag that was more like a briefcase in which she kept DeLevres' notebook and other references. It appeared to her that Mady was intending to transport not simply her clothes and some other belongings, but her entire room's worth of pots, storage canisters, utensils, and other working gear, along with a sack of rice and three shopping bags of various other foods. Doria let out an exasperated breath. It's OK, she told herself.

She got out of the car, looking for Mady, who appeared instantly as the group broke apart from their circle and formed a line. The Senegalese matron was giving instructions to the other women and when she saw Doria, she told her minions to be quiet as she greeted her newest friend.

The negotiation regarding what of Mady's they would carry took about thirty minutes. Nothing could be tied to the roof. Iba assisted his mistress, verifying whatever Doria said, often in Oulof. The food for Mady's family in the Casamance had to come, as did her clothes, so Doria made Mady prioritize the remaining items. At one point, Mady threw up her hands and claimed she would hire a small truck and go by herself. Doria stood her ground. In the end, around two-thirds of the pile fit into the Mercedes. Mady was all smiles, and Doria was wondering if Mady had just brought out everything she owned to see what she could get into the car. No matter. They were on their way.

The road to Ziguinchor either goes around or cuts through the country of The Gambia, a former British colonial enclave carved down the length of the Gambia River. The country's width on either side of the river had been determined by how far the British gunboat shells reached in the late 1800s. The French were annoyed for decades that the British established this penetration through the heart of Senegal, effectively cutting off the lower third of the country. As for the Africans who lived there, nobody had asked them.

If a traveler had enough cash to spend on both the border going into The Gambia and the border on the other side going out, the possibility existed of making the trip from Dakar to Ziguinchor in six to seven hours. To go around added nearly three hours to the trip— three hours that could easily be added on trying to cross the borders. Most travelers opted to go around and curse the British colonialists every time.

A kilometer before the junction, Doria asked Mady which way they should go. Mady didn't understand the question, since in her mind the taxis and buses to Ziguinchor always went around. A small argument ensued, Doria exasperatingly trying to get information from Mady, and Mady unable to contemplate why anyone would ask such a question. Doria asked Iba to choose. Around The Gambia they went.

It was nearly dusk when they passed the sign welcoming them to Ziguinchor. This was when Mady decided to tell Doria that she didn't actually live in Ziguinchor itself. She lived in a village about 25 kilometers outside of town and that was where she needed to be deposited. It took every bit of remaining daylight to drive there since the road was barely a road at all. The Mercedes could not travel faster than 15 kilometers per hour on the ravine-carved clay roads, interrupted with small ponds and short stretches of soft mud. When they reached Mady's village of Tchatsieng, the sun was below the horizon and illuminating the rain clouds with dark orange and purple splashes.

Doria told Mady they would come back to Tchatsieng the next morning as early as they could.

"Come when you wish," she told Doria. There was no more conversation and Mady dragged her unloaded baggage into the dusky shadows.

Their speed back to Ziguinchor from Tchatsieng was reduced further by the darkness. The fierce jostling of their bones and blows to the car made Doria question her sanity for believing she could do this alone. But she wasn't alone. Iba was with her. A man she hardly knew, yet trusted completely. It occurred to her how strange a notion that was: to trust a man, a foreigner, about whom she knew almost nothing, but in whose hands she had placed her life. Countless times, in fact.

"Iba, you are doing a wonderful job," Doria said. "I couldn't possibly have done this without you."

"Yes, Madame. We share this," Iba said.

She leaned her head sideways, then smiled and gently put her hand on his shoulder. Together they stared into the tunnel of light carved by the headlights. It was a nerve-racking last leg to a long journey. Eventually they made it back to the paved road and to the Hotel Du Sud.

Doria and Iba were both exhausted. Iba handed the bags to the bellman, who had to be awakened from his perch on the hotel steps. Doria thanked Iba and insisted he come by and have breakfast with her, for Iba's lodgings were in a local guesthouse a bit farther down the road. It was understood that Iba would be much more comfortable staying in that guesthouse than he could ever be, staying at the Hotel Du Sud.

Doria over-tipped the bellman, who had placed her bags in the room and showed her the bathroom and the armoire for her clothes. She placed her handbag on the lone table in the room and prepared for bed without bothering to unpack. Although she wanted to read some of DeLevres' notes again, fatigue overwhelmed her. She pulled back the covers to the bed and, as she slipped in, pulled down the large mosquito net around her. Within minutes she was deep asleep.

When she awoke, it was dark and raining. She could hear the heavy patter of a downpour like the drenching deluges in England. The bed was comfortable and the large mosquito net was like a canopy. Nevertheless, she rose, wiping sleep from her eyes, and gazed out through the large double French windows as the rain beat down onto the acacias and palms around the hotel. Her watch on the bed stand told her it was 5:40 a.m., too early to rise, too late to recover any restoring sleep. She picked up the leather satchel in which she carried DeLevres' notes and switched on a light. But there was no power. Unable to read the notes in the dark, she crawled back underneath the mosquito net, holding the case and its contents closely to her, and then drifted off until the sounds of cackling myna birds and howler monkeys startled her awake. Now the sky was a roof of rich, uniform black clouds blocking out any pretension of sunlight.

28. The Apprentice's Sorcerer

Mady Toula had expected the rain from the moment she arrived the night before. She knew its taste and its smell, its sentinel winds, how the voices of the insects and birds changed in anticipation. This morning, however, more important issues were at hand. The first thing was to divide up the money. She knew that all those to whom she owed some portion of her bounty were waiting for her: the two women who had helped gather the ingredients, remove stems and dirt, and place each component in its proper place. Then, of course, she would have to pay her brother's two wives for food and shelter, like a man would—give them money to help run the compound.

Most importantly, she had to pay Mbattu Sisay, the doctor, the man who had learned the traditional medicines from great Djiolla healers of the Casamance and had taken Mady under his wing when she was just a crazy little girl. Young Mady, in spite of the taunts and names hurled at her, and the taunts and beatings from her family, or the insults and threatening admonishments from other adults, fed her curiosity with a fearlessness that regularly tipped into recklessness. Sisay decided he would help her channel her gifts and befriended her simply by treating her as a deserving person.

It came naturally to Mady to try new things. Sisay had taught her ways to learn from her mistakes and to use that learning to do better next time, whether it was cooking yassa, catching elusive lizards, or matching herbs to get a particular effect. He mentored her about trial and error. He instructed her that while it is important to succeed, it is more important that you learn from each failure. He had insisted she attend the French school two villages away, knowing young Mady needed to have more of the world opened to her. As expected, she did extremely well in the subjects she liked—science and history. Mathematics had been too abstract for her and Mady didn't care to learn French. But Sisay, with his vision to her future, insisted that she apply herself, particularly in the subjects that did not come naturally. He told Mady that, at some point, the knowledge she would gain would help her unlock many secrets. Mady did not know what he meant, so she either ignored him or rebelled against his direction, making for a tumultuous relationship in the early years.

Mbattu Sisay was more father to Mady than her natural father, having given her encouragement when her family only shunned her as uncontrollable and different. He fed her when she had been denied food at her home and he healed her when she had been beaten by her father and then by her mother, until she could only limp and crawl out of the family compound. He had given her shelter and warmth. Most importantly, he had given her a belief in herself that she was not crazy but gifted. For that, she gave him a fierce loyalty that continued these twenty-five years. Old as he was, Mbattu Sisay was still a vibrant force in Mady's life. And though she struggled to be free of her master-apprentice relationship with him, never did she stray from her trust in him, nor from her sense of debt. She owed him for her life. The commission on all that Mady earned, heavy though it was, seemed fitting.

When Mady was ten years old, Sisay took her to the first village east of their own, from where a woman had sent one of her children to fetch Sisay. Her oldest son of nineteen years had been accused of stealing cows from a number of the local herders. They had banded together and dragged her son out of his hut and beat him nearly to death. His jaw was broken on both sides, his arms had been battered as well as his legs, his torso had several open wounds, and the young man was grabbing short breaths with great pain. There was no doubt he was on the verge of death. Mady had never seen a living person in such dire physical condition. Sisay set to work, first determining as thoroughly as he could the extent of the man's injuries. He then gave commands to summon additional people to help. He made them carry the bed with the young man outside, told two of the girls to keep fanning away the insects until he told them to stop. They brought both hot and cold water, wood for splints, and rags. Mady had carried one of his three bags and he told her what to fetch from it as she knelt behind him. Sisay took his time dressing the wounds, assessing each individually, and having Mady assist in mixing and stirring various ingredients together, which he applied with precision.

After more than half a day, Sisay stood up and declared that the boy would live. Sisay's work was complete. The mother hugged Sisay and kissed his hands, and then looked closely at her son, unconscious, breathing almost normally. Something was wrong.

"Your work cannot be complete, Master Sisay!" the mother cried.

Sisay had left the boy's right hand, gnarled by broken knuckles and blood, unattended.

"Did your boy not steal the cows, as the men say?" Sisay asked the mother.

"No! No! He did not, Master Sisay. He could not. It is not his way!" cried the mother.

As calmly as he addressed children passing in the street, Sisay said, "You know this is not so, woman. Your son has paid the price for his crimes. And you, you who benefited from them, have paid too. Your son will never steal again. And his work in your maize fields will be diminished. The sins are not the boy's alone."

"This cannot be! No!" The mother continued her wailing. "Who are you to judge! Who are you to say he is guilty? You must repair his hand!"

Sisay raised a hand. "Do not speak."

Three other women, who had arrived earlier to assist and to watch, came to the mother's side, holding her as she cried and begging her to obey Sisay. They counseled her in turn.

"Your son will live."

"He will walk again. He will work again."

"Do you wish it otherwise?"

The mother, kneeling on the dirt, crying inconsolably, could only shake her head.

"Be satisfied you have your son, who will comfort you in your old age. In payment for my work here, you will send your eldest daughter to my home every day after the sun rises, for three years. She will return to you each day when the sun sets. Do you understand?"

The woman crawled over the dirt of the compound and threw her arms over her son on the bed. She sobbed heavily. What price had she paid to save her son's life?

"Do you understand?" Sisay repeated, never raising his voice.

The woman, head down on her son's body which was now wrapped with cloth and splints and covered in muddy, oozing medicines mixed with blood, nodded without looking up.

* * *

Dressing in the early hours before what might have been dawn but for the heavily clouded sky, Mady wondered what her mentor would think if she told him about her bargain with the British woman. Perhaps she would not have to. Most likely, Madame Blake would not be able to tolerate all that was required to learn and make the medicines. Yes, that was most likely. Mady would say nothing to Sisay. Except that Mbattu Sisay could see things that others could not. Great care would have to be taken with Madame Blake, and the members of the compound would have to know what they could and could not say. Mady lit a candle, putting the future conversation with her mentor to the back of her mind while she recounted the money, wrapped each pile with the paper, and tied them with strings. With a piece of charcoal, she marked each one for whom it was designated and placed them in a latching metal box which slid under her bed.

29. A Walk Around

True to her word, Doria Blake arrived at Mady Toula's compound shortly after the morning meal. Doria walked around to take it all in. The compound entrance was flanked by two cinder-block buildings. Attached to each was a porch of concrete, protected by a thatched roof resting on twisted tree branches resembling driftwood. Single-room huts lined the back of the compound. To her right were exposed black iron cooking kettles with utensils protruding over the tops like spider legs. Three women, with babies wrapped to their backs, pounded the grain kernels into coarse flours ready to be boiled into porridge. They looked up at Doria, but did not stop their rhythmic pounding. Little girls were cleaning up as the boys went off to play.

Doria walked slowly, taking in the mixture of the moist air laden with wood smoke and the salty aroma of dried fish. She noticed at least three large trees in the compound stretching 10 or more meters into the sky and forming a canopy of shade and cover from the rain. Doria looked around for Mady, who emerged from the cinder-block building on the southern side of the compound.

"Madame Blake, please have some tea or coffee. Our morning meal is over, but please sit."

Doria was pleasantly surprised by this hospitality. "How thoughtful, Mady. Thank you."

Though she wanted to get to work, Doria knew it would be disrespectful to turn down Mady's hospitality. Mady seemed at ease. A young woman appeared with a plastic chair. Mady smiled at Doria, who returned the smile and accepted the seat. Mady spoke in a language Doria did not recognize. Two of the girls set to making tea for Mady and Doria.

Doria asked about the children and women, who they were in relation to Mady. It was new to Doria, how many of the residents seemed to be displaced from their original families, such as Mady's niece, whose husband was in the military; and an eleven-year-old girl whose father was the half brother to Mady's former husband and had been abandoned when the father went to look for work in factories east of Dakar. Doria noticed there were no males over the age of ten.

"Shouldn't the children be in school?" Doria asked, and then felt silly as she realized it was summer and school was not in session. Her sense of children's seasons was that of an outsider.

"School is over until September, Madame Blake. Two of the girls attend. They are smart and like school. Anything to get out of compound chores. The boys seem not yet to like school. We will see."

"Are there older boys living here as well, Mady? I see two teenage girls, but no teenage boys."

"This is still planting season," Mady said as she prepared her own coffee. "All the men, even those who work at other jobs in Ziguinchor, are in their fields, and have been for the past month. Soon, though, the planting will be over and they will return."

"Return?" Doria asked. "Do you mean they sleep in the fields?"

"I do," Mady replied.

Their tea completed, Mady rose and motioned for Doria to follow her into her house. There were all her bags, unpacked. She asked Doria to step into the adjacent room, which looked very much like the dark room she first encountered at Mady's house in Dakar: jars, bowls, bottles, tins, baskets with and without lids, all sitting about in no apparent order. Today, unlike a month ago, most were empty, and the room, even in the cloud cover, seemed airy and light.

Taking a notebook from her bag and placing it on the smaller of the two tables, Doria began what she had come to do: learn. She started with so many questions: What were the names to the most common medicines she prepared and what did they do? Which were from a single plant and which required multiple ingredients? Mady squinted as she listened, then threw up her hands.

"Today," she said, "we will concentrate on *ndaymou gar*, yes? That is what you wanted to know all about when you first came to me. We will do one remedy today and maybe still only *ndaymou gar* tomorrow too."

Doria put down her notebook and waited. Mady rummaged among her various supplies, pots, and jars, clearly looking for something. With a flourish of triumph, she emerged from the far corner of the room with a large glass jar. She struggled to remove the tight lid. When she did, she sniffed inside the jar and handed it to Doria, who cautiously imitated her host. There was a dense herbal scent, mixed with other scents of dirt and cooked oil. It was odd, yet not unpleasant. And the greenish substance inside, barely enough to cover the bottom of the jar, was powder dry.

"What is the name of this?" Doria asked as she took another sniff.

"It is half of *ndaymou gar*," Mady said, taking the jar from Doria, closing the lid, and placing the jar on the table.

"Yes, Mady, but does it have a name of its own? Surely it must."

"I will tell you later," Mady said, giving no reason why later was any better than now.

"Mady, please just tell me. I have to write it down." Doria opened her notebook and made as if to begin writing, hoping Mady would understand.

Perhaps she did or perhaps she did not. Either way, Mady went about finding and setting a bowl of gray seeds on the table, next to the jar.

"Mady Toula, you must tell me the names of these substances. That is how I learn."

"I know how you learn. You will write the names when I give them to you."

Doria stood her ground, explaining how she stitched bits of learning together in her head. It had a logic and steps. Each step was brick in the foundation and she couldn't understand what came next until she understood the prior step completely. Mady, never having a student or understudy before, was on her own learning journey.

They negotiated the names for Doria to write down. They were Djiolla names, the language of the Casamance. They made no sense to Doria.

"Mady, we must go and find these in the forest. I have to see what they look like before they are harvested. The names mean nothing to me."

Mady sniffed. "Of course they do not. You are more eager to pluck than to prepare, I see."

Doria nodded. Mady told her where these plants grew: a two-hour taxi ride, plus a one-hour walk just to begin their search. Doria offered her vehicle as a taxi, to save some time. They packed a bottle of water each and some bread. Doria brought along DeLevres' notes and a rain slicker. Off they went to the forested area close to the border with Guinea-Bissau.

The road was only slightly better than the one to Mady's village, but the flush of excitement and novelty made the voyage easy for Doria. Mady spoke to Iba in Djiolla, glad to be able to speak to someone in her first language. Though it had been years since Iba had worked in Ziguinchor, it turned out that he and Mady shared acquaintances. Mady occasionally slapped Iba on the shoulder, causing him to turn his head slightly and smile. This made Doria feel that perhaps her journey would have some unintended benefits for others in her life. Then she thought of Victor Byrnes. Here, hundreds of miles away on a mission to the deep forest, she felt safe to think about him and wonder how such a chance meeting should have been so disruptive.

Mady motioned for Iba to pull into a small clearing marked with large rocks on the side of the road. The two women descended from the car, stretched, and checked their belongings. Doria had a satchel to carry her notebook, water, half a baguette, and two oranges. Mady carried a large canvas sack slung over her shoulder, empty except for some small used paper bags for her collections.

Iba let the two women know they had to be back with sufficient time to make the journey both to Mady's compound and to the hotel by sunset.

Doria looked hopefully at Mady, who waved off Iba's concern and said in French, *"Pas de problème."*

Doria followed Mady to a path between acacia trees and thick grasses, still wet and overgrown. Like small animals, the women disappeared into the dense greenery.

30. A Logical Outcome

School had been far easier for David Semba than for any youngster in his village of Kaala. At St. Barnabas Catholic Missionary School, he came to the attention of the Jesuit principal, Brother Armand, and a quick-witted French nun, Sister Marie Chapelle, who taught David mathematics and science. The colonial education system, with its focus on rote learning and standard test scores, offered no teaching of critical thinking skills and precious few opportunities to use such skills. Sister Chapelle, in her diligence to assure her school was showing well at the district and national levels, took note of David's consistently high marks in all of his subjects and his nearly incessant questioning in class. She and Brother Armand supported his application to the Franciscan Brothers' lycée in Conakry, which provided education to the sons and daughters of Guinea's ministers and European partners. From there he was offered the opportunity to study in France for his baccalaureate, which he took in public administration from the University of Grenoble.

At the university, David learned more than simply how to turn his talent into a marketable skill. He studied public administration because, as most West Africans believed, it was through government, not private business, that a man could become rich—the kleptocratic rule of most leaders having been exquisitely mimicked from their European conquerors. But political leaders in Guinea came mostly from the military and from certain tribes. David had no notion of entering the army and was certain his minority tribe would not be the platform from which to launch a political career. He was certain, though, that he could get a job and learn how the levers of power moved.

After working in Marseilles for a shipping company for two years as an accountant, while enduring the constant racial tensions between the North Africans, the Sub-Saharan Africans, and the French, David returned home when his work visa expired.

Back in Guinea, David encountered a country he barely knew. He despaired as President Sékou Touré surrounded himself with like-minded thieves who looted the resource-rich country with impunity.

Bureaucrats and administrators of every station worked only for bribes. As dynamic as the rhythm of independent Guinea seemed, it was also corrupt, self-centered, and Darwinian. David was without a job for over a year, until he found work in the British embassy as a logistics assistant. When it became clear to the British foreign service facilities officer that David Semba could plan for all the chaos that is Conakry, yet make and keep deadlines, David was promoted to the role of logistics manager and sat at a desk next to the office of his direct supervisor, Tony Hume.

Today, at this moment, David had a conundrum. He was all too aware that his former diamond mule, Issa, was very likely working for someone else. That meant Issa could betray their operation. Before David could securely procure additional diamonds and take them himself to a new mule, Issa's whereabouts had to be determined and then ... what? What were the alternatives? David's analysis concluded with only one. Finding Issa of course would be the easier task, since David himself had recruited him. Like David, Issa was from the Malinke tribe. He knew who Issa's friends were, his likely places to seek refuge, and with whom Issa had most likely made a deal for just a single delivery of stones. Issa was a small thinker, David concluded, with a vision of the future that extended all the way to his next meal. As David glided through the crowds of a commercial neighborhood in Conakry, he cursed himself for having trusted such a slow-witted man with such critical work. Had Issa not owed David for his financial support during a year when neither of them held a job, it is unlikely he would have ever trusted Issa. But David had miscalculated. Now he had to avoid further damage.

It took David four days to locate Issa, all the while being careful not to contact any of Issa's friends directly. He followed a number of them daily, until one of them led him to a small local restaurant where Issa had just finished a bowl of rice and fish. David watched Issa from across a muddy alley, emerge slowly from the restaurant door. Issa looked right, then left, from the threshold of the entrance, donned his sunglasses, and walked away. This, David surmised, marked him as a betrayer. He would follow Issa for a few days and see if there was a repeating pattern to his actions and if David might turn that into an advantage.

To David's dismay, Issa strode over to one of the many mopeds parked along the sidewalk. He mounted the padded seat and turned the handlebars toward the street as he began pedaling. David now had an idea how Issa had spent his pieces of silver. The pedaling urged the moped engine to life and Issa started careening his way into the chaotic traffic. David hurried to the street to be certain of his quarry's direction. Although Issa could not speed away for all the cars, trucks, buses, taxis, and pull carts, he was not easy to spot in the sea of vehicles. David peered in the general direction of Issa's departure and ran through the throngs.

He spotted Issa weaving his way through the traffic, his feet on the ground for balance; Issa hadn't enough speed to keep the moped balanced on its own. A passenger panel truck, known by the gleefully ironic moniker of *car rapide*, pulled up alongside David and the conductor leaned down, shouting to David to hop on board, which he did. The car was no faster than anything else on the streets, weaving dangerously close to other vehicles. David pulled a coin from his pocket and gave it to the conductor. All of the seats and standing room inside the *car rapide* were occupied, which suited David. He needed to stand on the back step to watch Issa and be prepared to get off quickly. At one point the *car rapide* passed Issa, but was quickly ensnarled in traffic, allowing Issa and dozens of other moped riders to weave between the larger vehicles. As they passed the last traffic light before the north-east junction, which, like all the other traffic lights in Conakry, had not functioned for at least a year, the *car rapide* again passed Issa and began to accelerate. David looked back, keeping Issa in view, and breathed a sigh of relief as Issa motored just a few blocks past the light and turned down a dirt road. David smiled and slapped his hand on the roof of the *car rapide*, signaling it to let him off. It slowed without stopping, and David jumped to the shoulder of the road.

David recognized the street down which Issa drove and concluded a high probability where Issa was headed—to the home of Issa's cousin, Ditaba, and her three children. Though widowed by one of the countless traffic fatalities in West Africa, Ditaba was fortunate enough to have both a steady job as a maid with a Lebanese businessman and to have no claims other than her own on her former husband's small home. She lived quietly and peacefully, sending her eldest daughter, age ten, to a local Catholic school while her other two children remained at home. Issa was one of numerous extended family members who imposed regularly on Ditaba's good fortune and good nature, all of which she accepted as her duty. Issa had introduced David to Ditaba soon after the two men met, perhaps thinking David would make a good match for his widowed cousin. Perhaps in another life, David recalled thinking.

Although he wanted to observe Issa for a few more days, David was concerned that time enhanced rather than degraded the probability that Issa would divulge more information of the Blueprint to whomever he had switched allegiance. Issa didn't know much, but he knew David's name, where he worked, and the method of delivering the diamonds in the past, which could lead competitors with resources to cause serious trouble. David needed to act now.

Crossing the main street to the dirt road, David walked casually down to verify his belief that Issa was staying with his cousin. Passing on the opposite side of the street from Ditaba's house, David saw Issa's parked moped in the compound. He continued walking until he found a small shop. He bought a baguette and a "Coke-Cola," engaging the shopkeeper about business, the lack of electricity, and the neighborhood. David asked if there was a hostel close by for a room. The shopkeeper pointed out a white cinder-block wall a short distance away, in the opposite direction of Ditaba's house. David thanked him and left.

If Issa were not staying at Ditaba's, he would likely want to leave soon, since driving a moped at night in Conakry is like playing Russian roulette with three bullets. David guessed Issa would stay with his cousin, so he took a position near the guesthouse to observe the entrance to Ditaba's home. David hoped Issa would be there at least tonight.

As dusk settled and no movement came from Ditaba's home, David completed his plan. He checked into the guesthouse and ate a quick meal. He talked to the lone waitress and made his way into the kitchen, talking to the cook and looking for a specific tool, which he noted after a few minutes. He then went to his room and slept until around midnight.

When David awoke, he dressed quickly and went quietly into the guesthouse corridor and into the kitchen. There he found and lit a candle, recalling with little difficulty exactly where he had seen the ice pick. With care but without hesitancy David withdrew the instrument from the counter shelf and left the kitchen and the guesthouse. He heard drums in the distance. David happily noted that unlike more remote communities or even the outskirts of Conakry, there were no dogs in this neighborhood to bark at any passerby.

Entering the unlocked gate of Ditaba's compound, David took Issa's moped and pushed it out and up the road to the corner of the main road, laying it on its side so as not to attract attention. Even appearing to be in need of repair, it was likely to be stripped by morning if David did not return soon. He calculated that no one would steal it in the next hour.

Returning to Ditaba's compound he searched for a sleeping Issa. He thought to find him in the sitting room. But he wasn't there. A bedroom, then? Had he displaced one of Ditaba's children? David's search found the two girls together in one room, and the little boy slept in a space that more resembled a closet. Was Issa in his cousin's bedroom? Moving carefully down the short hallway to Ditaba's room, David slowly opened the door and peered in. His heart sank. Issa was sound asleep … lying next to his cousin, with his arm around her. David cursed repeatedly under his breath. His plan for Issa to have an accident did not involve Issa's cousin. That would rouse too many suspicions and was much more difficult. There was no need—yet—to involve Ditaba. She was a mother who happened to have a quisling for a cousin. She should not have to pay for his crimes.

Upsetting as this was, David had somehow to recalculate and suppress his frustration. He waited in the dark, not knowing what to do, thinking Issa must have manipulated his cousin with his short-term wealth, helping her with money, ingratiating himself, and finally having sex with her. The intruder stood in the dark, listening to the breathing of the sleeping people, listening for external sounds that might signal the need to flee. David would have to abandon his current plan and form another one. After thirty minutes he turned to leave, when fate intervened. Issa rolled over, wiped his nose with a hand, and clutched his groin. Swinging his legs with some difficulty because of his grogginess coming out from under the mosquito net, Issa slowly rose and headed outside. He had to pee.

The virtual nonexistence of indoor plumbing in all but the wealthiest of families worked in David's favor. Still scratching himself, Issa, clothed only in a pair of shorts, walked half-awake through the front door and headed across the compound to the latrine. As Issa reached for the latrine door, David swiftly grabbed him around the head, with his left hand covering Issa's mouth. With his right hand at virtually the same time, David jammed the ice pick into Issa's heart. David's first blow seemed to glance off a rib, so he withdrew the ice pick and repeated the jab. Although the adrenaline had snapped Issa fully awake, it was too late. David held his grip as tight as he could while Issa thrashed, bucking his head back against David, and suddenly stopping.

David whispered in the dying man's ear, *"Tu mérites pire, crétin."* ("You deserve worse, asshole.")

David had his own rush of adrenaline, as now the most critical part of his plan began. He hoisted Issa onto his shoulders, thinking that he probably should have taken one of Issa's shirts with him to soak up the trickle of blood that oozed from the wound. It might have had the added benefit of making Issa's moped accident more plausible. But there was no more time. With Issa over his shoulders, David trundled through the gate, straining with the weight, and up the slippery dark road to the corner of the main road where the moped was parked. Now the hard part of balancing Issa's body on the moped.

As the occasional *car rapide* spread some light when it whizzed by in the otherwise still night, David worked methodically. He leaned the body against the corner of the wall, propped up by a short stone column. Bringing the moped beside Issa, David raised one of Issa's legs over the seat, and then leaned Issa and the moped in that direction, hoping gravity would assist moving Issa's body into position. Unfortunately, it did so too well, the momentum of bike and body overcoming David's ability to stop it and all three tumbled onto the ground. Cursing erupted from David as another *car rapide* flashed by. He started again, propping Issa next to the moped with some difficulty, again swinging one of the dead man's legs over the saddle. This time David rocked the moped back and forth and Issa's body slowly jiggled into place and slumped over the handlebars. David arranged the hands between the brake cables, adding more stability.

The last part of the plan had no room for error. He would have to get the moped up to some speed and push it into the path of an oncoming *car rapide*. Because of their excessive speeds at night, David would have to be very careful himself as he ran the moped down the side of the road. He let two cars go by while regaining his strength, and used his knowledge of the cars' possible trajectory to plan exactly how he would run and jump.

Ten minutes later, as he was tiring significantly from balancing Issa on the moped, he saw the light of a car. With all his determination he began running the moped down the road. As the *car rapide* approached, David steered farther into the road. Just as the car was 10 meters behind him, David turned hard to his right and pushed the moped and Issa with all his strength, and hit the ground as fast as he could. Instantly David heard the squeal of brakes and the crash of the moped hitting the front of the car. In the now single headlight of the *car rapide* David saw Issa's body fly in the air from the impact in front of the car. The moped followed in a tumble down the street. David rolled off to the side of the road and lay still. The *car rapide* stopped and four people got out. The driver and the conductor both looked at the twisted, broken moped and approached Issa's body, yelling at each other as they did. They seemed not to have noticed David.

An argument ensued about what had happened and what to do next.

"He was drunk. He must have been drunk. I didn't see him at all. Neither did you," David heard the driver say to his conductor.

"He's dead," his companion replied. "Nothing we can do. Should we report this?"

The driver seemed to be thinking as he looked around. "Let's go," he said.

Without another word they ushered the other two passengers into the car. There had been little damage to the car, save the one headlight and possibly a few dents that they would tend to in the morning. They knew that even if someone had witnessed the accident, they would never be able to identify them or their car for certain. They drove off, leaving Issa the seeming victim of a late-night hit-and-run.

David crawled to the wall where he had propped Issa and used it to help get to his feet. Utterly spent, he staggered down the road toward the guesthouse, not noticing that the drums he heard earlier had stopped.

He unlatched the gate to the guesthouse and slipped quietly back to his room, not bothering to turn on the light. He stripped off his clothes and left them on the bathroom floor, then turned on the faucet. David was very glad just to have the trickle of cold water to splash over his face. He emptied his trouser pockets, and then put all his clothes into the sink and filled the sink with water. Naked, bereft of energy, and shivering as his numbness started to dissipate, David fell heavily onto the stiff bed. But he could not sleep. Perhaps it was due to the remnants of the adrenaline still coursing through his blood, or the vivid memories of the murder he had committed, or the tenacious construction of his justification, repeated like a mantra over and over until the twisted conclusion became reality, the only rock to which he could cling in a sea of self-recrimination: I had no choice, I had no choice, I had no choice.

31. THE MISSING

"I heard from David yesterday," Tony said. "It seems our former associate Issa Moleng was killed two days ago in a moped accident."

Silence.

After another moment Nigel replied, "Interesting. Given the fact that Issa had probably stolen from us and may have told the wrong people about the Blueprint, I'm tempted to call this a fortuitous coincidence, wouldn't you?"

"I'm not a big believer in coincidence and certainly not those of the fortuitous variety."

"What do you suppose happened, then? Do you think we need to be concerned?"

"Of course we need to be concerned! Don't be naïve!"

"How is David taking this? He would have told you, wouldn't he?"

"Yes, indeed. David. David was interested in getting on with business. He believes that to make the next transfer overland we will need to wait until the rains subside. He's gathering the statues and such and hollowing them out. He's planning to be up at the mines next week to see his cousins."

"If David is moving forward, then surely he believes Issa's death was accidental."

"I don't know. I don't think so. David doesn't believe in coincidences any more than I do. And he certainly isn't the kind of man to risk business as usual on a *hope* that the appearance and the reality are the same."

"Then he knows more than he's telling us, but either way, if David believes we should look ahead, then we are right to do the same, no?"

"What if David had Issa killed or killed him himself?"

"Chilling as that thought is, Tony, I can't see that it makes a difference at this point. You are the one who warned me that this effort of ours could get morally compromised. I'm not willing to change our plans because of a supposition that our partner had someone killed."

"I don't think David would have taken the chance of involving another person. If Issa was killed deliberately, David did it himself."

"It doesn't look like the rains are very good this year. Bad for the crops, but potentially good for us. I think the IMAME caravan is going to try their first extended run to the dam site next month. That should give David time to prepare the statues and get up to Tougue."

"Yes. The Blueprint is apparently back on track. What news do you have from Doria?"

"Oh … yes. … My lovely Doria. She'll be back tomorrow."

"That's good news. Have these last two weeks of heat, bugs, and mud disabused her of this fantasy of hers?"

"Quite the opposite, actually. On the telephone last evening she sounded breathless and giddy, like a girl who's been given a pony for her birthday. She wants to gather more of her things and return to Ziguinchor next week to stay for a few months. She says she needs to be there when most of the plants are ready to be harvested."

"Plants? What plants is she on about?"

"Apparently, DeLevres' notebooks and conversations have led her to what she thinks are new, or at least rare, discoveries. She went on for about ten minutes, talking about some small plant that, when mixed with some other concoction, is a cure for some types of dementia."

"Oh my Lord, that's quite a laugh. She's in the Casamance for all of two weeks and suddenly she's a savior of modern medicine. I'm afraid, Nigel, it's your girl who's got dementia!"

"She's quite serious and full of detail. It's all very amazing, and, I will say, puzzling. When she arrives, she wants to meet with DeLevres and discuss setting up some sort of plant laboratory down there. Her enthusiasm is quite … remarkable."

"Really? Good for her, then. Daft as it may be. She has been a bit sullen the last few years, Nigel, you have to admit. This junket of hers may actually be good for her. And you won't have to hide the Blueprint from her—she'll be off pursuing her world-saving botanical dream. I think this could work out smashingly for everyone, don't you think?"

"I miss Doria, Tony. I don't care if she's sullen or jubilant. Well, that's not true. I do want her to be happy and bright. But truly, I love her being here. She does such a wonderful job entertaining. The servants adore her. The garden is truly her making, you know, and … and …"

"Careful here, my dear friend. Your wife may be beautiful, but you know better than anyone that she's no ornament for your estate or career. It never struck me that you thought of Doria as your trophy wife. Rather unlike you, Nigel, I must say."

"No, you've missed my point. I …. She's been a rock for me. A sense of security and a reason for my wanting to be more. I'm the one who's traveled, business and all, for the most part, while she's stayed at home. This is the first time she's been away, not on some family visit, but on a journey that excites her, that seems to have awakened her. And frankly, I'm worried."

"Oh, come now. Worried for what? Worried she might enjoy herself? For her safety? She's with Iba, and I dare say she's an adult woman. She's not about to be stupid."

"It's not that."

"Are you worried that she'll get fed up and be morose all day long because she failed to invent a new cure for boils or old age? Is that it? Or is it you think she'll go back to not-so-merry old England?"

"Close, Tony. Very close … I'm worried that I'll lose her."

"Lose Doria? That hardly sounds likely, even when I say it. Aren't you being a bit dramatic?"

"Am I? Perhaps. But as I heard her voice last night on the phone, it was a voice I didn't recognize. Resolute, full of purpose and confidence. It was as though she had discovered why she was put on earth. You know, I was even a little envious, I'm sorry to say."

"It's a perfectly dreadful shame that all the qualities we admire in a man should make a woman difficult."

"Difficult, Tony, only when we need or love them. Do you think that's how women think of men? That we're difficult? That our lust for defining ourselves against our peers and for accumulating the spoils of one-upmanship make us unattractive, make us difficult?"

"I would only be guessing, Nigel. Who knows, really? You'd have to ask a woman, I suppose."

32. On the Job, Part 2

Although the rains prevented the IMAME team from scheduling trips to southern Mali and Guinea in August, there was plenty they could do in the north. With paved roads all the way to Rosso in Mauritania, Derek and Victor worked out a schedule with the teams to head out to Saint-Louis from Dakar, cross the border into Mauritania, and work the northern side of the river basin. Victor and Mammadu would head out, taking one Land Rover with ornithologist Leah Genescieu and forestry specialist Orson Limber, three days ahead of the rest of the other teams. They would spend two days in the richest of the northern ecosystems, the estuary of the Senegal River, counting and recording the species of birds and trees before joining the others, then traveling deeper into Mauritania. Victor was very glad to be getting back into the bush.

Leah had secured a meeting with the head of the Département des Eaux et Forêts, which was responsible for the Djoudj National Bird Sanctuary, a broad 14,000 hectare stretch at the mouth of the Senegal River that had been set aside by the French just before Senegal's independence. President Léopold Senghor, among the first democratic despots in West Africa, had the foresight to retain Djoudj in its entirety, and the migratory birds of Eurasia had been grateful ever since. Having persuaded the director of the park to escort the team through the entire conservation area for two days, Leah also secured a campsite on the grounds of the Eaux et Forêts compound, next to running water and clean latrines. Victor's respect for Leah continued to grow.

* * *

Amid the tall acacias next to a large stream, Mammadu and Victor pitched the tent and made camp after the six-hour journey from Dakar. Although both Leah and Orson offered to assist, Victor insisted that they use the remaining daylight to begin their explorations. Both scientists smiled and grabbed binoculars, field guides, notepads, and water bottles, striking out in different directions into the mangroves.

With the slow departure of the natural light, Mammadu lit four candle lanterns and two gas lamps to illuminate their work area. Orson came back to camp, babbling enthusiastically about the density of the trees in an area of such little rainfall. It was then Victor realized it was too dark to see in the woods and began to worry about the adventurous ornithologist. They began shouting her name. Mammadu retrieved two battery-powered lanterns from the trunk of gear next to their tent and handed one to Victor. They listened for Leah's call from the darkened landscape and brush. The land offered up an unexpected cacophony of responses. Insect noises of all kinds, clacks and whirrs, zings and zips of creatures on the ground and in the air. They called again and listened. The croaks and calls of frogs and other amphibians, and distant, unidentifiable screeches answered. And then even more distant, the high-pitched howl of jackals.

"Just great," Victor said out loud. "I'll go look for her. The two of you stay here. If I haven't found anything in fifteen minutes, I'll turn around and come back and we can organize ourselves and perhaps get help from our hosts." He said this in French to Mammadu and then translated for Limber.

"You should not go alone," Mammadu said. "There is a better chance if we go together."

"But you need to stay with Mr. Limber."

"Mr. Limber is fine—if he stays at camp. With two, we have a better chance of finding Miss Leah."

Victor and Orson agreed.

After a few minutes of searching, Victor shouted to Mammadu, who responded in easy earshot. They each shouted Leah's name. This was beginning to feel to Victor much too reminiscent of the encounter with the army ants. Here he was, traipsing through the West African bush in pitch-black night—Where was the goddamn moon, anyway?—not knowing where he was going nor how long it would take him to get there.

"This isn't a freakin' job," Victor said under his breath, "it's a recurring nightmare."

He walked slowly and watched his feet, knowing he wanted no part in disturbing a sleeping snake in the night. A large rodent scampered over his shoes. Victor yelped.

"Shhh. Shhh. And turn off that torch!" It was Leah, not more than three meters in front and to his right.

"What the hell are you doing still—"

"I said turn off that light! Please!"

Victor did as he was commanded and made his way cautiously in the direction of Leah's voice. Apparently reaching a narrow, focused objective, her sense of purpose made her oblivious to her own comfort, even the fact that she might have been lost.

On his hands and knees, Victor edged closer, until he heard Leah's shouting whisper, "Stop!" Victor stayed still, thinking he should insist that she come back to camp immediately, when a hand grabbed his ankle and he convulsed.

"Shhhhhh! Don't move a muscle," Leah ordered from behind him.

"What the fuck!"

"Crawl backward. Slowly."

Again, Victor did as instructed, until he was side by side with the prone scientist. She pointed in front of them. It was nearly impossible to see, even though his eyes had adjusted to the darkness. He discerned a silhouette of movement in front of them, two in fact. They appeared like miniature dinosaurs.

"Abyssinian ground hornbills," Leah said, as though the impact of this revelation assured Victor's complete understanding.

"How the hell can you tell?" he whispered back to her.

"Can you see the large hooked bill? Where it meets the head, there is the large bulge, a casque. No bird of its size other than the hornbill has this feature, and only ground hornbills nest in dry brush like this, and only the Abyssinian ground hornbill is found in the Sahel."

"Mammadu and I are out looking for you. You can't get lost in your work here, Leah. You're not in Texas!" Victor stood up purposefully, and the birds dashed away through the undergrowth. "Mammadu! I've found her. She's all right."

Leah let out a sigh of exasperation as she pushed herself upright.

Before she could protest, Victor took the offensive. He was shaking. "You don't do this again. Ever. I mean it. I am responsible for your safety and if I say you need to be somewhere before dark, you had fucking well better be there."

Leah suddenly understood how disturbed and angry her guide was. She remained poised. "Victor, I was clearly doing what I have come here to do and had no intention of causing you any concern."

"Of course you didn't. Because you didn't think of anything else. Just Leah Genescieu doing her expert shit—whatever you do. But here's the deal, Ms. Genescieu. You are part of a team. And the next time you do anything so stupid, you will be on the next bush taxi back to Dakar."

"Does this mean you are sending me to bed without my dinner?" she said.

Victor fought for self-control. He was about to grab the ornithologist by the throat, when Mammadu appeared at his side.

"Everything OK, Barbu? Ms. Leah, you are unhurt?" He put his hand on Victor's shoulder and all the tension dissipated.

Victor returned the gesture. "We just saw a bird, Mammadu, an Absinimth hornbill, right, Ms. Leah?"

"It's called an Abyssinian ground hornbill. And there were actually two birds and a nest. In fact, it is extremely uncommon to find them this close to aquatic habitats. And since you are now so interested, the literature claims that the Abyssinian ground hornbill has never been observed this far north in the Sahel, making this a singularly important observation. If I can verify it." She turned in a huff.

Speaking to her back, Victor said, "I'm sure if we walk single file and wear a path down back to camp, you'll be able to find your way back to this spot in the morning."

Leah made her way past her guides and headed in the direction of the camp. Mammadu overtook her and, shining his flashlight through the brush, indicated a slight course correction.

At camp, Orson and Leah sat outside the lady's tent and chatted away like sorority chums, until Mammadu called them to the table for dinner. The four sat around a sheet-metal camp table as Victor served.

"I hope I'll be able to find those two hornbills again tomorrow. I would very much love to take some pictures. We will have to be up before light so we can retrace our steps to the nest."

"We?" Victor said.

"Surely you will want to prepare my breakfast and coffee, yes? How could I go out into the deep bush without my morning coffee?"

"I'm sure the hornbills won't mind if I sleep in."

Orson came to the rescue. "I'll be up early making coffee, Leah. You won't go without."

"How gallant of you, Orson. No need, unless you are up. It would surprise our guide to learn I can actually start a fire and make coffee too."

"So, what makes these birds so special?" Victor said, prodding her.

"All birds are special, Mr. Byrnes, for varied reasons. Though the Abyssinian ground hornbill is fairly common in certain parts of its range, it is quite uncommon here. What does that mean? Could it be, for example, there are more of them and the habitat is changing? Is there more of what the hornbill likes to eat, like locusts or beetles? If that is true, what does that mean about how this area will react when there is more water in the river or a dammed lake the size of Luxembourg? More food for hornbills, perhaps."

"So they are insect eaters?" Orson queried.

"They are carnivores and insectivores, living off small rodents, eggs of other birds, and insects of all kinds. Also, these birds are special because ground hornbills mate for life. They are monogamous."

Victor said, "And that makes them special because ... they chose to be that way?"

"Good point, Mr. Byrnes. Monogamy is not a matter of choice in the animal kingdom. Either a species is genetically predisposed—I think you say hardwired, yes?—for monogamy, or it is not."

"What about Homo sapiens?" Victor said, having no clue why he had decided to ask this question.

"I think you will be better asking our anthropologist, whenever he arrives. Mankind's brain is not like those of the rest of nature's fauna. If I understand early history, monogamy and polygamy grew up together in our species, both as a matter of survival. Sex seems to be hardwired, but how we collect partners is not."

"But," Victor said, "if evolution is what made the hornbills monogamous, right, then couldn't there be some monogamy gene in humans? You know, brown eyes or blue eyes, light skin or dark."

Orson said, "Certainly, women tend toward monogamy and men don't. Sounds like it's an X chromosome thing."

Leah took him on. "If you mean that in Western society men are cheats and women are faithful, I'd say that's an exaggeration. The socialization of humans is quite complex when you consider the hundreds of cultures we have evolved. It could be said about humans that if one is very rich or very poor, monogamy is less important for survival. The human middle class seems very keen on the structures of monogamy, you know—Christian weddings, joint property laws, and such. You could make the case that most human societies are serially monogamous, more or less. But remember, the hornbills mate for life. Not one at a time. One, and one alone."

Victor considered this. "I don't think we are genetically predisposed to monogamy. It's all socialization. And those that have socialized differently have a different value, right?" He was thinking of Lamine and Claire, and how Lamine wanted his wife to be his and his alone. Yet, while Claire might love him, the concept of "his alone" or "hers alone" had no meaning for her. From Lamine's story, she seemed casually dispassionate to the very idea of a monogamous relationship. If Claire was wired, hard or otherwise, it seemed to be to polyandry.

"Any biologist will tell you," Leah said, "that sex practices are about survival. The ritual around sex—be it religious, cultural, legal, or even personal—is only to assure procreation and rearing of young, for the best chance of the progeny to carry on the species. Once children are born, it is all about economics."

"That's not possible," Professor Limber said. "I'm a biologist, but I wouldn't be prepared to say that all sexual ritual is about procreation. A lot of it is about fun!"

"If I may?" Leah said to him with raised eyebrows. "First, you may be a biologist, Professor Limber, but you are a botanist, not a zoologist. Second, you are a man with a man's reptilian brain. You think all ritual is about fun."

Victor wondered aloud: "What does it mean when a woman disregards the conventions of monogamy once she's already married? Is that about rebellion? Is it about survival? You may not be an anthropologist, Professor Leah, but you're a woman. What do you think?"

Leah paused and looked at Victor. "For a woman to burn the bonds of fidelity in marriage would mean either utter disappointment or utter security, or maybe some combination of the two."

"So," Limber chimed in, "it wouldn't be in a man's best interest to make his wife feel too secure. Is that what you mean?"

"Don't talk nonsense, Orson," Leah replied. "That's not what my answer means." Looking over at Victor again, she said, "I wouldn't know or understand such a woman, Victor."

Mammadu had not let his lack of English proficiency disturb his eating. He finished his entire plate and, with a big grin on his face, held his plate up to Victor. "More, Barbu. You're a very good cook."

"Only you think so," Victor replied, pointing to the plates of their two traveling companions who had barely eaten. "Help yourself," he said, nodding to the stew simmering on the camp stove.

The next morning Leah was as good as her word, up before dawn, making coffee. Victor was awake and, so, rose from his cot to start the camp stove. He took the kettle she had filled with water.

"It's instant Nescafé or tea," Victor said.

"Coffee, instant or otherwise, as long as it's coffee."

The stars in the eastern sky seemed dimmer than those in the west. In the distance, across the acacia trees and savannah scrub, the sounds of animals that foraged by day came alive: korhaans and guinea fowl squawked from far into the flat distance, and the rustling of awakened lizards and ground squirrels was all around the campsite. Toward the banks of the estuary lake the muted cries and squawks of unseen and unknown animals ascended like strange music.

The man and woman stood silently as they prepared and then drank their coffee. After a few minutes, the sky gave up the stars to the sunlight. Leah thanked Victor, promising to be back at camp by noon, and went off, binoculars and field guide in hand, to rediscover her hornbills. Victor was glad not to worry about her.

After a breakfast in daylight, the three men walked over to the office of the Eaux et Forêts. They presented their credentials to the director, Pappe Beng, a slender Senegalese man. Orson was offered a guide to take him into the records office and then into the surrounding forests and bush. The guide, originally from Cameroon, spoke English. After the forestry duo left, Pappe Beng said he would like to take the ornithologist on a boat tour of the estuary.

"It is reserve land set aside for the sole purpose of preserving natural phenomena that occur only here. Only in Senegal. Thousands upon thousands of migratory birds, species from Eurasia, stop here on their remarkable journeys to southern Africa. She will see nothing so wonderful as these sights. I can only take our boat out at three o'clock this afternoon."

Back to camp for a late lunch, Mammadu and Victor had just started to eat their sandwiches of sardines and tomatoes when Leah returned, hungry and excited. Her species count had reached fifty-five for the morning, more than expected. And yes, she had reencountered the ground hornbills. Victor extended Director Beng's offer to tour some of the remote areas of the estuary.

"Victor, that would be fabulous. Can we go early in the morning?"

"Apparently, we're going in about an hour. Director Beng has instructed us to meet him at the boat launch area at precisely 3:00 p.m."

"That's a bit silly," she said. "What is 'precise' anywhere in the country? And why would we go in the hottest part of the day, when the birds will be least active?"

"Well, maybe you can go again tomorrow morning, if you want. Dr. Beng seems eager to help out. I think it should be fun to be out exploring on the water this afternoon. What, you have other plans?"

Leah sniffed. "All right, then. We will meet the director at three o'clock. May I have some lunch, please."

Forty minutes later they appeared at the boat launch. The boat was practically brand-new; the open fiberglass hull was about six meters long and had a wide canvas canopy covering the center console. A Mercury 90 hp outboard engine was propped up on the rear gunwale. The dock itself was slowly disintegrating into the lapping waters of the estuary. Leah and Victor looked at its rotting boards and support posts tilted at the horizon.

"Hmm," Victor said. "Looks more than a little shaky!"

"Good! You have arrived," came a jaunty voice behind them.

Victor took Dr. Beng's extended hand and introduced him to Dr. Genescieu.

He took her hand, bowed, and kissed it. "What a pleasure it is to have a renowned ornithologist with us to see the utterly unique character of our estuary wonderland. This is a great honor for me, Doctor."

Leah glanced at Victor.

"I'm honored, Dr. Beng," she said. "Though I confess I am not renowned. Simply a hard-working zoologist with a few publications to her credit."

"Nonsense!" insisted Beng, and from his jacket pocket he pulled a booklet marked "Société de Conservation Mondiale" on the cover and turned to the middle, where he pointed to an article in French about the loss of forest habitat and the rise of parasitic birds in tropical areas. The author was Dr. Leah Genescieu. The article had been written during her early postdoctoral years and had been among the first to define the mechanism responsible for the decline of endemic bird species. Of course, her work had been in Brazil and Colombia, not West Africa. Leah blushed slightly as Dr. Beng continued to insist what a giant she was in the field of avian ecology.

He added, "Now it will be my honor to take you to see our jewel here in the north of Senegal. Who would think that such a lush and magnificent estuary could be found so close to the desert? It is a miracle of great scale, is it not?"

Victor and Leah nodded slowly.

Dr. Beng, like Leah, had a satchel over his shoulder and a pair of binoculars dangling from his neck. He motioned for Leah to proceed down the rickety dock to climb onto the boat.

She hesitated, and then looked back at him, saying, *"Pas possible!"*

He laughed and said, "Follow me."

Stepping precisely along the supporting beam onto which all of the dock boards were nailed, Dr. Beng led the way. The dock swayed and the support poles shuddered with each step. All four of them made it into the boat.

Dr. Beng proudly launched into a monologue regarding the government's latest acquisition of this modern watercraft as he slipped the docking tethers, fired up the Mercury outboard, and headed into the estuary lake.

As Dr. Beng steered the boat through a channel, startled birds cackled warnings to others. Black-headed herons and marabou storks climbed in physics-defying flights, until achieving a velocity that allowed their enormous wings to catch the upper breezes and carry them away. Dr. Beng cut back on the throttle even more when he veered close to the bank and came around a sharp bend in the lake.

There, as though from a lost kingdom, was a gigantic blanket of whiteness covering the lake in the distance. As the boat drew closer, Leah made out through her binoculars that this blanket was woven with the plumage of thousands upon thousands of white pelicans. Beng cut the engine completely and let the boat drift toward this monstrous raft of birds that extended as far back along the estuary lake as anyone could see. A cacophonous avian din suddenly filled the air as the pelicans noticed the approaching craft. Then, as if a shot had been fired, they decided all at once to take flight.

Pelicans do not just explode out of their sitting position in the water to get airborne, as would a small duck. Pelicans run along the surface of the water as they flap their prodigious wings and then take flight mere inches above the water. As all four humans watched, over ten thousand white pelicans did this simultaneously and headed directly toward the drifting boat. The vocalizations of the startled pelicans were overcome by the thunderous beats of their wings. As the birds approached the boat at nearly eye level, Leah stood up, possessed, and spread her arms, trying to touch the massive flock. The pelicans slowly rose into the air all around them, blocking out the sun. The wind from the pelicans' wings blew back their hair, their eyes, and their clothes.

Neither Victor nor Mammadu had ever imagined such a phenomenon and were paralyzed. Dr. Beng simply smiled as he watched the spectacle unfold. It was minutes before all the pelicans had passed over them, depositing feathers and guano into the boat. Leah turned to watch the last of them glide over the horizon of the estuary. She was holding her diaphragm and breathing as if she had just sprinted 200 meters.

Mammadu's face remained turned to the sky and a broad grin stretched across his face. "Barbu, *Dieu nous aime*—God loves us," he said.

"That was fucking amazing!" Victor noted, eyes still wide in awe. "Did you get pictures?" he asked of Leah, completely unaware that the ornithologist had been just as mesmerized as Victor himself.

"What an incredible privilege!" Leah said in a gush while still standing in the boat, her face toward the sun.

"I was not exaggerating at all, was I, Dr. Genescieu?" Beng remarked.

"Not in the least, Dr. Beng. How many pelicans would you estimate were in that flock?" she asked.

"At least ten thousand, and likely more," he said.

It was after seven when they returned to the dock.

* * *

Three of the four campers came brightly awake at dawn. A groggy Victor eventually joined them. As Mammadu rose to clean up, the rumbling of a diesel engine drowned their conversation. A Winnebago rambled into view along the dirt road, listing from side to side like an empty rowboat. A fully packed Land Rover followed. The mobile lab pulled into their camp clearing and halted a few meters from the breakfast table.

Dr. Hamilton Laird opened the cab door and bounced out like a Labrador retriever. "Good morning, boys and girl," he said. "It is sooo good to be out of the city, finally! I hope you've been having a good time waiting for us."

Smiling slightly, Dolores Knapp walked out, clutching her straw hat in front of her and smoothing her khakis.

From the Land Rover parked behind the lab emerged the remaining health team members. Gwen Wong was dressed like she was going to the gym—wearing running shoes. Denali Tekkendil looked the freshest of them, in a lime-green leisure suit that featured epaulets.

Can this be? Victor thought, blinking in the hope that the scene before him would disappear. Couldn't Tekkendil at least have worn beige and pretend he knew what work in the bush would be like?

Mammadu jabbed Victor in his side.

"OK, then," Victor said out loud. "Here we go."

33. A Convergence of Sorts

"Nigel, be a great dear and help Iba with the luggage," Doria said as she opened the rear door of the muddy Mercedes. She pecked Nigel dutifully on both cheeks and went back to the car to retrieve what appeared to be scrapbooks.

"Whatever have you got there, love? Here, let me help you with these."

Help, though clearly needed, wasn't the task Doria had in mind for her husband.

"No, no. Really, I'll get these. I'm fine. There's a metal trunk of samples I want you to pay particular attention to. I don't know how these plants will have made the journey. Most are already dead, I'm sure, but I don't want them deteriorating and I'm so worried this heat will have dried them to dust."

"Doria, what exactly do you intend to with these samples? If you're worried they'll dry out, I'm not exactly sure what we can do."

"Let's put them in the coolest spot we have in the compound. I was thinking the laundry room. It's behind the garage and almost never gets any sun. I know there's not much space, but Ahminta usually hangs the clothes outside, so there won't be any extra heat from the dryer. Besides, I'm hoping they won't be here long. I've got to get in touch with Professor DeLevres and see if he agrees with me."

"Do you really think so?" Nigel asked. "I mean, that you've found some special plants and all?"

Doria looked at her husband and decided not to tell him what had happened to her these last three weeks. At least not yet.

"I guess I'll have to find out once the professor has had his inspection," she said, trundling up the steps with a bounty of notebooks spilling papers from the sides.

Nigel scooped one up with his free hand and before he could make out any of the drawings or the writings, Doria snatched it from him with a quick "Thank you," and hurried into the house. Iba and Nigel carried the trunk to the laundry room.

Once the car was unloaded and Doria's luggage tucked into their bedroom, Nigel found his wife in the study, trying to organize the reams of paper she had brought back with her.

"Doria, do that later. Come have a drink with me. It's Sunday afternoon and you must be parched from the trip. When was the last time you had a decent glass of wine?" He came to her side and took a gentle hold of her arm to lead her to the living room.

She brushed his arm aside without looking up. "I'll be finished right away, Nigel. A glass of wine sounds delightful. Please go ahead and pour one, and I'll join you in a moment."

Nigel pursed his lips and nodded as he turned to comply. Pulling a white Burgundy from the fridge, he heard Doria on the phone, speaking excitedly to DeLevres, arranging for him to come to their home the next day.

Nigel watched her from the study entrance as she worked through each notebook, made additional notes, muttered loudly to herself in reprimand or reminder, oblivious to his concern.

The Doria he saw was new to him. Though his hard work and plans for true financial independence were stitched with dreams of life together, of his ability to offer his wife any material thing she might desire, his deepest motivation had been his own ambition. Had Doria made Nigel her highest priority, and, sublimating her own needs for so long that now, as she explored and embraced those needs, she could only accelerate her journey away from him? Nigel shuddered.

Sensing she was becoming fatigued with her cataloging and organizing, Nigel set the wine down on the desk where she was working. She stopped writing and looked up at him and smiled. He put an arm on her shoulder as she stood up and took her glass.

"This is so exciting, Nigel. I feel like I've rediscovered a part of myself, you know? That studious, excited girl who wanted to do something special, the one I left behind as life changed. I've reunited with her."

Nigel clinked his glass to hers. "Welcome to that studious, excited girl whom I hadn't known but believed all along was there," he said.

"This must seem so strange to you. It means a great deal to me that you've supported me, though surely you think I'm daft."

After taking a sip she put her wine on the desk, kissed her husband lightly on the lips, and hugged him. Nigel responded gently, but could not help feeling this was a hug reserved for a mentor or a father, not a cherished soul mate.

After their light dinner, they retired to bed early and Doria fell fast asleep.

When Nigel rose, he noticed that Doria was already out of bed and getting dressed. She took less than her usual time and care selecting her clothes and adjusting herself in the mirror. It dawned on him that he was, for the first time, intensely observant of his wife's behavior, as though he were now studying her and looking for … something. She waved at him as she nearly dashed out of the bedroom and down to the kitchen, where Ahminta had just arrived and was preparing tea.

It seemed like a routine morning as Nigel finished his breakfast, kissed his wife, and left for work, thinking he would tell her he'd be home for lunch. But he did not.

* * *

At exactly 9:00 a.m., Alain DeLevres appeared at the Blake residence. Doria welcomed him with excitement. She offered him a seat at the breakfast table, and Ahminta poured them tea.

"Professor, it was the most amazing journey I have ever taken. There were times when I thought I would die from exhaustion or the heat, and my guide was a most enigmatic woman. It was often very difficult to know if she was helping me find these incredible plants or leading me away from her secrets. We spent an entire week near the Guinea-Bissau border, hunting plants, some of which I vaguely remember, like *daturous* and *strophantus*, and so many which I did not know and hopefully you will. And also, Professor—"

"Please, Madame Blake, you may call me Alain. May I call you Doria?"

"Of course, of course. Yes. Well, I have a bit of a surprise for you, I think."

"Oh? I'm not surprised by very much these days, I must warn you," DeLevres said.

"I understand. Perhaps you will not be surprised, but I hope you will be pleased."

Doria led him to the study, where she showed the professor his own notes which she had meticulously reorganized and set next to her own, which were nearly as copious. "Your notes were such a great source and guide for me, Professor."

"Once more, it's Alain. I see you have augmented my research considerably," DeLevres acknowledged, paging through both sets of notes.

"I'm not really sure if I have, *Alain*, but I wrote down everything I could and then tried to organize it. Here." She handed him his notebooks and picked up the stack of her own. "I want to go through the specimens with you and we will need these. Are you ready?"

"This is why I am here, Doria. Please lead the way."

In the laundry room they pulled the green metal trunk from under the folding table and put it on top of the washer and dryer.

When Doria opened it, DeLevres' face showed a passing delight. He bent his head forward and squinted. A strong aroma of mulching vegetation hit them like wind. Inside the trunk were dozens of plant samples, some tied together with string, some in plastic bags, some in newspaper. All were labeled with numbers. Some bundles looked like herbs, others were plants with long, dangling roots; there were separate bunches of bare sticks, of bark, and of small branches with wizened leaves. Some plants had buds and others withered flowers.

"This clearly represents a good deal of work. I imagine, then, that each of the numbers corresponds to notes in your papers."

"Correct! And here," she said, reaching for a box in the back of the trunk, "is the surprise I told you about." She handed DeLevres a shoebox tied with sisal. "As you said, perhaps not a surprise," she said, smiling slightly.

DeLevres untied the box, lifted the lid. Inside the box were at least ten different types of fungi, maybe more, four of which he recognized as ones with which he had been experimenting. Others he recognized from his work, generally. But there were three he could not identify. One was a group of small, dark, morel-like buttons with banded stripes; another was a white-and-black ball the size of a brussels sprout, without any gills; the last resembled a tiny closed umbrella, with rings of red and orange. DeLevres could not stop studying them.

After a minute of his silent gazing, Doria asked, "What do you think, Professor? Is this something you can work with?"

DeLevres took a few seconds to let out a few deep breaths, and nodded. "You must tell me how you came to find these fungi, Doria. And why did you select these?"

She took the box from his hands, fitted the lid back on, and placed it back in the trunk. "I made a deal with Mady Toula—that's her name—that I would let you select only a few of these specimens for your study, Professor. The rest I will bring back so that we can make these tribal medicines I've been so consumed to learn. So, we can bring the trunk along with my notes and you can select a few specimens that are yours. Will that suit you, Professor?"

DeLevres rubbed his chin. "What do you know of these fungi, exactly? Did your mentor share with you the properties of each? If you have any information about this, you must share it, Doria. In what manner are these fungi used? Physical healing? Treating psychosis? Ritual? Are they administered alone or are they mixed with other substances?"

Doria noted that DeLevres was asking the same questions of her that she had asked of Mady. "There is sometimes too much to learn in too little time, Professor. Mady was constantly warning me that knowing these plants and where to find them had, at the end of the day, little to do with making or administering their derivatives. Most are—from what I have learned—mixed with other substances, and the results are used in healing and in rituals and ..."—she struggled for the word—"and, I believe, recreation."

This amused DeLevres, who half smiled. "Ah, yes, Madame Blake. We humans have so much in common, whether we are born in Avignon or Accra. Have you learned any of the 'recipes'?"

"Not a one, I'm afraid. Only the inferences I could take from Mady's inscrutable way. But I fully intend to learn more when I return." She repeated with conviction, "Yes indeed, Professor, my plan is to stay there until I learn how to create at least a few of these medicines. I would so enjoy showing the nurses at the orphanage that they can have local medicines for nearly no cost. Wouldn't that be wonderful?"

DeLevres looked at Doria with soft, faraway eyes. "I cannot say, Doria. But from my own experience, such medicines often come at a cost we cannot foresee." He fell silent, then clapped and rubbed his hands. "But that is a discussion for another time. With your permission, I would like us to take these to the laboratory now."

"We will put them in the trunk of my car," she informed him. "Iba and I will follow you to the university."

* * *

When Nigel arrived home for lunch, Ahminta handed him a note.

Visiting DeLevres' lab at the university. Minta has lunch ready for you. See you this evening. Love, D

"What the bloody hell?" was his first reaction at reading the note. But of course Doria would have taken her botanical treasures to DeLevres' lab. Nigel told himself he should have thought of that. It would do no good to go to the university. He would only make Doria wonder about him and would accomplish nothing. Having blocked the time for personal business, Nigel instead put a call in to Victor Byrnes who, like Doria, had recently returned from a trip into the West African bush.

Victor was not at the office when Nigel called, so he left a message with the secretary. When Nigel called Tony Hume, his partner had nothing new to report. As soon as Nigel put down the phone, he started to roam through his house like a burglar, looking for something of value, not knowing what it might be.

He recalled that last week he had received a letter from Simon Lasry, cryptically asking when some action from their conversation might be expected. Nigel sensed he was losing control of the many designs to which he had given momentum, now moving with independent, almost chaotic volition. His frustration simmered as he reviewed each loose end, each straying arrow. Finding himself on the patio steps he stopped abruptly, hung his arms down, closed his eyes, and faced the sky, taking in one deep, shoulder-heaving breath, then a second. He turned his head around and around to purge the tension knotted in his neck, and stretched his arms straight up into the air. When he brought them straight to his side, he said aloud, "Come on, Nigel. Keep thinking, lad, keep thinking."

* * *

Doria returned to her home, finding no indication that her husband had been there. Nigel had been home for perhaps ten minutes to make three phone calls, determined his wife was not at home, and left. Yet she had a sense, a tingle in her forehead, that Nigel had been there very recently, and she wondered why. She had processed some sign or scent only her subconscious could see, sending that signal like a wisp to her otherwise diverted thoughts. She shrugged it off, knowing what she should not have known. Doria did not puzzle or struggle with this awareness. Nigel's brief lunchtime haunt, however curious it seemed, was not important at the moment. There were critical plans to make.

* * *

DeLevres requested that Doria stay through the week, until he had completed his preliminary analysis of the new fungi. He also offered her opportunities to assist his work, to which she instantly assented. They settled on morning hours, before DeLevres' classes, and a few evenings. That left Doria time to go to the orphanage and see if she might present to the nurses one of the medicines she had brought back. This was not *ndaymou gar*, but something else, something Mady called *boppuday* or "clear head," made from two of the plants she and Mady had collected in the forest. Doria had already made up her mind to try the drug herself, before she even considered administering it to the children. But she knew that she wasn't the proper test subject. She could test herself for the potion's harmfulness, but not for its desired effect on disoriented and delusional children. She needed an accomplice, possibly DeLevres. But to distract him from his current task was probably not wise, even if the medicine worked as it should, focusing the mind.

Victor would do it, she told herself. He can come to the orphanage with me and he might even be my lab rabbit. She chastised herself. What an abominable idea! No! Victor might assist her, but to make him an experiment was absurd. Unless, of course, he volunteered. Doria was wondering if Victor could help her and Mady hunt for an ingredient that Mady insisted was found only in the freshwater swamps of Guinea. Apparently, amphibians ate it to acquire protective smells or poisoned skin—something to deter predators, in any case. Something called *fleur de feu*, fire flower.

The phone rang. She answered with a polite "Good afternoon" and gasped as she heard Victor's voice on the other end.

"Oh. ... Hi, Doria. It's Victor. How are you? I'm returning Nigel's call. Is he there?"

"No. No, Victor, I'm afraid he isn't." She was silent for the next few seconds to catch her breath.

Victor said nothing on the other end.

She said, "I was ... I was actually thinking of you a moment ago, Victor."

"I'm flattered. It must be the motorcycle you were remembering, or was it my poolside manner?" She heard a distant clap over the phone.

"Actually, it wasn't either of those. I was wondering if you might be willing to help me with a project I've started working on."

"How can I help?" he said.

Doria sensed his excitement, but hesitated. Nigel was trying to get hold of Victor for some reason related to his own project with the Guinean artifacts. If she were to invite the young man to dinner for that reason, she could find some opportunity to tell him more about the orphanage and ask him about chasing down a rare plant. Erring on the side of caution, she told Victor she had some ideas, and would speak to Nigel about having him over that week for dinner. She promised to get back to him the next day.

Doria thought how lucky that phone call had been, making her wonder if there was some larger confluence of forces at work. How could he possibly have called at the precise moment she was thinking of him? For his arrival in Dakar and elements of his work to exquisitely complement the direction and activities she was now undertaking spoke to Doria of fate. Not that their association was meant to be. Yet there was a connection between them, beyond the world inhabited through her senses, that thrust the two of them toward an unknowable destination. She was fascinated by this thought and cataloged it as more fancy than fact.

"We shall see," she said aloud. "We shall see."

34. The Soul of Rain

A messenger appeared at Mady Toula's threshold. The messenger was not a child, as Sisay often sent. This messenger was a tall, gaunt young man with scars around his eyes like Sisay's. It surprised Mady that she did not recognize him. Perhaps he was a family member from a distant village or maybe a slave from a family Sisay had saved from disease. Perhaps this waif owed Sisay his life. His lips resembled cracked plaster, and his cheeks, deep hollow bowls. In a place where one meal a day is considered well fed, this young man stood out as thinner than most. Whatever the nature of his connection to Sisay, whatever hold Sisay had on him, there was no doubt in Mady's mind that this man was himself part of Sisay's message.

He was standing in the rain outside Mady's doorway, not having knocked, but opening the door and standing still without entering. "I am Duba. I am bid by Mbattu Sisay to have you come to his compound."

Mady knew the messenger meant to come *now*—not tomorrow when it might have suited her, or later when the rains may have subsided, or in ten minutes when she finished repairing her curtains. He meant she should come with him this instant. She changed into a pair of plastic sandals and pulled an umbrella from her closet.

As she locked her door behind her, she saw the messenger moving quickly through the downpour toward Sisay's compound. She did not hurry to catch up. She knew the way. She also knew the reason she had been summoned: her apprentice. Sisay would want an accounting of Mady's independent activity: teaching a white woman the ways of the Djiolla healers. At the very least, she reasoned, he would demand a cut of the money Madame Blake was paying her. This thought soured her disposition and she began to calculate what she would tell Sisay, what he would believe, and what percentage of the fee he would exact.

Sisay's compound was larger than most and blessed with towering mango trees along the wood-fenced perimeter. With their fruit harvested months ago, they spread their shiny leaves in a dense canopy. Sisay was seated on a bench underneath the largest of these, next to his hut, which was in fact a four-room house. Rainwater drained in rivulets around the tree and away from the area where he sat, resting his hands on a traditional walking stick and looking directly at Mady. He did not appear to be agitated, nor had he been soaked by the slowing rain.

He did not rise to greet her, but motioned her to sit beside him. "Thank you for coming to see me, Mady Toula, on this perfect morning, full of rain and life."

"I am always glad to receive an invitation from you, Chief Sisay," she said.

Sisay continued for some minutes to ask about Mady's family, her health, and her work. Though this greeting was completely familiar, or perhaps because it was familiar, it put her even more on guard. Normally, Sisay was uncommonly direct. This extended salutation began to unnerve her.

"And your new friend, the good Madame Blake, how is she?" Sisay asked in the same pleasant tones.

Though Mady had never mentioned the white woman's name, she was not surprised that Sisay knew it, and replied with equal calm. "She left for Dakar three days ago. I believe she was well."

"Good. Good. And was her time in our humble part of the Casamance enjoyable to her? I'm sure you were a most hospitable hostess, were you not?"

Mady decided not to avoid the issue Sisay was probing. "She did enjoy herself, I'm sure. She helped me collect many plants from the Maylu forest that I will use to make more medicines to sell in Dakar."

"Indeed. And did you instruct her how important and rare this knowledge is? Will she now guard it safely and with humility?"

"She seeks to help the orphans near Dakar. She is serious and full of care, my Chief."

"This is all, do you believe? That she has no intention other than to heal our children? Do you not think she might use our precious knowledge for some individual gain? She has paid you handsomely, has she not?"

Mady was expecting this too. Sisay may not have had direct knowledge of any of Mady's dealings with the Blake woman, but he was a master of discerning patterns and connecting people and events. Most of all, he understood the personalities and motivations of those with whom he was dealing. She would only anger him with denial.

"Not handsomely, as you say, Chief Sisay. Mostly travel costs, a small amount for food, and something for my time."

"Mady Toula, I am sad that you did not take me into your confidence, that you did not bring her here and introduce us. What you have done is brought a stranger with no understanding, no connection to our way of life, and shown her secrets she can neither understand nor protect."

"That is not so, Chief Sisay. She is a good, though self-absorbed, woman. And I have not shared with her anything except where certain of our herbs grow. She does not know how to put these together, what other ingredients are required, or in what measure." This was not entirely true, but Mady was gambling that Sisay could not confidently infer otherwise.

"Did you know that her husband is the head of one of the largest commercial food companies in all of West Africa?"

Now Mady was shocked. How did he know such things? She could only shake her head.

"Of course you did not, because you did not think to learn. Now that you know, Mady Toula, can you tell me why this might be important?"

Mady thought quickly. This might be her only opportunity to recover.

"The Blake woman may tell her husband and he may want to bring his company here to ... to buy our crops!"

"With their Western paper money they would steal our treasure, and you, Mady, and many of our people would help them. Is this wise? Is this the reason I have taught you so much about our ways and given you leave to become a powerful healer in your own right? You know it is not. Do you now see the danger you have placed us all in?" Sisay stopped, and Mady remained silent, her hands in her lap. "Here is what you will do, Mady Toula. When the Blake woman returns, you will work with her as you have planned on the first day. On the second day, you will bring her to me and we will have *kertunang* to understand if she is worthy."

Kertunang was a ceremony rarely performed and only Sisay, for all the healers in the Casamance, was reputed to know how to perform it. It was a truth-telling ritual and ancient rite of cleansing for those who professed to become healers. Mady herself had never been through a *kertunang*, nor was she inclined to. The ritual was over a full day long and required fasting, meditation, and other physical privation of which Mady was only dimly aware.

"A *kertunang* for a white woman? Why would you possibly consider such a thing? She will refuse."

"She will not refuse if she is as serious and as good as you say. And it is you, Mady Toula, who have made this necessary. Can you discourage her to never return, to stop her hunger for the knowledge she seeks, stop a journey she herself does not direct? You cannot. Nor will you try. Madame Blake must go deep into her soul and find that she is Djiolla in spirit, or she cannot be allowed to continue. And for this, Mady Toula, you forfeit the full sum of what she has paid you. The full sum. Not one *sous* less."

Mady was distraught. She feared holding back any money, now thinking that he knew, somehow, the precise amount Madame Blake had paid her. And she was plunged with the white woman onto a new, perhaps dangerous path led by Sisay.

"I will do as you ask, Chief Sisay."

"I know you will, Mady Toula. Go now, go back to work, for you are a good healer. These events of the past and of the future are part of a single river. You have brought the Blake woman here for a reason. We will soon know that reason."

Sisay put his hand to his head and closed his eyes. His face contorted in pain.

Mady stood up quickly. "Chief Sisay, do you want water?"

He neither answered nor moved. Mady went into one of the huts to get a medicine.

Before she could open the door, Sisay said, "I am fine, Mady Toula. I was having a vision. Yes, water."

Mady obliged.

* * *

Sisay sighed deeply and ran his hand over a bulge like a small pancake on the back of his head. This, he believed, was the source of his visions. His ancestors were speaking to him. This woman of Dakar was filled with the strength of purpose, but she could be a great danger to the Djiolla. How would he engage Madame Blake to test her, to uncover the truth of her motives, and her ability to hold precious their powerful knowledge? The visions had instructed him: *kertunang*.

He himself had been through the ritual when in his third decade. *Kertunang* was a private ritual, reverent and solemn. There were no wild fire dances or mock battles. It was steeped in a religion that predated the written word. The ceremony had left Sisay purified and fully converted. He was scarred physically on his face, back, and arms where his mentor had deliberately opened wounds to mingle the lifeblood of a man with the life-force of the earth. These scars forever marked him as a healer. Purification arrived through the pain and the visions that came to him as he was left alone for two days in the forest, bound to a sacred acacia tree, full of *gnudu* tea, and fearing death for the last time.

He himself had administered *kertunang* only one time. It was to a young man who showed great promise. He had a highly developed aptitude for perceiving how life intertwined, how living things depended on each other in ways obvious and mysterious. This young man was tall for his age and thin like a stalk of maize. His questions to Sisay displayed thoughtful curiosity and insight. Sisay had no doubt this young man was to become a healer. His decision to initiate him through *kertunang* was not an easy one. But his vivid recollection of his own *kertunang* and how important it had been to him helped Sisay decide.

Only, something went wrong. Maybe he had made the *gnudu* tea too strong or cut the lacerations too deep, or maybe young Duba had been too sensitive to withstand two nights alone, lashed to a decaying tree in the middle of the forest, hallucinating and fearing death every waking second, unable to sleep or blot out his visions. Young Duba's soul fled his body during *kertunang* and left the vessel hollow, yet alive. Sisay did not know what had happened, but he knew why. It happened so Sisay would be humble: so that he would carry a pain so sharp, so resolute that it would unmercifully and unceasingly focus his mind on his people and his role, no matter how venial his thoughts or how craven his needs.

What had these new pains and new visions to tell him? Sisay knew. They foretold of the opportunity to atone for his carelessness and hubris; he should bring the visions and the mystical life-connecting understanding to the Blake woman and liberate her Djiolla spirit. Whether or not her flesh completed the journey with her was not important.

35. Small Talk

"It's about time," Tony Hume muttered as he put down the phone.

He was not exuberant. Perhaps the waiting and uncertainty had sapped some of his energy. David had seemed overly cautious, waiting if any repercussions followed Issa's death, not contacting his cousins at the mines, only now purchasing the primitive statuary to house their cache of raw diamonds. The situation at the mines and elsewhere in the interior of Guinea wasn't improving. David's original plan that a shipment would be ready in two weeks had now been two months. He needed Nigel to take a more active role in this part of their operation. In less than two weeks their next package would leave the mines in Guinea and make its way north with David. Which meant Nigel needed to make certain that Byrnes committed to the rendezvous within their window. Hume walked around his office, banging on his desk and the walls.

His secretary knocked and came in. Aishatu was born in Mali and had attended university in Ireland, of all places. She was not slender, with a smile that overtook her entire face. Hume never knew from one day to another if she would wear traditional African clothes or a thoroughly Western outfit. He gave her a compliment on her attire every day, which became the full depth of their social interaction.

Aishatu pretended not to notice Hume's agitation and presented him with trade delegation itineraries to review and approve. He looked up from his desk and noted Aishatu today wore a white boubou with sparkling embroidery. It draped her in a long flowing triangle. She looked like a priestess.

"Aishatu, love, please get Nigel Blake on the line for me. And I must say you're looking rather regal today. Is this just for work with us stiffs, or are you headed off to a hot date after work?"

Aishatu sniffed at him and curled her lips, which was both a smile and a sneer. "I'll have Mr. Blake on the line in a minute, sir." She turned away and returned to her desk.

Moments later Nigel was on the other end of the phone.

"We're ready," Tony told Nigel cryptically. "David will be in Tougue in one week. He'll stay there one full week. Can you get Byrnes there within ten days?"

"Shit, Tony, I don't know. They're heading out to Manantali on Monday, so I would say yes. Three days to Manantali, if they don't get diverted. Then Byrnes has to figure out how to get to Tougue. Tougue is the right place. It's a proper town. Tell David that Byrnes will be there. How shall I direct Byrnes to meet up with him?"

"He'll be the only Guinean in Tougue wearing a blue sports jacket. Don't worry, Nigel. David will find our mule if he makes it to Tougue in one piece."

"One piece? Is there more you need to tell me?"

"No, there isn't more to tell. But it's worth recalling that this excursion isn't just like motoring from here to Rufisque. Of course I would let you know if I knew of anything that could possibly jeopardize this operation. Christ, man, I'm not an imbecile. I'm just saying even with every precaution we can take, this is still dangerous stuff."

"It most certainly is, Tony, which is why we both agreed to use Byrnes in the first place. I would appreciate it if you would please stop trying to make things look worse than they are. Considering our short time frame, I'd say we've done improbably well. We're going to give this a proper fucking chance to work."

"OK," Hume said, "let's calm down here. I simply made a quip that was more about my own nervousness than anything else. You became a bit testy right quick. This isn't like you, chum. Not at all. My feeling, though, is that we both need to bloody make sure this mule of ours has the guts to see this through. He thinks he's working for some artisan co-op, for God's sake. Not exactly the enterprise most folks would be willing to risk their lives for, yeah?"

"You're anxious, I'm anxious," Nigel admitted. "I get it. So we'll both settle down and let this play out as we've planned. Yeah?"

"I'm just making sure you give our young transport specialist some sense of importance and urgency. We can't have him giving up just because he gets a flat tire 100 kilometers from a petrol station."

"Yes, yes, I get it. We need to make sure Byrnes has a sense of mission. Agreed. I will entertain him this weekend so there will be no doubt about his resolve."

"Let's get him to dinner together and—"

"No, Tony, no. I have more leverage here at the house. And you should not intervene. I think I know how we will steel our man for his task."

"Keep me posted, Nigel. David will be in Tougue in seven days. Seven days. After his week there, he will leave. Please, let's not fuck this up."

"We need to keep calm and alert. I'll let you know how Byrnes' visit works out."

In an instant Nigel was back on the phone to reach Doria at home. She answered on the first ring.

"Hi, Doria, love, it's me. How has your day been so far?"

"I've had a wonderful day with the professor," was the extent of her story.

"Super. I'm so glad that's working out for you. Look, if it's OK with you, love, I'd like to invite our young Mr. Byrnes over on Saturday for dinner. I've got a few things I need to go over with him, and I'm sure he could stand to get off the island for a few hours in the evening."

Doria held the phone receiver in front of her and looked at it as though it were a genie's bottle. How can this be so easy? she thought. She had been trying to think of exactly the right way to approach Nigel to invite Victor over. Now Nigel was suggesting to Doria the very thing she struggled to ask him. Fate was not fickle. It was direct, discernable, and real as sunrise.

"You know, Nigel, that's a fine idea. I was hoping to ask the two of you to help me over at the orphanage on Sunday. Do you think you and he would be up to that?"

"That might be all right, assuming Victor can make it," he said. "But I'm just talking about Saturday dinner for now."

Remarkable! That Nigel was game to accompany her on a chore he normally loathed was a curious surprise.

36. One Mission, Two Missions

Victor was not in any hurry to leave the serenity of Gorée. Too soon he would be back in wild West Africa, herding and chaperoning those single-minded professionals so utterly sure of themselves, as if their academic success gave them license to impose their limited reasoning on those who might know better. But he was committed to a curious venture with Nigel Blake that gave him an opportunity to be near Doria. He had even considered when he first returned from his last trip that maybe he should be the one contacting Nigel. But like so many other forces that overtook Victor's life, the Blake invitation came to him before he could act.

The ferry ride into Dakar Harbor was eminently soothing. Victor leaned on the lower deck railing and was cooled by the only breeze anywhere near the sweltering city. The steady rhythmic chug of the engine lulled him like a mantra. He closed his eyes expecting to find thoughts of Doria or Amelia, but finding instead a memory of the bizarre turn of events during his last sojourn after he, Leah, and Orson Limber had been joined by the health team.

* * *

It began with a near disaster when the health team insisted on taking the mobile lab through a rain-swollen streambed. The two Land Rovers made it through in four-wheel drive, but as Victor and Mammadu had warned, the lab stuck like a tar baby in the middle of the ravine. It had to be winched out. The cost in hours and emotional stability had been significant, although the health scientists finally realized they could not take the low-slung Winnebago where they needed. They had worked with Victor to create a lab-to-go that packed into and onto the Land Rovers. One more uneasy victory ….

* * *

The Gorée Ferry slipped sideways in its berth, rocking with the ocean swells, and bumped the docking timbers harder than usual, shaking Victor back to the present. He exhaled deeply as he disembarked and took a taxi to the Blake residence.

When Victor arrived, Doria joked how they had expected to hear his imminent arrival from a great distance, and praised his decision in favor of safety. Nigel extended a hand and shook Victor's energetically. Putting an arm around his wife's waist, Nigel kissed her on the cheek and glanced back at Victor, who was looking down with his head but up with his eyes.

"Your timing is perfect, young man. Let's have a cocktail before dinner, shall we? And we can talk a bit about your upcoming voyage into the heart of West Africa."

It was curious to Doria how her husband played with Victor. She considered it was likely some male ritual in which an elder lauds his treasures over a protégé, to ignite a need for the wealth, the influence, and, of course, the woman. Is this supposed to spur Victor on to deeds of grandeur? Deeds of daring and idiocy in which only young men can engage? This was as transparent as a stage play to Doria. She considered how she might protect Victor.

The three of them chatted sociably through a round of drinks. Victor relaxed slowly. He was eager to hear of Doria's trip to Ziguinchor, of which he had been unaware and was thrilled to learn that she had this separate adventure away from Dakar. As she told the stories of the forest near the Guinea-Bissau border and discovering plants she had only read about or ones she did not know at all, of getting covered in mud and flies while trekking through the wet forest, of Mady and her bizarre commanding behavior and dense, incomprehensible logic, Victor sat up noticeably.

"That's amazing, Doria! Your adventure in the bush really reminds me of so many experiences I've had. I remember this one time …." He looked up and blushed.

Doria's face was bright. She leaned toward Victor.

Nigel's gaze was cast down to his gin and tonic when he said, "Please, don't stop now, Victor."

Victor struggled to look at Nigel. Doria, sitting on the edge of her chair facing Victor, casually shook her hair and brushed it back slowly, but never back in place. She listened intently.

Ahminta announced dinner was ready. The three arose together and went into the dining room, Doria taking the arms of the two men.

Dinner was simple and fresh—salad and fish, with roasted leeks and couscous. Nigel poured a chilled Montrachet for Victor, who couldn't tell a Burgundy from bean curd, but who also had enough manners and sense to ask about the wine. Nigel was happy to oblige. The conversation turned to business in the middle of the main course.

"When do you expect to be in Manantali, Victor?" Nigel asked.

"Well, we're hoping to get an early start on Monday, but I really don't think we'll be able to leave Dakar before noon. Let me think. We'll make it to Tambacounda Monday night. Then continue on to Mahina, in Mali. We should be in Manantali by Wednesday, midday. But, you know, between flat tires, sick scientists, confused drivers, and bad cooking, it could be later."

Nigel said, "Do you know how far it is from Manantali to Tougue, in Guinea?"

"I know, according to the map, it's only about 120 kilometers. But as far as we know, there won't be more than trails to the Guinea border and not much more from there to Tougue. I'll go to Tougue with one Land Rover and probably take the forestry expert and our head driver, Mammadu—a lean, agile crew that knows how to get through tough terrain. The health team will either do it later or simply won't make it as far."

"Sounds eminently reasonable," Nigel responded. "When do you think you'll be in Tougue, then?"

"Say we arrive in Manantali on Wednesday ... maybe Monday or Tuesday. We'll start mapping the roads the day after we arrive. It's the main project for Orson. After the mapping, we'll count trees together."

The prospect of Victor going into the Guinean forest sent a tingle down Doria's spine. She was unsure if she should mention her hope that he would add one more errand on his manifold mission, but needed to know if it was possible.

"You know, Victor, you're going to be in a very interesting part of the world, botanically speaking. Many plants in that area have been only sparsely cataloged or simply not discovered."

Victor blurted, "Would you like to come along with us?"

Nigel's eyes went wide and his face reddened. Just as he was about to laugh off such a ridiculous notion, Doria responded, nearly blushing. "That is a most tempting offer, young man, but I cannot ... this time." She looked over at Nigel, whose color was returning. "I'm going back to Ziguinchor next week myself, with much work and exploration of my own to do."

Nigel said, "Doria has managed to extend her imposition on the good people of Ziguinchor, where she will, I understand, be collecting a slew of these medical herbs or whatever, chopping, cutting, and generally denuding the local forest. She's working with someone who knows the area too, a Madame Buddha. Have I got that right, love?"

"Toula, dear. Her name is Mady Toula, and yes, you have got this right. But I'll be doing more than just collecting, I'll also be preparing medicines from the specimens we collect. And working with Professor DeLevres, I've made some real progress, helping his research to find all manner of important attributes from some actually quite common weeds. And, hopefully, some not so common ones."

"Who is Professor DeLevres?" Victor wanted to know. A slight vibration entered Victor's words. He cleared his throat and sat back in his chair.

"He's quite an interesting chap," Nigel explained, smiling. "French born and bred, educated in Paris, and, if I recall correctly, Sao Paulo, Brazil. Has done research in Brazil, Borneo, and Vietnam. He teaches here at the university, and Doria's been spending an awful lot of time with him, haven't you darling?"

Doria tilted her head and glanced at her husband, then returned her attention to Victor.

"I'll give you an example," she said. "There is an herb called *blantum sterigis*. Alone, it's a bitter-tasting root that has a slight painkilling effect on aching muscles. But when this is ground and mixed with the oil from *thaumatococcus* leaves, the resulting paste apparently soothes the stomach lining and can stop diarrhea—though I must say it still tastes awful. When you consider how dehydration from diarrhea kills hundreds of children and that cholera kills in the same manner, this simple remedy should be available to everyone, in every village. And honestly, I don't know why it isn't. Well, that's not entirely true. It isn't available because it isn't well known and those who have the knowledge guard it secretly."

"Like your friend Madame Tuba?" Nigel asked.

"Not just Mady, Nigel, but all those people like her that intentionally mystify ordinary, natural mechanisms for personal gain. Helping others is secondary."

"Why, then, is she working with you, Doria?" Victor asked.

Nigel answered first. "Because, of course, Doria is paying her."

"Indeed I am. And I shall continue to pay her so long as she continues to work with me. And soon, Professor DeLevres will have a much richer catalog than he currently has. We've talked about publishing the work in a scientific journal."

"I don't know, Doria," Victor mused. "My experience, and I'll grant you it's not much, is that when the organizations of the West, whether governments or corporations, get hold of something like this, they do the same thing, just on a massive scale. They'll control, then exploit, then sell it to the West at prices the locals can never afford. I think maybe Mady Toula and her folks have it right, or at least righter than anything else I've seen."

Doria shook her head and said, "Because it has been that way, Victor, doesn't mean it must always be that way. There are good people who want to help and do what is best for others."

"*There* is most definitely the road to hell," Nigel quipped.

"Nigel?"

"I simply mean, my love, that exploring these plants with all good intentions and believing one knows what is best for others is rather like being a missionary and ending up in a boiling pot of your own making. The locals will resent it, you'll resent that they resent your good work, and the whole enterprise will be a muddle of misunderstanding. No one will get anything of lasting benefit. Except perhaps a lesson on whom to trust."

Doria persisted. "You're certainly correct that I may have entered this 'enterprise,' as you call it, with both good intentions and naïveté. But I want you to think, please. What if I can do this? What if I can work with Mady and her people and build a natural health practice that trains more people to do this work for themselves?"

"Assuming your tutor has similar motives, it's possible, I suppose. But Doria, if you are taking away this woman's livelihood by distributing her knowledge—that's what your plan is ultimately, no?—then you will have a battle on your hands. And even if you win that battle, you may be doing her great harm in the process."

Doria was momentarily silent, and then spoke. "Truly, I don't think there is a system yet for getting the right medicines or food or care to the neediest people. There are children dying in the forest because they don't have the latest miracle drugs from our Western pharmacology, and yet that miracle drug is almost surely something that is derived from a local plant or animal—like the secretion of the tiny speckled frog or the unfathomable digestive juices of a horned beetle. And whether these medicines are sold at prices no one in Senegal can afford, whether there is no road or transport for them to get where they are most needed, or whether they are hoarded and passed as magic to an ignorant population by self-serving shamans is all the same. The people in need are separated from help."

She waited for a comment. When none was forthcoming, she continued. "Besides, if Mady is smart, she can turn this into a business with more people working with her, or even for her, and making more medicines available throughout the region."

Victor asked, "Culturally, can Mady really start a business out of this? I mean, don't these traditional healers have some kind of code or secret blood oath or some practice like that?"

She replied, "I haven't seen anything to indicate that, and surely, would Mady be working with me if that were the case? Whether or not I'm paying her?"

Nigel interrupted. "Getting back to the business of collecting the artifacts for the co-op, Victor, you're going to meet a very good man in Tougue named David Semba. He's worked with Tony in the past, and is respected among the cultural leaders. He'll be in Tougue from Sunday until Friday, so it is very important that you get there no later than Thursday. Have you got that?"

"I do, Nigel. That should give us plenty of time."

Nigel said, "And please remember the sensitive nature of this venture. You must keep it confidential since the cooperative could be shut down and members prosecuted were word to leak out—to say nothing of what might happen to others who assisted."

Without looking up as she speared the remaining fish from her plate, Doria said, "Such as foreigners without diplomatic immunity?"

"Such as us," Nigel acknowledged. "Precisely."

"I'll be very careful, Nigel."

Doria wanted to ask Victor's help in both testing her *boppuday* and going with her to the orphanage. And even more, she wanted to ask him if he would be willing to look for the fire flower when he was in Guinea. She had an idea.

"Would you gentlemen be willing to accompany me to St. Michael's tomorrow in the late morning? I want to bring along my usual basket of food for the children, and I'd also like to see if the nuns are aware of one or two local medicines that might help the children study better. I was thinking maybe I could offer something as a nutritional supplement."

"Working on an experimental drug, are you?" Nigel kidded.

"No, no, not at all. Mady gave me something that's supposed to help with concentration. I thought it might be helpful."

Victor said, "I've got the attention span of a five-year-old. Maybe I could use some!"

"Maybe you could, both of you, but you haven't answered my question. Would you please accompany me to the orphanage tomorrow?"

"I committed to it earlier, so yes, I will, my love," Nigel said.

Doria was pleased, but Nigel wasn't the critical person. "Wonderful. Thank you, dear, so much. And you, Victor?"

"As much as I would like to, Doria, I'm going back to Gorée tonight, then coming back tomorrow morning, then back again. Logistically, it's a bit of a chore."

Doria was again undeterred. "You can stay the night here," she said in a matter-of-fact tone.

Nigel said, "Um, ah, … the man has a big week ahead of him. Don't make him feel obligated." To his guest, Nigel said, "You are indeed welcome to stay here tonight, if you wish, Victor. But don't feel you must."

"We won't be long there, I promise," Doria said. "And it would be something new for the children. But I understand if you can't."

Doria and Nigel watched Victor make his decision.

His shoulders lifted and he smiled. "The two of you are very kind. I accept."

"I have to go to the market first thing after breakfast, to get the foods for the basket. We'll go right after that."

She stood and picked up her empty plate to clear it, and reached to clear Victor's. Then she remembered to call Minta, who waited in the kitchen to help.

Nigel said, "I swear, Doria, you've been living here six years and you still aren't used to having servants, are you?"

"No, and I'm not sure it's anything I wish to get used to." She handed the empty plates to Ahminta. "Besides, it's just us here."

* * *

When Doria fell asleep, she dreamt vividly. She remembered upon waking: *Voices harmonized in wordless hymns. They emerged from the waves that rolled onto a coarse sand. The beach was full of shells and smooth stones. The waves deposited yellow and orange flowers with thick leafy stems, strewn along the beach. A green crow appeared, picked up one of the flowers, and flew away. Then another, and another, until the beach and the air were a deep green, thick with the wings of crows, dotted with the flowers. Doria picked up a flower and immediately rose into the air, holding a velvety stem with a giant orange blossom. She held the flower as close as she could, knowing it had given her the power to fly: above the water and the sand, above the forest, and into the striated sunlight—the power to fly above the earth. She descended to the forest but was unable to reach the ground, still holding the flower. Suddenly the flower became a chameleon that looked at her with eyes from which no light escaped, and the chameleon said, "I know what you are." Suddenly she was shivering.*

37. Beast and Guinea Pig

Doria hadn't slept well and was up much earlier than seven o'clock. Before descending to prepare breakfast, she went to the study to scribble in her notes as thoughts sprang to her about equipment and materials she would need to take to Ziguinchor. Her mind gushed with questions.

Entering the kitchen, she stopped abruptly to see Victor, looking as if he had slept in his clothes, rummaging around her kitchen countertop. Her surprise was replaced with ease and wonder as she tried to understand what Victor was about. He turned around sheepishly, knowing she was there.

"I, uh … I'm a coffee drinker in the morning. You wouldn't by any chance have any coffee, would you?"

"I'm afraid all I have for coffee drinkers at the moment is that Nescafé. I'm told it's dreadful, so I hope you'll forgive me." She walked toward the cupboard where the instant coffee was kept.

"Are you kidding?" Victor laughed. "I've lived on Nescafé for more than two years now. I'd be disappointed if you offered me anything else."

This fib had its desired effect. Doria stopped in the middle of opening the door to the cabinet above the stove and looked at Victor with one eyebrow arched.

"Liar," she called him.

He laughed and said, "Granted, it isn't exactly like the Café Paridiso's café au lait, but hey, I'm going with what you've got!"

"Are you hungry, by any chance?" she asked.

Victor suddenly was hard as a rock. Doria was totally oblivious.

"Hungry isn't the word … but actually … I'm … uh …. No, Doria. Thanks. I'm not big on breakfast. Coffee—Nescafé will be fine."

They both laughed. Victor prepared his cup while Doria heated the water and then opened the windows over the sink. The morning air, still cool, floated into the house carrying the songs of white-breasted sunbirds. They chirped a call that echoed throughout the house. It was as if a passing spirit had decided to stay a while.

When Nigel descended the stairs, stretching and farting, the light found him, too. As if he noticed something odd, he stopped on the stairs, looked out toward the patio. He smiled and inhaled. Dressed in shorts, sandals, and a Manchester United T-shirt, he sauntered up to the table, observed his breakfast perfectly prepared, looked at Doria, who was radiant and smiling, and said softly to himself, "I'm a lucky bastard, I am!" As he pulled out his chair, he noticed Victor, hunched like a drunk over a mug of steaming Nescafé, and reconsidered.

"I took you for a morning person, Victor. We didn't force too much wine on you last night, did we?"

Victor looked up cheerfully. "I do better in the bush than I do in civilization, I guess." He shrugged and smiled.

"And indeed, you are in civilization, make no mistake. Except perhaps for those daft noisy birds! Doria, are you headed to the market soon? I expect we are on our normal Sunday schedule, yes?"

"I am, Nigel, and we are."

"Jolly good. We can be at the orphanage by half eleven, yes?"

Doria nodded as she prepared her tea.

"Be a love, then, and take our groggy friend to the market with you. I think carrying your groceries might wake him up and give him some purpose this morning." Nigel was surprised at himself for making such a suggestion. But the thought of having Victor in or around the house on his Sunday morning while he read his paper and relaxed in his personal ways was irritating. "Though I must say, he doesn't look like he can be ready in thirty minutes."

"Oh, I think I can," Victor responded. He gulped his remaining coffee, pushed back from the table, and announced as he stood up, "A quick shower and I'll be good to go."

"Good to go, indeed." Nigel laughed. "Well, get on with it, man. Don't keep the mistress of the house waiting."

Victor took the stairs three at a time, heading to his room and the guest shower.

* * *

The silence that expanded between Nigel and Doria may not have seemed out of the ordinary to their usual Sunday morning as each went about some private moments while still sharing the kitchen or the living room. Occasionally conversation might have arisen as Nigel commented on something he was reading in the paper or a thought that Doria casually shared out loud. But this Sunday their silence had the underpinning of caution, each concerned that the other might glimpse deception, ulterior motives, or some deeper emotion in the most casual of comments that neither was yet prepared to share.

Doria took a seat opposite her husband and finished a second cup of tea, thinking how she might try the *boppuday* herself and maybe ask Victor to try it as well, to see if there were any unwanted effects.

Nigel, nose close to his *Sunday Times*, noted there was trouble in the world economy, ignited by Iran's taking of American embassy hostages, oil prices spiking in reaction, along with the prices of other commodities—commodities on which BBI's business depended. It was more important than ever to guarantee their financial security.

Victor appeared at the top of the stairs, his beard glistening with trapped drops of water. His wet hair was combed straight back. He buttoned his untucked shirt as he descended.

To Doria his eyes seemed jeweled with enthusiasm. Her stomach fluttered, accompanied by a sense of danger. Just how disruptive will this become? she asked herself.

Nigel saw his wife in a composed gaze toward the stairway and so turned to see Victor approaching. "You clean up passing fair for a ruffian," he commented. "Right, then, off you two go. You are my wife's beast of burden, Victor, and be forewarned. She lavishes food on these youngsters like they need a feast every day of the week. You will earn your bed and breakfast and then some."

"I'll do my best, Nigel. Beast of burden. You got it."

Doria, who drove herself regularly to the Marché Kermel on Sundays, fetched the keys for the Mercedes, along with five large cloth-and-sisal carrying bags. Victor looked at them with surprise.

"I warned you, I did!" Nigel laughed.

Victor took the bags from Doria and followed her as she headed for the front door.

Doria turned to face Nigel, and said, "We ... shouldn't be more than an hour ... darling."

The Sunday morning traffic in Dakar was mercifully sleepy. Through the years this ritual had allowed her a small moment of independence and confidence. Riding over the corniche road that curved in concert with the rocky coastline always provided a sense of calm and wonder. The ocean waves broke close to the road at high tide and the foam spewed gems of white into the air, sparkling against the sky and the dark green water. Doria took her time and, for this part of the trip, hardly noticed that for the first time, she was accompanied by someone. A stranger, mostly.

The silence they enjoyed spoke of the calm they both felt, no small amount of which was generated by their desire to be in each other's company, without pressure, without intervention, or interruption, regardless of the circumstance.

"So you do this every Sunday, I guess," Victor said.

"I do," Doria said. "I have a sense of purpose and a sense of freedom. There's no traffic to speak of, so I don't fear for my life being behind the wheel." After a pause, she said, "These children, Victor, they want for so much, yet they are such a delight. This is only a small thing, this weekly food basket I deliver. But I'm hoping to do more ... much more." She paused. "You used to do volunteer work here, didn't you? What made you give up your life in America?"

"Right ... my life in America. It wasn't much of a life, really. Being a philosophy major in college, it wasn't as though I had a lot of prospects, except more school, which would have been both pointless and expensive. I suppose I could have sold insurance or light bulbs or something, maybe worked in a grocery store. But there was no adventure in that. No future that I could see. Besides, I wanted to try and speak French. Otherwise, why all the courses in high school and college, right? And I really needed to get out of myself, you know? Concentrate on someone else's issues, particularly if I could help. I really wanted to see if that was possible."

"Did you think it wasn't possible?"

"Jesus, Doria. Yes. Yes! I was frightened to death that I'd be trapped in this shell of an ego, always imitating instead of creating, stumbling instead of running. All I managed to do in the States was screw up my life and other people's lives. Not because I meant to or anything, just because ... I guess I was just off-center all the time. When I think of the absolutely stupid, thoughtless shit I pulled and some of the consequences, never to me, of course, always to someone else ...." He shook his head and let go a rueful laugh. " 'How could a guy with all these brains just waste away?' I used to get that a lot, mostly from adults who thought being good in school meant you were smart. You know, all around me, people knew what they wanted, knew how to act, knew who their friends were. I never felt that. I was always in this sort of bubble, watching what my friends did and trying it to see if it fit. None of it did."

"Surely you must have done something that made you happy, something that connected you to the people you called friends."

"Lacrosse, mostly."

"Lacrosse?"

"Yeah. I played lacrosse in high school and for three years at Cornell, before I got fed up with the forced camaraderie, the hyper male bullshit that passes for friendship. Sorry. I loved the game, but it felt like being in the military. And these jocks just slept, ate, and injected the game. Turned out I wasn't much like them."

After more silence, Doria probed another thought. "Did you leave someone to come over to Africa?"

"She left me, actually. Gretchen. She thought she'd hitched her wagon to some hip, iconoclast star who was eventually going to be a lawyer or something and take on the world. I had no clue what I really wanted, except to get out and experience the world, to see more than the same old crap I'd grown up with. My adventure wasn't hers, I guess. She knew what she wanted. She had upper middle-class USA dreams."

"You don't know what you want out of life, Victor?"

"I didn't, really." He looked over at her as she concentrated on the road. "Until, well, recently."

"And what is that?" Doria asked.

"I want to explore," Victor said without hesitation. "I want to plunge into the unknown and be devoured."

"Explore," she said. "Explore. Of course. But to what end? What do you hope to discover and what purpose will it serve? Are you saying to me you lived for two years in the bush as a volunteer, getting parasites, drinking foul water, muddling through the corruption and the flies, just for the experience? At no time did you think you were actually helping the people you were serving?"

Victor thought about this. "I couldn't tell. Maybe I was, maybe I wasn't, but no one will know if I made a difference or not for at least a generation."

Doria stared at the road. "I see, I think. You were working with children, is that it?"

"Not exclusively and certainly not by design. That work evolved because the older people were the least likely to have any desire to learn from me. Did they want me to do work for them? Sure. Give them handouts? You bet. But learn from me? No. Maybe I was too young for them. But the kids and I got along really well. They helped me build a small vegetable garden and then kept it going themselves. They taught me how to play soccer—sorry—football. I educated them about the stars, the constellations as we know them, and they told me what they call them. If I made any difference at all, it was with the kids."

"Good on you, then. When we get to St. Michael's we'll see if you still have your touch." Taking her eyes off the road, she looked at him and gave him a broad smile.

The streets of Dakar were at rest. No young girls were waiting at the traffic lights with baskets of mangoes or guavas on their heads, eager for a sale. No boys were coming up to the car as it slowed down, to sell a belt or a blanket. The few people walking about stayed to the sidewalks instead of darting across the road. On Sunday, people were walking with purpose and patience, dressed for church. The street scene bore little resemblance to the weekday bustle that both frustrated and buoyed the people of Dakar carrying on their overheated lives.

Doria guided her car through the narrow back streets to the Marché Kermel, where she parked directly in front of the entrance. Though a mere whisper of its weekday self, the market was nevertheless open for business, mostly filled with late churchgoers picking up the supplies for Sunday dinner.

Before leaving the car, Doria reached into the back seat, took hold of the shopping bags she had brought, and handed them to Victor. "Let's go, my beast," she said with a laugh.

They clanged their car doors shut and walked into the market.

The selection of produce on Sundays was never wonderful, but Doria's regular presence interested a few of the vendors, who made an extra effort to have the kind of stock she wanted. Three of these vendors were lined in a rickety kiosk not far from the entrance. Two women and a man called out to Doria as she approached.

"Madame Blake!"

"*Bonjour*, Madame Blake."

"*Comment allez-vous ce matin?*"

Doria greeted them and, with a smile, asked, "What do you have that's good and fresh today?"

The women held up bunches of carrots and pointed to the red and green peppers. The man proffered eggplants in one hand and two large tomatoes in the other. As Doria looked over the vegetables for her decision, Victor greeted the vendors in Oulof.

The trio laughed and greeted him back. Victor asked why they worked on Sunday. They were Muslims, they said, so their day of rest was Friday. But they had to work every day in order to make money and feed their families. The women were large, older, wearing regal scarves and matching bright-colored dresses. They were jolly and well-fed. The man wore a tan leather jacket. They all smiled with incongruously perfect teeth.

Doria was amused at the scene and admired how easily Victor spoke to the vendors, less for his facility for the language than for his comfort with their company. She summed up the various items in front of her, inspecting their color and shape, shaking and squeezing them. Once she made her selections, Doria was ready to start the bargaining ritual. The vendors picked up the produce she indicated and put it on the wooden counter covered with newspaper.

Separating the piles by vendor, she called the man by his name and asked, in French, "Amat, how much for these eggplants, green beans, and potatoes?"

Amat weighed the produce carefully in an old hanging metal scale which had last been calibrated prior to World War II. He then placed the vegetables back on the counter.

When Amat said "Five hundred CFA, Madame," Victor laughed and said in English, "Doria, please don't spend any more time here. This is robbery."

Doria looked at Victor with disappointment. "Come on, Victor. You act as if I don't know that we're bargaining. You needn't worry. I come here every week. I have no intention of spending over 300 CFA for these."

"Three hundred!" Victor shouted. "A kilo of green beans is 40 CFA at most. Same with the eggplant, and you have two kilos. The potatoes are around 25 a kilo and you have three kilos. That's 195 CFA, tops."

Although he was speaking in English, the three vendors had no problem understanding that the Oulof-speaking stranger wasn't helping their business.

Doria was slightly embarrassed, but knew what she was doing and so explained it to Victor.

"I understand that I pay over the going rate for most of the food I buy here when I'm by myself. But it's only on Sunday. I shop here with Ahminta during the week and she has always helped me understand the prices. And I know what's in season, what's fresh, so please don't think I'm just some rube being taken in by the local merchants."

"Fair enough, I guess. But do you like being exploited? Do you like being singled out because you're a white woman with money and the reason they like you is because they think you're rich and ignorant?"

"Don't be offensive, Victor. And you know nothing whereof you speak. Amat has two wives and six children, plus an extended family including a brother who was made an invalid in a lorry accident, all living in his compound. Do you think the brother is collecting disability insurance? Amat is the primary supporter of fourteen people. You may have lived in this country in the bush for two years, but I have lived in Senegal for six years. Six years! And I've learned a few things along the way, which maybe you have yet to learn." She did not take her eyes from his face.

Victor blushed and lowered his head. Then he laughed at himself and shook his head. "I get your point, Doria, and I'm sorry for making an assumption of how you treat the Senegalese. But wouldn't it be far better to deal fairly with the transaction and at true market price, and then give Amat some extra money for his family, if that's what you want to do?"

Victor's apology was important to Doria. He recognized his mistake and, astonishingly, admitted it right away. She was unfamiliar with such behavior. "Look, just because so many people beg for money on the streets doesn't mean they wouldn't rather work. Why should I diminish this workingman's pride by bargaining him down and then offering him charity? Our 'arrangement' keeps everyone content. Did you see the quality of the vegetables at the other stands? Do you think it is by accident that these three merchants have the quality vegetables I'm looking for? The issues you may have encountered far away from Dakar are not at work here in the market today," she said softly.

"You're an amazing woman, Doria," he said, looking directly into her eyes.

"Please put the vegetables in the sack, and I'll bargain with the ladies for the rest. Is that all right?"

Victor moved his face forward, seemingly intent on kissing Doria. Her instinct was to meet him as her stomach fluttered. But she pulled away slowly and Victor stopped, bowing his head in a second apology. Doria smiled, took hold of his arm, and led him to Amat's counter to load the vegetables into the shopping bag.

After the transactions, they strolled through the market. Doria wanted to buy fish from one of the stands on the far side. They took the longest possible route, through dozens of empty stalls.

"I'd like to ask a favor of you, Victor," she said. "Please don't feel you must say yes. I just need some help and haven't much idea where to get it."

"Ask away," he replied.

"I'm going to Ziguinchor, as you know, to set up a workshop. I hesitate to call it a laboratory, though that's exactly what I'm hoping it will be. I'll be working to learn more about natural medicines from the local plants and perhaps even from different chemical compounds, to the extent we can isolate them cleanly and all. It's terribly exciting. This is something I've dreamt about since I was a little girl. I almost can't believe I'm doing it." She paused.

"I know," Victor confirmed. "It's as though everything you've done up to now has been leading to this."

She tilted her head and looked at him. "Yes, it has. You're exactly right." She continued. "There is a particular plant called a fire flower, that is apparently only found in the freshwater swamps of north central Guinea."

She averted her gaze for Victor to absorb this and come to his own conclusion. It wasn't difficult for him.

"Looks like I'll be working for the Blake family when I get to Guinea, won't I?"

"Do be careful. Whatever Nigel has asked of you, I'm sure it's risky."

"Since I'm smuggling art out of Guinea, I'd say that carries some risk. But really, Doria. The border there is completely unmarked and unmanned. People buy and sell local artifacts all the time. But transporting dangerous biological agents internationally? Now, that's risky business."

It took Doria a few seconds before she laughed. "I'm serious, young man. Do not take too many chances out there. Please. Please, Victor."

They continued to the fish vendor and the chicken vendor, the bread and cakes vendor, and filled all five sacks with food for the orphanage. Sweating and grunting, Victor put the sacks into the trunk of the Mercedes and settled into the passenger seat. Doria retrieved something from her purse before getting in on the driver's side, but it wasn't her keys. She held a small jar with a beige paste in it that had flecks of green. She sat in the car and held the jar up for Victor to see.

"This is my first medicine, Victor. I mean the first that I've actually put together. Mady Toula taught me how to make it. It's called *boppuday*."

"*Boppuday*?" Victor repeated. "Mother's head?" he said, trying for a literal translation.

"I think the meaning is closer to 'clear head.' This is supposed to help one focus and concentrate. I really want to see if it works, so I'm going to try some right now, myself. I'm not asking you to, also, but I thought you should know what I was doing. I truly don't expect any effect at all until we're home, since we still have breakfast in our stomachs. I don't know how fast it might be absorbed or if it will cause a stomachache. I want to test it before I consider administering it to some of the children." She unscrewed the lid and a not-unpleasant herbal smell drifted from the open jar.

Victor reached for it, and Doria handed the jar to him. He sniffed around the top, looked at the substance more closely, and handed it back to her. "How much should someone take and how long should it last?"

"That's exactly what I'm hoping to find out."

"Maybe we should consider two controls. Two different body weights and different sexes and see if there are differences for the same dose. What do you think?"

"I think you're thinking like a scientist. Are you willing to try some now?"

"Sure."

Doria pulled a wrapped tongue depressor from her purse. Pulling off the wrapper she scooped about a teaspoon-sized glob on one end and put it in her mouth. She then used the other end to scoop out an identical-sized portion and handed it to Victor, who swallowed the paste without hesitation.

"Oohh!" Victor puckered his mouth. "It tasted like lemon rinds and rotting grass. Shouldn't this be a suppository?"

"Very clever." She looked at her watch. "It's nine forty. We'll travel back to the villa now. When we get back, I'd like to take notes of any effects you feel, Victor. So please stay focused."

"Sure," Victor said. "I'll definitely stay focused to see if I can focus."

Doria chuckled. She started up the Mercedes and steered into the narrow street, heading back to the corniche and the Blake residence. "Exactly, Victor. Focus."

* * *

It wasn't a mystery to Nigel that he was edgy and uncomfortable. Doria never took longer than an hour for her Sunday trip to the market. Never. She had now been gone over ninety minutes with the doe-eyed American. Had Nigel been too eager to let them go off together? Had he really wanted to spend his Sunday morning by himself in a flatulent ritual that was more habit than nourishment? Or had he been overwhelmed by some perverse impulse to push Doria and Victor to mix their restive chemistries and dare them to spark? Either way, he was now feeling the fool, unable to concentrate on his newspaper and pacing from the effects of four cups of tea.

When the Mercedes pulled into the driveway and parked, Nigel's relief at seeing his wife get out of the car, followed by Victor Byrnes—heavily laden with bags of food—was insufficient to calm him. "Damn tea," he said.

He leaned into the doorway with his hands on his hips. "Well, finally you're back! I was getting concerned," Nigel said, to greet them.

Doria and Victor looked at each other.

"Oh, that sounded awful," he said, trying to recover. "What I meant to say was, 'So glad you're back.' "

He grabbed two of the bags from Victor and carried them into the kitchen. After placing the bags on the countertop, he leaned on it with both hands and shook his head. He could use a drink to straighten himself out and should have thought of that before Doria's return.

"Bah, man! Don't lose it over small things, for Christ's sake!" he whispered to himself. He walked slowly back into the living room.

Doria was pointing to her garden, pronouncing the names of the flowers and shrubs she was raising. Like the good student, Victor dutifully repeated each one, making sure he was pronouncing their names correctly. His brow furrowed with concentration.

"There you are, Nigel," Doria said. "I was seeing how much everyday botanical knowledge Mr. Byrnes possesses. And while I'm afraid he isn't equipped with much from his paltry American education, he seems an apt learner." She smiled.

Victor said, "You all have a lot of flowers and plants that I've never seen, that's for sure. But they really are pretty, and interesting. Not that I'll really need to know these things, ever."

"Don't sell the future short, Byrnes. You never know. Yes, Doria has a way with growing things, which I confess I have not. Her birds of paradise and clinging hibiscus are the envy of most in the area who care about such things. And it does rather sparkle up the bungalow. But look, now, shouldn't we be off to see the waifs at St. Michael's of Yoff?"

"Yes, you're right, Nigel. We were a bit longer than we'd anticipated. Mr. Byrnes was concerned for my ability to bargain properly."

Victor opened his mouth to defend himself, but Nigel spoke first. "No doubt Doria is regularly taken by the sharpies of the market. But you needn't worry about her, Victor. After a few years in the great contradiction that is West Africa, she's made peace with the gods of disproportionate wealth, haven't you, my love?" He moved quickly to her and kissed Doria energetically on the cheek. "Now let's carry on."

38. The Hopeful and the Resigned

Nigel drove Doria's car. Victor sat in the back seat, watching the sights along the out-of-town road as if for the first time. There were more vehicles on the road now, crowded blue-and-yellow *car rapides* with their messages of redemption or revolution painted gaily on the sides, churchgoing families walking along the streets—the little girls bright and blossoming in perfect white dresses, and young boys in dark suits, stern and purposeful.

The thirty-minute ride to St. Michael's Orphanage seemed like twice that as each passenger explored his and her thoughts.

St. Michael's Orphanage was part of the St. Michael's Mission, between Yoff village and the Dakar airport. Though located some distance from any of the major landing or take-off routes, the mission nevertheless experienced many moments each day obliterated by the thunderous crackle of jet engines. Was it any wonder the children found it difficult to study or even sleep?

Sunday was of course a day of rest and prayer. After church, none of the children were in the playgrounds, hence no small people greeted the familiar white automobile on this day of additional passengers. Two African nuns walked slowly to the car as it halted in the sand parking lot.

"Good morning, Sister Marie-Antoine and Sister Fatouma," Doria said. "How are you and how are the children today?"

"All is as well as can be expected, Madame Blake," Sister Marie-Antoine replied plaintively. "We survive on what the Lord gives us. And we thank him for giving us you."

"I've brought my helpers today, Sisters. My husband Nigel, whom I've spoken about, and a family friend, Mr. Byrnes."

"You are all very welcome," said Sister Fatouma with a slight bow. She motioned for them to come inside.

The stairs of the main entrance to the orphanage were three layers of whitewashed cinder blocks, crumbling on the edges and sides. The ceilinged portico was peeling paint or wood wherever one looked, and the columns holding the entrance roof looked like aging tree stumps from a burnt-out forest. Victor looked around and noticed to his right the gleaming church itself, its new roof and rich stained-glass windows, the magnificent steeple, the very specter of the pride in worship one expects of the Catholic Church. The mission, it appeared, did not itself lack for resources. Only the orphanage. Nigel put his hand on the back of the hesitating Victor, helping him enter. Victor straightened up, looked at Nigel, and shook his head.

In the main hall of the orphanage Victor and Nigel smelled stale cooking odors mixed with ammonia and the aroma of dank earth. It was like opening the door to a mushroom cellar after a fire. A single window at the back right-hand corner provided the only light. There were two doors on the right wall, one leading to the dormitory section of the orphanage, the other to a large storage closet. Neither door was closed nor looked like it could be closed properly. Five long tables with nondescript coverings were pushed to the back of the room, where thirty or forty chairs spilled around them as if they had been poured from a giant sack. Sister Marie-Antoine led the others through the large double doors on the left and into the kitchen.

"Where are all the children?" Victor asked.

Nigel nodded. "It does seem rather odd, doesn't it? Are they hiding somewhere? Still in church, perhaps?"

Doria answered for the nuns. "The children are in their rooms, on their beds, praying to make them strong in the lessons they learned in church today. Isn't that right, Sister?"

"Most certainly, Madame Blake, most certainly." Sister Marie-Antoine's reply seemed lighthearted. "And we will gather them momentarily to say 'thank you' to Madame Blake."

"May we play with them outside?" Victor asked. "Are there any soccer balls around, you know, footballs? Do they have a swing set, seesaws, jungle gym, something like that?"

"It is all we can do to school the children, put clothes on their backs, feed them twice a day, and give them shelter," said Sister Marie-Antoine. Her mouth curved steadily down and her voice became lower as she spoke. "We have received donations in the past of such things, but they don't last. There should be a few balls outside."

"Who does the maintenance around here?" Nigel asked. "Doria, this building doesn't seem healthy ...."

"The children do, of course," Sister Marie-Antoine said.

Nigel shook his head and continued to look about.

The kitchen was large but it, too, was in severe need of overhaul. Pots were scattered about the counter and sink, covered in a charcoal plaque accumulated over the years from the burnt remains of cooking oil and animal fat. Forty-kilogram sacs of millet were piled in a far corner, next to the large double doors of a walk-in refrigerator, which, as Sister Fatouma explained, had not worked properly in over five years. The defunct cold storage was functioning these days as an adjunct pantry. The dark brown floor tiles had paths worn from the sink to the stove and to the large refrigerator.

"But the electricity is out most of the time," said Sister Fatouma, "so it hardly seems worth the cost and time to repair what we can seldom use."

Doria unpacked a bouquet of flowers and a small sack of candied mangoes and papayas. "I should introduce you gentlemen to the children," she said. "Sister, may we roust the girls and boys now?"

She was cheerful, even as Victor and Nigel looked gloomily around the facility. Doria believed she was bringing more than vegetables and sweets into this parentless building. When Doria read aloud to the youngest of them, when she held them in a loving way that no one else ever had, she wanted them to feel that the world was not indifferent—not everyone wished to cast each of them away like a refugee. She also understood that she needed these children at least as much as they needed her. They were the underpinning for her own hope and ambition.

"Let me tell them you are here, Madame Blake." Sister Fatouma smiled and left the kitchen.

Doria pulled up a chair and motioned for the men to sit next to her.

Nigel fidgeted, glanced at his wife, and looked into his lap, shaking his head. "This is a grim place, Doria. I don't know how you do this every week."

Victor looked to Nigel. "You should get out more, Nigel. This may not be a picnic, but I can tell you from my experience, there are lots worse out there. Lots."

Sister Fatouma emerged from the hallway door, the children following behind calmly but in some disorder. Doria rose. When the children saw her, they shrieked and rushed to greet her. She knelt on the floor and embraced each child as they clamored around her. She called each of them by name, hugging one after another. They called her *Yaye*—Mother—and asked what she brought them.

"I brought you my family," Doria said without embarrassment. "This is my husband, Nigel. Ni-jell ..." and the children repeated his name, giggling.

Nigel stood up and gave a gallant wave, patting a few of them on the head.

Each week Doria designated one of the children to be in charge of distributing the sweets. She tried to choose a different child each time. When a boy was chosen, there was more fighting, and the boys always went first. When she selected a girl, there was some bickering, but somehow the treats got to boys and girls equally, but not in any particular order or hierarchy that Doria understood. She believed the treat distribution was based on some social organization the girls had figured out, in which the boys participated indifferently. Meesha, a tall five-year-old with a shy smile and calm way about her, was this week's treats distributor.

"And this other gentleman," Doria said, "is our friend, Victor."

"Is he your brother?" one of them asked.

"Do you have two husbands?" asked another.

Victor rose and stood next to Nigel, and spoke to the children in Oulof, telling them he was from the north of their country. The children had never encountered a white person who spoke Oulof. To a one, they beheld Victor with wide eyes. He picked up a small boy who was looking on, away from the main clutch of children. The boy allowed Victor to hoist him into his arms. Victor asked his name.

"Sulayman," the boy said after Victor prodded him with the question four or five times.

He then asked Sulayman how many noses he had. All the other children were shouting the answer as Victor held up two fingers from his free hand and little Sulayman shook his head. Victor then held up three fingers, and again the youngster shook his head, this time with a slight smile. Sensing a win, Victor held up four fingers, and Sulayman shook his head once more and put up his own single finger and placed it on his nose.

"Bena tannk," Sulayman said. ("One nose.")

Victor asked Doria and Sister Fatouma, "Do you think we can find one of those balls and play some soccer with whoever wants to play?" Then he asked the children, again in Oulof, "Who wants to play football?"

The hands of most of the boys shot into the air.

"Well, then, let's go find a ball!"

Victor placed Sulayman on the floor, but kept hold of his hand as he led a group of boys outside. Doria stood and watched him walk outside, trailed by his new fans.

When Nigel called her name she was almost startled. He said, "Are you going to read to them now? Is that what you do?"

"That's what I usually do, Nigel. Yes. But I think today may be better for some physical activity. I'm thinking the girls would like to play football as well, or maybe hopscotch."

She asked the girls if they wanted to go out and play. Naturally, they did, so Doria took the hand of a girl on each side of her and headed for the door.

"Come, Nigel. It will be good for us both. You might even enjoy yourself."

Doria and the children disappeared into the beckoning day. Nigel was quite glad to follow.

39. A Chance Encounter?

From Conakry, the road to Tougue led first to the mining city of Kindia, north of which was Kaala, David Semba's birthplace. David had traveled this route hundreds of times and not once did he enjoy it. After World War II, the French paved the route through Kindia to Mamou, where it forked northeast to Kankan and south to Kissidougou. David still remembered traveling this route as a boy, with his family, in bush taxis that roared along the tarred roads, getting to Conakry in little over an hour. But during the nineteen years since independence there hadn't been so much as a single pothole filled. Today the road was a dangerous obstacle course, pitted with holes into which an entire vehicle might be lost. The four-hour ride to Conakry was painful, particularly in the heat, particularly if it rained, particularly if the taxi driver sped through holes and over rocks believing speed would overcome gravity.

David was grateful to be leaving Conakry. As he'd predicted, there had been a quick conclusion by the police that the demise of Issa Moleng had been due to a hit-and-run accident with an unidentified *car rapide*. David's contacts revealed some confusion and disquiet among those people who knew Issa, but the trail to David and his colleagues appeared severed. He could now concentrate on his business with his cousins who worked in the diamond mines.

The taxi rumbled into Kindia, and David disembarked, gathering his two suitcases, two shopping bags, and a sack of rice. He found a driver going to his village, and sat on his pile of baggage, fanning himself with a *Jeune Afrique* magazine, otherwise still as stone while the remaining passengers assembled.

Much of his cargo comprised groceries: rice, a box of sugar, peanut oil, two cans of tomato paste, three dried barracudas for the family. He had clothes for the youngsters, all with logos of Western companies and words in English. He had a pair of blue jeans for his eldest cousin, Temu, a pit supervisor at the mine. David's suitcase also contained five stone statues, each the size of a small milk carton, one of which had been carefully hollowed out and plugged at the bottom.

The driver indicated he would help David pack his belongings into the back of the Peugeot station wagon and bind the sack of rice to the roof rack. As they did, the last passenger to Kaala arrived. The passenger was a boyhood acquaintance of David's, Mbaye Touré, who had introduced David to Issa Moleng years ago in Conakry, just before David worked at the British embassy. Touré sold hardware supplies for all manner of government and private projects. David greeted Touré with his usual reserve and asked about his family. David offered Touré to enter the taxi first, which he did without acknowledgment.

"Did you know, Mbaye, that Issa Moleng was killed in a taxi accident a few weeks back?"

"I did, David. Yes, I did. Very tragic."

"Yes, it was."

"Were you and Issa still working together?"

"Not for some months now. We had a good partnership for a year, but he wanted to move on to something … more grand."

Mbaye laughed and shook his head. "That was Issa. Always looking for something better than he had, never satisfied. I hope he has better now than what he had on this earth."

David stared straight ahead, nodding.

"And you, David Semba, are you still working with the British, then?"

"Yes. I'm a private consultant."

"And exactly what do you consult to them?"

"Commercial opportunities, mostly for private companies."

"Ah, you must have some very good connections, eh, David?"

"Some."

"I tell you, my friend, any commercial business is very difficult, very bad these days. You must pay off everyone you meet, or else you can get nothing done. My trading business is still just scraping by after six years. I have to pay off the police, the electricity company, the transport drivers. Everyone has their hand out. It is very discouraging."

David knew this to be less than accurate. Mbaye Touré's family was distantly related to President Sékou Touré and was accorded a number of contracts and back-door deals that others were unable to get.

Shooting a weary glance out the window, David shifted in his seat while the taxi lumbered along the dirt road to Kaala.

"Perhaps," Mbaye said, "you can introduce me to some of these British companies you represent, yes? They must certainly need hardware supplies, tools, pumps, generators. How can I help them?"

After a few seconds, David said, "It may be possible, once they decide what projects they find most appealing. One company is investigating a rice plantation. One is thinking of building a new cement plant. But I doubt they will invest, given the current climate. If you were not Guinean, Mbaye, would you be starting a business in Guinea?"

"Only with the government as a partner, my friend. But if your British investors do want to do business with the government, I can help."

"I'll make them aware."

"Yes, David, please do. And please stop by to see my family while you are here. My car is being repaired, so I will be in Kaala for a few days. Please."

"Thank you, Mbaye."

The taxi passed rusting carcasses of old trucks and huts for mango-picking migrants, now vacant until the season returned. A sheet-metal sign, hand-painted in faded black lettering, marked the turnoff to Kaala. Cattle and sheep walked languidly along the route, prodded by the sons of their owners, barely noticing the automobile as the driver turned from side to side to avoid hitting any hoofed village wealth. They went by a bar and a grocery store, and then came to a courtyard surrounded on three sides by family compounds and a mud-brick Catholic church at the far end. The courtyard soon flooded with people to see who the travelers were. Among them were David's cousin Temu and his son, Jean. The taxi came to a halt.

The two relatives managed to get all of David's cargo to Temu's compound in a single trip. This was David's home. He grew up and attended primary school here. By the time his father and older brother went to work in the bauxite mines of Tougue, David had already been given the chance to attend school in Conakry. The family had broken up, but David had returned regularly to Kaala. He brought back tales of school and academic competition at the university, of the great wealth of France, and the purple fields of lavender that blanketed the alpine foothills. He told young and old about the clean, mechanized society that ran with precision and purpose, the tarred roads, and trains that kept to schedules. He told of the distracted, distant people.

David took the next hour to walk around the village to greet everyone he could think of. He was comfortable with the greeting rituals that often devolved into repeatable pantomimes. They were nevertheless a social glue binding him to his extended family and community. He and Temu visited the compounds of nearby relatives.

For the village chief, David always had a gift. Today he presented a small portable radio with an extra set of batteries, to replace the old, green, shoebox-looking one that had been broken and idle for months.

The cousins returned to the Semba compound for dinner and business. Awaiting the evening meal, the men sat in David's two-room hut, Temu on the couch, David on the large easy chair, next to which was his bag with the five stone statues. David jumped up to latch the door.

"Did you have any difficulties?" David asked.

"One of the pit diggers may be skimming for himself, but he has nowhere to sell his stones without drawing significant attention. I don't trust him. Since I am the manager, I must investigate, and if I find stones on him, punish him."

Settling back in the easy chair, David said, "Do so without hesitation, cousin, but be measured. The owners must continue to trust you."

Temu nodded. He reached into his jacket pocket and took out a cloth sack the size of a man's fist. Pouring the contents onto the table, he looked at David with a smile and a puffed chest. The careful gathering of small, individual stones over the last four months had yielded an impressive collection. The stones seemed little more than a pile of dirty quartz, none larger than a finger digit. But David knew this pile of nearly forty rocks was worth more than half a million US dollars before they were cut. He was very grateful to his cousin.

"This is excellent, Temu. But I must again say, please be careful. Would this amount be missed?"

"You know me, cousin. I am a simple man and I, with you, am the provider for this family. It is only Dugue and me, and we only take one stone at any time. We do not select the best nor the biggest. We take only what falls into Dugue's hands. We do not choose."

Dugue was David's other cousin who also worked at the mines as a pit digger. Because he had worked at the mines for over ten years, like Temu, Dugue was in charge of a crew and a specific area of the pit. The exchange of a single stone was made after the day's chips and tailings were washed and sifted by hand. Dugue was responsible for pouring the sifted rocks into a metal box that would then be locked and taken to the inspection station, where armed guards oversaw the next stage of separation. Dugue was watched by the supervisor, in this case his cousin, Temu, during the process. When he poured the stones out, he had one hand on the bottom of the hopper and sifted small stones through the tops of his fingers, which then fell into the palm of his hand. After the pour, Temu would inspect his cousin in front of other mine officers and then send him back to the pit. As often as not, the stones they captured would be worthless.

As Temu returned the diamonds to the cloth sack, David opened his bag and took out a small zippered purse from which he pulled a single banded stack of one hundred US twenty-dollar bills, the true currency of Guinea. He handed the stack to Temu. This was twice Temu's yearly salary at the mines.

"Spend little of this, cousin."

"As you have told us, David, we will not be calling attention to ourselves."

David nodded.

"We have seen the results of greed and flamboyance," Temu said. "They will only get us killed."

David reached over and patted his cousin on the shoulder. The two men stood and hugged each other. David placed the sack of diamonds in the bag with the statuary.

A knock at the door was followed by a woman's voice. It was Geema, Temu's wife. "David Semba, you have a visitor."

This was to be expected. David was a local celebrity.

"We will be out shortly," David said. He placed the bag at the bottom of the armoire, next to his bed, closed the door, and latched it.

When the cousins walked out of the dark hut and into the light, David's taxi companion, Mbaye Touré, was standing in front of him, smiling like a cat, with his brother, cold-faced and large, next to him.

After a perfunctory traditional greeting, he said, "David Semba, I'm sure you remember my brother Moti."

David did, of course. Moti was a somewhat belligerent man, prone to anger quickly but also to settle down reasonably. He had been a bully as a youngster, though he was not slow-witted. His older brother Mbaye, who had always been the more ambitious and politically active, had schooled his younger sibling on how to intimidate without resorting always to violence, how to watch people, and how, from time to time, to leverage people. David trusted neither of them. Temu and Moti had been alternately childhood friends and enemies who, these days, respected each other and kept their distance. Moti worked as a truck driver for a contractor who transported supplies to the mines, much of which were purchased from his brother Mbaye Touré's hardware supply business.

Mbaye Touré continued his smile and addressed Temu. "We've come to pay our respects to you and your cousin, whom we have not seen in many months," he said with congeniality. "Moti tells me it is a long time since he has seen you, as well, Temu. And yet you both live here in Kaala. How is this possible? It is time to rekindle old friendships, I think."

They all shook hands without looking at one another. Temu welcomed the guests and bade them to enter his hut, located on the other side of the compound.

Mbaye hesitated, saying, "Would it not be fitting for the recent arrival to welcome us to his hut?"

Temu was perplexed and then annoyed. "Is my hospitality not worthy of your visit, Mbaye Touré?"

The smile never left Touré's face. "Not at all, Temu, not at all. I thought the occasion of his rare visit might offer David the opportunity to host old friends."

Temu started to protest again, but David spoke to his cousin softly. "Please don't be insulted, cousin. I'm sure Mbaye meant no disrespect." David looked squarely at Mbaye, inviting him to confirm the assessment.

"By all means, no disrespect at all, Temu," Mbaye said.

David continued his leveled look at Mbaye. "Yes, I'm sure you have other objectives, isn't that right, Mbaye?"

"Only to catch up with old friends, David. This is a social call, I assure you." Mbaye's smile edged down slightly.

"What? No business? And here I was, most certain you had business on your mind. Forgive me."

Moti was beginning to get impatient. "If you want to talk business, we surely can. You must need local partners since Issa Moleng is gone."

David had surmised as much. Mbaye was one of the people with whom Issa was most likely in contact and it was probable that Issa would have sold any diamonds directly to Mbaye or to a third party that Mbaye introduced to him. But how much did he know about the smuggling operation? Not much. If Mbaye was Issa's contact, he could still go no further in the chain than David himself. Nevertheless, this was a dangerous situation. David needed to understand it better. If Touré believed David was smuggling diamonds, it would be easy to connect the theft of the diamonds to his cousins who worked at the mine.

Touré said, "My brother is always hoping to find opportunity, David, but I don't think this is the right time to speak of business issues. Do you?" He castigated Moti with a glare.

David decided to learn as much as he could right now. "Temu, please ask Geema to serve us some drinks in my hut. Let's then speak socially, as you say, Mbaye. You must first tell me of your family. Please, come in."

The four men settled into the chairs where, moments ago, David and Temu had talked.

Stories of old friends and characters from their past came easily from Touré. He was relaxed and disarming.

The women came in with bottles of Fanta, plastic glasses, and a small bowl of ice from a nearby merchant who owned a kerosene refrigerator. After they poured their drinks, Mbaye continued, engaging Temu with questions of recent events, to which Temu responded pleasantly but with an unusual twitch in his shoulders. David listened, nodded, or shook his head.

"And how sad the death of our friend Issa Moleng," Touré said after a prolonged lull.

Everyone agreed.

"I sent Ditaba something to help cover funeral expenses," David remarked. "I was distressed that I could not attend his interment."

"How thoughtful of you," Touré said. "Alas, I was unable to attend as well, being away for business. I heard Ditaba was the very picture of poise in grief."

"I'm sure she was."

"Tell, if you will, David, what had Issa's arrangement been with you, exactly?"

"Issa was a logistician. He would help procure and transport various equipment and supplies as may have been needed by my clients. He was a freelance operator. I'm sure you must have done business with him recently."

"No, no. I'm sure I would have remembered. Issa and I hadn't spent any time together recently and certainly no business for over a year."

"Really. That is peculiar of him, I must say. When I told him that our project was nearly over and that the British company would no longer need his services, I'm sure he mentioned that he was fine since he would be working with the Touré Supply Company." David looked for any sign that Mbaye was nervous or confused by David's fabrication.

He only shook his head. "That could not have been the case. I would have known."

"One of your managers, perhaps, set him up with other contacts." David sipped his Fanta.

"Quite the opposite, actually, David. I thought he was working for you right up until his accident."

"Really, Mbaye. And why would you think that?"

"That's what I heard, anyway."

"But you just heard from me that was not the case. You now have your information from the source."

Touré scowled slightly. "Yes, I have. I always go to the source. That is exactly what I do."

"Good, then." David was convinced that Issa had told Mbaye something more than he should have, and that Touré was trying to leverage that information. David finished his drink.

It was Moti's opportunity to speak. He spoke slowly and glanced at his older brother. "David Semba, we are people of your village, people you have known most of your life."

David stared expressionless at Moti.

"If there is any business with which you need assistance, we are here."

Moti shifted to the edge of his chair and continued. "I work in transport, as you know, and my older brother is respected and knowledgeable, not just in the supply business, but in the people business. We hope there is an opportunity to work together. You are a man of action, David, as are we, men of action."

"Indeed," David said with only the slightest trace of scorn. "The truth, gentlemen, as I have said, is that the projects with my British employers are coming to an end. In the near future I would certainly like to uncover more business, so that is my plan at the moment."

"Are you intending, then, to return to Conakry right away, or will you look further afield, Dakar perhaps? And does that mean you will be leaving us soon?" the older Touré asked.

"After a week, maybe. It is difficult to say, of course, as I have, only hours ago, arrived. I very much want to spend some time with my family for now." David stood up. "We shall see each other throughout the week."

Temu in turn stood up. David stood silent and motionless. After a long thirty seconds, Mbaye rose to his feet.

"I'm certain there is more to tell us, David," Mbaye said. "And it can surely wait until we see each other through the week. I return to Conakry myself in three days. Perhaps if your family business is concluded, we could go to the city together."

"That is a thought," David said.

As the two brothers walked over the threshold where David was now holding wide the door to his hut, Mbaye gave David a crooked smile that made him cringe. The thought of doing business with such a man who looked out only for himself, for whom the fortunes of others were simply fuel tanks waiting to be siphoned, was distasteful.

After the guests took their leave, David spoke to his cousin. "Temu, I will need to leave for Tougue before the sun rises."

"Won't that make Mbaye more suspicious, cousin? I'm certain he will be back tomorrow. Aren't you?"

"Oh, indeed I am. But I am clear in my mind it was him Issa was working with, in one way or another. He knows we had business with Issa that we did not discuss. But it is hard for me to believe Issa told him very much. Issa was a craven, self-centered man, but he also knew that he could not give too much away to someone like Mbaye, who would cut him out at the first opportunity. Issa must have held enough back. Mbaye is still wondering exactly what we are doing and how we are doing it. When he arrives on the compound tomorrow, let him know that I had to leave for Faranah, where the British and the French are building the new technical university. I've gone there to find new business and have some contacts there. It is irrelevant whether he believes you or not. He will not try to follow. But he will try to use his contacts to see what I'm up to. I will return here by way of Faranah."

"That is a very difficult journey, David. I cannot go with you."

David laughed. "I'll be careful, cousin, and I'll use the time to think. Is the truck ready?"

"As you left it here last May."

"Let's check everything now and prepare while there is still light."

In the back of the compound was a small storage hut and a larger hut for keeping lambs and birthing sheep. The area smelled of dung and decaying earth. Between the two huts and at the very edge of the compound, against the wild banana trees, was a large mound covered by a canvas tarp. The two men pulled the tarp back, revealing an army-green General Motors Scout. It had two 40-liter jerricans of diesel fuel strapped onto rear-mounted cradles. The short wheelbase allowed for either passengers in the back or cargo, but not both. A winch was attached on the front, as well as a frame of black steel pipe on which were mounted a thick screen mesh for traveling through the bush and an extra set of headlights.

Temu went to his hut and returned with the keys to check the battery. David got in, pushed on the glow plug, and started the engine. With a slow, heavy turnover, the engine coughed to life and sputtered to a steady, chugging cadence. David looked at Temu and nodded. Temu opened the hood while David surveyed the tires and wheels, the undercarriage, and the exhaust, which was extended by an additional pipe rising above the cab. David silenced the engine and pocketed the keys. Temu closed the hood.

At his hut, David retrieved two small travel bags from his armoire and placed them on the bed. Into one, he placed clothes and toiletries. Into the other, he placed business needs including a machete, 10 meters of rope, two flares, a WWII pistol, and a box of forty shells. He then took the diamonds and the hollowed-out statue from his other bag and placed them on the table. David held the stone carving and looked at it with an understanding of the caricature it portrayed: a squatting man holding a cattle-herding stick in one hand and his penis in the other. How Fulani, David thought, referring to the neighboring tribe, to portray a man protecting cattle and his manhood. We Malinke are bound to the soil, not to hoofed meat and bones. David felt a sense of pride that the Malinke were at one time the most productive farmers in all of West Africa. But the hangover of colonialism had sapped their confidence and drive. Guinea was deteriorating every hour, every minute.

"I will never let myself nor my family down," David averred in a whisper. "Never."

Carefully removing the plug from the bottom of the statue, he observed that the space for the diamonds would not accommodate all the stones Temu and Dugue had amassed. Pouring the rocks into the cavity confirmed this instantly; the stones spilled around the filled statue, onto the table. David would have to make a hole in one of the other statues. He wished now he had kept the ice pick he had used to dispatch Issa. David's entire body shuddered as though a ghost had passed through him. He began to sweat. Taking deep breaths, he recited a poem to himself that he had learned in childhood while at St. Barnabas. It had become a sort of mantra for him as a boy, when his gift was treated by many as satanic.

The devil has no hold on me,
His bidding I reject.
My life remains a golden key,
God's blessings to protect.

David's belief in God had suffered greatly over the years. He had seen the slaughter of his fellow Malinke tribesmen during the rise of Sékou Touré, and knew God was an illusion. Had the vestiges of his belief metastasized into something else? Would he suffer for having taken the life of a venial, self-obsessed, and destructive man such as Issa? David could not answer. He could only endure the occasional convulsions welling from deep within and go on.

He searched for and found a small letter opener with which he scraped and carved out a space in the bottom of a second statue. He worked for thirty minutes, carefully avoiding weakening the statue's sides, before stuffing the last few diamonds in the bottom. He needed cement plaster to seal the cavity.

Rushing from his door, into the compound, David went to the storage hut where everything from sorghum to cooking pots to lambing ewes were kept. He spotted a small, half-used bag of Portland cement, which he picked up and brought to his hut. He prepared the cement and plastered the overflow diamonds into the second statue. Then, thinking that perhaps all five should look identical, he plastered the bottoms of all five statues and set them on their heads at the back of his sofa to dry. Satisfied for the moment, David rose from the chair and took off his shirt. He poured water into a basin and slowly splashed his head and face, taking long, slow breaths.

Geema called David to dinner an hour later as he was resting on his couch. On his way into Temu's hut, he passed the six children, circled around a large bowl outside, on the ground. Here, with his remaining close family, all healthy and bound for a better future, David felt a sense of accomplishment and peace.

After the meal, David said good night to all. Tomorrow before dawn he would make the journey to Tougue and meet for the first time a white man he was supposed to trust with results of his family's hard work and risk. This will not be a simple matter, David thought. The man will have to prove himself; prove that he can be trusted with the treasure he is to courier; prove he would not take greater risks than would David himself; prove he would divulge nothing of his association or activity to anyone, under any circumstances. Why, he asked himself, would a stranger agree to such things? How could he possibly know the meaning of this venture to David and his family? To know utterly that this man could be entrusted with his family's future, David needed a test to prove Mr. Byrnes had the fortitude and character to see this through. If he failed the test, David decided that Tony Hume and Nigel Blake would bear responsibility for their poor judgment.

* * *

At 4:00 a.m., the sound of a diesel engine rumbled through the forest like distant thunder. It pierced into the sleep of many in Kaala but did not awaken them.

When the muffled chug reached the sleep of Mbaye Touré, he became quite awake, though he remained still.

David Semba is leaving early, Touré surmised. He is a very elusive man, a clever man. But he will be exposed, Touré assured himself. Then we will do business.

40. Home Away from Home

Lost in her planning, Doria was oblivious to the bumps and jostles of the drive back to Ziguinchor. She wanted to tackle problems that on the surface, at least, appeared less severe and perhaps less difficult. So many ailments attracted little attention from Western pharmacology. Some of those ailments nevertheless had severe consequences for the sufferers: short attention span, inability to focus, dyslexia, delusional behavior. Doria was convinced that as the diseases had sprung from nature, so must the cures, even though they were inexplicably hidden. The mental disturbances of the children of Yoff remained heavy in her thoughts.

The heat and steady rhythm of the car passing over the thinly paved roads under Iba's steady hands occasionally made her drift into a fitful, dream-laden sleep. She recalled Nigel's fanciful good-bye, singing Cat Stevens' "Oh, baby, baby, it's a wild world. And I'll always remember you like a child, girl." Another man might have tried to restrain her or could have erupted with vitriol; another man might have succumbed to a lashing violence as the loss of control gnawed at his self-image. But dear Nigel had watched helplessly. He had tried so very hard to be happy for her. Doria was undergoing a change that must frighten Nigel, both for his powerlessness to intervene and for the distance this change seemed to take his wife—to a destination where he had not been invited.

She dreamt of Alain DeLevres and his role unlocking her resolve, providing a way to pursue her sublimated passion for medical botany. This round, curious man, intelligent and driven in much the same way as Doria herself, had much still to offer her work. He could be a mentor, he could be a cohort, or he could be difficult. Perhaps all of these.

Her dreams edged toward another man, full of energy and physical longing, full of adventure and chaos. A man who could help in so many ways. Doria felt a sense of warmth as she imagined Victor close to her, working by her side, neither acolyte nor knight. Doria allowed herself this fantasy without worry. It was only a dream, after all.

But quickly this dream dissolved into something different and unexpected. She saw the face of an African man, kind but forlorn, rising above her as she realized she was seated on the ground. This man put his hand on her head and said words she recognized but did not understand. She felt at ease in his presence, while brimming with an apprehension of something unknown. What is all this? she asked in her semi-awake state. What is this about?

The Mercedes bumped over a deep pothole that jolted Doria fully awake.

"So sorry, Madame," Iba said, gripping the wheel more tightly. "The road has turned quite bad here in the south."

"We're in no hurry, Iba," Doria assured him. "Please take it carefully."

Doria sat back and gazed outside. The landscape had turned from the muted green of the flat savannah, drying from the cessation of the rains, to the dense green of the hilled forests where the rains persisted. Nature's chemical plant, she thought, where the heat and the water and the minerals come together in imagination-defying combinations, driven by a principle, by an energy in all matter that vibrated to the frequencies of our universe. And those frequencies can only be the manifest will of the unknowable God. Doria was steady in her belief in the goodness of the world around her, derived from an all-powerful presence in everything. She believed it was the perversions of mankind's ego and lust of self that brought evil into the world. Most of the suffering endured by humans could be traced to our inability to reconnect with the natural world after our original fall from grace: the rise of self-consciousness.

But how was she ever to reconcile the existence of immense brutality with a permeating spirit of vibrant life? Doria found it difficult to form an idea; she nevertheless felt that nature is the result of an infinite number of infinitely small vibrating particles combining or not combining on the basis of a few undecipherable rules. Could it be that this universe, only one of an infinite number, had no predilection for harmony or reconciliation, no differentiation between good and evil? Wasn't it more likely that this universe was simply a machine, not governed or moved by anything other than the imperative to evolve sufficiently to know itself? She smiled and admitted to herself, I am completely off my nut.

She glanced at her fingernails and realized she would need to keep them much shorter than usual. The thought of neglecting them altogether was downright perverse. Maintaining her appearance in this near jungle of a town where she would be working with all manner of plant materials, making mushy liquids and pastes, might be written off as simple vanity. But keeping oneself kempt was a matter of personal organization and, in this land, critical to maintaining hygiene and health. Taking care of her appearance gave her a sense of dignity and structure.

The hills surrounding Ziguinchor were laden with the deep green of banana and papaya trees spreading like hands over the land. Too helter-skelter to be plantations but too collected to be random, the semi-wild vegetation dominated the land from whichever direction one entered the city. As densely interspersed as they were with stately palm trees and hulking baobabs, it was clear Ziguinchor was blessed with fertile soil, water, and sunlight. Iba steered over the main road and slowed the Mercedes. Though they had departed Dakar at 4:00 a.m., Iba and Doria both silently applauded the decision. Unlike their last trip when they arrived in the dark, today there was more than enough daylight illuminating the lush city.

Though she could stay at the Hotel Du Sud for months, it was obviously not possible to work there. And she had no intention of trying to set up even a rudimentary laboratory on Mady's compound.

"Iba, tomorrow our first order of business will be to find a place for us to stay and work. Once we have that moving, we will need to make sure the banking arrangements are satisfactory. Then we can start exploring the city of Ziguinchor. How well do you recall the city, Iba?"

"Well enough to start us, Madame."

"Good. Please take us to the hotel straightaway. We shall unpack and begin setting up shop." A sense of contentment fueled a playfulness that she couldn't remember feeling in quite some time.

With much daylight available, she focused on a place to rent. She had something specific in mind. The front desk clerk seemed to have trouble understanding Doria when she asked if he could direct her to a real estate agent. Eventually, with Iba's intercession, the young man understood and, without expression, motioned in a direction and mumbled the name of a street and a man, Monsieur Didier.

The only relation of Monsieur Didier's office to the directions from the hotel clerk was that both were in Ziguinchor. Iba and Doria searched for over thirty minutes, burning daylight as they stopped pedestrians and bicyclers, interrupted shopkeepers, and halted fellow motorists. Along the way they learned that Monsieur Didier was the product of a Lebanese father and a French Senegalese mother. He had been raised in Marseilles, France, coming to Ziguinchor some years ago. Eventually the pair found Monsieur Didier's office, advertised by a large white sign that read: *DIDIER – LOUEZ, VENDEZ, ACHETEZ, OU RENTREZ.* (RENT, BUY, SELL, OR GO BACK.) What a welcoming enterprise, Doria mused. She was beginning to think her first impressions of Ziguinchor as a friendly city might need updating.

As Doria and Iba approached the entrance, the door opened and a roundish man with café-au-lait skin and a crop of tightly curled dark hair walked through and turned to lock the door as he left.

Doria called to him, "Monsieur Didier? You are Monsieur Didier, yes?"

The round man turned without completing his task and stood as erect and tall as his five-foot seven-inch frame would allow. "Indeed, it is. Aziz Pasquale Didier at your service. And whom have I the pleasure of addressing?"

Doria did not recall the last time she heard such perfect and formal French spoken to her. "My name is Doria Blake, and this is my driver and friend Iba Yagg. I am hoping to rent a suitable lodging here in Ziguinchor."

"If I may, Madame, Ziguinchor has no lodging suitable for one so elegant and refined." He bowed slightly, and Doria thought he might take her hand to kiss it. He did not.

This shameless flattery, the opposite of her experience with the hotel clerk, intrigued her. She smiled politely and asked, "Might we come into your office, Monsieur Didier, and talk of the type of dwellings you have available?"

"Alas, Madame Blake, I am already late for an important appointment. Would you be able to return on Friday?"

Three days hence. Doria was not interested in putting this off. "Truly, Monsieur, there is a good deal of urgency to my request. Tomorrow would be far better and would mean a great deal to me. I would be most grateful. Please, sir."

"Quite impossible, I'm afraid. I am expected in Cap Skirring tomorrow afternoon, and the drive to the coast is still somewhat treacherous."

Doria had been with Nigel to Cap Skirring a number of times. It was a beautiful tropical refuge with two world-class hotels. During the rainy season it was accessible only by private plane. He could be going there for pleasure or business. Doria considered her options.

"Perhaps you could give me the addresses and descriptions of some of your properties so that I might explore them on my own? I truly cannot wait three days, Monsieur, without making progress. We were told you were the only man in Ziguinchor with whom we should do business."

Didier glanced at his watch and let out an exasperated breath. He glanced at the parked white Mercedes, then at Doria. "Please come inside, quickly then, and let me make a phone call."

Iba indicated he would stay with the car, but Doria insisted that he accompany her inside Didier's office. Crossing the threshold, she hardly felt like she went indoors at all. The air remained humid and thick. Vast green plants in brightly painted planters formed a tropical grove along the dark tiles. Overhead the ceiling vaulted in thick panes of glass covered with gauzy curtains to restrain but not restrict the light. The scent and sense of this interior brought Doria back to the forest.

Didier led them through double French doors, into a large office that struck Doria as schizophrenic. On one side was a beautiful ebony desk with legs carved as giraffes, atop a distinctive Persian rug. The desk held not one scrap of paper. The walls were interspersed with genuine and possibly exceptional African sculptures and European paintings.

On the Mr. Hyde side of the room, chairs were strewn helter-skelter around a table on which were four large stacks of blue folders, each spewing papers. Additional stacks of folders sat on the floor and on two small coffee tables. Books of various kinds sat in stacks rather than in bookshelves.

"And which office is yours, Monsieur Didier?"

He did not immediately understand her. He glanced around, picking up his phone, and smiled. "Alas, Madame Blake, it is all me. But I owe the serenity of this part of my office to the wonderful Madame Didier."

He tapped the phone cradle three times and dialed. "Margarite? Aziz. I am with a client and will be thirty minutes late. ... Yes, truly, only thirty minutes. ... No, please wait. ... Of course, I have. ... Thank you." He hung up and faced them. "Voila, I have bought us some time, though not much. Please sit and tell me what you are looking for and your price range."

Doria gave exact details of her imagined layout and size, the minimum amenities. Didier smiled and took notes.

"I think that covers it, Monsieur Didier. What do you have for me?"

"Alas, Madame, Ziguinchor is not Dakar, you know? There is little new construction, so the few good buildings are quickly taken, yes? And to get the space you are asking for ... I don't know. I will have to ask around. It is possible that from among older villas built by the French or the Scandinavians before independence, there may be something."

"I truly don't need a villa. I simply need good space for both my living and my work. And, of course, quarters for my ... for Iba."

"Precisely," Didier said, indicating that they did not understand each other.

Didier suggested that he take Doria to see a few properties that were or would be available, and she agreed.

The two places they visited were run-down concrete buildings with chipping plaster exteriors, questionable plumbing, yards that had been unattended for years, inoperable electrical switches, and roofs that looked as though they would collapse with the next gust of wind. Doria had been certain she would have seen the gem underneath the years of neglect from among these properties. But one was next to a tavern and another had an open sewer running by it.

"*Du courage*, Madame," he said, consoling Doria as he prepared to leave her. "Friday is another day and we will find you something, yes?"

"I hardly intend to give up on the first day, Monsieur. But I will certainly be searching on my own while you are away. Iba has some family and friends here, so we will continue to explore. Shall we agree to meet again Friday morning, say, nine?"

An expression resembling fear and then introspection crossed Didier's face. "If I can get away earlier, Madame Blake, how shall I reach you?"

"I'm at the Hotel Du Sud. Call or leave a note anytime, Monsieur Didier."

"Very good, then."

They shook hands, and Didier sped away in his rattling Peugeot.

Doria looked at her chauffeur. "Do you think, Iba, we can do better on our own? Can you reintroduce yourself here and help us locate a suitable place?"

"I can, Madame."

"Let's try."

Iba drove to the fabrication shop where he had worked when he lived in Ziguinchor many years ago. He was not surprised to see the industrial area still humming, neither larger nor smaller than when he had made the 14-kilometer bicycle journey from his cousin's village every day. The road was poorer, yet the businesses appeared intact. Scores of people were walking home from the plate glass manufacturer or the brick works. At the far end, the street dead-ended at a canning factory, and just before it, Iba steered onto a driveway flanked by a corrugated steel fence. FORGERANT D'EXCELLENCE read the sign (QUALITY METAL FABRICATION). And underneath: PAPPA CONTE, *PROPRIÉTAIRE*.

The grounds were filled with metal and asphalt scraps. Iba drove past bays of various works in progress: steel-frame beds, pots and pans, large metal gates, piles of door hardware. At the near side of the main building three men were welding and cutting large sheets of metal. Iba pulled up in front of the sign that read: GÉRANT (MANAGER). He walked straight in without knocking, and Doria followed while she glanced around.

Moving past an empty desk, Iba opened the closed door on the other side of the room. Seated at a cluttered desk was a man reaching for papers as he cradled a phone between his shoulder and ear. He was speaking at light speed, mixing three languages—French, Djiolla, and Oulof. He glanced up at them and continued his conversation, reading from a retrieved document and nodding his head. He managed to motion Iba and Doria to sit on the well-worn wooden chairs in front of his desk.

In a quiet tone, Iba said, "The owner is Pappa Conte, Madame. This is his son, Mustapha. Tafa, we call him."

"Does he remember you, Iba?"

"Oh yes, Madame. He remembers me."

Tafa finally hung up the phone and stood up. Everything about him was long: his fingers, his arms, his torso, his face. Tafa extended his hand.

"I'm sorry, I am very busy at the moment and it is late in the day. What can I do for you?" He spoke in French as he took Iba's hand to shake.

"Tafa, I am Iba Yagg. Do you remember me?" Iba spoke to him in Djiolla and held on to Tafa's hand with both of his own.

"No! It is not possible. Is it truly you, Iba?" He smiled broadly and pumped his hands furiously. His smile then turned to a deep frown. "But Iba Yagg, where have you been and why do you leave so long ago, so quickly? Were you being hunted by the police? We never saw you again. Very bad of you!"

While Doria sat quietly, understanding nothing, the two men spoke for ten minutes. Doria could see it was getting dark. She cleared her throat. Iba turned and recalled why they were there. He gestured to Doria, who extended her hand to Tafa as Iba introduced her.

"Tafa's father, the owner, is not well these days, and Tafa runs the operation. His family has been in Ziguinchor for many generations."

"Too many!" Tafa interjected. "What brings you to our sleepy city, Madame?"

"I'm doing research on medical plants and natural remedies found here in the Casamance, in Guinea-Bissau and Conakry. We need a place to stay for maybe a year, where I can set up a laboratory and where I can live, that has a place for Iba, as well."

"Iba can live anywhere he likes, Madame Blake. You, however, I think will have more limited choices."

"Can you help us locate something, Mr. Conte?"

"I am Tafa to my friends, Madame. And yes. Well, maybe. We will see. But you must come to dinner tonight! I invite you."

Doria was familiar with these impetuous and genuine invitations. They were hard to refuse and time would be completely elastic. But what better way to start building a local network and learning about Ziguinchor? They agreed to follow Tafa to his home, so long as he allowed them to drive to a grocery store first to pick up a few things.

* * *

The Conte compound was in a section of Ziguinchor inhabited by prosperous local families and European workers, mostly French and German, some of whom were international aid workers, others of whom were businesspeople with deep ties to the commerce of the region.

After Iba and Doria were introduced to the extended family, including the ailing Pappa, Tafa's young wife, Yessa, led Doria into the kitchen. Yessa was an educated woman, a mother of two boys, six and five, and a daughter, three, and with a dream to become an artist. She had designed and made the tapestries and tablecloths on display in the home. Doria held the daughter, Fatu, who played with Doria's hair and spoke the few words of French she had learned.

"So, when Fatu or one of the boys falls ill, Yessa, what do you do?" Doria asked.

"There is a clinic close by, where there are nurses and two doctors. They are very good."

"What do you do for medicines?"

"There is a pharmacy in the center of town, and the doctor will tell us what we need. They will write it on a piece of paper, and the pharmacist will find it. But often they do not. And it is always expensive."

"Do you worry about malaria?"

"We live with malaria all the time, Madame. Though many of us do not get very sick from it, others do."

"Do you and the children take anything to prevent getting it?"

"There are medicines, of course, that we take if we are sick with the disease. I'm told malaria does not kill us Africans the way it kills Europeans."

"That's not always so, I'm afraid. What I meant was, do you take any medicines to keep from getting the disease? Something you take when you are healthy, so you stay healthy."

Yessa looked puzzled. "We don't take medicine when we are healthy, Madame. What is the point of that?"

Rather than continue her explanation, Doria asked what she had wanted to all along. "Do you use traditional healers and locally made medicine?"

Yessa looked down and hesitated, not wanting to answer. "We do sometimes," she finally said.

Doria realized she had been playing the role of inquisitor, indulging her curiosity but forgetting her host. She changed the subject to the dinner they were about to have and how hungry she was. Yessa smiled and returned to the stove, where an older woman, Yessa's aunt, had been laboring over the meal.

Normally the women ate separately from the men. But in deference to their guests, the Contes set the meal around two large bowls in the center of the table, for the entire family.

Over the meal, Iba mentioned to Doria that Tafa and Pappa had some property ideas for them to investigate the next day. They included contacts for leases and consulting on the local laws and customs. Pappa warned that even the best people would try to take advantage of newcomers, particularly those thought to have money. A blond British woman with a chauffeur-driven Mercedes would certainly qualify as someone thought to have money. Pappa suggested using his name with the individuals they would meet in the coming days.

"And keep Iba close at all times," he advised sternly.

When the main course came to an end, Pappa placed his hand on Doria's arm, preventing her from rising to help the other women clean up. "It is good to have new people come to Ziguinchor," he pronounced. "Yes, I think it is very good. But it is not true that all people of Ziguinchor believe this. You have come a long way, Madame Doria, not just from Dakar, but from England. Why do you come so far?"

Pleasantly surprised by this straightforward question, Doria said, "I've come to learn how to create better medicines from the materials found here in the Casamance. I'm hoping to find the ingredients for these remedies among the plants of the rain forest."

Pappa Conte reflected on this. He said, "Unlike my neighbors, I am not a superstitious man. I believe what I can see, what I can smell. What I can taste and touch. But I know much is hidden to me. There are many things that exist in the world which I cannot see. What are the natures of these hidden things? That is difficult to say. Can they be unlocked and known? Many people claim they can. Some of these are good people of purpose and some of these are people in search of power and control."

At the other end of the table, Tafa listened to his father and said, "Pappa has become a philosopher in his old age. I believe that is the right of every old man, isn't it, Pappa?"

"Only those who actually think and don't just mouth what their neighbors tell them!" was the older Conte's reply. He returned his attention to Doria. "Why do you seek this knowledge?"

Doria would have thought this obvious. "To help the people, of course, particularly the children. There is so much poverty and disease across all of Africa, Pappa Conte. Western companies may donate doctors and nurses, but mostly they are selling medicines to governments and communities, that simply cannot afford them. And I also believe that Western drug companies aren't that interested in the afflictions of Africa, so there is little development of new medicines that can address things such as sleeping sickness or river blindness."

"Such indignation from a rich woman. And on behalf of people she lives among but isn't a part of."

The people at the table appeared to have no sense of the likely offense these words had conveyed. Doria suddenly had an overwhelming feeling of isolation. Except for Iba, not a soul within 200 kilometers of her chair spoke her native tongue, let alone enjoyed clotted cream with strawberries or had read D. H. Lawrence.

She took a moment to compose herself, and replied, "And shouldn't the Senegalese be the indignant ones, then? Why are there no organized African medical societies exploring and experimenting with new treatments when treatable and curable diseases take thousands of lives every year? Where are the African scientists passionate about uncovering the secrets of the land and creating better communal health? Am I just missing them, Pappa Conte?" She paused and put a fork full of rice and peanut sauce in her mouth.

The old man sat, smiling, as though he had heard nothing.

Doria continued. "You have traditional healers everywhere, selling herbs and concoctions in the markets, but the traditional healers act more like priests, or worse, shallow money-grubbers, it seems to me, protecting secrets, promoting themselves rather than the health of their communities. Or perhaps they're closer to charlatans, really, creating and feeding off the superstition *you* have admirably outgrown."

Pappa Conte sat back in his chair and looked at his guest with a smile that expanded over his entire face. "Bravo, Madame Blake. Though you are still learning, I see you are passionate. This is wonderful, of course, but I am curious. Why are you so passionate to help our people?"

Doria had never pursued the answer to this question. But she had looked deeply at her own motivations. Part of it was an acute sense of justice and fairness, so inequitably distributed in the world and in short supply. However, there was a more personal reason. From an early age Doria had believed in herself and wanted to pass along a capacity for reflective and honest self-confidence to her children—children that she had come to realize she could not have. Did she consider, then, the children of Senegal as her own in some way, or at the very least, as the outlet for her maternal instincts and needs?

Her answer to Papa Conte was simple. "Because so much is possible when children are healthy."

"And your children, are they healthy?"

"I don't have any children of my own, Pappa Conte."

"You are still young, Madame Blake. You have time."

"Thank you," she said, and smiled. "Thank you ... so much."

Yessa and her sister cleared the table, and Tafa revisited the issue.

"There are traditional doctors who are serious people, Madame Blake. But they guard their knowledge. It is used for power and money. And, as you say, there are the false doctors who prey on the weak-minded and desperate. Personally, I think your goal is a worthy one. But I would ask you two things. One, please forgive my father. He may not be superstitious, but he is suspicious. The French were very eager to take whatever they could from our land in the name of helping the poor Senegalese. The Chinese and Russians have proven no better."

"There is nothing to forgive, Tafa. Pappa Conte is a concerned and wise man. And a challenging one, I must say!"

"Second, please do not do your work in isolation. Please seek out an African and work with him or her."

"It seems your father is not the only wise one at the table, Tafa."

Doria considered that Mady Toula was more businesswoman than healer, and Doria wanted to work with someone with greater skill, who possessed a vision as wide as her own—wider, even.

That person, concerned for his own mortality and legacy, was in fact looking for Doria at that very moment.

PART 4:

CONFLUENCE

41. Into the Breach

As dawn slowly brightened the sky of southern Mali, the distant mountains appeared like smoke over the horizon, apparitions of splendor, mystery, and beckoning. Leah Genescieu was taking in the view from a flat precipice high above their Manantali campsite as she slowly stretched her limbs, banishing the torpor of her sleep. Her morning exercise routine was stabilizing, especially here, so far from home. The view made her long for the mountains of Romania, where the dense rock clusters and steep white carpets of snow suffused the Romanian spirit to a rugged, brooding mysticism. Here in the warm, moist air of Mali she felt it was too easy to float away, disengage from the gravity of her soul, and soar untethered, high into the wind and light, until she evaporated into a billion disconnected molecules. She inhaled deeply. This was indeed a dangerous land, she reasoned.

Her ritual served as well to stretch out the aches and stiffness of the long journey to the site of the future dam, a journey that took two weeks and included stops along the way to accommodate the other scientific teams, now four strong, in as many Land Rovers. Some of the stops had been quite interesting from her perspective as an ornithologist, and others, more interesting simply from the strangeness of the culture. Still others were interesting for the unfolding disaster one observes from a point of detached safety.

The entire camp awoke as the sun peered over the horizon. Victor stood beside the cooks as they prepared a breakfast of instant coffee and tea, baguettes, and peanut butter. He told them to try to purchase or barter for some eggs and fish at one of the surrounding villages. Their diet of dehydrated and canned foods was less than satisfying.

Victor looked around the campsite, hands on his hips. The four Land Rovers were parked in a neat row facing the river, about 15 meters farther from the bank than when he had last set up camp. He still shuddered when he recalled that trip.

With all of the scientists heading in different directions today, it seemed the right time to venture across the border, into Guinea, to meet his contact in Tougue and try to get Doria's fire flower. However, his sense of unease about leaving his primary duties and heading to a completely unknown area kept him from a firm decision.

According to Nigel, Victor had exactly three more days to get to Tougue, meet his contact, and pick up the package. The contact would be leaving on Friday, regardless of whether Victor showed or not. Today was Monday.

Events in Victor's life seemed like riders in a bicycle race, sometimes orderly, following one after another, but as often, overtaking and colliding with each other, distorting the order and realigning outcomes. It was only yesterday when the entire troop had been in Mahina early in the morning, and Victor thought it prudent to stop in on Chief of Police Swaray and swap information. …

* * *

This trip, Victor was charged with the safety of eight scientists, both men and women, plus the drivers and two cooks. Once in Mahina, the troop was surrounded quickly by the curious and suspicious. Many had likely never seen a white woman before, let alone three.

Leaving their charges to explore the town on their own, Victor and Mammadu paid a visit to the police station and to the chief, in particular. The desk clerk was joined by an upright man with an air of authority, who surveyed Victor and Mammadu. Victor explained why they needed to see Chief Swaray. The upright man announced that the chief would see them soon and to please sit down and wait.

Mammadu brought out a green apple from the side pocket of his smock shirt and handed it to Victor.

With a laugh, Victor said, in English and in a low voice, "How did you know, my friend?"

"Did you not tell me the story, Barbu, how you bought Swaray and his men with green apples when you first arrived?"

"You should keep your apple," Victor said, "and we'll see what Swaray does for us out of the goodness of his heart."

Mammadu laughed. "There is no goodness there, Barbu. He thinks only what can he get out of us and what will it cost him."

"Then we are on firm footing."

Mammadu smiled.

At that moment, Swaray shouted from his office, "Come in, come in, Mr. Byrnes."

Victor introduced Mammadu, who greeted Swaray in Malinke. Chief Swaray asked them to have a seat.

290 THE SIREN OF GOOD INTENTIONS

"So, your studies bring you back to Mahina with more people. And this time you have brought women with you."

Clearly, his spies had prepared Swaray while Victor and Mammadu had been waiting.

"One is a nurse. Another is a medical doctor and the third is a bird scientist," Victor informed him.

"What can I do for you this time?"

"I'm acting upon your wish to check in with you when we come to town, and we need your advice, Chief Swaray. We would like to know which villages you think could best benefit from our visits. And also, how do we explain to them that we need for them to give us samples of … their … well … their body fluids?"

Swaray cocked his head and stared at Victor for a few seconds. He pushed his chair away from his desk and stood up. At his metal cabinet, he pulled out a rolled-up map from among a dozen within. He spread it out over the desk. It was an administrative map, not a topographical map. It showed the serpentine Bakoye River and the villages on either side, all the way to the Guinea border and into Guinea itself.

"There are many villages along the river, though you will find none along the riverbank itself. Too many problems—bad insects, hippopotamus, I'm sure you know," Swaray stated.

"We know," Victor said.

"I suggest you consider Bao, here, just above the dam site. It has about eight hundred people. The others, here and here, too, have about three hundred to four hundred, depending on the season and how much work there is in the mines."

"Which mines?" asked Mammadu.

"The bauxite mines in Tougue. Also, there is another village … here." Swaray pointed to a village named Tchode, in Guinea. "That is about the same size as Bao."

Swaray sat down, put his elbows on the desk, and rested his chin on his clasped hands. "Gentlemen, what do you know of the border between Mali, here, right here, and Guinea?"

"Only what it shows on the map," Victor said.

"You, Mammadu, African man. What do you know of these borders?"

"I know, Chief Swaray, that they were not made by African men."

"Indeed, these borders were drawn by French surveyors in the early 1800s. This land extends from the north of Mahina, right down to the mountains of Guinea." Swaray stated this as one might read from an encyclopedia. "Did the French ask us what nation we were, what boundaries we wanted for our country? They did not. My people, Monsieur, are on both sides of the border. Those mines are in *our land*, and yet we Malinke derive very little benefit from them, save the slave wages paid for working there. Sékou Touré keeps all the wealth on his side of the Frenchmen's border. We, on the Malian side, get nothing."

"Then," Victor said, "perhaps this mythical dam, as you have called it, will be something for the Malinke to embrace as a source of wealth. It is supposed to bring electricity and many jobs to the region for many years."

"Yes, much of that would be welcome. But my experience tells me we must fight to get what we deserve. Otherwise, it will be taken from us."

Victor was getting uncomfortable, even though Swaray never showed a hint of emotion. It was important that he refocus so he could get the troop back on their journey.

"Thank you for all your help, Chief Swaray. And there is something we can do for you."

Swaray looked at Victor, leaned over the desk, and pressed his face into his. "You have brought a doctor, as I asked."

"We have," Victor confirmed. "But we can stay only one day. We'll need an hour to set up."

All three stood, shook hands, and the two travelers left.

* * *

Victor had remembered the policeman's request from months ago only at that very moment and hadn't confirmed with the health team that it was possible, let alone within their research parameters to conduct a one-day clinic in Mahina. He had to move quickly.

Gwen Wong was easy to find. The three women had decided to stick together. When Victor noticed a large group of children milling about the entrance to a small grocery store, he ran up to the entrance. Inside, Dolores, Leah, and Gwen were at the counter buying canned pineapple juice.

Victor needed to involve the entire health team, rather than just the co-leaders. He asked Dolores and Gwen to meet him at the vehicles to discuss a possible addition to the health team's plans.

They thought it was a very good idea.

Dr. Ham was more elusive. Getting directions had proven challenging for Dr. Ham since he spoke no French. Nevertheless, he persevered, gesturing to people walking along the street that he might be ill, holding his stomach as if in pain, hoping this would get him directions to a clinic. As people asked in broken French if he was hurt, they pointed him in a general way to medical help. He managed to zigzag his way to a small office front whose sign in French read: *Médecin traditionnel, guéris garanties* (Traditional doctor, cures guaranteed), below which was a list of the most common ailments one might seek from a local healer: headaches, stomachaches, impotence, infertility, and unrequited love.

Dr. Ham opened the door and walked inside, then nearly choked from the smell he encountered. Not that the smell was so bad, but it was intensely strong, like someone had burnt a powerful incense in a closet. His eyes started to water, and he turned around to get outside and catch his breath.

Mammadu caught up with him just as the doctor was dry heaving outside.

"Are you all right?" Mammadu asked in English.

"No … thank you …. Mammadu, I'm not … all right. Soon, I hope!"

Mammadu couldn't fully understand this answer, so he simply continued with his mission. "Victor needs to see you now."

"Well, Victor can damn well wait a few seconds until I can breathe and walk again!"

Still, Mammadu didn't understand Dr. Ham. But he did understand tone and he was not too appreciative. The doctor was clearly in pain, so Mammadu waited in silence while the doubled-over doctor recovered.

Victor found the other four men as they returned to the vehicles. They couldn't say where Dr. Ham was. Victor was also thinking of the clock. He wanted to get to Manantali before dark, thinking of some of the more treacherous parts of the journey. He went off in the direction given to him by Tekkendil, shouting Mammadu's name.

Mammadu eventually heard his name in the distance and shouted back for Victor. Dr. Ham lifted himself upright, putting his hands on his hips, but did not yet move forward. Victor found the two men standing motionless on the street.

"What the fuck …?" Victor said out loud.

When Victor reached them, Dr. Hamilton Laird was almost indignant.

"Are we leaving so soon? What's so important that you needed to send your man here to find me?"

Victor noticed that Dr. Ham's face was very pasty, almost green. "Are you all right, Ham?"

"Yes, yes, of course I'm all right. Just a close encounter with a voodoo effluvium, that's all."

"A what?"

Dr. Ham pointed to the office of the traditional healer. "In there. Go see for yourself. Well, *smell* for yourself. It's overpowering, Byrnes. I'm forewarning you."

Victor read the sign and became intrigued. "I wonder," he said as he walked to the shop and slowly opened the door. Although he did not immediately step in, the same invisible cloud started to wrap around Victor. He held the door open to let outside air mix with whatever it was inside. Leaving the door open, he took a few steps into the office and called out, *"Monsieur le Docteur! Monsieur le Docteur. Êtes-vous là?"*

There was a bit of rattling behind the wall at the far end of the reception area, and then came a response.

"Oui, je suis là. Qui êtes-vous?" ("Yes, I'm here. Who are you?")

"Travelers from America," he answered.

Without delay, a shirtless man with a gray goatee and shaved head walked into the room. Though Victor was squinting and holding his breath, he could see the man was dressed in traditional Chaya pants and sandals, with four leather amulets called "gre-gres" hung around his neck. The belief was these warded off evil of various kinds, kept people safe, or attractive, or made one potent. There was a gre-gre for nearly every human wish.

"Why are you here?" demanded the healer.

With this powerful aroma swirling in Victor's nostrils, thinking wasn't easy. He put his hand up to his face and took short breaths through his mouth.

He said, "I was told to look for a wise man who could help me."

"Were you, indeed?"

"I was. I am. I was told that only a wise healer could tell me where I could find a fire flower."

This produced a startled and puzzled expression on the healer's face. "Why would you, white man, want to find a fire flower?"

"Because a special doctor said that this fire flower can help make medicines of great strength. Medicines that can help many people."

"Yes, it can," said the healer, who seemed to relax. "Yes, it can, white man. The fire flower is a rare and powerful plant. Where is the doctor who will use it?"

"The doctor is in Senegal, in the city of Ziguinchor. Do you know where I can find a fire flower?"

The healer came closer to Victor, looking him over, his posture full of curiosity and suspicion. "They are very difficult to find, very few places, and two days' journey from here, into Guinea. Are you willing to make such a trip?"

"I am."

Pulling at his goatee, the healer paused and studied Victor. With a sniff, he said, "Then you will pay me 500 CFA, and bring a fire flower back to me as well, if I tell you where you may find them."

"Yes, healer, I most certainly will."

The healer took a few steps toward the greening Victor, threw his head back, and laughed. "So, you do not like my preparation of *shalla*, heh?"

"Of what?"

"*Shalla, shalla!*" the healer said, more loudly each time, as if that might improve Victor's comprehension.

"Oh. Of course … *shalla*."

"My *shalla* is quite potent, and women who have never had babies will come from villages all over just to get *shalla* from Siepo Deng."

Victor nodded and then returned to his point. "Where can I get the fire flower, Siepo Deng?"

"Come outside." Deng put an arm around Victor and led him into the fresh air, where he saw the waiting comrades. "Are these your friends, white man?"

"Yes, they are. My name is Victor."

"Veektoir. Yes, Monsieur Veektoir, will they help you find the fire flower?" Deng asked, pointing to Ham and Mammadu.

"Only the African man will. The other man is a doctor from America."

With narrowed eyes and down-turned lips, Deng regarded Ham. "Western doctors know little of the ways of the Malinke. They believe we are savages. Thanks to the gods they leave us alone."

"He is here to learn, Siepo Deng. We are all here to learn."

"You have promised to bring me back a fire flower, Veektoir. Say it again."

"I promise to bring you back a fire flower, Siepo Deng."

"Very well, then. There is a village in Guinea called Tchode. There is a woman named Mosa Deng. Like my name. She can take you to the only place where you can find the fire flower. You must pay her what she asks. Whatever she asks. Pay me my 500 CFA now, then come to me when you have your wish," said Siepo Deng.

Veektoir obliged.

Walking back to the Land Rovers, Hamilton Laird demanded, "What on earth was that all about? How did you manage to stay in there for so long?"

"I was forewarned, remember? Forget about that voodoo doctor for a second. I need to ask your team something."

Everyone assembled at the Rovers for a group discussion, with as many as sixty children surrounding them, standing silent and watchful.

"We have a request from the chief of police for the health team to conduct one of their surveys and clinics here in Mahina. I'd like to know if this is possible and, if it is, under what circumstances."

Instantly, Denali Tekkendil spoke. "I can see why that might be an appealing enterprise for some, but I can't say that it will in any way assist me in my work. Perhaps my epidemiologist colleague has a different view."

Dr. Ham said, "Well, a couple of things to think about. A humanitarian gesture as it may be, I don't think it will add greatly to our mission of collecting data in the immediate dam area. Also, we haven't coordinated anything with local health officials. How many toes would we be stepping on if we suddenly set up a free clinic for a day? And wouldn't we be overwhelmed?"

"Strictly from the position of supplies," Dolores Knapp said, "I can't imagine that we'd have enough to run our work for more than an hour or two in a large town like this. And frankly, if our material usage rate along the river in Senegal is any indication, I'd be surprised if we had any supplies left on the way back."

"And there's no chance of us doing it before we explore upriver," Victor said, in full knowledge that the mission couldn't be compromised by using a good portion of their supplies in Mahina.

"But," Dr. Ham said, "there must be something we can do. Perhaps we can do something in conjunction with the local clinic rather than on our own. Also, maybe if we focused on, say, maternal health, or children under a certain age, we could have some control."

"That sounds fine, Ham," Gwen Wong said, "but I'm thinking it would be very interesting to see if the disease reservoir profiles differ significantly in the town from those of the villages upriver. If that were the case, with all the new facilitated traffic from Mahina into the dam area, it could mean some significant changes in disease profiles, infection rates, and morbidity. Without a baseline profile for Mahina, it would be impossible to foresee. So, my preference would be to include as many people as possible."

"Assuming," Dolores Knapp reminded them, "that we have enough supplies to carry out our sampling."

"OK," Victor said. "We'll simply have to make that call when we head back in a week. If we were to do something on the health side—whatever that something might be—say, for one extra day, would that be a problem for the other disciplines?" He glanced at the group members.

"Not for me, per se," Doug Borden replied. "My work is exclusively in the immediate dam site and it's data and sample collection. No analysis, for the most part. If we were back here for an extra day, I could lend a hand doing something for the health team."

The rest of the scientists nodded in agreement.

Victor took a step away from the group and said, "So let's keep that in mind. Ham, would you mind coming with me to see Chief Swaray. If we're going to pull this off, we will need him to help coordinate with the doctors and nurses at the local clinic."

"I never did see the clinic," Ham said. "But what might be very interesting would be to interview the health professionals there and find out what they're dealing with—besides a tremendous dearth of resources."

After explaining the plan to the drivers, Victor and Dr. Ham disappeared into the police station, where they were given an immediate audience with Chief Swaray. Victor told the chief of the possibilities and willingness of the team to help, but that there could be no guarantees of any significant assistance.

Swaray smiled, appreciative of the effort the team was making. "Our little outpost of Mahina gets very little attention, save from the railroad people in Bamako. Please do what you can."

At Dr. Ham's prodding, Victor explained to Swaray the need for communicating and working in conjunction with the local clinic.

"We have one doctor, who is shared by the clinic in Djoudaba, about three hours away by car or moped. I will speak to the nurses, who will appreciate even the smallest amount of additional assistance."

Dr. Ham asked, "Will the local traditional healers be angry? Will they see us as taking away their business or spreading false or bad medicine?"

"A few will undoubtedly resent your presence, Doctor," Swaray said, as Victor did a simultaneous translation. "But many people, superstitious as they are, have not been helped by our traditional medicine and would welcome, shall we call it, a second opinion?"

This made Victor chuckle and he translated. Dr. Ham smiled and nodded.

"We will come by here as soon as we return, Chief Swaray. With your permission, we'll set up where we did the last time," Victor said.

"For a single night, yes," Swaray said in all seriousness. "We will look for you in eight days' time." Swaray rose and offered his hand to Dr. Ham, who took it and shook it vigorously.

Victor shook Swaray's hand and met the eyes of the chief of police. They were steady and dark.

"I wish you well," the chief said. "And for a safe return to Mahina."

* * *

The trek to the Manantali site with four Land Rovers took nearly half again as much time as it did ten weeks earlier. That experience paid big dividends. With his drivers and the help of Orson Limber's skill reading a topographical map, the logistics team flagged a different path, taking advantage of a wide crevice nearly a mile out of their way. The new road proved much more level and had only two large boulders and a few trees to navigate around. The extra two hours were well worth every second in unspent adrenaline for all travelers.

Victor and Mammadu estimated it would take four hours of nonstop driving to get to Tougue, bypassing Tchode on the way and stopping there on the way back. He doubted they could make it all in one day, even if they started before dawn. They would have to stay the night. Since they would need all the daylight they could get, they would leave the next day and use today to make sure all the scientists had everything they needed to be productive, fed, and safe until they returned.

Victor first let Leah know, since she was already at the table eating breakfast while the rest of the troop was still getting dressed. Her response was nonchalant.

"As long as the cooks have what they need for our meals and making fresh water, it sounds fine to me. Are you scouting out that village in Guinea the health team was considering?"

A perfect cover. "That was the primary reason. I'm also trying to gather a very specific plant sample for a botanist friend of mine."

"Should you not take Roger with you? He's an agronomist and all."

"I think his work is primarily upriver from here, rather than downriver. Also, I don't believe what I'm looking for is edible." But Victor really had no idea.

"I can observe birds in this surrounding area for a week. This is no problem for me."

Victor was able to get similar answers from the others, until he spoke to the health team.

"We're considering moving down to Bao in two days," Gwen said, speaking for the team. "You have to be back by then to help us with packing up the generator and our makeshift lab."

She was not making a request. She was informing Victor of his duty. He would have to supervise the packing with Tekkendil and Wong. With these assurances, Victor and Mammadu planned to leave very early the next day to rendezvous with David Semba.

* * *

While the track was level for the most part, it was overgrown with thick shrubs or disappeared over a field of boulders between the large trees that blotted out the sun. Mammadu insisted on driving. Victor was happy to let him. Every so often they would stop, clear brush away from the truck's radiator, and check to see if the way was clear or if the brush hid a tree trunk or large rock that might smash their vehicle. They saw families of baboons making their way through the forest. Thatched roofs of village huts occasionally appeared in the distance, but the path never led directly into a village.

They came to a large stream that fed the Bakoye River and stopped to be sure they could cross. A large splash echoed from the river, so they decided to investigate. After a short walk, they saw a man pounding a stake into the ground, to which was attached a long rope that disappeared into the deep part of the stream. Mammadu greeted the man, who smiled in a broad, dark-toothed grin.

"This man is a fisherman," Mammadu explained, "and he wants to sell us some fish."

"Yeah, that would be great. But we can't today. Will he be here Friday afternoon?"

After an exchange with the fisherman, Mammadu said, "He is here every day, Barbu."

"OK, then. Let him know we will definitely purchase some fish on the way back. What kind of fish does he have, exactly?"

The fisherman went to one of the lines he had in the stream and pulled it in. At the end of it was the biggest catfish Victor and Mammadu had ever seen. It was over a meter long and had a mouth larger than a man's shoe.

"Holy shit!" Victor exclaimed. "That will feed us for a week. Fantastic! Does he usually get fish this large, Mammadu?"

The fisherman beckoned to Victor to come over to the stake he had just finished hammering into the ground, and motioned for

Victor to help him pull it in. Not imagining it would take both of them, Victor picked up the line and tugged on it. It hardly moved. The fisherman laughed, then joined Victor with both his hands and the two men hauled in the line. Suddenly the maw across the glistening black-whiskered head of a gigantic catfish broke the surface.

Victor reeled back on his heels and fell flat on his backside. "My God! What a fucking monster!" he yelped.

The head and mouth were as wide as the other fish was long. The monster fish was two meters out of the water and still had more than a meter of tail in the water. The catfish was bigger than the sharks Victor had seen as a kid on the Jersey shore. Mammadu's eyes widened liked a child's. The fisherman let go of the rope, which Victor could see went through the monster fish's mouth, out the left gill, and was tied to a tree branch too large to slip back through the gill.

How could this fisherman possibly have done this by himself? Victor wondered. It was such a strange experience, Victor half expected the catfish to talk to him.

Instead, the fisherman looked at Victor, still on the ground, and, blocking the sun with a dark silhouette, he said in French, "Feed your whole village, 2,200 CFA."

Mammadu choked a laugh and said back to the fisherman, "Feed your own village, fisherman. And pray your monster fish spirit doesn't poison you all!"

"Never poison, my friend. The fish spirit lives mightily in the Bakoye and is older than my grandfather's grandfather. You will buy the other fish?"

"When we return, fisherman. Two days."

Mammadu extended a hand to the still-sitting Victor, who had barely grasped what he had just seen. The two walked back to the Land Rover and climbed in.

"Every day is another surprise, Mammadu. Unbelievable. How do you think that fisherman caught and threaded that gigantic fish?"

"He hit the fish on the head, Barbu."

"But how did he get the strength to pull it out of the water and thread that gill line in him?"

"He never pulled the fish out of the water, Barbu. When the fish was unconscious, he went into the river with the line and put it on him."

"Of course. No mystery at all."

Fording the stream with steady acceleration, Mammadu guided the Rover through the fast water and up over the bank. Victor consulted his topographical map. They were very close to the Mali-Guinea border.

As Victor imagined, there was no way to reckon where exactly the border was until they were about two or three kilometers past where they believed it to be, marked by a stream on the map, but which was inexplicably a feeble drip meandering through a wide and, for the most part, dry riverbed. Since the rains had been substantial in recent years, including the present one, Victor could only surmise that somehow the drainage geology had changed and the water that fed this stream in the past had been diverted.

A few kilometers farther, they approached a small mud-block building with a corrugated tin roof. Near a flagpole with no flag leaned a faded hand-painted sign that read TCHODE, GUINEA. The two travelers exchanged a knowing glance and kept driving.

The road in Guinea had clearly seen more use than what they had traveled in Mali. And for the first time, people were walking along the side of the path with bundles on their heads or in their hands. Some people waved, either in friendship or in an attempt to get a lift. Others stared. Mammadu stopped to ask one of them if this was the right way to Tougue. He learned that most of these people lived in Tchode and other small, unmapped villages nearby. There was only one road and it led to Tougue, about 20 kilometers' distance.

Eventually, the road became strewn with pedestrians, and the travelers saw the first moped since Mahina. The road went from rocky and grassy, to a wide swath of hard mud, not enough to require four-wheel drive, but enough to cause the occasional fishtail when Mammadu accelerated. Clusters of small huts appeared, as did crossing paths marked by automobile tires. Like a fortress, the Fouta Djallon mountains rose in the distance, behind the deforested hills. Multiroom buildings, some with signs indicating commerce, became the norm. They had arrived in Tougue.

"This looks larger than Mahina," Victor observed.

"And different."

The perpetual sense of mold and decay of Mahina was gone. Tougue was a remote jungle town, but with a hint of prosperity, more than its train-stop counterpart 150 kilometers north. Along the road a number of pickup trucks and larger cargo vehicles hauled food and construction materials. It had the chaos and energy of a boomtown, without any obvious signs of wealth.

Mammadu stopped in the middle of the road and looked at his companion. "We are here, Barbu. What do we do next?"

"A great question, Mammadu. I wouldn't mind looking for a place to get something to eat and drink, would you? We've traveled nearly the whole day without any rest."

"I'm hungry. Let's get something to eat. Then we must see where we can make camp."

They asked a man holding onto a bicycle piled high with bananas where they could eat. He recommended the Restaurante des Voyageurs, farther down the road.

The mining town of Tougue swirled around them.

42. The Test

Perpetually restless and ever more so these days while waiting for an American stranger, David Semba paced the compound of his cousin. This compound had belonged at one time to David's father, who had died after nine years of working in the mines and sending money for David to go to school. His mother held on to the compound and had hoped in vain that her sons would join her. Five years later she herself passed on, so the property fell into the hands of the only male relative living on the compound, his cousin Fen.

For all of Fen's incessant tales of woe, he was industrious, working his way up at the mines so that after twelve years, he was a foreman. Fen was family and would work with David in nearly any endeavor David asked. But he did not trust Fen as he did his cousin Temu. Fen's loyalty, David assessed, did not extend beyond any economic benefit he obtained from David or anyone else. Fen was an independent agent, and family blood was simply one of the currencies in which he traded.

When one of the three boys David had employed to be his eyes on the streets approached the compound at a quick gait, David's nervousness subsided. Someone has arrived in Tougue. But there was a twist: two men, not one, in the Land Rover with a Senegalese license plate. One of them was an African man. This was concerning, but not yet suspicious. It was time to meet Mr. Byrnes and determine if this relationship was going to work. David left his diesel Scout on the compound and walked the kilometer into town, with his messenger following eagerly behind.

Naturally, Byrnes would go to the Restaurante des Voyageurs. David had eaten a few meals there over the last week and knew the clientele to be a mix of truck drivers, mine workers, and expatriate managers, mostly Russian and Scandinavian. The white men thought of themselves as the overlord class, acting like they were saving Tougue from hell by dragging it into purgatory. The Russians kept to themselves and hung out at the restaurant bar, insulting the locals at any occasion and becoming surly drunk three of the five nights David had observed them. The Scandinavians drank as well, but never behaved any differently than when they first entered. From what David observed, the Algerians didn't drink at all, nor did they treat the Guineans with any greater respect than the Russians.

David identified the Land Rover parked in front of the restaurant. He parted the red, blue, and yellow strips of plastic hanging in the doorway and stepped inside. The dining area was empty except for a white man and a black man sharing a table and drinking bottles of pineapple soda. The white man's face was wreathed in rust-colored hair. He was clearly young and seemed fit. The black man had on a sleeveless undershirt and his arms showed the precise definition of every muscle. His neck was sleek and his head shaved. He and the white man were speaking in French, and the black man laughed heartily, showing the most brilliant smile David had ever seen.

Mammadu noticed a well-dressed black man standing just through the doorway. The man seemed to be staring at him and Victor. Mammadu tapped Victor on the arm and nodded in the direction of David Semba. When the two seated men looked in David's direction, the Guinean man walked over and introduced himself.

In English, he said, "Good day, gentlemen. My name is David Semba. May I presume that you are Victor Byrnes?"

Victor stood and extended his hand. When David did not take it immediately, Victor used his gesture to offer David a chair at the table. Only when Victor confirmed in French, "Yes, I am Victor Byrnes, Mr. Semba," did David accept the offer and sit down.

Mammadu eyed him with indifference.

"This is my colleague," Victor announced, "Mammadu N'Diaye."

"N'Diaye *wye*," David said as he extended his hand to Mammadu.

The familiar rhyming greeting of his last name made Mammadu tilt his head. David continued his greeting in Oulof, asking about Mammadu's family, his fields, his cows, how was he sleeping, were his legs in good walking form. David's over-the-top greeting may have put Mammadu at ease, but he never smiled. The facility for language practiced by both David and Temu Semba was not lost on Victor, who surmised that David was every bit as out of place here as were the two of them.

David continued in French. "You have just arrived and you must be quite exhausted from your trip."

"To be honest, the road was long, but we've had much tougher journeys, haven't we, Mammadu?"

"Three flat tires on one trip between Bakel and Matam last year," he said. "But I think, Barbu, the new vehicles make a difference."

"So yes, we're a bit tired, but we still have enough steam to set up our lodging for the night."

David didn't understand.

"We're going to set up a tent outside of town. That's where we'll sleep and get an early start in the morning."

"That would be foolish," David said. "Tougue can be a rough city. People who have lost jobs in the mines are resentful—for good reason, to be sure. Because of the mines, Tougue is an oasis of wealth. This leads certain elements to resort to crime. The police here lift no finger to safeguard anything but their own pockets. If you camp out of town, you will be dangerously exposed."

This had the ring of truth for both travelers. "Where do you suggest we stay?" Mammadu asked as his eyebrows knotted and his eyes squinted.

"There are two guesthouses as you continue on the road out of town to Mamou. The one with the French name, Girideau, has a guard all the time, as well as a wall completely surrounding it. It is clean and has a good reputation," David told them.

"We can check that out later, Mr. Semba. Thanks. When would you like to conduct our transaction?"

David glowered at Victor and asked, "Are you having lunch here?"

Victor chuckled without humor. "Yeah, we'd like to, but it doesn't look like they're serving at this time of day. We were lucky to get these soft drinks. We haven't seen the waiter for fifteen minutes."

"If you can hold your hunger for another thirty minutes, why don't you try the guesthouse I suggested and you can return here for dinner together later."

"You will have dinner with us then?" Victor put a 100 CFA note on the table to cover the drinks.

David pushed it back to him, saying, "The official currency is the syli. The real currency, however, is this." He pulled out a money clip which he held below the table, from which he pulled a single US dollar bill. "You can use your CFA at the guesthouse, Byrnes, but if you have dollars, you will make more friends."

David rose from his chair. "And the answer to your question is no, I will not be joining you for dinner. But I will meet you at your guesthouse at dawn, just before you leave."

Victor nodded.

Mammadu and Victor stood up, Mammadu saying, "Thank you for the drinks, then."

David simply bowed in his direction. As the trio walked from the table, David pulled Victor aside as Mammadu continued to the Rover.

"What exactly are you expecting here, Mr. Byrnes?" David asked in English.

"I'm picking up some artifacts from you and taking them to Nigel Blake. I've got nothing to give you. I'm just transporting some statues, I guess."

"And what does your comrade know of your business here?"

"He knows that I'm picking up something for a friend. He doesn't know anything about the co-op or that we're trying to get art out of the country because of this new law. Nothing like that."

"It is very important for all of us that it stays that way, Mr. Byrnes. I tell you that the authorities could take this very seriously. The fewer people who know, the better."

"OK. Sure. I get that. Mammadu is not a problem. If anything, he's a great guy to have on your side. He not only speaks Malinke, but he was a champion traditional wrestler in Senegal. I wouldn't tell him anything to get him in trouble."

"That is wise. Now tell me, what of your route back? Did you encounter any border guards or soldiers?"

"We saw hardly a soul until we got just outside of Tougue. What looked like a border crossing at Tchode was deserted. But even if there are guards there, I don't think there's anything to worry about, David. I've got the border passage papers giving me permission to cross Guinea, Mali, Mauritania, and Senegal."

"So you believe, do you, that guards at one of the most remote border posts in the country, where everyone is exceedingly poor and the soldiers themselves haven't been paid for months, wouldn't demand some *baksheesh* to let you pass?"

"I'm not new to this, Mr. Semba. I know what it takes to get through shakedowns of all kinds, unmolested. I've been held at gunpoint by police. I've talked my way across borders all over this part of West Africa. And I know when I need to pay someone to get on with the show."

"But you *are* new to this, Mr. Byrnes. Until now, you have nothing for which the authorities could legitimately arrest you, am I right? Once you carry my package, you have crossed into unfamiliar territory. Your very confidence might be altered because now, you *do* have something to hide. You cannot make a mistake. Do you understand?"

Victor shifted his weight back and forth on his feet, and a shiver passed through him. At the Land Rover Victor took hold of the door handle without opening it.

"Look. We're not arms dealers here, right? We've got a benign package, easy to hide, and I have legitimate, official reasons to be anywhere in the river basin I want. If you think you can get someone else with a better chance of success, be my guest." Victor looked directly at David, who remained motionless.

David saw something in Victor he needed to see—a belief in himself. But it wasn't yet enough for trust. "I don't know that I can, Mr. Byrnes, and I have to know to whom I'm entrusting a rather important cargo."

Victor opened the door. Mammadu was sitting in the driver's seat, tapping on the steering wheel, anxious to get to the guesthouse.

In Malinke, David shouted, "And you, Mammadu N'Diaye. Would you trust this white man with something very important of yours?"

In French, Mammadu replied, "David Semba, you are wasting our time. If you have business for us, please, let's do it. If not, we will return to Mali. And you should know this: I trust no man with any ease."

David smiled at Mammadu. This block of a Senegalese man appeared stern and implacable. David thought how righteous and how simple he must be. So straightforward and understandable. David considered the virtues that earned the loyalty, the love, of such a man: courage, perhaps intelligence, willingness to act, all of which David possessed. But what of honesty, humor, and compassion? How important might they be to a man like Mammadu, and how did David measure himself in these? As he held Mammadu's glare against his own smile, David forced back a deep sense of need. So uncomplicated these two men are, he thought. So in love and so completely unaware of it. David pushed back a slight shiver. Were these men softer than they appeared?

For all of Issa's other faults, David thought, he had been very alert to the chaos in which he found himself and could navigate well through and around it. Were it not for his greed and arrogance, he might still be working with David. Another shudder passed through David Semba, leaving a sniff of remorse.

After his couple moments of consideration, David told them, "There is not much to do at night in Tougue, I'm afraid. But you can be safe and comfortable at the Girideau Guesthouse. We will meet there tomorrow at six fifteen, when the fresh bread is delivered."

David stepped away from the vehicle and watched the Land Rover back up and head in the direction he had sent them. Though he had no intention of personally joining them for dinner at the Restaurante des Voyageurs, he was certain their meal would be memorable.

* * *

A guard slid back a heavy steel gate to let the Land Rover enter. Mammadu parked in one of the spaces marked with large painted stones, next to a new Renault sedan. A number of large mango, bamboo, and acacia trees shaded the grounds. Victor and Mammadu ascended a short flight of stairs onto a stone porch protected by a thatched roof. They heard the rumble of a generator in the distance.

No desk clerk appeared when they entered. The temperature inside dropped enough to raise goose bumps on the arms of the men still sweating from the midday heat. Even after their eyes adjusted, it seemed dark inside. A still ceiling fan hung over a sitting area with a glass-and-bamboo coffee table, chairs, sofas, and cushions. Straw mats covered half of the stone floor. The other half glistened with moisture.

Mammadu clanged the service bell on the desk.

No response.

He repeated his chime after a minute. A few more quickly spaced requests, and then a small woman emerged through a beaded doorway. She smiled brightly and waddled up to the desk. In her best African French, she greeted her two guests.

"You come far, gentlemen," she said in jolly voice.

"Yes, Madame, we do," Victor said.

"You stay long?"

"Just one night."

"Wise. One night, plenty."

Victor looked at Mammadu. "Is there something we should know?" Victor leaned across the counter slightly, so that she could tell her secret safely.

"You have come from Manantali. One night in Tougue plenty." She chuckled to herself.

The two companions shrugged. She beckoned them to follow as she led them back behind the counter, to a corridor illuminated by a single incandescent bulb that was no more than a night-light. She indicated two rooms opposite each other and a shared bathroom at the end of the hallway. The whirr of the generator was louder here.

"When do you turn off the electricity?" Mammadu asked, knowing they would not waste precious fuel, running it through the night.

"Twenty-two o'clock," she replied.

They decided to eat their own provisions for lunch and then rest.

When they reconnected, they drove to a filling station on the main road, filled their tank, and headed back to the Restaurante des Voyageurs for dinner.

Three men wearing work clothes, looking as though they came from one of the mines, munched lazily on some chicken bones and argued over a bowl of fried manioc. The three of them stopped their interaction and looked up when Victor and Mammadu entered.

The newcomers took the table where they had been seated earlier and looked around for the waiter. Not only was there no waiter, there was no noise behind the doors leading to the kitchen. Then, as if a signal had been given, the clang of silverware from the other diners stopped. Victor noticed the three men had their arms on the table and were staring at Victor and Mammadu. Victor asked Mammadu to call for a waiter in Malinke.

"Waiter!" Mammadu shouted in French, and laughed. "Waiter!"

"Christ, Mammadu, I could have done that."

"Waiter," Mammadu yelled a third time, letting the word die in the humid room.

"Don't think he's coming," said one of the three Guineans from the corner table.

"Really?" Mammadu asked. "And how did you get served?"

"We're friends of the owner."

"Could you help us, then? We're hungry and just want some dinner."

The three Guineans stood up in unison and walked over to Mammadu and Victor's table.

One of them said, "No food here for you, I think. Maybe you should leave."

The hair on the back of Victor's neck stood up like wire. He looked around quickly, then got to his feet slowly, saying to Mammadu, "Maybe our friend here is right. Maybe we should go."

Mammadu didn't budge and nodded his head and eyes, indicating that Victor should sit down. He did so slowly, glancing at the three men who had now taken positions to surround the two friends. He noticed that two of them had machetes dangling from small rope belts at their waists. Adrenaline was starting to knot Victor's stomach. Mammadu sat expressionless and motionless.

The one of the three doing all the talking looked at Mammadu. "You, Senegal man. You want to stay and eat, do you?"

How, Victor wondered, did they know he was Senegalese?

The leader removed the machete from his belt and tapped the table with its tip. "You know, this is a very unsafe place. Bad things can happen to strangers who have no business here."

"We *have* legitimate business here," Victor stated. "We're looking for sites to set up a clinic, a medical clinic. And we're—"

With a *whack*, the man brought the flat side of his machete down hard on the table.

"Shit you speak, white man. You are like the others. You come to Guinea to take what is not yours, to make yourselves rich and leave us in stinking poverty. You rob our land, you foul our women, and leave us with fuck-all!"

As he finished, the man standing to the left of the table lifted his foot and kicked Victor hard just below the shoulder, knocking him to the floor. Victor rolled twice and brought himself up quickly, ready to run or fight, his heart pounding. The man with the machete raised it menacingly and turned to face Victor. Mammadu had seen enough.

Faster than Victor had ever seen him move, Mammadu thrust his chair back, knocking the third man over. As the machete-wielding leader turned to face him, Mammadu grabbed his opponent by the crotch with one hand, by the back of the collar with his other, and with one motion lifted the man over his head and held him there. As the man who had kicked Victor over started to pull out his machete and move to aid his leader, Victor stepped in quickly and elbow-punched him on the side of the head with all his force. The man's feet lifted off the ground and he fell in a heap. Mammadu shook his captured opponent up and down and then threw him directly on top of the third man, letting out a primal scream as he did. Victor grabbed the machete from the man he had knocked to the floor and held the point pressed to the man's throat. Walking with controlled rage to the heap of the other two men, with both of his hands Mammadu pulled the leader up by his head. The leader swung the machete wildly and hit Mammadu's shoulder a glancing blow. Mammadu brought his knee up swiftly to the man's groin and the fight was over.

"Shit!" Victor yelled. "Shit, shit! What the fuck is this all about!"

Victor handed Mammadu the machete he had taken. "We need to get the police. Where is the goddamn waiter or the cook or the owner, someone!" Victor ran to what he believed was the kitchen door, opened it, and yelled into the void. "Someone come here and help us, please!"

The empty kitchen returned barely an echo.

"What the hell is going on here?" he shouted to himself.

"I think, Barbu, we should leave," Mammadu said. He squatted on his heels next to the men he had vanquished without raising a sweat and held the two machetes in his hand in front of their groaning faces. "I will keep these as souvenirs. Come and take them back when you think you can," he said.

"Mammadu, leave them. Just leave the machetes, and let's get out of here."

"It is only right that we take weapons from the defeated, Barbu. We did not start this fight. We did not want anything but the peace of an evening meal. These cretins wanted to fight and now they have lost. I will keep their worthless claws."

Holding the two machetes in front of Victor as if for inspection, he took the smaller of the two in his right hand and put the larger one on the table. He grabbed the shirt of the leader, still recovering on the floor, and ripped it off him. The man stirred in protest, but Mammadu put a foot on his knee and the man gave up. His companion was slowly crawling back toward the kitchen door. Mammadu wrapped his right hand in the man's shirt and, holding the smaller machete in front of him with both hands, he began to bend it. The blade was rusty and brittle, bending hardly at all, until Victor heard a crack and saw that Mammadu had actually broken the blade in two. Mammadu tossed the broken top of the blade to the floor and tied the wooden hilt with the short, broken blade to his own belt, gaining his victory trophy. He then picked up the larger machete. When it refused to bend, he put the blade in the kitchen doorway and asked Victor to push as hard as he could against the door. As Victor did, Mammadu pushed the machete hilt toward Victor and slowly the large machete bent, splintering part of the door in the process. Mammadu continued pushing until the blade resembled a harpoon gaff. At the feet of his adversaries who were now slowly rising, he dropped the useless machete to the floor.

Mammadu looked the leader straight in the eyes, raised his index finger, and moved it back and forth as he shook his head. In Malinke, he said, "This was a crazy thing to do. Next time, I will not let you stand up ever again. Recover your brains. Go back to your family." The Guinean spat onto the ground.

He walked up to Victor and took his hand, at first to shake it, but then held on to it much longer. Victor's pulse was returning to normal. He put his left hand around Mammadu's shoulder, and the two companions walked out of the restaurant, into the steam of the evening.

From inside the hardware store across the street, David Semba watched and heard the two men walk into the fading daylight, holding each other and speaking in animated, terse sentences. Not one of the three men David had paid to put some fear into them had emerged. David was at once relieved and nervous. Victor and his Senegalese friend apparently passed this test of their ability to handle unexpected confrontation. It was reassuring. He could trust their courage and ability. Could he trust their character? Still, the package must leave with them tomorrow morning.

* * *

Victor and Mammadu went looking for the police station to report the incident, not with any expectation of action, but with the desire to be the first to tell their story before the locals had any opportunity to twist the account in their own favor.

The two friends told their story to a desk officer, who seemed to be the only person on duty. He raised his eyebrows a few times as the two men recounted the incident. A one point the desk officer closed his report book and turned to put it away among the piles of other report books.

"Don't you want to ask us a few questions?" Victor called after him.

Mammadu elbowed Victor in the side.

The desk officer turned back to face them. "Did you forget to tell me something?" he asked.

"No. No. I don't think so."

"Thank you. I have no questions to ask you." He turned back and placed the report book on one of the piles. The report had been filed.

Victor and Mammadu left.

Back at the guesthouse, they ordered sandwiches in the tiny dining room and consumed them voraciously.

"How did that guy know you were Senegalese?" Victor wondered aloud.

Mammadu shrugged. "People see. They assume. They talk. Our license plate is Senegalese."

"I guess," Victor said while still harboring the feeling that it wasn't enough. Next, he began to wonder about their contact, Semba, and what he might know. That would wait until the morning.

* * *

Victor awoke in total darkness. Without moving, he tried to recall a strange dream about a woman sitting in a huge yellow blossom like a cabbage. When she opened her mouth, crows flew out. Slowly he realized where he was. He glanced at his watch but couldn't make out the time. He was awake now. Throwing off the mosquito net and rising from the small bed, he went to the lone window in his room and opened it. The air outside had cooled slightly. Stars blazed in a glittering belt from horizon to horizon, disappearing into the contours of the treetops. Victor listened. There were no human or animal voices, no drums, no hum of distant engines. No guard, no lights that he could see. The black peace of nothingness. Victor shuddered. Thoughts of his own death slid into his mind. He wasn't just on some adventure in an exotic land, living heartily and strong from one event to the next. He was in the middle of forces of which he had no understanding, like a feather in the wind.

He listened again for the guard or intruders, but heard nothing. Then the sounds of the forest grew in a distant rhythm that was both reassuring and lonely. Victor closed the window and crawled back under the mosquito net, sitting up for a few minutes to try to feel what he was thinking, to try to touch and hold this strange and indefinable sense of immersion into ... what, exactly? What had his dream told him?

* * *

Mammadu awoke, claiming the shared bathroom first. Thirty minutes later, when the sun was not yet above the trees, Victor opened his door and shuffled to the bathroom. When he was dressed, he walked into the reception where Mammadu was speaking with David over coffee.

"You are up and ready, then?" David asked Victor.

"Up? Yes. Ready? Not until I've had a cup of coffee and some bread."

"I told David Semba, Barbu, of our visitors at the restaurant yesterday. They seemed very angry for no reason."

"There are many local people," David explained, "men, mostly, who have lost their jobs in the mines or have moved here hoping to find work, and learned life is very difficult in Tougue. They become desperate and lash out in different ways, mostly in crimes of violence. Robberies, beatings. It is quite terrible sometimes."

"And the police?" Victor asked.

"Yes, of course. The police," David said with a nod. "They are among those who get regular 'consideration' from the owners of the mines. They focus on protecting their interests. Did you really expect something different, Mr. Byrnes?"

"No, I sure didn't. But getting rousted by a trio of thugs. ... I guess I was a bit more hopeful, you know?"

"I can tell you that your reputations will only be enhanced in the town. Should you decide to return," David added.

Victor looked at him curiously. "I expect that once we complete this transaction, Mr. Semba, that will be entirely up to you and your associates in Dakar." Sitting down next to Mammadu, Victor helped himself to some instant coffee, a piece of fresh baguette, and some quince jelly from Belgium.

"I'm always amazed," he said, after swallowing a bite, "that you can find some of the strangest trappings of Western civilization in some of the most remote places in West Africa."

"Tougue is not so remote as you think, Mr. Byrnes," David said. "You have seen very little of this large village. The mines have brought prosperity to many, misery to some, and we have many 'guests' from all over the world—Russians, Chinese, English, Dutch, Swedes, Canadians, and of course the occasional American. They bring many amenities with them. Enterprising Guineans find opportunity when they can among this traffic."

"And you are from here, Mr. Semba?" Victor asked.

David replied, "I have family here, as do many Guineans."

Mammadu and Victor finished their breakfast. David left his coffee unfinished.

Mammadu was the first to stand. "It is time to go," he stated flatly.

Victor stood and David, as he rose, reached for a cloth satchel sitting beside his chair. Having settled their bill when they checked in, the three men exited the building and stood next to the Land Rover, ready to take each other's leave.

David held the satchel close to Victor. "This is more precious than you know, Mr. Byrnes. There are five small statues. They must all arrive together. Where are you going to keep them during transport?"

"Are they fragile?" Victor asked.

"No. Nor are they as sturdy as a cooking pot."

"I'm going to keep them right here in my bag," Victor told him, picking up his vinyl overnight bag from the ground and showing David an inside zippered pocket.

Victor took the satchel from David. It was every bit as heavy as Victor thought it would be, and perhaps heavier. It took all the space in the zippered pocket.

"They must arrive intact and together, Mr. Byrnes. Do you understand?"

"Yes, Mr. Semba. Yes, I do." Clutching the handles of the overnight bag, Victor climbed aboard the Land Rover. Leaning from the open window, Victor informed David, "I will deliver them to Nigel Blake. And Mr. Semba, I know you find it difficult to trust us. But I honestly don't know how far to trust you, either. I was recruited for this. I didn't volunteer. Let's just say that if this works out for all of us, we'll expect a warmer welcome the next time we see you, yes?"

Mammadu backed the Rover out of the guesthouse compound and left as David answered, "One thing at a time, Mr. Byrnes."

43. Lest Ye Be Judged

It wasn't exactly what she'd had in mind, Doria mused, but it would do—so long as she and Iba and perhaps her new friends, the Contes, could fix it up. The dwelling she had liked turned out to be offered through Didier. But it had been Tafa Conte who told her about the property. A concrete wall surrounded a compound of less than an acre, on which two long-neglected buildings stood. Nevertheless, a number of attributes attracted Doria. In particular, the two buildings made Iba's quarters reasonably independent. An old and flourishing flower garden circumnavigated the larger of the two structures, along with ample room for additional plant beds against the security wall. It had thatched roofs that appeared sturdy. The main house connected to a large storage and work space that would be ideal for a laboratory. The piping existed for the indoor plumbing, but Iba's tests revealed that much would need replacement. The stove was gas and the two empty propane tanks could be filled locally.

Doria had a difficult time getting Didier to convince the landlord to invest in the property to meet her minimum standard. The absentee owner lived most of the year in an apartment in Marseilles and took little interest in her deteriorating property. Didier, seeing a commission slip away, ran up excessive phone bills getting the owner to come to terms. In the end, Doria had agreed to pay for the walls and some new appliances, and the landlord would pay for exterior and interior repair to the structures.

The agreement, however, was only the first battle. Getting workers contracted, showing up on time, or at all, and keeping to a minimum level of workmanship was daunting. Were it not for the continued help of Tafa Conte and Iba, Doria might have given up.

When she was not project managing the construction, Doria organized her newly acquired worm-pocked desk with her files and DeLevres' notes. She set up a table next to the desk at an L to provide space for writing and consulting references simultaneously. She proclaimed aloud each day how grateful she was that Professor DeLevres had allowed her to take one of his notebooks to Ziguinchor. This was more generosity than Doria could have hoped for, causing her to speculate occasionally on his motives. Most often, however, she honored the favor by devoting herself to the work and keeping scrupulous records.

In addition, Doria spent time on her makeshift laboratory—the "jungle kitchen," as she called it. The space was dark, humid, and destined soon to be crowded with vegetation. She also expected to be "cooking" all manner of brews from her plant collections. A large window next to the door afforded a view of the garage and a much smaller window at the opposite end opened out to the barbed-wire-and-concrete security. Outfitting this space required replacing and augmenting the overhead lights, installing shelves on the rear wall, along with a sink and a gas burner in the existing workbench. Though the work was significant, Doria saw a near-perfect finished product in her mind.

During the second week, as she was carrying a box of recently purchased vessels and tools from her car, she noticed a man just beyond the iron gate, sitting beneath a eucalyptus tree and watching the activity inside the compound—watching *her*. She gave it only a fleeting thought, believing there was precious little entertainment or new activity in this subtropical town, so what was an old gentleman to do? Also, knowing that people are generally nosy, she was actually surprised there weren't more people clamoring along the perimeter of her new home, looking for work, looking for discarded household items, or just looking to see what the white woman was up to. Doria could barely make out the countenance of the old man, but she thought his face looked oddly blank, as if he was blind.

She saw the man every day thereafter, sitting calmly, staring into infinity. She never saw him arrive or leave. He was either there when she looked or he was not. It was odd that Doria didn't feel in the least threatened. Quite the opposite. She found it amusing and tried to see when he arrived or left. One early afternoon at the beginning of the third week, on a particularly hot day, she noticed the man under the tree and decided to bring him a cold drink and introduce herself. In the few minutes she went into the kitchen to pour a glass of cold guava juice and return, he had vanished. She vowed that she would simply approach him the next time she saw him.

Though Doria was certain that Mady Toula would know of Doria's return to Ziguinchor, she was relieved that the medicine woman had not come to visit. This gave Doria time to get organized, both physically and mentally, before plunging into the next round of plant collection and processing, and for coping with the irascible Mady. She hoped Mady's absence did not mean she had abandoned Doria, but if that was the case, Doria would deal with that once her other preparations were complete. She felt it an extraordinary coincidence that within hours of deciding that her structures were in place so she could begin the true enterprise for which she had uprooted her old life, Mady appeared at her gate in the company of the old gentleman.

Doria threw up her hands and greeted Mady. "Mady Toula, *ini chay*?" ("How are you?") She held Mady by the shoulders and bussed her on each cheek. Mady smiled and hugged Doria as a child might hug an aunt she was forced to visit.

"Madame Doria, how good to see you. I am well, thank you. And you?"

"I'm a bit tired, I must say. There's been so much work to do. Please come in and let me show you around. And who is this fine gentleman you have brought to my house?"

Mady made no move forward. "Madame Blake, this is Mbattu Sisay."

Doria extended her hand as she brushed some of her hair from her face with the other. "How do you do, Monsieur Sisay. You are welcome. Please come in."

Neither guest moved. Sisay did not extend his hand. Instead he tilted his head and stared at Doria.

She put a hand to her throat and took a step back. "Dear me. Well, would you … care for something to … to drink?" she asked.

Sisay moved his cane from his right hand to his left and extended his hand to Doria. "Madame Blake, I am honored to meet you. Mady has told me much about you."

As she shook his hand, she looked straight at him. "And you must certainly have made some observations of your own as well. Did you enjoy watching the progress as we tried to transform this old compound?"

"Yes, I did, Madame Blake. You seem a very determined and energetic woman."

"How well you know me already, Monsieur Sisay. Would you like to come in and have something to drink?"

Mady looked at Sisay, whose gaze fell only on Doria. He continued to hold Doria's hand and now placed his other, still holding his cane, on top of their clasp. "We cannot stay, Madame. We are here to invite you."

"Invite me indeed. That sounds delightful. Yes. Might I extend the invitation to my friend and driver, Iba?" She turned and gestured with her free hand to the yard, where Iba was directing two workers installing pipes underneath a large plastic water tank.

"Perhaps Iba may join us another time, Madame. I would first very much like to get to know you."

"How thoughtful," Doria said slowly. She gently pulled away from his hands, noticing how worn and cracked they appeared yet how soft they felt.

Mady said, "Mbattu Sisay, Madame Blake, is one of the most respected elders in Ziguinchor. He is a master healer. Some say he is the most knowing healer in the land."

Sisay bowed as Mady spoke the words he had instructed her to say.

Doria's eyes widened. "Dear me! Well, this is certainly an honor, Monsieur. I have so much to learn from someone as wise and experienced as yourself."

To this, Sisay simply nodded and continued to hold Doria's eyes with his own. She was now very curious about this man and returned his gaze with near equal intent.

"Where and when would you like me?" she asked.

"Mady will come for you after sunrise tomorrow and lead you to our compound. Please plan to spend the whole day with us. I promise you will find it most educational as, I'm sure, will I."

Doria gulped. "Monsieur, that is such short notice, really, for an entire day. We have scheduled to finish and test our water system and meet with two other contractors—"

"It is time, Madame Blake, to learn what you have come here to learn, no? Your man Iba is capable to carry on for a day, I'm sure, while your true journey begins. Mady will be here after sunrise tomorrow."

Sisay turned and began to walk out the gate as Doria watched without further protest. Mady looked at Doria with a hard-set mouth, but with eyes that seemed plaintive and uncertain. Doria stared back at her with an unformed question on her lips. Before a word could pass between them, Mady turned and fell into a slow gait behind Master Sisay.

What a strange encounter, Doria thought as she walked back to the house. Seeing Iba from the corner of her eye, a thought occurred to her. This man had investigated Doria long before he introduced himself. It might be wise if Doria undertook an investigation of her own before attending whatever event Monsieur Sisay had in mind.

Taking Iba aside, she recounted the details of the meeting and dispatched Iba to ask in town and elsewhere, what sort of man Mbattu Sisay was, what he did, what he cared about, what did people know of his ethics, what about him was rumored, and what was observed fact. Though there was very little time for this task, Doria felt that any information Iba uncovered could blunt surprises that may lay in store for her. Iba understood, and went into town on foot.

The clear western horizon was turning a soft purple when Iba returned. Doria was still in her work clothes and putting tools away. The workmen had long since departed for the day. She welcomed her companion-servant.

"Iba, you've been gone such a good long time. I was beginning to worry what I might do if you did not return shortly after dark."

"I am here, Madame Blake. And I have learned things of Mbattu Sisay."

"Indeed," Doria said.

"Mbattu Sisay is indeed a powerful man."

"Is he really?" Doria led Iba back to the veranda, where they could sit as he recounted the fruits of his investigation.

"Tell me, Iba, to whom did you speak?"

Iba had started with Tafa Conte, who knew the name and something of the reputation of Mbattu Sisay, but had no first-hand knowledge of his skill or character. Tafa then had sent Iba to a local traditional healer named Dr. Dia, at an office in the middle of town. Dr. Dia was quite suspicious of Iba and had asked why he was seeking to learn of this secretive and powerful man. From Dia, Iba learned that Sisay was indeed revered and feared throughout Ziguinchor. He healed many people who ended up paying for many years afterward. Dia also told him that Sisay could make people ill from the distance of his office, without a visitation or contact. He wasn't just a healer, he was ... something else: a man wielding the power of unseeable forces and forcing his will upon any whom he wished. From Dia, Iba obtained the names of two people who claimed to have been cured of life-threatening diseases by Sisay. He was able to visit one.

Sharay Bontu was a single mother of two teenage sons, living on the outskirts of Ziguinchor. Iba had taken a bush taxi to her home. He found Sharay and her sons in a two-room hut with a corrugated steel roof. The interior was a prosperous contrast to the impoverished exterior and the rest of the neighborhood. Iba noticed it was the only hut with electricity. The interior had a tile floor rather than broken linoleum, concrete, or dirt. A small gas stove stood in the corner rather than the usual space reserved for wood-fire cooking. When Iba told Sharay Bontu he was asking for information about Mbattu Sisay, she had asked Iba to leave. But he persevered.

"She seemed to me," he said to Doria, "to want to protect her benefactor. Dia seemed envious and fearful. Sharay Bontu was not."

Iba had stood in silence for nearly fifteen minutes as Sharay Bontu took his measure, asked him to leave many times, introduced him to one of her sons, gave him a cup of water, and ignored him. Finally, exasperated but no longer concerned, she decided to tell Iba of Mbattu Sisay, so long as Iba promised to leave afterward.

When Sharay was a young woman of fourteen, she had been raped by an elder in her village and had become pregnant. The elder refused to acknowledge his act. He had piled public vitriol upon Sharay, humiliating her and causing her to be shunned by her family and community. With nowhere to turn, she sought help from Sisay. She wanted to abort the fetus swelling her belly, but Sisay said that would be a shame; that her child would be male, would come to love her as his mother, and would provide for her as he grew older; that she should have the child and move to town. Sisay had been the only person who believed her or cared for her. Sisay told her the elder who had raped her would provide for her. Sharay could not believe that would ever happen, but in a matter of weeks the elder fell gravely ill and repented the wrong he had done to Sharay. Before he died he gave her thirty head of cattle and twenty goats, which she sold for enough money to move to town.

Months later, at Sisay's compound, she bore male twins, one of which died immediately. Sisay had given her medicine that took away her pain, and her remaining baby boy had continued to grow in health. Sisay had fathered a second boy a year later. He helped her find housekeeping work and assured that her sons attended school.

When Iba finished his story, Doria was puzzled and concerned. "So in effect, Iba, this man may have killed the rapist and set the young woman up as a concubine? How is this traditional healing? How, in any sense that I understand, can this man be something like a doctor or ... someone of decency?"

"This is not England, Madame Blake."

"Oh, I know so well this is not England. So, so well." She let out a heavy breath. She had wanted so much to believe that not only could this man lead her to the knowledge and skill she craved, but that he shared her values as well.

"The medicine of this man Sisay is powerful, Madame Blake."

"If this man is a murderer, how is this better than the rapist himself?"

Iba looked puzzled. "Madame, in your country, do you separate wisdom of different kinds?"

"Iba, I don't understand your question."

"We believe that justice and healing of the body are part of the same ...." He stopped, appearing lost for words. "The same force."

"You believe this doctor meted out justice? No. No, I can't see how this makes sense. It doesn't change the fact that he likely killed another man."

"In our villages, Madame, justice for those with no power is rare. If Sisay has given justice to the powerless, is that not healing?"

"It's not justice. It was murder!"

"Perhaps Sisay was able to look into the future. Sharay Bontu did not lay the death of the elder at the foot of Mbattu Sisay."

As interesting, troubling, and important as the information was about Sisay, Doria was learning more about the man who had driven her around Dakar for the last six years. She looked at Iba, realizing how little she knew of this loyal and dedicated man. This schooling from Iba, of the Djiolla worldview, was fascinating.

"Iba, do you think this man is honorable? From what you have learned, can he be trusted? And is he really a healer, or, or ... something else?"

"Sisay helps people who have little or no power, Madame. I do not know if you call this 'healing.' You can trust that he will do what he believes is right."

Doria fussed. Iba's investigation had actually made the situation worse. Assuming the few details were true, the man had a reputation as a powerful healer and soothsayer. If she were to learn enough from him to apply his knowledge of natural medicines to her own world, then she had to take a cultural journey for which she had not prepared herself. It had been easy to accept, embrace, even, the challenges to Western medicine that tribal cures posed. But the challenge to her value system, the challenge to her sense of right and wrong, of justice and revenge, had awakened her to new dangers of her quest. She began to feel cold and instinctively brought her arms up around her shoulders. For the first time, the true risk to her life, to her hold on her beliefs, to her body, and to her very sense of self engulfed her, not with dread, but with wild animal wariness. At any instant her heartbeat might cease.

* * *

Green-headed parrots announced sunrise with a chorus of chirps as they flew from their perches. Had they not startled Doria awake, she might not have believed she had slept at all during the night. She wondered what she had gotten herself into and admitted that part of her was fascinated by the day's possibilities. While she could hardly bring herself to believe in healing or hurting at a distance—through the air, as it were—it would be interesting to find out from

Sisay himself what had happened and how. But Doria kept reminding herself, never forget who you are. I'm here to discover and to learn.

She arose from bed and dressed today as she dressed nearly every day: in khakis and a simple cotton blouse, her feet clad in running shoes. She put her hair up and went into the kitchen.

She prepared a pot of tea and could hear the roosters calling from deep in the town. When she sat down with breakfast, she felt very alone once again. She enjoyed her new independence from Nigel, no longer a woman in his shadow. Doria was proud of herself for following her passion that she had yet to fully unlock. Yet this morning, her sense of being alone was accompanied by a loneliness that she hardly recognized until she let it seep into her thoughts. Longing. Victor. Her stomach tightened and she closed her eyes. Something uncontrollable about her sudden need for him thrilled and terrified her. Never had her body reacted so strongly, so independently to another human being, that her mind, like a hostage, could only watch. She sipped her tea and waited for the wave to pass.

When she walked outside, she saw Mady Toula sitting outside the gate, her back turned to the compound. Doria heard sounds of Iba washing in his quarters and called to him.

"Iba, I'm going. I don't know where exactly. Iba?"

She waited, and eventually he came from his room to the outside, dressed only in his jeans.

"Yes, Madame Blake."

As she opened the gate and Mady rose to her feet, Doria asked her, "Mady, please tell Iba where we are going."

Mady looked stern-faced and shook her head.

"Mady, it is quite simple. I'm not going anywhere, either without Iba or without him knowing where I will be. Please tell him."

Mady spoke to Iba in Djiolla. "I can only tell you where we are going. I cannot tell you where we will be."

Iba translated, and Doria shook her head.

"Well, then, where are we going, Mady?"

The Senegalese woman spoke now in French and described their journey to Mbattu Sisay's compound. A walk of some two hours.

"Why can't we have Iba drive us? Surely that would be the sensible thing to do."

"Master Sisay was clear, Madame. You and I are to walk to his compound."

Doria turned to Iba. "Do you think you could find that compound, Iba, if you had to?"

"I can, Madame," Iba said.

"In that case, let me get my water and my bag."

They managed to keep to the main roads for the first hour, and shortly afterward Mady took a path into the brush. Doria followed as she had when the two had been flora hunting on the edge of Guinea-Bissau. The trail bent and turned into a footpath of red clay. Doria was sweating, yet not wilting. Insects buzzed everywhere. The awakening forest hummed and churned as beetles, dragonflies, locusts, ants, spiders, and mantises went about their forage, their home building, fighting predators, and preying on lesser beasts. Bothered as she was by the sheer inconvenience of it, Doria developed the appreciation of a keen observer watching little battles or construction taking place. These active insects attracted the attention of hundreds of birds, all eager to feast and feed their offspring. Such a beautiful, brutal world, Doria thought.

The forest thinned out gradually, until they came to a meadow of sedge grass growing in mounds the size of beach balls, forcing the women to zigzag. They ducked under the broad leaves of a small grove of banana trees. When they stood upright they were in a clearing with a large mud-brick house set toward the back, from which the rest of the compound sloped. A monstrous mango tree stood in the middle of this clearing, throwing shade over the entire compound.

Doria surveyed the clearing and said to Mady, "This is the place, isn't it?"

Mady looked back at Doria, but said nothing. She went and sat on the ground underneath the mango boughs.

Doria noticed a number of small buildings, constructed, she thought, of wood or bamboo. She counted seven in all. Six were about the size of a single room and had thatched roofs. The seventh was a bit more difficult to understand. It looked more like a big basket. There were no windows or doors, from what Doria could see, and no roof. How very peculiar, she thought. She noticed, too, some benches near each of the huts, not for sitting, but high like a countertop.

As she walked toward Mady, the color of the ground changed from the bright rust-red of the clay, to a smooth, light brown, hardened almost like concrete, unforgiving to her steps. Looking back over her shoulder she noted the edges of the compound were lined with garden beds. She turned and went to inspect them. Each was about three meters long and a meter wide, and all were filled with thriving plants. Many were flowering in multicolored blossoms, many were growing tall or wide. One squat plant had long silky leaves that seemed to wave even in the absence of the wind. Another, tall and chaotic, had leaves like sheared wool and a stem that looked like a dark brown corncob.

Doria sniffed as she approached, hoping to find something utterly out of her experience.

"It is a unique garden, Madame Blake," Mbattu Sisay said, standing, impossibly, right next to her.

Startled, she drew back instinctively.

"I did not mean to frighten you, Madame Blake."

Doria looked into his eyes and said, without any reservation, "But of course you did, Monsieur Sisay. You very well meant to put a start in me. And well enough you succeeded." Her smile was simultaneously gracious and challenging.

The old man looked at Doria intently and nodded. "Surprises come in many forms and for so many reasons, Madame Blake. I hope you will forgive me."

She said nothing to this and turned back to the garden. She asked if Sisay would explain what these plants were and why he had selected this particular structure for the garden.

"I intend, Madame Blake, that you will have the answers to your questions and more. Perhaps you may come to know what these plants can do. Which ones like to be together and which hate to be together, unless a third is brought in. But that is for later today. Please come and sit beneath my lady."

"Your lady? Oh, you mean the mango tree."

"I do. Come sit with Mady Toula and me. You must be very thirsty from your long walk. May I offer you some water."

"I've brought some with me, Monsieur. Please don't go to any trouble. I would actually prefer to drink my own bottled water, if you don't mind."

"I don't mind. It is very sensible of you, who have not grown up here, to keep healthy with water you know. May I get you a cup?"

"Please, Monsieur. That would be very nice."

Sisay made a call like the cry of a wolf. From the doorway of the house emerged a young Senegalese man, tall and rail-thin. Doria wondered if he was on drugs. The only people she had ever seen who looked like this young man were junkies in Manchester City—people who forgot to eat, people who had forfeited their living spirit.

"Duba, please bring Madame Blake a cup for her water."

Duba returned to the interior of the house and reemerged with a tin cup. He went over to Doria and placed it in her open hand. She thanked him and watched him walk back to the house, listing to one side. She turned her attention to Sisay.

He said, "Mady Toula has told me much of your desire to learn our traditional healing and how we prepare our medicines. She said you were very strong when you went into the forest in search of *szhelel* and *gar*. But please, I would like to know from your mouth, why you come to us in this need."

"Curious you should call it my need, Sisay, but I suppose you have it right. What should I tell you, then? Well, ..." She paused, wondering exactly how much she wanted to reveal. He was measuring her, testing her. A good bit of the truth had to be told if she was to learn from him all that she hoped.

"Ever since I was a little girl, from my very first memories in England, plants seemed so remarkable to me. In England, do you know, our garden plants die off in the autumn, are covered with snow and spend months in the frigid earth, only to be reborn when the spring returns. It is all so wonderfully different than we humans, isn't it? They grow magnificent flowers of every color, they have so many different shapes and textures and scents. And certain of them feed us, clothe us, warm us in winter. Without the plants, there simply would be no human beings."

She paused to sniff the air and brush back her hair. She stretched out her cramping legs and leaned back on her arms. "Even before I went to university, I learned how photosynthesis turns sunlight into food. No human has yet been able to duplicate that process. I learned that plants have microscopic chemical engines working every second of every day, producing the most amazing substances. I remember reading about the aloe vera cactus and pestering my mum until we went to a plant shop and bought a tiny little aloe in this thimble of a clay pot. It looked like someone had buried a tiny green octopus by its head. Mum bought me a book on how to care for it, and I followed the instructions religiously.

"One day I decided I had to see for myself how the aloe vera could heal a wound, so I went into the kitchen and chose a sharp knife from the cutlery drawer and brought it back to my room. I cut just a tiny tip from the top of one of aloe's fingers. And I saw it bleed this clear liquid, a syrup, really, and I quickly decided to cut the top of my own finger the same way. Strange little girl that I was, it seemed natural to me that mixing my blood with the plant's blood, we would become, you know, sisters. Of course I did not come remotely close to a neat, precise cutting job on my own finger ...."

Doria held up her left index finger that bore the tiny scar of her childhood experiment. "I really butchered my poor finger. I hadn't even thought of all the blood my finger might produce. In any case, I finally stopped cutting myself and used a sock to wipe the blood. When I held the little stem of aloe against the open wound, there was such a rush of cool tingling, I'll never forget it. Within seconds the tip of the aloe became the tip of my finger and I was in heaven. I ... I can't really describe it any other way." Doria looked at Sisay to see if there was a glimmer of understanding—that this simple act of the child was a seminal experience in the life of the woman.

Sisay smiled. "You became sisters with the aloe," he said. "Are you sisters with other plants?"

"Many, Monsieur. Many. And what they tell me is that we know so little of them, of what they are, and of what they are capable. I studied botany at the university. Do you want to hear more?"

"I want to hear only what you want to tell me."

"Until the next question," Doria mumbled with a laugh.

" 'How well you know me already,' " Sisay quoted her from the prior day. "But please tell me more. Why are you not a doctor of plants, from your studies?"

"That's a fair question, Monsieur Sisay, for which I have no answer. I'm sorry to say that it didn't seem like the proper thing to do back then. Mum—as dear as she was to me—was so very interested in my getting married to a 'man of substance,' you see, and however was I to meet one, wasting my time in a botany laboratory. But, as things do from time to time, it worked out. I began to volunteer in the children's ward at St. John the Divine Hospital while working full-time as a lab assistant at Barrow & Bean. It was in that hospital that I discovered the link I had been looking for, that connection between the astounding properties of plants and the needs of mortally ill children. Do you understand, Monsieur? I watched children die in the hospital because our medicine and probably our whole way of caring for them was not enough. It wasn't what they needed. We had no cure for them."

"Do you think, Madame Blake, that you are here to learn how to cure them?"

"I don't know. That's a great hope of mine, yes indeed. A great hope." Doria hung her clasped hands in front of her and felt her eyes well up slightly. "I know I am not a true scientist, but there is great, vast power locked in the cells and the DNA of these plants. And I don't want to be mixing bloody perfumes or discover a new way to package thyme to last ten years on a bloody grocery store shelf. And ...." She hesitated, not wanting to blurt out loud that she could no longer stand being the ornament wife. "I want to do something important. I want to heal in ways others have ignored. I want to give everything I have in order to bring down the arrogance of modern medicine, and build a more natural medical practice based on a relationship with the earth." She paused. "Listening to myself, Sisay, I wonder if I'm not the arrogant one."

Sisay heard something he had been hoping to hear: the depth of Doria's need. This was the fuel to sustain her through her trial. It was more than simply a desire to help others. She needed a power, not over others, perhaps, but over herself. Sisay believed her passion was real and flowed from her spirit naturally.

"Let me show you what I have here. May I?" Sisay rose from his squat on the earth and beckoned to Doria.

"Mady?" Doria said, turning around. Mady remained still. "Mady," Doria repeated, and held out her hand to help Mady off the ground. Mady looked at Sisay, who nodded.

He began with the garden at the entrance. Kneeling at the midpoint of one of the beds, Sisay reached in and cupped a thick vine of spiny, dark leaves clustered around thorns and dense flowers like amethysts. He broke off a small piece and crushed a flower between his thumb and forefinger, bringing it to his nose and inhaling. Doria knelt beside him, and Sisay handed her his tiny bouquet. She studied it at first, noticing the thickness of the stem, the coarse green of the leaves, the size and danger of the thorns. Finally, she took the crushed flower exactly as Sisay had and noticed the glycerin texture. Putting it to her nose, she sniffed tentatively and was rewarded with a scent so strange, so new, that she opened her eyes wide. The smell was tart and pungent, like decaying meat but supported by a soapy licorice scent and something like pepper.

"How strange this is, Sisay. So utterly different from what you might expect. No hint of sweetness or perfume."

"It is called *poot* and it protects the skin against fire."

"You mean it heals burns, Sisay."

"No, Madame. Hear me. It protects against fire. And when it is married with *dokhokete*, it protects against blows to the body of any kind."

"Truly?"

The healer nodded.

"This I should like to see before I leave today. Can you arrange it?"

"It is already arranged, Madame Blake."

"Splendid. This is so very exciting." She tittered.

Sisay stood up, as did Doria. The two of them walked slowly along the edge of the garden as Sisay pointed out all manner of plants to Doria, to whom it seemed none was ever duplicated. Mady followed. This disturbed Doria, who had always thought of Mady as someone with whom she might eventually be a friend.

"Why, Sisay, is Mady so despondent and removed? She has always been so lively and engaging. Have you done something to her? She is most certainly not herself today."

"Mady is learning today, the boundaries of her word and of my affection for her."

"She has been a friend to me. If you have her controlled, somehow, I beg you to release her."

"How exactly do you control another human being, Madame Blake?"

"Oh, many ways, Monsieur. Fear, for example. Fear of bodily harm or harm to a loved one. Money can be used to control another person. It is done quite regularly throughout the region, surely. And what about social pressure and other ways used to convince people they should act in a certain way. My husband believes in marketing to sway mass tastes, for example. There are many ways to control another human being, both direct and indirect, no?"

"You are a thoughtful woman, Madame. And you have little fear. Is this not so?"

"Oh, I've got plenty of fear. Plenty. More than my share, I would say." She laughed as she thought of her fear of not being a proper British wife.

"Of that, we will learn more later. Please follow me."

Sisay continued through the plant bed, then took Doria across the compound to the first of the six one-room huts.

Entering the first hut, Doria was again assaulted by an array of scents and sights: dozens of harvested plants—some in bundles, some in jars. It very much resembled the hut where Mady preserved her plants, except these seemed larger and more organized, with three times the number of plants. It was clear that the organization had meaning beyond the need for order. There was a relationship between these components that Doria could sense.

"This is where I store the basic plant ingredients after harvesting them," Sisay pronounced. "You see *poot* in the bowl away from the window? That is because once the flower is taken from the mother plant, it quickly loses its potency in sunlight. But after two days in partial darkness, its power is concentrated and ready to be mixed with its allies."

Doria walked through the harvest hut exploring many of the plants with her touch. Small branches tied with vines and piled together looked coarse and rough. But to her touch they were as soft as new wool. Stick or stalk, flower or leaf, Doria approached each with the idea of submitting it to her senses, holding a sample in her hands and inhaling.

"I recognize many of these, Sisay, but I don't know all their names. And of course, there are many here I've not seen before. I should so much like to learn all their names and write them down. I could never remember them, otherwise."

"I hope you will have that opportunity, Madame Blake, but that will depend on you."

Doria ignored Sisay's inscrutable remarks, focusing on her exploration.

"Let us go and look at the next stage of the preparation," he suggested.

Doria turned and walked back into the sunlight. She immediately felt the heat, and paused. There were no flies. How odd. Flies were part of the heat, part of the daily experience of living in West Africa. Why were there no flies in the compound?

The second hut was the preparation room. Mady waited outside, near the entrance. Here were the tools of a chemist: a small burner, knives and grinding stones, pottery flasks of different liquids. It was all in impeccable order. Doria remarked that there were no labels of any kind.

"Sisay, how ever to you keep track of what you have here? You have not written anything down or put labels on your containers. How can you know what to mix and when, how long anything has been stored? It all seems unfathomable to me."

"Time and place is the order of all things, is it not?" Sisay asked. "I know by the time of the sun or the moon, by the arrival of the swallows or the rains. I know also because of this." Sisay went over to the table and lifted a small flask. Underneath was carved a symbol. He did this for successive jars and bottles and under each one was a different symbol. The Djiolla man smiled.

"Very clever, Sisay!" Doria exclaimed. "You are an old fox, aren't you?"

Sisay bowed. He proceeded to show Doria the tiny markings on the clay cylinders and how each represented a particular measure for a particular ingredient: this much of the powdered *tremsi* leaves, a different amount for the bark of the *gomtu* bush. Measured, yes. But for what? Where were the recipes?

"Sisay, how do you remember how much of which ingredient goes into which medicine? Surely, you have something to help you remember, particularly as you grow older, no?" She laughed softly.

"Mady Toula," he called out. "How do you remember how to make *ndaymou gar*? Come in, tell Madame Blake."

Mady stepped into the crowded hut and, with a nod from Sisay for assurance, said, "I learn from Master Sisay, and I restore my memory every week."

"Restore your memory? You mean Master Sisay teaches you again and again?"

"Yes, Madame. Master Sisay is very patient. But first I restore my memory with this." She looked at Sisay, who again nodded, and Mady took a small leather sack out from the folds of her clothes. The sack was tied to a leather string that went at least twice around her waist. Mady lifted the sack, pulled off the wooden stopper, and held the sack out to Doria as she loosened the leather strings that fastened it to her body. Holding the sack delicately in her hand, Doria sniffed the opened top carefully. At first, she could only detect the mustiness of old leather and wood, but slowly a different scent made its way to her brain, like sandalwood and pine, with a hint of black pepper.

"It is called *khatreng udaye*—the strength of mothers," Sisay explained. "It helps those who use it regularly, to hold all experience fast in their waking mind."

In a slow whisper, Doria exclaimed, "Utterly fascinating!" She now could not move her gaze away from the little leather pouch. "And taking this allows you to remember all the recipes of the medicines? How does it work? How long does it last? Sisay, this is magical, if what you tell me is true."

"It is true, Madame Blake," he said, taking the pouch from Doria and handing it back to Mady.

"Please excuse me if I seem incredulous, Master Sisay. I have no direct knowledge of such medicines and would very much like to understand *khat, kato* ...."

"*Khatreng udaye.*"

"*Khatreng udaye.* Yes, indeed. I shall have to say this a number of times in order to remember. Perhaps I need a slight nip of *khatreng udaye* myself," she said seriously, looking directly into Sisay's eyes.

Doria noted that everything to which Sisay pointed had been a single component and not a finished compound. Sisay explained that many medicines did not last long, some no longer than a few hours or even a few minutes.

Ah, Doria thought, what a wonderful line of research, to extend the life of these medicines. Though she knew she didn't have the expertise for such work, she might enlist the help of someone who did.

"It is time to see the next hut," Sisay said.

Back into the muggy heat and the unexpected absence of flies. How could this be?

The third hut was altogether different. There were no plants anywhere, some light, and oddly, noise: motion and clicks and hisses mingling like soft, distant voices. She did not need her eyes to readjust to the dark to tell her she had entered a hut full of insects. Doria shivered and stopped, feeling slightly nauseated and, for the first time, fearful.

Sisay put his hand on her elbow. "This is a new realm for you, perhaps, Madame? Do not be afraid."

"I'm not afraid, Master Sisay. Unprepared, yes, but I'm not afraid." This became more true when she said it out loud. She began to see the jars filled with creatures, alive or dead, desiccated and stiff in their storage pots. Sisay took Doria's wrist and led her to a glass tank covered with perforated cardboard. He slid the cardboard back slightly. Putting his hand into the tank, he bent down on his knees, looking to see something in the tank.

Even with her eyes adjusted, Doria could only make out vague details. How could the old man see what he was searching for, she wondered.

After about ten seconds Sisay stood upright and pulled his hand out. In between his thumb and forefinger, he held a beetle about two centimeters long, with antennae twice that length. The carapace was a fluorescent blue, dotted with tiny spots of white.

"She is quite fast and has no bite at all," the master said.

Now fascinated, Doria looked as closely as she could. "So beautiful, Master Sisay. How do you use her?"

"This is *Selle Drom*. Light into darkness. Behind her antennae, here," he said, pointing, "is a gland which produces a chemical allowing one to see at night as though it were dawn. She is very powerful and stingy. Using the glands of three *Selle Drom*, this ability lasts only thirty minutes for a human, and using more than three does nothing to enhance the effect."

Doria touched the smooth, hard back of the *Selle Drom*. Sisay placed the beetle back into the tank.

"Know this too, Madame Blake. If I combine the secretion of *Selle Drom* with a certain amount of the pulverized bark of the *zholay* bush, I can take away the sight of a man or woman for a day."

Doria was not at all prepared for this revelation. She stood in silence as the ramifications of Sisay's pronouncement cleared in her mind. Her thoughts swirled with questions both technical and ethical: How would one administer such a *poison*? Why would one even create such a thing? What were the implications if the doses were not exact? How could a person of healing and knowledge use such a force against another person? Doria took a step backward, putting her hand to her mouth.

Sisay watched her intently, moving his head to see her face from different angles.

Her mind raced. She did not doubt for an instant the truth of what Sisay had told her. What then? Was this the knowledge she wanted to possess? Was it equally important to know the ill these potential medicines could cause? But Sisay had not mentioned the ability to remove the sight of another human being as though it were a mere side effect for which to be cautious. This was a power of the drug that could be wielded by those with the knowledge. But equally, Doria rationalized, it didn't have to be used. In fact, the knowledge of the potentially malevolent applications was critical to keeping them in check.

Doria spoke. "Why, Master Sisay, would a person of healing ever wish or need to use such a power on another person?"

"Let me give you an example, Madame. A woman comes to a healer and tells of her husband, who is a good and smart man in his heart, but is constantly seeking the praise of others, to the neglect of his family. He gives away his grain, gives his labor to help others, but his children rarely feel his touch, nor does his wife feel the conjugal contact for which she longs. How does the healer help this woman? Is it possible that if this man were to lose his sight for a day, he might come to appreciate his family, lie down with his wife, and use his remaining senses to learn from her, feel the warmth of his family, and their importance to him? Might he learn a lesson that only the loss of his sight could teach him?"

"That is a very, very tenuous leap, Sisay," Doria said. "It could as easily be used to frighten, threaten, and coerce an individual. Extort money, force another to do one's bidding. At its core it seems wrong."

"That is why such knowledge is shared with so few. Nature is not right or wrong, it simply is. Right or wrong is what we people do to each other and how we treat the gifts given to us."

Though unconvinced, Doria nodded. "There is more, isn't there?"

"There is."

"I'm interested in healing, Sisay, not harming."

"And did my example not tell of healing a family?"

"But how to know to apply such a difficult and potentially hurtful cure!"

"If you are to learn from me, Madame Blake, it will require your full attention and time."

After another thoughtful silence, Doria asked, "What are the abilities of all these tiny animals you have assembled here?"

Sisay looked at Doria with a thin smile. "The strength and breadth of the forest's treasures cannot be understood by one not willing to walk into fire for the sake of that knowledge."

Doria was willing, yet she didn't feel the fire she must walk through. However, she knew it was coming.

On the table before them was an assemblage from an entomologist's hunt. Beetles, worms, flies, and other bulbous and flying insects impossible to identify, were either live captives in old jars or dead and drying carcasses. Sisay explained how each one had a chemical protective mechanism honed for specific survival needs over eons of evolutionary stress. One might produce a surface discoloration and distortion when heated to body temperature, another a foul and debilitating odor, another a convulsive nerve toxin when ingested, still another that stimulated the generation of blood cells. All of these natural defenses were locked in the bodies of the tiniest of creatures. Moreover, Sisay explained, they could be combined with other mixtures distilled from local flora, to produce effects that were as astonishing as they were dangerous. Some could enter the body through the skin, others required ingestion. A few could simply be inhaled.

Doria was fascinated and repulsed. As she began to explore the insects in the same way as she had the plants, she was more tentative, unsure about the effects but wanting to identify each with a sensory memory. She looked at Sisay as she picked up a glass tube full of centipedes. They were iridescent purple and squirmed around each other in coils. He gestured that she was safe. She removed the rubber stopper and poured a centipede into her palm. A paroxysm of revulsion swept over her, yet she could not stop. The centipede uncoiled in her hand, slowly explored the grooves separating her fingers, and crawled onto the back of her hand. She held it up close to her eyes, her pulse quickening with fear, and yet, when she beheld the dark insect eyes and the barbed mandibles that tore other insects apart, she was overwhelmed with a curiosity. What could this creature teach me, she wondered. The centipede felt cool as she picked it off the back of her hand and placed it in the glass tube.

"That caterpillar has a powerful chemical on its mouth that can paralyze an animal five times its size. Had it bitten you, Madame Blake, you might have lost the use of your hand for the rest of the day."

"You allowed me to inspect it, Sisay. You wanted me to put it on my skin, didn't you? All the while knowing I could be hurt."

"But I knew you would not be hurt. Not if you are who you say you are. Let's continue."

The fourth hut was exactly as Doria had expected—a table with insect parts in jars and small bowls on top of symbols carved into the wooden table. Just like the preparation hut for the plant material. Doria got the idea.

The fifth hut, however, was very curious. As they stepped in, Doria felt as though she had entered a cemetery. Little wonder. This hut had no living thing inside. Everywhere were the carcasses and body parts, mostly heads and internal organs, of forest reptiles, mammals, and birds. Very few were preserved in any way Doria understood. And while the stench was perceptible, it was not overwhelming—another oddity, given so many decaying animal parts. To her left, an unidentifiable assortment of organs lay on a table, without any covering or attempt to keep them from rotting.

"Good Lord, Sisay, what is this?" Doria pointed to a drying series of small fleshy pouches, pairs of which were attached to each other.

"The stomach acid of this creature can be recreated only when attached to the rest of the immediate entrails and only for about ten days after it has been extracted."

"For what purpose do you use this acid?"

"It is used exclusively to mix with an extract from the *doldadde* flower, which binds the acid indefinitely, and can be used even to melt metal."

"Like hydrochloric acid? Do you just pour it on the metal and it slowly dissolves?"

Sisay looked perplexed. He continued. "Depending upon the proportion of the *doldadde* extract, this mixture may be applied and nothing may happen for an hour, or a day, or a week. Is this what you mean?"

A time-release acid? Curious. Probably more useful for conflict than for healing, Doria surmised. Her own clinical assessment suddenly made her gag, a convulsive reflex to the nearly sinister nature of what she was, up until then, so calmly absorbing. It took her by surprise and she had to leave the hut immediately, dry heaving as she stepped through the doorway.

Sisay and Mady joined her outside, seeming more curious than concerned. Bent from her heaves, Dori slowly righted herself and pulled a tissue from her pocket to wipe her mouth. Once she regained her composure, she looked squarely at Sisay.

"What I just saw in there was not a medicine, it was a weapon. Is this how you heal? Using the earth's secrets to tear and hurt?"

"Is healing for you only a matter of putting a bandage on a wound or a serum into the body? To heal the body is easy, for the body mostly heals itself. But to heal the body and the heart and the mind, and the whole person, this takes many tools, many medicines, as you say. And sometimes, to heal one person you must heal many. Do you understand this?"

"I believe I do, Sisay, yes. But tell me, when healing one or many, is it also true that one or many may be hurt as well?"

Sisay nodded. "Sometimes that is unavoidable, Madame." Sisay paused, then asked, "Do you believe in evil?"

Without hesitating, Doria answered, "Evil, as you said, is a construct of humans. Individual people and man-made things can be evil. But I don't believe evil is inherent in the earth, in nature."

"So when a fever destroys a whole family, or a flood destroys a whole village, or a drought slowly causes the starvation of an entire country, this is not evil?"

"No, it is not. These are forces of the earth that people endure everywhere. How we react to these forces is what is important."

Again, Sisay nodded, and beckoned for Doria to follow him to the last hut. Doria recovered enough of her strength and curiosity to follow him, ridding her mind of expectations for what she might learn next.

The final hut was anticlimactic. It looked more like a pantry than a primitive laboratory for the concoction of dark secrets. Bowls and jars lined shelves made of bound sticks and cinder blocks. As many of the vessels were empty as full. She noted the table with the symbols carved onto the top, yet it was bare—not a single tool, bowl, or jar.

She smiled, turned, and went back outside, not needing to see any more of the pantry. She addressed Sisay over her shoulder: "There is much to learn. So much, that I believe it will take years."

Doria was fascinated but overwhelmed. Was this truly what she wanted to learn? Was this path leading her to an ability to apply natural medicines to ailing children, or was it something different, something larger and barely grounded in her original desires? This no longer seemed the simple botanical exploration she had envisioned. It was a longer journey with many forks and junctions, for which her own moral compass was searching to regain its magnetic north. She reasoned: It will require great faith to continue. No. Not faith, but its opposite: an absence of preconceptions; a complete clearing of my mind that would allow these strange concepts to engage my embedded values and views of the world in a way that would create a new vision for developing and wielding these locked-up natural forces. But, Doria worried, what if I'm completely wrong? She began to feel like a small open boat, loosed from its mooring just before a storm.

Sisay gently took Doria by the arm. "Madame, it is time to rest a bit. We will have something to eat and then we will talk over tea. You have much to think over, but not much time. Some fish and rice will be good for you."

44. Flowers and Other Gifts

Mosa Deng was expecting visitors. She felt it would be today. These guests would not be her normal visitors: customers from the villages who asked for a *gregre* to ward off evil spirits, or for an incantation to thwart a rival or heal a sick relative. These visitors would be different, searching not for a solution to a problem but for a thing. Something rare. Mosa wasn't clear about that. Only that they were close.

As she swept the dirt floor of her hut, she knew she had to be ready to receive them soon. How many would there be, she wondered. And would one of them be the right one? She would have to prepare a welcome meal for them and dress properly. After she started the charcoal fire in the cooking area of her compound, Mosa set about preparing a celebration, like she had for her sister's wedding. When all the ingredients were simmering in the cast-iron pot, she went to bathe and dress.

* * *

Victor and Mammadu were making good time traveling back to Mali. They were feeling a residual confidence boost from having overcome bad actors. They relived the Tougue encounter in conversation as Mammadu kept the Land Rover steady. Victor's thoughts, however, were never far from his next task to retrieve a fire flower for Doria.

"We should be at the turnoff for Tchode soon, don't you think?" he confirmed with Mammadu, who glanced at the odometer.

"Soon, Barbu. Less than eight kilometers now, I think."

The midmorning sun was barely penetrating the forest canopy, yet the day had already reached the temperature of a kiln. The breeze through the open windows was no more than a fan of hot air. Mammadu saw the pole with the sign for Tchode first. He pointed, then made the turn.

"I hope this is easy, Mammadu. I'd really like to get back to the Manantali camp before sunset."

"There is no telling, Barbu. It will depend on how important your plant is to you."

"And the kind of welcome we get."

"The villages are always friendlier than the towns. We will be fine."

Although there was a turnoff to Tchode, there was no road in any sense. A footpath seemed to have enough room on either side to let a vehicle pass, but there were no vehicle tracks. After about two kilometers, the path went between two large boulders. Mammadu halted the Land Rover to the side of the path, pulled up the handbrake, and turned off the engine. Without a sound or thought to alternatives, both men got out of the Land Rover, each taking a satchel with a banana and a canteen of water.

There was no indication how far they had to go to reach the village. After hiking thirty minutes over the hilly terrain, they encountered two women walking from the direction of Tchode. Victor pressed Mammadu to ask them how far it was to the village.

As though grateful for the diversion, both women lifted the full wooden bowls from their heads and placed them on the ground. They began to speak in a fast, clicking dialect of Malinke.

Mammadu scratched his head. "They surely think I'm slow-witted," he confessed to Victor.

They frowned and poked Mammadu with their fingers, exhorting him to some heights of understanding. Mammadu laughed at first, but as the prodding continued he became annoyed. He grabbed one of the women by both her arms, just to stop her from poking him. She shrieked like she was being murdered, which startled Mammadu into letting her go. Victor stood motionless, dumbfounded. The companion woman laughed and gestured as if to strike Mammadu, from which he half-jokingly recoiled.

The two women chattered at Mammadu and then looked at Victor. They both wagged their fingers at him. Then they put their bowls back on their heads and continued on their way.

"What the hell was that?" Victor asked with concern and amusement.

"I'm not sure," Mammadu said. "They said that we had better hurry up. I don't know what they meant."

"Did they mistake us for someone else? Do you think there's a ceremony or something?"

"Truly, Barbu, I don't know. But the women said we were expected and to hurry up!"

"Expected?"

"That is about the only thing I understood from them. We are expected."

"Crazy shit! Well, let's not keep them waiting!"

They walked for thirty minutes more, passing solitary men with walking sticks and small bundles and one with a small cardboard suitcase, who greeted them politely but didn't stop. At a steep incline leading to a broad, tree-lined plateau they could see outlines of huts and small billows of smoke from cooking fires. They heard the steady *dub-dub-dub* of women pounding grain and the high-pitched squeals of children. Pied crows glided through the trees, cawing and roosting in every branch like spectators.

As the companions walked into the village, both men were struck at how little attention was paid to them: children ran up to them, giggled greetings, then disappeared; women looked up from their work, many of them smiling, some waving, and simply allowed the men to walk on. Having passed through half the village, enjoying the sights, smells, and sounds, Victor realized they had no idea where they were headed.

"Mammadu. We have to ask where we can find Mosa Deng."

They approached a group of women seated on straw mats, who were winnowing ground sorghum while singing. After both men greeted the women properly, Mammadu asked for the compound of Mosa Deng. The five women looked at each other, chattered, then one responded.

"Why are you asking us? You have been expected for weeks now. Just go!" She waved dismissively in the direction the two men had been walking.

Mammadu shrugged. "That way," he said, pointing and laughing.

Eventually they arrived at the far edge of the plateau and the main part of the village. A path turned left along the ridge, leading up a grade and into a grove of trees. They followed the path to a compound with one very large hut and two smaller ones. Though no people were visible, a cacophony of pied crows erupted as they entered. The men stood motionless now and looked questioningly at each other.

Mosa Deng walked into the sunlight through the beads that served as her door. When she straightened up, the two men stared at her. She was wrapped in an embroidered white cloth that clung like skin to her body, from the tops of her breasts to the tops of her knees. A shawl of red-and-yellow stripes covered her shoulders and hung down to her thighs. Her hair was piled in thin braids on top of her head, with occasional tendrils hanging just over her forehead and down past her ears. Her face was flawless except for the four shallow scars that lined both sides of her face. Victor thought she was no more than twenty years old.

She said, "You are welcome guests in my home this day. I am Mosa."

Victor extended his hand. "It's a … true pleasure to meet you, Mosa. I am Victor."

Mosa shook his hand pleasantly and looked directly at him. "You are on a mission, Victor. Do you believe I can help you?"

"I … I don't know. I hope you can."

"If I can, I will." Mosa now turned to Mammadu and spoke to him in his native Djiolla. "You, sir, are most welcome. You are not here on a mission, are you?"

"I am here with my friend. I—we … have traveled much together." Mammadu's gaze was fixed on the beautiful woman.

"And your name, sir?"

"I am Mammadu. Mammadu N'Diaye."

Instead of extending her hand to be shaken, Mosa touched the side of Mammadu's face. Switching back to French, she said, "I have prepared a meal for you. Please come and sit down in the shade. You are hungry, yes? And thirsty?"

Both men nodded as they took seats on a colorful sisal mat lined with small stiff pillows at one end. Mosa called into her hut, and immediately two older women brought out a chair for her, placing it at the opposite end of the mat. When she sat, the men had to look up at her. The sun radiated behind her.

The servant women disappeared and returned with a drink of sour milk mixed with water and sugar served in wooden cups. It was impossibly cold.

"Monsieur Victor, you are not from our African countries. Where do you come from?"

Victor explained how he came to be in Africa and why he was here now.

Mosa nodded. "But there is more, surely. You have not come to me because you are studying my village or the trees or the snakes."

"I have a good friend who is trying to help children in Senegal. She is learning everything she can about how the plants of the forest and of the desert hold secrets that cure illnesses. She has asked me to find you."

"Find me? I do not think that is possible. To find what I know? Yes, this I believe. And where is this friend of yours today?"

"She is in Senegal, in Ziguinchor."

"Monsieur Mammadu N'Diaye," Mosa said, redirecting without another thought. "You are an athlete, yes? You have the arms of a wrestler."

"I was a wrestler in Senegal," he said softly, almost embarrassed.

Victor spoke for his suddenly reticent friend. "Mammadu was the champion of the Casamance and wrestled in the National Championship of Senegal."

Mosa glanced at Victor with a smile and a slight tilt of her head that told him he should let her conduct the conversation.

"Tell me of your family, Mammadu N'Diaye."

"My parents live in the village of Bundell in the Casamance. My father was a fisherman who died at sea when I was a boy. My mother still lives in Bundell with my two sisters."

"Do you have a family of your own?"

Mammadu looked at his beautiful inquisitor and stopped speaking. Victor knew Mammadu rarely spoke of his family. If this subject arose in conversation, Mammadu always became quiet.

"Tell me about her," Mosa said, as if she knew something she could not have. "Tell me about your wife."

Mammadu glared at his host as though she was forcing the information from him. Then slowly and softly, he spoke. "Seemtay was much younger than I was. When we were married, I was a fisherman, like my father, gone all day at sea, sometimes three or four days. We had a son who was very weak at birth. Seemtay could not care for him enough, though she tried. He was less than two years old when he died. My wife could not take this pain. She was sad and crying every day. She begged me not to go to sea. She said she wanted another child, but was afraid. Children die in the village all the time. It was only right that we have another child. But she would not ...." Mammadu took a few breaths.

Mosa said, "You were a good husband, weren't you? You stood by her, even though she did not have sex with you."

"It wasn't right," Mammadu said, shaking his head.

"When you forced yourself on her, how did she react?"

Mammadu looked up with a combination of amazement and anguish. "How could you know?"

"You must say what happened, Mammadu N'Diaye."

Mammadu shook his head, and Mosa simply waited. Victor had never known why Mammadu's wife left him, and he had never probed. Now he was fascinated to hear his friend's story and at the same time uncomfortable to watch this painful history pried from his lips by a delicate yet irresistible force.

"It was her duty. She was my wife. She could not deny me sex even if she was frightened to have another child. And I wanted another child."

"Another boy, you mean."

"Yes. Another boy. ... Afterward, she cried and cried. She screamed she would not have another child. I tried to calm her down, but she would not stop. I left the house. When I returned, Seemtay was still in bed but now she was sitting up, looking as though she could not see me. As I prepared for bed, she rose and attacked me with a knife. She cut my shoulder. I hit her hard and knocked her to the floor. She begged for me to hit her again, to beat her until she could not stand. I was going crazy. I hit my own head many times and cried for her to rise and come to bed. She crawled over to the knife on the floor and picked it up and started stabbing herself. I grabbed the knife from her and slapped her face. Then I held her close and wrapped her in our sheets and carried her to the clinic."

"How far away was the clinic, Mammadu?" Mosa asked.

"I do not recall. Two kilometers, maybe three."

"And you carried her the whole way?"

Mammadu nodded.

"You loved her. You must not blame yourself. Ever."

Looking up at Mosa, tears brimming his eyes, Mammadu posed a simple question: "How can I not?"

Mosa smiled at him. A breeze raced through the compound, evaporating the sweat on the foreheads of the men, cooling their bare arms, and taking the sting of the heat as it fled.

After many minutes, Mosa rose and went inside her hut. Upon her return she announced that their meal was ready and would be served shortly. She went back inside.

Victor stretched all four of his limbs and knelt close to Mammadu, putting his hands on his shoulders, and then patted his back. Mammadu stood and started a calisthenics routine. He dared Victor to keep up. Soon the two were stretching and sweating in earnest, puffing in short breaths as they pushed each other in a wrestler's warm-up. Victor had learned these maneuvers from Mammadu a long time ago, but never would he be a match for his friend.

The food arrived, mercifully, before Mammadu forced Victor to the ground. They put an arm around each other's shoulders before they sat back down on the mat.

One of Mosa's servants offered a bowl of water for the two guests to wash their hands. Mosa joined them on the mat around the bowl of savory rice, cassava, and chicken. No conversation passed during the meal.

After they washed their hands at the end of the meal and the food bowl was carried away, Victor decided it was time to make his request.

"Mosa, we thank you so much for this wonderful meal. I still do not know how you knew to expect us, but we are very grateful."

Mosa smiled and nodded. "It is I who am grateful for this visit, Monsieur Victor."

"You are very kind. You recall when we first arrived, you asked me why I was here. I told you I was asked to find you, or, as you more accurately stated, to find your knowledge."

"Yes, of course."

"My friend has asked me to find and bring back a rare and very important plant that she believes will help with her medicines. It is called a fire flower. Do you know of such a plant?"

"The fire flower is a rare and fussy plant, Monsieur Victor. It does not easily give up its secrets, nor does it travel well."

"Nevertheless, I'm told that you are the only person who can help me."

"This is the trade," Mosa said. "I understand. Please come with me."

"What is the trade, Mosa Deng?" Victor asked, recalling the Mahina healer's advice that he was to give her whatever she asked.

She rose without a response. The men followed her to the back of her compound and out a small gate. She led them through a series of paths that wound down the side of the plateau. Victor was amazed how easily Mosa navigated the steep slopes and rocks in her tight clothes. He then noticed that she was barefoot and keeping perfect balance. As they descended, the air became densely humid and hot. It seemed to Victor they had come lower on this side of the plateau than the point from which they had hiked up. When the ground leveled, they entered a swamp. Mud oozed over their ankles. The air was a thick wet gas smelling like rot. They had walked into a completely different environment.

Mosa stopped and pointed to a log as thick as an automobile and longer than a bus, partially digested by the swamp. Mammadu and Victor tramped over to the log and stopped. They heard a single hiss, then many. Slowly, they were able to differentiate the hundreds of hisses and eating sounds of tiny animals composting the ancient tree. Beetles, worms, mites, millipedes, and flies collided and battled through this mini ecosystem. It was teeming with hundreds, maybe thousands, of creatures—a world unto itself.

Mosa came alongside Mammadu. Placing a hand on his shoulder, she pointed to a rotting limb inside a crevice. The men could see the blossoms of nearly a dozen small plants. Each had dark green leaves like small coins and a single orange flower in the shape of a flame, the only seeming bits of color in the deep brown.

"If you are to take a fire flower, you must also take a deep cut of her soil. It can only survive in the heart of the decaying wood and the presence of the ants," Mosa told them, almost in a whisper.

"Ants?" Victor gulped. "Please don't tell me we have to transport a bunch of ants along with the plants themselves."

"Fire flower will not survive without the insects that carry water and food up the roots and to the tips where the stem becomes flower. See?" She bent close and pointed out the many ants—the smallest either man had ever seen—running up and down each plant. "The ants are life-givers to the fire flower."

Victor looked at Mammadu, wishing again he had been at Manantali that first time. "I'll need some help with this, friend," was all he could say.

From his pocket Mammadu pulled a military knife and, as directed by Mosa, separated two of the fire flowers with cuts as deep as the blade could make. With a stiff reed gathered from a cluster nearby, Mosa tried to make the incision deeper still. The reed wasn't up to the task, and she directed Victor to get a long rigid stick from one of the trees on the edge of the swamp.

Carefully he walked to the nearest tree and pulled out his own knife to cut a single branch. This tree turned out to be particularly sinewy. As Victor redoubled his efforts, he shook the tree harder. Something fell out of the tree, into the swamp mud next to him. Victor glanced toward the ground. He couldn't make it out in all the dark water, so he concentrated on amputating the branch as quickly as he could. Wiping sweat from his eyes, he saw the lump that had fallen out of the tree begin to move toward him … a green mamba, one of the deadliest snakes in Africa.

Victor surprisingly calmed himself with a feeling of inevitability. Of course, he thought. This was way too easy. It's only fitting that I face this goddamned angry snake. But he knew he needed help. Fast.

"Mammadu! Green mamba. Need your help now, please!"

The snake was only a meter away and could move much faster in the swamp growth and mud than Victor thought he himself could. Dropping the branch he had just cut, along with his knife, and holding onto the larger branch, he pulled himself into the air, wrapping his legs around the tree just as the snake lunged to bite him.

"Jesus Christ!" he yelled.

The branch was sturdy enough to hold him, but it bent precariously under his weight. The mamba fell to the ground under Victor and lay there.

Mammadu was sloshing his way toward Victor when he stopped and asked how far he was from the snake.

"You're still a good five meters. It's directly in front of you on a straight line to me. He doesn't seem to want to move. I'm going to work my way to the trunk of the tree, OK?"

Victor tried shinnying along the branch he was on. But there were several other branches the size of the one he had cut that made it nearly impossible to move toward the trunk of the tree. Victor started to lose his grip as he tried to navigate around and down. He was losing strength quickly. With caution, Mammadu continued to approach the position of the mamba.

Suddenly behind him, Mosa made her way, high-stepping through the mud and holding her white wrap high above her knees. She went past Mammadu and stopped within half a meter of the mamba. She looked up at Victor, and then squatted close to the snake and began to make a series of clicks and hisses. After about a minute of this, the mamba slithered off into the depths of the swamp.

"It is gone, Monsieur Victor. The mamba will not harm you now."

Not quite believing what he had witnessed, Victor hung onto the branch for a few more moments. Mammadu came up beside Mosa and confirmed that the snake had left. Dropping from his sloth-like hold on the tree, Victor recovered his knife and the cut branch. He caught up to Mammadu and Mosa, already heading back to the fire flowers.

Mosa asked Mammadu to shape the branch Victor had secured, with a blade at the end. With the new tool, she extended the cuts into the log, then slowly pried out the segment containing two of the small fire flowers. The whole chunk of the log was about the size of a cinder block. Victor could see hundreds of tiny ants darting around every square millimeter of the thing.

"This must be planted in a similar environment in two days," Mosa stated, the warning clear in her tone, "or the plants will lose any ability to bleed."

Victor looked at Mammadu, who shrugged.

She saw the look of bewilderment in the eyes of the two men and frowned. "I trust your healer, Monsieur Victor, knows of what I speak."

"It is I who am ignorant, Mosa Deng, not my friend."

"Let us return quickly, then. You have something you must do for me before you leave."

"Anything," Victor said.

Upon reaching the compound Mosa went inside one of her smaller huts. She emerged with the flower brick wrapped in a wet cloth and wrapped again with old newspaper, holding it close to her body.

"You have been a most wonderful host, Mosa. How can we ever repay you?"

"It is simple. You can give me a child."

Victor thought he misunderstood. "Did you say a child, Mosa? You would like us to give you a child? Do you mean take one from the village or a nearby village?" Victor in fact feared she wanted something more, that she wanted him to bring back a white child for her to raise or perhaps keep as a servant.

"I do not want you two to give me a child. I want Mammadu to give me a child."

Mammadu cocked his head, bewildered. Victor understood.

"Oh well, that shouldn't be too much of a problem, should it. Uh, Mammadu, my friend, what do you think. Wouldn't you like to give Mosa a child after all she's done for us?"

"I have no child to give this woman," shouted Mammadu. "This flower is for you, Barbu. You pay the woman what she asks."

"Mammadu," Mosa said. "Do you know what I am asking?"

"You want me to bring you a child from somewhere, my village, maybe. I do not know. This is wrong, what you ask."

"No, Mammadu. I want you to give me your child. A child that will be yours and mine."

Mammadu's face went from a deep frown to absence of thought … then to a broad smile, then back to a frown.

"This is the return favor you must have? You want to lay down with me."

He stepped forward to look much more closely at Mosa: how beautiful her eyes, the fullness of her lips, the smoothness of her skin. He moved around her as she held his eyes with her own. Mammadu looked at her buttocks, perfectly round, leading up to a slender waist and down to strong, extended legs. She smiled at Mammadu, keenly aware of her own beauty and its effect on men, on this man.

"How do you know you will conceive?"

"I know," she said.

He went to put his hands around her waist, but she held up her own arm to stop him. "No, Mammadu. You will not touch me here. Will you give me a child, Mammadu, yes or no?"

For the life of him, Victor could not understand what was taking his friend so long to say "Of course I'll shag you, you totally hot vixen!" or something to that effect.

"And will you raise this child without his father?"

"I will raise the child, and the father will be welcome at all times."

"Why do you want a child from me? Why do you not marry a worthy man of Tchode or a rich man from Tougue? You could have your choice of men."

"If I can have my choice of men, Mammadu N'Diaye, then I choose you. You have come to me in a dream. Our child will be a boy who will grow to be a healer and a leader. He will have a large, brave heart and care for our people. I have dreamt this. I know it will be true."

He said, "What kind of woman are you, Mosa Deng, who would have the child of a man she has only known for three hours?"

"One who has known you in dreams for many years. A woman who has learned many things of the unseen world and who knows what she must do."

Victor was getting annoyed with the conversation. He stood there, trying to be polite. After all, Mammadu was paying Mosa for the favor Victor needed. But enough, already! This foreplay was nauseating.

"It's agreed, then?" Victor interjected, trying to take the brick of flowers from Mosa's hand as she cradled it.

They both turned to Victor with scowls.

"Oh, good grief!" Victor said, exhaling. "Fine. You two sort this out. I'll have a seat over here in the shade." He turned around, went over to the mat, and stretched out. "Please. Carry on." He pretended to go to sleep.

Mammadu's face appeared confused and vulnerable. But his body was reacting very much in favor of the proposition. He nodded to Mosa, who placed the fire flower in the shade of the porch and took Mammadu by the hand. She led him into the cool of her large hut, where they lay together for nearly an hour. When they came out into the daylight, Victor was truly asleep, oblivious to the flies buzzing around him.

The walk back through the village was similar to their arrival. People greeted them with smiles and laughter. The two men smiled and greeted them in return.

* * *

Rumbling along in the Land Rover, Victor and Mammadu were quiet. As they approached the Guinea-Mali border, they noticed that, unlike yesterday, it was manned by two uniformed soldiers, though it was not clear which side of the border they were protecting. Mammadu stopped next to the tin-roof shack and asked which government the soldiers represented. They were from Guinea, they replied, pointing to their flag with insistence.

One of the soldiers said, in halting French, "There is a tax to leave the country, Guinea." He came up close to the car on Mammadu's side.

"That may be true for tourists," Victor replied, "but we are not tourists. We are here on official business for your government and the government of Mali." He retrieved his OEUFS official document, passing it over to Mammadu, who showed it to the soldier. It was unclear that the soldier could even read the document, let alone understand its content. When the soldier walked away with Victor's papers, Victor got out of the car, slightly annoyed, and walked purposefully up to him.

Hearing Victor come up behind him, the soldier turned to face Victor. "There are no exceptions to the tax, Monsieur."

"Yes, Commandant," Victor said, hoping the unmerited title would put the soldier more at ease. "It actually states that we have an exception to all transborder taxes. Right here." Victor pointed to the phrase and began to read it for the soldier, who glowered at Victor with squinted eyes.

"But just to show you that there are no hard feelings, Commandant," Victor said, taking the paper from the soldier's hands, "let me give you and your fellow guard, here, something."

Victor climbed back into the Land Rover and retrieved two apples for the border patrol. He gave Mammadu the sign to take off. As Victor closed the door on his side and Mammadu pulled out, Victor tossed an apple to each of the soldiers.

"Hope to see you next trip," Victor shouted out of the window. He waved good-bye.

The stunned guards could only wave in return to perhaps the only vehicle they would see that day.

With plenty of daylight left to make it back to the Manantali camp, Victor and Mammadu remembered the catfisherman. They found him sitting on the same shaded bank. There were no monster fish this day, but they managed to purchase a single fish to feed the team.

Pulling into the camp before dusk, they found Leah writing in her notebook at a table. Orson was napping in the shade. There was no sign of the health team.

"Welcome back, strangers," Leah said. "You clearly took all the excitement with you. It's been very calm and, I must admit, a little boring these last two days."

The two men smiled as they handed the fish to the cook.

"And you've brought fresh fish. What fine providers you are!"

"Are you expecting the health team back soon, Leah?"

"We are. They know you're due back today, so I expect to see them shortly." She brushed back some of her dark hair from her face and smiled at Victor. "Did you find what you were looking for?" she asked.

"That and a bit more."

When Victor failed to elaborate, she asked him directly, "Aren't you going to tell us your stories?"

"I will, Leah, another time. Right now I have some prep to do. It's great to see that you and everyone are all OK."

"Yes, Mr. Byrnes, we are all OK, and ready to go upriver now."

"Well, I think we'll go downriver instead, and come back when there's less water everywhere. It's very tough going, and I think a second trip in, say, six weeks' time would be easier to get around. Also, there is likely to be a greater concentration of animals and birds, right?"

"Perhaps," Leah answered, not understanding why Victor would want to postpone a trip into Guinea for the team. "Wouldn't it be a good thing to get some baseline data for this part of the year, as long as we are here? I'm sure the health team isn't interested in turning around at this point."

"As I said, we'll definitely come back, and there is lots to do in the basin on the Mauritanian side that is drier now and more accessible than these boggy footpaths in Guinea."

Victor wasn't at all comfortable letting the team members know of his personal urgency to return to Senegal. With two critical packages, neither of which had any relevance to his job, he had reached a crossroad he could not ignore. He might send the artifacts back with Mammadu and catch up with the team before they made it back to Dakar. That meant he'd have to take another driver with him to Ziguinchor.

Continuing without him wouldn't be very difficult for the team, Victor rationalized. Each Land Rover had a copy of the border pass from OEUFS, and Mammadu would be in charge of the camp. They had radios. There was no other choice because, above all, he had to get the fire flowers to Doria immediately.

Doria Blake overtook Victor's thoughts. She was the wife of a man who had conscripted Victor into a plot to smuggle cultural artifacts across multiple borders, a man clearly of situational ethics. And what did that make Victor himself? A man who, without a firm moral code, was easily coerced to subvert local laws. And now, as he pushed aside his commitments to Nigel and the IMAME team, all for the prospect of seeing Doria in an environment without her husband, what did that say about Victor? The reason he had plotted with Nigel, the reason he was ready to take company resources and travel hundreds of kilometers away from his work, was because he was obsessed with Doria Blake. Victor's stomach churned. Once the drug was consumed, body and mind focused solely on the high. His imagination was running wild. Would Doria, when presented with the gifts of his exploits, see him as a noble partner or as some lovestruck sap, a retriever ready to do any reckless thing she asked. However honest he was being with himself, he would not do anything other than go to her, if for no other reason, to discover if he was a complete fool or a man lurching toward destiny.

Leah's insistent tone snapped him out of his self-absorption. "Victor, what are you saying? Have you heard a word I just said?"

"There is something very important that I must do, Leah. Please. If you want to take an extra day to go across into Guinea, that's OK, but you should really consider what I said. We'll come back later and take a good three days on the other side of the border. If you go back now, there is still a great deal you can do."

Leah looked at him carefully. "It's personal, isn't it, Victor?"

He nodded, looking her in the eyes, and turned away to prepare for his trip.

45. KERTUNANG

The effect of the tea was quite pleasant. Doria noticed that Sisay and Mady were not drinking the same tea Sisay had poured for her. She was unconcerned. The fascinating things she had seen and the idea of learning so much from Sisay thrilled and frightened her. Imagine a compound that could make flesh impervious to flame! Even if it were only for a few minutes, the possible uses were endless. And what of the mystical fire flower? Doria needed to ask Sisay more about this plant. Hopefully, Victor would be able to bring one back for her. Victor! Such deep green eyes, such gorgeous russet hair, such a look into her heart each time her eyes met his. Such a boy.

Why were there no flies in this compound? Like a hangnail, the question came back to bother her. She needed to understand this.

"Sisay, please tell me. Flies are everywhere in Senegal, but I have yet to be bothered by flies in your compound. Why is this?"

"Because, Madame, I do not allow them. They contaminate and foul the medicines. And the plants do not rely on them for pollination."

"You don't allow them? And they obey this restriction, apparently. How do you make them obey?"

Sisay smiled. "Flies have enemies, just like all creatures, Madame Blake. If you can raise an army of the enemies of flies, they will shun your place."

"You will have to teach me who the enemies of the flies are and how you can raise an army of them."

"Perhaps later. You must understand too, that such an army brings hazards of its own. Nothing rewarding is without a consequence. A successful life greatly depends upon how one addresses that balance. Does this make sense to you?"

"It does, but I must also understand the details. The balance of the compounds you make is so important. If the ratios are wrong, much harm can be done. When can I begin to learn from you?"

"After your tea, Madame, perhaps tomorrow, or the next day."

Sisay smiled and Doria saw something hidden and deceitful. Still, she was more curious than concerned.

Sisay shifted on the mat. He took a few deep breaths, as if preparing to do something that concerned him.

"Madame Blake, this is a very important time for you."

"Yes, Sisay, you are right about that."

"More important than perhaps you know. In order to become a healer and to learn the healers' ways, receive the knowledge of the elders, you must go through *kertunang*. Yes, I will explain. *Kertunang* is a ritual of truth and cleansing of the mind. The mind is opened by drinking an infusion made from *zhole* bark and the *rokhart* mushroom."

Doria looked at her cup of tea. She had enjoyed its earthy texture and aromas. Now she understood that this was more than just a relaxer. Recalling DeLevres' notes she wondered if the *rokhart* was one of the species the botanist had been investigating.

"This is the tea you have made for me, isn't it?"

"Yes. But please do not be alarmed. This is a critical point. I will be your guide through *kertunang*, but much of it you will travel by yourself. Once you are opened to my guidance, you will see things you have never seen before, images like dreams will be real for you. You must be courageous, Madame Blake. You must know that this passage will mean whether or not you may learn from me, whether or not you have the strength to control and contain the knowledge you would wield in a world that is filled with superstition, envy, and fear. This is your proof to me and to yourself that you can be a true healer. Do you understand?"

"I understand that I am about to suffer the effects of some hallucinogenic drug, and that you need me to go through this in order to believe I am worthy. I have to somehow show you that I have both courage and strength of mind. Do I have this right, Sisay?"

"It seems that you do."

"How long will it be before the effects of the tea take hold?"

"Soon. Very soon."

Doria adjusted her seat on the mat and started to breathe deeply and slowly. She closed her eyes. Beads of sweat popped over her face and arms. Well, she said to herself, this will most certainly be a test. She swallowed down the fear that was crawling up her esophagus, making her tongue feel like dust. Was this an effect of the tea or simply of her mind understanding what was about to take place? She concentrated on her breathing and began to feel light, almost weightless. It was pleasant. The sounds of the forest became extraordinarily clear and differentiated, as though each chirping bird, each humming insect had a distinct and knowable voice. Even the wind evoked different songs as it glided through the reeds and grasses. Doria hummed a note she heard in this music.

Sisay said to Mady, "Go into the hut, Mady. Ready my pack, but do not return outside until I summon you."

Mady went quickly into the hut.

Sisay said, "Madame Blake, tell me what you sense at this moment."

"I hear music, not music in the sense of melodies from instruments, though. It's more complex, layered with thousands of different rhythms! Astonishing!"

"Good," Sisay said. "Stand up and walk with me." Sisay held out his hand.

Doria opened her eyes and rose to her feet with ease. He led her back to the hut where he had prepared the plant mixtures.

"You remember this, Madame, yes?"

"I do, Sisay."

"Show me what you remember."

At first puzzled by this request, Doria recalled when Sisay had first led her into this workroom. She thought about the questions she had asked and Sisay's answers. She picked up a small covered bowl. "This is *dokhokete*. It protects against blows. It strengthens the skin when mixed into a paste." She did the same with two other small containers, giving precise descriptions of each. But even as she spoke, Doria wasn't sure if she was accessing memory, or something else, like a reference book streaming into her mind. It was very curious.

Sisay led her to the hut where the live insects and other animals were kept and asked Doria to name as many as she could. At first, she could think of only two or three. Then more came to her, and as she concentrated, still more, until she had listed almost two dozen of the collected specimens.

"Now, reach into the jar with the brown mantis and pull one out."

Without hesitation Doria carefully removed the lid and, rather than grab one of the sticklike creatures, she allowed it to crawl onto the back of her hand. She pulled out her hand and covered the jar. Without any direction from Sisay, Doria grasped the mantis with her other hand and held it close to her eyes and nose to study it.

"He is speaking to me, Sisay."

"What does he say?"

"He says that he has secrets he will share with me if I let him go."

"Do you believe him?"

"We both have secrets to share, I told him. We will heal the wounds."

"Wounds?"

"Yes, wounds."

"What secret does the brown mantis hold, Madame Blake?"

Doria held the mantis even closer, the compound eyes of the insect dimly reflecting the light from the door, its face alive with mouth parts and secretions. "It can halt the flow of blood and deaden pain," she said again, having no notion how this information had entered her brain.

"You may replace the mantis now."

When the insect was back in the jar, Sisay led Doria back outside. He asked Mady to bring the satchel and accompany them out of the compound. With Sisay in the lead, holding Doria's hand, the three of them walked into the forest for about fifteen minutes, until the path seemed to end. Sisay guided them through a dense cluster of prickly bushes, arriving at a small baobab tree. He helped Doria sit at its trunk and pulled cloth swatches and a rope from his satchel. Doria allowed her hands and legs to be bound and her torso tied to the tree. Sisay then pulled a knife and a small jar from his bag. He bent down in front of Doria and, with his knife, made two incisions about two centimeters to the side of each of Doria's eyes.

She winced in pain and shuddered from the mere surprise, but she did not cry out. She managed to say, "Why must you do this?"

Sisay made no reply. He applied a black salve that stopped the bleeding. He used it to paint the side of Doria's face. Backing away slowly, Sisay put the knife and jar back in the satchel, motioned for Mady to turn around, and the two of them disappeared into the forest.

Doria was alone—with no indication of when or even if her would-be mentor might return for her.

Her fear returned like a geyser and she cried out in a mournful sound of anguish and despair. The release of this cry purged some of Doria's fear, though it did not entirely dissipate. She took breaths in short gasps. Already, she was thirsty and had to pee. Good God, she thought, how long will I be here? A few hours, a few days? Will I die out here after a week of torture? She tested her bonds. They were very tight. Doria leaned back against the tree, closing her eyes, trying to breathe deeply. Soon the noises of the forest became the natural symphony she had heard only moments ago, only now they sounded richer, more distinct. Doria realized that the forest and its creatures were speaking to her.

While she knew in some part of her brain this was not possible, the foremost part of her consciousness grabbed hold of this idea and explored it. What were the voices saying? And could she speak to them in return? She tried to clear her mind. Soon Doria's legs started to tingle. She opened her eyes and saw her legs were crawling with ants. They scurried about in their frantic food search, sending queasy shivers up Doria's spine. But she soon realized the ants would not hurt her. They continued to explore other areas of Doria's body, yet without a single bite. After some time, only a few ants remained. How curious, she thought. Not enough food on me, I suppose.

She turned her focus to the small plants around her: grasses, mosses, weeds with heads of bristling spines or tiny flowers. What secrets do you hold? Doria asked. What wonders are you making? A hot breeze blew over her, pushing the grasses and the very air to bend and waver. When the breeze left, the flies came. The treacherous, annoying flies. Doria closed her eyes, pulled tight her lips, and shook her hair with a bowed head to cover her ears. Still they came. Doria concentrated. She thought of an enemy of the flies ... lizards, perhaps, or insect-eating birds, or a horde of centipedes feeding on fly maggots. She kept thinking of the enemies, the enemies, the enemies of flies. Her thoughts drummed in this way for over an hour. Then at some point the annoyance of the flies disappeared. Still she kept on imagining and saying in her mind with a mantra-like focus, "the enemies of flies."

As the sky dimmed to purple, new sounds developed. The mosquitoes emerged with their high-pitched whines. Doria concentrated on the insect-eating bats and nightjars with a fierce belief that she could summon them to rid her of the masses of swarming bloodsuckers. The predators took their time, arriving as the last light of the sun gave way to the pinpoint illumination of stars. Doria was not prepared to believe these creatures came strictly of their own accord. She was beginning to believe she could call into the forest for help and that the forest would respond.

* * *

At his compound, Sisay remained alert, on guard. He expected to hear more cries of the Blake woman pierce the night, calling from a place of deep fear. During his own *kertunang* he had called out in pain when the animals of the night accosted him: rats and snakes and the insatiable mosquitoes. But this night the dark forest delivered no sound other than the cacophony of creatures. None had the voice of a terrified Englishwoman.

"What does this mean?" Sisay said into the night. He called upon all his senses to sustain his overnight vigil. Not until the full light of morning, when the sun topped the tree canopy, would Sisay venture to his apprentice and determine if she was fit to continue, if she had faced her deepest fears and not allowed them to drain her confidence or her belief.

Mady rose before the sun, prepared tea for Sisay, and fetched a fresh loaf of bread from the baker in town. Sisay was coiled on his mat, sleep having overwhelmed him in the early morning. After Mady nudged him awake, he became alert instantly and again listened for any sound that might have indicated how Madame Blake had come through the night. He stood up so quickly he lost his balance, sitting down hard on the mat. He looked back at Mady, who set down his tea and bread. But he did not eat.

When he judged the hour appropriate for the ritual, he rose and walked slowly, with Mady trailing him, carrying his satchel. When they arrived at the tree where Doria had been bound, Sisay stopped abruptly as his mouth fell open.

There was no sign of Madame Blake. Sisay bent down to examine the rope no longer binding Doria to the tree. The rope looked as though it had been gnawed away, eaten in several places. The strips of cloth he had used to protect Doria's wrists and ankles were unwound and lying next to the rope.

"Argh!" Sisay cried out loud.

Mady stood still and wide-eyed as Sisay surveyed the small clearing around the tree and saw footprints. Hundreds of footprints. Only a few of which were human. They were of different animals. Sisay walked in wider and wider circles from the baobab tree, looking down, then up, then down again to read the tracks, then up to see where the tracks led. As he reached the perimeter and was ready to walk into the undergrowth, he noticed a small opening recently made through which the human footprints disappeared. Following this clue into the undergrowth he came upon Doria, curled on some matted ferns.

Sisay put both hands on his head and shook it violently. He rushed to Doria's side, checking to make sure she was breathing. There were bruises to her legs and arms, and scratches on her face. Her slacks and blouse were torn. The wounds made by Sisay's knife were still prominent but seemed to have healed rapidly.

"Madame Blake, Madame Blake, are you all right? You've survived a painful and telling night, haven't you? Madame Blake …!"

Doria stirred awake abruptly, but no orientation entered her brain. Where in heaven's name was she? What happened last night? She was aware of an overwhelming dryness in her throat. "Water!" she tried to yell.

Sisay brought a skin of water from his satchel, and Doria lifted her head, drinking quickly. The bruises over her body swelled and oozed. She looked at the African man offering her water, but could not recognize him. Something strange and hurtful had taken place. But what, exactly, she had no idea.

Her legs were unsteady as she attempted to rise, only to fall down. And then again. With help from Mady, Sisay managed to lift Doria to her feet.

"Madame Blake, how did you undo the restraint?"

She looked confused, so Sisay pointed to the tree. "There, where I bound you yesterday afternoon. What happened to the rope?"

Doria gazed around her as if looking for the answer in the tree branches or in the passing clouds. "I don't know," she said in English. "May I sit down, please? I ... I really do need to .... How did I ...?"

Sisay did not understand a word Doria said. He signaled Mady to help bring Doria back to the compound. Doria was nearly dead weight to them, each step a struggle.

All along their way, the metallic hiss of locusts surged and ebbed. Taking advantage of the gathering insects, shrikes and other birds flew and darted in remarkably intricate patterns to collect their winged meals. The locusts sometimes flew into the air as if to surrender to their pursuers. Doria looked on in wonder, while Sisay and Mady strained to keep her upright.

In the compound Sisay and Mady put the barely conscious Doria on the mat underneath the giant mango tree. Mady prepared a tea of *gar* and mint while Sisay did his best to make Doria comfortable on the pillows. After forcing her to drink some of the tea, the two Senegalese decided that if the Englishwoman could sleep now, that was probably for the best.

When Doria awoke five hours later, the sun was low and orange in the sky. She was famished. She looked around as she wiped the sleep from her eyes and began to recognize where she was.

"Sisay," she called out in a low, cracking voice. "Sisay, are you here?"

The Senegalese healer emerged from his hut. A smile lit up his face. "You are back, Madame Blake. How do you feel?"

"Honestly, I feel as though I have been traveling in outer space. I ... I feel .... Do you, by any chance, have a meal ready? I am positively starving!"

"Dinner will be here very soon. Are you thirsty, still?"

"God, yes! Where is my bag? I've got water there."

Sisay pointed to her oversized bag sitting behind her, in the same spot from the prior day. She retrieved a bottle of warm water and gulped it down.

Her senses were reassembling. "What did you do to me yesterday? What went on? This is too strange!" She shook her head slowly, her hair falling over her face. Overwhelmed by the exertion and her inability to grasp the events themselves—let alone their meaning—Doria burst into tears, her shoulders heaving with each deep sob.

"You have done something very remarkable," said Sisay. "I myself do not know exactly what this means, but there are no stories having told of anyone loosening the bonds during *kertunang*. And many do not survive with all of their thoughts intact. I do not know yet how to interpret this. Please, Madame Blake, this is important. What can you recall from your night? Try very hard."

Mady brought out a large bowl of rice with fish and peppers. The aroma captured Doria and she salivated to the point of drooling. Wiping her tears away, she took the bowl from Mady and started to eat. Mady smiled. Sisay and Mady joined Doria on the mat, around the bowl.

The fog in Doria's mind lifted slowly, and she was grateful that Sisay didn't pressure her to recount last night's events. She believed they would coalesce at some point. Until then it was impossible to pin them down. What she could more easily access were her feelings throughout the night. Fear, abandonment, anger, curiosity, wonder, connection—all arriving in succession like the elements of a childhood story she had heard often yet always wanted retold. Slowly she remembered the events themselves. Yet so different were these memories from Doria's sensibilities, she didn't trust them. Was it truly possible that the ants covered her arms to keep her warm? That the mosquitoes were kept at bay by a swarm of bats? That a puff adder curled next to her back to stay warm, neither threatened nor disturbed by Doria? That a family of rats, instead of feeding on her helpless limbs, actually ate through the rope that bound her? Was any of this true? She could not find her voice to tell Sisay these things. They were all too otherworldly.

Of course, she thought. The tea. It was clearly hallucinogenic and anything that happened she obviously interpreted through a psychic haze, a distorted egocentric logic. If that was true, maybe the tea had let her pass through these events like air or allowed her a different place within the environment, as natural as a shrub or a resting animal. It was all very bizarre, as though she had floated into a meadow where the connective tissue to each and every living thing was visible. As she thought about this, she giggled. She was conceiving a child's fantasy. And how right it seemed.

Eventually she spoke about her memories and asked for help to understand them. Sisay didn't offer explanations, only encouragement for her to explore the memories as deeply as she could. It was dark and moonless by the time she completed her journey of recollection. Rising to signal the time to rest, Sisay asked Mady to prepare a suitable sleeping area for Doria.

"Tomorrow, Madame Blake, we will begin your training as a healer. Please rest now. The weeks and months ahead will require all your strength."

Doria's eyes widened and a small surge of joy went through her veins.

I've passed the test, she thought. All I managed to do was survive and that was enough. Oh, I have so much to learn. Can I do this, really?

Doria's self-doubt rose like a nitrogen bubble. How could she possibly commit her life to so strange and unknown an environment?

46. Never As Easy As It Sounds

"I don't know these roads, Monsieur Victor," Dante Sen confessed as he steered the Land Rover on the dirt paths just across the border from Mali into Senegal.

Having left camp in the morning darkness and dropping off a fire flower at Healer Deng's office in Mahina, Victor figured it still was unlikely they would reach Ziguinchor before dark.

Much farther south than the route Victor had traveled with the ailing Alan Broca months earlier, these unmarked tracks required the same routine: stopping at villages along the way to assure they were on the right path. The first significant hurdle was to cross the Falémé River, a major tributary of the Senegal River. Though the Falémé was not nearly as low as it would be later, in the dry season, Dante and Victor found the wide, shallow bend that the villagers had identified as the crossing. The men decided to head north, to travel the graded road that came down the end of The Gambia and turned southwest to head to Ziguinchor. Though it was not a direct route, it held the promise of better roads and quicker time.

Victor and Dante both knew there would be at least two river crossings to negotiate. The topographical map was mercifully accurate, allowing Victor to make reasonable estimates of their time. They reached the first by late morning. At the police station next to the river crossings, they stopped to ask how best to cross. Victor learned that the ferry made the crossing only with a full load.

The ferry was a flat barge with thick ropes looped through iron couplings on both sides. The ropes were fastened on each side of the river to massive poles sunk deep into the muddy banks. Two semis or four normal-sized vehicles could fit on the ferry at one time. Once it was full, all the passengers would assist the workers by pulling on the ropes to take the barge across. The problem was that once on the other side, it would wait again until it had a full load before returning. It wasn't uncommon to wait an entire day to get across.

When Dante and Victor arrived at the debarkation point, they thought they were in luck. The ferry was halfway across the river, returning from the other side. Their Land Rover was the third vehicle in line. The ferry floated up to the assembly of rotting planks and trusses that served as the pier. The *garçon de bac*, the boatman, threw the soggy tie-down ropes to a boy on the pier, who looped them over the tops of the two unsteady poles on either side.

After the last pickup truck rumbled off the ferry, it bounced like a cork at the river's edge. The boatman signaled to start loading the vehicles for the next crossing. The first truck, a Volvo flatbed, lurched onto the ferry and pushed it out into the river slightly, bending the poles of the pier and straining the old ropes. The Volvo's rear wheels churned in the mud as the driver tried to power his way over the pier and onto the ferry. The boatman and his helpers started shouting at the driver to back off in order to take the strain off the ropes and let the ferry float back to the pier. The driver refused, apparently believing he was very close to getting his truck on board. He was wrong. The truck suddenly gained traction as the rear wheels edged onto the short pier and lurched. This had the effect not of propelling the truck cab onto the ferry, but of pushing the ferry farther into the river, so much so that one of the mooring ropes snapped, allowing one side of the ferry to float freely into the river. The driver jammed on his brakes a second too late and the Volvo cab's front wheels slipped off the ferry, banging its bumper on the loading ramp and crashing into the river. The cab jackknifed over the edge of the pier into three feet of river water and blocked the path of the ferry to return to the dock and load the other vehicles. Victor and Dante looked at each other, knowing instantly that no traffic would move on either side of the river until this predicament was resolved.

"*Purée de merde!*" Dante yelled. "Unbelievable, Monsieur Victor. We will have to help them move the truck if we are to get across this morning."

"Shit! *Shit!*" Victor screamed, thinking of the time they were losing. "You're right, Dante, but how exactly can we help? It's going to take a tow truck or a tugboat to get that flatbed out of the way."

Dante cast Victor a puzzled glance, Victor reflecting his confusion. Dante dashed out of the car and ran through the mud to the ferry.

By now the air on the dock was crackling with recriminations and accusations in several languages. Fists punched the air, the driver and his apprentice blaming the bac workers for not mooring the bac properly; the boatman accused the truck driver of arrogance and incompetence, and, clearly, nothing was getting resolved.

Dante bounded onto the pier and, ignoring the fracas around him, inspected the wreck.

The driver's apprentice noticed him and came over. "It's a proper mess," the apprentice muttered. "Those crazy bac men didn't tie up the bac like they should have. Lazy Guineans!"

Dante glanced disdainfully at the apprentice but said nothing, preferring to continue his inspection to see if his idea would work.

"Please get a hammer and a tire iron from the cab," Dante said to the apprentice without looking up.

The younger man hesitated, and then did what he was asked. The argument to their right continued in full force until the driver noticed Dante inspecting the wreck and his apprentice rummaging about in the capsized cab.

The driver yelled over to Dante, "You there! What are you so interested in, heh? You like accidents, do you? Get away from there!"

Victor walked over to the truck driver, who had started to approach Dante. "This young mechanic is a brilliant problem solver. I'm sure he can help," Victor told him.

The driver ignored Victor and continued over to Dante. The bac workers were silent and still.

Dante sensed the driver's approach and stood up to face him. "We can get this fixed very quickly, Monsieur."

"Really? And you are an expert in transport crashes, are you?"

Without a flinch Dante said, "Yes sir, I am. I'm a master mechanic and have studied many auto accidents."

This had exactly the effect Dante sought. The driver hesitated, not knowing if this was simply a punk liar or someone who could actually mastermind the resolution to the problem. Pressing his advantage, Dante explained quickly. Victor watched and listened.

"We're going to separate the cab from the flatbed. We will then tow the bed off the pier with our truck. We will then push the rest of your tractor off the pier into the river—it isn't deep here. With our tow to assist, you should be able to restart your engine, back up onto the shore, and reconnect to your trailer. Do you understand this plan?"

When the driver started to argue, Victor stepped in. "This is a good plan, Monsieur. Think about it."

The apprentice returned with the tools, and he and Dante set to the plan while Victor convinced the driver of its soundness. The ferry workers watched Dante hammer out the iron pin connecting the trailer to the cab. Travelers and others waiting anxiously on the shore moved out of their vehicles and closed in to the pier to see what was happening.

Though the trailer didn't separate once the pin was removed, Dante saw that the connection was held together only by the notches of the hitch. If the apprentice were to pull the release lever in the cab, Dante could pull the trailer off the pier with the winch of the Land Rover. More leverage could be supplied by some helpful jostling from the drivers and the boatmen. He smiled confidently.

Though not as easy as Dante had envisioned, the trailer separated from the cab with the assistance of his minion, grunting and grimacing from the strain of their pushing and twisting. He maneuvered the trailer off the pier as Victor provided coaching and a bit of brawn. Keeping the Land Rover on tractable ground, Dante backed the trailer off the pier and onto solid ground away from the path, for vehicles to load onto the bac.

Free from the trailer, the jackknifed cab was pushed over the side of the pier. Although it stood in only a half meter of water and started easily, there was no traction on the muddy river bottom. The driver continued his tantrum when he tried to reverse onto the shore and only managed to spin the wheels in the mud. Victor took the winch line off the trailer and signaled to Dante as he waded into the river to attach the line to the cab. Coordinating Dante and the driver, Victor motioned for the workers to get into the water and push the cab, which they did with glee.

Thirty minutes later, Victor and Dante were on the other side of the river and back on their way to Ziguinchor.

"We did really fine, didn't we, Monsieur Victor?" said Dante, with a giddiness Victor couldn't share.

"You, my man, did very well. Thanks for that great work," Victor replied with a false calm. "We need to reach Ziguinchor in under twenty hours, Dante. We cannot let this fire flower perish. Understood?"

"Understood, Monsieur Victor," Dante replied, his happiness drained by Victor's dark face.

47. REUNION

The half-moon was partially obscured by wisps of high clouds, otherwise undetectable in the night sky. There was no electricity that night in Ziguinchor, so Doria was hunched over a set of six candles burning in a semicircle on her dining room table as she reread her notes of her "initiation." Something strange and remarkable had taken place, Doria knew. But the nature of that event and its implications were only a dim notion. Sisay had been deferential to the point of doting on her the last two days and Mady had become a servant to her instead of a guide and friend. What Doria noticed most about herself was acute awareness of her surroundings. It was wonderful at first, as colors, scents, and textures all revealed new intricacy. Within a day, however, her senses provided a constant intrusion, not allowing her to think or study as the motion of a beetle or the whisper of a breeze or the distant conversation of neighbors became simultaneous events in the forefront of her mind. All the events of her world, normally registered only by her subconscious, now became conscious. Doria struggled to understand how she could take advantage of this new awareness—or suppress it.

She searched through Dr. DeLevres' notes, hoping that concentrating on another topic would help clear her mind. DeLevres had cataloged an astounding array of local fungi. He had also created extracts that he had apparently experimented with, on himself. Most of these extracts proved inert or benign, but in the later notes DeLevres had isolated compounds that he believed responsible for various reactions such as pupil dilation, quickness of breath, and local skin anesthetization. He had combined these with compounds that caused more dramatic reactions, such as heart palpitations, nervous system spasms, and hallucinations. But to what end? Doria wondered.

His notes contained precise descriptions of extracts and other preparations. He had given descriptive names to all his new compounds, such as Pasty Alkaline 17, or Powder Stromonium 05. More interesting were the notes of many experiments he had carried out on other plants, test animals—mostly cats—and himself. Doria shook her head. DeLevres' experiments on himself had been at once brave and foolish, jeopardizing his ability to view results dispassionately and possibly even coherently. Nevertheless, his insight to the power and strangeness of some of these materials could have come only from firsthand experience, not just observation. How should Doria interpret this for her own work?

A fresh pot of tea was in order, but without electricity Doria needed a charcoal fire. It was still early in the evening, so why not? Taking a candle lantern from the table, she went into the kitchen and prepared a fire in a small hibachi on the stone counter. The charcoal crackled and sparked as the flames brightened the kitchen with flickering light. Doria looked out the window and saw a pale incandescence opposite the moon, like green phosphorus on a black sea or what she might have imagined the aurora borealis to look like. The strange phenomenon brought her outside, where Iba was sitting peacefully at the far end of the compound, finishing his dinner.

"Iba, please," Doria said, walking over to her driver, "what do you make of that mist or light or whatever, next to the moon?"

Iba stood and stretched, opening his eyes wide and cocking his head in curiosity. "I don't see, Madame. What light is there other than the moon?"

"Really, you don't see? That green sort of shimmering light over there." She pointed. "It looks rather like gauze in a breeze, don't you think?"

"Truly, I don't see this light. Do you see it brightly?"

"No, no, Iba. It's a pale, wavy light ... right there! Do you mean to say you don't see this?"

"I'm sorry, Madame. I see the moon. I see a few stars, though I do not see as many stars as I am used to. Perhaps this is a hazy night."

After a long pause and a continued gaze at the strange phenomenon, Doria told her driver, "I don't know what it is, Iba, but it is something. It is most definitely something."

Over the wall a different kind of light appeared, a vehicle. Rare as it was for cars or trucks to pass by her house at night, Doria knew the source. Victor had arrived. And he had with him the fire flower. Her certainty of this startled her.

"I believe that will be Monsieur Victor, Iba. Please open the gate for him. I'm sure he has no idea which house is mine."

If Iba wondered why Doria gave him no advance warning regarding Victor's arrival, he showed it only with a shake of his head on the way to the gate. Stepping into the middle of the entrance, Doria was bathed in headlights. The oncoming truck stopped abruptly, and then continued slowly up to the entrance, stopping a few meters directly in front of Doria. Victor descended from the passenger side of the Land Rover and walked to the front of the car, becoming a dark silhouette. To Doria he was awash in light.

"I see you found my compound all right, Mr. Byrnes," she said, extending her hand.

"Actually, this is the third time we drove by. I was about to start knocking on doors." He came to within a few centimeters of Doria, his heart suddenly racing. He looked at Doria's hand, not knowing what to do with it. She smiled at him, took him by the arm, and guided him through the gate.

"You must be extraordinarily thirsty and hungry—and your driver. Please come in and get cleaned and have something to eat."

Victor waved Dante in to park the Land Rover inside the compound.

Her smell and touch calmed and excited Victor. "We'll do that, Doria. But first I have a present for you ... well, not so much a present, but something you asked for."

He loosened himself from Doria's arm and ran to the Land Rover. Opening the rear door, he gathered the package of wet wood wrapped in newspaper.

"I hope we made it here in time for this thing," he said, handing the fire flower to Doria.

She held it up to her nose and sniffed the package multiple times. "I'll need to take care of this right away, Victor. I've prepared a special place. Thank you so, so much!" and she kissed Victor on the cheek. "Iba, please help Monsieur Victor and his driver. Show them inside."

Doria took the fire flower to a potting shed in the back of her compound. She had prepared the soil days ago, had watered it, filled it with the debris of swamp-rotted trees, and turned it over and over. It was time for this earth to receive its charge. With great care, Doria unwrapped the paper from the fire flower, keeping the root log complete and setting it into a hole she had dug with her hands. Hoping she had done everything right, she stood up.

What had Victor risked, what had he done to bring this gift, this precious ingredient to her? And what would this blunt-edged, frighteningly earnest male creature want of her in return? But no, he hadn't searched out this plant and driven God knows how many kilometers out of his way for anything more than the fact that she had asked him. Doria thought of his huge smile and started to feel warm and relaxed. Dear Lord, that's all so physical, isn't it? Was it that alone which attracted her and what she wanted of him? He wasn't Nigel, was he? He had none of Nigel's sophistication or perfect sense of irony, none of Nigel's understanding of the world or easy charm in it. But these were things that Doria had come to appreciate in Nigel, not endearing traits that she loved deep in her heart.

Nigel had always found a way to make her feel special and important in his life in the beginning, but when she didn't conceive in their first two years of marriage, he became less attentive, more work focused. Perhaps these events were just coincidental. Yet it seemed to Doria that it was soon after she received confirmation that she could not bear children when Nigel had become more distant. Nor did they ever talk about their infertility, not so much by mutual consent, but by a reflexive avoidance of pain. Even with her consuming interest in medical botany and his compulsive work, they might have bridged this gap and spoken to each other how they missed a child in their lives and how each coped alone and sought other fulfillment. Caring for each other as they did, why didn't one of them ever overcome his or her fear and put this single most significant trial of their marriage in full view—to bring them closer and help each other with the profound ache. Had that happened, they might have adopted a child. But that time was passing quickly. With every day, Doria was moving further from thoughts of her own children and thinking how she could heal so many children of others. And now there was this young American, raw, fascinating, and less threatening than her husband.

* * *

Iba had taken excellent care of the guests, finding leftover fish and rice in the refrigerator and setting it before Dante and Victor in large bowls. Victor remarked how fortunate it was that guests had arrived when the electricity was off. No food would go to waste. The two travelers ate like hyenas. The candlelight made for dim viewing of the table. They banged with their plates, their cutlery, and each other, reaching for bread, knocking over water glasses, and losing their knives on the floor. Had they been drunk they would not have been clumsier. Doria arrived in time to watch them rise from their meal and clear the table.

Victor came up to Doria. "So, give me the word, Doria. Please tell me we got it here on time. The fire flower is going to be OK, isn't it?"

"Time alone will tell us, Victor," she answered. "It did look rather stressed from the long journey. But you needn't fret so soon. It was to be expected. You can fret later." She touched her palm to his face, noticing his raw concern.

Doria's touch sent waves of electricity through Victor. His stomach knotted and his leg muscles clenched. He felt a sudden chill. They pulled away simultaneously, as they had when Doria had fed him the candy, fearful of the intimacy that came so easily, so tangibly.

Iba knew that Dante would be staying with him in the guesthouse. Without a question or announcement, Iba held Dante by his upper arm and motioned with his head to follow him to their quarters for the night, leaving Doria and Victor to clean up.

When Victor cleared the dishes and walked them into the kitchen, he slipped on the stone tiles and began falling to his side. Doria reached out to him instantly even though he was in the doorway and moving away from her. He recovered his balance by rushing forward, and slammed into the kitchen counter with his shoulder.

Wincing but not crying out, Victor straightened up, placed the dishes on the counter, and turned to Doria. "Ta-da!" he sang.

Doria halted her rush into the kitchen. She smirked at Victor and clapped. "Jolly good dance moves, Mr. Bushman."

She smiled and went over to the sink. As she did Victor took a step toward her. Her eyes were turquoise, clear and soft. There were no lines on her face except the tiny parentheses on either side of her mouth, and two tiny scars to the side of each eye, visible only when she smiled. She had a mole under her left ear, but her skin was otherwise perfect, smelling slightly of citrus. Then, as he inhaled the scent of her breath, Victor started to leave his body.

She looked directly into his eyes with only the slightest smile. Victor could not move. Doria reached up and touched his face with her open palm. He found himself able to turn his head into her hand and drink in the scent of her skin, and put his lips to the contours of her fingers. She lifted her other hand, holding his face, and gently pulled it toward hers. When their lips met, Victor pushed in more quickly than he intended. He wiped his hands on his khakis and put them on Doria's shoulders, kissing her deeper as her mouth opened. Doria moved into his arms and held his face immobile to hers as she kissed him with a strength and a passion she felt for the first time. She kissed his cheeks, his chin, and then his mouth again, pulled by a delicious, consuming gravity.

In the back of her mind Doria wondered why there were no alarms ringing into her thoughts, no warnings that she was in dangerous and altogether improper territory. In the rarified air of her passion these wonderings evaporated.

Victor was barely conscious as his body found its own initiative. His hands moved from her shoulders to her waist, then wrapping around her body, pulling her closer as his mouth reached into hers with tenderness and longing. He felt the supple softness of her skin as he ran his hands underneath her now loosened blouse. She started to unbutton his shirt with a nervous clumsiness that made them both laugh as their mouths stayed connected. He unhooked her bra and brought his hands under the cups to massage her full breasts and explore her beautifully erect nipples. When Victor's shirt was finally open, she moved her hands up and down his core, from his navel to his shoulders while marveling at his sturdy chest and moving her kisses there. Without bothering with the buttons, Victor tugged her blouse over her head with her help, freeing her breasts, to which he now bent and kissed with hunger and transporting pleasure. When he unbuckled the belt of her slacks and cupped her warm, covered vagina, she exhaled a loud moan, pulled him hard to her, and returned her mouth to his. Before he could completely loosen her pants, she pulled his hands up back to her breasts, leaned into his neck, and kissed it with abandon.

Then she whispered, "Come with me, Victor." She took Victor's left arm and put it around her waist.

"Take the candle," she told him, pointing with a nod at their light source.

When he had picked up the lantern, they walked with arms around each other's waist as she led him from the kitchen, through the small dining room, to her bedroom.

Victor placed the lantern on the single dresser in front of the mirror, magnifying the dancing light. They completed undressing each other as they kissed unselfconsciously, needfully.

"I hadn't dared let myself dream of this, Victor. I-I ..."

"Shhh. You are magnificent, Doria. So beautiful, so beautiful," he said, burying his head between her breasts.

She watched Victor in the mirror as he wrapped himself around her. When Victor bit her swollen nipple, it caused a surge of excruciating pleasure and she pulled his head harder as though it were possible to pull him inside of her. She ran her fingers through his hair, bending to kiss the top of his head as he continued to explore her. Victor went to his knees, caressing her belly with his tongue, the sides of her waist, the inside of her upper thigh, finally rubbing his cheeks and mouth over her wet mound.

At that moment she became aware of her nakedness as never before. It both thrilled and frightened her. She pulled Victor up, wanting to see and feel his manhood. As he stood, she put her hand around his erect cock, stroking it, and looking back into his eyes. He put his hand on top of hers.

She loosened her grip slightly. He reached down and rubbed her vagina with his whole hand and slowly parted her lips, inserting two fingers into her.

She closed her eyes and let her head revolve on its own, still rubbing him "Ohh … ohh, please, Victor."

His head was at her shoulder, sucking on her neck, her cheeks, her ears. She let herself be lifted into an unguarded sensuousness she could not remember.

"Come to the bed, Victor. Come into me."

They moved together, falling onto the bed as if guided by a single mind between them.

But just as Victor was about to enter her, a thought of care and curiosity flew into his mind. "Doria, what about … I mean, can you get pregnant? I should …"

Pulling him inside her with a light in her eyes, for the first time happy she could not conceive, she shook her head. "Come into me."

After Victor's powerful and youthfully fast orgasm, Doria guided him on how to pleasure her with his fingers, bringing her to an orgasm that shocked her and made her laugh. "Oh my God, that was … was … oh, my!"

They were now in the throes of satisfaction, though not yet sated. Separating to adjust the mosquito net, they returned to the center of the bed to hold each other and continue the exploration.

"I couldn't believe how beautiful you were the first time I saw you, Doria. Floating in your pool. Just so perfect. Whew."

"I remember that, Victor. I remember that your deep green eyes went completely through me. My stomach came into my throat and I thought I'd eaten a bad oyster!"

They laughed and fell into a pensive, comfortable silence.

He asked, "What do you make of this? This thing between us. It's pretty powerful, isn't it?"

She stroked his stomach. "It is that, all right. Overwhelming, I would say. But wonderful, really."

"What happens now? I mean, where do we go from here?"

She looked up at him quizzically. "Really, now! Am I not the one who should be asking those questions? Hmm, let's think about this. Victor, we've just made love one time here, out of the light, you understand? Away from anything that might interfere, do you see what I mean? We are completely dark to anyone who might peer in," she said. Then, after a short pause, she asked "Where do you want this to go?"

"OK, I guess that was really dumb of me. I sure as hell don't know where we can go. The only certainty I have is that I really don't want it to stop. I've just never felt like this before, you know?"

"You're young, my love. You may yet again feel this way. But let's not think about anything other than now, shall we?"

"And you, Doria? Have you felt like this before?"

She knew the answer, but couldn't bring herself to say so out loud right away. She pulled herself on top of him and put her head on his chest. After a deep breath, she told him, "I wanted to feel like this, but I never thought I could or that such a feeling really existed. I haven't been unhappy in my life, but I haven't been fulfilled, either. It's just recently I've discovered I can be fulfilled, or at least I can do more of the things that make me feel good about myself. Build some sense that I am a complete person, not just some dutiful spouse to a successful man. I've taken an active role in my own life recently, and you, somehow, are part of this new me."

"But doesn't this—the way we feel about each other—doesn't this change things? You know, change your life in a way that, well, you can't turn back from? That's kinda the way I feel right now."

"That's precisely the point, my dear, dear brute. Things were already changing. We're just catching up." She kissed his chest and moved down to his navel, and to his belly, then licking his soft sex back to attention, eventually taking him completely into her mouth. It wasn't for another hour that their lovemaking stopped and they slept in the cradle of each other's arms, a dream rising between them.

A little girl held on to Victor with one hand. In the other she held a string that bound a canary perched on her shoulder. The canary tried to fly away, but each time could only hover at the end of the string. Then he would return to the little girl's shoulder. The sky became dark with rain clouds and a wind blew up. From a glade in front of them where the trees bent like grass in the wind, Doria, dressed in shorts and a white T-shirt, walked toward them, saying, "Do I know you?" The little girl looked up at Victor, who nodded. When he did, the little girl let go of the string and the canary flew up into the black sky.

Miraculously sleeping through the incessant rooster calls at 5:00 a.m., Doria awoke first and nuzzled closer to her lover, comforted by his deep breaths and slow heartbeat. Victor stirred and reached dimly for Doria, happy to find her shoulders resting on his chest. They began to move together more earnestly as sleep gave way to touch and then to passion.

After showering individually in the tepid water, they watched each other dress, exchanging an occasional caress.

They went into the kitchen together to prepare a breakfast, finding Iba and Dante making tea and toast.

"Thank God for Nescafé," Victor pronounced.

Victor asked Dante if he was ready for the journey back to Dakar, knowing full well his young driver was eager to get on the road. When the two Africans left to pack the Land Rover, Doria stood up and led Victor by the hand, through the back door and into the garden.

"I have seen and learned some extraordinary things since I arrived here, Victor. Things which I cannot explain. There exists here, in this place, the real possibility for me to do something that I have wanted to do my whole life. I can learn more about natural healing and medicine than I ever could in Dakar or England. I can't possibly return now or, quite honestly, in any near future I might foresee."

Victor looked puzzled, then downcast. "When can I see you again?"

"I'm here. I want you to come when you can." She lifted his arm and wrapped her shoulder with it. "Tell me about your project. How long is your contract for and will your work take you close by again soon?"

"Doria, Dante and I drove 800 kilometers off our path the get here. It's going to be a real trick to get here again soon. I don't know. I-I just want to be with you." He pulled her gently into a long kiss.

When their lips parted, Doria broke from his arms. "You have to go, then," she said in a low, distracted voice.

"Christ. The team has probably already made it back. I need to make sure that Mammadu delivered Nigel's package."

"Of course, you're delivering something to Nigel, aren't you? Whatever is it, he told me nothing of it. But then, that's not surprising. Tell me, Victor, what have you done for him?"

"He's trying to help a group of young artists, a co-op, I think, get their work out of Guinea without the new cultural preservation law binding it up in bribes."

"Nigel Blake helping a band of native artists? Rubbish. Nigel is a good man in many ways, but he hasn't an altruistic bone in his body. Are you certain that's what you're doing? Delivering artifacts?"

Victor shrugged. "Mammadu and I both saw them, Doria. What's the harm in taking a few statues out of the country to help a group of hungry sculptors?"

"Even if it were the case, which I sincerely doubt, he is still enlisting you, my soldier, to break the law for him. And before you say another word, it makes little difference that this law is a corrupt and silly one. I don't like it. You really should be careful, Victor. Nigel is a clever man, but Tony Hume is more clever by half *and* more devious. The two of them dream up all manner of schemes, most of which they decline to carry out. Or they get someone else to do it for them. I repeat, be very careful." She placed her palm on his cheek and gazed into his eyes as if he were about to go to war.

"You don't need to worry, really. Mammadu and I have seen more than our share of the dangerous and strange. We can take care of ourselves. In fact—." Victor stopped like a man suddenly listening to himself talk bullshit.

Lost in a new and concerning thought, he turned his head away from Doria. She asked him to share what he was thinking, but he would not.

"I need to get up to Dakar and make sure the statues arrived safely, Doria. I don't know when I'll be back, but I'll make it as soon as I possibly can."

"I know you will, Victor."

They circled to the front of the house, where Dante was standing next to the Land Rover. Assuring himself that everything had been packed, Victor kissed his new love and got into his seat. When Dante started the engine and backed the Rover out of the compound, the pit of Victor's stomach clenched and his heart pounded. No longer was this the anticipation to be with the woman of his obsession. This was the pain of loss taking hold of him like a parasite.

Doria watched the gray vehicle leave in a cloud of red dust. She was worried for him. She had so much of her own work ahead of her. Still, she could not help the gnawing sensation that Victor would need her protection.

48. A BOUNTY OF STONES

The headlines in *La Presse* were depressing. Nigel wasn't sure he wanted to read about the airliner crash in Bogota killing 164 people or the resurgent Polisario who, eleven days ago, kidnapped six French tourists in the western Sahara, killing two of them. It put him off his midmorning break, which otherwise was one of the highlights of his days while Doria was away. It was so comfortable to arrive at Le Café des Rois and smell the ground espresso, hear the hissing steam as it blasted the cold milk into a warm froth. Was there a better way to complete a morning? He had a favorite table too, sitting in the corner closest to the sidewalk, one of three tables without an umbrella yet shaded for the few hours of the morning. And they always had the daily paper. So few places did.

The charming Lebanese waitress recognized him and always greeted him with a coy smile. Nigel found it energizing to simply nod, sit down without having to order, knowing his perfect café au lait and croissant would be set before him in minutes. Even as November moved to a close, these mornings still warmed up quickly and Nigel felt comfortable. Why should it be that the unsettling tragedies around the world, so fervently reported as though such loss belonged to everyone, should today make him feel that loss? Perhaps it was only this gnawing anticipation for the delivery of his diamonds.

He walked quickly back to his office, still puzzled by his reaction to the news. As he entered his office, Nigel's secretary nodded to the couch in the vestibule, where a thickset Senegalese man sat, stoic and large.

"Mr. N'Diaye says he has business with you, Mr. Blake. He says that he is a colleague of a Mr. Victor Byrnes."

Nigel looked at the man with utter bemusement. Is this some shakedown? Has Victor discovered what he was really transporting and decided to up the ante? No, not possible. Nigel could not have misjudged the simple youth so completely. So, now to find out what was going on.

"It's fine, Jeanne. I'll see him."

Without a smile or a word, Mammadu followed the secretary into the office of oblique angles, thin metal, and light wood.

Closing the door behind Mammadu, Nigel offered him a chair in front of his desk, and extended his hand. "Nigel Blake."

Mammadu offered him a surprisingly limp handshake for such an obviously powerful man. "Mammadu N'Diaye," the driver said.

"My secretary tells me that you are here on behalf of Victor Byrnes."

Silently, Mammadu reached into the faux leather satchel he had slung over his shoulders and brought out a bundle the size of a pumpkin, wrapped in newspaper. "Barbu asked me to deliver this to you," said Mammadu, depositing the package loudly onto the desk.

"Barbu? ... Oh, yes, of course. Mr. Byrnes." Nigel picked it up and inspected it, noting that the strings binding the paper appeared intact.

"Well, thank you very much indeed, Mr. N'Diaye. And what of Mr. Byrnes himself? I was expecting him, actually, to complete our arrangement."

"Barbu has gone to Ziguinchor for another delivery. He should return soon."

"Today, perhaps, or do you mean tomorrow?"

"Soon."

Nigel and Mammadu stood up simultaneously, recognizing the end of the meeting. Again Nigel extended his hand and again Mammadu offered an indifferent handshake.

"Thank you, Mr. N'Diaye, and when you see Mr. Byrnes, please do ask him to drop by. I should very much like to speak with him after his journey."

Mammadu nodded and walked out of the office.

Victor had gone to Ziguinchor and entrusted this delivery with a worker. What was going on? Of course, he's gone to see Doria. A pit formed in Nigel's stomach that took up residence like a troll. Good Christ, what could that mean? He was certain of his courier's attraction to his wife. And Doria had shown a discernable liking for the scruffy American, though *why*, Nigel could not fathom. Had Doria made some arrangement with Byrnes to stop by and assist her? The Senegalese man referred to another delivery. How long would they be together, alone? Nigel tried to bury these thoughts and refocus on the package. He found it difficult. Sitting back down, he picked up the phone.

"Jeanne, please get me Tony Hume on the line."

"Yes, Mr. Blake."

A moment later Hume's jaunty voice rang through the phone. "What's up, old man?"

"I've received a delivery, though not from whom I expected. David told you that Byrnes had showed up in Tougue with a driver, did he not? I think I just met him."

"Is everything there, Nigel? Is the package intact?" Tony was oblivious to Nigel's blurry statement about the delivery man.

"It seems to be."

"Well, open it, for fuck's sake, and tell me what you find."

Cradling the phone with his shoulder, Nigel took a letter opener from his desk and snapped the strings that bound the statues. He unrolled the package on his desk blotter like an ancient scroll, until he beheld the five statues, just as David had related to Tony. Nigel inspected the bottom of each one and recognized where they had been plugged. Using the letter opener, he pried the mortar away from the base. The first two statues revealed nothing. The third uncovered a chamber that, with some further scraping, revealed a cache of small dull stones that Nigel poured into his hands.

"How many of these statues actually have diamonds in them?" he asked into the phone. "Two, right?"

"Two of the five, exactly. What have you got there, man?"

"I've got one so far," Nigel said as he scratched the fourth and it too had a small chamber with rough-washed opaque stones. "Now, two. I think we can count this a success, Tony. What was the count of the stones David gave you?"

Thirty-six in one and thirty-three in the other. A total of sixty-nine uncut diamonds. He estimated that the smallest was about three carats and the largest about six. Average it at four uncut carats a stone, at about 2,500 quid a carat ... that would be around 690,000 quid, or slightly over $1.5 million. A right tidy sum for our third run, wouldn't you say? Are they all there, Nigel?"

He counted slowly, three times, letting the silence over the phone convey his concentration to Tony. "Sixty-nine, three times. OK. Come to my place tonight after six. We'll go through what we've got and plan for Antwerp."

"I'll let David know our boy came through. Well, well, Nigel, it seems your plan worked like butter and toast. We should consider another go in a month's time. David is concerned there's increased scrutiny of his family at the mines. And other things. It's likely we'll have only one more bite at this apple."

"What other things?" Nigel's pulse rose.

"I'll tell you tonight. Look. Why don't we plan to meet Byrnes tomorrow and get him scheduled as soon as possible, assuming, of course, he's still up for it."

"He's not back yet."

"Say again. He's not back yet? Where the bloody hell is he? And how did you get the delivery?"

"I told you. His driver. Byrnes apparently went to Ziguinchor," Nigel said flatly.

"That's not exactly on the route back to Dakar, is it? What bloody business does he have in Ziguinchor, I wonder."

"I can't say for certain," Nigel said with a frown. "His man said something about another delivery Byrnes had there. It could have something to do with Doria, you know. I don't like this, Tony."

Hume was silent for a moment as he pondered his friend's assessment. "Christ, Nigel. Don't go jumping to any conclusions, mate. Byrnes is just the new Blake delivery boy or handyman or something. I suspect Doria's got him working at an orphanage or hospital, or in her garden or something, yeah?"

"Most probably."

"When's the bastard supposed to get back to Dakar, anyway?"

"Soon," Nigel said.

49. CANARY DREAMS

Je n'aurais jamais dû laisser mes notes avec cette sirène! (I should have never left my notes with that siren!) DeLevres said to chastise himself. He was laboring into the night, combining isolated derivatives of various local fungi and deciding how best to test them. His notes contained information of past experiments regarding dosages that caused specific reactions in his field mice, including death. Mushrooms could easily do that without any assistance from DeLevres. But he was very interested in the exact doses per body weight that could cause a specific reaction in a predictable length of time. And how varied these reactions were! With different amounts of the same compound, a mouse might lose its sight, lose motor coordination, become energized, run in circles, learn how to open its cage, or try to escape by biting at the metal cage bars until its teeth fell out in a bloody soup. In the notes he had allowed Madame Blake to borrow, he had details of over 180 experiments that he was desperate to cross correlate with his work this night. His copies were not as faithful as he recalled.

So there was no other way. He would have to drive to Ziguinchor tomorrow and retrieve his notes. As he considered this sojourn, he realized that he would love to spend time with the alluring Doria Blake and see her work, if indeed she had done anything. She was not a professional researcher, after all. But she was a fine-looking woman with intense passion for the work, so it seemed. Perhaps she would surprise him.

DeLevres vowed to call Nigel Blake in the morning to ask for directions to his wife's hotel in Ziguinchor or wherever she was staying. As this plan jelled in his mind, he did something unconsciously that he had done no more than a few times in his life: he began to whistle.

PART 5
Discovery

50. My New World

I don't think I have ever felt such freedom. I've stepped into a different world where limits, unspoken rules, the notions of this social order I've lived in for so long are upended.

I wonder if I'm fooling myself, though. My husband is a day's ride and a phone call away. Is there a point when I must return to that place, that life with him, at his side, be again his loyal companion, and abandon this wonderful experiment? But why? Too much may have already happened. Were I to return, even that old numbing world would be different, more constricting. I would become a crazy woman. Good Lord, I don't know. Things have changed so fast and are still changing in ways I can't foresee. This is so thrilling and yet so very frightening. I so hope I'm up to this.

Victor's faint spirit lingers—a scent in a towel, my teacups in disarray. I feel his presence, but I don't mind that he's away. He's so unlike me. I'm not terribly sophisticated myself, but Victor has the sensibilities of a boy off the farm. When I spoke to him of my family, he seemed not to understand at all, how we children had our roles so clearly defined and how my world as a little girl was centered around our mother's chores and support of our men and our home. It is such a pity he did not grow up with a sister.

Oh, but I do love his curiosity and his willingness to do seemingly anything. Is there no line he wouldn't cross, I wonder. This must be why I feel he's in danger all the time. He seems not to have any sense of the horrible things that can happen, nor has he any compunction against trying the silliest or most dreadful task. How can this be so endearing and at the same time so troubling? Best not to think about that, Doria. It can't lead to anywhere good right now.

I've reserved today for testing, though I'm not really sure how to go about it. DeLevres' notes clearly show that he was missing some critical component for his distilled fungal compounds. He wasn't able to regulate the reactions of his mice. And nor did the dosages seem to coincide with the length of time the mice were under the influence of the compound I've discovered.

Iba was so funny when I told him I needed test animals. Poor dear just could not grasp why I wanted to pay the local children to bring me live mice. But wasn't he wonderful, finding three large boxes and making them into little mouse colonies? It was fascinating, and to be expected, I suppose, that once the word got around that I was paying five CFA for a live mouse, a cottage industry was born. Little boys who never went into fields except to play football are now mouse rousting at every opportunity. No surprise that they brought in the occasional field rat. There was certainly no reason to turn them away, but we discovered that we needed to keep the rats and the mice separated. The rats would tolerate the mice for about four or five hours, and then they would kill and consume them if left together. Grizzly business, this test animal stuff. Iba continued to find the materials for housing them. I was able to locate a few old aquaria with the help of Tafa Conte, and the odd kitchen pot was rejuvenated to house my experimental mice. And of course I had to devise a way to tell them apart. Iba to the rescue as always, mining his friends for some small bottles of black ink, unavailable at any local stores but regularly supplied to the schools, even if books or teachers are not.

Not only did I need to keep the mice fed and disease free, but I had to make sure my mice were protected from the local cats that, like baboons, get into everything. The good news is that I don't believe I will have to kill and dissect any mice for these experiments, though I'm certain that the dosage tests will claim a number of them. 'Tis a higher purpose to which they are called.

Sisay continues to be very keen that I learn the traditional compounds from him, for which I am so grateful. But since that night of the *kertunang*, he has been much more deferential, and I suppose the only word for it is happy. I'm still trying to piece it all together, though it leaves me shuddering sometimes. I asked Sisay what the ritual was telling him. And why am I different in his eyes, having come through it … whole? As he often does, he became coy. He told me that few are honored to participate in the ritual and fewer still come through it able to continue their learning and work. I could only deduce from this that I am very fortunate to have come through *kertunang* at all. I don't feel it's changed me in any substantive way, other than perhaps this chill up my spine when I think of spending the night hallucinating among all the creatures of the forest. Yet they seemed so, I don't know, protective of me. Is that what it feels like now? That the forest protected me? Ha! I won't be doing that ever again to find out! How dangerous was that, and foolish of me! And yet the results have been all I could have wanted.

Today has been fascinating. Sisay taught me how to assemble the compound which helps people with what I can only call hyper-mental instability. This elixir seems to calm them down to where they can function almost normally. It was a remarkable demonstration, really. Two women and a man, all probably in their late sixties, came to Sisay from a nearby village. They seemed very agitated and overeager for intervention. After they left, Sisay told me their history.

One of the village boys, Guamy, had been born mentally deficient, yet, as is the custom in many African cultures, he was considered unique and was tolerated, no matter what he might do in the village— up to a point, that is. When he would sit down at a neighbor's meal and take food without courtesy or even acknowledgment, he was eventually escorted out of the compound. As the boy grew to become a man, his mind could not grasp what his body was doing. He attacked girls and women in the village. He smeared himself with his own feces. He accosted people in the streets, shaking them and shouting gibberish to them. He'd been beaten senseless by some of the village boys many times, and Sisay had been called more than once to set his broken bones. About a year ago the same delegation had come to Sisay requesting greater help. Guamy was too much to care for or tolerate. He was bankrupting the family, who had to repay neighbors for damage he had caused. He could no longer be controlled by his mother or sisters, as when he was younger. Something had to be done to settle him down, make him docile. Could Sisay do this? If Sisay could keep the young man calm and docile, the delegation promised Sisay three cows, one from each household making the request. Sisay agreed.

His intervention was swift and effective. He gave Guamy a spoonful of the concoction I was about to learn. Then, once a week, as instructed, the young man's mother administered a single spoonful in his food. For the first six months it worked perfectly, and Sisay got his three cows. What was happening now was a bit of a mystery, but Sisay had his ideas.

"They have stopped giving him the medicine," Sisay told me with some gravity.

"Why on earth would they stop, Sisay?" I asked him.

"Laziness, forgetfulness. Maybe they are selling the medicine to another family. Come with me, Madame Blake, and we will learn the truth."

I was delighted to go on this medical investigation, though I didn't much fancy the walk, recovering as I was from continued sleep deprivation and muscle aches that surely came from that night's ordeal—or was it Victor's visit? I wanted Iba to drive us, but Sisay was insistent. By walking these long distances we earned the privilege to heal the afflicted, he told me. This sounded all too Christian and martyr-like for my sensibilities, but there you have it. Sisay was keen on keeping his status with the community. I did admire him for that.

After a two-hour march through the boggy forest, swatting at flies, avoiding snakes, and trying desperately to conserve energy and water in the sauna that was the Casamance autumn, we came upon a small village. There could have been no more than a dozen huts, including those reserved only for cooking. Children with few or no clothes on poured from the huts to greet us, and Sisay smiled as they rushed toward me with delighted squeals. Then they stopped, looking diffident and unsure.

"They have never seen a white woman, Madame. You are their first."

"Really?" I answered.

Ziguinchor may not be Zurich, but it certainly has had its share of Europeans working there. It seems quite unfathomable that I should be the first white woman these children—some certainly fifteen years of age—had ever seen. Well, if that was in fact the case, I should be on my best, hadn't I. And these children were so adorable, and though nearly naked, were remarkably clean. I knelt beside three little girls, two of whom had baby siblings swathed to their backs. I slowly picked up a hand of the smallest, who thought to pull away but decided to allow me to hold her. I put her hand to my cheek and had her stroke the side of my face. I wanted her to know I was flesh and blood, not some jinn, come to eat her. She wasn't sure at first, but with persistent soft stroking with her hand, I got her to smile and touch my face on her own, including my Gallic nose. Very soon thereafter, more children gathered around us, and I could see real hunger in their bellies, blotches on their skin, and runny noses with flies running in and out of their nostrils. Heartbreaking.

Adult women, each, as the youngsters, swaddled with a child, accompanied by a few old men with barely five teeth between them, approached us, or I should say approached Sisay, each taking a turn to greet him and shake his hand. They took Sisay over to a large acacia tree in the middle of the village and bade him sit on a mat in the shade. Sisay beckoned for me to come and sit beside him. Listening patiently to one of the older men tell the story of how the medicine Sisay had supplied disappeared over a week ago, my mentor would stop them and translate for me, and then have them continue.

He asked them, "What have you done to locate the missing medicine?"

"We have searched everywhere for it, Master Sisay. It is no longer here," answered an older man, tall and gaunt, with a thatch of gray hair encircling his face.

"Do you agree that the medicine could not disappear by itself?" Sisay asked in his fatherly way.

"We do not know, Master. It is not normal."

"Not normal indeed. So, if the medicine did not disappear by itself, how did it disappear?"

The downcast looks of the ten villagers and their reluctance to speak gave Sisay a clear path for his inquiry.

"Someone has taken the medicine, is this not true?"

Three of the village men, addressing their esteemed elder, answered almost as a chorus: "We do not know, Doctor. It could be as you say."

The women, all still standing, nodded in agreement.

"You, mother of Guamy," Sisay said, and pointed to a haggard woman who held a basket of sorghum. "You have been in charge of the medicine for Guamy. Where did it go? Did you take it and sell it?" He accused without any change in the soft tone of his voice.

"No, Master, no. I would never take my son's medicine. It is the only help he has! Not me. I could not!"

Sisay asked, nearly in a whisper, "Who, then?"

Everyone looked at the ground as if the guilt of a person unknown was theirs.

"You may not have seen anyone take the medicine, but you know that someone did," he told them. "Who could it have been?"

No one said a word.

"I have brought another jar of medicine for Guamy. But why should I give it to you if you cannot protect it? Mother of Guamy, where did you keep the medicine?"

"In a clay pot in the dark part of the hut, Sisay, as you instructed."

"And did your husband know where you kept the medicine?"

"Of course, as did my other children."

The teenage girl next to the mother of Guamy, who, unlike the older women, had no scarf on her head, started to paw the ground with her left foot. Sisay looked at the young woman directly for a few brief seconds that held the attention of the entire gathering. Though she had defiance in her eyes, she could not hold Sisay's gaze for more than an instant. I saw her look up and then away at least three times. At that point I was certain it was she who had taken the medicine.

But why? Did she sell it to buy something for herself, for someone else? I wondered if Sisay knew, or if not, that he would discover the girl's motivation.

Sisay slightly squinted as he continued to stare at the daughter. He said, "Where is Guamy now? Take me to him."

There was a flourish of activity as the men rose from sitting. They spoke to each other and called for some young boys from farther away in the center of the village. Guamy's mother and sister moved quickly toward the interior of the village as well. The older men signaled for Sisay to follow them. Sisay took me by the arm and together we walked through the center of the village, to a livestock pen where a number of people were now gathering.

When Sisay and I reached the simple enclosure made of decaying logs and thorn brambles, we saw no livestock. However, at the far end, fastened to a pole with ropes of cloth and gagged, was a man of indeterminate age, dressed in mud-caked rags, sitting on the ground and staring stone-eyed at nothing in particular. Guamy. As the crowd pressed in on the barriers of the pen, he seemed to become aware of their presence and stood up quickly as if not recalling his binds. He thrashed around trying to gesture, his screams and shouts muffled by the gag. He was now extremely agitated and was kicking up mud from the pen at the crowd. Some of the boys laughed as they picked up clods of mud and threw them at Guamy. The older men raised their walking sticks and chased the boys, who were still laughing and pushing each other. Guamy continued to struggle against his constraints. Soon he was coughing so forcefully that he had to stop his thrashing and he slumped to the ground in convulsions. His mother threw down her basket and ran through the mud to her boy. He fought against her as she tried to comfort him, cradling his head. For a few seconds his wild eyes looked through her with no recognition, only primal fear. Then, as if a new person took over his body, Guamy's eyes softened, his body stopped convulsing, and he began to cry. Guamy's mother rocked him in her arms in the filth of the animal pen.

What a strangely moving moment, I thought. I felt a wave of compassion well up in me and my eyes watered, to hope that I, like Sisay, could help these desperate people. Then I managed to get a glimpse of Guamy's sister from the corner of my eye and noticed her lips tighten and her fists clench as her mother caressed the forehead of the deranged brother. I could see the girl's body shiver slightly with what could only have been rage. The girl was intensely jealous. Of course! Her brother was terribly afflicted, not only unable to contribute but consuming the family resources and reserves. Yet the mother gave her firstborn son the full measure of her affection, while her eldest daughter was emotionally starving.

When I turned to look at Sisay, his gaze was already on me. He nodded once and then turned his attention back to the mother and son, walking to the fence as the crowd huddled around him.

"Mother, I know you do not want this for your son. You must do two things," Sisay told her. "Stand up, Mother of Guamy, and walk to me."

The mother did not move or react in any way.

Sisay was patient but insistent. "If you want my help again, Mother, stand, leave your son for now, and come here to me."

Sisay's words reached her agitated mind and she rose slowly, making sure her son was sitting upright, still bound, and came over to Sisay. From beneath the inside of the dark Western jacket which he wore over his traditional boubou, Sisay pulled out a jar of the medicine he had prepared.

"Give him one spoonful now in a cup of water or a bowl of porridge. It will take a few moments for the medicine to work. When you are sure he is calm, wash him, clothe him, and the two of you come to me at the chief's compound. Do not let the medicine out of your care for a single moment. Do you understand?"

She nodded quickly multiple times.

"Good."

Seeing the exciting moments had passed, the enthusiasm of the crowd melted away and the people dispersed back into their routines. Sisay and I were left with three of the village elders to walk back to the shade of the acacia tree where we had met earlier.

We took our places on the mat, sitting there in silence. Sisay said nothing to me, though I had expected some additional explanation from him. I sensed we were waiting for the mother to complete whatever tasks Sisay had given her. After a good half hour of doing absolutely nothing except wave at flies and try to be at peace with my own thoughts, I saw Guamy's mother appear from the village with a clean Guamy calmly in tow.

Sisay later translated for me their agreement.

"Your daughter has stolen the medicine I gave you for Guamy. Do you know why?"

The mother sheepishly shook her head.

"It is because you have given her very little of yourself and she is jealous of Guamy."

"But, 'Bye Sisay, Guamy is my firstborn son. He needs me!"

"Yes, and the rest of your family needs you, as well. Look to your daughter and work side by side with her. Show her you are her mother, as well. And if you safeguard and use this medicine wisely, Guamy will not be such a burden. Do this and live a more peaceful life."

The mother nodded submissively, perhaps not understanding all she needed to do, maybe resolved, maybe not. I couldn't tell. She retreated back to the center of the village with her son.

Sisay spoke to the three village elders. "See that she protects this medicine. If she does not, there is no more that I can do."

They looked at each other, shaking their heads in agreement.

I wondered if they would do anything themselves, really. What could they do? It all seemed so open and unresolved, yet everyone seemed to believe it was time to carry on.

Sisay rose, and I heard the chirping of birds at the top of the great tree as we left its protective shadow. I looked up to see two birds of shimmering blue and violet. How they came to be so joyful in the heat was a mystery to me, but the song was comforting and, in my hopeful state, optimistic. Isn't it odd how we humans will interpret the slightest phenomenon in nature as supporting our own state of mind?

* * *

Two days after Sisay and I visited Guamy's village, I feel isolated and, well, a bit forlorn. As I try to develop anything that remotely assists the people of Senegal, I feel so inadequate and stupid. The effect on Guamy of the potion Sisay prepared was real and thoroughly helpful. But I can't seem to find anything helpful for the children of Ouakam orphanage, or for anyone at all, really.

I so wish I had access to my old texts and a real laboratory. How can I ever distill an important compound or create a new natural medicine in this primitive setting? Or how could I have ever done it? I've deluded myself completely, haven't I? Oh, Doria, how could you be so carried away, so full of yourself? But I'm not trying to cure cancer, am I? I want to relieve suffering by better understanding and combining what elements nature has given us. It's so important that I hold on to that. It's not an impossible dream, but really one—be honest, Doria—that will take most of my life to realize. Is that truly what I want to do right now, at this time? It must be. I cannot give up on myself. I can do this, I can. I must. Good Lord, if we could just find one straightforward, simple medicine for those desperate children. Something to stabilize their emotional swings or to neutralize some other chemical chaos in a brain misfired. Wouldn't that be such a huge victory? I cannot let one down day overwhelm me. Not now. If I don't try, how can I say I have lived my life, been what I hoped to be? Oh God, and what is that, exactly? … It is so tiring always questioning myself. Slow down, Doria ….

I realized, of course, that I had neglected Alain DeLevres' notes—neglected in the sense that I hadn't tried to apply them to anything I was learning from Sisay. Certainly, there was no obvious or intuitive connection that I had yet discovered, but I started to feel there might be some value in making a stronger effort.

So, over to my makeshift laboratory I went. The first thing I did was go over my own notes, seeing if I could recall enough of DeLevres' direction that would let me identify something similar to what Sisay had taught me. After at least two hours I felt I was getting nowhere and losing a bit of hope. Then I realized that the compound the old healer had given Guamy might be exactly the kind of thing that could be combined with DeLevres' work with psychotropics extracted or derived from certain mushrooms, the alkaline compound being key. But my mycology, never particularly strong, was totally insufficient to go into the forest and identify the species described in DeLevres' notes. What I did learn from rereading the professor's work was his method of distillation and extracting what he needed, testing it chemically, and then on animals. Well, I did have my mice. But what was I trying to do? Perhaps if there were a way to increase the potency of the medicine Sisay gave to Guamy, then what? Might it provide a longer-lasting result? A stronger result, restoring more normal behavior? Might it put the subject into a coma? And if I could increase the potency, would it actually help? There is only one way to know. I must keep going forward.

Since DeLevres' mushrooms—at least the ones with extensive notes—were basically medicinal but mostly lethal, I had to believe that Sisay knew what some of these were. I took the two books showing the mushrooms I was interested in, *pluteus salicinus* (next to which DeLevres had put a series of question marks) and *inocybe haemacta* because they had high alkaline and psilocybin concentrations. His notes indicated that these chemicals could be almost instantaneously absorbed, quickly stimulating specific neurotransmitters. However, I doubted the professor's rather crude drawings would be enough for Sisay to determine the location of these fungi, assuming he had ever seen them.

To my complete surprise, Sisay took one look at the flattened dark top and thin stalk of *p. salicinus* and seemed to know instantly where these mushrooms grew.

"This is not their season, Madame. They will come when the rains begin again and the cattle are well fed." Which I understood to mean that the cows will defecate more profusely and provide a "home" for these mushrooms.

"Have you collected any of these, Sisay?" I asked him with great expectation.

"And if I had, Madame Blake, what would you do with this mushroom, heh? Start a garden, make a stew?"

His defensiveness was rather startling. What nerve had I struck?

"I would, Master Sisay, learn all I could of its secrets. I wonder if it would be possible to—"

"This is called *njin doram*. It means the 'devil's hat.' It is an evil plant that will not let itself be used for healing. Do not seek this out. It will not serve you."

Sisay turned around and went into his house, expecting me to leave without even a proper good-bye. Very cheeky, by Djiolla standards, but Sisay has his own way about him. Rather than stand there dumbfounded, I left.

As I turned to close Sisay's gate behind me, Mady Toula rushed through the exit as if blown by a gust of wind. She closed the gate behind her.

"Madame Blake, *njin doram* is not like other plants. Sisay is afraid of it because it defies his understanding. I am afraid of it too, Madame, and so should you be."

"I have great respect for the medicine of this ... of *njin ... doram*," I said. "But great power does not mean it is evil, Mady Toula. It means we need to be more careful and go more slowly in order to understand and uncover the secrets to use its strength for good. No?"

"You are a magical person. No one has survived *kertunang* with their thoughts still their own since Sisay himself, so long ago. And he fears your power, as well. Perhaps you could tame *njin doram*. I will show you where you may find it, but I cannot go with you. It grows all year long, Madame. But often it simply cannot be found."

"Where, Mady? Tell me where."

I was surprised that the fungi could be found so close to town, but I shouldn't have been. We were in a rain forest. The real problem, Mady said, was that they lived for only a day and only where the cow dung perfectly formed into solid-like clumps. Mady tried to give me precise directions, but I couldn't understand. Her description was peppered with Djiolla that she couldn't translate into French. Mady touched my shoulder and said, with a longing in her eyes, something else in Djiolla.

"What, Mady, do you mean. What do you want to tell me?"

"Your destiny, Madame, is to unearth the strength of our world. You must be very careful." She turned quickly and disappeared back into Sisay's compound.

* * *

With Iba's help, it turned out to be less difficult to find the general area where the *p. salicinus* mushrooms grew. But finding the actual plants took three days of searching. I finally found a cluster of *p. salicinus* inside a molding tree trunk half submerged in a bog and covered in dung. By the time I reached it, I was covered in mud and, I discovered later, leeches.

But what an interesting specimen! The top was a deep translucent blue-green with brown stripes. Before I harvested them, I pulled from my canvas satchel DeLevres' notes with his illustrations and assured myself I had found *p. salicinus*, though I confess I did not understand the question marks in the notes. DeLevres' renditions were as accurate as I could have asked for. Iba had not ventured into the swampy area with me but kept watch from a distance. He must have thought me mad as a hatter, traipsing through the deep muck just to find some mushroom.

Now then, what are my next steps? DeLevres' notes said that heat was not the way to extract the compound, but to make a slightly acid solution with lemon juice and ... aspirin? So I soaked two of my specimens overnight, as his notes instructed. In the morning, the mushroom had shriveled considerably, the liquid had taken on the color of the mushroom cap and had thickened. I measured the syrup and set out four combinations of liquid *p. salicinus* and Sisay's medicine, which I've named *guamy*, after the village boy. I kept the amount of *guamy* constant and changed the amount of *p. salicinus*, starting with 10 milliliters, up to 40.

I couldn't attest to the specific mental conditions of my test mice. I did note their ability to eat, find their way through the maze to get to their food, and their interactions with each other. But I was not at all certain that I would be able to identify any response based on the new mixture. I would see.

I started with the lowest dosage first and gave it to the first pair of mice. After an hour, there was no appreciable behavior change that I could note. Having marked each mouse with stripes to identify them, I gave the second dose to mouse pair #2. Still nothing after over an hour of observation. Likewise, mouse pair #3 with dosage three.

Finally, I administered mouse pair #4 with the highest dosage. This one, labeled p-g40, was a disaster. Within minutes of eating the dosed grain, both mice began to jump about madly, flipping onto their backs, lying motionless for seconds as if dead, and coming back to life in a fit of circular running. The behavior of both mice was so similar it was as though they had received a single set of instructions. Their frenzy went on for more than twenty minutes. I grabbed them numerous times, difficult as it was, to see if there were other signs to note: foaming at the mouth, change in eye color, skin heat, any other manifestation to identify this particular reaction. I could discern nothing as they quivered and fought in my gloved hands.

Back to the beginning. I suppose my little experiment was just not theoretically sound. After all, why should this combination lead to anything other than chaos. I really hadn't looked at the chemistry of both *p. salicinus* and *guamy* to glean anything of how they might react together. But then, this is how ancient knowledge was developed in the first place. Simple experimentation. Think, Doria, think! And it dawned on me that maybe that universal additive Sisay told me about, the plant that Victor had so earnestly delivered to my door, the fire flower, might make some difference.

I reviewed my notes from Sisay's conversation about the fire flower. All it said was "to harvest the 'tears' at sunrise, before the ants begin their work." So, eyedropper in hand, I collected the tiniest nectar of the fire flower, and sat with it for half a day while I tried to decide exactly what to do with it. In the end, I opted to use the entire collection with the strongest dosage, p-g40, since it was the only one that produced any reaction. I administered the concoction to two untested mice and waited. It was a very different reaction altogether. These mice started to become more active, not in a frenzied way ... almost in some collaborative game where they stood on their hind legs and leaned on each other, and then raced through the maze together even though there was no food. How extraordinary! I needed then to check on any of the outward physical changes that I had looked for during the previous test. When I extended my hand to pick up one of the mice, it disappeared. As in, it vanished from view!

Instinctively I looked around for the mouse, completely disbelieving what I had just seen. But the mouse was gone. I shook my head and blinked at least three times. I stood up from the mouse house and then, suddenly, right in front of my eyes, the mouse reappeared. What on earth!

51. Intrusion

I wasn't just shocked when Alain DeLevres showed up at my gate on Tuesday morning, I was mortified. Having borrowed his notes and used them as if they were my own, without giving him so much as a thank-you note or some letter of appreciation, I felt a pang of guilt such as I had not experienced in ages. So, my greeting might have been more than effusive. Iba was asking him to stay at the gate after the insistent knocking. I hoped Alain wouldn't misinterpret me.

"Professor!" I called out as I walked quickly toward him with my hand extended. "Iba, please let Professor DeLevres in. He is more than welcome! How did you find me this morning, Professor? You did not telephone, did you? I would surely have known if you had. And it seems my 'spies' from town have let me down," I said.

He himself appeared a bit disoriented.

"I, uh ... yes, Madame, I did arrive last night and stayed at the hotel de something or other. The university driver and I tracked down your location with the sparse information the desk clerk could provide, and by process of elimination ... voila! The driver dropped me off somewhere, over there, on a corner." He waved his hand high and limp, as though this indication to a corner would be meaningful for me to understand his ordeal. "And I walked to this address."

"Well, now that you're here, let's get you some tea—or is it coffee?—and some toasted baguette, yes? After you've had a chance to settle, we can then talk about our work. I have so much to tell you—and to ask you!"

I put my arm through his to guide him to the entrance and was surprised that he resisted. He was looking glassy-eyed as he surveyed my little compound, and then stared at me. I looked back at him with my best innocent smile.

"Whatever is it? Please. You've made it to my house. Come in and sit down. Are you all right?" I was as solicitous as I could be.

"The truth, Madame, is that I can scarcely believe I'm here. I don't know why I should feel this way, of course. It's just that—"

"Why," I said, leaning in to him, "you've been imagining coming to my house for some time, haven't you?"

He turned the cutest shade of red, and I knew I was right. He probably had been fantasizing for days about finding me here. That was an advantage not to be wasted, so I pulled a bit firmer on his arm and this time he allowed himself to be led inside. Iba closed the gate behind us.

When Alain was seated at the kitchen table, I put on a kettle for my tea and his coffee. He relaxed.

"I hope instant Nescafé is good enough for you this morning," I said. "It really is the only coffee available, and since I don't drink it myself—"

"Yes indeed, Madame, Nescafé. Best invention ever to come from Switzerland," he stated. Then he added, "Have you been able to put my notes to valuable use down here?"

"Oh my Lord, I certainly have! I can hardly wait to show you, Professor. You won't believe your eyes!" I laughed at my own cleverness. It was thrilling to think, though, that someone else might witness what I was still finding so difficult to believe. And not just anyone. It was this earnest, renowned, and eminently corruptible scientist.

Since that day last week when one of mouse pair #5 literally disappeared, I think I've discovered how it happened, in a manner of speaking. Professor DeLevres' arrival could not have come at a better time. However, I sincerely doubt whether even he will fully understand the mechanism at work. Its implications seem beyond my own belief!

We chatted away for a few minutes about Dakar, how dry and hot it had become. He told me about the President's Charity Ball for Health and how miserable he had been, watching all the rich Africans and expatriates congratulate themselves. He railed on about how failures in the through-the-looking-glass world of development politics—full of corruption, incompetence, and neglect—are painted as heroic successes.

I knew, of course, looking upon all this as a bit of an outsider, that he had a point. Nevertheless, I was quite put off by this rant of his, triggered simply because I asked for news from Dakar. It was the cheeky French in him to arrive unannounced and then pour out some radical views on development. I often find it amazing how people of talent have so many peccadilloes and blind spots that the rest of us tolerate because of their brilliance. Ah, woe to those of us with little talent and a surfeit of bad habits. Anyway, I gave my surprise guest his soapbox. Not only did I need him, I suddenly seemed overcome by my own shortcomings.

"Things will look ever so much brighter, Professor, once you've finished your coffee. And once I show you the most extraordinary thing you have ever seen in your life." I leaned over the table and opened my eyes as wide as I could. "I'm not the least bit joking with you or exaggerating. What I'm about to show you will shock you!"

I worried that I might have overdone the buildup a bit. No matter. As long as I was certain I could duplicate what I saw last week, I knew he would be amazed. The real question would be, "What next?"

Having filled the professor's stomach and rejuvenated him, it was time to show him what the mice could do with the chemical assistance of my new brew that I've called "Blink."

* * *

At first I had thought the mice actually dematerialized and rematerialized of their own volition. But that was so farfetched I could not on my life believe it true. I then thought that somehow the mice became invisible, which, though still not possible in my world, was nevertheless a more palatable theory. So that same day when it had first happened, I asked—well, frantically begged is more accurate—Iba to come and confirm what I saw. That was when I began to understand what was happening.

"Come, Iba! Come quickly! I need your help! Please, now!" I was screaming while looking at the reappeared mouse.

Iba rushed in, fast and flustered. "Madame, what is it? What do you need?"

His eyes were wide and he was ready for battle, I'm sure of it. Never had I seen him in such a state of agitation. But then, I don't believe he had ever heard me scream in such a state before, either. The poor man was shaking.

"Iba, I'm OK. I'm fine. I need your help." I put my hand on his shoulder, hoping to soothe him. It was slightly awkward because Senegalese men often take a physical gesture of this type from a woman as something more. One learns these things the hard way. I slowly withdrew my hand and waited for him to regain his calm. As he was centering himself, I led him over to my experiment.

"Now, Iba, I'm going to reach in to pick up this mouse and I want you to stand over here." I placed him where he could view the mice and me but not be in the way of anything. "When I try to pick this mouse up, I want you to tell me what you see."

His quizzical look informed me that I would need to be very explicit. So I went over thoroughly with him what I would do and what I wanted him to observe. He finally nodded his understanding of the instructions, if not their justification.

The two mice were at rest in their box. When I reached down to pick one up, they both scampered away, yet remained visible. Finally, I had one cornered and just as I was putting my hand on it, it vanished. I stopped my hand.

"Iba!" I shouted, though he was no more than a meter away. "What do you see? This instant!"

"I see that you are about to catch a mouse, but you've stopped."

"Do you still see the mouse?"

"Yes, of course I do, Madame."

I, however, did not see the mouse. This was very curious. I moved my hand away and backed up one pace. The mouse returned, still shivering and afraid in the corner of the box.

"Please come over here, Iba. What I'd like you to do is pick up one of these mice. Is that all right?"

"Pick one up and hold it? Is that all?"

"That's all."

He faced the box and decided which mouse he would go after. I stood back to watch. As he was about to catch one of them he let out a surprised grunt and then started looking about as though he had lost something. He saw the second mouse and decided to try to catch it. Another surprise as he stopped. But I saw them both clearly. All Iba had to do was continue to extend his hand and grab the stationary mouse. But he could not because he couldn't see them.

"My God, Madame, what kind of mice are these? They disappear as you try to hold them." He backed away, still looking at the box and suddenly he pointed nearly hysterically at the interior. "Now they are back. They have returned from thin air. This cannot be. This cannot be." He was shaking his head as he turned to me with a worried expression on his face.

"It's OK, Iba, it's OK. I think I know what is happening. These mice have evolved a very advanced optical defense mechanism, like camouflage of the walking stick beetle or the lizards of the forest."

I didn't want Iba to start doubting his own senses or believe that some evil force was at work. And the explanation did have an element of not just plausibility, but truth. Now I knew that the mice became invisible only to the person trying to catch them. Blink had provided the mouse a way to send a single to the brain of the aggressor that the mouse was no longer there. Utterly, utterly fascinating! A directed brain function signal triggered by fear! Could this be true? What had I discovered?

I thanked Iba, bidding him not to concern himself with this strange one-time occurrence, and sat at my desk to write feverishly until well after dark.

* * *

After DeLevres finished his meal and calmed a bit, I led him to my makeshift laboratory. Explaining the objective of Sisay's medicine, *guamy*, and my thoughts on combining it with the *p. salicinus* mushroom, I told him about the fire flower: how, by itself the nectar seemed to have no special properties. It was a bit like glycerin to the touch and had no discernable smell.

"Please show me this fire flower, Madame," DeLevres said.

I led the professor around the back of the house to my potting shed, where I pointed to the lump of rotting wood sitting in the mud. He bent down as low as his wobbly legs would allow to get a closer look, but eventually he had to get on his hands and knees, so small were the plants.

"There are hundreds of tiny ants on all three plants," he observed aloud, pointing to them.

"Three plants?" I said. There had been only one, originally. I bent lower myself and, to my delight, indeed saw three tiny scarlet blooms atop three individual stalks, all glinting with busy ants.

"One can only harvest the nectar at dusk when the ants have finished for the day," I informed him. "However, last night I did mix a small sample of my new concoction, thinking I would experiment more today. And to think, I had absolutely no idea you would be here. Isn't this quite fortuitous, Professor?"

"Uh ... quite, yes, Madame." He grunted as he rose, mud caked on his hands and knees.

As I contemplated running the experiment a third time and in the presence of Professor DeLevres, I wondered what could go wrong. Did I mix the right proportions? I had scrupulously followed my notes, which matched my memory perfectly. How long, I questioned, does Blink retain its potency? I needed to understand that as soon as possible.

From my original experiment I was able to deduce that the effects of Blink lasted on the mice between three and four hours. I wanted to make batches of varying strengths, but I would need to harvest more *p. salicinus* mushrooms and make more *guamy* in order to do that. But now I had three little fire flowers instead of just one. I am indeed a lucky lady.

"You wish me to see some experiment you have completed, Madame?"

"I do, Professor."

Back in my laboratory I pointed at the stack of his notes next to a stack of my own. Thumbing through his old notes first and then picking up a book of mine and appearing to study it, he mused, "You have been busy, Madame Blake, very busy. It pleases me to see that you have used my notes and added many of your own."

"Here is what triggered my latest work, Professor," and I pointed out to him his work on the *p. salicinus*.

"Interestingly," he said, shaking his head, "I was not quite correct about this. You see this question mark near my sketch? That means I was not certain I had identified the genus properly. And it turns out I have not. *P. salicinus* is not native to this area and does not grow here, as far as I can determine. This mushroom, which I have seen only once and only in Guinea, is a different and quite probably a new species."

"Well, this is interesting all around, I must say," I said, wondering what this all meant. "This mushroom here, Professor,"—I went to my cold box and removed the glass jar holding the six remaining mushrooms—"is the one whose essence I distilled and used for my … potion," I blurted, for lack of a better word.

"Potion? Yes indeed, potion." DeLevres laughed in a gust of condescension.

I ignored it. "Sisay, my traditional medicine man—he's been such an immense help to me—has called this mushroom the 'devil's hat.' He says it is dangerous and difficult to control. How did you come to locate it?"

"The usual manner. I used my university colleagues to put me in touch with a mycologist doing work in Guinea, who, when I went there, put me in touch with two other Guineans who knew of various plants used ritualistically or known to produce psychotropic responses. Most were just poisonous. I catalogued a number of species over the course of five months. Unfortunately, I couldn't conduct extracts for all." His explanation descended into a pensive silence. Rousing himself, he said, "Please tell me more about your … your potion, Madame. What exactly are all the ingredients and in what measure?"

I explained *guamy* and how it was made of a specific tree bark and extract from a yellow spotted beetle. I did not mention, though I would certainly tell him in due course, that it was bound with a few drops of fresh menstrual blood—moon blood, Mady had called it.

"That sounds rather simple and traditional, doesn't it? And this traditional medicine is then used to treat seizures, did you say? Episodes of high mental agitation or perceived disorder?"

"That's correct," I replied as I set about preparing to test Blink for the professor. "Sisay has been my traditional medicine mentor, as I said. I watched him give *guamy* to a young man who had been restrained because of his uncontrollable and menacing behavior. Within minutes, literally, after ingesting it, the boy calmed down and was able to be led back to his home."

"A simple tranquilizer is all," DeLevres said with a huff, applying his scientist's skepticism. "Or possibly even a placebo. Many factors, such as the presence of the boy's family, a white woman stranger, how much he had eaten and when, all might have contributed to the reaction. A controlled environment would help to understand the true effects better."

"Yes, yes. I'm sure it would, Professor. But I observed a profound change in the lad's behavior. Whatever combination of effects was responsible, it worked."

I did not want to discuss the efficacy of *guamy* when I was about to shock the professor out of his scientist's wits. "Come observe as I prepare the mice." I wanted him to see me catch the little dears and administer my Blink, which I had put into a syringe, not to inject them directly, though I might try that another time, but to squirt it into their mouths. I had painted numbers on the backs of each mouse and took hold of #4 easily and squirted 10 ml of Blink into his tiny mouth. I did nothing to mouse #7, his mate in the maze. I stood back and carefully placed the syringe with the remaining 30 ml of Blink on the counter behind me and waited. The professor had one of his own notebooks in hand, reading it, and nodding.

After ten minutes, I reached down to grab #4 and was shocked myself. Mouse #4 stood up on his hind legs, waiting for me to grab hold of him! What on earth was this? Dismayed and a bit confused, I picked up #4 while he remained starkly and annoyingly visible.

"Why, you silly little creature!" I said, admonishing #4. "Why don't you disappear, like a good little mouse?"

My slight outburst caused DeLevres to look up from his notes. "Difficulties, Madame?"

"I-I'm not sure yet." Clearly, this little mouse was not frightened. Quite the opposite. On a whim I opened the palm of my hand to let #4 climb along my arm. Which he did not. He stood up once again, now in the middle of my hand, and pawed the air in a gesture of ... of ... play? I laughed in spite of my frustration and brought up my other hand to tickle this amazing, fragile creature. As I touched his stomach, he immediately rolled onto his back and started to disappear and reappear, disappear and reappear. I was so startled I nearly dropped the poor thing onto the floor, but caught him with both hands and this time he was gone. Fortunately, I could still feel him in my loose grip and returned him quickly to the maze, whereupon he reappeared.

"Professor DeLevres, I need you to come over here right away."

He pushed back his chair and lumbered over to my side.

"Please try to catch mouse #7 for me."

He looked at me as though I had asked him to stand on his head, but he eventually shrugged and, after a few missed attempts, had #7 firmly in hand.

"Very good. Now please return him and try to catch #4."

Curiosity certainly drove him, rather than simply indulging me, for his peevish frown turned into a smile as he replaced #7 and reached for #4. Almost immediately, he shouted, "Good God in heaven, what is this!"

I couldn't help myself. "Why, Professor, where has your sense of dispassionate inquiry gone?" I said with a playful laugh and no small sense of self-congratulation, I admit.

He, like me and like Iba, pulled back, saw the mouse reappear, and made a second attempt. When the mouse disappeared this time, DeLevres extended his hand, believing the mouse hadn't moved. But I could see #4 scurrying through the maze so that when DeLevres stopped his futile attempts to grab a mouse he couldn't see, #4 reappeared at a far corner of the maze and stood up on his hind legs as if to signal victory.

DeLevres adjusted his position to move closer to where #4 stood. Rather than attempt to catch #4, the scientist stood there and observed the mouse intently. I had seen #4 the entire time, so although I knew what had happened, I didn't quite have the same sense of astonishment as DeLevres.

Until #4 started to blink in and out of sight.

"Professor, do you see that!" I exclaimed while approaching the edge of the box maze to observe #4.

"I believe I do. Our mouse friend is somehow flashing in and out of view. Did you see him disappear when I attempted to catch him? How is this possible?"

"No. He was visible to me the entire time."

DeLevres tore his gaze away from #4 to gape at me. "So," he said, "our mouse made me believe he was no longer there since I was the threat. A very precisely directed defense mechanism. And now,"— he returned his gaze to the continuously flashing #4—"we are both subjected to what is no longer a defense mechanism, but a broad and consciously directed display of … of …?"

"Of power, Professor. He's playing with us. How on earth did a mouse become this … smart?"

The professor was immobilized, gawking in amazement at this creature. I was doing exactly the same thing.

52. Life Finds a Way

The truth is I'm not certain that pursuing this new investigation will lead to my dream of finding cures for mental illnesses and learning deficits. What has happened to these mice is so challenging, not just to my rationally thinking mind, but to my very imagination. I am having terrible difficulty even believing what I have seen and documented. Will this lead to the unlocking of mental abilities that can turn damaged children into brilliant students? And why only damaged children, and why only children? Arrgh! This stream of events has raised questions so much larger than I had ever hoped or feared. I can say with the utmost certainty this new awareness and strength of my mice is at the same time wonderful and dreadfully frightening. The need for much more experimentation to duplicate and understand the mechanisms is so far beyond me. But it is oh so exhilarating! Yet, since the demonstration, DeLevres barely turns his head away from his writing and his plant expunging. Is he not awestruck as well? Such a strange man.

* * *

Good gracious *God*, this is not possible—not in this lifetime. My breasts are aching like just before my period and my whole body feels strangely different. Am I suddenly fertile! It makes no sense that during a single night of passion with Victor, I have conceived. Why now? Could all of those tests revealing Nigel to be reproductively perfect have been flawed? How can this be happening? Oh Christ, am I truly *pregnant*?

It's not logical. And yet I should have had my period two weeks ago. There is another explanation, surely. I wonder if my cycle has been interrupted or affected by these experiments we've been conducting. More precisely, that *I've* been conducting while DeLevres feeds me bits of information from his detailed analyses. I dare say he doesn't know quite what to make of this collaboration of ours. I scarcely do myself. I do wish he would be more communicative and interested in my experiments with the mice, these super creatures who've now become like pets. Oh, Doria, how awful is that?

But I can't really be pregnant. It must be something else, something in my own body mocking me or just cruelly indifferent, storing up my menstrual blood for some other purpose. Filling my endometria and holding all the nutrients in storage ... for what purpose? What purpose is there other than to nurture new life? Each morning I hope to see the evidence that my life will be back to normal. But in truth there is only one explanation, isn't there, Doria? I am, as mother said sarcastically about my cousin Irene, 'surprisingly with child'! Delicate Irene, my lovely, unsophisticated cousin who had three children by three different fathers by the time she was twenty-four. A life-force of her own, I would say, but not in any willing or self-conscious way. She had such a calm way of embracing the old destiny of nature, while I avoided it and then, well, it avoided me. Maybe it is my time to connect to that nature, to a biological destiny I thought unreachable. Oh God, I don't know what is happening! How will this all unfold?

I cannot let this stop my work. Discoveries are coming quickly. It's oddly comforting sometimes to watch Alain hunched over his notes, mumbling to himself as he writes or fumbles and curses around this poor excuse for a laboratory, looking for the hand-cranked centrifuge, or graduated cylinders, or a simple flask. As a houseguest, he's actually more useful than one would expect. He cleans up after himself and takes direction easily if he happens to be in the kitchen and hungry. But he's often frightfully bad at remembering instructions that don't require immediate action. Why he can never remember to reset the water tank valve after washing up and draining the tank is beyond me. Worse, of course—and if I'm honest with myself, it should not be surprising—is that he's an awful lab partner. It's more than the fact that he becomes transfixed and impenetrable when he works. On some level I envy that ability of his to concentrate so completely that the rest of the world is shut out. But I often need his advice when I'm trying to match compound properties to their compositions and his inscrutable notes aren't clear enough for me to use. There is no doubt of the importance for him to go as deeply as possible into the chemical mechanisms of these new properties we're discovering. But I find it much more useful to understand the details of the effects on our mice. I'm less interested in the "how" and very much centered on "what." Of course that means our work and interests are complementary, doesn't it? Perhaps this is for the best.

I was terribly sick this morning. The nausea easily overcame my normal desire for a morning tea and I shuffled into the bathroom, dry heaving at the door and finally emptying into the toilet. I was in such pain. After a while and a full liter of Evian later, I wandered into the kitchen where DeLevres had made a pot of tea and had toasted the leftover baguette from yesterday. I wasn't hungry, and the tea, though tempting, would have to wait.

If I'm no longer be menstruating, how do I collect the blood I needed to mix with some of the new compounds? It was never much, of course, but I had learned that the nutrient-rich blood infused some mixtures with strength and others with altered properties. And, of course, there were those—most in fact—for which the blood made no difference. Still, I now fretted that an important ingredient was no longer available. Good Lord, Doria! Listen to yourself! This pregnancy is remarkable beyond imagining, and you, you're worried that you won't have a period! What if I'm not fit for motherhood? Oh Lord, how this child—Victor's child!—will change everything. And everything has already changed once.

* * *

Sisay has been avoiding me. I've asked Mady Toula many times to tell the shaman that I want to see him and ask for his advice. Mady shakes her head and turns away. No explanation. Just a blank acceptance of some circumstance I cannot fathom. I resolved myself to go see him at his compound early in the morning. It occurred to me that he would know of my plan, so I expected him to be elsewhere when I arrived at the entrance to his compound. Of course I was wrong. Sisay was standing sentry-like, arms at his side, watching with a glare as I approached.

I greeted him respectfully, and his responses were less than the perfunctory phrases normally poured into these encounters. He merely grunted.

Finally, I said, "Master Sisay, I need your advice."

"You do not know what you have become, Madame."

I thought about this. It would surprise me only slightly if he knew I was pregnant. Rather than try to interpret, I asked, "Whatever do you mean, Master Sisay?"

"You do not see yourself from outside any longer. Only inside."

"If this is so, is it wrong? Have I offended you, my tutor?"

He had something to tell me, so he ignored my questions.

"There is nothing more you can learn from me. You have chosen a path I cannot see. But it is not a sacred path, not a path of honor you have chosen. You are daring the earth to reveal herself too quickly."

Really? I thought. Folklore platitudes when I'm trying to learn what is happening to my body, and, oh God, to my very world! "Sisay, I have seen things I cannot explain. I would truly appreciate it if you—"

"I have not the power to be at your side, Madame. Do not come here again." He turned his back to me and walked into the compound.

What on earth ...? Why would he suddenly behave like a wronged child? I wondered what he thought he knew about my work and about what DeLevres and I were doing together. Did he simply not care for the fact that I had brought this strange white man into the mix of learning the ancient cures? Did he fear something I couldn't understand, something that may have happened that night when he left me tied to a tree in the forest? Or was it more likely that I had forged ahead, advancing the knowledge? Was he struck down that a woman should have passed him by? Was the master now unable to communicate because of his bruised ego? I had thought he was so much more self-confident and genuinely interested in the craft, not merely in his own power. And I needed him. Now I understood that he would not rise beyond whatever frame of culture and self-image bound him. He could not see me as a friend who wanted his help.

I ran after him, calling his name. "Sisay, Master Sisay. You are a part of this. You schooled me, believed in me. Why must you abandon me now? Are you not strong enough to complete what you have begun?"

He stopped and turned to me. "You say that as though it is mine to complete, Madame. It is not. Your powers and your gift are rare and beyond me. But you do not have the respect, the awe, or the fear of what you would become. You only see the journey and you believe it will lead to a place of your choosing. It will not." He turned his head away, shutting me out with his absurd, oracle-like pronouncements.

"Sisay," I said, "you have been my light along this journey. Please do not abandon me when I need you the most. You shared little with me as you tested me, nurtured my curiosity, and helped me discover this gift, as you call it. For the very fact that I am not of your ways, that is all the more reason for you to help me still." At that moment I decided to share with him my newest and maybe my most critical dilemma. "Sisay, I am pregnant."

His eyes widened as though he'd swallowed a hot pepper. Then he closed them and cast his head down upon his chest. When he opened his eyes to look at me, he seemed sad, like a parent lamenting the departure of a child still too young to be independent, but too eager to be denied.

"It may not be as it seems, Madame. Please come with me."

He did not wait for me, of course. He resumed his path back to his compound. I hurried slightly to catch up, wondering why indeed my being pregnant should have changed his mind. "It may not be as it seems"? What on earth did he think was going on here? I had blurted out that I was pregnant so I could get some sympathetic action from the old shaman. However, the fact that he could think it was something other than pregnancy causing the loss of my period made me feel uncertain and deeply cold, as though I were caught in one of those bone-chilling winter rains of Manchester. Involuntarily I hugged myself.

When we reached his compound, Sisay went straight to the back where the sheds of medicines and aging ingredients were kept. He became a flurry of work. Looking for things, picking up flasks and bowls, sniffing some. After about thirty minutes of my standing aside watching this, he had assembled five different substances on his work table and set about combining them in a bowl, stirring, smelling, adding more of this or that. He completed his task in total silence.

I asked him more than once, "Sisay, what are you making?"

He never even raised his hand to silence me or pay me a stony look. He worked as though I were not there.

He rubbed a bit of the compound between his fingers, sniffed it, and spread it on the back of his hand. It looked like a cross between a cream and bread dough. It was hard to tell. When he left it on the back of his hand it turned from orange brown to white. This made him nod. He then gathered what he had made and put it in an old jam jar and presented it to me.

"When the pain becomes too great, you must take this, all of it."

"Sisay, what pain? When I deliver the baby? Is this a painkiller?"

"If you carry a child, you will not need this. But you will know in one more cycle of the moon if you are truly pregnant or if you are growing something else."

"Something else? Sisay …. Is this cancer, you think?"

"I think, Madame, that you are growing in your belly a medicine more powerful than you or I have seen. It is a medicine that can only be made in a woman's body with a man. It is only for you. You will use this in ways I do not know. Take this for the pain." He held out the jar. "Take it all at one time, only when the pain is so fierce you think you will split open."

"You are frightening me. I won't take it. What do you think I have? Why do you think I'm not pregnant?" I was crying now, confused and scared.

"Madame, from when we first met, I knew you were very special. Healers pass down the knowledge of how to recognize the gift in others. We learn that the most special healers are women who cannot bear children. But these women are so rare that generations may pass before one is born. And even then, she may not recognize her gifts. Though they cannot have children, their womb is nevertheless a factory, a place where a very powerful medicine can be made. I have never seen this myself, Madame Blake, but I know you are one of these special healers." He pushed the jar into my hands and wrapped his around mine.

I was shaking. "Sisay, what will happen? How will I know what to do? Please! You have to help me! Tell me what I must do!"

"This is where my knowledge ends. Only you can know what will happen."

"But I don't know! I have no idea. Please, can you be with me, help me understand what this is?"

"No. It is not for me. But I will be here to learn when you are through. If this is as I believe."

He reached out as though to touch my stomach, but only allowed his hand to hover there like a blessing. "I have not seen a woman with child who had your abilities. We have only heard the stories from our history. But though you are most probably a magic person, Madame, you are also very strange to us. I cannot trust all that you will do. I cannot know what you will do, just as you cannot know. If you and I are guided by the same hand, your purpose is far different than mine. Please. Go now. Go."

Tears were still streaming down my face. I was truly frightened. Here I was, pregnant when I shouldn't be, listening to a tribal medicine man telling me I wasn't pregnant but that something else was growing inside me! Was I going mad? I clutched my stomach instinctively, then turned and ran back out of his compound, barely able to breathe.

It wasn't until I was nearly a kilometer away, down the forest path, that I stopped and bent over, drenched from tears and sweat, desperately trying to catch my breath and not be violently ill. After a few moments bent over with my hands on my knees, it came to me as simply as though I had just awakened.

There must be a European doctor in Ziguinchor, there must. I should go see him or her and hopefully find someone who reasonably passes for an obstetrician. Of course! I need to revert to *my* traditional medicine. What have I been thinking?

I righted myself and wiped my face with the sleeve of my blouse, adjusted my bra, and strode off with a sense of, not relief, so much as direction. Gracious Lord, this whole business was absolutely horrifying, incomprehensible, maddening!

PART 6

UNTETHERED

53. Solitude in a Sea of Company

Victor was not looking forward to meeting with Nigel Blake. He had avoided Nigel for nearly two weeks since Mammadu had turned over their smuggled artifacts and delivered the payout to Victor at the IMAME offices. So as not to appear to be avoiding him, Victor had sent over a quick note to Nigel's office, via courier:

> *Just got back yesterday. I'm glad your package was*
> *delivered as you expected. I also delivered some plants*
> *to your wife in Ziguinchor.*
> *Take care,*
> *Victor*

He had debated whether or not to let Nigel know that he had visited Doria. He concluded that a truth half told is far better than a lie.

All had seemed fine. Victor was working with the team members, planning their next excursion into the bush. Glad to be focusing on the upcoming trips, Victor got a chill one morning when the IMAME secretary found him in the back, inspecting the Land Rovers.

"Mr. Nigel Blake is on the phone for you, Victor. Would you like to call him back?"

Actually, Victor would have preferred never to see or hear of Nigel Blake again, but such a bleak fantasy only made him feel worse.

"I'll take it, Miriam," Victor said. "But not at my desk. Transfer the call to Alan Broca's desk, please." Broca's phone had the advantage of being in a real office. The man himself was back in the States, rehabilitating. Victor closed the door and sat at Alan's desk until the call rang through. Victor blew out a full breath, picked up the receiver, and said hello.

"Victor, this is Nigel. How are you, good fellow?" He sounded as buoyant and positive as ever.

"I'm fine, Nigel. Good to hear from you. I've been really busy at work. We've got three major trips planned, starting next week, and the preparation is killing us. We had a lot of wear and tear on more than the vehicles that last trip to Manantali."

"Precisely the reason for my call, chap. I wanted to discuss another run, hopefully the last, for some very ancient statues. Are you still in?"

"Sure, well ... uh, you know, things didn't work out exactly the way we'd thought. Some guys tried to rough us up in Tougue. Your man David Semba is nice enough, but completely creepy, and the extra wear on the Rover was significant. Fuel and maintenance alone cost us a fortune over our budget."

"Nice to see a young explorer like yourself has a healthy respect for budgets. But here's the story, Victor. The co-op is willing to pay additional for those things, those additional expenses of yours. We understand it is the price we must pay for recovering such a treasure," Nigel stated easily.

"The co-op. Of course. I'm sure they are," Victor replied.

"You're sure?" Nigel sensed Victor's suspicion. "Of what, exactly? That the co-op will pay? Only if you know precisely the costs associated with that part of the trip. Do you follow? Fuel and food are straightforward enough to calculate. How many additional kilometers did you travel? What extra did you spend on food and lodging? I'm willing to bet you that much more was spent on your detour to Ziguinchor than you expended recovering our statuary in Tougue. Am I right?"

Victor hesitated before answering, feeling trapped. "That's true," he said.

"So then, enough of this nonsense about additional expenses. We will be able to cover your extra day or two in Guinea. When are you next planning to be in the vicinity of Manantali?"

"Probably in eight to ten days." Victor could see clearly where this was headed and wanted nothing to do with it. But he couldn't just tell Nigel the whole thing was off. Why on earth couldn't he say "No, I can't do this." The words never formed in his mouth.

"That's a bit soon for us, I think, but we could be ready in, say, two weeks. Could you possibly retrieve eight more statues for us?"

"Let me think it over and get back to you, Nigel."

"I have something else I'd like you to do, if you're going back in this time frame. I'd like you to deliver a package to Doria from me. I won't be able to get away and visit her for the week I promised, at least until June. If you wouldn't mind, that is?"

Mind? Victor thought. That's just too good to be true. Slowly, Victor's welcome surprise gave way to suspicion: Nigel knew this would be an irresistible motivator. "Sure, I guess. I mean, I'd be glad to deliver a package for you, Nigel. Hopefully it won't be perishable because I would only be passing to Ziguinchor on the way back, like before."

"Well, young man, I'm afraid it is perishable. Couldn't you see your way to leaving a day or two earlier, pass by Ziguinchor, and be on your way?"

Victor hesitated, not because he didn't want to see Doria as soon as humanly possible, but he wasn't certain he could keep the logistics working in his favor. Goddamned Ziguinchor wasn't on the route to anywhere except Bissau, Freetown, and Conakry. It would take him a day to get from Dakar to Ziguinchor and then another day or two over to Kayes, and another half day getting upstream where the hydrology team wanted to launch their research boat.

"You're the one who wanted me to delay, Nigel, and now you want me to start early? I'm not sure. I'll see what I can arrange."

"The early start suggestion is just to give you the time to get to Ziguinchor without affecting your own schedule. But if you can do it with your original departure date, then splendid. So if you would, Victor, pop over to the house next Saturday morning and pick up my present for Doria. We can discuss the trip over to Tougue and, hopefully, David can make certain you don't have any more brutish encounters," Nigel said with a brightness that angered Victor.

For the rest of the day Victor found his concentration frequently broken with thoughts of Doria and the excitement of seeing her again soon.

Mammadu, even with his head stuck under the hood of a Land Rover, noticed his friend standing motionless, staring.

Victor could sense in himself that it wasn't the anticipation of so soon a rendezvous with Doria that made him light-headed and dim. He discovered that he loved the feeling of being in love, perhaps more than the woman herself. This isn't what love feels like, is it? he asked himself. When he had a troubling thought of his meeting any obligation to Nigel, or the condescension he endured from his professorial colleagues, he would think of his love for Doria and hers for him, and suddenly little else mattered. Never in his life had he felt anything close to this. Yet it was so disorienting, complicating, and fuzzy. How could he trust this feeling when it took away his caution and sense of his surroundings?

"Barbu!" Mammadu barked from his perch.

Startled back to the present, he shot back to his friend, "What? What now?"

Mammadu looked at Victor with an icy stare and said nothing.

"Like you're so perfect!"

Still no more words from Mammadu.

"OK! OK, I get it. I need to focus."

Mammadu nodded, and as he turned back to his own work, a smile rose quickly on his face and then vanished.

The rest of the afternoon passed with the echoing clanks and whirrs of a mechanic's garage in full work mode, until Victor received another call.

"I'm in Dakar for the next three days, Victor," came the deep, soft voice of Lamine Volant through the receiver. "I'd like to get together if we can find a mutual time."

Victor noticed a new distance in his Canadian friend's voice, as though his words were spoken from inside a cave.

Without pausing to reflect, Victor invited Lamine to dinner at his place out on Gorée, sweetening the deal by offering Lamine a bed for the night and breakfast early. They agreed to meet and take the next ferry over.

* * *

Lamine was already at the dock when Victor arrived. Victor greeted Lamine with a sturdy embrace. Lamine's shoulders hung low and he simply patted Victor on the side of his waist, telling him how good it was to see him. Victor knew something was wrong and what the something likely was. His diaphragm contracted as if he had absorbed a body punch and his own shoulders slouched in unconscious solidarity.

"It's Claire, isn't it?"

Lamine nodded, his countenance turning downward until he looked as if he were about to cry. But he did not. Instead, he sent away the wretchedness by making two tight fists that vibrated like plucked violin strings and closing his lips like a child refusing to speak.

Victor led his friend onto the ferry and decided to wait until the boat had shed its mooring lines and chugged into the bay before saying another word.

Looking out at the bay, Lamine spoke. "She says she loves me, Victor, but she refuses to end this affair. It is eating me from the inside out."

"Lamine, you have to save yourself. You need to get out of this relationship as soon as you can. You haven't yet had children, so it should be easier to make a full break." The ferry bobbed calmly as the engine chugged.

Lamine looked at Victor with something resembling contempt. Victor became startled and a little frightened. He could only stare open-mouthed and mute at Lamine.

"You have no idea what you are saying. None." Lamine was raising his voice. "You don't just stop loving a person, you don't just stop wanting to be with someone because they have crushed you. God! It would be so much better if that were true. If only I could stop wanting her. But I can't, Victor, and I don't even want to stop. I want *her* to stop! I want Claire to stop fucking that fucking Ukrainian asshole!"

"Whoa, Lamine, hold on. ... He—"

"Don't fucking tell me to hold on. That's exactly what I'm doing. I'm holding on to the life I've got. My life and my wife!"

Victor's mind raced. Should he tell Lamine what he thought and try to talk his friend down from this burning perch? Should he agree with him that he deserved better than he was getting?

"I don't know what to say, Lamine. If it were me, I'd leave. I'd have to. I couldn't take what you're going through. But you're a different guy. You take this thing inside of you and you can't let it go. But, man, I'm worried for you. This is going to eat you alive."

"It's already done that. I was able to put Claire's tryst out of my mind at work. When I'd come home, sometimes she'd be there and we'd have a nice dinner together, and sometimes she wouldn't be there. If she wasn't, she'd always leave a note so I would know where she was. What, so I shouldn't worry? This is so goddamned perverted! Last night when I got home, she told me dinner was ready, and that she was going to go over to be with Darius that night and she'd see me in the morning. I grabbed her by the hair and threw her to the floor. I held her down and asked if she knew what she was doing to me. Had she any idea how stabbed I was? And then as I let her go, suddenly realizing I really didn't want to hurt her, she stood up, brushed back her hair, and said, 'At least the stabbing was in the stomach and not in the back.' She said to me, 'Lamine, you need to be a man about this.' What in God's name does that even mean?"

"It means, to me," Victor said, while hoping his advice would be right, "that you need to know what's best for you, Lamine, and move on it. You aren't going to change her. You have to do whatever it is for yourself. Be every bit as selfish as she is being. I don't mean revenge. Shit like that never works."

"Like you know anything about revenge, Victor!"

"Right. You're right, I don't. But focus on how to put this behind you. She's not coming back to the life you had before, OK? So what do you do? How do you move yourself forward?"

Lamine put his face in his hands and sobbed.

Victor put an arm around his friend and looked up into the direction of Gorée Island. It was his refuge, Victor thought, and he would help it become a refuge for his friend, at least for tonight. He could see no resolution for Lamine, other than complete extrication. He had to leave Claire, not just for his dignity but for his sanity, for him to have any opportunity of recovery. Anything else was just a descent into hell. But he wouldn't say that tonight. Tonight, Victor resolved to make it an easy getaway, pasta and salad for dinner, put Lamine to work in the kitchen—horrible cook that he was—and take in just enough alcohol to numb the pain, but not enough to kill it. Some company would probably help, too.

Recovered but sullen when the ferry docked at Gorée, Lamine rose with Victor and disembarked. Thinking of his friend Jules Tamara, Victor asked Lamine to take a short detour around the beach, to Jules' striking domicile overlooking the bay.

* * *

The white flagstone walk was flanked by meticulously kept red hibiscus and scarlet birds of paradise. The men stepped up three wide stairs to a slate porch. The front of the house featured a giant set of French doors, providing a nearly unbroken wall of transparency and reflection.

Victor tugged the bell cord, and shortly, Jules appeared at the door with a large bottle of Perrier and an even larger smile. Victor was thinking he'd made the right call. Jules extended his arms in an expression of pure welcome. Victor was enthralled and a bit transported, even though he'd spent many hours here. Having brought a friend in need of emotional support, and to have Jules so open hit Victor with humility and awe. What makes a man like Jules magnanimous, caring, and inclusive? There was so much at work here, for which Victor felt grateful.

Through the white marbled foyer and into the sunken living room, Jules led the guests to a set of white leather couches. Between the couches, a glass tabletop sat on a solid bronze leopard. Thiery, Jules' steady companion of the last six years, rose from his seat, greeting Victor with a smile and a powerful handshake. Thiery, a former professional football player in France, had lost little of his lithe athleticism of the last decade, since leaving Marseilles to promote trade with the former colonies. Victor introduced him to Lamine, and the four of them settled into the rich serenity of Jules' home.

After handing the guests their drinks, Jules sat down, saying, "I'm so pleased you stopped by, Victor. Another friend of yours will be joining us, probably on the next ferry. She called me after she said she tried a few times to reach you at the office, apparently. The line was busy, of course." Jules' eyes danced with an impish smile over the rim of his glass as he sipped and looked at Victor.

Victor's first thoughts were of Doria, but of course that couldn't be who the caller was. It could only be Amelia. Yes, indeed.

"Ms. Amelia Jensen," Victor said.

Jules nodded, delicately setting down his Perrier. "She just returned from Côte d'Ivoire and has some great stories of bungling bureaucrats."

"She always does." Victor nodded, wanting and not wanting to see Amelia.

"Tell us about yourself, Lamine. Are you Dakarois or just visiting us?" Jules asked.

"Just visiting," he answered. "I'm living and working in Saint-Louis as deputy director of the trade school."

"And what brings you to Dakar?"

Lamine hesitated and looked down. Then, with a deep breath and an attempt at a smile, said, "I'm looking to place promising students into jobs here in the capital."

Jules nodded and fell silent himself.

"Thiery," Victor said, "are you here for long? Aren't you usually traveling about every month?"

"Much as I love to travel throughout West Africa, you know, even I need to rest and unpack my suitcase for more than a week. I'm taking a month off to rediscover home."

"I thought home for you was any francophone capital on the continent," Victor joked.

"Home, Victor, is not necessarily a place. It is where you are yourself, unguarded and at equilibrium. Where you have a sense of belonging. This is where I am at home, though Jules might say it has taken me too long to realize that."

"Not at all, *mon cher*," Jules said. "But perhaps I realized this was your home before you yourself, no? You returned here even though you still have your home in Aix-en-Provence and the corporate apartment in Tunis. But you who travel so much, you must have a way to find home wherever you are, do you not?"

"Sometimes yes, sometimes no," Thiery replied, and smiled. "So much depends on your emotions, you know? Did I have a good day or a bad day? Were the people in the market friendly or sour? Have I cemented a deal or did I screw things up? If things are going well, it is easier to feel at home, I suppose. Perhaps home is nothing more than good brain chemistry."

"You are too faithless, Thiery, too modern," Jules said.

Thiery shrugged. "Home is where we are together. Let that be enough for now."

Jules punctuated the thought by raising his glass to his lover. All joined in the toast, Lamine extending his arm slowly at the end.

Jules was interested to hear the latest news from IMAME, and Victor was happy to talk about his work, praising Lamine's protégé, Dante, which, though genuine, was meant to bring Lamine into the conversation. Looking at his watch and then staring out over the harbor, Jules rose, noticing the arrival of the ferry. The sky, purple from the setting sun behind them, blended seamlessly with the water along an invisible horizon. The running lights of the ferry floated in the distance.

Lamine rose as well. "I think I'll just take that ferry back to the city. I've got an early start in the morning. Thanks for your hospitality, Jules."

With a glance to Victor, Jules shook Lamine's offered hand and said, "Are you sure you won't stay, Lamine? There's plenty of room, good food, and an early morning ferry."

Victor said, "Please stay, Lamine, really. You don't have to be back tonight. And you have to admit this is pretty decent company."

"Thanks, no. I need to be getting back."

That was the end of the discussion. Victor looked to Jules and Thiery, a plea in his eyes.

"Let us at least walk you down to the dock," Thiery said, standing up, drink in hand, and coming up quickly to Lamine's side.

Lamine didn't look toward him or slow his walk in any way. Jules and Victor hurried to catch up. Thiery opened the glass door, and Lamine stepped through as though Thiery were a valet. Victor was embarrassed by his friend's preoccupation, but Jules was understanding.

"It's all right, Victor. He must clear his mind at some point. Today is too early for him, whatever it is."

Victor thanked Jules.

The quartet retraced Victor and Lamine's path to the dock, remarking on the freshness of the night, the merciful absence of tourists, and the smell of roasting fish on the grills of the nearby restaurants. They each asked Lamine one more time to reconsider. He thanked them but would not change his mind.

The ferry eased into the dock while some thirty or forty awaiting passengers going to Dakar stood in a group, chattering and jostling. The four men hung at the back of the small crowd, Jules craning his neck to see the disembarking passengers. As he predicted, Amelia

Jensen was the fifth passenger to come down the gangplank. She held both a garment bag, draped over her shoulder, and a straw satchel in her right hand. Her other hand carried her large purse. As she approached, she blew once, then another time at a strand of hair dangling across her eyes, to no effect whatsoever. Jules waved to her as Victor and Thiery focused their attention on Lamine.

"Oh, Miss Jensen," Jules called in a singing voice, "your entourage is here for you!"

This made Victor turn his head in Amelia's direction. She looked at him in surprise, smiled brightly, and then stopped. The expression on Victor's face wasn't a happy one. She strode over to Jules and accepted three kisses on the opposite cheeks.

"We're just seeing Lamine off and our timing seems to be exquisite," Jules told her.

"I'm so tired, Jules," she said with a long exhalation. She dropped her bags to the dock. To Victor she exclaimed, "Well, look who's here! Victor Byrnes, late the conquering logistics chief. Mr. Byrnes, how nice to see you." She offered her hand to be kissed, and Victor took it and shook it and then leaned in to kiss her. Amelia turned her head away, then shook it. "Victor, don't you know when a lady offers her hand to be kissed? Show a bit of chivalry, please."

Though confused, Victor, still holding her hand, brought it up to his lips and kissed it on the inside of her palm and then put a long kiss on her wrist. Amelia's whole body shivered.

Victor mentally slapped himself. Goddamn it! Why did I do that?

"That's more like it, Mr. Byrnes," Amelia purred.

The departing passengers were starting to board. Lamine moved with the crowd, and Victor, dropping Amelia's hand absentmindedly, raced up to Lamine.

"Are you going to be all right, Lamine? I'm not sure it's a good idea for you to be alone right now. I've-I've, uh, never seen you like this …."

Lamine regarded Victor and took his hand, shaking it firmly. "I'm going to be fine, my friend. I know what I must do," he said, showing no emotion. "Thank you for being here. I really needed this interlude, short though it was. Thank you. I'll be going back to Saint-Louis tomorrow. You take care." He placed his other hand on Victor's shoulder, looked into his eyes, then let go and walked onto the ferry.

Victor wanted to hug him, but just watched him board. Thiery put his hand on Victor's shoulder where Lamine's had just rested.

"Your friend has something very heavy on his back, yes?"

"He does, Thiery. Very heavy. Too heavy, I'm afraid."

"You've done everything a friend can do, Victor."

"You think so? I don't know. I hope so, but I'm worried for him."

Thiery steered Victor back to Jules and Amelia. Jules stooped to pick up Amelia's garment bag, but Victor moved quickly to get it first. He slung it over his shoulder and a new quartet headed off the pier. Amelia put her arm through Victor's without a look or a word.

"There's wine, cheese, and dinner, chez moi," Jules informed everyone.

"Fantastic!" Amelia exclaimed. "I'm starving! The only food I've had all day were some peanuts I bought when I arrived in Dakar."

"You didn't want to just collapse at your apartment for a bit?" Victor asked.

"Of course, dummy. That's exactly what I did. Today is a travel recovery day for me. I got back and collapsed for about two hours. But what I really want to do is relax with friends. Besides, Jules invited me."

Victor shot a quick stare at Jules, who smiled back and said to her, "Well, you couldn't be expected to cook for yourself or dine alone on your first night back from such a long trip. And, I know how comfortable you are here on Gorée, Amelia. Thank you so much for coming."

"So, what's for dinner, Jules," Amelia said, "and did you cook, or did you have that splendid chef of yours concoct something special?"

"Thiery and I are quite good together in the kitchen, you know. Tonight will be a labor of love. No chef other than the proprietors."

"I can't wait," she said, and smiled.

Victor was reeling. He cared about Amelia, certainly, but couldn't feel the depth of that care; it seemed to bob up and down like a buoy on a turbulent sea. He knew he didn't have that visceral desire, the consuming need that he felt for Doria. How would this emotional ambivalence manifest tonight? He would have to tell Amelia something soon. Did Amelia already assume she would spend the night at Victor's?

He let out a deep, pensive sigh, and Amelia shot him an inquisitive, unhappy glance.

Suddenly Amelia Jensen turned stone-faced. She tightened her lips and faced forward. Her steps became more regimented and stiff. Her eyes opened wide as if in a realization and she took several deep breaths.

"Amelia," Victor asked, "are you all right? You must be exhausted. Look, I'm not sure why you decided to come out here tonight, but … but I'm glad you did. It's good to see you."

"Really, Victor? You don't know why I came out here tonight?" She stopped walking, her mouth open and quivering, and then separated herself from Victor, who gave her a blank look.

Behind them a few paces on the walkway, Jules and Thiery also halted.

"You wanted to see me," Victor said. "You know you should have called the office. I didn't know when you were getting back."

"I did call. A few times, in fact. It was always busy."

"Yeah, we've been really busy. Amelia, I'm sorry that—"

"Please, Victor, *please* do not apologize. It's belittling to both of us." She fixed an unrelenting gaze on him.

Victor's mouth dropped open while he was trying to understand if Amelia's look was a challenge or a prayer. He pursed his lips and nodded. "So let's relax for a few hours, OK? You just got here. Let's get you a glass of something—"

"Something stronger than wine, please."

"Gin and tonic, then, and we can all hang out in the kitchen." Turning his head over his shoulder, he said, "Does that sound OK, Jules? Can Amelia and I help you and Thiery in the kitchen?"

"I can't imagine that the two of you would be anywhere else, since we would insist on your company, but—and I speak for myself only, here—I think most of the work will be handled by the hosts. What do you think, Thiery?"

"Um ... we might make one of them *chef apprenti* and the other the dishwasher."

"Or the bartender," Victor chimed in hopefully.

"*Mais oui, mon cher.* You will be responsible for keeping us refreshed."

"That's my job. Keeping the professionals content so they can do what they do best."

Entering the house, Victor put Amelia's garment bag in a hall closet, where it could stay without any assumption where she might spend the night. The four of them went into the kitchen, and Jules orchestrated the work.

Victor poured wine and made Amelia a gin and tonic, and the four settled into a groove of common purpose.

"What's up with Lamine?" Amelia asked. "Why didn't he stay for dinner? He looked really strange."

It was Victor's question to answer. "Lamine's going through a pretty rough time right now. He and Claire are in a bad place."

"That's a shame. They always did seem like an incongruous couple, you know? She's always this free spirit, almost like a revolutionary, and he's such a serious, straightforward guy," Amelia observed. "They're a striking couple to look at, really, but …'"—she put a slice of the bell pepper she was chopping into her mouth—"I guess I'm not too surprised, given how different they are."

Victor twisted at the counter. "That makes a lot of sense, Amy. How do couples survive such differences, huh? Claire told Lamine she was having an affair and that she both wanted to continue the affair and stay married to Lamine."

"No shit!" Amelia exclaimed. "Wow! That's something I might expect a man to do. No, I take that back. A man would probably never be that honest—unless he wanted to leave, of course."

"That's a bit unfair," Jules responded. "Not all men have the prevaricator gene. And when it comes to extra-relationship sex, well, that's a very sensitive area. What exactly is the right communication? It all depends so much on the circumstances."

"And don't you think, Amy, it's really awful that Claire can feel like she's doing the right thing just because she told Lamine the truth? She has set herself free and caged Lamine! He might be free, you know, to pursue an affair of his own, but that's not what he wants."

"So the roles here are reversed, for a change," Amelia replied. "Men have been having affairs in marriage forever. Hell, in many societies, Claire's actions are sanctioned for men. Isn't polygamy for some societies the codification of men having multiple, simultaneous sexual relationships? Four wives for a Muslim or a Mormon man? Imagine a woman with four husbands. Good God! On second thought, what an awful idea! Yuk!"

Thiery had his own ideas. "Certainly there is a discussion worth having about the norms of any society and how it treats men and women differently. But bringing it back to the personal level, Lamine is staring at the upheaval of his world. He must be wondering if his love or Claire's has been built upon a lie, or an inability to understand or know her. And in that upside-down world, where does he land?"

Victor said, "I told him he should just end the marriage, but he couldn't see that as an option. It's like Claire was his emotional home and that home has been ransacked. I'm trying to think what I would feel in his shoes and I honestly don't have any idea. It's pretty scary."

"Revenge," Thiery said. "That would be my first response if my home were ransacked."

"That's an ugly thought, Thiery," Jules said.

"Perhaps. But an emotion I've no doubt Lamine will go through."

"He's known now for over a month," Victor said. "I guess he's trying to work it out, not so much with Claire, but with himself."

"I hope he's not digging himself a deeper hole," Jules said.

"He's a strong guy. It will take some time, but I think he'll eventually decide he can't be in that marriage."

"Why not suck it up like women do every day?" Amelia said.

The men were all silent, until Jules asked, "Amelia, please tell us about your travels. How was the Côte d'Ivoire?"

Amelia told of her attempts to work with the ministries and the local offices of her foundation, the problems with projects to treat and prevent malaria, and more. The three men listened intently. As the meal preparation progressed and the drinks circulated, the subject of irreconcilable relationships disappeared like a shipwreck.

By the time the quartet completed the meal and cleanup duties, it was near midnight. A workday awaited Amelia and Victor, yet they both seemed hesitant to decide when or even how to end the evening. Amelia eventually tugged on his elbow, taking him out of the kitchen and onto the patio. The humid night air, full of fresh sea scent, begged to be inhaled deeply, which the two did easily and for more than a few breaths.

When they resumed their normal breathing, Amelia turned and faced Victor. She fought the urge to take his two hands in hers. "You don't look happy, Victor. What's wrong?"

He didn't want to talk to Amelia about his feelings, at least not now, so he said, "I'm thinking about Lamine. It's going to be a rough ride for him for the next few months."

"Really? Is that what you're thinking? Look. I can make this easy for you, though God only knows why I bother. You like me, but you don't love me. I know. And you think I want more from you than what you're willing to offer. OK. That's true, and damn you for making me say it and not saying it yourself."

"Amelia, I—"

"Ba-ba-ba!" She held up a hand, shushing him. "I had some time to think this over and you know, Victor, it's OK that you don't love me. No, really. It's helped me understand some things about myself. What kind of woman keeps coming back to a man she knows doesn't love her? Well, if that man tries to love her, even if he can't, that effort is worth something, right? And you have tried. I know you wanted to, but you couldn't. You really like me, and we have very fun sex together. But in the end, you don't feel it in your belly, you know, here," and she placed a fist on his stomach. "I'm not sustenance for you like you have been for me." She sniffed back a sob as this reality, finally spoken, became the irrevocable truth between them.

"I'm ..." Victor started to say, "I'm sorry," and then realized how hollow and insufficient it sounded. "I'm ... coming to grips with this myself, Amelia. You're right. I wanted so much to be able to feel for you what you've ... expressed to me through your ... what? Your relentlessness."

"Oh my god! You horrible person!" She simultaneously laughed and cried, and struck his chest.

He pulled her to him. She resisted, but hadn't the will to sustain the fight.

Resting her head on his chest, she said, "I'm going to spend the night here, Victor. With Jules."

"Yeah, we both have to work tomorrow," he said.

54. RITUAL

The rest of the workweek was occupied with accelerated preparations for the support team's next trip to Mali. Unlike Monday when he was mooning over Doria, Victor was now driven. He consulted Dante and Mammadu for repair and maintenance of the vehicles and other equipment. He debated new routes with Derek and the team leaders. He revised the budget to account for more risks. He remained at the office each night until just before the last ferry back to Gorée, arriving at his unshared apartment with a weariness born of his new obsession with work.

After dinners of sliced mango and two-day-old baguette and peanut butter, consumed while listening to one of the cassette tapes he already knew by heart, he would collapse into bed, nursing a vague sense of accomplishment. He rose by five thirty each morning and caught the first ferry into Dakar, to do it all again. Until Saturday.

Victor awoke at his normal time on Saturday morning, the dawn barely hinting its arrival and the song of the Muslim first call to prayer floating dim but welcome. The only mosque on the island was at the far end, opposite the harbor, near where Victor and others liked to dive for cowry shells. The entire structure, except for the terracotta roof tiles, was plastered-cement white. One of the minarets had a loudspeaker from which the imam's praise to God was broadcast faithfully at the appointed hours. It must be powered by a car battery, Victor reckoned. Against his own beliefs and cultural moorings, he found himself oddly comforted by the simple Islamic traditions as a call to prayer. He rolled over and tried to recover his dreaming sleep.

An hour later, apprehension swelled in his head like a blister. He had to see Nigel this morning.

The day was starting out like every other day: cloudless and warm. He dressed quickly in sneakers, khakis, and a blue T-shirt with the slogan "Veteran of Foreign Peace," and got onto the next boat to Dakar. As with his weekday routine, he walked quickly through the debarkation turnstiles and up the street for about a kilometer, to the office.

Today, instead of settling down at his desk or scrutinizing the big calendar sprawled on the conference room wall, he went directly to where he kept the Norton, checked it for fuel and inspected the exterior, and then fired it up. The surge of the Norton engine boomed through the still of the morning, sending a rush through Victor's arms and legs. He cranked the accelerator up and down a few times to listen if there were any sputters in the engine or the exhaust. Satisfied with his ride and resolved for his meeting with Nigel, Victor glided the motorcycle out onto the street and down the corniche to capture that incomparable sense of freedom sharing the road with no other vehicle, the rushing air like the cheering of a crowd. Wings could not have enhanced this feeling.

* * *

Nigel was humming. When he caught himself, he could not, for the life of him, understand why, except that perhaps it was nerves. He was neither anxious nor cheerful regarding the pending visit from Victor. Doria had been down in Ziguinchor now for nearly three months. He had no reason to be humming like some blissful dolt. Nigel missed his wife in ways he could barely express, even to himself. It had nothing to do with the orderliness that Doria had maintained in their household. Ahminta had been capable of not only taking direction, but in carrying on without orders. She had learned well from Doria, and Nigel saw his wife's distant hand tucked into the maid's work. Sitting alone on work evenings or on weekends, he read up on the diamond market and news, drafted different plans on paper and crumpled them up, and poured stiffer gin and tonics than normal.

With Doria at his side, Nigel never doubted himself—at least not in any way that lingered or led to fear of making good decisions. Her mere presence, her beauty and calm were, he could now see, a foundation for his own courage and an enabler of his ambition. Neither his successful work nor his project to establish his own independent wealth filled the void she left. Not his facility to charm ministers or his ability to get the best work from his subordinates were sufficient buoyancy for his life, now bouncing on the top of the waves, fending off the moment when he might disappear below them. Why then, in God's name, was he humming?

As on the day when Doria and Nigel had first met Victor, the sound of the young man's motorcycle cracked the air with blunt energy. After parking the Norton next to Nigel's Range Rover, Victor climbed the residence stairs. He was greeted at the door by Nigel's extended hand and convincing warmth.

"Victor, Victor. Good of you to come. Punctual as always, heh? Come right on in. Would you like a coffee and a scone, by any chance?"

"Some coffee would be great, Nigel. Thanks."

Around the dining room table they made jokes at the expense of the Minister of Trade and Commerce.

Victor was first to address their business. "For that delivery, I'll be able to squeeze out a day ahead of schedule, which I can use to get to Ziguinchor. Assuming you still have a package for me to pass on to Doria."

"I have, Victor. And I'm sure you can guess, it's a plant. Something Doria actually brought here many years ago from Essex. How it actually survived here is a miracle, but then, Doria's talent for wresting miracles from her flora is not to be underestimated. It's a flowering vine related to honeysuckle. I haven't the foggiest notion what it's called. Sugar flower or something like that. But she said it reminded her of home, and since she's making Ziguinchor her temporary home, well, I thought it fitting she should have some reminder of some things dear to her. Dear to both of us, actually."

"Really?"

"Certainly. I remember when she announced that this sugar bloom was actually growing, after six months of nursing it like a sick child. She cut a few branches and placed them in vases around the house. The sweetness of the air became very pleasant and for nearly two years we had that scent in the house every day."

"And then what? She stopped cutting them and filling up the house?"

"She moved on to the next experiment, I guess you could say. She was breeding new flowers, trying to graft some hybrid, you know. She moved on from one success in search of the next."

"Do you think she'll be able to make it grow down there as well?" Victor blanched visibly but Nigel took no notice.

"Who knows? Truly, it's more to give her a reminder of home. I'm sure she has all she can do with her own work. Did you get a chance to see what she's been doing when you made your delivery? She's been quite bubbly on the telephone when we get a chance to speak, but she hasn't told me any real details."

"I didn't see much while I was there," Victor said, glad to be able to answer honestly. "I know she was working in a greenhouse-like structure where she kept different plants and things. Also, she mentioned working with a local medicine man of some kind."

"That would be Sisay. He's been her tutor in all things related to indigenous medicine. Mostly poppycock, in my humble opinion, but she seems to believe there's something to it."

Victor drew a breath, about to tell Nigel stories of the unexplainable things he'd seen these past months. But he believed Nigel would not be interested. Astounding encounters are just boring exaggerations to some.

"Well, I suppose she's fast into the swing of things with her newfound mentor from the university here in Dakar."

Victor arched his eyebrows. His mouth drooped.

"Our friend Dr. Alain DeLevres, a plant physiologist or botanist, I believe, has gone down to Ziguinchor to help her unlock these mysteries." Nigel's smile was wistful.

Victor's abdomen contracted.

Nigel went on. "He's quite a likeable chap, no doubt. Bit eccentric for my taste, but he is world class in his field, I'm told. Doria did some work for him at his lab here in Dakar for a few months, before heading to Ziguinchor."

"Is he, you know …. What's he like?" Victor asked.

Nigel stood up and looked down at his visitor, allowing himself a snort under his breath. "What's he like? He's dashing and sophisticated. That's what he is. Dr. DeLevres is an expert in a field Doria cares about deeply and he's planted himself in Ziguinchor just to be near her. Ha!" Nigel shook his head and smiled. "Victor, your affection for my wife is plainer than your own nose."

Nigel sipped his coffee as Victor turned red and lost the ability to speak.

"Oh, come now. You're certainly not the first. Don't be embarrassed, lad. Doria is a beautiful woman. You think I wouldn't understand a schoolboy crush?" As if to break the tension, Nigel slapped Victor on the shoulder. "God, man, you'd scarcely be male if you weren't attracted to a woman like Doria. It's how you respect her and her station that's important. And you act respectfully and honorably toward her, don't you, Victor?"

Victor was still having trouble making his body do anything. His gaze started darting around the dining room, then rolled to a stop. He stood up and walked over to the buffet table to pour himself another cup of coffee, unable yet to speak.

"Yes, of course you do," Nigel mused, answering his own question. "Look here, it's all how we behave, not what we believe, that makes us who we are. So far, you've behaved like any sensible and honorable man, and I should think that would carry the day. Shall we have a chat about your next meeting with our man Semba?"

"Nigel, what do you mean by behaving honorably? Is it some British notion of sublimating your feelings, carrying on as though nothing has happened, adhering to a set of unwritten rules so rigidly that you misplace yourself in some—I don't know—some made-up world where emotions and individuals don't exist?"

Nigel's face contorted slightly. He said, "I say, Victor, that was the most singularly obtuse thing ever to come out of your mouth. Have you any notion of the painful centuries of progress, the wars both civil and abroad, and the blood spilled to bring order and a way of life to a brutally competitive world? These rules, as you call them, are the cultural inhibitions that kept neighbors from sinking ax handles into each other's skulls and allowed intellectual inquiry and scientific progress to flourish."

Nigel walked over to Victor and faced him. "Even you must know that the contribution of the British to the civilization of the world is without parallel in human history. And honor is not some meaningless code of conduct that keeps people controlled. Quite the contrary. It is a belief in the nobility in each man, that regardless of your station in life, you treat your fellow men with respect and afford them dignity. Honor is the wellspring of sacrifice, Victor, without which we humans are little more than clever beasts. You should learn a bit more about things you dismiss so easily." He sipped his coffee.

Neither man moved.

Nigel restarted. "Do you not know what sacrifice is, either? Have you ever sacrificed for something, the way, say, that Doria has sacrificed for me these past six years? Do you know what it takes to give years of your life to another person, all the while indulging yourself only in small bits, intense little episodes of loneliness that occasionally burst into a vignette of personal expression and then fade? I've seen that from my wife, Victor. She sacrificed for me and for us. Her honor for me and for our marriage is manifest in nearly everything she does. And you would do well to understand that."

Victor took a deep breath and nodded. "Right, OK. Nigel, I spoke out of turn. But looking at your society from mine, you all seem to be wound so tightly and unable to be who you want to be. You mentioned something about nobility, regardless of your station. Well, I don't believe in stations. I believe in steps. A person may be born into a station, as you say, but they can fall back or climb up in *my* society. And what about this notion of sacrifice? What is the good served by the sacrifice, anyway? Stability? Avoidance of chaos? That isn't sacrifice to me, that's fear. Fear of being yourself. Of trying to be more than yourself."

"What do you love?" Nigel asked Victor, who fumbled with his cup and spilled some coffee into its saucer.

"Wh-what, what exactly do you mean?"

"It's not a trick question, you know, and was not meant to upset you." The hair on the back of Nigel's neck bristled, yet he continued. "I ask what you love so you can envision something for which you would sacrifice your time, your labor, your very life. And if you did, would you not be ennobled by it?"

"I suppose I would."

"So now you begin to understand. And I must say, right now, I too am beginning to understand." Nigel's expression turned hard. "I spoke of Doria's sacrifice for me, my career, and for us, for our marriage so that we could be together. Stay together. Did my dear wife sacrifice too much for me, I wonder. How much of herself and of her own dream for fulfillment did she simply let go so I could have my role as this commercial sultan in Africa? Shit. ... A neocolonialist if ever there was one, wouldn't you say, my Yankee friend?" Nigel placed both hands on the table and looked down into his coffee cup.

Victor offered nothing.

"And as Doria recovers from that role of giver—the good wife and all—will she be able to say it was worth it? God, I never thought otherwise until this very moment. Perhaps it is my turn to sacrifice something." He sipped from his empty cup and placed it on the table. "Would you care for anything stronger than coffee, Victor? I know it's early, but suddenly I need the brace of a good single malt."

Without waiting for an answer, Nigel went to his liquor cabinet and grabbed an unopened bottle of Glenmorangie. He poured generously into two crystal glasses and offered one to Victor. "Can you drink it neat, man?"

"I'm not much of a whiskey drinker, Nigel," said Victor as he rose and tentatively took the glass from his host.

"Never touch the stuff myself," Nigel said, and drained half the liquid from the glass.

Victor put the glass to his lips and took one swallow. It burnt his esophagus, yet it wasn't unpleasant. It had an aftertaste like raw wheat. They finished their drinks without speaking. Nigel took the glass from Victor and placed both empties on the cabinet top.

With his hands in his pockets Nigel stepped away a few paces, and then turned and said, "David will be in Tougue exactly two weeks from tomorrow. Can you be there and collect the statues from him? He says there could be as many as ten this time."

Victor shifted his weight a few times and looked directly at Nigel.

Nigel crossed his arms at his chest.

"I think I can, Nigel, but don't forget I've got a real job that takes me to that area. These are single-minded scientists who will need food, clean water, need their noses wiped, and who couldn't care less what I might need to do for myself, you know? They could make demands on me that would make it really hard to keep to the exact time frame we're talking about."

"Here's the problem, Victor," Nigel said. He was used to managing subordinates to do work they didn't want to do. "This isn't the type of operation that has any slack built in. It is dangerous, as you already know, and if we miss our window, then some very bad things can happen. David Semba is a man of extraordinary commitment and capability. If he says he will be there at a certain time, he will be there. I'll bet you don't know too many Africans you can say that about, yeah?"

"I know a few like that," he said flatly. "My friend Mammadu, for one."

"The point is, dear fellow, that this operation takes commitment. You showed that you're made of some stern stuff, and you delivered the goods, which is why, in large part, we believe it's the right time to put together one large crate of statues and be done with it. No more after this, understood? The risk will be too great later. That's David's assessment, and everyone wants to be alive and well at the end, don't we?" Nigel took a step closer to Victor. "We need you to be there in exactly two weeks and if you can't, man, you need to tell me now. We will pay you $3,000 US."

Victor turned and walked toward the buffet, then turned around abruptly. "Commitment on my part isn't a guarantee. I can move lots of pieces around and go toe-to-toe with my IMAME friends. But if we get into real trouble, like needing to medically evacuate one of the scientists because he or she got bit by a snake or fell over a cliff, then we're going to have a problem. That's *we* are going have a problem— you, me, David. All of us. It seems to me you should have a backup plan or, like before, a window of two or three days. Without any way to communicate, Nigel, the risks go up. Any chance David could carry a broadband radio or transmitter? Or how about a low-power shortwave radio?"

"It's a little late for that, I'm afraid, and besides, those types of communications carry the risk of being intercepted. We haven't got a code language or anything like that. We're just amateurs trying to do the right thing."

"Amateurs, we are," Victor said. "Give me a two-day window after next Sunday. What's that date? The 18th. Mammadu and I will be there."

"I'll let David know."

They shook hands, and Victor moved to leave.

"Don't rush off now. You don't want to forget my gift to Doria. After all, you haven't any other reason to visit her, do you?" Nigel met Victor's surprised stare with a curled smile and squinted eyes. "Look, I'll be speaking to Doria tonight and I'll let her know you're coming. You can meet Dr. DeLevres. And hopefully I can get there myself, very soon. Perhaps while you're with David in Guinea, I'll finally take that trip to Ziguinchor."

Victor nodded. "I'll come by with the Land Rover on our way out, to pick up the present. I can't exactly take a potted plant on the motorcycle, can I."

"Oh, I suspect you could if you tried. But don't concern yourself. It will be here waiting for you next week, when you leave. I probably won't see you until you return with the statues. Keep your wits about you, man. Stay safe and sane, yeah?" He slapped Victor on the shoulder.

"You too, Nigel. And tell Doria for me that I hope she's finding that cure for psychosis or whatever it is she's curing."

"Indeed, I shall."

* * *

As Victor sped away, up the corniche road, Nigel pondered: I really do need to get to Ziguinchor and see Doria. No more of this nonsense. Damn it all, I should be the one traveling there and delivering my gift in person! I have scads of leave days saved up. Why in hell haven't I taken them?

"Well, that settles it, old boy," he said to himself. "You need to get there in two weeks."

He wondered if he should surprise Doria or tell her of his visit. He would figure that out when he spoke to her tomorrow. What would he find when he got there? His inability to even speculate an answer made him cold and disoriented. The blood rushed out of his head and into his stomach. He wasn't worried, he realized. He was afraid.

55. A Crash of Values

Lamine liked to travel as early as possible, which meant being on the road as the sun was hinting it might rise. That avoided the dense traffic that began an hour later. But the real reason Lamine liked it was for the sense of aloneness. The convenience of avoiding the snarls of trucks, pickups, taxis, and sedans was welcome. The solitude of the highway, a tunnel of light carved by the headlights of his Peugeot pickup, gave him a sense of peace and place in his mind, where neither the mistakes of the day before nor the difficulties ahead could intrude. Or so it had been all the other times he made this trip. Today, however, there was solitude, yes, but no peace, no refuge from his nightmare, no ability to unburden his mind from his thoughts. He gripped the steering wheel of his pickup until his hands cramped. And then he gripped harder. His mind would not let go of the images of his wife, naked in bed with another man, closing her lips over his cock, her wet sex craving for their joint release.

For over two months now, Lamine had often been overwhelmed by a drenching sadness overtaking him at unexpected and awkward moments—in the middle of teaching a class or during lunch with colleagues. Tears would flow and he would feel disemboweled, unable to process his own saliva or even air, suspended like a skinned sheep. If Claire was there, she might ignore him or stroke his hair as he was unable to pull away. Or she might snort dismissively. Or she might get up, get dressed, and leave the house, not returning until the next evening.

In the past few days, however, these waves of despair grew less frequent and were replaced with an anger that scorched his skin. It was directive, decisive. Whereas before he was bereft of his organs, now he was cleansed of his human shell, burnt away by a righteous fire. He turned the pain of Claire's open infidelity into fuel.

It was noon when Lamine arrived home, a day earlier than he had told Claire and his LOMA colleagues he would. He had not intended to mislead them, but had no desire now to inform them. He parked in the sand parking lot behind their apartment building and sat in his pickup for some moments, breathing and trying with some success to clear his mind. When he opened the door and pulled his travel bag up to his shoulder, he was calm. With the ease of a soldier, he mounted the three flights of stairs to their flat.

* * *

Why was there no chalk, ever, in the classrooms, Claire muttered angrily to herself. Taking off her glasses, she placed a rebel strand of hair neatly back on her head and fastened it in place with her barrette. It was difficult enough trying to teach Baudelaire to trade school students near the heart of Bedouin Africa. Was it really necessary, even after purchasing the chalk and other classroom materials herself, that she be tested by their constant disappearance? Oh, well. *Les Fleurs du Mal* was better read aloud than diagrammed on a blackboard. She selected one of the few female students to read from Claire's book, the only text available, and helped her through the arcane French of the mystic poet.

Finished for the day, Claire was looking forward to an evening with Darius. He was so easy to be with. He made no demands, was nearly always in a good mood, or when he wasn't, he never directed any of his ire toward her. He was handsome and a little goofy, but not as intelligent as Lamine nor as sensitive. She and Darius would have an easy night of conversation, dinner, and lovemaking, and then she'd be back at her apartment when Lamine returned. She left school to change into something more appropriate for a casual evening and to take a change of clothes for work the next day.

As soon as she opened the door, without closing it and without looking or stepping into the apartment, she knew Lamine had returned. Preparing herself mentally, Claire walked nonchalantly into the living room apartment and, as she suspected, Lamine was sitting in the rattan armchair near the sliding doors to the balcony.

"You're back a day early," she said, going over to plant a kiss on his cheek.

Lamine turned away, saying, "I hope I spoiled your plans."

"Not at all. I'm going to gather a few things for tonight, and I'll be back tomorrow evening. I'll see you at school during the day, though. Maybe we can have lunch," she stated.

Lamine jumped up from his chair and screamed, *"Va te faire foutre! Foutre le déjeuner!"*

Claire not only heard the explosion of rage, she could see he was shaking from head to toe. Never had she seen him like this. Then she noticed a bright reflection at his side. Lamine was holding a long unsheathed machete.

"Lamine, no," Claire said, trying to take command as she stepped slowly backward.

Lamine was instantly behind her, locking the door to the apartment. He looked back at her as terror crept into her eyes.

"You can't go out tonight, Claire," he told her. "You can*not* go *out* tonight!"

"Lamine, calm down. Please. Please, Lamine. You're frightening me."

"Am I?" He raised the machete and looked at it, then back at Claire. "You should be frightened, dear Claire. Gaze upon your work, your creation. This is the person you have turned me into." He took a step toward her. "Do you think this is what I want? Do you think I like being this betrayed crazy man, sick with love and hate, hate for myself for what I've let myself become, hate for you for your not caring enough to stop your wanton behavior. Cursing myself that I should be so terribly in love with you?" Lamine looked at her with desperation. Spare my life, he seemed to implore. Save me.

"My own, my dear Lamine—"

"Don't call me that! Don't you dare call me your dear!"

"But you are my dear," she insisted. "You have always been. But you have never understood who I am, Lamine. Who *I* am, beneath these ... these clothes and this skin." She slapped her arms and her thighs. "Deeper than these breasts and this vagina, who is this woman you have shared your life with for the past five years? Have you ever wondered if I was truly happy here? Do you think we put off having children just because I wanted to be free of that anchor? Could it possibly have been something else? Something more? Do you hear me now, Lamine? Do you hear yourself?" Claire was now shaking. "I have loved you for who you are and for what you dream. You are so smart and dedicated. But you are so self-absorbed, sometimes I don't know if you see me."

"See you? Of course I *see* you. I see you working hard, day in and day out. I see you exhausted and coming home to me, also exhausted. You cannot punish me for that. We both work hard, and we chose this life. It was purpose, it was giving to a part of the world we wanted to explore! But you, you have ... you ..."

"You wanted to explore ... is that it?"

"We decided this together, and if you've been unhappy and unfulfilled, you should have told me. You should have ... said something."

Claire shrugged carelessly. "I did, many times, but I know now it was not in a way you could understand. Well, I'm telling you now, in a way you absolutely understand, yes?" She looked at him defiantly.

"You cannot—you have no right to make me suffer like this. I'm the self-absorbed one? Truly? I'm not the one having sex with someone else. I'm not the one shitting where we work, you craven bitch. Having sex with that simpleton. Everyone knows! Everyone sees what you are, Claire. You have—"

"And what am I, exactly. A whore? A slut? Words used by men in a male-dominated society to put women down. That's all. And what does that make you? Another oppressor, that's what! Another weak man who can't 'tame' his woman?"

Lamine struck out with a force and speed neither he nor Claire knew he possessed. He didn't just slap her. He hit her with his fist, knocking her hard to the stone tiles, blood spurting from her mouth. It was all she could do to stay conscious.

He screamed, "You see! You see! Is this what you wanted? To be crippled in your own apartment by a madman? You did not foresee this consequence did you, Claire? Now you will understand what you have done."

Weakly, Claire looked at Lamine. "You think this is all about you, don't you?" She gurgled on the blood. "Your pain and your rage. How you will be looked upon by the people we work with. Once more, you understand nothing about what I am going through, nothing of what I need. You are not the Lamine I married."

"And you are some monster, a foul, disconnected woman who can only bring misery and death!"

Lamine raised the machete as Claire watched helplessly, her mind a whirl of horror and pity.

"Lamine, don't. Please, La—ahh!" Claire opened her mouth to scream, but she coughed on the blood.

Lamine grasped his other hand onto the hilt of the machete and brought the blade down with all the force of his anger and loathing. He hit the floor tile next to Claire with a deafening clang, sending shards of stone in all directions, many of them hitting Claire in the face and arms. She instinctively turned away from where the blade had struck. He brought the weapon up as if to strike again. Claire could only put her arms up in a futile effort to protect herself.

In the next moment, as if another consciousness had overtaken him, Lamine dropped his arms from over his head and let them hang at his side. Tears streamed from his eyes. He shook his head, though his expression of rage and bewilderment didn't change. Letting go of the machete, he folded his arms at his chest. "Get out, Claire," he told her. "Go to your lover, have your fun, your simple, inconsequential love affair. Go."

Claire was still on the floor in shock, but as she tried to speak it was clear she was in pain. She slurred her words. "I ... I need ... a doctor." She put both hands to her face, where Lamine's blow had broken her jaw.

Lamine looked at her and then closed his eyes, shaking his head. "My dear God, Claire. What is all this?" he asked as if unable to recall or understand what he had done. He shook his head "I-I ... oh, fuck! How has it come to this?"

He bent down and took a handkerchief from his pocket, holding the cloth against her cheek to wipe the blood.

Claire winced in pain, but found the strength and will to hit at Lamine. "You animal!" she screamed. "Do *not* touch me!" She squirmed away on the floor, avoiding his attempt to help her up.

"Claire ... for Christ's sake, let me help you!" he cried as if somehow that act would put them on a path of reconciliation.

"Help me? Help me? You are the one who did this." She could barely speak through the blood rising in her mouth. "Help me by leaving. I will take care of myself!"

Lamine knelt at her side, picking her up slowly. As he did, Claire unleashed her own fury. She flailed at him, her fists hitting him full in the face, again and again. Her volley hurt him much more than he expected, eventually drawing blood from Lamine's nose. But he managed to get his arms under her armpits and lift her off the floor. He ripped off his shirt and held it to her jaw to slow the bleeding. The floor was red and slippery. Lamine lost his balance and fell hard on his butt, letting go of Claire. She turned and kicked him once, but as she went to kick him a second time, she too lost her footing and fell, screaming as she landed next to her husband. The two of them moaned and rolled for a few seconds on the floor, each searching their pain for clues to how seriously they were injured.

Claire sat up slowly and started to cry. Lamine crawled over to her and put his arms around her from the back. She tried to slap them away, but he held steady. Eventually she put her hands on top of his and started to rock and, as she rocked, she stopped crying. They stayed like that for minutes. Lamine loosened his hands from her waist and stood up, the blood brown and clotted on his shirt. He breathed a slow liquid breath in and out while repositioning his hands under Claire's arms, lifting her again. This time she put an arm around his waist.

Though her mouth was filled with blood, she told him, through clenched teeth, "You must be brave if you are going to love me, Lamine. Braver than you have been. More open to me." She paused as the pain surged. But Claire persevered through it. "And I must be careful if I am going to love you."

"Just be quiet, Claire. Let me take you to Dr. Lucien right away."

What the hell just happened, Lamine asked himself as he continued to support a wobbly Claire. Am I so ignorant, so stupid, so utterly hurt that I could have killed her?

As though reading his thoughts, Claire said aloud, with no hint of sarcasm, "Thank you for not murdering me."

"The day isn't over," he answered, wondering if he was truly capable of committing the act he had contemplated for days.

56. REVELATION

Being around Doria Blake was like being a drone bee, DeLevres concluded. He was compelled to work on her behalf, not simply for his own objectives, but so that he could retain his composure. Surely it was his imagination, but since a few weeks after his arrival, Doria Blake seemed to radiate a faint but visible aura. Very disconcerting! As Doria's work with her potions and her mice continued, she had become somewhat of a mystic to him, engaged in something half science, half faith, and all mystery, with results that were not only bizarre, they were not of the real world as he understood it.

Yet the mechanism for these otherworldly occurrences was almost perfectly rational. They could be duplicated and empirically verified. The psychotropic properties of all the plants he studied, and particularly the fungi, could be enhanced and amplified depending on any number of factors, including how susceptible a particular host might be. Cats, for example, reacted much differently and stronger than dogs or rabbits. Rats were different still and offered experimental results that could very often be used to model human reactions. Experimental results on mice were less easy to scale. What was new to DeLevres was the whole idea of combining the alkaline derivatives from, say, *p. serperisi*, with another substance such as one of the many plant extracts he and Doria Blake had produced, or more strangely, the secretive blood mixtures she sparingly prepared with the sap of the fire flower and from small earthenware jars she kept in her refrigerator. Never did she confide in him the source of the blood, but DeLevres was convinced it was Doria's own.

Whether he understood it or not, DeLevres admitted to himself that the results Doria had produced were unknown in the biological sciences and seemed more in the realm of theoretical physics. What exactly was the mechanism that allowed the mind of a mouse to create a defense that affected the perception of a human? Looking for analogs in the natural world was almost futile, though he thought sardonically of the effects of royal jelly on honey bee drones.

* * *

Unfortunately for Doria's work, her preoccupation with her presumed pregnancy inhibited her preparation of compounds and tests. And if her condition was not sufficient distraction, Nigel had phoned, letting her know that Victor Byrnes was on his way to see her in a week and that Nigel himself would probably follow, "looking forward to seeing her in her new element." These developments did not make her happy, though the thought of seeing Victor was soothing. But the soul-searching dilemma of what to tell the two men in her life, whom she had easily shunted aside even yesterday, was now upon her like a fever.

What was worse, she despaired that a rabbit might have to die. How else could she conclusively know if she was pregnant or not at this stage? It seemed corrosively venal—to kill an animal so a woman could know early on if she was pregnant. Moreover, she wondered if, in her case, it might not be a false marker. If her womb was a "factory," as Sisay had said, might it not be possible that the hCG hormone was there, regardless? She decided that her knowledge was not going to change anything. Even if the local French doctor knew how to perform the test, she would not be the instigator of one more instance of this barbarous medical practice. Her body would eventually tell her all she needed to know.

Work for Doria was an incomplete distraction from thinking about her physical condition. She found it difficult to concentrate at times. Tiny tears would form in the corners of her eyes for no reason and silently roll down her cheeks. She wondered if there were any chemicals in her tears which might have useful properties when combined with her other compounds. Over the course of four days she had saved enough to fill a petri dish. Her ensuing experiments to see if her tears, like her blood, produced a new condition or capability in her mice proved fruitless. Perversely, this failure made her feel better, allowing her to believe she might actually be pregnant and that Sisay's pronouncements had been pure rubbish. But nothing was conclusive.

The following Tuesday, at midday, she received Victor's call.

"Doria, I'm in Ziguinchor. Did Nigel get in touch with you?"

"He did, Victor, yes. How nice to hear your voice. Are you at the Hotel Du Sud?"

"Exactly. Good guess. Shall I come on over? Nigel has sent me with a gift. A token of his feelings for you, I would say."

"No, let me come to the hotel and let's have lunch there. I'm certain you're ravenous after your journey. When did you leave Dakar?"

"Yesterday morning. It was a madhouse, Doria. Our next expedition is headed to some pretty remote places in Mali, mostly for the public health team, but also the new agricultural specialist. They were squabbling over drivers, camp stoves, tents, even which Land Rover they would take—all kinds of crazy stuff—like they were evacuating Berlin or something. I'll tell you all about it when I see you."

"I'll be right there."

Hanging up the phone, she slowly placed her flat palm below her navel, watching herself as though a stranger watching from a distance, knowing exactly what was happening, but having no influence. She felt Victor as a presence in her life: a man and a lover, certainly, yet there was something else, something elemental and perhaps even transcendent, neither fully understandable nor fully welcome. The feeling in her belly was these days no longer a manifestation of her attraction to Victor or a sign of hope that a happy miracle had occurred. When the pain swelled or her abdomen gurgled, her thoughts would, as often, turn dark, fearing she had precipitated an increasingly complex and dangerous chain reaction. She went into the laboratory, where DeLevres was busy titrating a fluid and marking color changes in his notebook.

"Alain, a good friend has arrived with a gift from Nigel. I'm going to the Hotel Du Sud to meet him for lunch. We'll return directly, and he will spend the night here. Shall we try to make some time this afternoon to compare notes?"

"If you are ready, Madame. I've uncovered a few interesting puzzles on which I would like your perspective."

"Right, then. I'll be back in a few hours."

She located Iba, who was tending to the gardens peacefully. Since the car was used very little, his job had been to make sure it didn't deteriorate in its idleness and to help as best he could with the upkeep of the compound. He was glad to drive anywhere.

* * *

The weathered mahogany stairs of the Hotel Du Sud creaked under her, another reminder of the slow decay that was claiming the structures of the colonial era.

Seated near the large window looking out over the veranda and directly underneath a still ceiling fan, Victor was staring into the steaming outdoors. Alone in the vast dining room, he rose as soon as he saw Doria. As his arm curled around her waist, Doria kissed him quickly on the mouth, then on both cheeks, releasing his arm as she took her chair. Victor seemed confused.

She whispered, "You may not see anyone but the waitstaff, Victor, but I assure you we are watched. Please don't be cross. I'm not ready to announce to the world that I'm having an affair with you."

Also keeping his voice low, he replied, "It's been hard not seeing you, Doria, not talking to you. Not knowing how you're doing or if you're happy with your work. And there is this longing, you know?"

"I do know, dear, I most certainly do." She reached to brush his cheek, but pulled her hand back slowly into her lap. "It is wonderful to see you. How long will you be here?"

"I have to get on my way and join the ag and geology guys in Mahina by Friday. That means an early start tomorrow."

"Do you have a room here?"

Again, Victor looked puzzled. "Well, no. I thought ... oh, boy," he said dimly. "I-I thought I would stay with you."

"I need to explain that I have a gentleman staying with me right now, and I'm not certain we can ...." She completed the thought with a quick raising and lowering of her eyebrows.

Victor turned away. "Yeah, of course. The professor that Nigel told me about. What has he got to do with us?"

"Dear Victor, he has nothing to do with us, but he has so much to do with my work, literally, our work. Alain and I have made some truly remarkable and—hard to believe, myself—utterly world-changing discoveries." Doria's face barely revealed the excitement she was exclaiming, but her eyes brightened like exploding stars as she spoke. "I cannot, I will not risk losing our momentum."

Victor's shoulders softened and he looked at Doria, hands hung along the sides of his chair.

"What are you thinking, Victor? I know this must be so terribly new and strange for you. Please know that it is for me as well."

"I'm humbled by you. Humbled and more than a little frightened." He exhaled audibly.

A waiter came to their table, and they learned that less than a quarter of what was offered on the menu was actually available. They both ordered the fish and rice.

Doria described her work with DeLevres, leaving out the reactions of the treated mice, and explained how important it was to continue without letting up. Every day there were new and potentially critical discoveries to be made, new compounds to test. There were theories to develop which might explain what they were seeing, and then they would figure out how to test them again to break the theories as well as see where they held.

When they had finished lunch, Doria gazed at Victor. The physical rush returned, and she bit her lip.

"Victor, are the rooms here as spacious and comfortable as they used to be?"

"I … I … don't know," he said slowly as understanding emerged through his smile. "It might be worth a look to see if they're up to your standards, Mrs. Blake."

"Indeed. Would you be kind enough to show me?"

He gestured toward the hall stairways as he stood up and pulled Doria's chair back with mock chivalry. She placed an arm through the crook of his elbow, and he led the way to the front desk, where he ordered a room for the night and she agreed to inspect it.

Their lovemaking was hungry and full as they took turns moving around each other's bodies. Doria glowed in Victor's unbound need for her. Standing against the bathroom door, he turned her around and pulled her backside tight against him. He reached around to cup her breasts fully, slightly twisting her hardening nipples and drawing her tighter to him. Doria responded with her hips pulsing, her juices flowing freely. She reached back and grabbed his butt cheeks and squeezed as hard as she could, pulling him into her, shaking from the electricity of the initial penetration and then the deep thrust that lifted her up onto her toes. As Victor grew larger inside her and his thrust quickened, Doria pulled herself away and turned to face him. She drew his head and mouth directly onto hers, and Victor again found his way into her and they kissed with a deep and ancient hunger. Victor moved his mouth over her body and to her aching breasts. She cupped them, inviting Victor's ardent sucking and licking as they both arched. It was electric and glorious. Doria could tell that Victor was close to orgasm and, wanting that for herself as well, she disengaged and pulled Victor by the hand, over to the bed. Instead of climbing onto the mattress, she simply bent over with her elbows on the blankets and beckoned Victor to enter. She guided him easily with one hand, and as Victor moved in and out, she placed a finger against the top of her sex and rubbed herself in the rhythm of Victor's pulses. When Victor erupted inside her, she quickened her pace and before he was spent, felt her own orgasm mount and overtake her in a wave of energy and pleasure. Doria exclaimed in a voice deeper and louder than she had ever heard herself, as if some power, long stored away, was released.

When they finished bathing, Doria became pensive. She wondered what Victor's reaction would be when she told him of her pregnancy. How would this knowledge change him, change them? And could she possibly tell him of a strange and fretful pronouncement from a local shaman, that she might simply be creating a new medicine inside her body? It wasn't even comprehensible to her, so how could she possibly make it comprehensible to Victor? And for all the love she felt for him, she did not truly know him. She had no idea how he would react to this new and unpredictable future. At the end of the day, how might she want him to react? In her heart of hearts, she did not want him to react at all, and decided, therefore, to tell him nothing for now.

They agreed that Victor would not spend the night at Doria's, but that he would drive over with Mammadu and have dinner. Whether DeLevres suspected their tryst or not should have little consequence, so long as Victor returned to the hotel that night and left early in the morning. Victor remarked that the electricity between them would be difficult to disguise and impossible to turn off. Doria chastised him for his lack of discipline.

* * *

Alain DeLevres was deep in thought when the cars entered the compound. He managed to break himself away as the sounds of two cars rather than one pierced the air. He turned off the Bunsen burner, stripped off his gloves, and went into the living area in time to see Doria lead a red-bearded man carrying three potted plants into the room. DeLevres also noticed Doria's fluttering animation and the young man's wide-eyed fumbling.

Victor turned around to check on Mammadu, who was already laughing and slapping hands with Iba. His friend motioned to Victor to carry on and that he and Iba would take care of themselves.

When Doria introduced DeLevres, the two men shook hands. Victor's shoulders relaxed visibly as he eyed the disheveled botanist. Doria offered tea, and Victor chatted on nervously about his project. He told Doria how Nigel had presented the carefully nurtured English honeysuckle to provide a sense of connection for Doria while she stayed in Ziguinchor. Doria smiled wistfully, looking over her shoulder at the foreign weed sitting in a corner, out of the sunlight.

Victor said to DeLevres, "Doria told me you have been working hard together on some potentially groundbreaking discoveries. It's really cool that you're working on the better use of local plants in medicines."

DeLevres nodded casually and sipped his tea.

After a few seconds without pleasantries, Victor said, "How did you set up this lab, anyway, you two? We have to special-order so much equipment and supplies from the States and Europe for our project. How do you manage here, in the deep Casamance, to find all the tools and chemicals you need?"

"Truly, Mr. Byrnes, that is an extraordinary challenge that … Doria … has endured far longer than I."

Doria stood and took Victor by the hand. "A quick tour, that's all. And I'll introduce you to my talented mice."

DeLevres' eyes grew wide. "Doria, there's a great deal of clutter and I've left my last experiment rather in the middle. Perhaps there is a later time better suited for a visit to the workshop?"

"Just a quick tour, Alain, I promise. Is there something you need to complete or tidy up before we barge into your domain?" Doria asked.

"Please give me about fifteen minutes, if you would," DeLevres said, rising and leaving his teacup half full on the table.

"Very well, then. I'll introduce Victor to the real talent of our work."

"The mice?" both men said.

"Yes, just so. My wonderful, brilliant mice."

As soon as Victor closed the door behind them in the office, he put his arms around Doria's waist from behind. She leaned back, turning her head to join him in a series of lingering kisses. She turned away eventually, to the workbenches in front of her, leaving her right hand on Victor's neck for a few moments.

She pointed out the jars and flasks of different compounds, explained her notes and her logbook. She showed him how various results from one test led her to consider different mixes and quantities for new tests. She had been searching for differences in the learning responses of the mice, which she stressed in a maze that was never the same. Victor had to admit it seemed detailed and dull.

"How do you possibly keep this up?" he asked.

"But Victor, this is why I'm here. This is precisely what I've been meaning to do for many, many years. How sad and, well, weak if I had just gone to university and never used what I had learned, or not set out to do what I wanted. This experimentation may seem boring and inconsequential to you, but really, it is ever so much more than you imagine. Come look. Over here." Her whole body shimmered as she led Victor by the hand over to the mice. "Come and have a look at my colleagues, won't you?"

Victor could see six mice in a clear box with plastic wrap over the top, poked with holes. "Really, Doria, couldn't the mice get out of there pretty easily?"

"So true, yes. But that's the beauty, Victor. They no longer want to!"

"So, effectively, you've drugged them."

Doria thought about that for a second. "That could be one way to look at it. Another is that they have decided that these surroundings best support their lives."

"Oh, really? Will you be teaching them genetics and Kant as they get older?" he teased.

"Ha-ha. Seriously, these mice have shown me that we know so little of the world around us and that if one is willing to go where the information takes you, willing to loosen oneself of preconceived notions, there is no limit to the doors that can be unlocked."

Victor arched his eyebrows and took a step back from Doria. "You sound like a convert to a religion, Doria. What are you talking about, exactly?"

"What, exactly," Doria said, tapping an index finger on her right cheek. "Yes. What indeed."

She slowly turned back the plastic top of the mouse crate. She looked around the box before extending her hand in and saying, "Oscar."

One of the mice in the corner stood on his hind legs for a second, turned, and scampered onto Doria's hand and up her arm.

"A mouse that comes when he's called!" Victor shouted. "That's amazing, Doria, that's beyond amazing, isn't it? I mean, has anyone ever gotten a mouse to respond to a verbal command before?"

"I don't know for certain, but I know these three all know their names and respond to a few simple verbal commands. The other three I keep as control, to be sure these differences are real. And I have another two dozen mice over here." She led Victor over to the area where the other mice were kept. Oscar crawled up onto Doria's shoulder and stayed there.

Victor was amazed. Like a cat, he thought. Without thinking, he extended his hand to the little creature to see if he would climb onto his hand. To his astonishment, he didn't simply climb onto his hand, Oscar leapt like squirrel, directly onto Victor's shoulder and over his neck and up to the top of Victor's head. Victor was so startled he swatted at Oscar, who was moving away faster than Victor could strike. Doria turned, mystified and horrified to see a flailing Victor terrorized by a tiny mouse.

"Oscar, come here this instant!" she shouted.

To which the mouse leapt back onto Doria's shoulder and stood up, waiting for the next command.

"What the fuck!" Victor was still checking himself to see if the mouse had bitten him or shit on him.

"Victor, what happened?"

"What happened? You saw what happened, right? Your pet came at me! One moment I was thinking how much he was like a cat, and the next, I was—"

"You were thinking Oscar was like a cat? Why?"

"Why? Hell, he was perched on your shoulder like a kitten. Should I have thought he was a parrot or something? What the hell is going on?"

Doria held Oscar in the palm of her hand and looked at him inquisitively. Victor could have sworn he saw the mouse turn red, as in blushing, and then start to fade from view. Doria turned away from Victor, hiding Oscar, and quickly went back to his crate, placing him among his fellow mice.

"That was the strangest thing. ... I could have sworn I saw that mouse—"

"It's all right, Victor." Again she took him by the hand, leading him out of her work space.

When they were in the living room, they sat together on the sofa.

Victor looked at Doria with a question written on his face. Doria took a deep breath and recounted her experimentation and the subsequent characteristics now resident in her mice. Different behaviors seemed to come and go and different stimuli produced different traits. Some, she could predict, but others she could not, nor could she even, with DeLevres' help, fully explain the neurochemical mechanics at work.

Victor looked at her in near shock. "I don't know enough to advise you in any way, but this isn't just another discovery you've got. If you can prove this and reproduce it, you've got something that is bigger than electricity! I mean, the implications are mind-blowing!"

"I'm so very excited myself, but I dare not reveal this beyond the bounds of these walls. I'm far too unsure how this all works and where it might lead. I'm certain, however, that were this to become public, I'd have the international news media, perhaps even religious extremists, either wanting to burn me at the stake or hail me as the next Joan of Arc."

"Well, she was burned at the stake, don't forget. But I think you'd have to be a virgin. Sorry."

Doria smirked. "To say nothing of the pharmaceutical companies. Oh God, my very own husband would swoon if he saw the commercial value of this. Victor, please, you must, you must help me. This information cannot go beyond this compound. Tell me you understand. Tell me you are with me. Please! I need to hear you say you're with me!"

"Wow! I've seen some strange things, Doria. Some really interesting things. Hell, when Mammadu and I got that fire flower for you, I thought we were going to end up as totems for the medicine queen. But this? This is in a different category altogether. I promise I won't tell a soul. Hell, who'd believe me?"

"There are many, many people willing to believe the fantastic. And just as ready to fear it, I think. People could easily want to destroy this work. Your complete confidence is vital, maybe even to our very lives." Not until this moment had Doria thought what would happen when her work became exposed to the greater world. She was now shaking, worried how to protect it—and how to protect herself and Victor. Suddenly she sensed a distant violent chaos set in motion already. Doria shivered, wide-eyed and silent.

Victor pulled her to him. She resisted at first, but her need not to be alone, her need to trust this man and for him to trust her, pushed her doubts away for now.

A sense of urgency came over her as she hugged Victor and planted soft kisses on his ears and cheeks. It didn't matter if DeLevres or her husband knew she and Victor were lovers. There were much more important things to which she must attend, and time was no longer her ally.

By the time DeLevres returned to the living area, Doria and Victor were speaking quietly on the sofa. They greeted his return warmly, but with a bit of distance.

"So, what do you think of the work of Madame Blake, Monsieur Byrnes? Impressive, no?"

"I would have to say that what I witnessed was a few steps beyond impressive, Professor. More like earthshaking!"

"Then you have seen maybe more than is really here," DeLevres stated. "What did you see, exactly, and what does it tell you?"

Victor gazed up at DeLevres. "Is that really possible, Professor? I mean, I'm still catching my breath. I'm still trying to figure out if what I saw was illusion, magic, evolution …. You guys are working on something that is out there, no question. And, you know, I'm barely hanging on." He looked over at Doria. "I'm fascinated by the little that Doria's let me see. But as you can tell, I'm still really shaky." Victor extended his right arm so DeLevres could see the quavering of his limbs. "I'm not even sure I can stand."

DeLevres nodded. "You can most certainly stand, Mr. Byrnes. This is scientific experimentation, not alchemy or voodoo. Come, then, and let me show you the process for analyzing the chemical compounds of what Madame Blake has gathered and brewed."

"That's a kind offer, Professor, but I was thinking that I need an early dinner and an early sack time. If it's all the same to you, Mammadu and I will head back to the hotel and maybe you two would like to join us for dinner."

Victor shook DeLevres' hand. Then he and Doria went outside to the waiting Land Rover.

She looked at her lover in the dimming light. "Victor, I know Nigel has you involved in a scheme of some kind. I'm certain you're a courier for him, just as you were for me."

Victor started to say something in his own defense, but his lost voice confirmed Doria's pronouncement.

"Shhh. Don't say anything yet. You must be careful. Nigel likes others to take risks for him. He's not a bad man at all, but he is a bit … maybe just a bit greedy, and it makes him ignore his big heart."

"All that stuff is between you and him. He asked me to do him a favor and I agreed to do it. That's all."

"That's never all. Between him and Tony, they have ambitious plans for a mining and mineral company, becoming a force in the world cocoa market, and who knows what else. I'm asking you to be careful. Please. You think you're invulnerable, but you're not."

"A mere mortal, I?" Victor joked. "Doria, I saw something today that shook my world. The woman I love has made a reality-shifting discovery, and I'm along for the ride. How could anything else measure in importance to that?"

Doria nodded and held Victor's forehead against hers. They kissed good-bye.

* * *

She had more work to do with her mice. What was happening? Oscar hadn't had a taste or injection of any mixture in over ten days. How had he developed something new? And what was it, exactly? She rushed back into the house and then to her lab. Where was this going? she thought. Suddenly, the answer to the "where" didn't seem important. It was the journey now: the exploration and the wonder that fueled her energy. Her original purpose dimmed in the shadow of these new discoveries and the pursuit of their meaning.

"I don't know where this will lead at all," she murmured to her mice.

Why was she not more concerned that she was willing to abandon a goal that had nourished her spirit and given her a sense of purpose in the world? What kind of woman was she, who could so easily cast aside a lifelong dream to follow a strange and thrilling path that had no foreseeable outcome or even benefit? And odder still was that the answers to such questions were themselves unimportant. What was happening to her?

57. Decision in Reverse

The house on the corniche was dark. There was no hint of a breeze this night. Ahminta had cleaned up the kitchen after preparing dinner and had departed. Nigel was still sitting at his dining table as night descended. When he repaired to his office to review two new local contracts, he did so begrudgingly, knowing he could do it in the morning while feeling that some work at home helped him deserve his standard of living. However, he read the same paragraph in the first contract three times. He gave up, rubbing his eyes and thinking he should go to bed. But he wasn't tired. He was restless.

Pushing back from his desk he stood up straight and put his arms in a high stretch over his head. He bent low to touch his toes, hanging like an empty overcoat across a railing, feeling the blood move to his brain. When he straightened himself up quickly, little pinpricks of light dazzled his eyes and he became light-headed. He shook it off and stretched again, and then went into the dining room and poured himself a Glenmorangie. Its scent of peat and alcohol sent a ripple of electricity through his arms and face. He drank two quick gulps before settling the glass in his left hand and holding it at his side like a pistol.

Nigel walked out onto the patio stairs and sat down. He could hear the familiar beat of drums in the distance. Even on a weekday, the people of Dakar gathered as family around a fire, after dinner, whether they lived in a grand compound or in a seedy shack with a sand floor, and played traditional drums, socialized, and connected. Nigel felt immensely alone. He could have headed back into town and mingled at the High Commission Social Club or the Bar Ponty with the other Brits and expatriates consuming life as though it were a bottomless through. How often had he tried to recover the swaggering warrior of his youth, to imbue this middle-aged professional he was now. Nigel shook his head as he looked into his drink. He would never be the man he could be. He was seriously flawed by a vestigial force to be animal rather than spirit. He took another gulp from his crystal cup and contemplated how many brain cells he might destroy in the next twenty minutes if he really put his mind to it.

Until a few short months ago, Doria had been this subdued backlight illuminating nearly everything except the hard-edged details. She managed to soften the hot days, the sweaty work, and the abhorrent politics and corruption that seemed to make up the bulk of his life and to which he had succumbed.

"You've really boxed yourself in, haven't you, old chap," he murmured to himself, swirling his glass absentmindedly. This business with the diamond smuggling wasn't really a shot at financial independence, was it? No, damn it all. It was a fucking self-indulgence of the first order. It was a not-so-cheap thrill, out across the boundaries of propriety, a pure play of one-upmanship and a tongue sticking out at the highborn—except for the fact that none of the imaginary dons of British virtue ever took note of his schoolboy rebellion. It was nothing more than a thumb in the eye of a dead man.

He finished his whiskey. "Fuck me," he sneered.

Nigel was having difficulty trying to understand how he had arrived at this stage. And now here, he could see it was time to do something different. He would see this last bit of smuggling through to its conclusion and hopefully come out of the whole affair with the £500,000. Not the millions he fantasized about when he and Hume first conceived of this enterprise. It surprised him to feel that this was now much less important than recovering his wife and finding a way to renew what they had. Nigel shook his head. Renewing what they had was not it. Doria left because she didn't like what she had. She was unfilled in her life, unfulfilled in her relationship with Nigel. The only way forward was not a renewal but a rebirth. They had to start completely new, or else there would be no relationship. The clarity with which Nigel saw this made him feel better. He had a destination that illuminated a path to act. He had to go to Ziguinchor and be with Doria. Talk to her from the deep recesses of his heart, which itself was brand-new. So resolved, Nigel picked up the phone and dialed his business partner.

"Tony, it's Nigel."

"Isn't it, just. Past your usual bedtime, I should think. What are you plotting now, my friend?"

"I'm going to Ziguinchor tomorrow. I've got to go be with Doria and put our marriage back together. I've been just an idiot about her, letting her go down there by herself, with that crazy botanist for company. Then sending that naïve Byrnes down with a present. I should have gone myself. And so I shall. Tomorrow morning."

"Don't you have some important business you should be attending to? Aren't the introductions we made for BBI supposed to bear some contract fruit tomorrow or soon thereafter? Nigel, think about the timing. That's all I'm saying."

"Thinking about the timing has been my problem. Never a good time to do something difficult, particularly when there is so much to distract, yes. But that's what I'm talking about. This work, these contracts, hell, even our arrangement with David and Antwerp are all distractions. Doria has been gone for the better part of three months, and I've become more wretched by the day. Functional, oh, yes. Cordial and engaging, most of the time, I suppose. But before I'm no longer able to sustain those tricks, before I become so miserable and preoccupied, start to babble in front of clients, I must be with Doria. Do you understand?"

"Of course! A part of me understands and wants you to be happy in your marriage, but another part of me is saying this is something that Doria has to work out for herself, and you should be concentrating on your career and your finances, both of which are in the position to aggrandize substantially in the next two weeks."

"To hell with my career and my finances, damn it! Why am I doing this, anyway? To accumulate more money than the Crown? To have my great success as visible as my nose so that passersby nod their heads with admiration? To be a financier? A man of leisure? What shit it all is!"

"You're not serious, man! What other yardstick are we to use to judge our success, except by the size of our bank accounts and the clever ways we can put that capital to use? Come, Nigel. I know you must go to Ziguinchor. I truly do. Just remember, your ambition has served you well to this point. Don't let that fire be doused by a brief torrent of loneliness."

"Has it served me so well, really? I feel I was greedy for the wrong things. I'm not just lonely. Doria is incredibly special and, gads, I can't remember when I told her as much. So I wanted to let you know. I'll make arrangements in my office. Please let others know for me, won't you?"

"What will you do when you get there? How long will you be?"

"I can't answer that now. Two days, two weeks, two months, I have no idea."

"We're expecting Victor back in two weeks. You have to be here then to get our stones to Antwerp. That's not negotiable. Do not waver here, old man. It's far too important. Do you hear me?"

"I hear you, Mr. Hume. Now, you listen. If necessary, you can take four days' holiday and fly to Antwerp yourself. You have all the information you need."

"You built the relationship with Lasry, damn it. This isn't some business meeting between global corporations with interchangeable vice-presidents. This is an under the table, and, might I remind you, highly illegal arrangement that is both delicate and time sensitive. You need to be back to see this through. You *must* complete this."

Nigel nodded in silence, conveying nothing of his acquiescence to his partner. "I'll be back as soon as I can. That will have to be good enough for now."

"It bloody well isn't good enough. Do not fuck this up for us. I expect you back here in less than a fortnight. Now, buck up and remember you have done more than anyone to put all these bits in motion. David and I are depending upon you, damn it! Keep your word. Keep your bloody word."

"Keep my word, indeed. How appropriate that you should remind me of my word. And keep it I shall. Good night, Tony. I will contact you as soon as I can from Ziguinchor."

"Go safely, Nigel. Our business is messy enough. Don't kick any shit into it, all right?"

"All right."

PART 7

Event Horizon

58. Interruption

M baye Touré knew the time to act was now. He had fired one of his six shopkeepers two days ago not because he was stealing from Touré, but because he refused to provide information to him from his brother who worked at the diamond mine. Touré was becoming fixated on the movement and projects of David Semba and had begun his inquiries in earnest, trying to find out where he'd gone, how long he'd been away, and what he was buying. But surprisingly, people were not talking, regardless of the bribe. It wasn't simply that David was secretive and elusive. Touré interpreted David's inscrutability for an attitude of superiority; David Semba believed himself to be smarter and above everyone else in his village. Touré sniffed, telling himself, "I'm the shrewd businessman. I'm the one with six simultaneous projects, of which no individual knows of more than two. I'm the smartest man in the village!" It was all the more infuriating to him that Semba showed no sign of understanding that he was in competition with Touré. David virtually ignored Touré and did his best to avoid contact with him. That had to change, and soon.

It was time to raise the stakes. Semba's family working in the mines had to be his contacts and even his sources, considering Semba only deigned to come home to Kaala once a month or so. How could the Semba cousins be coerced into betraying their clansman? Touré wanted to give his brother Moti the opportunity to find out what was going on, but Moti was too blunt an instrument. He was all power and intimidation, no guile, nothing that would disarm an unwary opponent, just bludgeon him. A direct frontal assault would trigger instantaneous defenses in the Semba clan. He had to find a more subtle approach, at least at the beginning. Having given careful consideration to all risks, Touré landed on an idea. He needed assistance from some specific individuals in his own family. An indirect approach, soft and on the tangent of family life, might be the right entrance into the Semba fortress.

Shena was the seventeen-year-old daughter of David's cousin Dugue. Shena was fourteen, walking home from school one day, when three older boys from her school attacked her, dragging her screaming into the dense roadside brush. They beat her into silence and tore her clothes from her body and raped her, two of them holding her down as she struggled. By the third, she didn't struggle at all.

It was days after when Dugue heard of this atrocity, told to him by his second wife and Shena's mother. Dugue's first thoughts were of his daughter's health and state of mind. But if concern came first, revenge came strongest.

Shena's trauma had been sufficiently deep and indelible to force her complete retreat into a cocoon of her mind, unable to speak or make eye contact, let alone identify any of her assailants. Dugue was beside himself to the point where his daughter's violation became more about him than about Shena. After weeks of significant entreaties from both his wives and his brother, Dugue solicited the help of his cousin David.

When Dugue told David of Shena's degradation and torment at the hands of her classmates, David himself became nearly silent, speaking in three-word sentences, asking short questions. "Who were they? What time was this? Did no one help? They will suffer."

Dugue was against reporting this to the village chief, but David insisted. The chief, however, was not particularly sympathetic to their desire for justice and did nothing. Rape of a Malinke woman was not uncommon or nearly as serious as stealing a cow. David told Dugue his plan to uncover the culprits and exact justice.

Shena exhibited little signs of recovery, while David formed an affection for his distant cousin in her vulnerability and need. He visited her often, telling her nothing of his plans on her behalf, and telling her the same stories he had told to her as a child, stories of faraway places where streets were all paved and where such things as snow, street lights, and dancing in great halls booming with rhythmic music were daily occurrences. But Shena never spoke. She could only stare through deep, woeful eyes.

In the end, David's victory was bitter and unsatisfying. Having befriended the weakest of the cohorts that it had taken a short time to identify, David had asked the young man to show him his favorite place to go swimming. Dutifully obliging to an elder and a man reputed to be wealthy and helpful, the young man led David to an isolated swimming hole. As they swam, David spoke to the young man of crimes he knew people had committed and how they had to own up to these crimes before God. As the boy's attitude went from confusion to curiosity to comprehension and, finally, to fear, David was close enough to take the boy by the shoulders and push him under the water for over thirty seconds. When he let the boy up, spitting, coughing, and gasping for air, David was clear and direct. The boy would tell him everything he wanted to know and he would agree to a punishment for his crime or else he would die there. It had taken only one more dunking to convince the youngster that he wanted to live.

After the boy's confession at the police station, the reluctant commandant arrested all three boys. Their parents went to David and Dugue's compound to protest. They sneered their displeasure and spat on the ground in front of them, calling young Shena a whore whose life was not worth the limb of one of the three boys, let alone their subsequent beating and incarceration. But David was calm, telling the two fathers that if they ever set foot on the Semba compound again, they would each lose a leg in the middle of the night. That was enough to send them back to their remote part of the village, never to return.

The family turned their attention to Shena for the next many months. Although David traveled frequently on business, he remembered her as the smart child he had cared for, and always brought her clothes or jewelry from his travels. Whatever David brought Shena, she accepted it in silence and wore from that point forward, until there was little adorning her entire body on any day that David had not given her. As she slowly gained the use of a few words and phrases, such as "thank you," David felt ever more protective and hopeful that Shena would become the person she could have been, growing through the dirt of her trauma like a new sprout.

Shena could be the perfect fulcrum by which Mbaye Touré would get leverage over David Semba.

During David's long absences, Touré had instructed his second wife, Loda, to befriend Shena's mother, Toli, for the express purpose of getting to know Shena, and eventually asking if Shena might be used for some simple tasks at the Touré compound.

Loda did as her husband requested. "It will do the child good, Toli. She does the same few things day in, day out. Have her do something different. She may begin to speak."

"Shena does everything around here we ask of her, Loda. She is nearly mute, yes, but she has not lost her mind, only her will to speak."

"If she is capable, then all the more reason to give her opportunities to work with others. She can be genuinely useful and could make friends outside of her sisters. You must want that for her."

"Perhaps, but I don't know if Shena would want that."

"Then let me start her an hour each day, working with her in your compound. I could bring laundry and millet to grind. Maybe if we work together, she will learn to trust me and we can see if she continues to improve."

"This is very generous of you, Loda," Toli said, her eyebrows arching.

Loda responded cheerily, "Not at all, dear. The poor child has been through so much, and I'm sure that some new people and work in her life will help her recover. Can it hurt?"

Over the next two weeks, Loda was as good as her word, bringing new chores for Shena, who dispassionately addressed them without even a nod of permission necessary from her mother. And Loda stayed close to Shena, instructing her as though Shena did not know how to do laundry or make porridge. Loda's voice was pleasant and she occasionally sang, asking Shena to join in. She didn't at first, but eventually began to try and sing a chorus of a familiar childhood working song. Toli saw the slow yet real progress Shena was making.

After two weeks with this success, Touré decided it was time to get Shena into the Touré compound. Loda was pleased with her success and even more with her husband's rare praise. She was ready to sink her claws into the girl who had given her trust so easily.

As Toli's suspicions subsided, the invitation to Shena to visit the Touré compound seemed like a good next step for her daughter's rehabilitation. Loda arrived early on a Tuesday morning and led Shena out of her family compound without a single look back. When she arrived at the Touré compound, Loda continued her apparent care as the two of them worked together. But the conversation was different. Loda raised suspicions about how much Shena's family actually cared for her. Were they the right sort of people to have a daughter who they had allowed to be violated so and were then unable to properly care for her? Why had her mother prevented Shena from working with Loda for so long? Why was her father never home and caring for her the way a good father should?

Loda couldn't be sure this was working on the girl, difficult as it was to communicate with her even in the most straightforward of issues. Nevertheless, Shena was beginning to speak with increased frequency and in direct response to Loda's comments. After nearly two weeks of this every day, Shena's trust of Loda had become familial. Loda conferred with her husband as to what she should do next.

Mbaye's plan was ready. "We want to learn the movements of her father and her uncle in the mines, and we want her to tell us when

David reappears. I'm sure he won't announce anything to me." Touré sneered, as his wife empathized. "I need to know how he is stealing diamonds from the mine. And make sure she understands her father and her uncles are stealing!" he finished emphatically.

"Calm yourself, Mbaye," Loda told him. "The girl trusts me, but she doesn't say much. Let's try to see if her father and uncle store things secretly. Let's ask her to tell us if they hide something after they come back from work, and, if yes, to find out what that something is."

Loda gave Shena a task to watch for specific movements of her father and her uncle, particularly if they returned home and appeared to protect small bundles and to note where these bundles were stored. For two weeks Shena reported nothing to Loda. Then one day she did have something to report. Her favorite uncle, David, had come back. Loda had enough savvy to know that they needed to be very careful, and asked Shena to go and stay home the next few days while Uncle David was visiting.

It was with little surprise but much consternation for Mbaye and Loda, when David paid them a visit the next day.

"I wanted to extend my thanks to the two of you, and especially to you, Loda, for caring for Shena for such a long period and helping her heal. Who knows how long it would have taken otherwise?"

"Yes, how long indeed," Loda said as she twirled her hair and looked at her husband. "Won't you please come and sit, David?"

Normally, David would never stay long enough to accept this offer, but today was different.

"Thank you, Loda. Yes, I will."

Husband and wife exchanged glances.

Under the covered porch David took one of the two goat-hide chairs. Touré sat in the other, opposite David. Loda hovered behind her husband.

"It is remarkable the improvements I have seen in Shena," David said. "She is speaking almost as she did four years ago, before her rape. She still doesn't have much eye contact, does she, Loda?"

"No, David. No, she doesn't. Not yet."

"No, not yet. But then, she seems to have her curiosity back. Why, just yesterday she was asking me where I had come from and if I had any small bundles. I was rather amazed, I have to tell you, to see her so engaged. Apparently, she had asked her father the same questions—repeatedly, actually."

A bead of sweat formed on the nape of Loda's neck and trickled down her back, causing her to shiver. David noticed her slight convulsion, but said nothing about it.

Touré responded easily, "There's no understanding sometimes, where a child picks up notions that pique their curiosity."

"Quite true, Mbaye Touré. Yes, very true. And sometimes, of course, there is," David countered.

"Oh?" was all Touré could manage.

"Well, Shena has been spending a great deal of time here. But it's so hard to know for certain, as you say, Mbaye. On a completely different matter, I will be traveling with her father tomorrow, and Toli will be going to stay with her mother, taking the children with her. So I'm sorry to say you won't be able to see Shena for a few weeks, anyway. I can only imagine how fond of her you must have grown over these last several weeks."

"So true, David," Loda said, finding her voice.

David smiled slightly. "I must go back and make travel preparations," he said. "But it was important for me to see you before I left, to let you know how much I appreciate your care of Shena."

"David, if I may, what trading are you doing and where?" Touré was bolder now that David had seen through his ruse to gather information.

"Mineral rights in the south," David answered.

Touré opened his mouth to ask more questions, but David was already standing and turning to leave.

At the gate, David turned toward Touré and extended his hand. He looked into Touré's eyes. "We hope to return within the next few weeks. My whole family extends its greetings for your continued health." David pulled his hand back and wiped it on his trousers.

After the gate closed behind David, Touré was seething. Making his way back to his house and pounding his left fist into his right palm, he muttered, "I know where David is going. If his cousins are involved too, this is important. They are planning an exchange of diamonds and that brazen shithead thinks he's outsmarted me!"

* * *

David returned to his family's compound with renewed understanding of Mbaye Touré's treachery. The seed he planted regarding the family trip south should push Touré into a mistake. If that happened, David and his cousins must be prepared.

Shena approached David with her head down. Placing his hand lightly under her chin, David lifted her face for her eyes to meet his. Then, in a gesture he had not made in years, he hugged his young second cousin tightly. Small streams of tears escaped him. Feeling David's tears fall on the side of her face, Shena looked up, pulled the bandana from her hair, and dried his cheeks.

59. Forcing the Issue

Work in the diamond mines of Kaala was a singularly hazardous and unrewarding job. Armed guards patrolled the edges of the steep walls made jagged by the uneven cuts of mechanical shovels. These beasts tore into the stony shelves of Mount Lucius to cleave chunks of mountain, often loosened by the repeated blows of sledgehammers wielded by local men. These villagers all began as strong men, capable men. But their bodies were made brittle and frail by the incessant heavy impact of iron on stone, hundreds of blows a day, turning sinew and ligament into strings barely roping elbows and shoulders together.

Dynamite was rarely used, precious as it was, not because it was expensive. It wasn't. But it was hard to get and harder to keep, prized by everyone from fishermen to bandits to renegade soldiers roaming far from their barracks in search of a payday. What little dynamite there was on hand was used sparingly and kept under a single manager's watch.

Until he became that manager, Temu Semba, who had broken or bruised nearly every bone north of his navel, begged the foreman at least twice a week to dynamite the brutally unyielding stone. The response never varied: "Do your work, Temu. We make the decisions. Do as you're told and maybe in time you'll do something else."

Temu did as he was told and, in time, he got to do something else. As he got older and his muscles recovered more slowly, he was removed from the dreadful steel pounding on stone and became a hod carrier, taking hand-gathered loads of stones to the crusher and sorter, a vast belching array of three interconnected machines dubbed the "Ball Breaker." The mine owners had purchased it years ago and maintained three full-time mechanics to keep it running. Its only true advantage over the labor it replaced was that the machine had no interest in stealing the diamonds that were revealed and liberated from the anthracitic rock.

Temu poured hods of stones into the maw of the Ball Breaker every day for three years, before once again being promoted. This time it wasn't that he had become less physically capable, but that he had proven himself reliable, pliable, and just smart enough to replace a manager who thought himself more clever than the owners. Sufficiently so, in fact, to believe he could take and hide small amounts of raw stones *and* sell them in Conakry. One morning his severed head appeared on the light post next to the Ball Breaker. That afternoon, Temu became the counting house manager.

Upon his return home that evening he excitedly told his family, including his visiting cousin David, about his good fortune. But David was not happy for Temu. He was worried.

Weeks later David approached Temu and his brother Dugue with a plan to remove diamonds safely, without being detected, and after another fifteen months, Temu and Dugue agreed.

* * *

If it is true that an army operates on its stomach, then the Guinean army was an emaciated baby, starving at its mother's breast. The government of Sékou Touré, which had in the early days of the regime, paid and fed the army handsomely, had grown increasingly complacent regarding the needs of its partner in subjugation. But what would eventually signal the end of the Sékou Touré regime was pure opportunity for his relative, Mbaye Touré. Soldiers would go for months without pay, even years. Touré saw in every officer, particularly those charged with "protecting" the European and South African miners, the opportunity to create an ally and perhaps even a dependent. Through his carefully distributed largesse to the families of soldiers and the men themselves, Mbaye Touré had amassed the loyalty of the local garrison and beyond. It was within this web that Touré lured Temu Semba.

* * *

This day was like all the other days, flowing into rote hardship for all the men working the mines. Temu oversaw two loyal tribesmen in the disgorging of the Ball Breaker into a wheelbarrow. Between the armed soldiers, the men wheeled the dense, barely glinting stones up to the counting house and into an open garage where the weighing and hand separation took place. A gaunt Frenchman representing the owners made notations on a clipboard and waved them on.

In a tiny office with no door Temu sat at a makeshift desk, weighing two-kilogram measures of the stones and putting them into sacks with tags, on which he wrote the day and time of the collection and the names of the people carrying it out. Temu signed the first, and then the second, as he always had.

As he tied off the third sack and dutifully marked it, he heard a conversation strike up at the garage entrance. Touré's brother Moti was speaking loudly to the soldier that he needed something. Temu continued his work without a missed beat. After the weighing and tying off of the sixth sack, Temu saw an armed soldier and Moti approaching.

The soldier spoke to him. "Go with this man now."

"Sir, I am not yet halfway completed," Temu said, indicating the work.

The soldier looked at Moti for what to do next.

"Someone will take your place, Temu," Moti said with a sneer.

"Really?" Temu asked. "Who would that be, exactly? You, Moti, with your superior mathematics skills?"

Moti looked at Temu with his head cocked to one side, wondering why this small man would say such a thing. His lips curled and he snorted. "I'm sure the commandant will arrange for someone of your skill to take over," Moti replied.

Temu said, "Is that so? Please tell me who you think that might be. Kitwake? God, he can't even remember to buy food for his children. Sugu, maybe? I'm sure he'd like a break from the prison cell you have him in for doing nothing but speaking his mind … drunk! Maybe you, soldier, or you, Moti," he said, noticing Moti's growing impatience.

Moti and the soldier moved rapidly up to Temu, and Moti, pulling the sack from his hands, stated in a loud voice, "The director wants you in his office, now."

Temu remained seated and dusted himself off. "Thanks for telling me that, you numbskull." The last word, Temu said in Fulani, knowing the soldiers at the mine were almost all of the Malinke tribe and would most likely not understand. But even if they did understand, Temu thought, what's the worst these cretins would do? Maim me? Torture me? Temu stood up and rubbed as many creases from his trousers as his summoners allowed.

"Where are we going, precisely?"

"My brother would like to ask you for some information. We're going to his car."

"He could have come here himself, and I would have told him exactly what I will tell him in the car."

"I don't think so," Moti mumbled to himself, sure that Temu would confide things he didn't even know he knew. "Mbaye has his reasons, Temu. Be wise. Come with me." He motioned with his head, as if Temu and he shared a secret.

"What is wrong with you, Moti? You get an armed escort and suddenly you act like an owner. Everyone gets an armed escort. Until Mr. Seduru, my immediate supervisor and the one responsible for my work, tells me to go with you, I have no intention of leaving my job. Tell Mbaye to meet me here."

"How diligent you are in your duties, Temu. Are you so diligent when keeping your family safe?"

Temu lost his composure. "What did you say to me? What … you … who are you to say such a thing to me, you thug! You motherfucker!"

This made Moti smile. "Let's pass by Mr. Seduru's office to see Mbaye, yes? I'm sure he'll give you fifteen minutes to attend to a family emergency."

Temu rushed at Moti, but the soldier stepped quickly between them. Temu's momentum turned the three of them into a human sandwich, Temu shouting invectives at Moti over the shoulder of the guard, who was having difficulty pushing Temu back. Finally, the guard gave Temu a strong shove with some help from Moti, who was pushing the soldier from behind.

Temu was drooling with anger. He wiped his mouth. "I'm going nowhere with you, you goat's ass. And you don't go near my family. Do you understand? You stay away from my family!"

Moti realized that his brother wouldn't be happy if Temu didn't show up. But to subdue him and cart him over to the car like a sack of groceries would draw too much attention. Moti stepped back to leave the small office, turning to Temu before he left. "Stay here, then. Don't move. I'll be right back."

The soldier and Temu shot puzzled glances at each other. Moti lumbered his way down the steps, across the yard separating the compound of offices from the pits, through the inner security gate, and over to his brother's car.

Mbaye Touré rolled down the window on the passenger side and asked in exasperation, "And Temu Semba is where?"

"He refused to come with me, Mbaye. I was mad enough just to pick him up and carry him over, but I didn't want to do something stupid."

"You didn't want to do something stupid. How much I appreciate that, Moti. Please keep that thought with you at all times. Where is Semba now?"

"I left him in the sorting house, with the guard. He says he won't come unless Mr. Seduru gives him the OK."

"I will go speak to Seduru myself."

Mbaye Touré left the car and indicated for Moti to sit in the back seat to wait. Touré strode through to the inner security, passing with relative ease, and entered briskly into Seduru's outer office.

The secretary looked up and recognized him. "Yes, Mr. Touré?"

"I need to see Mr. Seduru for five minutes."

The secretary went to the open door of Seduru's office. She told her boss who was there to see him. Seduru rose from his creaky leather chair and came to the door. Without a word he waved Touré into his office and closed the door.

"What can I do for you, Mbaye Touré?" he asked.

"A very small favor, Bedu Seduru. I need a moment rather urgently with a family friend and worker here, Temu Semba. With your permission, I would speak to him for about fifteen minutes. He seems ... reluctant to do so without your blessing."

"Understandable. Semba is a very responsible and a conscientious sorter and counter. But I'm sure your business is important." Seduru looked at Touré in the silent question of compensation for this small favor.

Touré nodded nearly imperceptibly. A future favor was deposited.

"Ruta!" Seduru shouted to his secretary. "Please have Temu Semba come to my office. Send one of the guards."

"I would prefer, Bedu, to speak to Temu privately at my car, which is parked in your visitor's space."

Seduru nodded. Mbaye went back to his car, where Moti was waiting. Mbaye retook the front passenger seat and looked over at his brother. Then he saw Temu, escorted by a soldier, walking toward the car.

Touré got out of the car and when Moti started to do likewise, Touré signaled him to stay put.

"Well, Temu Semba. How are you?" Touré said. "I'm so pleased you are able to speak with me. How is your wife? And how are your children?"

To Temu, the traditional greeting from Touré about his family had become menacing. "They are well, all is well at home. And your family?"

"God continues to smile on us. Temu, I need your ... I need your help."

"Yes?"

"Your cousin David and I have some unfinished business of some urgency, and he has apparently departed before we could complete our arrangement."

Temu stared at Touré and shifted his weight from one leg to the other.

"I simply need to know where he is now. You see, I have some … concerns regarding our agreement and it's very important that I meet with him as soon as possible."

"David didn't share his business with me, Mbaye, and he will likely be back in a week's time or so. I'm sure you will be able to do your *business* when he returns."

"I'm afraid this matter cannot wait. And you must have some notion of his travels and where I can find him."

"No, I cannot help you, Mbaye. He does not confide in me all his comings and goings."

"Oh, but I think he does, Temu. You are his connection here at the mines, and I'm sure he wouldn't conduct his other business without your involvement. Please tell me where I can find him."

"Perhaps you should ask Dugue or Shena, even. They would know better. I cannot help you."

"Let me be very clear with you, Temu. I'm aware that you and David are stealing from the mine. You have been very clever, there is no doubt. You have done well here and you would like that to continue, I'm sure."

Temu started to seethe and then doubt crept in. Could Touré really be aware of their so very careful system? Or was he simply guessing and trying to trick Temu into revealing something from which to hang himself?

He said, "Mbaye, I am offended by what you say. There is no truth to this. Ask anyone here at this place where you seem so well informed and knowledgeable. Ask if Temu has been anything but diligent and loyal to the mine where I have worked these many years. Do not insult me further!" Temu crossed his arms and widened his eyes as he looked directly at Touré.

Touré laughed. "You believe you are so clever," he said. "Perhaps you are, or perhaps you are telling me the truth. But it doesn't matter. You will tell me where I can find David. Yes, you will. For the sake of your future and the future of your family."

"Why would you do such a thing? You simply want to know where David is and if I don't tell you, then what? You will hurt my wife? Spread lies about me to my employers? Who will they believe? You are a big man, Mbaye. But I have done nothing wrong and have been a good worker. You threaten me for information I do not possess, with accusations that are not true. Where is the wisdom here? Where is the payoff for Mbaye, the businessman?" Temu was loyal to his cousin and had learned many things from him.

"Temu, Guinea is growing more lawless by the day. No one can predict from one hour to the next from where prosperity or grief will come. But we can take precautions. We must choose to keep our families whole and safe, yes? But wrong choices would mean devastating outcomes."

Touré made a sweeping motion into the air and said, while pointing, "Do you see those soldiers circling the pits, armed with automatic weapons? Do you think they are well paid? Do you believe they are loyal to the mine owners? To the commandant colonel who cannot guarantee their wages from one month to the next? They are loyal to whoever can pay them, Temu. And I can pay them. It matters little that I prove or not that you are stealing. I know that you are. And if I decide you are no longer worth information to me, then it would not be difficult for you to have an accident leaving work, or for your wife to be beaten and raped as she fetches water. Do not trifle with me, little Semba, for I can break you simply because it is my desire." Touré was not willing to spend more time enticing Temu to divulge David's whereabouts, and he could sense the young father was buckling. He signaled for Moti to come over and assist.

"My little brother, here, enjoys fighting and proving his strength. Moti, would you like to show Temu how strong you are?"

Temu had no illusions. He was no match in a fight with the hulking brother. But Temu did have an advantage over both his adversaries: he was very fast. Instinctively he decided to run. But instead of running away from the mine toward home, where Touré would merely overtake him in his automobile, Temu charged back into the mine compound before Moti could grab him—first slipping though his legs like a child. By the time Moti and the soldier escort turned, Temu was through the security gate with a flash of his ID and moving quickly along the rim of the large pit. The guards regarded him quizzically, not used to seeing anyone running at full tilt in their direction.

Touré, Moti, and the soldier trotted to the security gate where they were allowed in after a flash of their passes. The escort soldier went to report to Mr. Seduru. By that time Temu had made it to the far rim of the open pit, stopping to catch his breath and speak to one of the senior guards.

"That man down there, those two men … they just tried to bribe me to steal for them. They must be stopped."

The guard cast a skeptical gaze on Temu.

"It is true, I tell you. Why else would I be running here, into the mines?"

The guard peered down and across to the entrance of the great pit, where Touré and Moti were being restrained by two guards. Moti gestured wildly up at Temu, who stared defiantly back at his pursuers and then resumed his run back along the muddy rim of the diamond pit, stopping to catch his breath when he reached the administration building.

He charged into the outer office of Mr. Seduru, completely ignoring the secretary's meek protests. She hurried behind Temu with no thought other than to excuse herself to her boss. Oddly, Mr. Seduru was not at his desk. Temu turned to the secretary. His rage and fear swirled like hot air masses building a hurricane over the ocean. He shrieked at the secretary as he rushed around the room trying to find the boss who wasn't there.

"Where is your boss!" Temu shouted. "I need his help now. Don't you know where he is?"

The secretary shook her head and could only stammer. "I-I ... thought. I ... didn't see him leave. He must have gone to fetch a tea or to the WC."

"Incompetent cow," Temu muttered. "Find him!"

The secretary bristled at Temu's words. She was used to it, however. She moved like a sloth to her desk and picked up the phone to call the guardhouse.

Temu looked on, twitching like a mongoose. "This is ridiculous," he said. "Put down the phone. Go and find him!"

"And leave you here alone to sift through his files and God knows what else? I will not, Mr. Semba. You go look for him, and I will try to find him with this!" She shook the telephone handset at him.

"Damn you!" Temu shouted as he bolted through the office doorway and onto the porch overlooking the mine operations. He scanned around for his tormentors and immediately found them, not just past the guards but accompanied by them, moving toward the administration offices with purpose.

Temu had to get away and then find a way to warn David. Thinking quickly now, it dawned on him that he might never be able to return to his work in the mines; whatever he did now, his future and that of his family were lashed to his actions. A remarkable clarity settled on Temu as he ran to the back of the administration building and bounded down the steps to the sorting house. It was time to cut his ties to the mine and move his family. His only doubt was, could he do it fast enough? He slowed down to greet the guards at the sorting house, where Temu was a familiar figure. Managing a demeanor akin to normalcy, he chatted briefly about their families and then moved deliberately to the small office in the back of the chambers, past another guard who saw Temu every day, and into a single-entry room where he kept his written records in stacks upon stacks of dirty, ink-filled notebooks in uneven wooden shelves. Behind the notebook with the spine marked May 1976, he removed a wooden knot from the back of the bookcase with his pocketknife, lifting his left hand as the knot fell to the floor and a cache of eighteen tiny, perfect diamonds fell into his palm.

Temu heard the shuffle of a guard's feet stopping at his open door. Temu opened the notebook to give the semblance of studying the records, the stones mixing with the sweat of his clenched hand. Temu nodded meaningfully and, with a grunt, slammed the book and placed it back into the bookcase with a flourish, letting his other hand fall naturally into his pocket.

"I thought as much!" he exclaimed for the guard's benefit. He rushed past the guard, who adjusted his AK-47 and yelled, "Mr. Semba!"

Temu slowed but did not stop, turning his head over his shoulder to see what the guard wanted.

"Is everything in order?" the guard shouted, holding his AK like a security blanket.

"That is exactly what I intend to find out. Please don't let anyone in here until I return with Mr. Seduru."

He readjusted his gaze forward and resumed his pace. Once outside, Temu sprinted for the far perimeter of the mine, knowing the approximate location of a very small vulnerability in the delineating chain-link, barbed-wire fence. But guards would be patrolling there as well.

Temu was taking Mbaye Touré at his word. He had the wealth and the connections to pay off the guards and others in the mine, but probably didn't have the ability to squirrel out any diamonds himself. Was this why he was so obsessed with catching up with David? Never mind. Escape was the objective now and Temu needed to focus.

Although he might well be able to outrun the guards and escape, and even though he might well dodge the bullets from all the poorly maintained weapons, any ensuing alert would have the mine authorities at his home before he himself could reach it. Therefore he had to escape undetected. And he had to make his move now.

Temu's small size became a distinct advantage. Staying hunched low and moving as fast as he could, he doubled back to the main administration building and moved along the foundation until he came to a small vent window that provided air into a basement storage room. He tried to open it, but it was locked. He kicked out the glass and squeezed through headfirst, cutting his chest on some remaining shards. His adrenaline helped him disregard the pain as he fell onto the concrete floor. He looked around in the darkened room and bumped into crates and a metal shelf as his eyes adjusted. He needed to make his way to the sewage drain in another section of the basement. He tried to open the door to the main section. Locked. But above the door was another vent window, this one open. Temu moved quickly, pushing a crate over to the door and stood on top of it to peer out into the dimly lit hall. There were no sounds of movement, just the coughing whir of a generator in the far end. He lifted himself up and backed through the opening, dropping to the floor in a crouch. Still no sign of anyone. He hastened down the hallway, dodging into the equipment room. The sewer discharge in no way resembled modern industrial plumbing. Four different-sized pipes converged to a large overflow tank which had a discharge pipe to the outside, just large enough for a man to fit. Temu opened the valve cover where the pipe left the building, and hesitated. The stench caught him by surprise. A stream of fetid liquid reflected the dull light enough for Temu to see that there was only a trickle. He summoned his courage and dropped himself in, pulling the valve cover over him.

Temu knew this building. He'd worked here for years. He knew that he had only the length of four cars once outside the building, to where the discharge pipe dumped its waste into an open canal. The canal could take him under the fence and help protect him from the sight of the guards. Unless an alarm was sounded, which Temu reckoned was not something Mr. Seduru would do simply at Touré's request, he had hope of getting out.

Temu crawled like a wounded rat, holding down his own vomit, as his chest and stomach reflexively contracted, the putrid sewer engulfing him. Then a pinhole of light ahead gave him renewed energy. With his chest and elbows raw from crawling over the pitted steel, he emerged out of the sewer pipe and into the canal, coughing and blinded by the sunlight. At first he lay there motionless, face down as the pipe poured a steady stream of waste onto his back.

A guard was walking away from the sewage outlet, patrolling the perimeter fence. He heard a disruptive splash behind him, which made him stop and turn around. He could see nothing out of the ordinary; the sewer simply continued to pour into the small channel. There was no other sound. He chuckled to himself and continued on his patrol.

Like a fish in an oil spill, Temu slid down the canal and passed under the chain-link fence to freedom. All that remained was to make his way through the swamp created by the discharge and the rain, back to his compound. As he forced his way deeper into the swamp, the leeches pressed onto his pant legs and his belly. The smell of blood from his wounded chest attracted the little beasts in droves. He stood up, hidden from view of the compound by the swamp forest, and he lunged through the waist-high water, plucking leeches from his abdomen.

He passed the much larger discharge canal, the tailings from the mine itself, frothing like a seizure as it disgorged its wastewater, stones, and chemicals into the swamp. From this point, Temu knew the distance to the dry forest and moved as swiftly and quietly as he could. From the swamp to the forest; from the forest to the path to the road; from the road to his house, Temu finally arrived at his compound, exhausted and reeking. He pushed through the gate and collapsed to his knees.

Geema was outside preparing sorghum and fish for the evening meal. "My God in heaven, what has happened to you?" Geema shrieked, surprised to see him home at this hour, yes, but far more surprised to see him in such a state.

"Geema, listen to me. We are no longer safe here. You must take the children and go to your family in Semdra. Pack only what you need and go immediately."

"Temu, you are in such a horrible way! Tell me what has happened. Please. Are you hurt? Please, take off those clothes and bathe!"

Temu had been only dimly aware of how wretched he appeared, spent as he was. But the idea of a quick douse and fresh clothes was too much to resist. He stripped as he spoke.

"I will, but you must listen. Mbaye Touré believes we are stealing from the mines and has told this to Mr. Seduru. I will be hunted down and so will Dugue and David. Here is what you must do. Geema, listen to me!"

Geema grasped that her life as she knew it was coming to an end. She howled as loudly as she could, like the bale of a dying animal. "No!" she screamed. "No, Temu, *no*! How can this be! We are doomed if what you say is true."

"Shush, be quiet. For God's sake, do not bring any attention to us." He held his wife by her shoulders and stared into her eyes. But Geema could not be consoled.

"My God, Temu, what will become of us? How will we survive?"

"Geema. Do as I ask, for the love of God. Pack only what you can carry and do it quickly. Bring the children with you and go to your mother's this instant."

He dashed inside his house, stopping only when he reached his daughter's bedroom and removed a brick in the outer wall. Behind the brick was a coffee can full of cash. Temu took out nearly all of its contents, replaced the can, and rushed out to Geema, pressing half of the cash into her hand.

"You must take the children and go. There is no choice, not if you want to live."

Through her sobs and sniffles she nodded and went into the house to start packing. "What will you do, my husband? Will you leave us to fend for ourselves?"

"Goddamn you, woman. I have just put six months of food and shelter into your hands. Please do as I ask. The goons will be here soon!"

Geema called to the children and herded them into their single bedroom to gather a few belongings. A wave of sadness came over Temu. How could his plan with Dugue and David suddenly come to this? And what had he done to his family? My God! What will happen to us? He ran to Geema and, from behind, hugged her with all his might. Tears rolled down his cheeks.

"Oh, my sweet Geema, we still have life to live. You must go to your mother's place, and I will come to you later. I will."

Geema reached back and stroked her husband's face, felt his tears. She turned to him, kissed his face multiple times, then pushed him away. "Go!" she yelled at him. "Go, Temu. Stay safe and come back to us."

She returned to her packing and directing the children, who were confused and feeling the tension of their parents. The smallest one started to cry.

"Hush, little one. We're going to Grammie's. It will be all right. Get your toys, and we'll head there straightaway."

Temu rinsed himself with a bucket of water and quickly dressed in clean slacks and a T-shirt. He packed only a small shoulder satchel that held a bar of soap and a towel. Lastly he retrieved the clutch of stones from the pocket of his soiled trousers. He went back into the room where Geema was shouldering a bag of her own as she strapped a small schoolbag onto her eldest daughter.

"I must go warn David," Temu said gravely. "The rest of our lives depends on this, Geema. Please come away now."

The family pulled the last few items of meaning and survival that they could in the last few seconds—a doll, a framed family picture, and the Bible—then flew out of the compound together. They trotted to the main road. Temu was out in front. Geema held the hands of her two daughters as the son tried to catch up to his father.

At the road, Temu flagged down a bush taxi. There were three other passengers. Temu pulled out enough cash to purchase a ride for his family to go to Conakry, but they wouldn't need to travel that far. He negotiated with the driver, securing his word not to pick up any more passengers and deliver his family to Geema's mother's village some thirty minutes' ride away. He beckoned for his family to come quickly and they trundled into the Peugeot station wagon. Through the open window, Geema extended an arm to Temu, who kissed it hard as he closed his eyes. Then he let go, and turned away from the direction the taxi took.

He jogged, pacing himself, down the dirt road to the intersection of the tar road, where he flagged a ride from the first transport that stopped—a small flatbed truck carrying charcoal and workers north to Tougue.

* * *

Meanwhile, the car carrying Mbaye and Moti Touré had rounded a bend and stopped at the Semba compound. The brothers disembarked and entered the compound. There was a cook fire smoldering and doors left ajar, but all was silent.

"Back in the car," Mbaye ordered. He reasoned that without a car of his own, Temu would have to find other transport, probably at the main north-south junction.

They sped away and came to the tar road in time to see Temu climb onto a truck heading north.

"He's going to warn his cousin," Mbaye said. "Moti, I want you to follow him until he stops. Do not let him see you. He must lead you do David." He opened the door to disembark. "When you know where he is going, and only when you are sure, I want you to call my office from a police station or anywhere you can find a phone. I'm going to prepare to travel north as soon as you send word. I'll bring some assistance. Go now and do not lose him."

Moti sped off without a word. Mbaye smirked to himself. This might work out even better, so long as Moti kept to the instructions. Mbaye would bring a few of his workers to assist in his confrontation with David. If I were David Semba, he thought, and I had a cache of stolen diamonds, I'd be heading to a place where I could smuggle them easily out of the country. Someplace on the border with Mali, perhaps, where there was little fear of customs or border guard interference. He will be in Tougue. That's where I will take him and his mules. Touré flagged down a taxi to return him to his office.

60. Preparations

Temu shook himself like a retriever emerging from a swamp when he descended from the over-packed bush taxi. He had no belongings, only the clean clothes on his body and a residual dirt-sweet smell of excrement to remind him of the urgency of his mission.

But Temu couldn't be sure where to find David. His only thought was to contact his distant cousin Fen. Temu hardly knew Fen, but felt David would at least have contacted the one family member in Tougue they both shared. Without any idea where Fen resided, Temu set off through the dusty taxi park and proceeded to ask the keeper of a local hardware shop if he knew Fen Jubay and where he lived. Temu was rewarded; the merchant gave him directions, telling Temu he had but a few hundred meters to walk. Temu knew that meant at least two kilometers.

Temu had never been to Tougue and was surprised to see it was every bit as bustling as Kindia, where he worked the diamond mines. But nothing so precious as those stones was mined here, he thought. What is the world so interested in that they should spend such time and money in this outpost of Guinea? Temu noticed white men, not just in the Land Rovers and Peugeot pickups that many of them were driving themselves, with Guineans at their sides. These white men, with hair on their faces but not their heads, with arms thick and red resting on the sills of car windows, were not drivers. All the trucks were filled with construction materials: bundles of thin pipes tied together with rags, lashed to the gunnels of rickety white trucks; bags of cement that loaded down the flatbeds like a seated elephant; cables and wires, big tools with gas engines having no use that Temu could fathom. Were it not for the drier climate and lack of palms trees, it could be Kindia. The shops had all their wares outside, so close to the road that whatever was for sale—furniture or shoes, cartons of milk or stacks of tomatoes—was covered in dust carved into strange runes by the wakes of the speeding vehicles. Temu thought he saw words spelled on the surfaces, unrecognized words that signaled caution, strangeness, chaos. As Temu walked farther to the intersection where he had been directed, his sense of urgency rose. He broke into a trot, then a run.

He crossed the road to the blare of horns and ran quickly up a hill and onto a level path that had seen more cattle traffic than automobiles. The house of Fen was undistinguished along the row of cinder-block wall connecting each compound to the next. A wooden gate, crookedly set but firmly closed, displayed the number six. Temu pounded on the gate, stopped, waited. Pounded again. He waited longer and was rewarded with the sound of footfalls. An opening appeared when the individual inside pulled back a small covering and demanded, "Who is there, and what do you want."

"Is this the house of Fen Jubay?" Temu asked in short breaths. "I'm Temu Semba, come to find my cousin David."

"Are you, now?" came the reply.

"If this is not the home of Fen Jubay, please point me there. I must find my cousin."

The window shut with a force that surprised Temu, followed by the sound of chains clanking against wood. The gate opened enough for a man to peer out.

"You're looking for David Semba, you say? Your cousin?"

"That is so. Do you know where he is?"

"And you are who?"

"I am his cousin Temu. I bring news from his family in Kaala."

"Temu Semba. Well, well. We are related, then. I am your cousin by marriage of David's sister." Fen opened the gate wider and extended his hand. "This is unexpected, to be honored by two men of the Semba family in such a short span of time." Fen turned inward to the compound and shouted, "David, do you have a cousin Temu, or should I send this imposter on his way?"

From the main door already open, David stepped into the daylight, squinting and looking with disbelief at Temu.

"Temu, come in quickly. Fen, close the gate," David commanded. He walked over to Temu, unable to conceal his disbelief or his displeasure.

"You should not be here at all. Temu, why have you come? What is wrong? Is your family safe?"

"I don't know, David. I hope they are safe. But there is trouble for you, cousin—for us."

David took Temu by the hand and led him to the concrete veranda shaded by a thatched roof. Fen looked up and down the street for other potential visitors before locking the gate. The three men sat on white plastic chairs in a semicircle. Temu looked with suspicion at

Fen, wanting to be certain he could speak in front of his unknown relative. David nodded, so Temu began.

"Mbaye Touré. He approached me in the mines, claiming to know about something, some scheme or robbery that you were planning. He threatened me and said he had paid off the guards. He wanted to know where to find you. I told him nothing, but he threatened me, he threatened Geema and the family, David. He's a terrible, ruthless man."

"How did you escape?" David calmly asked.

"I outran him and was able to get out through the sewer system. I know those buildings like I know my own compound," Temu added, puffing his chest.

"He did not give up, Temu. You know this. Where are Geema and the children?"

"I sent them to her mother's. It is far enough away, and I don't think Mbaye has any business there."

"Do not underestimate the serpent, cousin." David stared pensively into the compound and then stood up. Fen followed his lead, but Temu rested in the chair.

"Is this man dangerous, David?" Fen asked.

"He is. Mbaye Touré is a very clever, very direct man whose only ambition is to make himself more powerful than the people around him. He and I haven't been enemies so much as occasional antagonists. How Mbaye sniffed out that there was something to my travels other than my own consulting business is a mystery. But if he could do that, he could surely have had Temu followed." David considered this a moment and uttered something he now considered a fact. "He will be here soon. Yes. Mbaye Touré will be in Tougue in less than two days. And with men in his employ, maybe even police or soldiers. We must assume he believes our venture is worth such an investment from his precious purse." David spat on the ground. "He does, curse him to hell!"

David mused: How to prepare for this man and his small army and deep pockets? He could spread enough money in Tougue to get all the information he wanted about David and his meeting with the American. The American. There was a wild card. He and his Senegalese man. They were not due in Tougue for another two days, plenty of time for Mbaye to arrive and stir up trouble. David needed a plan.

Elements of the plan came together quickly in his mind, but he couldn't see the full winning strategy. He had too many variables, too many unknowns making every step-by-step approach highly risky.

"There is but one thing to do," said a resolved David to Temu and Fen. "We must prepare for multiple scenarios. We will need many decoys and some people we can trust. Fen, do you know five men who can defend themselves well and would not ask too many questions?"

"Three perhaps, no more. Most people you can trust only if you know you are the highest bidder."

"That's understandable. We also have to know beforehand who Touré will make contact with here first. The chief of police? The army commandant? A businessman, maybe one related to his family? We must find a way to preempt these contacts—poison his well before he arrives. My brothers, we must move swiftly."

PART 8

Intersection and Collision

61. The Only Way In

Leah Genescieu was in awe. Walking the banks of the Baffing River—two football fields ahead of where the great dam at Manantali was to be constructed—she found remarkable how large and old the trees were and knew they must shelter many, many birds, many species, even. The spiny, squat acacias had all but disappeared when the group of scientists left the savannah just north of Mahina. Here the trees were dense and tall, with broad leafy canopies providing refuge from the heat and other predators. They could have been oak, but more likely were related to mahogany. She would have to ask Orson when they next traveled together. For now, the grey parrots darted about, squawking of warnings or food. With her binoculars, she scanned the roof of the forest, looking for the silhouettes of birds keeping cool in the shade and saving energy until near dusk, when hunting for food would begin anew. With methodical precision she mapped the forest top like a grid, occasionally writing in her notes, trying not to frighten the birds, who frightened nevertheless whenever she moved too quickly. Her efforts were rewarded when she saw a darkened shape directly under the highest set of branches. It was as tall and as wide as a cinder block, with tiny tufts on the side of its head. She could not see its color, beak, or eyes.

It has to be a Great African River Owl, she thought. "So majestic and calm," she whispered to herself. "Utterly amazing. It's a privilege to see you, Great One." As she gazed through the Nikon lens, she saw the bird's head twist around, surveying its surroundings, exercising its ability to view impossible angles from a sitting position that humans could but envy. She watched the great creature for another ten minutes before jotting notes and moving along.

Victor was acting strange, she suddenly recalled. What was it he had said? Something about making sure everyone stayed together for the next few days. Now, why on earth would he insist on that when he knows all the scientists have separate agendas. Why is he trying to keep us wrangled like steers?

He did seem a bit agitated when he connected with the group in Mahina. She, along with geologist Doug Borden, sharing a Rover, had dutifully waited for him there for two additional days, which were not at all wasted. She got to know a local farmer who knew the Malinke names of all the birds and who could imitate most of their calls. Such a person, in her experience, was rare anywhere in the world. People seemed to pay birds little heed—until they raided the crops or were suspected of transmitting a sickness. And while habitat destruction was an enormous problem, she was grateful that people generally left the birds to their own devices—unless, of course, they could be eaten.

The same productivity proved elusive to the two health team members who were anxious to investigate disease vectors directly along the river. Barry Snead, in particular, was impatient. He had arrived only a month prior and exhausted the literature research quickly, politely insisting that he get to the field and verify or debunk what he had read. Dolores Knapp was eager to learn more about insect vectors of the diseases she identified colonizing human fluids, and volunteered to act as his technician, seeing that the rest of the health team was preparing preliminary reports and her lab work was on hold. After the second day in Mahina, the two were bored.

It wasn't until near dusk on the third day that Victor and Mammadu arrived from wherever they had detoured. It did not go down well with Snead, who had met Victor only briefly in the office in Dakar. The two latecomers parked the Rover and unloaded their gear, and then set up a tent next to the other two. Barry and Dolores came over and gave Victor a cordial handshake, voicing their concerns and that they were looking forward to an early start in the morning. Victor was genuinely sympathetic, though less forthcoming on how to make up for it. He excused himself and sought out Leah, who was busy at her camp table, writing out notes as she constantly referenced a field guide.

"Hi, Leah! You seem to be making the most of your workday. I take it you had no problem being in Mahina for two days, right?"

"I was fine, Victor, as was Doug. In truth, with a little imagination, there is a great deal of applicable inquiry that any of us might do. You shouldn't worry about the newcomer. He's just getting used to things."

"You're looking forward to our trip to Manantali tomorrow, then."

"I certainly am. It will be nice to see it a second time, in a different time of year, and venture a bit farther afield."

This made Victor laugh. "You are about the most 'far afield' person I know, Leah. I'm surprised you weren't already camped halfway down the river by yourself."

She looked up at him and asked, "You aren't insinuating, are you, that I'm a maverick or something?"

"Absolutely."

With an exaggerated "Hurumph," she returned to her work.

* * *

The road to Manantali was by now a well-traveled passage extending to the border with Guinea. But "well-traveled" had little to do with maintenance. It was easy to follow but still difficult to traverse. Barry Snead was the only one of the group making the trip for the first time; he seemed to enjoy the controlled adventure of it all. Leah and Dolores both tried to do some reading in the back of their Land Rover, but soon gave up the idea since the trucks lurched and bumped for the better part of the four-hour trek.

Setting up camp was a rote exercise as well, but the memories of the first trip haunted Victor, informing his selection of camp and meal sites. At lunch Victor was fidgety. When Doug Borden asked him why, he explained he was worrying about ants and hippos, baboons and snakes, and just about anything that might impede their work or safety. Leah looked at him quizzically.

In the late afternoon, after Leah returned from her successful birding, the cook was preparing for dinner by butchering a locally purchased goat. Mammadu was resting on a cot pulled outside the tent, in the shade. The medical duo was still out catching flying insects and digging for dirt-residing bugs. Geologist Doug was taking flow measurements in the river. Victor was writing in his journal. Leah went over and sat on the ground, facing him.

"This is a wondrous area," she said. "It's so unspoiled, so remote. It's hard to believe that in a few years, that will all change."

"You think?" Victor said, not looking up.

"Victor, I've read the project documents. They have the money lined up and lots of big companies chomping at the bit to build this dam. All four countries stand to gain from the electricity. The low-flow regulation can make Kayes a port for small cargo ships. It's going to happen, don't *you* think?"

"I suppose."

"My whole reason to be here is to take full advantage of this opportunity. I want to see as many new species as possible because whether it is in three years or ten years, many of them will be gone from this area. And it's unlikely many others will migrate here, save scavenger species. Perhaps if the agriculture benefits from larger irrigated farms, some pest species will emerge. That's one of the potential consequences I will need to predict. But now, there is so much to learn, so much to explore. I feel like a graduate student, excited to be on her first field trip of substance. I'd love to stay here and document the natural histories of as many birds as I can." She fell silent, and Victor continued writing.

"And you, Victor Byrnes, what is it that moves you about this place?"

Victor put down his pen and sighed. "Me? Well, for one thing, I just want to be able to say that when I was in the prime of my life, I was out pushing my envelope, you know? Not sitting around eking out a career in some traffic-snarled city. Nope. I want to be able to look back and say I took some risk with life, to try and live it more fully."

"Weren't you a volunteer of some sort before you took this job? Didn't that mean something to you? Something more than being an adventure tourist?"

Victor sat still. "You know, Leah, I volunteered to get out of a rut. I wanted to do good things, assuming that was possible, assuming my degree in philosophy and my … energy gave me something to offer. I have no idea if I left that village better or worse for having been there. And you know, at the end of the day, what did it really matter? It was only two years and then I left."

"But you might have done something good there and just don't know it."

He looked at Leah, then lowered his head and shook it as he laughed.

"I'm serious!" she pleaded. "I know it's possible to have an indelible effect on someone's life and never know it …." She turned away from him and stopped talking.

"Really? Can you give me an example, 'cause I'm not sure I really get what you're saying."

Leah heaved a grunt, and said, "When my father left my mother, me, and my three brothers, we were a mess—poor, uneducated, angry at the world. My brothers coped in different ways. One became a gangster and one became a girl. No, not literally. But I suppose my father's leaving stripped Rokai of his need to fight who he was. I coped by withdrawing and reading. I escaped into vast worlds and hated to leave them except to go to bed and sometimes to eat. But a neighbor down the street, a young woman who desperately wanted my mother's friendship for reasons I will never truly know, came to help my mother cook and clean and take care of my brothers and me. She was perhaps the kindest woman—kindest person—I had ever met. At least she seemed that way to me. Lord only knows what she was really like. But that young woman, Nadia—she had two little ones of her own, just so you know—that woman Nadia was a godsend. She didn't just help my mom make sure we had food and clean clothes. When my mother couldn't cope and would disappear for two or three days at a time, with the car and a bottle of cherry schnapps, Nadia always came around, every day right around 2:00 p.m. Sometimes she brought her two children, but more often she didn't. She never engaged us much with games or great feats or even good cooking ... but she was steady, secure, you know, Victor? Like a tree in the wind that never breaks, but bends and bends and bends. When Nadia read to me, she would always stop somewhere in the middle and tell a story of her own. And always, those stories were about common women she admired, who had accomplished amazing things, like resuscitating a drought-riven farm to prosperity or taming a wild boar who had been a scourge to the people during harvest time, to eat out of her hands. She told me I could be like them if I wanted. That I could do something important, something big. It was hard to believe Nadia, but she was so sure, so positive, that I came to believe it too. So tell me, Victor. Did you encourage anyone in your village while you were a volunteer? Did some young person look up to you and think, maybe, that they could be like you?"

"Hell, I don't know. Maybe I did. But it's just as possible that maybe I didn't."

"You should choose to believe that you did, not the reverse. Maybe you'll know for certain when you return in fifteen or twenty years."

"Maybe," Victor mumbled.

"Are you going farther south tomorrow?"

Victor's senses prickled to alert. "Why would you ask?" he said.

Leah explained. "I need to investigate the baseline species all the way into the Fouta Djallons. I need you to take me right up to the foothills."

"Sorry, Leah, I can't do that this trip."

"You didn't answer my question. Are you going south tomorrow or aren't you?"

"Well, I was ... thinking about it. ... I didn't have anything definite in mind, but maybe I was going to go."

"Oh, for heaven's sake, please don't act like you have no idea. I know you're going. I heard you and Mammadu discussing it in the Land Rover."

"How ... when was .... Really? You speak French?"

"Of course I speak French. I was educated in Bucharest and Sofia, where French was the language both of science and diplomacy. Now it is my turn to be surprised. You did not know that I speak fluent French and never thought to ask? So uncharacteristic of a man who prides himself of preparation."

"You could have told me," Victor shouted as he sulked.

"Irrelevant. Answer my question, please. Are you planning a trip south tomorrow or, in fact, anytime while we are here? I would like to continue my investigation as far into the mountains as time and resources permit."

"You can't come."

Leah was now convinced that Victor was planning something that he didn't want the rest of the team to know. It had to be dangerous and, possibly, unethical or even illegal. Leah wondered to herself if Victor was even capable of such a thing. Whatever the odds, it was possible Victor might be putting them all in danger. Leah wanted to know more and was aware that as the senior scientist she could probably get Victor to change his plans altogether if she so directed. But did she want to stop him from going into Guinea or did she want to make sure he took her with him?

Leah settled on a course of action. "Not only can I travel with you, Mr. Byrnes, but I can direct you where to go. As it is, I need the observations from Guinea and you will take me there."

Victor was starting to feel helpless and a bit angry all at once. "We can go after I return. I have to pick up something in Tougue," he said with all the conviction the truth would allow him.

Leah pressed. "That's just not sensible. And it's not like I'm asking you to babysit me the whole day. We'll do as we always do. You will drop me off and pick me up at a designated area. I don't see the problem."

"Shit, Leah, you can't come. It-it … Christ, it could be really dangerous, OK? You could get hurt."

"What are you doing, Victor? Are you putting this group at any risk?"

"Not if you stay here and work!"

"And if you and Mammadu don't return, then what?"

"Then you take Dante and go back."

"That is the most stupid, unaware thing I have ever heard you say. Do you think we would not come looking for you? Do you think we would not find ourselves in danger anyway?" Leah threw up her hands. "How can you be so foolish? Oh yes, of course, you're a male in your twenties. How silly of me to even ask."

"Stop it, will you. Look. It's not all that … dangerous. I just wanted to do this without bothering anybody."

"Do what, exactly?"

Victor was exasperated and decided it would be better to let her accompany them into Guinea if she was dropped off before they reached Tougue. "OK, Leah. We'll go together, like you said."

"Fine." Leah punctuated her victory with a quick turn and a stiff walk back to her tent.

* * *

The morning held an unwelcome surprise for Victor. Barry Snead had spoken to Leah and decided it was a splendid idea for him to investigate the river area upstream of the proposed dam as well. When Barry announced his decision around their sunrise breakfast table, Victor nearly choked on his stale baguette and peanut butter and spewed his sip of diluted coffee across the table right at Barry.

"Good God, Byrnes! What's that all about?" Barry demanded.

Victor rose sharply out of his chair and stomped around, muttering to himself out of earshot: "Shit, shit, shit, shit …. Fuck."

"Calm down, Byrnes, for Christ's sake," Leah said. "He has every right to accompany us and it only makes sense. What are you so upset about, anyway?"

Mammadu laughed aloud at his friend's distress, not certain himself what was happening. "Barbu, we can all go together. We will have safety in numbers, yes?"

Although this was said in French, Leah understood it and asked, "Safety? Do we have any reason to think it will be less safe where we are going? What do you mean 'safety in numbers'? *Mammadu, qu'est-ce que vous voulez dire, 'plus de sécurité'?*"

Victor recovered quickly. "He simply means that Guinea is a lot less hospitable to strangers than either Mali or Senegal. The border guards are more likely to shake us down, the people in town are suspicious, and there are marauders who prey on people who can't protect themselves."

Barry puffed his chest. "Come on, Byrnes. You went there yourself, your last trip out here. We all know. You seem to have made it back in one piece. Are you afraid we're going to be too much work for you? Too hard to protect? Well, suck it up, sonny! That's your job, as I understand it. Am I wrong, Leah?"

Leah shrugged at Barry's logic and smirked at Victor. "As I see it, you don't have a choice. There are two scientists here and we both say that we need to get into Guinea. Today. So, please. Let's not waste any more time discussing and let's start preparing." She pushed herself from the table and, walking toward her tent, she came up to a frozen

Victor Byrnes and patted him on the chest. "We're not babes in the jungle, Victor. Let's all handle this together, shall we?" She looked him in the eyes with complete confidence and ignorance.

"Leah, this isn't a good idea. Really."

"I think you're wrong and you should make sure you do everything you possibly can to assure you are wrong."

"Aside from lashing to the two of you to a tree, you mean."

"Aside from that, yes. Come, now. You're the trek leader. Let's not linger anymore."

As she disappeared into her tent, Mammadu came up to Victor, full of reassurance. "Do not fear for them, Barbu. We will all be fine. We will let them wander outside of town and gather them up as we leave."

"Mammadu, my friend, I have a bad feeling about this." He looked at Mammadu and put both hands on his shoulders.

"Trust yourself, Barbu," his friend told Victor.

The four travelers were on their way to Guinea by 9:00 a.m. Doug Borden and Dolores Knapp waved good-bye and happily attended to their own work. Dante was grateful for the time to himself, to check and tune his Land Rover.

62. Revelation Redux

The phone call came in the middle of the day, as Doria Blake and Alain DeLevres were separately engaged in their work. The clang of the old French phone was not a welcomed intrusion, but it rang so infrequently that Doria thought she had no choice but to answer it. It could only be her husband.

"I'm at the hotel in Ziguinchor, Doria. Do you want to come and fetch me, or give me directions?"

"Nigel, yes dear, of course. Well, let me see. I'm concluding a test at this very moment and shan't be much longer. Let me come to you in, say, thirty minutes. Would that be all right, Nigel? Yusef, the bartender there, is very accommodating. I'll be along as soon as I can. Did you drive yourself or were you driven?"

"I couldn't very well have Joseph lying about and paying him while we spend some time together. I must say, I could have used him, navigating around The Gambia, but truth be told, I did just fine on my own."

"Very good then, dear. I'll pop on over to the hotel in half an hour."

"Thanks, love. See you then."

Doria hung up the phone and wondered how she was going to react to Nigel now. She knew she was no longer the compliant wife he had lived with these last six years. Would Nigel see this immediately or would he see her through the gauze of their past, discerning similar shapes and movement, but with no ability to view the details of her emerged self? She worried, too, that she would be too honest with him. At what point would she tell him that she did not love him as she had—that she now was his wife only by a decree carried on a piece of paper, signed many years ago in an overcast island country from which they had both escaped.

* * *

Nigel paced around the hotel bar like a caged fox. He was finishing his second gin and tonic when Doria flowed into the dark-wooded barroom. His smile at seeing her was genuine, warm, and subdued. He held out his hands to her, which she accepted into her own.

"Darling!" he exclaimed. "How utterly grand it is to see you. You look smashing! I was certain I would find you slung over a microscope or something, covered in an old bathrobe for a lab coat, mussed hair, and dark eyes. Yet here you stand, as radiant as ever."

Doria blushed slightly and let go of her husband's hands as he kissed her on the cheek and then on her lips.

"In truth, I *have* been using an old robe as a lab coat, Nigel. It is so dear of you to say those things. I know I look quite the fright. You are looking as full of life as ever, aren't you? All those enterprises that you move around like a chess master ...." She turned her head away. "Let's have a drink here, shall we?"

Nigel paused. "I could do for one more, dear. Is that what you'd like? Don't get out much, eh?" He turned his head toward the bar and bellowed, "Yusef, another round for me and a white wine for the lady." He turned toward Doria. "You are still drinking white wine, I trust?"

Again she blushed slightly. It had been months since she'd had a glass of wine. "I .... That would be lovely."

They stood in the center of the hotel bar, neither moving initially. After a few moments, Nigel led Doria to one of the many empty tables. Yusef came over with Nigel's gin and tonic and said to Doria, "We have no white wine, Madame." No apology, no suggestion for anything else, just a statement of fact.

Nigel looked up as incredulous as if the man had said "We have no air today." He couldn't hold back. "Well, you might have bloody told us before you brought—"

Doria's hand was on his shoulder. "A sparkling water will be fine, Yusef. Thank you."

Yusef bowed and disappeared.

Incensed, Nigel said, "I'm continually amazed at the utter inability of the Senegalese to comprehend even reasonable service. Was it so difficult to inform you immediately, before he brought my drink? Don't they understand that—"

"Hush, Nigel," Doria said. "It doesn't matter. Are you going to change in a single visit what one hundred and fifty years of colonial rule could not?"

Nigel stared at her for a moment and then laughed. "Perhaps you're right, dear. Still, I can't help but wonder if it is hardheadedness or the fact that our two societies—"

"Nigel. It is immaterial."

"But it speaks to me of something that isn't immaterial. Is it inability to learn or rebellion? Is it a complete disconnection of standard values?"

"Living among them, rather than above them, might help answer that question, Nigel, if indeed you really do want to answer it."

Nigel leaned his head forward, frowning. "Doria, I need to know something. Something about you and what you're doing here."

She took a slow, deep breath, which instantly disturbed Nigel.

"What is it you need to know?"

"All of it. Every bit of what drives you to be here in Ziguinchor. Why exactly are you here in this, sweltering, mosquito-infested backwater of a town? And exactly what is Alain DeLevres to you? Honestly, I find him such a fastidious, secretive prig. I can't imagine how the two of you are getting on. And exactly what is he doing here? But more than anything, Doria, I want to know this. Are you coming home soon or are you drawn into some misadventure of your own, something over your head and possibly deadly, like our friend Byrnes?"

Nigel let slip a curled smile, which Doria thought oddly mean. Her stomach jumped at the thought of bringing her relationship with Victor into the conversation. Though her point of no return had been passed weeks ago, Doria had not deeply contemplated the impossibility of going back to the life she had known the past six years. Now, with a clarity illuminated by her husband's presence, she accepted that her future was new and unforeseeable, which gave her the fortitude to speak to Nigel dispassionately, as though she were simply telling him of a luncheon she was preparing.

"The Casamance is the rain forest of Senegal, Nigel. You know that. And close by is Guinea-Bissau and Sierra Leone. Within this region are scads of uncategorized plants with chemical properties and uses about which Western science has very little or no knowledge. I believe, and so does Alain, that from these plants we can harvest new medicines and oh so much more. We can harvest new ways of looking at our world and how it works!"

"Doria, you're talking bloody nonsense. You can't tell me—"

"Listen to me." She looked into Nigel's eyes with a certainty and calm that made him stop in mid-sentence. "What we are discovering and creating here has the potential to change the lives of tens of thousands, maybe millions, of people. Think of the possibilities of eliminating some of the world's worst diseases or treating disorders that now have no known causes or cures. This is what I've wanted to do all my life."

"Really? All your life? And which part of all your life was last year, or the year before, or the year before that?"

She paused and looked down for a second, and in an exhale of relief, she told him, "The part of my life that was on hold."

"I see. Well, frankly, I don't see. We've been having a very good life here together, I thought. We don't want for anything. Not one bloody thing, save maybe more time with your mum, which is, of course, on both sides of the ledger."

Doria was stone-faced at Nigel's attempt to lighten the mood. He moved on.

"I want to support you, dear. Truly I do, but I need something from you. I need you to look me in the eyes and tell me there's a chance, a good chance, we will come through your search for meaning, this new life on which you've embarked, together."

Doria looked Nigel directly in his eyes, but did not answer. She was puzzled and it showed in her expression.

Nigel said, "Did you not think I want to be with you? Have you mistaken my selfish ways, my time at work, my dull conversation as an indication that I didn't want you? That I didn't want to be with you or make love to you?"

"Nigel, it has been recent, truly, but you haven't been attentive to me, to us, unless you were feeling jealous or left out. I am surprised, a bit, that you care as much as you say. You've always been so driven, so focused on your success—your upward mobility and respect from people with … people you admire. Could it be that you see my taking my life more into my own hands as your own failure, rather than my evolution and growth?"

A crater formed in his stomach. He began to sweat. "I don't believe I've ever seen you quite this cold and direct, Doria." He paused. "So let me be equal to the task, love. You've been living a lifestyle that my income alone has provided. You have been the perfect wife, of course. The consummate hostess, the perfect homemaker, keeping our servants in line—you know, those people we pay so that you don't have to lift a bloody finger!"

"But Nigel, I've not been …. I've never been a mother," Doria uttered with a bitterness she could not control. A quirk of biology had removed the possibility for their own natural children, upon which were piled decisions and indecisions that together became the shackle of a shared destiny.

"Yes, of course. How could our childlessness not be somewhere in this equation?" He looked down. Then, as a reflex, he resurrected the rest of the topic as if they had not discussed it a thousand times until it had died of ambivalence and neglect. "Doria, we can still adopt. We haven't had that discussion in such a long time. But it could be the time. It could be the precise time, dear. Very soon, I'll have a completed deal that would make us financially independent. We could even adopt one or two of the—"

"I'm pregnant, Nigel."

He looked up, open mouthed, unable to utter a word. He couldn't grasp all the implications at once. Were they both miraculously cured of their defects? When could this have happened? Then came that ancient, visceral, and debilitating question. It was this last question that sapped his energy. His shoulders slumped. He looked at Doria almost mournfully.

She began to look away, yet found the courage to look at him. Feeling his pain, sympathy welled up in her chest. She began to reach out to him.

"Don't!" he shouted. "This child is not mine, is it?"

She opened her mouth to answer and realized she didn't know for certain. As the realization struck, Doria felt tears gush, unexpected and unwanted, and they streamed down her face. Nigel interpreted this as a confirmation and stood up. Doria put her hands up to her face.

There was a long silence. Doria quickly dried her tears but didn't look up at Nigel as he circled their table, hands on his hips, gazing at the ceiling and letting whispered expletives escape his clenched lips.

Doria eventually looked up at him. "You should sit down," she said gently.

"Really? Is that what you think? I should sit down? Bloody right, I'll sit down. Bloody—oh, Christ ... Doria, Doria. What have you done? Fuck."

"I've changed, Nigel. That's what I've done. Or maybe I've emerged. Does it matter? I'm not the woman who left Dakar three months ago. I've done things, seen things, discovered things—"

"Of course you have. That's exactly what this is about, isn't it?"

"If you could see past your wounded pride, you would see this isn't about another man, it's about me. I'm doing things I've barely imagined, all because I finally decided to make my own way."

"Your own way! My income, my work, my choices have made 'your own way' possible. And this is the way I'm rewarded? I encourage your freedom, your self-exploration, and I get what? I get a sucker punch in the gut, a fist around my heart." Tears were rolling down his face and he nearly collapsed into his chair.

"You're right. I could never have done this without you. But do be honest. This grand bargain we struck was exactly what you wanted, even if it wasn't at all what I wanted."

The silence between them grew.

She spoke next. "I confess I didn't really know what I wanted for the longest time. But now I do. So ..." Doria felt deeply cold, as though the heat of her blood had been drained in an instant. She began to shiver uncontrollably.

It took Nigel a moment before he looked up. His wife had turned paler that he had ever seen her. She had wrapped her arms around her stomach and was shaking, not like she was cold or with fever, but as though she was strapped to a jackhammer, without control. His bewilderment and hurt turned to panic. What in God's name was happening?

63. Setting the Snare

Mbaye Touré trusted his instincts without question. A fleeing Temu Semba confirmed what his instincts had told him: the Sembas had figured out a scheme to steal diamonds from a heavily fortified mine armed with blood-lusting, unforgiving killers. Few dared attempt such an enterprise and fewer, still, succeeded. The Sembas had succeeded. The method of their enterprise was the real treasure. Mbaye did not want to take a single clutch of stones which David must surely be smuggling out of Guinea. He wanted to understand the scheme and take it over. For that, at least one of the Semba family must remain alive. Probably not David.

Having taken the better part of a day to plan and gather his resources, Touré contacted his wife's cousin in Tougue: a large, affable, and venal customs lieutenant who considered the border crossing into Mali his own personal enterprise—when he was sober enough to care about it. Touré's plan was to let this cousin Bouba know he had a personal interest in the comings and goings at the little-used border control area, and that if things worked out favorably for Touré, Bouba would be rewarded. He should look out for and report anything out of the ordinary.

It wasn't uncommon for days to pass without a single vehicle or individual crossing in either direction. The occasional pickup trucks carried produce, rice, charcoal, and other local commodities to villages, and recently a few empty trucks made the trip to Mahina to gather merchandise shipped by train from Dakar. Distinctly uncommon was a Land Rover with three white people coming from the wilderness of southern Mali, into the forests of northern Guinea.

It was a bit of a surprise to Victor and Mammadu to see anyone at the border, given their experience of three months ago. Victor brushed the dust from his satchel holding all his paperwork and casually showed it to the customs official, who studied it with feigned diligence and some officious mumbling.

As he inspected the group's passports, Bouba waved his subordinate agent toward him and gave him instructions to alert

Mbaye Touré that there were Europeans in a Land Rover crossing into Guinea for purposes Bouba did not know.

"Why should we tell Touré?" questioned the disinterested agent.

"Because I tell you to do so! *Now!*" Bouba barked. "He is waiting at the Diallo Guesthouse. Go."

The agent looked at Bouba with narrowed eyes and a snort, then went away.

Mammadu, Victor, Leah, and Barry looked at each other, not comprehending the little scene. Bouba saw this as an opportunity to extract a border crossing fee, which would have the added benefit of giving his subordinate enough time to alert Touré.

"There is a 100 syli charge to enter into Guinea. Each. Plus 150 syli for the vehicle." You can pay that here," Bouba said, pointing to the dilapidated guard shack.

Mammadu and Victor exchanged knowing glances. Victor nodded and took the lead.

"These papers give us the authority to cross into Guinea at any time in order to conduct research for the Manantali dam. We aren't required to pay any border entry fee." He stated this as a fact, not threatening, but clearly understanding his authority. "We've crossed over before and never been charged."

Bouba was a proud man, and not particularly happy to be put in his place by some white visitor who would return to Dakar or wherever, to continue some privileged life. He decided to use Victor's revelation to up the ante. "In that case, you will pay me 200 syli each and 500 for the vehicle. You can't just come and go to and from Guinea as you please."

Victor realized his miscalculation, yet persevered. "But that's exactly what these documents say we can do. We can come and go as we please, in order to conduct our research. Please let us pass." Victor sat back in his seat, and Mammadu continued his unblinking stare forward.

Bouba reassessed. Perhaps if he made it more difficult for them, they would pay him just to end the annoyance.

"You must all descend from the vehicle now. Please get out of the vehicle and come over to the guardhouse."

Incredulous and angered though Victor was, he translated this for his fellow scientists and made a move to open his door. Mammadu reached out and grabbed Victor's thigh. Still looking only straight ahead, he released his grip and wagged a finger below the dashboard, signaling not to leave the Rover. Victor sat back. All four occupants sat stone-like. The only sounds were those of the flies buzzing like a tiny engine in the distance.

Bouba looked back from his saunter to the guard shack, only to see no movement. Letting out a loud wheeze of exasperation, he returned to the Land Rover.

"Did you not hear what I said? You will all come with me and pay the required fee to enter Guinea. Come, now. Come, all of you."

No one moved.

Bouba's level of annoyance rose. He shook his finger at Victor, but it was right in Mammadu's face. Just as he went to yell at Victor, Mammadu spoke.

"Do not insult me and do not insult us, *douanier*. Remove your finger from my face and let us pass, as we are legally allowed." He said this in Bouba's Malinke tongue.

Bouba was startled, and then laughed. "You, Djiolla man, you like these Europeans? You think they should come into our country and not help out the people?"

"They come to help. They come to bring transport ships and electricity."

"That is a small vehicle for such large cargo!" Bouba laughed heartily at his own joke.

"Let us pass. You know you must. Let us pass."

"Let you pass and not have some small something for Bouba? Something for Bouba's small children and hungry wife. Come now, Djiolla man. Surely they can spare something for a hungry Guinea family."

Mammadu smirked. This man was clearly overfed. "You and your family are not hungry," he growled.

"We have not been paid in months. Months, I tell you."

"Let us pass, Monsieur *douanier*."

Finally fed up with this missed opportunity, Bouba turned around and simply waved them on their way. The party of four jointly exhaled and a brightness came into the Land Rover.

* * *

Mammadu parked the Land Rover at the precise spot where he had parked it months earlier—in front of the Restaurante des Voyageurs.

Victor looked at him, somewhat cross. "Are you sure we want to park here, Mammadu?"

Mammadu deadpanned, "I have heard this is the best restaurant in all of Tougue."

Barry, tired and thirsty, opened the back door and jumped out. "A toilet and a beer. That's what I need, for a start. Just a toilet and a beer."

Leah stepped down from the Rover and dusted herself off. "Some pineapple juice and a snack that won't give me the runs. Is that too much to ask, Victor?"

Victor closed his door and looked around nervously, hearing but not responding to Leah's question. Mammadu was already through the door to the restaurant as though he was ready for a fight. Barry followed immediately, clapping and rubbing his hands together. Victor stepped aside to let Leah enter ahead of him.

Before following her in, he looked around trying to assess the environment, searching for a sight or a sound that would give him some indication of what lay ahead on this day. All seemed normal for a sleepy, forgotten mining town in the sweltering heart of West Africa. A car horn blared in the distance. A woman wrapped with indigo cloth, carrying a baby on her back and a large metal bowl on her head, looked directly at Victor but did not stop or change her expression. Pied crows fluttered from one mango tree to the next, noisily looking for a meal, nesting material, or a mate. It was all normal.

Victor stepped into the restaurant and unconsciously put up his collar as though he were protecting himself from a chill.

* * *

The news of Europeans coming across the border didn't immediately interest Mbaye Touré. His vision of David Semba's plan was something more surreptitious, a clandestine meeting with an unobtrusive African who would pass unnoticed through borders. As he contemplated this, Touré thought it might be difficult for David to trust such a courier. He recalled that the recently departed Issa Moleng had worked with David years ago, when David managed projects for some English construction companies. Issa and David were of course working together before Issa's death. In which case, two things were certain: David and his cousins had been smuggling diamonds from Guinea for at least two years and their little enterprise had come into jeopardy with Issa's death. Of course! Touré rubbed his chin and nodded.

"Moti," Mbaye shouted to his brother, "let's pay our respects to the chief of the *gendarmerie*. If there are any strange and suspect activities in town, it might be our duty to inform him."

The home of Touré's wife's cousin provided their meeting place. There were more than a dozen men in the room, sunken-eyed and tapping machetes in boredom. Moti had gathered these relatives and acquaintances—cousins and third cousins whose moral fiber was as dense as a dollar bill. They shared the fantasy that they deserved a better life. Too often, this belief combusted with jealousy and alcohol, plunging families and communities into cycles of violent uncertainty. Most of these men were former soldiers or police who had neither talent for law enforcement nor discipline for the military. Nor had they been paid for their service, however brief and reckless. They were eager to assemble for whatever project Mbaye Touré might pay them.

"What for? What is your plan?"

"I am thinking that our own eyes and ears are as reliable and insightful as those for which we pay. I am also thinking that there is perhaps a chance that the arrival of these Europeans from Mali is not an everyday occurrence and merits our attention until I'm certain it does not." Touré paused, to let Moti absorb Touré's meaning. He continued. "Moti, who, among these men, knows David Semba and can recognize him?"

"Only Charity and Diuba. The rest only know him by name or not at all."

"Know him by name, do they? How curious that he should have any name locally, don't you think?"

"David Semba is no stranger to Tougue, brother. He has contacts and friends here. Whatever you are thinking, also think this: our adversary is cunning, and he is connected."

Touré turned in surprise, looking at his hulking enforcer brother with bemusement. "That is good counsel, Moti. You impress me." He tapped his brother's shoulder on his way to the door. Moti beamed.

Over his shoulder, Touré ordered, "Have Charity and Diuba posted on either side of the main road for the next two hours, until I release them. If these Europeans—or most likely, one among them—is the mule for Mr. Semba, he will try to contact them soon."

Moti dispatched the two mercenaries and had the rest follow him in a deployment along the ridge that paralleled the main road. Marching like a platoon, they carried their machetes on their shoulders.

64. From Wreckage to Havoc

Nigel had been paralyzed for many reasons in the Hotel Du Sud, none of them physical. To understand that his wife of twelve years, childless in all that time, was now pregnant by another man was stupefying, debilitating. Watching his wife convulse in uncontrollable spasms took him so far out of his known world— already shattered—that he could only look upon her as a shepherd might look upon a nuclear reactor losing coolant.

Doria regained control of her body; she wiped the flowing perspiration from her forehead and arms by using every napkin from the tables within reach. She took a series of deep breaths and sat upright as a Victorian servant. She looked at Nigel and saw a stymied, overcome being, more animal than man. She reached out and took his arm in a grasp of viselike strength.

"We must go to Guinea," she pronounced. "Victor is dying."

Nigel repeated the words, "Victor is dying?"

"We have to go, Nigel. It will take us a full day to drive to Tougue. We have to leave now."

Doria and Nigel rose from the table together, and suddenly Nigel whirled as his faculties returned. "*We* do *not* have to go to Guinea!" he shouted.

But his wife was already running out of the hotel restaurant and signaling her driver. Nigel raced to catch up. Just as she reached the door of her white Mercedes, Nigel grabbed her arm.

"You are not going to Guinea. You are going to stay here and explain yourself. You are—"

She pushed him in the chest and pulled away violently. "You have sent a young man to his death and not cared a bloody fig, haven't you? You sent Victor into Guinea and now he is in peril of his life, and you, you bloody fool, haven't the slightest idea. You disgust me!" She pushed him once more and nearly dove into the car, giving Iba instructions for home.

Nigel stood there in the dust, furious and confused. How could she possibly know the arrangement between him and Victor? Surely, she would have said something before this if she had known. And how dare she yell and insult him when it was she who strayed, she who betrayed, she who had become a strange and defiant beast! Nigel ran to his car, turned the key until the engine ignited in a grinding start, and sped off in pursuit.

By the time he reached Doria's house and got through the gate, climbed out of the car, and stormed in to confront his wife, Nigel had regained self-control but was still reeling, unable to make sense of his situation. When he entered the kitchen, Doria was packing jars and other containers into a large cloth bag. He thought she was packing food for her trip to Guinea. It was something else.

"Doria, this is ridiculous. You can't seriously go off traipsing to Tougue on a whim. This isn't—"

"It isn't a whim, Nigel. Look at me now and tell me that Victor Byrnes isn't in mortal danger."

She studied her estranged husband as he struggled to answer. Nigel resigned himself to the fact that Doria knew. Maybe Victor had told her.

"I don't know what that damned fool American told you. And I have no idea what danger he could be in!"

"Don't you? Really, you are such an ass. And he told me nothing. He wouldn't betray you. He's better than the lot of us for that."

"I never intended for him to be in danger, Doria. Certainly, no more than he was already in taking those scientists into the bush. And he's no child! He knew precisely what he was doing. It was a simple working operation with our man David in Guinea." Nigel had second thoughts as he said this.

Doria glanced at Nigel as she packed and saw the uncertainty on his brow. She sniffed at him as she threw a pair of shorts and clean underwear into her cloth bag. She completed her packing, hoisting the bag onto her shoulder, and strode with purpose through the bedroom door and toward her lab. Nigel ran after her and grabbed her arm. She pulled away with a renewed strength.

"You are *not* the man I married! You have become some self-centered adolescent on some quest I cannot understand." She continued to the lab.

Nigel hurried after her, saying, "Nor are you the woman I married, you know. This life of international travel, tropical living, smart and important people around you, no material worries, suddenly no longer interests you? I did everything a man could to care for you and keep you safe. Doria, I love you! I have always loved you."

Her voice was serious and conciliatory. "In your way, you did. And I loved you in the way that I could, I suppose. But we are not enough alike. You could not fathom that I was something different from your image of me. And I could not understand how a man who had everything he could want, could want more."

"You are bound to go to Tougue even though you don't know what awaits you or even if there is any real danger?"

"There is real danger. And yes, I'm going. Now."

In the lab she began searching for something she had been working on that, if she could take or get Victor to take it, would protect them. She found two small jam jars filled with a liquid that looked like drainage water. Scooping them into her bag, she turned and faced Nigel, who stood between her and the door.

"I'm going now," she declared, expecting him to move.

He didn't. He was looking forlorn but angry, unable to grasp his own culpability for the turmoil they now inhabited. He grabbed Doria by her shoulders and pulled her to him.

"I-I can't let you go."

"Yes you can. And you must."

He tightened his grip. "Doria, stay with me. I'll make you happy, I swear. Are you going to have this baby? I will be the father."

Her voice softened, knowing that Nigel was in great pain. "It's too late, Nigel. Our time is past. Please don't make this more difficult." She lowered her head to look at Nigel's hand on her arm.

He started to let go. As she moved, his grip tightened again quickly with greater force than he expected. "Doria, you are not leaving!"

She looked at him in horror and anger. Nigel had never lost control.

He pushed her backward. "You are my wife, mine. I love you and I can't have you leaving. Not to chase after some young cock whom you don't know and can't love! *No!*" He shoved Doria with his full strength, and she tumbled to the floor, landing on her bottom, her bag crashing down on her belly.

Nigel dropped to his knees and crawled to her. "Oh my darling, I'm so sorry. I was so .... Please forgive me. Please, Doria!"

He got to a crouch and held out his hands to help Doria to her feet. She recoiled like a cornered cat, staring at him with fear and rage.

Without a word she shook her head, parrying his supposedly helpful arms, and rose to her feet. As she did, she traced a semicircle around him, slowly making her way to the lab's exit. At the threshold she turned and moved swiftly through the house.

Standing at the opened front door, she shouted, "Iba! Iba, I need you. We have to travel right away!" She looked over her shoulder quickly and saw Nigel approaching her cautiously. Turning back to the outside, she emphasized her command. "We must go *now*, Iba. Please hurry."

Iba emerged from his apartment, pulling a short-sleeved khaki jacket over his T-shirt. "*Toute de suite*, Madame Blake."

Before she could turn to go inside, she saw the headlights of a car swing toward her gate, stop, and honk to request entrance. It took her eyes a few seconds to adjust before she recognized the silhouette of Alain DeLevres' ancient Citroën. A sigh of exasperation escaped from her and she shook her head. "Not now," she muttered. "Please, not now."

Iba left his preparation of the Mercedes to open the gate for the professor, who bounded out of the car, full of excitement.

"Madame Blake, *j'ai eu une révélation*. I believe I know how to form a stable combination of the *d. stromonia* and *t. phosfeseum*, using the fire flower extract."

Doria understood that he had solved a problem they had both been working on to temper the psychosomatic effects of the *deturos* with the tranquilizing effects of the *telleos* in dosages that allowed them to be complementary rather than self-annihilating. The right combinations were always unstable, and the solution continued to elude them. It was therefore not the news, but the horribly unfortunate timing that accounted for Doria's sullen and perfunctory welcome. So smitten was DeLevres with his own thoughts and cleverness, he barely noticed.

"Please, may I come in. I want to go directly to the lab—with your permission, of course. I just don't want this idea to fade in a tropical night slumber. I promise to be quiet and gone before midnight."

"Of course," Doria said, long ago accustomed to her colleague's strange habits and odd hours.

As DeLevres entered he encountered Nigel, who appeared worn and uncomfortable. DeLevres turned to Doria. She returned his look with uncertainty and annoyance.

He was undeterred from his purpose. "I'll show myself to the lab, then." Shuffling quickly into the back of the house, he disappeared into the lab and shut the door behind him.

Doria and Nigel looked at each other and shrugged simultaneously. Dropping her bag by the door, Doria went into the pantry and took several bottles of water for the journey. Nigel came up to her side.

She turned to him with a bottle of water in her hand, brandishing it in warning. "Don't you dare touch me. Leave me alone. Go back to Dakar."

"I can't leave you alone, Doria. I won't. You could be hurt on this journey. I can't let you go."

"Haven't you learned anything? You cannot just order me to stop now. This is not your decision. Do whatever you want for yourself, but this is something I must do and I will do." She rushed past him, with the last of the water now staged at the front door for Iba to put into the Mercedes.

"Doria, it's already dark. How far will you go? Where can you go?"

She ignored him, saying, "Iba, can we get safely to Kedougou tonight?"

"Tonight, Madame?"

"Yes, tonight."

"We would have to drive all night. We would ...."

Iba lost Doria with his explanation of the route, but she understood. It was worrying. When Victor had described the journeys, they were so much shorter. "Then we need to move quickly. Iba, we will probably be away for four or five days. Can we bring extra petrol?"

"Yes, of course, Madame. I'll bring two jerricans. Is Kedougou our destination?"

"No, it's Tougue, in Guinea."

Iba looked surprised, then puzzled, and suddenly flushed with an idea. "We should travel south through Guinea-Bissau and across. There are truck routes that travel across and it is much more direct. Let me show you on the map."

Iba retrieved a map from the Mercedes. As she and Iba pored over it under the interior light of the car, Nigel looked on, lost as an orphan. Watching Doria and Iba connect with each other, it seemed to Nigel they were conspiring, united for some purpose in which he could never participate. Or could he?

"The roads through Guinea-Bissau are dreadful," he nearly screamed as he rushed to the Mercedes. "Bloody awful, they are. Look, if you can't be talked out of going, at least consult with someone who knows about them." He pulled the door of the Mercedes fully open and put his head and shoulders through, grabbing the map from the laps of the surprised occupants and leaning it on the car to trace a route.

"Our trucks, or more accurately, our contractors' trucks, use these routes. There are lots of papaya and mango growers just over here." Nigel pointed to an area in Guinea across the Bissau border. We should really spend the night here. It will probably take us six hours, maybe a little longer."

Doria bolted out of the car and faced Nigel. "We? There is no 'we,' Nigel. You are not coming on this journey. I'm not having it."

"Is that so? Perhaps you should reconsider. Those aren't paved roads you'll be traveling over. They are probably not even graded. Just dirt and rock paths rutted by regular truck use. How long do you think your ladyship's white chariot here, will last?"

Even without the imploring look from Doria, Iba spoke up. "These are difficult roads, Madame. The Mercedes might have problems."

"Fine, then," Doria declared. "Loan us your Range Rover and take the Mercedes back to Dakar."

"No. That's not the right thing here. Surely you can see that. For one thing, Iba and I can share the driving chores, and for another, if you get stuck, the grates I carry take at least two men to maneuver. And think! If you are really going into trouble, Doria, you might just need me."

Doria supplied another reason for Nigel to accompany her. "And you do have an interest in whatever Victor is transporting, don't you? … Don't you?"

Nigel shook his head. "I truly care that you've lost your trust in me. But lost or not, you know that you need me with you. I can help you get there, help you survive. Help do whatever you think you're going to do."

"You don't believe he really is in danger, do you?"

"I don't know. It's absolutely possible. What I do know is that you believe this vision of yours. Maybe it's a psychotic episode or a spiritual connection to your lover." Nigel's own words rose unexpectedly in his throat and he throttled his anger. "Whatever the fuck it is, tea leaves or trance, I don't give a bloody fuck. It's completely unimportant what I believe. But you, Doria. You believe. You are so certain you're right. And once you are right, you won't be stopped. I don't believe anything unless I know it. I'm a sceptic and a pragmatist."

"A pragmatist wouldn't volunteer to go with me on this trip."

"As you said, I'm joining this trip to protect my interests, Doria."

She shook her head. "You're too late," was all she muttered. "I need to check on Alain and then we leave."

* * *

In the lab, Alain DeLevres was indulging his appetite for mixing mind-bending plant extracts, muttering to himself, "Mice were able to disperse mind-altering chemicals to protect themselves. Two have shown remarkable intelligence that could only be attributed to an unforeseen consequence of the drugs we developed. Too much serendipity, though. I have to contain and control these reactions!"

He found it curious and obstinately frustrating that so many of the compounds could not remain stable longer than a few days. At least not the ones with the most astounding effects. The simple headache remedies and lesion closers could stay on the shelf for years. But a compound that allowed a tiny rodent to become invisible to potential predators lasted about three hours before it broke apart. DeLevres had been experimenting with the fire flower and now was certain that a particular amount unique to each compound would be used to extend its longevity. Time was of the essence.

When Doria went in, she was clearly flustered but in control. DeLevres tried to engage her in his work, but she had more important issues on her mind.

"Never mind that now, Alain. When I return, we can spend all the time we need to perfect the binding agents, but for now,—"

"Return? You're going out of town soon?"

"Tonight, in fact. To Guinea. Alain, this place is yours for the next few days. Feel free to come and go as you desire, but please, please, look in on it regularly. Will you do that for me?"

"But of course, *chère* Doria. As if this were my own. I swear."

"Thank you, Alain, this is very important."

"Are you in trouble?" DeLevres asked.

"Not that I know for certain, but I could be."

"Hmm. Tell me, have you taken the latest batch of C26? I cannot find it and I want to experiment with keeping it fresh longer."

"I have taken it. I may need to conduct our first human trials."

Wide-eyed, DeLevres looked at Doria. "That's not … that's …. No, Doria, you should not try this on yourself."

"Alain, I can't explain how I know, but I know I'm going into violence. Victor is in severe trouble and only I can help him. I need everything I can bring for my advantage."

"You would administer C26 to yourself in an uncontrolled environment? Even you cannot believe this is a good idea."

"It isn't, but it might be the best idea. I don't know. These dreams are so vivid, so real. They leave me feeling certain, like a believer. I have to do this."

He scowled at Doria. He reached for a small tube of red powder that he'd been working on. "Take this with you and add a small pinch to the C26 within the next five hours. It will help to keep it potent, I think. Try it." He pressed the vial into her hands.

She nodded. "I will, Alain. Thank you. I have to go now." She kissed him once on each cheek and passed through the door, out of the lab like a swan.

By the time Doria gathered her clothes and medicines, Iba and Nigel were already in the Range Rover, with Iba at the wheel.

"We loaded all the water and two extra jerricans of petrol," Nigel said. "It's going to be a long ride, Doria. I hope you're right about this."

"I hope I'm wrong about this. But I'm not. Damn it, I'm not."

Iba pulled the Range Rover into the road and stopped to close the iron gates. As he descended from the driver's seat to the ground, Doria gazed out of the window to see two familiar people in the dark of the forest edge, on the far side of the road. Sisay and Mady Toula were standing like totems, barely visible. Confused, Doria watched them and rolled down her window, waving and calling to them. Though their expressions didn't change, they started walking along the side of the road, away from the Range Rover, and toward town.

It was odd, Doria thought, but no more odd than other dealings she'd had with them. She shook her head. Nigel looked back over his shoulder at the two locals disappearing into the night. He could make sense of nothing, it seemed.

Iba returned to the car and they sped off.

65. Detention

Into his third beer, Barry Snead was not the slightest bit buzzed. Leaning on one elbow, he was trying to catch flies as they lifted off the plastic tablecloth as fast as they landed. All the little disease carriers escaped unmolested save one. Barry perked with surprise at catching the nimble beast and inadvertently squeezed its pus-like insides into the palm of his hand.

"Shit," he whispered, wiping his hand on his khaki shorts.

"Agreed." Victor nodded, watching Barry.

The minutes had toppled into hours with no sign of David. A few patrons had come in, eaten, and left. Two older working types lingered longer than the others at a table in the far rear corner, keeping to themselves. Mammadu was sound asleep in his chair, snoring softly, hands folded in his lap. Leah was sitting at the bar, nursing a can of pineapple juice.

Something isn't right, Victor said to himself. We should go.

As though waiting for this moment, a slender African man walked through the doorway, flanked by two others just behind. These companions looked more like bodyguards than friends. They weren't a whole lot larger than the first man, but they were not dressed nearly as well and both carried two machetes, one slung through their loose-fitting belts and one in their hands. The leader did not move to sit or talk to the barman. He looked directly at Victor.

Victor kicked Mammadu under the table and grabbed his leg. Mammadu awoke with a start and stared at Victor. Victor nodded toward the tall stranger and tightened his grip on Mammadu's leg to assure he remained in place. It didn't work. Mammadu stood up quickly, at the ready.

Victor whispered, "It's OK, Mammadu, no problem."

Mbaye Touré took steady steps toward them. "Yes indeed, *toubob*. There is no problem at all. We are all waiting for David Semba, are we not?" He pulled a chair from the table where Victor and Mammadu were seated, sat quickly, and crossed his legs and arms.

Barry looked up from his boredom and wondered what the heck was going on. At the bar, Leah sat still, her eyes widening.

Mbaye Touré looked around the room slowly. The mention of David Semba's name alerted Victor.

"David who?" Victor asked.

"David who?" Touré shot back. "Do not take me for a child, Monsieur whoever you are—a child yourself, it seems. Look at me here, in my face,"—Touré leaned forward—"and tell me you are not here to meet David Semba."

Victor saw certainty and determination. Victor's Adam's apple rose in his throat. He tried to swallow but couldn't. Mammadu looked as his friend with a fierce readiness. Suddenly he leapt to his feet, fists clenched. The two men with machetes ran up to their boss, ready for a fight.

Mbaye Touré smiled. "There is no need for any violence, big man," he said. "Nothing good can come of it, I'm sure you can see that. We should all wait here patiently together for a while, and greet Mr. Semba. Then I'm sure we can all part ways peacefully."

"Barbu," Mammadu said to Victor while keeping his eyes on Touré, "who is this featherweight with his two monkeys?" Mammadu spat on the floor and glared at the bodyguards, one of whom had moved back to block the door.

"Featherweight? Most unkind, big man. And not all that accurate," Touré said, standing up while holding Mammadu's glare with his own. He shouted an order to the other of his men, who instantly made an about-face out the door and shouted something else.

In a matter of seconds three additional machete-bearing men trotted into the restaurant, halting just inside the threshold.

Touré moved closer to Mammadu. "Do not take me for another of your simple overmuscled opponents, big man. Your friends will be of no use to you in this fight. My men will slit the throats of your little party and wash their faces with their blood while you watch." Touré spat onto the floor and stared back.

Mammadu seethed to the point of shaking. It was enough to disengage Victor from his own fear. He stood up and put a hand on his friend's shoulder. The touch sent a shudder through Mammadu, who relaxed.

"We aren't here for any battle, for God's sake. Look at us," Victor pleaded. "We're just a group of researchers. How about you let us return to our truck and we leave, heh, Monsieur …?"

"Touré. Monsieur Mbaye Touré. And I'm afraid I cannot let you leave yet, Monsieur …?

"Byrnes."

"Monsieur Byrnes. I will be glad to let your party be on your way as soon as we have our meeting with David Semba."

Barry Snead didn't speak great French, yet he had no trouble understanding that this was a very threatening situation. Horrified and confused, he took a few steps forward. "Mr. Touré," he said in halting French, but changed to English, "we are as Mr. Byrnes here has told you. We are doing primary research for a very large project that could benefit this entire region. We need to get on with our work. You must let us return. Please."

"Your work has you waiting in a restaurant in Tougue for three hours, does it?" Touré said in very good, if heavily accented, English. "I don't see that research as very useful for a project like you mention. Don't you think, Monsieur, that perhaps you are here for some reason other than science?"

Barry looked at Victor, visibly confused and shaken. "Byrnes, this side trip was your idea. What the hell is going on?"

Victor knew he was over his head. He looked at Barry helplessly. "I tried to get you to stay in Manantali, for Christ's sake. Fuck. I don't know what's going on. But try to stay calm, OK?"

"Stay calm? You bring us into Guinea to be shanghaied by a bunch of thugs and your advice is to stay calm!" He he grabbed his hair and began to pace.

Leah Genescieu had been unobtrusive in the back of the restaurant, but her fidgeting made Victor look over his shoulder at her. She glanced around for a way out the back of the restaurant, as though looking to run. Eventually she put her hands on top of the table and closed her eyes. She remained motionless.

Barry puffed up his chest, but otherwise didn't move. He said, "We are United States citizens traveling under the authority of three governments and have diplomatic status—ah, protection. You can't hold us here. We haven't done anything wrong. Now please release us. Now. Right now."

"You will sit and wait with your friends. If you try to escape, my cousins here will be forced to assure you do not have any opportunity to make a second attempt. *Du calme, mon ami.* I have no wish to do anyone any harm. I mean only to get a package that Monsieur Byrnes was going to transport out of the country for my kinsman, David Semba. This package will not leave Guinea. And until I'm in possession of it, you will remain here—or you will lose much more than time."

66. Counterintelligence

With only a day to prepare for Victor's arrival—and a near certain collision with Mbaye Touré—David, Temu, and Fen had managed to secure the services of two former mine workers who knew the city well and had their own contacts for information. They were not very concerned that their duties might include some fighting, though they were very interested in who they were fighting, how many, and for how much money. David said that the only way their work could be successful would be if they kept any violence to a minimum. And as far as payment, they were fighting for 500 French francs each, more money than they could earn in three months.

One of the two proved useful right away; his network brought him information of men from the south buying muscle and information about newcomers to the town. It was as David feared.

He believed there was very little Touré wouldn't do to thwart David and enrich himself. This was puzzling. David did not doubt that Touré harbored a seething jealousy for David's ease in the world, for the people who cared for David without fear or threat. Perhaps Touré believed, without evidence, that David had accumulated sufficient wealth to make himself very powerful. For whatever reasons, Mbaye Touré needed to see himself at the top, better than everyone else, and to bind others to his will. In pursuit of this consuming need, Touré had displayed no restraint. His methods were brutal and cunning. For all his avarice and vanity, Mbaye Touré was also intelligent. His goals were strategic and his plans long-term. That must be it, David thought. Touré was not interested merely in stealing the diamonds destined to leave now. He wanted to humiliate David and his family and take over their careful diamond smuggling operation. How to use this against him, David pondered. How to neutralize the beast for good? Can I get near enough to him to take his life?

Deception and diversion. Outnumbered and outmaneuvered by the authorities and the terrain, David and Temu conceived a plan that should draw Touré out into the open, if not out alone. They would need to find some important supplies quickly and then move at exactly the right moment. To do that successfully they would need eyes on Touré and his gang, and get that information back to them.

I will have to take the night lookout, David figured, negotiating with himself. He would have only as much water, food, and sleep as was absolutely essential to keep clearheaded and energized. His will would have to dominate his biology.

67. Escape Vector

The heat did not subside as the tense day slipped into night. Though the incessant flies had disappeared, different and all-too-familiar pests began their nightly blood theft: mosquitoes. It made little difference now, in the dry season, that their numbers were but a tenth of what they would be in four months' time. It took only a single nearby marauder to destroy sleep, to prick one's skin in the most protected and often sensitive of places, and transmit malaria. Touré and his men didn't interfere with the restaurant operations, so, as the dinner and drinking hours arrived and passed, the proprietor and the bartender completed their normal routines and had closed windows and doors by ten, stilling any air movement which had kept most of the tiny attackers outside.

Nightfall also meant to Victor that David Semba had sensed the trap and decided not to make the rendezvous. Maybe now the local mobster would let them leave.

"Monsieur Touré," Victor said. "Monsieur Touré. Look. Whatever you thought was going to happen, didn't. Can we please go to the hotel, at least, and get some sleep? I'm sure the restaurant owner would appreciate it if we left and let him get on with his business." A silly statement, considering they were closed. But Victor was more than a little nervous.

Mbaye Touré was perched on a barstool, speaking to a large man with a high, sloping forehead and close-set eyes. The large man kept nodding, then would speak to Touré, unlike the other men who mostly stood guard silently and did what they were told. This big man was Touré's enforcer. Touré didn't acknowledge Victor in any way, so the American stood up and walked slowly to the bar.

The big man immediately disengaged from Touré and moved between Victor and his boss. The enforcer puffed himself up with a big breath and stopped short of bumping chests with Victor, an act which undoubtedly would have put Victor on his backside. Sweating but determined, Victor repeated his request.

Although Touré continued to glance straight ahead while cleaning his long fingernails, he answered slowly. "You do not know the mind of this man as I do, American. He knows you are here and he will find a way to reach you. Perhaps even tonight, as you pretend to sleep. He might try to slip in at the earliest hours before dawn and slit our throats. Oh yes, yours too. The man is ruthless and has no morality, no respect for life. I, on the other hand, know this about him and am ready to capture him and protect you. Protect you all."

"Protect us?" Victor cried incredulously. "Protect us? You don't know for sure he's even here. You don't know if he knows you're here. You're keeping us hostage for no reason. David S—whoever you said—isn't coming and you need to let us out of here!" Then, staring at the huge face of the enforcer as it turned from stone to anger, Victor calmed himself. "Please, Monsieur Touré. We've done nothing. We have nothing. All we want to do is leave."

"I'm sure you do, American. Just as I am every bit as sure that Semba will contact you, try to set you free, and usher you on your way to Dakar or Paris or wherever you are headed. Or if not, he will kill you as a nuisance and inconvenience, so he will never have to bother with you again." Touré stopped talking and continued to clean his fingernails.

Victor had seen little of what David Semba was capable. He wouldn't really kill them, would he? He had no reason to. But if Victor, Mammadu, and the others were devalued chips in whatever game he was playing with Nigel, there was no way to know. Enemies on all sides, Victor reasoned.

"We will spend the night here, American. Sleep. My brother Moti and his men will make certain no harm comes to you."

Victor glanced into the eyes of the big man still standing in front of him. "Moti?" he asked.

The big man shook his head.

The energy left Victor in a rush. He turned and walked over to his three companions. Mammadu and Barry were fidgeting in their chairs, semiconscious, kept from dreams by the aches in their bones and the dried sweat that needled their eyelids. There would be little rest tonight.

Leah stood up and walked over to Victor, her anger long dissipated and replaced with a mounting fear. "What in the world is happening, Victor!" she demanded in a loud whisper. "Are we supposed to sleep here on the floor? In this stinking, godforsaken bar? Shouldn't we at least try to escape?"

"Shit, I would love to get us all out of here, Leah. I really would. But you see these guys. There are at least six of them. If we disturb even one of them, we're screwed." He paused and an idea formed.

"I wonder if one of us could slip out first and get to the Land Rover without being noticed. It seems really risky, but maybe there's a way out the back."

She said, "Are they going to keep the lights on all night? That will make it impossible."

Victor heard the anguish in her voice. The lights! Why were the lights still on? Power in Guinea was notoriously unreliable. Even in Conakry, where there were embassies and banks, it was lucky if electricity was available for any random twelve hours of a day. Yet here, in the farthest reaches of an infrastructure-less country, power had been on steadily. How and why was that possible? They heard no generator. It could only be coming from the bauxite mine. That had to be it. So long as they were running operations, the lights would stay on. Did they stop or did they go twenty-four hours a day? Victor looked at his watch: eleven eighteen. Maybe they stopped at midnight. Or, at least stopped sending electricity to the town around then. Why would the mine owners waste such a valuable resource if it wouldn't be used? Not that logic, as Victor understood it, was the key decision-making tool in Guinea. Still, no one is going to throw money away. They have to cut the power soon. "They have to," he hoped out loud.

Leah looked at him quizzically.

"The electricity," he said to her. "It has to come from the mine. And they will cut it soon. They won't waste it powering a town. Then, at least, we'll have some darkness. Let's think about this, Leah."

The two of them plotted. One of them would crawl slowly to the back of the bar and scout the escape route. Victor thought it should be him, but Leah reasoned that she was smaller, lighter, and, if caught, might not be badly beaten. Victor wasn't so sure about that, but it did seem to offer a marginally better chance to succeed. If Leah made it out, she should get to the Land Rover. And then? They argued about what she would do next and what Victor might have to do if Touré or any of his men saw or missed Leah. It was terribly risky. Silly, even, with virtually no chance of success. Yet they couldn't sit like penned animals. They wouldn't.

Sometime before midnight the lights flickered once and died. Touré shouted something in Mandinke and soon a flashlight which he called a "torch" appeared, as did three kerosene lanterns, lit by Moti's men and placed on the bar. Touré grabbed one and held it high, walking over to where the four travelers were trying to sleep. He counted: two in chairs and two in near fetal positions on the floor trying to sleep. Touré snorted.

"Moti, have two of your men take these chairs here and watch our guests as they rest. Take two-hour shifts."

Across the sticky cement floor, Leah and Victor looked at each other in the dim light of the lantern. Leah nodded. She was not retreating from their plan. She was the one who would try to get to the Land Rover, so it was her call. Each second suddenly boomed in his head with his pulse. He visualized Leah's escape ten times each minute, none ending successfully.

* * *

Leah was planning when and how she would make her way slowly across the floor, behind the bar, into the kitchen, and from there through either a door, a window, a vent, a loose sheet of tin siding, anything she could squeeze through, and get to the Land Rover. If she really got that far, there wasn't a plan from that point. Once daylight arrived they would realize she was missing and the search wouldn't take long to find her. Or would it? She was an experienced hiker and trekker, often for hours scouting new birding behaviors. Maybe she could lead the searchers away from the restaurant and give Victor, Mammadu, and Barry a chance to escape. Really? Even if this were feasible, it wasn't likely that Victor and Mammadu would leave her behind. A shiver of despair shook her. Tears formed in her eyes. She pushed both away. Foolhardy or brave, doomed or inspired, she was not turning back.

Barely able to make out the luminescent dials of her watch, Leah reckoned that the second shift of the guards came around 2:40 a.m. The new shift had to shake the departing shift to consciousness, so Leah felt that within the next hour or so the time would be best to make her attempt. In the dark she heard the sounds of fitful sleep— limbs folding and unfolding uncomfortably over the furniture and on the floor. Oddly, in the distance Leah could hear drums beating. Was there a party going on somewhere? she wondered. Maybe I could make my way to wherever the drums were playing and join in, dance with the children, still awake and oblivious that curfews existed anywhere in the world. Eventually, though, Leah drifted off to sleep herself.

She came awake suddenly to the grip of a hand on her calf. Startled, she rolled away, ready to defend herself when she realized it was Victor, his head of curls glinting in the dull light.

"It's me," he whispered as loud as he dared, and gripped her leg even harder.

"I know," she whispered back. "Shhhh. Keep your voice down."

"Those two guards in the chairs keep nodding off. I'll bet if you make it slowly around the bar, you won't be bothered. I think there is at least another forty minutes before the next shift comes on. Are you ready?"

"Of course I am," she said. Yet as the moment arrived, fear rose like hot gas in her throat. Leah swallowed hard.

Victor whispered, "The last shift came on and didn't even check to see if we were all here. They just sat down. This could work!"

"It had better work," Leah said, "or I'm a dead lady."

"No, Leah. They won't kill you. And you can make it. I know you can."

Victor didn't see Leah's sad smile as she turned away from him and started a very slow, silent crawl on her stomach. It was a wonder the guards weren't startled awake by the roar of her pulse.

68. Narrowed Choices

Uncoordinated yet somehow concurrent with Leah and Victor's escape activities, the plans of David Semba were stitching together in the early morning. If David himself was the only "bait" that Touré would take, then David would present himself at dawn in front of the restaurant—but at a distance hopefully safe from the crude men and weapons surrounding the entrance. His cousin Temu would be at his side and both would be armed. Meanwhile, Fen would be at the back entrance of the restaurant. David would pretend to negotiate and then, at an opportune moment signaled by David, he and Temu would run to an old Peugeot station wagon staged behind the buildings opposite the restaurant. Temu would lead any pursuers over to the bauxite mine, whose labyrinth of roads, fences, and machinery even outside the security gate would give Temu the opportunity to evade and escape—they hoped. David planned that he would leave Temu, hide and evade, or, if necessary, incapacitate Touré's foot soldiers while moving closer and closer to Touré himself. David's endgame was to eliminate the threat once and for all. Fen's job was to get to the IMAME party, put the diamonds in their hands, and help them escape as quickly as they could once the diversion began. David thought this through over and over again. While his plan was limited and had too many variables, it was the one way to put events in motion. Victory would be owned by who could best improvise. "That must be us," David averred to his team. "That will be us."

At three minutes past four the first rooster crowed some distance from the house, and David awakened his cousins. Fen was dispatched with a machete and a small sack full of the largest uncut diamonds David's family operation had ever taken, to put into the hands of Victor Byrnes. If we are to end this, David thought, the American must get back to Tony Hume and Nigel Blake. David's own trust in the two Englishmen was an anomaly, he mused. Because he and his family had grown rich beyond the standards of his village, he needed to trust them one last time. But this American in the middle of Mbaye Touré's madness—could he be counted on when the chaos erupted? No. Byrnes would only defend and run for his life.

Fen was shaking. He kept whispering a chant to himself in a futile effort to still his body. David's information said there were two white men held by Touré. Fen must be sure the one with the beard got the bag. He was to guide the Americans and their driver quickly out the back of the restaurant as soon as David and Temu started to run and draw off the bullies. Fen had to steer the captives to their vehicle and fight off anyone who tried to stop them. As soon as the Land Rover was moving, Fen needed to run away as fast as possible.

A cold wind of dread passed among the three cousins. They looked at each other, ready to begin. Fen hugged David, who accepted the embrace with a tenderness that surprised him. Fen's eyes caught David's as they released. A sense of balance and courage returned to Fen instantly.

"Even should I die this day, David, I will succeed. We will succeed."

David nodded. "Our families depend upon us. After today we will all live with dignity and without fear." David swallowed hard. He paused and closed his eyes. His lips moved silently and he stiffened his entire body. When he opened his eyes, David Semba had become iron.

69. Determination and Consequence

"You can't be serious, Doria," Nigel complained with bitterness and incredulity. "It isn't sane to attempt this road in pitch blackness."

They had reached Mahina in under twelve hours, having passed into Guinea-Bissau and back up into southeastern Senegal, crossing the Falémé tributary into Mali. They had at least another five hours to travel south, past the dam site, into Guinea. Nigel knew the town for the exchange between Victor and David, but had no idea where it actually was or how to get there. Though he had shared the driving duties with Iba and had managed some fitful sleep, he wanted to have at least six hours of rest before tackling the next leg. Doria thought otherwise.

"This is not a discussion, Nigel. We mustn't wait any longer to refresh. An hour, no more. Please, please believe me that I know it must be this way. If we arrive by noon tomorrow, it may very well be too late."

"If we arrive at all! Have you any idea how dangerous it is to drive this road at night? We could easily get a flat tire by not seeing an avoidable object in time. We could do ourselves more harm than good." He paused and wiped the sweat from his forehead with a dusty handkerchief.

They were standing outside the Range Rover at the only petrol station in Mahina, which was always open. The proprietor's family lived in the small compound attached to the garage and never turned a customer away at any time, as long as there was petrol or diesel to sell—which was the case about half the time. The fuel pump was operated by hand, so the dearth of electricity made no difference. The petrol station was also a place to buy provisions, although bottled water was not among the available goods. After Iba topped off the truck's tanks, he went inside to supplement their drinking water with cans of warm pineapple juice. Nigel accosted him as he returned to the truck.

"Iba, you can't think it's sensible to attempt this next leg to Guinea tonight, really?"

"It has been traveled well lately, the station manager told me. The Americans have used the road many times now and even local pickups travel into Guinea with goods from the train and make it back in a single day."

"That's all well and good, man, but it doesn't mean that it is smart to travel on it in the dead of night. Am I making sense?"

The two debated the risks of large animals and potential breakdowns. In the end, it didn't matter. Iba worked for Doria and would do as she asked. Nigel thought of using his ownership of the Range Rover as leverage, but that would only offend Doria and make her ever more committed to this lunacy. She did offer that they should try to get some real rest over the next hour, but after that they would be on their way.

Nigel threw up his hands and huffed. "Fine," he said. "I'll just curl up here next to the petrol pump on one of our blankets."

"Nigel, don't be silly. You'll be eaten alive by mosquitoes. Come into the car." She held the door handle for him. He came up close to her, very close, inhaling her scent of sweat and resolve. She was unbelievably intoxicating. Nigel touched her arm on the door and ran his hand up her arm, to her shoulder.

"Please don't," she told him, not pulling away.

Nigel put his other hand gently behind her neck and invited her to move toward him with a slight pull. She shook her head and looked straight at him. Her breath was steady. Nigel dropped his chin and shook his head as well, then got into the car.

Iba drove to the start of the road to Guinea, pulled over and killed the engine, but not the parking lights. He locked all the doors and, like his two English charges, leaned back for a little bit of sleep.

There was a gaunt African man pushing a very large broom over the dirt floor of his family compound, pushing people and animals aside as he swept. He stopped at one spot where the dirt had hardened into a mound. He then concentrated on sweeping the mound harder and harder, until slowly his sweeping revealed a nose, a mouth, and then two closed eyes and a beard. It was a man. He opened his mouth and orange smoke billowed out.

The image startled Doria wide awake and reinforced her conviction that she could not wait to get to Victor's aid. She switched on the Rover's overhead light to read her watch. They had been resting for just over an hour. She roused her companions, who were less eager than she to be on their way.

Iba negotiated the ruts and rocks slowly as adrenaline pumped into his brain, keeping him alert. The Rover's lights illuminated not only the twisting mud road but also hundreds of small creatures crawling, running, or flying across their path. No one spoke in the cab except for the occasional gasp as the Rover hit an unseen ditch or quickly braked.

They were two hours into the journey when they encountered the steep, gravel-strewn path going over the mountain. Iba put the Rover into the lowest gear possible and started up the trail. Even with the tires responding with the powerful torque, stones spit out as the wheels grabbed, then gave up, then regained purchase with the road. In fits and bumps they made their way to the crest of the ridge. When the trail flattened out Iba sped up slightly and then stopped. In the horizon of the headlights the ridge abruptly disappeared into blackness.

"Iba?" Doria asked. "Are we all right?"

"The road has vanished, Madame. We have to find it to continue." Engaging the brake and leaving the motor running, he stepped onto the gravel road. Nigel got out and followed him in the headlights. Doria's anxiety mounted.

Iba and Nigel walked to the edge of the ridge where the road appeared to vanish. The headlights showed that the road continued down the ridge, but at a steeper incline than on their ascent. Iba went back to the Rover and returned to Nigel with a flashlight, peering as far as possible down the continuation of the road. It appeared to extend straight and long, at least 100 meters. Judging what lay beyond exceeded the limits of their light and vision.

"We can make it at least that distance, don't you think, Iba?" Nigel asked.

"It will be difficult and slow. You and Madame should walk behind until we are certain the road is safe." He handed Nigel the flashlight and went back to the Rover. Nigel followed closely.

"Iba," Nigel said, swinging the light to illuminate beyond both their footsteps, "we could wait for daylight. Right here. That would be the prudent course, man. Spend the rest of the night—what thankfully little is left of it—right here."

"If Madame Blake agrees. This is her expedition, I believe."

Nigel looked at Iba as if he had turned into a lizard. "Iba, is it possible you actually condone my wife's madness? Do you believe this vision of hers?"

"I do, Monsieur Blake. Madame has performed miracles. I have seen them myself." He opened the door to the Range Rover and climbed in behind the steering wheel. He leaned back and told Doria, "It is best that you and Monsieur Blake walk down slowly, Madame, and I will get the truck down as best I can."

Doria grabbed her bag, saying, "You are the pilot, sir."

Iba eased the Range Rover forward as the Blakes walked at an identical pace to the left and slightly behind. He stopped at the edge and as carefully as possible put the front wheels over. The grade was so steep that the edge hit the undercarriage of the Rover, high as it was. But it did no damage. Iba continued. In four-wheel-drive low, he proceeded steadily down, the headlights revealing a sharp left turn as part of a switchback. It looked very tight. Nigel and Doria dropped back as Iba picked up speed approaching the turn, and slowed again. Iba expertly steered the Rover around the turn and stopped on the steep straightaway.

He rolled down the window. "This may have been the worst. I think it is safe for you to return to the Rover."

Relieved, the couple picked up their pace. They were no more than five meters from their transport when they heard rocks and boulders rattle and crash against each other ahead of them. In the beam of the flashlight they saw the ground underneath the rear of the Rover disappear. The Rover sank back like a boat slipping under the waves. It jerked sideways to the right and disappeared over the embankment. The noise was now of metal on trees and rocks, and the Rover careened over the steep side of the mountain, coming to rest in a tremendous crash.

"*Iba!*" Doria cried. "*Iba!*"

Nigel went white. "Oh dear God in heaven!"

The two of them rushed to where the road had crumbled. It was all silent now, no motor running, no lights from the Rover. Before she could step to the edge, Nigel held Doria back and he flashed his light down the side of the mountain. The Range Rover had come to rest against a large outcrop of bare rock. It looked surprisingly intact, given the noise of the crash. He looked at Doria with the shared hope that Iba was not seriously injured.

They hurried with caution down the side of the mountain, slipping and falling, banging into shrubs and bruising themselves. When they arrived at the Rover, Iba was lying on his side, unconscious but clearly breathing. The Rover's windscreen was broken, though most of the damage appeared to be to the sides and top of the vehicle. They tried to open the door but couldn't. It seemed too badly damaged. The window was up, and Doria pounded on it in an effort to awaken Iba. He didn't move.

"Hand me the flashlight, Nigel."

He did so quickly. "Is he all right? Is he breathing?"

"I can't tell. I can't tell! He seems to be breathing, but I have no idea how badly he's injured. I see scratches on his face, but no pooling blood."

She pounded on the window with the flashlight in an attempt to break it and again she tried to open the bent door. To no avail. Tired and disbelieving, she backed away from the Rover, and looking at Nigel, she broke down and cried. Her shoulders drooped and then heaved as she was overtaken by a forlorn wail.

She was responsible. She was the one who had insisted. Iba's loyalty and unquestioning duty to her wishes had come to this. How could she have done this to someone for whom she cared so much and who cared so much for her? She cried inconsolably as Nigel tried to put his arms around her. She banged on his chest, needing to strike at something. Then she banged the sides of her own head until the strength in her arms dissipated and she collapsed. Nigel managed to encircle her with his arms.

"My God, Nigel, what have I done? What have I done! I've killed us, that's what, and left Victor to fend for himself. Stupid, vain, stupid woman!"

Nigel released his arms from around her as the reality of their situation began to sink in.

"Doria, we can't stay here. We have to go for help." He walked around the Range Rover, inspecting the damage. The jerricans of fuel had been jettisoned during the roll down the hill. Nigel did not smell gas. Though the danger of an explosion seemed remote, Nigel knew they had to get back to the road and down the mountain. Their only hope was to walk back to Mahina for help.

Nigel walked past his wife on his way back up the slope, not stopping to see if she was following. Her sobs dabbed the air, despair creeping between them. Then Nigel saw something distant and low, down the mountain. He peered into the night, squinting and momentarily unable to connect his mind to his eyes. Yet the hallucination persisted.

"Doria, am I imagining that?" he said, pointing.

It was a light. A light moving and jittering in the faraway night. Was it coming toward them?

Silently he stumbled back to Doria and turned her shoulders so she too could see this light. Numbed and despairing, she didn't recognize it for anything until they both heard it: the low guttural chug of a diesel engine.

* * *

It was boring at the campsite, with nothing to do except check the Land Rover, swim in the river, and cook for himself. Dante Sen was no longer happy having been left behind. The two scientists seemed impossibly strange and they didn't speak French. Dr. Knapp always cooked for herself and seemed eager to disappear for hours and then sit for nearly the same length of time by the river, writing in two notebooks. Doug Borden left the camp early and returned only at dark. The language barrier between them was small, compared to the fortresses of their cultures. The few times they attempted to communicate ended in frustration and renewed isolation. Effectively, he was by himself. And he wasn't very happy to sleep in the middle of the forest and be considered the night watchman and protector, the expectation from both Americans. Early that prior morning after making tea with the water Dante had boiled for his Nescafé, Dr. Knapp brought a machete to him and beckoned him to walk with her along the river's edge. At first he thought she wanted him to chop firewood. But after covering some distance it became apparent that she wanted a bodyguard, someone to protect her from snakes and baboons and whatever other creature managed to spook her. It bored him to near misery.

That evening Dante cooked up a meal of rice and catfish that he had caught on a toss-line baited with peanut butter. He offered some to Dr. Knapp, who declined, preferring her freeze-dried package of beef Bourgogne. Doug Borden was only slightly more adventurous, trying a few bites before returning to his stale sandwich. They both retired to their respective tents with no more interaction.

The sound of a vehicle crash was the last thing any of them expected in the dead of night. Dante was groggy, but there was no mistaking the sound and what it meant. Some fool transporter or smuggler was trying to get to Guinea before daylight. He could easily be hurt or worse, but the rules of the road in the jungle were that you didn't let anyone in danger fend for themselves if you could help it. He dressed quickly and checked on the Americans, who remained sound asleep. He considered waking them but did not. He fired up the diesel Rover, actually glad to have something to do.

The sound of the engine shook Dr. Knapp awake. Thinking it an odd time to do maintenance and not wishing to consider more dire alternatives yet, she remained awake and listened. When it became clear that Dante and the Rover were leaving camp, Dolores Knapp awoke with a start and a tremble. She ran out of her tent in time to see the Rover head north toward Mahina. She had no idea what was happening or when he would be back. She trusted he had left for a good reason, but could not puzzle out what it could be. She wanted to awaken Borden, deciding instead to try and recover her sleep. She lay back down on her cot, head covered, and got comfortable. Sleep did not return.

* * *

Though Dante knew the sound was close, he wasn't sure from which direction it had come. He reasoned correctly that the road to the south, toward Guinea, was flat and relatively obstacle free. The ridge road, with its constant shifting and lack of maintenance, was another matter. From the campsite, he veered the Rover north and headed for the switchback up the ridge.

As he climbed, he stopped to look for any stray lights through the darkness or sounds of people or an engine. Noticing nothing, he continued his climb until in his headlights he saw a white man and a white woman huddled together at the edge of where the road had clearly fallen away. They waved at him frantically. The woman came rushing toward his door, slipping but recovering each time on the loose dirt. It struck him very odd that he recalled her, however vaguely.

Grateful beyond words, the Blakes rushed to Dante's door and began explaining over each other what had happened and what they needed. Dante nodded when he saw the mangled Range Rover leaning against a rock wall when Doria focused the light down the embankment. He got out and, with the Blakes, surveyed the damage and the terrain, assessing what was possible and what was not, especially in the dark. He walked down to the wreck.

"We must get Iba out of the truck immediately," Doria said with authority.

"We don't know that, Doria," Nigel said, his voice shaking. "It could be that he can't be moved."

She moaned and said, "We can't even open the door to learn more."

Dante returned up the embankment.

"I'm Dante Sen, working for IMAME's dam surveillance project. Our camp is only a kilometer farther, once you get to the bottom of this mountain."

"You work for Victor Byrnes!" Doria exclaimed. "Where is he? Can he help us?"

"I do … y-yes, Madame," Dante said. "Monsieur Victor is in Guinea and will return tomorrow, I hope. He was supposed to have returned today."

Doria's face drooped and she looked as though she would cry again. But she didn't.

Dante said, "I might be able to tow the Range Rover out tomorrow if we are able to push it upright."

"We have to do something tonight, man. Our driver is injured and we do not know how badly. We can't open his door. It was damaged." Nigel was moving down the embankment as he raised his voice. "There's no time to delay. We have to get him out now!"

Dante thought about this and flashed the light to the Range Rover. "If my winch cable will reach, I should be able to pull the truck upright from here and perhaps the winch can pull open the door."

"Nigel, we have to try. Please. This may be Iba's only chance."

"Doria, we don't know. Please stay calm and let's think."

She paid Nigel no more attention and directed Dante. "Please, let's try this. Here …" she said, walking where she believed Dante's Land Rover would have the shortest distance to the wreck with the greatest purchase on the deteriorated road.

Wordlessly, Dante got behind the wheel and steered his Land Rover off the road to a small, nearly flat area. Most importantly, it had two large sunken rocks on which Dante nudged the Rover's front bumper.

"Brilliant!" yelled Nigel, who hurried over and up to where Dante's Rover sat, and grabbed the winch cable to bring it to his own battered vehicle. The slight angle concerned him because it would pull Dante's vehicle to the left as it pulled the heavier Range Rover up. Still, it was probably the best they could do. To turn the Range Rover upright, Nigel decided not to attach the winch hook to the door handle but to the roof rack. Dante got out of the car.

"No, no, Monsieur, smash the window with the winch hook, then attach it inside, to the right of the door."

Looking puzzled and unsure, Nigel hesitated. Dante gestured as though he were swinging a bola. Then Nigel understood. He wound up and heaved the heavy winch hook against the driver-side window, smashing a hole in the safety glass. Nigel used the hook to break away the rest of the glass, doing whatever he could not to get it all over the unconscious Iba. He tried to open the door again, but there wasn't the slightest give. So Nigel set the hook over the window ledge and through the lining until it struck the metal inner frame of the door.

"Take up the slack," Nigel yelled.

Dante backed the winch cable taut. Then, gesturing Nigel out of the way, he put the Rover in reverse and eased on the accelerator. The Range Rover shuddered and then jerked upright with surprising speed. The cable went slack for a fraction of a second and pulled taut again in a forceful jerk, and the door of the Range Rover flew open and bent on its hinges just as the truck completed its righting with a thump.

"Oh my God!" Doria screamed, rushing down to the Rover to attend to her injured driver.

She could not tell the extent of Iba's injuries, but he was breathing. There was matted blood covering his head and his right forearm seemed bent in the middle. Struggling, the three of them pulled Iba slowly out of the Range Rover and onto a blanket they used as a litter to transport him to Dante's vehicle.

In another thirty minutes they reached the dam site camp. A nervous and shivering Dr. Knapp, wrapped in a bedsheet, and a pacing Doug Borden, in his jockey shorts, met them as the Rover drew to a halt.

They lay Iba on a cot inside Dante's tent, restrained his arm with a tree branch lashed to the cot frame, and washed his head. His wound was a large gash from which the blood continued to flow. Dolores gathered whatever was in camp to staunch the blood and bandage the wound. Iba's breathing was labored yet constant. Finally, Doria stood up from the cot and thanked the Americans for their help.

She explained to them briefly the journey they were on and the reason for the accident. The Americans looked at each other in disbelief, even though Doria left out most of the motivating events to get her, her husband, and her driver so deep and nearly stranded in the forest. Doria could tell they would be no service to her from this point except to care for Iba. She returned to her plan.

Outside, Dante and Nigel were hunched over a fire, not moving or talking.

Doria walked out of the tent and said in French, "Dante, can you drive us to Tougue? Tonight?"

Nigel was astonished. He didn't turn around. He shook his head and stood up. "Goddammit, Doria! This obsession you cling to has nearly killed our driver and it has stranded us in the middle of the West African jungle. For what? For a foolish boy you aren't even certain is in any danger. Give this up, woman! More havoc is all that will come of this!"

Before Doria could answer, Dante spoke up. "I will go," he said, surprising them both. "I had a sense they may need help when they did not return today. You think they are in trouble, Madame?"

Dolores requested a translation into English, which Doria provided, ending by again addressing Dante. "I'm certain of it, Dante. They could be killed. Please, you must help us."

"Us!" yelled Nigel. "To what 'us' are you referring? You are delusional if you think I'm going with you from here."

"Fine. Then please stay here and tend to Iba. Dante, do you have enough fuel?"

"Fuel is not a problem, Madame. Tougue is not more than two hours, three at the most, from here, and you have already traveled the most difficult stretch of road."

"Monsieur Victor told you he was going to Tougue, yes?" Doria said to complete her confirmation.

"That's where he said they are all going," Dante replied.

Nigel's interest piqued. "They were *all* going?"

"Monsieur Victor, the bird lady, Monsieur Barry, and Mammadu," Dante replied.

"Shit!" Nigel exclaimed under his breath, suddenly concerned that the nature of his enterprise would be disclosed.

"We should leave now, Dante," Doria stated. "They are all in great danger, and we must go to assist them."

"How do you know this, Madame? Did you have a vision?" Dante asked with fascination.

"More a sensation. I sense very clearly that lives may be lost if we are too late to help."

"Then we must go, Madame."

Doria was amazed at the trust and belief of this young man. How easily he understood the urgency.

"Besides," Dante added, "these Americans are boring and treat me like a servant."

"I'm coming as well," Nigel unexpectedly stated.

"What the hell is going on!" shouted Dolores, feeling left out of the French conversation.

"Dante is going to take us to Tougue and help the rest of your party get back here safely," Doria said with a distance that separated the Americans from any counter decision.

"What? No, he's not. No!" Borden shouted. "He is staying right here until the party returns. You have no proof they are in danger. None. Besides, he can't go off and leave Dr. Knapp and me with your injured man. We have work to do. You need to stay here and tend to him until the team gets back to camp."

"Unless we go to help them," Doria said in a calm voice, "no one will be returning to this camp, and you will have to go find them yourself or return to Mahina when your provisions run out. We would have to impose on Dante Sen to take us to Mahina, in any case. Would you feel right, leaving your work and the camp to help us?"

Borden replied, "You can stay here until they return. We have enough provisions for you."

"Consider this, then, Doctor. Let us take your driver on this mission. If I am wrong, all parties will return here tomorrow, safe, and there is no harm. If, however, I am right, there is no other choice but to find them and bring them back to this camp. Otherwise you are alone and what decision would you make in three days when they haven't returned? Letting us travel to Tougue as soon as possible is the most prudent course."

Borden and Knapp agreed that her logic was sound even if her premise was totally flawed.

"We will stay here with your driver, then. You all go off on your godforsaken mission. But Dante,"—Knapp turned to him and wagged a finger in his face—"you return here tomorrow before nightfall, regardless of what this woman tells you. You must promise."

Nigel translated. After a bit more discussion, there was a meeting of the minds.

After they looked in on Iba and provisioned drinking water, Doria gathered her bag to her lap and sat on the front passenger seat. The men took their places around her. The earliest light of the new day was still an hour away as the Rover moved out of the IMAME camp, toward the rendezvous in Tougue.

Dolores Knapp peered through the tent flap to check on Iba and heard his breathing. She looked at Doug Borden, sitting on his cot and shaking his head.

"Have we gone mad?" she asked him.

"Actually, Dolores, I think we've entered into a completely mad world."

70. Time to Move

The sunlight eventually turned the sky above Tougue to gray. It was time for David and his cousins to move. He dispatched Fen to secure the rear of the restaurant. He and Temu walked quickly and carefully as their adrenaline began to stir. They crept past their escape car, a Renault panel truck. Temu patted his pocket holding the keys. Before they came to the crest of the hill overlooking the main street, from his trouser pocket David removed a rope he had fashioned from a ripped sheet. They stopped next to a Peugeot station wagon and unscrewed the gas cap. Assuring by smell that there was sufficient fuel for his fuse and bomb, he stuffed the cord into the tank and waited until the petrol had wicked to the top. He replaced the gas cap without screwing it down. David signaled his readiness to Temu and they moved forward.

At the top of the hill the cousins stopped. The street and shops below were dim in the predawn haze. David surveyed the old buildings, searching for the best perch from which to call out Touré. He signaled with a nod the direction they would go and take up their positions. With the palm of his left hand David wiped the beaded perspiration from his brow.

He and Temu walked down to the street, hunting for signs of the mercenaries. Two were asleep, leaning against a storefront across from the restaurant where Touré held the Americans. David and Temu hurried over to the sleeping men and bludgeoned them before they could wake up. They would sleep much longer now. David signaled Temu to move to the position in front of an alley that led back up the hill they had just come down.

"Now it begins," David said.

Fen made his way, unmolested, to the rear of the restaurant and saw something unexpected: a white woman crouched, carefully making her way around the back of the building. Fen hesitated, then continued on his mission to find Victor Byrnes. Fen cracked open the door he presumed the woman had used to exit. Silence. He slowly made his way inside. There was a kerosene lantern still lit, on the floor.

Fen could make out two men asleep near the lantern, not African. He crept silently closer to them and tried to awaken them.

"Psst … psst … psst." Fen crept closer and repeated.

The fitful sleep on the hard floor accounted for Victor's semiconscious state. It took him a few moments to realize that someone on the floor was trying to get his attention. He looked in the direction Leah had left and saw the silhouette of a man crawling toward him. It didn't make sense. The man inched closer and said something Victor couldn't make out. It was evident at least that this guy wasn't part of Touré's posse, but who the hell was he?

He was motioning for Victor to crawl toward him, calling, "Monsieur Victor? Oui?"

Victor moved cautiously. When he came alongside Fen, the Guinean man leaned in and asked if Victor was physically OK.

Victor gulped. Had Fen seen Leah? What were he, Mammadu, and Barry supposed to do?

Fen reached into his inside jacket pocket and withdrew a sack the size of a large grapefruit. "You take these and leave. You take them now!" Fen said, clearly desperate to hand the sack to Victor.

This package was the reason Victor was here, the reason he had put himself and his friends in jeopardy and for which they might lose their lives. He hesitated, pulled his arm back, and then reached out slowly and took the diamonds from Fen. He tied the end of the sack onto his belt and stuffed it inside his pants. Now he had to alert Mammadu and Barry without disturbing the sleeping sentries or their vigilante boss.

Fen gripped Victor's arm. "David will call Touré to come outside. That is when you escape." He let go of Victor and crawled like a crab back toward the door.

Victor hesitated. There were three others. If they all tried to escape as the light was growing, they would have no chance. Victor crawled back toward Mammadu, and suddenly the kerosene lantern rose off the floor in the hands of Mbaye Touré. The deep scowl on his face was outlined by the flickering yellow flame of the lantern. Malevolence oozed from him like sweat.

"You should not be so far from your comrades, Monsieur Byrnes," Touré said as he kicked the chair where his hired guard was dozing.

Victor used his grogginess to stall. "I … I … was just trying … to get comfortable. My whole body aches."

"That is truly a shame," said Touré. He feigned to return to his chair but turned quickly and kicked Victor in his abdomen with all his force. Again, then again. Victor groaned and doubled over trying to protect himself. The noise woke Mammadu, who got to his knees. Barry sat up and froze. The two guards rose from their chairs, brandishing their machetes.

"You and your accomplice, Semba, are making this worse with every passing moment. Your attempt at escape was pathetic and won't be tolerated!" Touré said, surveying the room. "Where is the woman!" he screamed.

At that instant a yell from outside pierced the morning.

"Mbaye Touré, this is David Semba. Come out and we will bargain!"

Touré turned and walked toward the door. To the guard on his left, he signaled to follow him. To the guard he had awakened, he snarled, "Find the woman now, or you will share her fate." The guard jumped up, looking at Victor, seemingly incapacitated on the floor. He raised his lantern and began searching the floor for Leah.

There were two more guards and Moti guarding the restaurant, wiping sleep from their eyes and peering across the street. When Mbaye Touré stared outside, he started to drool.

David and Temu were standing on the porch of the shop across the street. The unconscious bodies of two of Touré's guards lay in front them, while a third, glistening with either sweat or blood or both, was on his knees as Temu held a machete to his throat.

Mbaye yelled back, "Here is the bargain, Semba. You will turn your contraband and your operation over to me, and I will let your family live." To his brother, Touré said softly, without taking his eyes off David, "Moti, get the other men to surround those goat-turds on their flanks and kill them."

Moti nodded. "What do we do about our man they are holding hostage?"

"Be strong, Moti. Do not hesitate," Touré told him.

Inside the restaurant the lone guard was seething. Despite shoving tables and chairs aside, he had found no trace of the woman. He went to the back door. It was unlocked. He flung it open and looked outside. The woman was gone and could be anywhere. He came back into the restaurant, furious and fearful, striding over to Victor, still on the floor, and kicked him.

"Where is the woman!" he demanded. "Where has she gone! Bring her to me now!" As he kicked Victor again, the American reached out and grabbed his foot. Mammadu, who had been in the ready position for minutes, leapt at the guard and landed his full weight into the small of his target's back. With Mammadu on top of him, the guard's head snapped onto the floor with a loud crack. He was still and limp.

"Holy shit!" Barry cried out. "Holy shit!" He rose and looked at the front door, believing Touré and his other guards would show up at any moment.

Mammadu grabbed the machete on the floor and helped Victor to his feet. In a loud whisper, Mammadu said to Barry, "Help me. We need to move now. Come over here!" To Victor he said, "Barbu, can you walk? Are you badly hurt?"

He replied, "We need to get to the Land Rover. Through the back door. Come on." As Victor stepped forward, he bent over, groaning in pain.

Barry got under Victor's right arm and, with Mammadu, raced for the back door.

71. Breakaway

David knew Touré would eventually come after him personally once the small army had failed to capture him or his cousins. He could see Moti gathering the remaining hired thugs and spreading out in an attempt to surround them.

So David changed the stakes.

"Mbaye Touré, I have another bargain. You will let the American and his people go, you will let my family alone, and I will work for you. If you do not, I will burn your entire enterprise to ashes. Everything you own, everything you think you control, turned to dust. And you will watch all of it crumble." David voice trembled as he spoke, nearly spitting his words.

"Do not insult me, Semba. You and your cousins are losing time."

"Then come collect me yourself, Touré!"

David nodded once, and Temu hit the kneeling guard on the head, using the flat side of the machete like a baseball bat. The man tumbled over, and David and Temu fled in different directions.

Touré screamed, "Moti, they're running. Go. Go now!"

The two flanks of guards took off in a dead run after the cousins. As David disappeared around the corner of the building, he took precious seconds to light the fuse he had planted earlier and then doubled back behind the building.

Touré turned his attention back to his hostages. The image of his paralyzed guard on the floor and the open door in the back infuriated him. He raced to the door and saw the trio, hobbled by Victor's injury, making their way around the building.

Touré raised his machete high and yelled, "Stop or I will kill you all!"

The trio stopped. Mammadu let go his friend's side and turned to face Touré. Beholding the sight of the Senegalese wrestling champion holding his own machete and with a look of pure hate fixed on Touré made the Guinean pause. His backup was gone, and as sharp a fighter as he was, he was not going to take on this man by himself. Touré fled back into the restaurant and at the sight of his fallen guard, kicked him swiftly for his incompetence. Stopping outside the front entrance, he took a moment to think. He had to disable their vehicle. Could he puncture their tires in time? Block it in. Yes. His own Mercedes truck could smash the Land Rover, maybe even push it onto its side. He knew he had time to get into his truck before they rounded the back of the restaurant.

At that moment the Land Rover's engine started. He rushed back to the rear doorway. Squinting for a better focus, Touré could see the driver. It was the woman! "She *did* escape earlier," Touré cursed under his breath. He sprinted over to the Land Rover and yanked on the door.

Leah, having seen the disabled trio coming toward her, had not reckoned on Touré and only at the last moment did she see him leap at the truck. Touré reached in and pulled Leah out hard, snapping her arm back as she tried to hold on to the steering wheel. He jumped into the driver's seat and put the truck in reverse.

Victor and Mammadu couldn't believe their eyes. Their escape thwarted, they turned to run back down the alley. Touré saw the opportunity. He thrust the gearshift into first, popped the clutch, and gunned the engine. The Land Rover almost stalled, then revved furiously as all four tires spun in the dried laterite street and lurched forward. Running for their lives, the three men moved as quickly as they could.

They were nearly at the corner of the building when Mammadu yelled to Barry, "Hold on to Victor, *hold*!"

Mammadu pushed himself into the side of the building and swung with all his might, sweeping Victor and Barry off their feet and around the corner of the building just as the speeding Land Rover shot past. However, the human whip was not fast enough and the front corner of the Rover hit Barry's legs as he went airborne, breaking one shin so badly that it tore through his flesh.

He screamed in pain as he landed. "Oh my God! Oh my God!" he yelled, his face contorted as he grabbed his leg.

Victor yelled, "We have to go back inside, Mammadu!"

The big man nodded. Victor grabbed Barry on one side as Mammadu hoisted him from the other and the two friends dragged the injured scientist as fast as they could back to the door through which they had moments earlier escaped.

Having shot past his targets, Touré couldn't turn around quickly enough. He jammed on the brakes and backed up the Land Rover. He reached the opening in the alley in time to see the three men fall through the back door to the restaurant. Touré sped backward all the way to the main road.

Leah, who had originally started to run after the Land Rover, thought better of it and turned to the main street. She saw perhaps a dozen or more men with machetes and two with rifles running between, in and out of buildings. She needed cover. She went back into the restaurant as her only option. She pulled the door hard behind her and locked the deadbolt. There was a clamor behind her. Her three traveling companions had collapsed onto the restaurant floor. Mammadu and Victor, wincing and clutching his ribcage, stood up and carried Barry toward the front of the restaurant. Leah rushed over. When Victor and Barry were sitting, Mammadu pushed a table under the handle of the front door to slow down those trying to get at them. He did the same for the back door. Leah and Victor moved Barry onto the floor. He was delirious with pain, yelling and crying.

"What the fuck are we going to do!" Leah shouted. "Jesus! Barry! This shit—this is really bad."

Victor said, "We need to stop his bleeding and wrap his leg as tight as possible. It's going to hurt him even more than it does now. Also, Mammadu, grab a bottle of whiskey from the bar so we can have something to disinfect this!" Victor knew he was grasping at the slimmest of hopes. There was no way out of this. Mammadu returned with the bottle as Victor removed his shirt to tie up Barry's leg. That's when they heard a very loud, very close explosion.

The three who could, ran to the front window of the restaurant and a saw a huge plume of black smoke circling behind the building across the street. Men and women were running in different directions and one of the men with a rifle was kneeling and firing toward the explosion. Then they saw something far more menacing. Directly in front of the restaurant, in the middle of the street, sat their Land Rover with Mbaye Touré still at the controls, now with four men behind the vehicle. With the same maneuver as before, he gunned the Land Rover, aimed directly for the restaurant window.

Without thinking, Mammadu pulled Victor and Leah, with all his remaining strength, toward the back of the building just as the Land Rover crashed through the walls with a deafening roar.

72. The Trial

D ante knew they had entered Guinea because they passed the silhouette of an empty border kiosk. Then the path become nearly a road. For an hour, Dante, Nigel, and Doria traveled into Guinea as the night brightened into morning twilight. The sparse tiny homes along the route became larger and clustered. The hand-painted sign, tilted and old, announced their arrival: Tougue. At the same time the three travelers noticed a cloud of smoke behind the buildings, formed from two columns. It was a thick, billowing, unnatural smoke. A smoke of chaos. Dante swallowed hard.

Even Nigel's throat tightened. "What in God's name are we going into! Doria?"

Looking sternly forward, she said, nearly in a whisper, "I don't believe God has visited here recently."

Doria clutched her bag containing the creations of her last year of work. Was this in fact the worst case? Had she been right? And what if she was? Was she truly going to save Victor? How was that even possible? The courage she needed at this point was not to face whatever lay ahead. She knew she could do that. What she needed at this moment was the courage to live in the belief that she was meant to be here, was meant to prevail, and she would do absolutely and exactly what the situation needed. But now, in the prelude to meeting her destiny, doubt surged into her psyche.

As they came closer, they noticed people running away in all directions. Dante slowed slightly, hoping to make some sense of the scene. Doria was the first to notice the end of a Land Rover sticking out of a building, the dust of the collision fresh in the air. She opened the case in her lap and withdrew a jar filled with her latest experimental brew. Holding it ever so briefly in front of her eyes, Doria stripped off the lid quickly and drank the entire contents.

"Are you mad!" Nigel yelled. "Doria, how can you even think this is ...!" He stared out at the smoke and scurrying people in front of them, then at Doria. "Dante, stop this car. Stop it now!"

"No, Dante!" Doria shrieked back at him. "Head straight for that car smashed ... sm ..."—she struggled for breath.

Her stomach was roiling. She coughed and held her abdomen. Her eyesight grew dim and the closest blood vessels, in her arms and face, began to throb, turned dark purple, then bright red. Nigel could see them pulsing through her increasingly translucent skin. He grabbed a canteen on the floor to make her drink some water as Dante propelled them toward the wrecked car and building ahead.

Dante could plainly make out four men, three with machetes, trying to open the door of the Land Rover, which was wedged in the shattered wall of the bar. He stopped their Rover less than twenty feet from the scene, not knowing what else to do. He turned around to ask Doria for instructions and saw a woman in transformation. Nigel was trying to get her to drink, but she held his arm away. Her entire body had turned ashen and her skin turned to leather.

"Doria, please!" Nigel shouted, desperately trying to get his wife to drink some water.

Her expression seemed composed as she pushed Nigel's arm away with more ease than either of them expected. Without looking at either man in her car, she opened her door, got out and stood motionless, taking in the scene in front of her.

A siren sounded in the distance and was coming closer. The police were coming.

Victor must be inside this building, Doria reasoned. She walked calmly to where the crashed Land Rover, cement debris, smoke, and clamoring men were converged. Nigel and Dante both got out of the car and started to run to Doria. As they did, she vanished before their eyes. She was no longer there! Nigel pulled up, completely baffled, turning in two full circles before putting his hands to his head.

"Doria!" he shouted at the top of his lungs.

73. Wrath and Rebirth

The men who were trying to extricate Touré and recapture those inside were startled by this shout and turned to see from where it had come. They saw two men in complete confusion, standing by another Land Rover. Touré's men did not see the woman who walked right past them, paying them no heed, who looked through the gaping hole in the building to see three men and a woman huddled on the floor, all covered with debris.

Doria saw that she could climb over the top of the Land Rover and squeeze through the hole where the building had collapsed onto the roof of the truck. The falling rubble and the noises she made seemed perfectly normal to the men about to resume their work to save Touré. Before they could do so, however, Doria had slipped through the opening, climbed down to the four wounded travelers, and stood before them, facing Victor. She was completely visible to all four, who were in utter shock at her daring and presence.

Victor looked at Doria in disbelief as the other three looked to him and then at each other.

"I-I can't believe what I'm seeing! Doria?" Victor asked.

His friends began to shout and pull him to the rear door.

Between sobs, Leah said, "We have to get out of here now. Please!"

Barry was in too much pain to consider much of anything. Mammadu was confused, but signaled the need to escape out the back.

"Oh, Victor," Doria said, and sprang into an embrace. She kissed him about his face and forehead, touching his ribs gently. She looked into his face and saw profound disbelief and confusion.

"How could you possibly …?" Victor uttered in a near panic.

"Please!" Leah implored. "The back door. We must go!"

Victor regained some self-control and beckoned to Mammadu to hoist Barry up between them. Victor winced from the pain in his ribs, and Barry howled and then set his teeth hard, bracing against the fire raging in his broken leg. The five of them scrambled out the back door of the restaurant again.

Touré could see this plainly and yelled for his men to stop struggling with the door and cut off the escape route of the fleeing foreigners. As they left him, Touré tried again and again to start the Land Rover. When on his fourth attempt he succeeded, he jammed the gear lever into reverse and let go the clutch. As the truck backed away from the destroyed entrance, bricks, mud, and concrete poured into the space, virtually collapsing the front wall of the building. The Rover stalled and Touré cursed. He couldn't restart it. He jumped out to catch up with his men just as a police truck skidded to a halt behind him. Ever proactive, Touré jumped to the side, pointing frantically to the alley into which his men had disappeared. The local captain, in the passenger side, nodded knowingly and motioned with his AK-47 to his driver to block off the alley and arrest the outsiders. Touré ran along the side of the police truck, hoping to regain control. Nor had he forgotten about David Semba.

* * *

The group of desperate travelers believed their only hope was to reach Doria's vehicle. When they saw four men round the alley entrance blocking their way to the road, their bodies halted and sagged, thinking recapture and worse were likely. The four men were immediately backed up by a blue police truck and three policemen with rifles raised. While Victor and his companions froze, the police disembarked and attempted to take over from Touré's mercenaries. They argued for a bit until Touré arrived, breathless and steel-faced. He took the captain by the arm and explained how these foreigners had robbed him, colluding with a Guinean man, David Semba, who his men were tracking down this very moment.

The captain nodded. "They will come to jail now. Then we will look for their accomplice," he added.

Slowly Doria stepped forward. She didn't shout out, she didn't threaten, as far as the armed men could tell at first. Two of Touré's men with machetes stomped forward menacingly, intending to grab and drag her to the police vehicle. But when they were within only a few steps of her, they stopped as if on command and looked ahead, disbelieving. The white woman had disappeared. One of them looked at the other and he saw, not his colleague but the woman standing next to him. He lashed out and grabbed her, hitting her head with the butt of his machete. Taken completely by surprise, his cohort could not fend off the blow, but he managed to strike one of his own, cutting his companion's thigh. Now the two men were fighting fiercely, striking blows at each other with their machetes. The police captain grabbed Touré, who shouted at his men to stop. They didn't. Everyone stood dumbfounded as they witnessed two of Mbaye's men bludgeon each other into bloody mounds. The dust under their bodies coagulated into a dark red mud.

The captain shouted to his men, "Take the foreigners now. If they resist, kill them!"

The three police pointed their weapons and, with the two remaining mercenaries, advanced on the group. Almost immediately they themselves lost sight of Doria and began to look around as if she had moved too quickly and was about to attack them from the side. In fact, Doria had not moved. To her companions she remained visible and calm. But their would-be captors experienced something else.

Two of the police pivoted quickly to their left, spotting the white woman running away. They fired their weapons, spraying bullets on the wall and forcing their captain and Touré to hit the ground.

The captain was apoplectic. Rising from the dirt and spitting sand, he screamed at them, "Baboons! Stop shooting! You nearly killed me!"

But his men weren't listening. They were confused, frightened, and in full fight mode. One of Touré's men saw the white woman appear next to him with a knife in her hand. He quickly thrust his machete into her midsection—only to discover the third policeman standing next to him. Seeing this, the captain lowered his AK-47 and put six bullets into Touré's man for killing one of his. The two police who had fired at the sight of a fleeing Doria turned their attention to each other. Looking into the eyes of the man next to him, both men screamed in terror as they fired their guns, cutting each other nearly in half. A fountain of blood sprayed the captain and Touré. The captain jumped into the driver's seat of his vehicle and roared off in reverse, never changing gear, accelerating in a blind panic back up the street. Touré shrieked and ran across the street, his heart in his mouth and his brain unable to comprehend the hell he had just seen. Upon reaching the closest building, he collapsed on the porch and clung to one of the wooden columns. He heard more gunfire coming from behind this building. The fight continued.

Victor, Mammadu, Leah, and Barry had seen seven men kill each other without the slightest detectable provocation. Through it all, Doria had stood in front of them, bizarrely unafraid, still as a tree. Blood continued to ooze into the sand from the mutilated bodies, coagulating in crimson puddles. In the near full light of a sun sitting on the horizon, the morning had surrendered to an unnatural stillness. The buzz of flies and the hush of distant vehicles allowed for a few seconds of recovery. Then closer, gunfire.

"We have to go. Now!" Victor screamed.

Leah Genescieu was shaking as with a terrible fever. Barry Snead was in too much pain to absorb the reality. Mammadu's eyes remained bulging from his skull.

"Come this way," Doria said as she took Victor's hand and pulled him forward.

The others followed without hesitation. Barry was on the verge of passing out from pain, barely aware that Mammadu and Victor were carrying him forward.

At the intersection of the alley and the road, through the light dust in the air, Nigel appeared, worn and worried. He came directly over to Doria and put his hands on her shoulders. She kept hold of Victor's hand.

"What on earth, Doria! Have you lost your mind!" he yelled at her.

"Let's leave. These people are hurt. We must hurry."

Nigel saw the bodies behind her, torn into unrecognizable meat from a battle too illogical to contemplate. He quickly covered his mouth and looked at Doria in horror. She walked hurriedly past him toward the Land Rover, followed by the four beaten-down travelers.

74. SACRIFICE

Moti found his brother holding tightly to the wooden column supporting the thatched storefront roof. At first Touré did not respond to his brother's continued shouting of his name and shaking of his shoulders. Finally, Touré blinked and looked at his brother with an expression Moti had never seen before. His eyes were wide but distant, his mouth open, and with no sign that he recognized his brother. Touré's world had become alien and incomprehensible.

"We have Semba trapped behind the flour mill," Moti said. "He cannot escape. What shall we do, Mbaye? Shall we move in and kill him and his lizard cousin? Mbaye? Mbaye!"

"Kill him? Kill who? Kill Semba? No, no, no. We want Semba alive, yes, we do. Do not kill him. No!" Touré struggled to his feet.

"Brother, what in Allah's name happened to you?"

"What? Never mind that. Let's attend to Mr. Semba. Yes, that's what we must do!"

"Where is the police chief? I heard his car. Can we get more policemen to help us bring Semba in?"

Touré pointed to the opposite side of the road, to the alley where a pile of bodies could barely be made out. Moti squinted and shook his head.

Continuing to point his extended arm and shaking as he spoke with a barely contained rage, he said, "They killed themselves. They turned on each other and killed themselves. It was the woman, that yellow-haired jinn. Let her go! Let her and her wretched party go. We need Semba alive. He's cornered, you say. Help me, brother!"

Moti saw the look of unreality in his brother's face and knew what he had to do: he, Moti, would have to lead and command. His brother had lost his mind and was incapable.

Moti took his brother by the shoulders and shook him. "Yes, Mbaye, we have Semba trapped. But we cannot let the foreigners escape. They may have the diamonds."

Touré hesitated. Moti was probably right. But did that matter, if the yellow-haired jinn made them kill each other? He barely heard his brother's command to the men who had gathered around the brothers.

"Sila, take two others and go with Mbaye to stop those foreigners. They must not be allowed to leave. They remain here in Tougue, alive or not. Mbaye, take these men and take what we came here for." He signaled, and the men began at a trot toward the direction of the Westerners, distantly moving toward another vehicle. Touré still had not moved. Moti shouted at him to lead the men, to stop the foreigners.

Stiff with shock, Touré slowly grabbed his brother's arm. "We must get Semba. If he is still trapped. Yes. That's what we must do, Moti. Attack Semba."

Moti knew precious time was being lost. "Mbaye, you go after Semba. Dowit will take you up there. I will take Sila and the others to get our stones." He turned toward the men trotting away and joined them before Touré could comprehend what was happening.

"*No!* Moti, *no!* You cannot. *Stop!*"

But Moti did not stop. So Touré ran to stop his brother.

Moti and three men quickly descended upon Nigel, Doria, and the others as they were trying to load themselves into the last working Land Rover. Victor and Mammadu had lifted Barry into the back seat. He was racked with pain and barely conscious. The two friends then piled themselves into the back seat after Leah had opened the rear hatch and settled into a near fetal position next to the spare tire. Dante sat nervously at the wheel as Nigel and Doria raced around the rear to enter the passenger side.

A shot rang out and Nigel let out a desperate scream. He'd been hit in the high back of his left leg and went down hard to the ground. Moti fired a second round into the side of the Range Rover, where it safely lodged in the back door. But his point was clear.

Doria turned back to Nigel, calling his name and kneeling to help him. Moti and his men were upon them, and Doria looked up at Moti with a seething glare. Moti leveled his gun at Dante, who raised his hands. The other men opened both doors on the driver's side and pulled Mammadu and Dante onto the ground.

Moti turned his attention to Victor and shouted, "Hand over the stones now, you motherfucker, or you will die right here!"

Doria screamed, "Leave us alone, you murderous piece of filth! Leave us now!"

Such defiance got Moti's attention. He pulled Victor out of the car and struck him hard on the side of the head. Victor fell to one knee, yet remained conscious. Moti marched to the back of the car, where he found Nigel sitting on the ground and supported by Doria.

"Give us the diamonds now," Moti demanded, "or none of you leave alive. Now, I said!" and he drew aim on Doria.

"I have the diamonds," Victor said, coughing. "Take them and leave us alone."

Moti looked over as Victor took a pouch from his vest and threw it on the ground. Moti took two fast leaps and picked up the stones as quickly as he could. He shook the pouch to hear the rattle of the rough diamonds. He threw back his head and laughed. Then, as quickly, his face collapsed into a frown.

"Kill them," he calmly commanded his men.

One drew up on Mammadu and swung his machete hard on the back of his shoulders. Mammadu took the full force of the blow but still rose to his feet and tackled his assailant. Moti fired two shots into Mammadu's back. Victor screamed at the top of his lungs in agony as his friend's life bled out into the dirty sand.

Doria had risen from her position caring for Nigel and ran to the other side of the truck where Mammadu had been shot. "Oh dear *God*!' she cried. She covered her mouth and looked directly at Moti with a hatred she had never felt for another human being. As she did, Moti froze, just as his brother caught up to him, still shouting his warning.

One of his men asked, "Moti, what is wrong? Moti? Cousin?"

He walked over to Moti, who dropped to his knees, expressionless and stiff. A wound formed on his forehead, oozing blood that dripped over his face. He shook for a brief instant, and then there was a loud crack as Moti's skull opened like a pistachio and he fully collapsed into the sand next to Mammadu. His terrified men screamed defiant cries, raising their machetes to strike Victor and Dante—then stood still, unable to move a single muscle. When they each began to bleed on their foreheads, Victor, kneeling in the sand, looked over at Doria and shook his head.

"No. Please, Doria, no!" he said, crying.

The men fell to the ground, unconscious and bleeding.

Touré had limped up to within a few meters of the Land Rover, stopped and put both fists to his head, hitting himself slowly, then quickly, and then screaming like a banshee as he hit himself faster and faster. He could not take his eyes from his dead brother—the head cleaved, blood draining, brain slipping out onto his shoulder.

Doria came to Victor and helped him to his feet. "Help me get Nigel into the back of the car," she said.

Dante moved faster, racing to the back of the truck and opening the tailgate. A bewildered Leah unfolded herself and helped pull the wounded Nigel into the back with her. Doria asked Victor to remove his T-shirt, which he did, painfully. Doria used this to wrap around Nigel's leg to try and stop the bleeding. It was a bad wound. She had no idea how long he had before the bleeding became life threatening. They had to move now.

Victor went back to the body of his friend Mammadu and knelt beside it. With tears streaming, he looked up at Doria. "We have to bring his body home."

"There's nothing we can for him, Victor. We have to leave."

"We can't leave him here. Not like this. We can't. I won't!"

A crowd had started to gather, discreetly at first, but soon began to press in to see the gruesome details, to frighten themselves and let their deepest superstitions roam free.

Doria bent to pick up Victor from his mourning. He resisted, throwing off her arm and slowing standing. He tried to pull Mammadu up off the ground and grimaced in pain. He refused to let Doria touch him, repeating his struggle, and his tears and blood comingled in rivulets of grief running down his face.

Dante came to his aid. He brought with him a tarp that had been used to wrap equipment carried on the roof rack. The two men rolled Mammadu's body into the tarp. Dante, seeing the diamonds next to Moti's corpse, quietly retrieved them and placed the brown sack under Mammadu's arm. He and a depleted Victor dragged Mammadu's body to the back of the truck. Doria, conscious that the crowd encircling them might turn brutal at any moment, nevertheless helped Victor and Dante load the body into the back, crowding Leah and the fading Nigel to the side. A small dark stain emerged on the tarp. Victor touched it. Clenching his fist, he banged his head once, again, and still again on the wrapped, bent body. Doria put her arm around him and pulled him back to the passenger seat behind the driver. Dante needed no instructions. He climbed into the driver's side, fired the Rover to life, and with little heed to the bumpy road, made as fast an exit as he dared.

The crowd remained, unable to take their eyes away from the head of Moti, the insane grief of his brother, and the other unconscious men strewn like hunted doves on the sand. A few gawkers, wide-eyed and fearful, lifted their heads to watch the Land Rover disappear toward Mali.

75. Almost Unscathed

Neither David nor Temu could understand why there had been a letup in their pursuit. One moment they were breathless and cornered, and the next, there was silence around them … while in the distance, guns rattled and howls of men in pain pierced the air. What had the American and the Senegal wrestler done? Had they managed to find weapons and fight their way out? Had they eluded Mbaye Touré and the police, or were they dead on the streets of Tougue? Suddenly there were no sounds at all. Temu peered around the corner of the building against which they had flattened themselves, ready to fight or flee. David stopped him with an outstretched arm, deciding to take the risk himself. Crouching and craning his neck around the corner, he could see nothing. No men with guns or machetes. No smoke in the distance. Just the dusty back streets, tin roofs, and scrub palm trees. He motioned for Temu to follow him forward.

"We have to find Fen," he said. "And the American."

Slowly, deliberately, the two men came to a ridge checkered with small concrete buildings looking down on the main street of Tougue just before it disappeared north toward Mali. David and Temu stared across to the far side of the street, to the restaurant where he had encountered Victor Byrnes. The front was smashed in and Byrnes' Land Rover was backed out onto the side street, the front caved in, covered in concrete dust and debris. Then David saw something that registered in his eyes, but his mind rejected: a series of bodies lay to the side, away from the Land Rover and in the alley. It had been a terrible battle. But why? Was Byrnes and his cohort in that pile of broken bodies? Was Fen?

Temu tugged at his cousin's sleeve and pointed down the road, in the direction of a distant cry. The men who had been pursuing David and Temu were walking toward a man on his knees, surrounded by two, no, three more bodies. Was that Mbaye Touré with a small crowd of people gathered behind him, keening like an abandoned child next to the corpses? Cautiously the duo descended the ridge to the street and inspected the restaurant. There they found Fen, covered in rubble and barely conscious. They lifted him and determined he was not badly injured; he managed a wobbly walk on his own. Leaving the wrecked building, they moved hesitantly toward the side street to view the pile of body parts scattered in the sand. Temu turned away and David put his hand to his mouth. Fen could barely see. But he could smell. He swiveled his body to one side and vomited.

David forced himself to look. The American was not among the dead here. But three police were, he thought. It was so hard to tell. And there were four other men, one of whom David recognized, barely, as a cousin of Mbaye Touré. From what David could piece from the hellish puzzle before him, these men had killed each other. But that could not be. Had they not all been working together?

David and Temu stepped backward in unison and turned their focus down the road, where the small crowd had become much larger. Two pickup trucks drove past them—one marked with a police insignia—and pulled up to the crowd. As the drivers got out, one of them started yelling at the crowd of people, who backed away a few steps only, enough for David to confirm that the man on his knees, sobbing, was his enemy.

David looked past the crowd, to the road north, staring perplexed and worried in the direction where moments before, the Land Rover had sped.

He pulled Temu to him and said, "We have to go now, cousin. Let's collect Fen and leave this place."

Temu looked at David, hoping for an explanation, some logic on which he could hang his untethered imagination. But David offered none, pushing Temu, mouth agape, toward Fen's home.

76. Return to Dakar

D ante drove with near abandon, ignoring the relaxed guards at the border crossing into Mali and continued with more haste than he normally would have dared. Both Nigel and Barry lurched in and out of consciousness, sometimes groaning, sometimes screaming in pain, and then lapsing into silence. Victor put his hand on Doria's shoulder as he struggled to hold back tears that overtook him in waves of grief. She placed her hand on top of Victor's, but could not bring herself to say a word.

When they arrived at their Manantali camp, Dolores Knapp and Doug Borden greeted them almost cheerfully. Wearing a weary smile, Dolores approached Doria's side of the Land Rover and started to relate that Iba was stable, but it would be best if they could get some real medical care down to the campsite, with splints for his bones.

"You don't know how good it is to see you back, saf—" she started saying while taking stock of the passengers. "Oh my God! What on earth happened to you all!"

Doria got out of the vehicle, as did Victor, on the other side. "Some of us are gravely injured, I'm afraid, Dolores. Please help us. We need to stabilize them. Can they make the journey to Mahina?"

Doria was forming a plan. She discussed it with Dolores, the only medical professional.

Leah swung the door open until it nearly broke off its hinges. She sprang out of the back of the truck and onto the ground, rolling over and jumping up. Before anyone could say a word to her, she was walking hurriedly away with her hands in the air, waving in frenzied, senseless gestures.

Doria asked Victor to join her conversation with Dolores. First they would tend to the wounds of the three injured men as best they could, to stabilize them for the journey to Mahina and the infirmary, where there was the possibility of acquiring some medical supplies and putting the injured on the train to Dakar. Dolores and Leah, hopefully, would accompany them. Dante and Victor would ride in the Land Rover to take Mammadu's body to his home. With but a single vehicle now, the question was how to accommodate everyone.

Victor came up with an idea. With a great deal of rope, they tied Mammadu in the tarp and used the remaining rope to hoist his body onto the roof of the Land Rover. It was the only way the two wounded men, three women, Dante, and Victor could all make it out.

They spent the next hour cleaning Nigel's and Barry's wounds, assessing their travel worthiness, deciding what to leave behind, arranging the vehicle, and finally hoisting the body to the roof. It wasn't easy. Even with Leah's return and help, and with Victor swiftly overcoming his own bruises, it took a series of lifts and tying down of the rope. Victor climbed onto the roof and rolled his friend's body, finally, between the roof racks. And as he did, the bag of stones Dante had placed in the tarp rattled onto the metal roof. Victor picked them up and drew his arm back, ready to throw the diamonds as far as he could into the Mali jungle. He remained in that position long enough for Doria and Leah to look up and wonder whatever was possessing him. They watched as he slowly recoiled and plopped down to sit, elbows on his knees, tears pouring down his cheeks. Leah turned her head slowly and walked away.

Doria called out, "Victor, please come down, we must hurry. Please. There are two other lives, plus our own, at stake. Dear Victor, please. Come down."

He looked at this woman he had come to love, who had killed a dozen or so men by some mental force Victor could not understand. "Or what?" he yelled. "You'll split my head in two?"

Then he let out a primal scream, so loud and so forlorn that the birds scattered from the trees above. Doria shrunk from the cry. When the echo of Victor's scream evaporated, she stepped onto the door ledge, putting one hand on the roof rack and the other on Victor's leg.

"I love you, Victor. I love you in a way I don't understand, but I know it with all my being. Please come down to me. We have to finish this." Her voice was soft, tinged with remorse and a vulnerability that Victor recognized. He put his hand on top of hers, and came to the ground to finish what they had started.

* * *

No more than an hour of daylight remained when they arrived in Mahina. Dante drove straight to the clinic, finding a gaggle of would-be patients suffering from afflictions ranging from acute mental illness to severed fingers to tuberculosis. The relationship with the presiding medic got them seen in less than fifteen minutes, but there was little the willing physician could do. He dared not remove the bullet in Nigel's leg, nor would he attempt to set the bones in Barry's leg. He dressed the injuries as best he could to assure a minimum of movement, gave them whatever he had for infection, and suggested they take the train to Dakar. The train was due later that day, so it seemed a risk worth taking. Dakar was the only place to get the type of medical help that gave the two men a chance at mending and recovery.

Doria and Leah wanted everyone to go, but Victor refused. He had to return Mammadu's body to his family in the Casamance. He and Dante would take the Land Rover back to Ziguinchor in the morning, while the others went to Dakar on the train. When the train stopped at Tambacounda, they would make phone calls to the British embassy and IMAME to alert Tony Hume and Derek Planck, who would have medical help ready when they arrived.

Doria was suddenly torn. Should she go to Dakar to take charge of her husband's recovery as they originally planned, or to Ziguinchor, where her future would take its next leap? She weighed her sense of duty to Nigel against her love for Victor and found the decision surprisingly easy. Nigel's life was in jeopardy. Victor and Dante had all the means to complete their solemn mission safely without her. Nigel needed her at this moment.

When the train pulled into Mahina a mere half hour late, enough first-class cabin seats were available for three women and three men. Two young Malian men heading to Dakar helped get the two injured men onto the train.

Last in line to board the train, Doria stopped and turned to Victor, reaching up and gently taking his head into her hands. She brought her mouth up to his and covered it with hopeful kisses. Without warning she burst into tears.

"My sweet Victor, you must be careful. Promise me. Promise me you will not get trapped into any more violence or insanity. Do you hear me?"

"I promise I'll do my best. But this is West Africa. There are no guarantees."

This made Doria's eyes widen like glass orbs, as if a threat, safely bottled, had been released.

Victor saw this and laughed slightly. "Dante and I will do everything possible to be safe. I promise. You, Doria. I'm worried for you. I don't know what you've become or how you will cope with all this. I do know I want to be with you."

He pulled Doria to him and kissed her with a force he couldn't contain. For a moment the universe dropped away.

When it returned, Victor brushed a smudge of dirt from her face, and then hugged her and whispered in her ear, "I've only just found you, Doria. I need a lifetime to love you, so I will be safe. Call the Hotel Du Sud and leave a message for me there, of how to contact you and when. I'll come to Dakar the instant I've delivered Mammadu to his family."

With a hand lingering on the face of the young man who held her captive, Doria boarded the train.

77. Aftermath

It wasn't the loss of blood that took Nigel's life, but the level of infection that had seeped into his bloodstream and spread throughout his body before it could be contained. At Dakar Hospital, they amputated his leg, hoping to stop the infection. But after the days turned into weeks of a steady deterioration of his condition, Nigel died in his sleep, with Doria at his side.

Victor and Dante arrived in Dakar only three days after Doria and the others. He went back to work the same day he arrived and reported everything that had happened—such as could be believed by those not directly involved. IMAME suspended operations pending an investigation of the events leading to the death of one of their drivers and the serious injuries sustained by others. Barry Snead was medically evacuated back to the US, and Victor Byrnes was fired for his reckless endangerment of IMAME staff and property. He retreated to his apartment on Gorée and filled his days swimming and thinking.

For reasons he and Doria both understood, their contact was limited to her weekend trips to Gorée, where they could be themselves, for the most part. Victor introduced Doria to his friend Jules.

On a hot afternoon, as Victor and Jules sipped Heinekens at a Gorée beach café, Jules said, "Really, Victor, your relationship to that gorgeous woman is about as secret as a rocket launch. The electricity between you two simply crackles in the air even when you're not in the same room. If you want to be low-key about this, and I gather from your out-of-character silence you do, then just don't be in public together. It hurts to watch you pretend you don't want to jump her bones every second she's within calling distance."

Victor bristled for a moment, then relaxed. "You're right, Jules. Thanks."

"And when do you expect to let Amelia know you are no longer available? She's away for the next week, but she knows you're back in Dakar. And that things went bad in Guinea."

"Jesus Christ, does everyone know what a fucked-up disaster that was!"

"I'm just trying to help you do the right thing before two people I happen to be fond of, end up breaking things over each other's heads. Or worse!"

"I know, I know. I'll get to her next week sometime."

"Like a neglected chore, yes indeed. Victor, this young woman has been in love with you for some time. You need to treat her with that in mind."

"I will, Jules. You're right. But please understand. Shit didn't just go bad in Guinea. I saw horrible things I can't make sense of, at all. Not just that they were horrible. But how, in the universe I thought I understood, could these things have even happened? I can't explain them and I don't know if I'll ever be able to explain them. And I have this sense of a world off its axis that twists my stomach every day, every waking moment. You're asking that I suck this up to do the right thing for Amy. I don't know, my friend. I don't know."

Victor stood up, put money on the table, thanked Jules for his company, and ambled back to his apartment. When he arrived, he locked his front door behind him and went into his bedroom. From the lowest drawer in his dresser, he pulled out a paper bag and placed it on the top of his dresser. Withdrawing the dusty sack from the bag, he poured its contents onto the top of the dresser. There were thirty-eight stones, ranging from the size of a pea to the size of a thumbnail. He looked at them again, as he had every day for the past month. Can any good come of this? he wondered. Then the resolution came to him.

The next morning Victor sorted the stones differently. He dropped twenty-four at random back into the sack, putting aside the remaining fourteen into a hand-carved box on his dresser. He put the sack in his jeans pocket and hurried to the Gorée dock to make the eight o'clock ferry to Dakar. Jumping into a taxi upon disembarking and drawing a deep breath, he gave the address to the driver.

The protocol for a visitor not on the guest list of the British embassy took hours. Victor was unconcerned about time. It was midafternoon, and as Victor was thinking he should make an appointment for another day, a Senegalese embassy administrator came up to him and said, "Mr. Hume will see you."

Until now, Victor's only contact with Tony Hume had been twice during Nigel's hospitalization; during neither time had there been any discussion of what really happened or if there were any diamonds to be delivered. It had all been so tragic, so full of loss and retreat. Victor approached Hume's office with nerves and gloom.

Tony Hume rose from his desk when Victor entered, but did not come around it. He extended his hand, which Victor shook unenthusiastically. He sat on a leather chair facing Tony's desk.

"I apologize I could not see you earlier in the day, Victor. I'm glad you waited. I confess, however, that I simply couldn't conjure what might have brought you here." The attempt of a smile crossed his lips and faded.

Still without speaking, Victor took the dirty sack of stones from his jeans and held it across the desk. Hume was frozen. He stared at the sack, not trusting it was real. Victor shook it, hoping the movement and clattering stones would make it visible to Hume. Still no movement. So Victor placed the sack on Hume's desk and rose from his seat.

"I kept less than half," Victor said.

He paused and looked blankly at Hume, whose lips moved but no words were forming. Hume shook his head and put his hands over his face. His shoulders heaved. Victor turned and walked back through the office doorway and into the sweltering afternoon.

* * *

Doria returned from England after what seemed an eternity for Victor. She had accompanied Nigel's body home, attended to the funeral arrangements, fulfilled all her familial and estate responsibilities with care and poise—and a detachment that her family could neither understand nor penetrate. She did not tell her family that she was pregnant.

BBI had been very generous with the Dakar property; Doria had six months to arrange her affairs and determine her future. Iba was back on the job as her driver, recovered from his injuries except for a permanent crook in his left arm. He had gathered her from the airport as he had always gathered Nigel in the past. She was home no more than an hour when she asked Iba to take her to the port to catch the ferry to Gorée.

Victor knew only approximately when to expect Doria, so he was at the dock to meet each ferry of the day. She showed up on the third ferry, looking fresh but vulnerable. He gathered her in his arms the second she stepped onto land and held on to her with a will and a need that nearly crushed her. This led immediately to Victor's bedroom, where they spent the next two hours making love with urgency, moving from release to buildup, to release, and on and on in an oceanic rhythm that neither could nor would halt.

Later, they lay naked on the bed, touching only at their toes and fingertips, looking into each other's face, searching for confirmation

... determination ... searching for belief that this moment and their future would be worth the enormous price. Their conversation focused on the last few weeks while they were apart from each other. Had it not been for the two phone calls, compliments of the embassy, their contact would have been nonexistent.

They prepared a simple meal—pasta, salad, a bottle of wine—and fell silent as they ate.

Before the meal was finished, Doria said, "Have you thought about what you will do next, Victor?" She asked without any suggestion that she was looking for a particular answer.

"I thought we'd talk about this together, Doria. You're going to have a baby in four months or so. My baby. Did you see a doctor while you were back in England?"

"I did. And I will have to go back to England if I want to give this baby the best chance I can. I—." She fell silent.

"Is the baby healthy? Tell me. Do you know if our child is healthy?" He was raising his voice.

"It was too early to know for certain, but something could have happened to the fetus when I ... when ... I experimented on myself." Shame flushed her face and she looked down at the table.

Victor was at a loss.

"Looking at those horrible events, Victor, they seem like a dream—a nightmare. I see those images again and again. Things that I did. People I killed and was glad for it!" She began to cry. Her chest heaved reflexively when her sobs dissolved into a low mournful keen.

Victor rose from his chair and knelt on one knee beside her. Doria's shoulders slumped and shook. Victor put his arms around her.

After a minute, her breathing slowed and she pulled herself upright, embracing Victor like a life preserver.

Later that evening Doria told Victor, "I have to go to Ziguinchor. It's been a month since I've had any contact with Alain DeLevres, and ... well, all that research and work is there. I can't ignore how big and potentially important it turned out to be. Alain has been feasting on it in some fashion all this time, and I dare not imagine what difficulty or breakthrough he's experiencing. To my knowledge, he's not once tried to contact me since I left for Guinea to find you."

"Have you tried at the university?" Victor asked.

"I will, first thing tomorrow, but I tell you I have an uneasy feeling. I hope I'm wrong."

"Hope has just recently returned to these parts, Doria. Let's not overburden it yet."

She looked at him quizzically.

"I mean, let's not jump to conclusions or buy more trouble. Let's find out what we can, when we can."

"Certainly," she answered. What else *could* one do?

* * *

As Doria predicted, Alain DeLevres had not been seen at the university since his departure for Ziguinchor some months ago, nor had any of his colleagues heard from him. With this understanding, Doria prepared to go to Ziguinchor, and Victor, unemployed and in love, made plans to accompany her.

Iba seemed fully recovered, but reluctant when Doria asked him to drive them to Ziguinchor. She asked Victor if he wouldn't mind driving, a task he readily embraced with such good nature that Doria literally tingled as her heart lifted on the journey.

Ziguinchor was its usual combination of tropical torpor and dense crowds. As they drove through the center of town, masses of people on their way to the market, to church, to anywhere, clogged the streets like syrup. The couple navigated slowly and finally to the neighborhood where Doria had rented the house and where she firmly believed she would encounter the delinquent DeLevres. However, what Doria and Victor saw when Victor drew the rented Range Rover into the driveway, drove them back into a world of disbelief.

The tin roof had completely collapsed. The few remaining roof timbers were charred logs. Every window in the house was smashed, the front door was off its hinges and in pieces on the walk. Shards of burnt furniture lay about the yard in small heaps. From these and other piles of ash everywhere, acrid smoke escaped like ghosts. Doria gasped and put her hand to her mouth. Victor stared at the wreckage and looked down, shaking his head. They descended from the Range Rover slowly and took slightly different paths through the rubble, to the front door.

Victor did a slow 360-degree turn. "This can't be more than three or four days old," he observed.

Doria nodded. The house was a ruin. Faint sounds of disintegration gathered in their ears. Doria grabbed Victor's hand when they crossed the threshold.

The little that remained in the house was barely recognizable. Everything had been taken outside and apparently burnt or stolen. The smell of charred decay overwhelmed them, but they persevered. They entered the area that had been the lab, where the destruction seemed eerily organized. A pile of smashed glass must have been the beakers and vessels. The mouse cages were piled on top of each other.

Peering into one of them, Doria looked for charred remains of her test subjects, but found none. Perhaps they escaped, she thought.

Stepping through the broken and burnt debris, Victor spotted it first. His eyes widened and involuntarily he sucked in a gulp of air. Doria turned and saw it too: a charred corpse.

"Oh no!" Doria whimpered. "Not Alain, too!"

They edged closer to the slumped body. As they timidly examined it, Doria noticed something odd. The corpse seemed small for DeLevres, even in this burnt, decomposed state. She lowered herself from the waist, trying to take in the details. There was a sandal on one foot. Alain never wore sandals, she said to herself. And then she looked at the hands. There were rings on the middle three fingers of both hands.

"Oh my God!" she exclaimed.

She bent her knees into a crouch next to the body, covering her mouth and nose. She stood up and hugged Victor.

"This is Sisay, the man who taught me so much about the local medicines. I don't understand what happened here! Victor! I don't understand what happened! Where is Alain?" She pulled away and lunged into the middle of the room, looking for the remains of her other mentor. Nothing.

"Victor, help me, please. Help me find Alain's body. It must be here! *He* must be here!"

But he wasn't. There was no sign of Alain DeLevres. Nor were there any indications, burnt, charred, torn, or otherwise of his and her vast array of notes. Alain and their documentation could not be accounted for.

The couple searched for the better part of the next two hours. Inside, outside, behind crumbling doors. Victor used sticks to turn over some of the larger smoldering piles.

Dripping black sweat, he at last turned to Doria and said, "He's not here. And we shouldn't be, either. Doria, there's nothing more here. Let's go. Please."

He reached for her and she gave him her hand. When he pulled her close, he extended an arm to her belly and rubbed the barely perceptible mound where their new life had formed. She put her other hand on top of his and leaned in to kiss him, tears streaming over her smiling face.

"Take me back to Dakar, Victor. Now. Please."

ACKNOWLEDGMENTS

A manuscript taking twelve years to complete requires help, encouragement, and resources from many places. First and foremost, I want to tell my wife Robyn how much her support, enthusiasm, critical reading suggestions, and organization have made this publication possible. Beyond Robyn, others have believed in me and inspired me at various times over the years: Marji Wallach, Michelle Allison Poonwah, Regina and Sam Christiansen, and Joe Roy.

My son-in-law Sam Christiansen has been my graphics designer. Along with our daughter Regina, he has provided the unique and compelling artwork for the book cover and elsewhere.

And then there are those who, early in my life, believed I could be a writer, even when I did not believe in myself: my brother Paul Mooney, my post-college roommate Paul Orleman, my college writing professor James Mitchel, Sima Gabrielian and Carolynda Maitland.

Finally, I thank those who have helped me professionally, to get me started on this latest self-reinvention: my content editor Mary Ann de Stefano, my copy editor Beth Mansbridge, and my book and publishing consultant Fran Keiser. Were it not for these people, individually and collectively, this book could not have been written, let alone published.